WAR OF THE FOUR

THE TWIN SCHISM

⊢ BOOK ONE ⊣

D.J. DEMPSEY

MIRAGE MEDIA

Original cover art by Jackson Wrede

Cover design by Ebook Launch

Map by Chaim Holtjer

Library of Congress Cataloging-in-Publication Data

Library of Congress Control Number:2025917111

ISBN 9798998682605 (paperback)

ISBN 9798998682629 (ebook)

To Madeline and my family, thank you for always being there.
And to all who helped make this work possible, thank you.

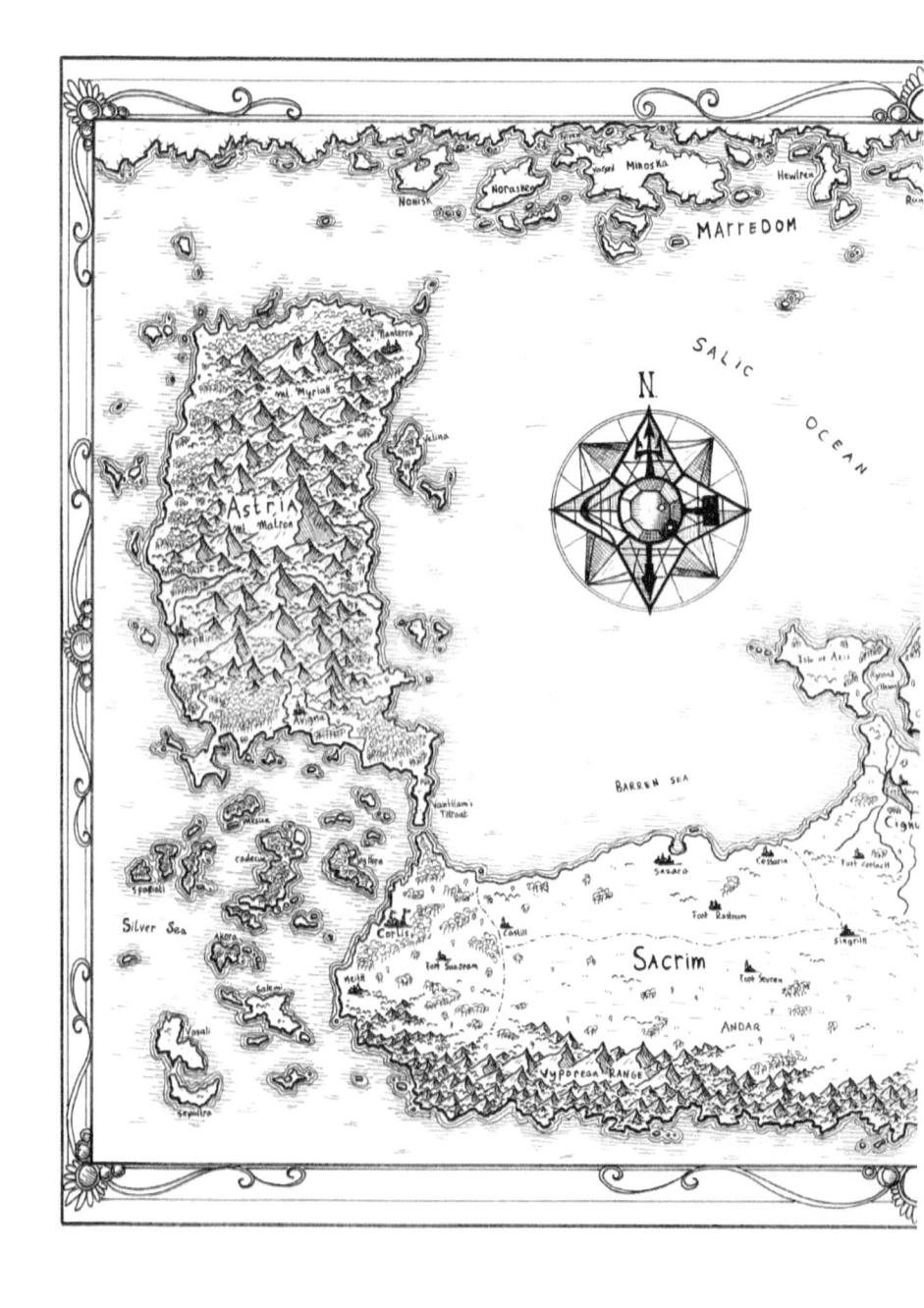

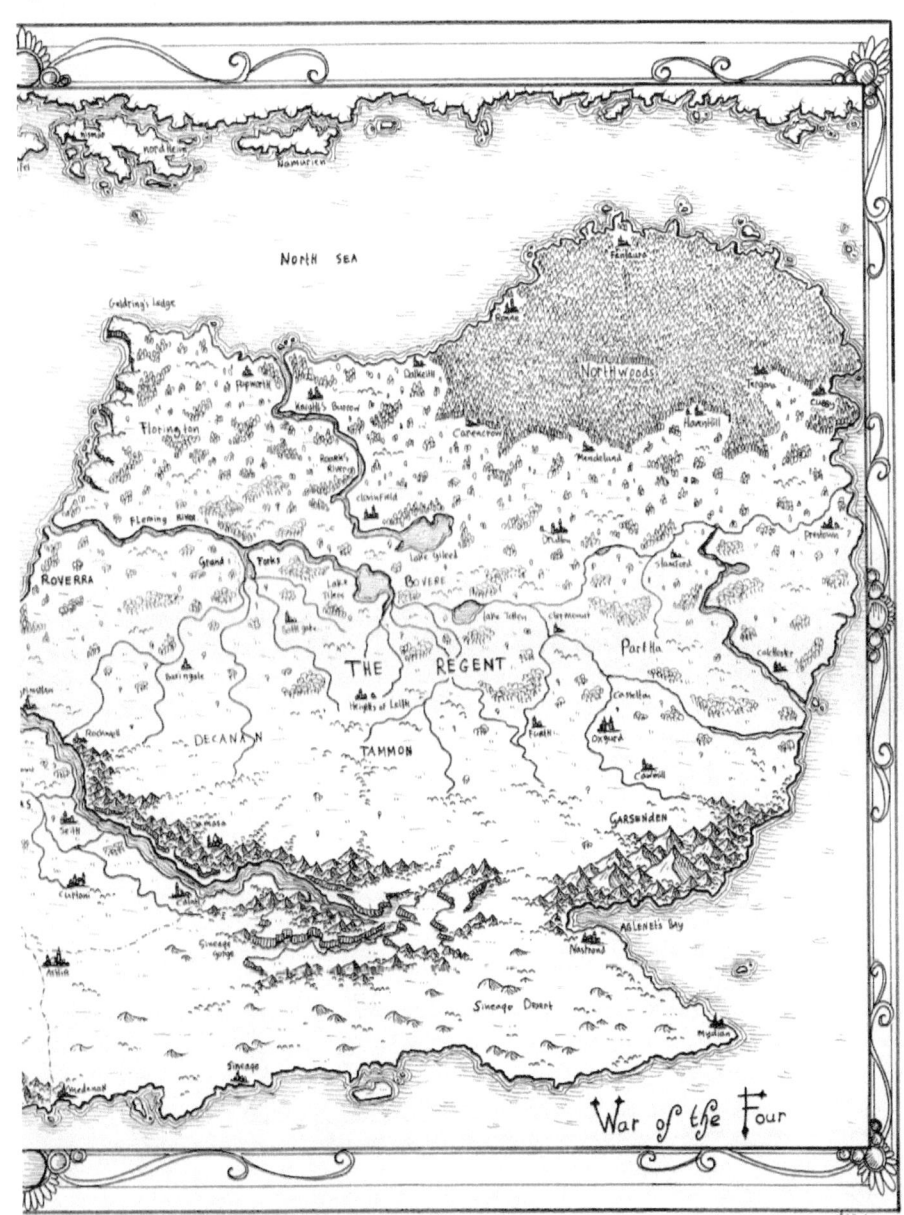

CHAPTER 1

SUN

Fire burned endlessly atop twin-pillared lighthouses that split the narrow inlet of Sazara's harbor. Cleo Scordisci sat at his polished desk, gazing out at the flames through the open window of the villa's third-story study.

"Have you finished?" Vident Lement asked from across its short stream of grains. For most of the afternoon, during Cleo's studies, his preceptor stared unwaveringly at his sheets of ordered parchment and moved only to adjust the folds of his burnt-orange vestment.

Cleo broke his trance that once stretched above the city's ceramic-tiled roofs back to their candlelit room. "No, not yet."

"Those pages won't transcribe themselves, you know. I'm aware of tonight's events and of those tomorrow. Just try to focus on the present if you can."

Cleo nodded and turned back to his work of translating and recording historical texts from sacred scipyrian into the Plane's common tongue, roalish. Little did he accomplish, however, before his wandering thoughts retraced the winding path of anticipation. "Will you be there tonight, at the hall?"

"Of course. Your father would demand most of his payments back if I didn't show up to celebrate your eighteenth solurn. You know, Cleo, you still have time to rethink joining the Guard. The vident could use some more youth with sharp minds these days."

"I think my father would really demand his gold back if that were to happen," Cleo said with a light laugh.

"Fair enough. You all can fight with your swords. We'll keep to fighting with our quills," Vident Lement responded with his baggy eyes still hidden behind his parchment.

If only I could fight today, Cleo thought.

Most days, after his morning routine of studies with Vident Lement, Cleo would continue his training as a cagerman with Kladden in the courtyard behind the general's villa. At the age of twelve, select young men across Sacrim's five partitions were sent off to attend a physical school that transitioned them from boys into capable men of war. After two turns of the solar season—more commonly called *solurns* across the Plane—of rigor and warring trials, they returned as *cagerman*, Sacrim's junior guardsmen. To maintain their standing, they were required to keep their fitness and skills in battle by training, typically in sessions paired with past guardsmen of high experience or those of command. Today, however, was Cleo's last as a cagerman.

"*Fine*. I give in," Vident Lement said. He released a sigh after finally looking up from the desk to catch Cleo staring off into the distance. "You have that same young look I used to have—one of eagerness, as if you're ready to conquer the Plane. But you should be reminded, Cleo, that to become a man, you must first conquer yourself... *Discipline.* I'll handle the rest of it on the morrow. I should be off to the square soon, too, anyway. Neither of us should want to be late."

Cleo fumbled his work back into its hard-leather bindings with a smile, then snatched himself out of his seat to place it on the shelf. Without another word, he hurried out of the study before Vident Lement could change his mind, skipping down the slick marble staircase by the brace of its rails until he became burrowed at its tiled bottom.

"I thought you would never be done," a familiar voice came from around the corner.

Cleo veered into the villa's main sitting room. "*Clara?* What are you doing here?"

"I couldn't miss my brother's final day as a little boy," his older sister and only sibling said.

Little boy, he scoffed to himself. *Or is it that you couldn't miss a party?*

She stood up from the cushioned chair near the window and made her way slowly across the room to hug him. "Look at you, all grown up. It sure has been a while since I last saw you."

"I see you're already dressed for the night." Cleo watched with a moment's regret as Clara fluffed out her long, auburn hair in reply to his comment.

"Do you like it?" She looked down to inspect her rosy-red dress that ruffled tightly to her waist, then spun around to show off the white-stitched wings of a swan that flared out from behind her back and around her sleeveless sides.

"Sure. You look nice," he replied without really taking notice. "I don't think any of us were expecting you to make the trip in from home. I could at least have had the villa's maids ready a room for you."

"It's fine. I already took to my old room. Most of the things I left are still there, surprisingly," she said, continuing to look down at her dress. "Coming here was a late decision anyway. Commander Giganti convinced me, so I rode in with him and some of his escorts from the Fourth Brigade. By that time, sending a courier with a post would have been useless."

"I guess he couldn't convince Mother to come either."

"You already know that would never happen," she responded, releasing a drawn-out groan. "The two of them in the same room together? It'd take one of them to pass before we see that again."

"You shouldn't joke about that, you know." Cleo's smile faded as soon as he turned away from his sister's green-eyed glare. "I just hope I get stationed back home in the Fourth Brigade, near you all. Maybe somewhere in the first battalion with the cavalry would be nice. I wouldn't be too far from Cignus, and I'd be able to see her more then. *And you.*"

"Don't take yourself too seriously," Clara responded, patting him a few times on his exposed shoulder.

"One of us probably should."

"Oh, that reminds me. Mother wanted me to give you something." Clara went back to the chair by the window, then returned to hand him a package wrapped in white cloth. Cleo untied the strings that looped around its sides to reveal a long over-gown, the same color as her dress. Two white swans were embroidered on the gown's chest, and ornamental gold laces hung from each shoulder.

"This is...nice," he stated reluctantly, glancing over the gown with the hope that one more look might make it change. "I was planning on just wearing my cagerman's ceremonial uniform."

"*Go put it on!*" Clara insisted. "We should be leaving soon anyway. As you can see, I helped Mother design it!" Clara spun around in her gown once more, smiling at Cleo, whose face frowned into a meandering growl.

Oh, I can tell, he thought.

Despite their differences, Cleo shared many similar features with his older sister. When they were younger, they were often mistaken for twins. Both had olive-tanned skin stretched smoothly over their muscular builds and strong cheeks that contoured sharply to each side of their long noses. Though Cleo's short hair was now shaded more in the color of copper and his shoulders far broader, seeing his sister for the first time in a while felt like he was looking into an old mirror—a mirror he wished would have remained fogged.

"You would." Cleo threw the cloth packaging to the ground beside her feet, then walked past the stairs and into his room near the opposite end of the villa. He unclasped the straps of his leather-padded vest and tossed it, and his linen undergarment, on top of his bedpost. He grabbed and dressed in a fresh white top, then slipped his bulky head through the collar of his new over-gown.

There's no way I'm wearing this, Cleo thought when he moved to stand in front of his actual mirror. In the reflection, he looked unfondly at his mother's gift, inspecting its long and sagging sides and shaking his head in disapproval. "*I look like an old lady,*" he whispered to himself, the thought fleeing from his mind.

For quite a while, Cleo sat alone in his room, debating what he should wear. There would be many dignitaries at the hall tonight, most of whom he hadn't seen in many solurns. The last thing Cleo wanted was for any of them to get the impression that he wasn't his father's son. But on the morrow, he'd no longer be a cagerman, and it could be seen as untimely—or too youthful, even—to don his old ceremonial garb. Through all of Cleo's doubts, however, there was a single thought his mind wandered the longest to consider: the possibility that his old friend Scarlett Calegri would be in attendance, too. And, to Cleo, Scarlett's opinion mattered more than anyone else's.

"Let's see it!" Clara shouted from the opposite side of the closed door.

Cleo stepped back out warily. "This? Really?"

"What? I told them you might want their input." Clara stood between four of the villa's maids, who were huddled under the arched frame of the hallway. Cleo continued to shake his head while they looked him up and down, trying to hold back their laughter and stares of bewilderment.

"The swans are a nice touch, sir," the maid to Clara's right stated.

"Really, Fronsa?" The other maids, dressed in black gowns beside her, struggled to contain their amusement as they covered their mouths with their hands and forced themselves to turn around. "I'm not wearing this. It's a gown with kissing swans on it!"

"Yes, you are! *You have to!* It's a gift!" Clara dragged her demands with enthusiasm. She rushed over and grabbed Cleo before he could retreat into his room and change. "It's a formal event. There will be plenty of men dressed finely, just like this. I promise. Plus, the swan is the insignia of our partition."

"Men might have worn this a few centuries ago, but not today," Cleo said as he was being pushed back into the main room from behind. He braced his legs against the tiled floor as if they were logs lodged in mud to resist her current of eager pushing. "Also, the elegant swan of Cignus has its wings spread wide in a showing of power. It isn't the dancing or kissing one. And it's our insignia because our ancestors hunted the lions that preyed on them, not because they were pretty."

"Well, now you're the one who looks pretty. Let's get going." Clara continued to push Cleo toward the front door while one of the villa's maids hurried to hold it open.

In the middle of the curving brick-laid road was their carriage, led by two draft horses. The coachman, dressed in a short crimson robe, moved to open the side door. Cleo grunted as he took a seat at the back, while Clara sat in the cushioned seat beside him. "Anyone else?" the coachman asked through the open window.

"No," Cleo answered with a gulp. *Unfortunately.* With a nod of readiness, the coachman took his seat at the carriage's fore and whipped the horses into stride.

The day turned to dusk as they traversed the outskirts of Sazara's winding streets. The farther the carriage traveled downhill, the denser and taller the city's limestone and red granite buildings became. Children dressed in faded gray and dirty white garments began to clutter the street's center, playing their games by throwing rocks against the weathered walls and into oddly shaped potholes. "*Move out of the way! This is a consolate carriage,*" the coachman had to shout often after snapping his fingers or clapping his hands to get their attention. Cleo gazed out of the open window as they traveled, watching the children of Sacrim's First Partition spread like beetles under an overturned boulder as they flung themselves out of the way.

"Sazara sure has changed a lot since I left," Clara commented with an undertone of sly disgust.

"How long has it been now? More than a decade? I thought your move back to Cignus might have made the city better."

"*Very funny*," she said, curving the brim of her lips. "But no. You can tell by the smell alone—it's bad. And every visit I make back here, it just seems to get worse. When Father was first elected as Sacrim's Consolar General, and we moved here fifteen solurns ago, I used to run up and down all these same streets. There isn't a chance I would let any children I might have do that today."

"*Might*," Cleo scoffed under his breath. "I remember. Sort of. But I rarely come down to the square now anyway, even with Father practically living there."

"You've still been in Sazara with him this entire time. What do you think went wrong?"

"Maybe it was always like this. I mean, not this dirty—or smelly, even—but still. Maybe we were just young then and ignorant of it all." Cleo stared out at the flat-sided buildings with open-air windows that shaded the narrow street. Growing groups of barefoot children lined up against the dirt-stained limestone walls, trying to earn a gaze into their carriage.

"No, I don't think it was. There's still enough wealth in Sazara to notice the difference. With all the gold that Consolate Chamber spends, you'd think we'd be able to see it, especially here."

"Well, it's these people's gold that they're spending, so maybe not," Cleo said.

"Where are all the parents of these kids anyway?"

"The ones with their heads on straight probably left just like Mother did and moved somewhere safe with real work—work, at least, that didn't involve selling their bodies or fighting over the scraps that come in off those damned nork galleys."

"You thought that's the reason why Mother left?" Clara asked with a mocking laugh.

But Cleo wasn't sure. He'd been young when his mother, Corianne, and Clara had moved back home to Cignus. And though he still tried to visit them when he grew old enough to travel, he never thought it was his place to investigate the enmity between his parents.

"Eh, you might be right. If Father weren't in dual command of Sacrim or even still in the Guard, I doubt you two would be living here either," Clara stated with a smirk.

That statement, though, Cleo knew, was correct. If there was anyone in Sacrim who despised its capital city the most, it would certainly be his father. It was dense with chaos and overflowing with fanatics devoted to the Temple of Sciron. And its impoverished enclaves were always *littered with the filth of pleasure*, as their father would so often describe it. But of all the reasons to dislike Sazara, none, Cleo knew, were as disdainful to his father as the Consolate Chamber of Sacrim and those who ruled from it.

As their carriage began to take tight turns in and around the sharp corners of the grassless city, they caught a view down the alleys that served most of Sazara's black-market trades. Scampish men and women wearing hole-ridden rags for clothes, similar to the children they'd seen earlier, looked at their carriage as it passed with stares that screamed of jealous disgust. The two of them could only sit in silence as their carriage continued down the side paths and alleyways that wound between the broadest segment of Sazara.

After a right turn and then a left, they passed through one of the many entrances to Arcus Street, which curved in a half-arch to surround Sazara's square. Grand buildings of limestone and red granite, with fancifully carved facades chiseled high to their crimson roofs, stretched along its curved extent. There, and still bustling with people, stood Sazara's burgeoning bathhouses, markets, and artistry shops, as well as workplaces for the wealthy.

"Finally, *a view*," Clara said, sighing in relief. Older men and women, dressed in robes easily distinguishable from those they'd seen earlier, stuck to the street's side paths as they chatted and ate meals under the shade of storefront canopies.

When the carriage reached the end of the street, near the water's edge, they took a right turn, allowing Cleo to see the long piers that branched into the mouth of Sazara's harbor. Along the street beside the seawall stood a long row of waterside homes. Through the gaps between them, which flashed quickly as the carriage passed, Cleo saw the same twin flames burning incessantly in bowls atop the lighthouse's pillars. Breakwaters built by stacked boulders stretched out from each of their opposite bottoms, winding to meet Sazara's wall and encircle the city and its harbor like a ring. But even from a far distance, Cleo knew their size to be misleading. Other than the Cathedral in the east, the two lighthouses were the tallest structures of any across the Plane. And more often than Cleo would like to admit, he found himself gazing out at their magnificence.

They continued to travel east along the coast until the carriage slowed to enter the most populated center of the city—Sazara's square. Closest to the water was the Temple of Sciron, by far the broadest and most grand of the square's surrounding buildings. It stood tall and wide, a perfect circle with marble columns placed evenly along its rounded edge to support a golden-tiled dome roof. At the peak of its cupola was a massive ornament shaped like the sun, crafted from pieces of mustard-stained glass. Pouring out from its supporting meridian were ten rays stained dark in shades of yellow to signify the ten deacons of the temple. In the center of the square's vast courtyard, the ornament of the Benevolent Sun overlooked a bronze sculpture of Claros Sciron, the first man to wield the Sunspear.

"Just like the good old days, right? With you here?" Cleo wondered, his eyes pinned to the towering sculpture. "Reminds me of the time Mother used to drag us all down here for the Midsun Festival."

"I thought you used to hate that?" Clara asked.

"I still do. But I guess it was sort of cool, seeing everyone's reaction when the sunlight reflected from the ornament, up there, onto Claros's Sunspear."

"So, you like parties after all," Clara stated while readjusting her auburn hair.

"No—at least not the way you do."

To the side of the temple and adjacent to the square was the Consolate Chamber, poised opposite the First Partition's Court, which provided working estates and offices for Sacrim's elected officials, magistrates, and chambermen from each of its five partitions. Both were equal in size and brandished symmetric limestone columns that stood tall to support their overhanging shallow pediments. Farthest from the water within the square was the Consolate Hall, the second tallest building of the four.

Their carriage stopped at the front of the hall's grand doors just as the sun began to set in the east. The coachman attended their leave, and Cleo and Clara were greeted promptly by doormen scrambling to welcome them in. The two of them were escorted into the hall's long corridor, which had life-size oil paintings of Sacrim's past consols hung on its walls by frames etched of gold, mounted between sconces of dimmed candlelight. To Cleo's left were portraits of prior Consolar Vizars, each appointed by the five magistrates to be the executive legislator of Sacrim. To his right were paintings of Sacrim's prior Consolar Generals, each of whom, at one point, led Sacrim's Guard. But every figure Cleo saw within the paintings posed with what appeared to be an obscure glare, staring directly down the long passageway toward the entrance doors and right into the eyes of them both.

Cleo and Clara continued down the gold-and-white-tiled floor, almost too anxious to look anywhere but forward. It wasn't until they were near the corridor's end that the doors to the hall's lavish gallery were opened.

"Well, we definitely aren't early," Clara said with a smirk, watching as people dressed in the fanciest of outfits glided across the floor in dances and groupings of chatter.

"No—no, we aren't."

The vaulted ceiling rested upon four marble columns near the gallery's center. Within the small square it formed, most attendees danced with chalices of wine in hand, while others mingled around the surrounding tables.

"I look like a fool," Cleo tried to tell Clara, though she had already begun wandering off to have a look around. His first instinct was to drift to the outer tables and join the elderly crowd, away from all the dancing and attention.

"*I'm going to find the wine,*" Clara finally turned back to him to scream over the chatty racket and stringed tunes, drifting toward the center of the hall.

Cleo's eyes flitted around in search of a familiar face, though all they seemed to fall upon were other men's outfits. Most wore the ceremonial uniform of the Guard—buttoned garments of deep royal red and gold, with white-pillowed pants. Others wore the Guard's working uniform of bronze-plated vests and spaded leather skirts. Scattered scarcely throughout them all were formal robes, typical of Sacrim's chambermen. But none wore an ancient gown like his own. Despite Cleo's growing sense of embarrassment, he stumbled his way toward the center of the hall's packed dance floor.

"Cleo! How are you, son?" a man asked, hidden behind his back.

Startled, Cleo whipped his shoulders around abruptly and knocked them into the chalice the man once held, spilling his wine onto the floor. Without hesitation, Cleo reached down to retrieve it. It wasn't until he straightened himself back out that he realized who the man standing before him was. "*Jern?* How are you?" he asked with a smile.

"Good, son, good. And you, Cleo?"

"More than well."

"Last time I saw you, you were just a little boy, following your father around in the Fourth Brigade," Jern said with a drunken slur. He waved over one of the servants to clean their mess and asked for another drink. When the bald man with a bearded face turned back to Cleo, he looked him up and down, paused for a moment, and then let out a rolling laugh. "And now you've grown into a fine woman!"

Cleo laughed, smothering his humiliation at the comment. "It was a gift from my mother."

"*Ah*, that woman. On the day you become a man, too. What a shame." Jern reached over and grabbed two chalices from the server's plate, handing one to Cleo. "Here, this should help."

"So, what have you been up to, now that you've retired from the Guard?" Cleo asked, sipping on the sour wine.

"I'm a salutor now for the Fourth Magistrate. Practically his personal lap dog. You think you can leave the Guard and live a life of peace, but everything today costs a silver, and my sword is the only skill I have still worth a damn."

"You don't like it?"

"The pay is better than it was in the Guard, that's for sure. And now my orders come from a man without a clue of what we do, so that's been somewhat nice," Jern replied with a smirk, leaning down to Cleo to speak above the commotion. "But you'll be on your way to join the Guard now, too. Is that right?"

Cleo scanned the gallery again. "That's the plan. Hopefully, somewhere out east, away from all the politics here in Sazara."

"East, huh? As long as you aren't placed in the Fifth Brigade. Sineaqe is dreadful. But then again, with your father serving as the Consolar General, anywhere will be dreadful."

"*Thanks*," Cleo said with a gulp. He knew Jern was right.

"But if you're half the warrior your father was, or even Kladden still is, then the Sixth Brigade is where you belong. They're the best of the best."

"That would leave me too close to Sazara," Cleo responded, clearly unamused. "And they wouldn't place me in the first battalion with the cavalry, which is what I want."

"The spearmen and swordsmen of the second and third battalions are a prideful bunch for that very reason. You'd fit right in," Jern slurred his words to say. "But if the cavalry is what you're after, I'm sure your father could put a word in with Cresden."

Cleo shifted his face with contention. "That also isn't something I would want."

"Well, I don't blame you." Jern took a heavy sip and lifted his eyebrows in agreement. "General Sepatus is just as much of a father to all the guardsmen as he is to you."

That sure is the truth, Cleo thought.

"Wouldn't want to go making your new brothers jealous now, wouldn't we?"

But Cleo didn't know what to say. If anything, he was jealous of the time his father spent with the Guard, away from him. He shifted his attention away from Jern. The first few sips of wine made the surrounding chatter around him grow numb, and Cleo's eyes tunneled to find his old friend, Scarlett. Between the shoulders of the talking crowd, he saw her entertaining a circle of men much older in age. As he stared on, she lifted her chin and caught his gaze.

Cleo twitched, trying to avert his admiration. But it was too late.

Jern gave him a quick pat on the back. "Good luck with the Guard, Cleo. *And with that one.*" As his father's friend drifted off into the crowd, Cleo sipped nervously on his wine, watching Scarlett walk toward him. Her gold-plated flats clanked against the tiles with each step, just loud enough for Cleo to hear her approach above the surrounding chatter and music.

"Look who finally decided to show up to his own party," Scarlett told him. Her hair was as orange as fire and pinned up seamlessly, with curling strings in front of her ears that fell to the top of her low-cut, crimson-red dress.

"Looks more like my father's party to me."

"Your father's party or your sister's?" Scarlett pointed across the packed inner square. There, Clara stood dancing wildly near the center of the floor.

"And I thought I'd be embarrassed by this outfit."

"You should be embarrassed by both," she responded with a soft giggle.

"At least someone's having fun."

Scarlett's glare turned incredulous, as if Cleo's pity wasn't to be believed. "You should feel lucky to be hosted here, at the hall. There aren't many who get this honor."

Cleo rolled his eyes but nodded in agreement. "I guess this sort of luxury is something we both share. You would know all about that, with your father."

"I'm the lucky one who gets to have an important brother, too." Her ocean-blue eyes glanced over to the raised stage at the opposite end of the hall's doors. On it was a long marble table headed by two golden thrones raised above five chairs on each side.

"I see Cayen hasn't changed much. I'm surprised he even came."

"Me too. You would think finally achieving his dream of being elected as the Consolar Vizar of Sacrim would have eased him up a bit," Scarlett drawled with sarcasm.

"To be fair, dealing with both the chambermen and the temple's deacons must be quite exhausting." Cleo followed Scarlett as she glanced up at her older brother, Cayen, who sat on one of the two thrones in the middle of the raised table. Behind him, on one shoulder, stood the Vice-deacon of the Temple of Sciron, dressed in his crimson satin robe with its sashes laced in golden scripts of sacred scipyrian. Behind Cayen's other shoulder stood his personal salutor.

"*Trust me*, they are a lot better than them." Scarlett nodded her freckled face toward the group of old men she had just walked away from. "They're the real reason I spend so much time away from the city."

"Still out east, along the coast, then, huh? The summer home?"

"When I can. It's only a half-day's ride away, so I'm forced to come back here more than I'd like."

"I'll never forget that place," Cleo said with a smile, remembering the time when he and Scarlett were both young. "The few times I was allowed."

But Scarlett didn't return his smile. "Right. But I guess I should probably thank you for saving me from them. All the men who work in the chamber's commerce are only interested in one thing."

Cleo's grin grew lofty as he looked up and down at her low-trimmed dress. "I'm not so sure I can blame them."

"*CLEO!*" she said aloud, slapping him softly on his shoulder. "*I meant gold!*"

"Oh, right."

"They only talk to me because they're too scared to talk to my father...*or him.*" Scarlett glanced back up at Cayen only to roll her eyes.

Then I really don't blame them, Cleo thought.

A loud horn rang twice over the tune of strings, which slowly softened with the crowd to silence. As the entrance doors to the hall opened, all who sat stood. All except for Cayen.

"*Thank you, thank you. You may all sit if you so please,*" Cleo's father, Sepatus, said loudly to the quieted crowd as he walked slowly through the center of the columned square. The two consols of Sacrim wore matching white robes with royal-red-and-gold cloaks draped behind them. Sepatus's hair flowed below his shoulders like that of Clara's—auburn but peppered with gray, the same as his scraggly beard.

In his hand, General Sepatus raised the Sunspear, tipped at its head by gold-azilian, just enough to lift the bottom of its staff off the ground. The candles, which were once dimly lit along the walls and columns, doubled in size to fully illuminate the hall and its attendees. He walked slowly between the splitting crowd to reach his throne to the left of Cayen.

Cleo drifted to that side of the hall and noticed the table where several of the vidents, including Vident Lement, were sitting patiently. Vidents were forbidden to speak publicly, but Cleo did manage to catch the attention of Lement, who kindly waved his way.

"Thank you, everyone, for joining us here tonight," Sepatus stated loudly so the hundreds inside the hall could hear him. "As all of you know, we are gathered here tonight to celebrate my son Cleo's eighteenth solurn. In his short time on this Plane, Cleo has grown into a fine young man and has decided to follow in his father's footsteps and join Sacrim's Guard."

Cleo could feel his broad cheeks turn the color of ripe springberries as everyone inside the hall joined in and clapped. Sepatus took a sip of wine and then placed the delicate chalice back onto the table. Cleo thought hard but couldn't remember the last time he saw his father drink.

"Again, it is an honor for all of you to join us in this festivity. Our cooks have prepared a fine meal of roasted geese, long-cooked mutton, and salted crisps. And, of course, we have casks filled with the finest wine across Sacrim." He paused to scan the room, ensuring he still had the crowd's attention. "But before we celebrate, I have an announcement to make. Upon my salutation, the most honorable Commander Jorad Cresdan of the Sixth Brigade has been promoted to the rank of assistant general and will join me here at the chambers in Sazara."

Murmurs from the crowd lifted throughout the hall as soon as his father had finished his statement. Cleo looked around, trying to figure out why.

"In his place, I name my son, Cleo Scordisci, as commander of the Sixth Brigade," Sepatus stated proudly.

Commander? Me? I can't be a commander… I'm only a cagerman. Cleo's eyes were fractured white and wide. What were once whispers erupted into loud buzzing chatter, as if swarms of birchbees now flew from one mouth to another across the hall, zipping back and forth with pollinated gossip. Cleo's face and cheeks turned from the hue of springberries into that of Vyporean lava, hot enough to melt through the hall's tiled floor.

Sepatus glanced down at Cleo from the table above with a confident yet mischievous grin, then turned to the corner of the hall and invited the cooks in with their trays of food. Ignoring the rumbling chatter from the crowd, Cleo's father took his seat and gave his final announcement of the night: "*Now, let us feast!*"

14

CHAPTER 2

SEA

Sometimes, it's necessary to suffer, Dane thought as he awoke before sunrise. It was an answer his father had always given him when he was young and would ask his fill of aberrant questions. At the time, it seemed like an answer that lacked substance, as if it were just a lousy excuse for the desperate situation his family was continually in. But the older Dane grew, the more his father's answer came to resonate with him. That persevering thought, first thing in the morning, was all Dane had to pull him through the days.

The prior night's chill carried a fresh layer of frozen dew, leaving his morning legs numb with a frigid stiffness. His sleep had been broken in the middle of the night by the howling of wolves near his mother's tiny wooden shack. To Dane, life in the small coastal town of Niven was a never-ending competition of hunger, one that questioned who would be the first to starve—his family, the roaming packs of wolves, or their rusted-iron stove in the corner of the shack that heated its only room. It was this race to survive that kept him awake and alert, day and night, cold season after long cold season.

To make light of their situation, his mother frequently lied to her four children by telling them that tiny things were often the best things—a tiny shack needs little wood, a tiny stomach needs little food, and a tiny wolf needs a little knife. Dane, however, was no longer tiny and had grown out of the young phase of comforting tales. Although frail, he was a few solurns past his initial sprout of growth and had some frost-tipped golden hairs on his face to prove it. He was yet a man, despite that being all he knew. And regardless of his actual age, he always felt older. That was the role he had to fill after his father was taken in Minoska when he was just a boy.

But a few solurns before he was taken, Dane had helped his father, Domus, build their family's only form of protection—a doddery shack strewn with shaven splines of timber and dried mud to hold its nimble walls together. Near the heat from the stove within it slept his mother, Amel, and his two little sisters, Ellian and Alva, on a hay-padded bed. He and his brother, Maven, had converted the shack's only attached closet into a tiny room just big enough for their double bunk.

"*Maven, wake up*," Dane whispered, giving his younger brother a slight shove on his shoulder. "We need to get going."

"Let me sleep."

"You can sleep when the fish sleep. *Or you can sleep with them*," Dane whispered back. He grabbed the thin, feather-filled covering Maven had clasped in his clutches and dragged it from the top bunk down to the lower post. "Get dressed and meet me at the shed out back. *Oh*, and try not to wake Ellian or Alva up this time."

In the night's dark, Dane changed into his hole-ridden trousers and slipped on the same gray undergarment he'd worn for the past moon. He wrapped his arms into his fox-pelt coat, one he'd grown out of two solurns ago, and then tiptoed his way quietly out of the shack. His temper subsided as soon as he stepped outside and felt the morning breeze slice a thin blanket of frost across his pale face.

At least the heavy snowfall should be over with, he reassured himself. *Spring couldn't come quickly enough.*

Between the thin trunks of the wooded spruce and birch, Dane could see the earliest sign of sunrise light the western sky into the color of a skimmer's beak. He walked a few short steps across the crunching frost toward the woods behind their shack. There, he dropped to his knees and reached his hands into the shallow split of rocks where a tiny stream trickled. Cupping his hands together, he splashed the water over his face and took a few refreshing sips.

Dane stared at his reflection in the little stream. His days in Niven were long, so he'd learned to cherish these quiet moments alone each morning. The sight of his icy-blue eyes became a reminder that there was still someone else he needed to care for inside. He ran his wet fingers through his long, rustic-blond hair before looking back down at the stream one final time. With a fresh splash of conviction across his narrow face, he brushed his knees and headed back toward the shack.

"*Still not awake yet, I see,*" Dane whispered to himself as he walked past the shed and saw it still unopened. He and his brother, Maven, had spent most of last solurn's summer building it. Inside its walls, assembled from scads of rounded stone stacked between four wooden posts, were the only tools his family had for survival. It was where he kept their chopped wood dry and his line, hooks, and poles for fishing hidden.

Dane skipped around the frosted puddles and opened the rotted door of the shack. As quietly as he could, he walked through and grabbed Maven's feet. With a twist, he slung them off and left them to dangle from the top bunk.

"*Okay, okay.* I'm up—I'm up," Maven grumbled while rubbing his eyes.

"Get ready. I'll handle the rigging. You grab the sack. And make sure you have your boots on straight. Meet me at the pier," Dane told his younger brother, then walked back out to grab their rigging from the shed.

Sharp air continued to slice between the bark, smothering Dane with a chill as he headed toward Niven's only pier. With each step he took along the rocky ground of the worn-over trail, the scent of pine from the fallen needles lifted with the breeze. Though Niven's westernmost shoreline wasn't far from Dane's home, it was still far enough to hide the sea and its condition. As he passed through the denser segment of the woods, Dane soon saw the breaking split of the horizon. Above it, dark clouds from a distant storm shadowed the rising sun.

Rough seas again. Maven needs to hurry. Dane reached the short pier and dumped his line and posts into their small wooden boat that pitched with the coast's emerging waves. He looked out along the rocky shore and spotted a snow pelican gliding low to the water. With its white wings spread wide and its orange beak lofted open, it swooped down to splash into the sea. In the deep pocket of its mouth, Dane could barely see the tailfin of a fish still flopping as the pelican turned and flew toward him. It landed at the farthest plank of the pier and pointed its beak to the sky, swallowing the fish.

"At least you get to keep your catch," Dane told the bird.

"*I'm coming, I'm coming,*" Maven's voice echoed in the distance, startling the snow pelican away. Dane watched its wings flap majestically, flying back out to face the wind and the sea with ease once more.

Must be nice.

Through the gap of the trees, Maven came jogging briskly down the path. He dumped the linen sack he had draped across his shoulders at the edge of the pier and heaved with his hands at his knees to catch his breath.

"Got everything? We're already behind, and it looks like that squall out there is headed toward us," Dane croaked.

"I think so," he replied, searching through the sack one more time.

Dane undocked the line from the far post and stepped onto the foremost of the two benches inside their tiny boat. "Grab the aft line." Maven tossed the sack next to Dane's foot, untied the line, and then hobbled onto the aft bench. His brother gave the boat a solid push off from the pier, then reached for the wooden oars that were tucked under the boat's sides, handing a pair to Dane. They placed them onto their crutches and began to row.

Sweat dripped from Dane's forehead to join the breaking waves that occasionally splashed over their tiny bow. His sight became blurred by its salty spray, his feet and bony bottom soaked by the puddling seawater. Together, they rowed farther out, past the shore's breaking waves, until they began to roll more smoothly with the sea.

"Who's been swimming with the fish now?" Maven shouted to Dane with the crackled voice of a growing boy.

Dane turned around, half-soaked, and shoved his younger brother, cutting his laugh short by yanking at his long, golden locks. "Just get the lines cast out. Looks like we'll only have time to make one pass to the knee today before we'll have to make our way back. Hopefully, we can beat this storm," Dane said while he rang out the cuffs of his gray trousers.

Maven picked up the four shaven tree branches and tied the lines at their ends. He opened his sack and grabbed a few tinfish, slicing a hook through each. After tossing the lines behind them, he set the branches between a stepped knock on the boat's floorboard, and the two of them began to row again.

The passage to the knee over the rolling waves was smoother than Dane had expected. Their father, Domus, was the one who gave the small island its colloquial name. Its rounded top poked high enough out of the water to look as if a man of stone were relaxing submerged beneath it. The knee was his favorite spot to fish. It was close enough to the shore and had shrubs surrounding its bottom, like the hairs of a leg, attracting schools of fish below. Dane moved both his oars to his lap as the boat slowed toward its ledge. "We're almost there. Do we have anything yet?" he shouted back to Maven through the growing wind.

Maven lifted his oars back into their boat. "No, I don't think so, but let's stop here and cast again."

"I had hoped that squall might bring the torsks in."

"Doesn't look promising. But then again, we haven't had a good bite in a few days."

"I'm just worried we won't meet our allotment," Dane said.

"Those tributars can rot under the sea for all I care."

"Well, if we don't meet what we need to give them, we'll be the ones rotting under the sea."

Maven sneered. "*We already are.*"

At first, Dane took his younger brother's comment as an insult. It was his duty, after all, to provide for his mother and his younger siblings. And the past winter season was rough on them all. But the more he sat and looked out into the morning sea, the more he could feel the pit of his empty stomach roll with every wave. *He's right,* Dane knew.

"Which reminds me…Narien told me yesterday that we could borrow his rake," Maven added. "But only after nightfall."

"Good. But those beetroots will take a season or two to grow. The fish, now, are more important." Dane cracked his knuckles and looked to his left, out across the sea and into the dark clouds that were gaining on them. "We don't have long before we cut this trip short. Check the lines again."

"Dane—*look—look*—this way," Maven stuttered like a rattle rolling downhill.

Dane turned around and saw a tribute galley off in the distance, forcing its way around Marredom's northwestern coastline. The long row of oars that protruded from both of its wooden-planked sides swung in unison as it headed for Niven's bay.

"It's only the third day of the quarter-moon. Why are they coming to collect?"

"*Dane.* We need to go back—now."

"I know. It's just odd."

"*No*, now. We need to go back. I think I left the floorboards in the shack open," Maven stated reluctantly. "I took a bite before I left, and—and…I don't know."

"*What?*" Dane's heart bellowed beneath the sea; his face turned as pale as the wings of the snow pelican. *Mother. The girls.* "Forget the fish. We need to beat that galley back to Niven," Dane commanded, rushing to swing their tiny boat back around. With each row they slapped against the growing waves, Dane grew angrier. Fury for his brother filled him as he powered their boat through the swirling wind. "Why didn't you close it? Do you know what will happen if they find the food we have stored down there?"

Maven answered with silence. *Here I was, worried about the wrong storm*, Dane thought in despair.

In their rush to reach the coast, Dane could barely see the oared tribute galley sitting still past the break of the woods. *No—the galley is already anchored*, Dane frowned in thought as they came upon the short pier. The two of them sprinted into the woods without securing the boat. Rain from the growing storm clouds began to fall, its drops dancing down through the dangling branches. Dane could taste them as they fell like tears across his face. *Salt from the sea, or the sky, or from my soon sorrow.*

Dane led Maven to the edge of the wooded tree line that surrounded the few shacked homes in Niven. "*Wait here*," he whispered to his brother while he circled around a large trunk, trying to catch a view of the closest one. His neighbors, Narien and Mikoal, an older couple, stood outside their own tiny home with their hands on their faces, sunken to the ground. *This isn't fair. They aren't supposed to collect tribute today.*

Dane glanced back at Maven and put his finger to his lips, signaling him to keep silent. He sprinted across the open patch between his neighbor's home and the woods. When he reached their only window, he crouched. Dane followed slowly along the edge of their circular stone-built shack until his own was in sight. Their front door hung from its bottom pin, swung open. Dane searched around but saw no sign of his mother or sisters. *Why aren't they outside waiting like Narien and Mikoal?* A sharp bang rang from inside their home like wood snapping through its splinter.

Through the rain, Dane sprinted across the span of muddy slosh to reach their broken door. His eyelids sprang open as soon as he turned the corner and peered into his home's open entrance. Two men dressed in long black overcoats stood in the shack's only room. On their knees beside them were his mother and sisters, with their hands tied tightly together by frayed line.

"Who are you?" one of the officers with a missing tooth and straying blond hair asked. He took his silver helmet off and placed it on the table against the wall.

"Her son. Whatever the problem is, it was my fault, not theirs," Dane said. He staggered cautiously inside.

"Look at this. We've found some more dirty, thieving hands," the other, much shorter, man jeered.

"One of our tributars had received a tip the last time we were here, from one of your own, here in Niven. Said someone might have been keeping more than they should have. Turns out, they were right. Stealing King Mordin the Fourth's property is a high-order offense. At a quarter-sun to midday, we seized *this*." The officer pointed to the pile on the corner of the table wrapped in cloth.

"I counted in excess: one loaf, nine torskfins, and a pack with five rotting pomes. What is your name, again?" the shorter man asked.

"Daneus."

"Daneus, you are aware of the King's Decree of Tribute, correct?"

"I am."

The taller officer strolled to the side of the room, near the table, and leaned against its corner post. "Tell me, Daneus, what rule of that decree have you broken? What does it state?"

"All shall give to Marredom so Marredom may give to all," Dane snarled, striking their nerves.

"The rule exists for our people's survival. It makes it difficult to provide for all when some choose to be selfish. *Correct?*" the snobby and missing-tooth officer retorted.

Selfish? The King himself is the selfish one. Dane's mind spun with thoughts he didn't have the courage to speak. Instead, he just gave a brief nod, refusing to maintain eye contact. The rain that belted against the roof of the shack began to sync with the pounding of his chest.

"Last time I was in Minoska, I saw no decree from King Mordin the Fourth for these extra food items to be in your allowance. Our King has been gracious to give what he can. And you've chosen to keep more than you're allowed. The decree states that allowance shall be distributed on the first day of the quarter-moon and your tribute collected twice in that period. The penalty for stealing from our King is lashes, equivalent in number. Nine plus six, by my count. That makes for fifteen lashes at the King's Pillars," the taller officer stated with pomposity. Although they stood a distance from Dane, the odor of their unwashed, sea-sweated uniforms coated the shack's cracking walls with revulsion. "Now, you said that this was your doing and not your mother's. The lashes will be yours, then."

"Wait, don't ruin the fun, Ivar. I was looking forward to *this*," the shorter officer said, grabbing Dane's mother's face.

"*Don't touch her*," Dane thundered from the depths of his thin chest. His jaw tightened, and his fists hung heavy, clenched at his sides.

"Who are you to give orders to me—an officer in our King's Navy? I'll do as I please." The shorter officer licked his dirty, stubby fingers, then lurched his mother's head back until her soft chin pointed directly at Dane. He could see the crescent of his mother's eyes flash blue, trembling as she struggled to look away. Or in any direction but his own. The officer ran his wet fingers across her pale face until they reached his mother's lips. Lips, once thin and pink, were now purple and swollen. He continued down her neck until his fat fingers nuzzled inside the top of her raggedy gray dress and onto her chest.

"*Stop!*" Dane shouted, rushing at the short officer. Drawing his right elbow back, he swung it forward and threw his heavy fist into the officer's jaw. The stubby man stumbled backward; his hands fluttered up from his side as he fell to the floor. Dane's fury raged inside, forcing him to charge for more.

Wail after wail, Dane leaped on top of the man and lashed out. He threw his fists in rapid spurts, clipping the officer's chin until his mouth oozed with blood. But when he raised his right elbow to throw one more, it wouldn't move. Whipping his head around, he saw his fist stuck in the air, gripped at his wrist by the taller officer's hand. In the blink of a moment, all Dane could see was the other officer's fist headed straight for his face, growing in size.

Daylight dazed into a dimmed darkness as Dane's body crashed to the floor, his eyes snapped shut. A loud scream in the fading distance became drowned out by the gushing of rain, pounding on what felt like his head, swollen to the size of the shack. Rain or blood, he couldn't tell. The pain continued to strike him from shoulder to stomach as he lay motionless on the broken planks of the shack's only room.

In the blackness of his memory, Dane saw his younger self standing beside his father as they trekked east across the muddy and snow-smothered tundra. Their pilgrimage to Minoska was a journey they took every solurn to render their tribute and receive the King's offering. Inside the city, they traded for things they couldn't find anywhere besides the populated port. Fishhooks, twine, and a tiny copper kettle—that was the list that fateful day.

To Varjord they hiked, stopping only for a night to sleep at their makeshift camp. From Varjord, they found Arnis Rov, the thin river that flowed near Minoska. They followed the trail along its bank until they caught sight of the rocky mounds—the landmark surrounding Marredom's oldest city.

The memory of his father's face flashed vividly when the graystone walls of the city's buildings first came into sight. Instead of the expected look of satisfaction, or even excitement, Dane's father looked saddened and stunned. Domus's eyes were as worried as his own and shook frantically in all directions. When he finally looked back down at Dane, his father told him, "This isn't good. Minoska has never had this many marines and officers on Norkatis Street."

But before his father could turn back toward Arnis Rov, the two of them were shoved and escorted into the chaos. Dane, as young as he was, struggled to keep up.

"We aren't cattle," he heard his father scream angrily as he poked his head above the crowd, looking for any way out. Grown men wearing silver bowls for helmets and long black overcoats rushed back and forth, keeping the arguing crowd in line.

"Come with me." Dane's small hand was clasped tightly with sweat, yanked left, right, and forward until his back was pinned against a frozen stone wall a few alleys behind Norkatis Street.

In a way Dane knew not how, his father had managed to sneak him away from the shouting officers and marines. Domus, who had always been stern and strong, trembled like Dane had never seen him do before. His father crouched in front of Dane's younger self and gathered his breath. "Listen to me, Dane. Run home now and give this to your mother." He handed him a torn rag from his garment, scribbled with charred letters. "Don't talk to anyone on your way. Especially not anyone wearing those silver helmets. They shouldn't bother you at your age. Follow behind these buildings, down that way, and it will lead you out of the city. From there, find Arnis Rov. You remember the way back home, right?"

The younger Dane nodded. "But where are you going?"

"I'll be here—away for some time. Just give this to your mother," his father responded, turning his head back and forth to check the growing voices between the alleys. "Don't worry. I'll meet you again at home."

"When?"

"Soon. I hope. I'm sorry, my son." A tear fell from the crest of his father's eye. "Tell your mother that I love her."

The last memory Dane had of his father's face was one engraved like a bust, forever in his mind. The younger Dane had to be pushed by his father to finally comply, scampering away. From alley to alley, he turned between Minoska's corners, running down and through its snowy, graystone paths. When Dane was far from the chaos of the city, he pulled out the torn cloth his father had written on and read:

We have become tribute.

Chapter 3

Sky

"Down."

Vanna reached between the buttons of her black half-cape and grabbed the small flute laced by a cord around her neck. Pressing the end of its wooden slit to her mouth, she blew two quick, screeching notes. Wind whistled past her fluttering double-braided hair as she emerged from the clouds to descend. She yanked her leather saddle to the right, then blew once more into the flute. Spreading its wings wide to drift down, the rook she rode landed gently on a flat segment of cliff that surrounded Astria's only city, Mount Matron.

"This should do, *Little Wing*."

Vanna unstrapped her legs from the saddle, then slid a short distance down from her large, brown, and black-feathered bird. She unbuttoned her black half-cape and dressed out of her silken hose, swapping them for a dress from the pack strapped to the back of her rook. Vanna donned the long, bland gray dress that covered her from neck to ankle and undid her braids, brushing her dark hair straight. She wrapped a black scarf around her head and neck and traded her boots for flat-strapped sandals.

"Stay," Vanna commanded her rook rhetorically. She reached back into the sack for her telson—the primary weapon of the Sisters of the Silo. Vanna, however, was not yet a Sister. She was still just a Child, raised under the training and tutelage of the Grand Dame.

The telson's leather-wrapped handle was long, longer even than her forearm, and the double-sided blade at its end was just bigger than her hand. At the handle's bottom was a knob that, when turned left, loosened to release the thin chain of steel connected to the blade, hidden within its handle. The Sisters were trained to kill with the telson by use of either method—like a whip with the blade at a distance or by using it as a long-handled dagger. Vanna tightened the knob and tucked it into the sheath behind her waist, at her spine. She gave Little Wing the command to stay by a note from her flute, then grabbed the ledges of the rocky cliffs and lifted herself onto the mountaintop's expansive plateau.

Gusts of wind passed under the overcast sky as Vanna found one of the three outer district paths that led to Mount Matron. The bruised clouds above lifted like a blanket as she walked closer, displaying the steeple-pointed windcatchers that stood tall to surround the city's center. There, the separating ring stood between Mount Matron's outer and inner districts. Most of the city's workers lived and transited in homes and shops nestled below the plateau's flat expanse. The outer district's buildings were carved out of the mountain, shaped by bulbous stone, resembling the nests of wormwasps. Despite some being stories tall, none rose above the level path Vanna walked along.

She kept to herself as she made her way down into the outer district, the harsh wind no longer pelting across her face. At the harvest market's shop, Vanna took a left turn and walked down a narrow alley. She avoided looking into the eyes of the few Astrians she passed, trying her best to blend in with their cold and unwelcoming demeanor. That was until she found the only brightly colored door that stood at the alley's intersection, brandished by a steaming pot painted the color of indigo under its lone window. Written above its door was a series of aruks that read *steam*, from the ancient language of Astria, varukian.

The lady with a straw broom in her hand met her at the table outside. "Anything to drink? The usual?"

"Hmm, yes, that's fine. And a peppered pastry perhaps." Vanna took a seat in one of the small wooden chairs. Crossing one leg over the other, she waited, focusing her attention on the people who traversed the opposite path.

Telling one from another was a difficult task anywhere in Mount Matron. Both men and women wore similar capes and dresses that covered their bodies like a single sleeve. Most wrapped their necks and heads with thick sashes or scarves to block the heavy and frequent winds that gusted the mountain's dust down into the city. Some wore hooded garbs or sleeved kirtles for protection past their ankles. But most clothing worn in Astria came from the same weaving house, one owned by the matrilineage of Queen Helera, which controlled the most prominent export of the Western Plane.

From face to passing face, Vanna sat watching the people walk with a discerning stare. Feeling a bump against her leg, she turned her head and noticed a hooded figure moving swiftly through the traveling crowd. Before she could catch the hooded figure's face, she saw a folded piece of parchment lying on the table next to her wrist. She took her time to open it and saw the glyphs written in ancient varukian that read:

Execute.

Over the past few moons, Vanna searched through the various enclaves of the inner and outer districts to track and collect information on a woman assigned to her by the Grand Dame. Like most Astrians, her target had long black hair, fair to pale skin, and was of medium height, making her prior tasking a challenge. Fortunately, Vanna had been given informational tips from her teaching Sisters, which detailed when and where the woman lived and worked and how she was distinguished by a freckle to the right of her eye. Vanna had gathered enough information to know where to wait for her target, who walked the same street at the same time each day through the crowds of people returning home from work in the inner district. On the first day of every quarter-moon, her target would enter the rundown building across the tea shop where Vanna sat.

Vanna didn't know who she had tracked or why, and it certainly wasn't her place to ask. The Sisters of the Silo dealt with many assignments directly from Queen Helera, most of which involved capturing and imprisoning those at Her Majesty's request. Though crime in Astria was rare, the Sisters primarily dealt with capturing those who tried to leave Mount Matron, or those who cultivated and smuggled vilova, a flower grown in the Astrian mountains that had been banned by queens long before her time. Regardless of the likelihood or cause, Vanna's interpretation was clear: her mission had changed, and her target was now to be eliminated.

"Here you are." The lady returned from the shop and placed a clay plate and cup on the table.

"Thank you."

"If you need anything else, I'll be inside." The lady walked back through the faded yellow door. Vanna lifted the fluffed, swirling pastry and divided it in half. In one smooth movement, she placed the folded parchment within its airy pocket and took a bite to swallow them both. Sipping on her smoldering hot tea, she washed down her new instruction.

There she is, as expected. Vanna sat still, as if constraining vines had sprouted from the wood of her chair to wrap around her body, following the woman's path with only her eyes. Today, however, her target did something Vanna hadn't expected—she walked past the door of the rundown building across from the tea shop and continued her stroll down the street. Vanna sprang her shoulders up and turned her head quickly to track her movements.

Where is she going? Why didn't she go in?

In a panic to follow the woman, Vanna stood up and placed two copper coins on the table, then left to cross into the half-filled path of people. The lady's head was left partially uncovered, which made her long hair distinct from the rest of the moving crowd and revealed the freckle to the right of her eye. As she walked, her target's black hair frolicked above her shoulders, bobbing up and down, then left and right, as she turned down an alley unfamiliar to Vanna, away from the flow of people.

Vanna passed timidly across the alley's opening, moving slowly enough to be certain she could sneak a solid glance. Sure enough, her target had entered through an open door to the right of the alley's bulbous corner.

Should I go in? Does she know I'm trailing her? Vanna was tempted to push ahead and follow her inside. But she knew the risk of exposure, however, was too great. As a Sister of the Silo, or even a Child of them like she still was, Vanna was taught to be as invisible as a shadow to the wind and as silent as its still whisper. And Vanna knew this was one of their many tests. The Sisters were always watching, waiting for her to fail. She needed to be alert and cautious, careful not to fall for any of their traps.

So, instead, Vanna walked along in confused hesitation, continuing down the broader street. When she felt that enough time had passed, she turned back around. Down the same bare alley, Vanna moved, this time with conviction. Through the open door she went, entering a long, dark hallway. At the far opposite end stood a set of broken stairs that led up and through the center of the building, spiraling to the top. Just enough light shone down from the center above to guide her cautious steps. The last thing Vanna needed was for her target to be warned by a creaking noise.

By the third flight, Vanna had noticed a door left open, swung halfway so the window's light trickled onto the staircase. She peered in and saw two young children, one toddling around and the other playing in the central room in front of the open doorway. Just as Vanna considered moving, her target walked into the central room to hand a blanket to the smaller child on the floor.

She must be a mother, Vanna thought to herself after ducking down. Crouched between the stairs, she waited a moment, listening for the sandal steps of the woman to leave the room. With the lady out of sight, Vanna hurried up the steps as quietly as she could, until she reached the final, fifth flight of the building. Next to the window in the ceiling was a door that opened to the roof. Vanna entered back into the striking wind and walked toward the building's edge, swinging her feet down first. She grabbed the protrusions that stuck out from the curve of the wall and crawled down.

Above the third-story window, Vanna paused her nimble feet. *This is it,* she thought to herself, trying to muster a breath of confidence. In one quick motion, she flung herself through the window's curtain and landed inside the room's kitchen.

Careful and still, she reminded herself. In front of the basin across the kitchen's room, her target stood with her back to Vanna, her shining black hair draped to her waist. Vanna slowly slid the telson out from the sheath at her back and softly crept a few steps closer. Just as Vanna lifted her telson to pounce, the woman turned around.

Her eyes.

A look of terror had pitted the lady's gray eyes open. She dropped the clay plate she once clasped, breaking the tense air into shattering shards. Vanna's instincts seized control. She plunged the blade of her telson into the woman's chest, struggling to keep her from squealing as her wide cheekbones squirmed her chin in every direction. The woman fought, her arms wailing from side to side as she gasped for life and for air. Vanna felt her heart slamming against her chest in slow, pounding beats, unsure of what would come next.

The flailing lady's arms fell weak, wilting below her limp body. *My first kill... That was too loud. I need to leave. Quickly.* But Vanna couldn't move. Her face was struck still as she stared into the lady's unflinching eyes, struggling to escape their lifeless gaze. Vanna returned the telson to its sheath and placed the body flat on the floor. She took a deep breath as she stood, closing her eyes to recall her training. But when they opened, the lady's eyes still stared back.

Gray, they once were.

Vanna ran down the stairs, hurrying to reach the alley. *Breathe. Focus,* she reminded herself. With slow steps, she entered back onto the street and did the best she could to hide her pounding heart from the rest of the walking Astrians.

Images of the two children being left alone replayed in Vanna's mind as she traveled back to the plateau's edge. With each thought, she found herself back where she'd stood, standing over the lady as her lifeless eyes stared back. Vanna could see the lady's essence trapped behind those emotions as they flashed across their glossy reflection. In her final moments of life, they told a story of terror, of misgivings and regret, of pain and then relief. But it wasn't Vanna's place to question why it had to be her—a woman who seemed to be just a mother.

Vanna gathered herself like she'd been taught and climbed down the cliff her rook was burrowed against, asleep. She blew softly into her wooden flute, her hand completely covering its shortened spout, and Little Wing awoke.

"Time to go."

Vanna changed out of her dress and back into her half-cape and hose, then climbed into the saddle of her large king bird. Blowing once more with a high-pitched sound, both of her rook's wings unfolded from its side. With each heavy flap, Little Wing lifted the mountain's dust into the air. They continued to gain altitude until Mount Matron became no more than a speck from the sky, half hidden by the haze of clouds and the setting sun. Vanna used her flute to guide Little Wing back from where they had come—the Children's Silo.

Before any of her recollected memories, Vanna knew the Silo as her home. Cold and dark, its pitted cave stretched from top to bottom, elongated by its entry hole above. It was just one of many within a series of large mountains that ranged west of Mount Matron. The Silo and its connecting tunnels were kept a secret from the Plane, hidden from all who were not Sisters or Children of the Sisters, as Vanna still was.

Blowing twice again, her rook glided down beneath the clouds until the entrance of the Silo came into sight. Vanna had learned to spot it by the distinct bushy groves and mountain trees that grew along its circular rim. But only from directly above was its gaping hole noticeable.

Little Wing lofted its wings wide to drift down into the Silo's opening. The encircling wall around Vanna turned dark. The light from above became just a glimmer, like the moon in a starless night sky. Her rook slowed as they descended to the bottom, flapping its wings just enough to brace its large talons into the dirt as they landed. Vanna debarked from the leather saddle and used a torch to guide Little Wing into one of the caged nooks embedded within the Silo's wall.

On the other side, three open tunnels were separated by lanterns hung between them. Vanna walked toward the central entrance and continued down the winding path meant for the elder Children. After a short but shallow walk, she reached its end, where an iron door stood locked.

"*Uvala,*" Vanna pronounced the varukian word clearly.

The iron handle rattled open. "There is a message awaiting you in your grot," the Sister at the door told her.

Vanna nodded, placed the torch on the hook by the inside of the door's latch, then walked up the railing-less steps that were carved against the cavern's wall. The grot where she slept was on the upper level of the Children's cavern, along a hallway left half open to the entrance room below. Vanna entered her small grot on the left and reached for the folded note on her desk. She opened it and read:

Dress proper. Mudin Spring. Half to night's mid.
Wyndulum.

Vanna lit the candle at the corner of her desk with kindling from her spark rock, then held the note over it to burn. *Did I do something wrong? Was I spotted?* she questioned. *Dress proper...maybe that isn't the case.*

Her grot had little space for anything but a single bed and a desk. Along each of the walls were a few strings where her clothing hung. She changed into the only nice dress she had—a long purple gown with a sleek bottom and even sleeker sleeves, which was laced along its seams with satin string stained the color of silver.

Above her desk and leaning against the rocky wall was a cracked mirror. Vanna stared into her reflection as she ran her black hair out and twisted it back into her usual double braids. Tying off the last strand, she moved her face closer to the mirror and turned her head to inspect the freckle on the side of her neck. Vanna brushed whatever dirt she could from her sharp cheeks and narrow chin, then walked back into the cavern's entrance room. Only two Children of Vanna's age stood near the door.

"We've been waiting for you to leave," Alice told her. "Hurry, we shouldn't be late."

"Do you know what's going on?"

"We aren't sure. But we're all wearing this dress, so maybe it isn't as bad as I first thought," Alice replied.

"We were hoping you knew. We both had the note," Elaine added.

"Hmm, I came to the same conclusion," Vanna said, joining them near the door.

"I guess Veronica and Norrel didn't get one," Elaine pointed out. Unlike Alice and Vanna, Elaine was short and strong-bodied with wide hips and a flattened nose. Alice had often assumed that Elaine was jealous of her and Vanna's kinship, as the two had grown the closest among all the Children in their age group. "I get the two of you getting one, *but me?*"

"Don't sell yourself so short," Vanna told her with confidence, trying to make it sound like she believed the words herself.

"I'm just surprised, is all."

"*Me too,*" Alice whispered so only Vanna could hear her.

"Should we go, then?"

With a stern look, the Sister held the door open and instructed the three of them to Mudin Spring. Vanna held the torch and led them out of the winding path. At the Silo's bottom, they turned left and walked through the right of the three tunnels—one Vanna had never been through before. It was longer than the one that led to the Children's cavern, or even the tunnels of the Silos she'd trained and studied in. With turns left and right throughout its length, its surrounding sides shrank into a narrow arch the farther they went. When they reached the door at the end, Vanna stated aloud, "*Wyndulum.*"

The door to Mudin Spring opened, and the three of them entered cautiously. Tall walls with jagged-edged crystals protruding down from the ceiling hung high above a central walkway. Along each of its sides were pools of spring water that were clear to the bottom. From the crystals above and below it, spectrums of purple, pink, and green shone bright enough to light the beautiful cave's path as they walked in a straight line toward its far end. The narrow walkway led to a raised platform mounted in front of a glowing waterfall. Men in hooded black capes that draped to the floor stood along each side of the path, aligned with candles between them, as they chanted deep, wordless hymns that echoed throughout the cave.

Vanna saw two women standing on the platform. Between them was a table where incense, with smoke flowing from its rims, burned in a large chalice. Vanna walked to the left, Elaine to the center, and Alice to the right.

"Bow before your Queen," the Grand Dame spoke above the chanting melody, to which the three of them obeyed.

The Queen of Astria? Here? For us?

"Congratulations to each of you. It is no small feat to make it this far as Children of the Silo," Queen Helera stated from the opposite end of the table.

Vanna peeked up to look at her Queen in awe. She wore a tight, purple dress that hung down to her ankles, with gemstones sewn along its front spine. At her pale chest hung a necklace—a large pearl sliced in half. The Queen's hair was black and perfectly straight, split at the center of her scalp like curtains opening to reveal the sharp contours of her face. In her hand was the Skybow; its curving brims of amethyst-azilian stretched the length of her legs.

"The Grand Dame tells me your group began with twelve Children. You three should all be proud to make it to this day."

Queen Helera turned to the Grand Dame and nodded. The leader of the Sisters then grabbed the golden handles of the chalice and carried it in front of her. The Queen snapped at her necklace and dropped it in. Dense pillows of smoke lifted from the chalice as the Grand Dame placed it back onto the table. Vanna caught a whiff of the burning incense, which made her legs begin to feel weak and nimble. With it, though, came a sense of calmness that floated her head high above her thoughts.

"*Kneel*," the Grand Dame commanded, to which the three of them again obeyed.

The head of the Sisters was a strong and muscular lady who had a single looped braid behind her fierce and brawny face. She picked up a small cup, which looked as if it were made from an overturned skull with the bones of a spine as its stem, scooped it into the chalice, and then walked over to Alice, at the right, first. She dipped her thumb into the cup and smeared the oil across Alice's forehead. She lowered it and did the same to her lips. The Grand Dame moved in front of Elaine to repeat the ritual before she finally stood in front of Vanna.

Don't flinch.

The Grand Dame lowered the cup and dipped her thumb into the hot oil, smearing it across Vanna's forehead. After slithering it like a snake, she wiped her thumb across Vanna's lips. At that moment, everything had changed. The smell from the oil had gone from floral spices to that of rotten death—the colors from the crystals that surrounded her began to blur her vision. Vanna's body had become frigid and stiff. She closed her eyes, trying to focus.

A vivid image flashed in Vanna's mind. She saw a faceless girl surrounded by darkness, alone. Figures smothered by shadows emerged from the ground, slowly stepping toward her. Vanna saw the worry on the girl's face as it spun in circles, looking for an escape. But the girl couldn't move. Her feet were planted in the darkness. One by one, the figures approached, stabbing the girl's body repeatedly. In Vanna's mind, she tried to scream, telling the girl to run. But no sound came. The figures ceased their stabbing, and the girl breached the madness, rising above them like a child saved from drowning. But as Vanna watched on, the girl's face slowly became revealed. It was her own, crying out for help.

With the shadowed blades in their hands, the figures turned Vanna's way.

No…no.

Each of their eyes was a piercing gray orb, mimicking the dying gaze of the woman she had killed. Vanna's fear soared as the figures began walking toward her. She tried to move and run, but her feet were as still as the girl's, rooted in the darkness. One by one, the figures lifted their shadowed blades and struck them down—the pain from each stab suffocating her to death.

Vanna's eyes struck open, though she couldn't move.

The waterfall poured behind the raised platform as the Grand Dame returned the oil from the cup back into the chalice. When she turned to face the three Children, Vanna's vision had cleared, and the putrid smell had vanished. She felt an eerie sense lift from her body, slowly bringing her back to where she knelt. What Vanna saw, she couldn't fully remember. But what she had felt remained.

Death.

"All three of you were selected from birth and trained with a set of skills unmatched anywhere across the Plane. Earlier today, you each completed a special task. A task that has broken the only bond of your past. You have each ended the thread of life that connected you to your birth mother. Now, four solurns past your bloom into women, you have each been anointed with the secretion of the first mother—Mother Moon, the sacred egg that bore all life to the Plane, under the witness of the First Sisters that soar in the sky beside her. By this oil, you shall commit yourselves again to the vows you once made as Children—one to your new mother, the Queen of Astria. Each of you shall be born anew in duty to her service. It will now be your life's honor to rise from Children and stand as Sisters of the Silo."

Queen Helera stared intently at each of them. "*May you fly among the stars that never rest.*"

Vanna lifted her head and stood as a Sister. Inside, though, her mind echoed like the chanting walls of Mudin Spring with a harrowing thought: *They were my own eyes. I murdered my own mother.*

CHAPTER 4

STONE

"Your patterns are off," Roth said to Ludwyn across the rattling table. "*You wish.* You haven't beaten me once today."

"It's this damned box-cart carriage. You'd think that with all the people coming to watch this fight, they'd at least fix these craters in the roads."

From the bench seat beside Roth, his twin sister, Ruth, looked up from her leather-bound book to ask, "What did you expect?"

"It took a couple of solurns of savings for us to make this trip… I'd expect to ride a little more smoothly than we are over these lumps of dirt," Roth replied. "It's not like Bovere doesn't have the gold for it."

"These roads aren't Bovere's to fix," Ruth told him.

On their diamond-shaped board, Ludwyn moved one of his three white pieces wide, turned the gold stone around, and then slung it into Roth's corner. With a proud smile, he reached across the table within the carriage and clapped his hands in front of Roth's face. "It's just an excuse, Ruth. He knows it."

"We're playing again."

"Do the two of you have to keep playing?" Ruth asked. "If either of you took a moment away from your stupid game, you would have seen that we've already passed Lake Gileed. We're almost there."

"When the coachman up front stops his horse, we'll stop playing," Roth replied without paying his sister much attention.

"I don't know, Roth," Ludwyn said with a chuckle. "She has a point. Just because we keep playing doesn't mean you'll ever win."

"Nonsense. I've taken six games off you so far. And she's the one who hasn't looked up from that book this entire ride," Roth grumbled back.

"And I've won nearly twenty," Ludwyn refuted.

36

"Unlike the two of you, I didn't come to Bovere to watch the bondfight. I—"

"Came to see the Cathedral," Roth finished her sentence with a mocking sigh. "Trust me, I know."

"Well, then, some peace and quiet would be nice so I could finish my chapter." Ruth brushed her brother off as she turned a page of her book, *Emanations*. She flicked her long, chestnut-colored hair back over her left shoulder to block his view.

"You do know that the Cathedral doesn't let women become divine sages, right?"

"There are ways women can serve the Cathedral of the Divine One, *Roth*. Some of the greatest honorary knights the Regent has ever had were women. And many of us help in their sceptories, as mother and I do every other moon in Prestown."

"Sure. But you'd need to be smart and have the pockets to become one of those," Roth replied, pestering her growing irritation.

"Why do you think I read so many books?"

"*You're still missing the wealthy part*," he said under his breath, cautious not to push her further. "Fine. I'll stop playing Cornerstones and give you some peace if you come out to grab a few drinks with us when we get to Bovere."

"*No*," she replied sternly.

"Oh, come on. Loosen up. Back home, you'd spend all day inside. Even when you're at work in the mill, your head is in those books while I'm out in the woods. Have some fun for once," Roth insisted. She looked up from the bench seat and stared out of the carriage's open window as if she were contemplating what to say. "Come on, Ruth. It's our first time in Bovere. We're finally grown. Let's have some fun!"

"*Fine*. Just so you'll stop annoying me, I'll go."

Roth glanced at his best friend, Ludwyn, who mimicked his smile.

Ruth turned back to them both, her broader forehead and thin lips straining to withhold what it seemed she really wanted to say. "But not a word more until we get there."

"Deal," they both said.

"*And* I get to pick the tavern."

Roth ruffled his short, messy brown hair. "You? Pick the tavern? No way."

"Roth, just let her have it. We'll be in Bovere for a few nights. We can go where we want after the bondfight. And we'll catch the horse races after," Ludwyn said.

Having grown up together in the small town of Tergona, near the Northwoods, which covered most of the Regent's northern coast, Ludwyn had always tried to act as the mediator between the two twins. He was a ranger, like Roth, and the two had spent nearly every day together out in the woods, protecting the lumber mill's forestry from competitors, the lumbermen from dangerous wildlife, and catching any criminal hide hunters. But even then, Roth had always known Ludwyn was partial to Ruth, despite his insisting that she was like a sister he never had.

"*Okay...*fine. I could use a good drink or a few, anyway, regardless of where we'll be." Roth placed the seven black, white, and gold-painted stones into a small leather sack, then folded his thin wooden board in half and tucked it away. Opening the curtain of his window, he looked out at the fields of tall grass that sloped with the hills across the open meadow. The three of them rode in silence for the rest of the duration into Bovere. Occasionally, Roth had turned to his twin sister to ensure she was still reading.

"*Look!*" Roth shouted, elbowing Ruth in her side. "You can see the three spires of the Cathedral."

Just over the grassy hill was the expansive city of Bovere, the metropole of the Regent and most populated of any in the Plane. In front of the extent where the city's tall timber buildings began, tents of white and shale were erected to encircle the fields around it. Wind pelted through the window onto Roth's face, though it didn't curtail his strong-jawed gleam of excitement. After more than a half-moon's journey from Tergona, the three of them had finally arrived.

"We could stop here if that's okay with you two," Roth said as he pulled his bouldering shoulders back inside the carriage.

"We aren't even inside the city yet," his sister said.

"Yeah, but look at how much fun they are all having out here. I'd be happy to stop." Along each side of the dirt road were masses of people drinking and dancing to the sound of drums and stringed music being played under the shade of their tents. One man, drunken with delight, stumbled his way to follow their carriage, handing Roth and Ludwyn mugs filled with burnt-stout. "*See.*"

Roth turned to Ruth and watched her shut the curtains of her window, shoving her face back into her book. "We aren't there yet," she said, her face forming a stern frown.

Roth drank the burly foam and continued to watch the people of the Regent party. Their carriage soon traveled along the loud cobblestone roads of Bovere. From canton to canton they went, inspecting the signs that marked the division of land ownership from one block of buildings and roads to another. Most homes, taverns, and markets were closely knit, side by side, and framed with timber or clay walls topped by thatched roofs. Others of more prominence were tall remnants, or mimics even, from the Age of Knights—square holds and wide keeps built of mortared stone that stood tall within the center of the cantons.

Even Ruth had reopened her window's curtain to take in the historic ambiance of Bovere. In the cool breeze of the busy streets, most people Roth saw, men and women alike, wore green or brown trousers and longer skirts, with thin white garments laced loosely around their tops. The wealthier Boverian men dressed in clean-cut tunics and leather-buttoned vests fit with top hats cushioned like a pillow. And the affluent women wore gowns with tight girdles embroidered with the finest tapestry and broad caps that shaded their often-exposed shoulders.

As their carriage slowed to a stop, Roth struggled to squeeze his large frame out of the wooden door. Ruth paid the coachmen the rest of their fee in copper and silver coins while Roth and Ludwyn grabbed their belongings from the back. He glanced down at his own rumpled outfit before brushing off his thick-soled boots and dirty black trousers. Roth wore what he always had, his clover-colored shawl of dense wool—the garment of a ranger. He was proud of where he came from, regardless of whether he stood out from the more cultured Boverians.

"This is it—the Motley Inn," she stated proudly.

"Looks fancy to me," Ludwyn commented. The inn's outer walls were weathered white, and its windowsills had soiled beds of yellow and green flowers mounted at their bottoms.

"I'm just surprised at how short they all are," Roth snorted with a laugh, looking left and right down each side of the busy cobblestone road. As they walked toward the two-storied inn's door, Roth couldn't help but notice that he, Ruth, and even Ludwyn towered more than a head's length above all the people strolling by.

"And I'm surprised by how loud this place is," Ludwyn noted as another carriage rolled past them.

Roth listened to the horse's hooves as it trotted across the stone. "We certainly aren't in the Northwoods anymore."

Before they entered the inn, Ruth pointed to the three tall spires of the Cathedral, just above the roofs ahead. "We're still a few cantons away from Bovere's central plaza, where the Cathedral is. The pit and horse track are down the creek that follows it—near the far end of this street to the right. So, if either of you gets lost, this is where we'll be. Be sure you remember it."

Ludwyn nodded along with Roth, who moved to shake his head in an annoyed fashion. "How do you know all of this when none of us have ever been?" Ludwyn asked.

"Must have been in one of those books." Roth chuckled.

Without commenting on their mockery, she led the two of them inside and got them checked into the rooms of the lodge they split. Roth and Ludwyn quickly stuffed most of their belongings away, then headed down to the bar below to refill their mugs. There, they drank and waited for Ruth to ready herself and join them. Four fills later, she finally walked down the dimly lit staircase, dressed in a long skirt the color of a fern and a white shirt patterned with daisies at its collar.

"Looks like someone came prepared to fit in," Ludwyn commented.

Roth laughed to himself as she walked closer. "I expected nothing less."

"Are you two ready?" Ruth asked, fidgeting with her long hair that she had brushed smooth.

"We've been ready for a half-moon now."

"Not the usual plaid… You look really nice," Ludwyn told her.

"*Oh*, hush," Roth said, shoving his elbow into Ludwyn's side. They followed her out of the inn, then took a left down the cobblestone road until they reached one of Bovere's many creeks that ran throughout the city. "Where are we going?"

"The Applewood Tavern," she answered bluntly without turning around. "It's one of the oldest in Bovere, in the Appleston Canton, east of the plaza."

"Sounds exciting," Roth replied sarcastically.

"I wouldn't expect too much," she turned to say. "It certainly won't be as rowdy as the taverns or parties in Bovere's outer cantons."

"*Great.*"

"But your stout will still be there."

"And the women?" Roth asked with incipient interest.

"That, I can't promise you. The Appleston Canton is known for its history and wealth. I'd expect most of the women there to be older or already married away," Ruth replied. After a long walk under lantern light, Ruth stopped and pointed across the short arches of a stone bridge. "There it is."

Roth turned to Ludwyn and complained, "Our first time in Bovere, and we're going to a dusty relic."

Ruth led the two of them across the small creek toward the tavern. It was wider than it was tall and framed by broad, square-cut timber beams. Stained-glass windows of red apples and their accompanying trees were displayed along its facade. Roth looked over at his twin sister and saw her round face gleaming with a bright smile as soon as she opened the doors and walked in. Its shallow ceiling was dimly lit by oil lanterns that hung in the room's corners and along its broad columns of support. Round wooden tables were scattered along the slick and shiny floor, most of which, to Ruth's earlier confirmation, were filled with finely dressed old men and women carrying on quiet chatter among themselves.

"Well, Ruth, you weren't wrong."

"You said I could pick, so I did."

"There," Ludwyn said, pointing toward the bar. "An open table. I'll grab the stouts."

"Lud, can you grab me one too?" Ruth asked. Ludwyn broke a faint smile of surprise at Roth, who followed her toward the table, gazing at the illustrious paintings that clustered to decorate the tavern's walls.

"It is pretty," Roth admitted when he took his seat at the table.

"History, when preserved, tends to be. That one there," Ruth said, pausing to point at the painting behind his shoulder. "Is a Ferdinand Elaire, a master at his craft. He had a cabin by Lake Gileed that he loved to sit by and paint. And that one, there, is a Dravinican. Thomas Dravin made mountains of gold from his old portraits of the royal families back during the Age of Knights," she added, pointing back by the door.

"They are beautiful," Roth admitted again after turning to scan the rest of the paintings. Ludwyn returned from the bar with fists full of burnt-stout, handing them two mugs each.

"The keeper was a nice fella," he said. "Don't think he pours much of these here, though."

"No. No, he doesn't." Ruth giggled and took a sip. "You two brought your board, didn't you?" With a look as if they'd been caught, Roth nodded, then reached for the straps of his small satchel. "Care if I play?" she asked. "It's been a while, so you may need to reteach me how."

Roth laid the board out with a glad smile and turned the colored corners to face them. "White or black?"

"White."

"Here." He handed her three smooth pebble stones painted white. "Set them up in a flat line like mine to protect your corner. The gold stone goes in the middle. With each turn, you can move one of your three stones along the gridlines to each connecting point. When one of your white pieces has possession of the gold stone, you can spin it in all four directions along the lines. But you only get one pass or one sling at a corner score per turn after moving. Play first to five corners?"

"So, protect my corner and shoot into yours?"

"Yes. And if you steal the gold stone, you get back-to-back turns. Corner scores reset to the center, and the losing player moves first."

Ruth took a heavy sip of her burnt-stout. With a mustache of pale foam, she said, "*I'm ready.*"

Late into the night, Ruth played Roth and Ludwyn game after game, growing in skill and confidence until she began to beat them both handily. As competitive as Roth was, he was happy that Ruth was out drinking with him and Ludwyn, regardless of who won. It was a side of his sister he rarely saw. A few times, even, the keeper at the tavern's bar had to come to their table to remind them that they needed to quiet their voices down, or they'd be asked to leave.

They spent the night sharing drunken laughs until Roth felt a hand touch his shoulder from a figure hidden behind his back. At first, he thought it might have been the bar's keeper again. But instead, a deep and drunken voice snarled, "*Cornerstones?*"

The man moved to Roth's right and leaned against the open chair at their table. He was stocky but short and wore a padded vest under a green tabard. At the center of his chest was the stitched pattern of a silver pine tree. And on the left side of his belted waist, Roth noticed a sheathed longsword. *A sentinel,* he recognized, this time without needing Ruth's explanation. "Yes."

The thick-browed, beardless man ignored Roth's answer and kept his stare on Ruth. "Care if I play?"

"We're in the middle of a game," Roth said, half annoyed.

"I haven't played Cornerstones since I was going through my commissioning back in Florington," the sentinel said proudly. With his gaze unwavering from Roth's sister, he asked, "May I get you something to drink?"

"No, I'm okay," Ruth answered without looking up at him.

"Not even a fine wine? My friends and I are sitting on the opposite end of the tavern over there," the sentinel said, pointing to a group of men dressed like him. "We drink only the best, imported straight from the harbors of Sazara."

"No, thank you."

The older sentinel drifted around the circular table until he stood behind Ruth. He lifted his hand and rested it on her shoulder. "You don't know what you're missing."

"You can go now. She isn't interested," Roth told him when it seemed like he was about to reach for her hair.

The older sentinel locked his eyes on Roth's; his smile flattened sharply into a drunken smirk. He pulled his hand away and rested it on his sword's pommel, the blade sheathed at his waist. "*And you are?*"

"Roth Fendorse. This is my sister. She doesn't like you, and neither do I," he said, his fists clenched under the table.

"Which slum did they drag you here from, *Roth Fendorse?*"

"The Northwoods."

"Ah, that explains it. Being from the Northwoods, I find it hard to believe this beautiful young girl knows yet what she likes."

Roth glanced at Ludwyn and Ruth, who both looked unsettled. "I think she does. You should leave."

The sentinel reached for the pouch at his waist, then tossed a handful of copper coins onto the table in front of Roth. "Grab a few drinks from the keeper for the two of us. Sacrimian wine will do."

Drunken and angered, Roth grabbed the coins and stood up to face the bar. He took a deep breath, then swung his broad shoulders around to stare the older sentinel down. In the man's eyes, Roth saw a glimmer of fear as if he hadn't expected to be dwarfed in height by a boy from the Northwoods.

In the snap of a moment, Roth sidestepped the table and threw his right elbow back, slinging his coin-grasped fist straight into the sentinel's jaw. Teeth flew through the air as the man's head lurched backward. His shoulders bobbed from side to side as he stumbled to catch his footing. With blood dripping from his mouth, the sentinel unsheathed the longsword from his waist. Roth heard the sound of the wooden chairs scraping against the planked floor as the finely dressed people around them scattered.

"Scared to fight fair now, are we?"

"*You woodrat*," the sentinel gnarled.

Without hesitation, Roth lunged toward him. He closed the distance before the sentinel could breach his longsword back far enough to swing. Punch after punch, he pounded his tight fists into the man's face and stomach. Roth continued to swing with all his might until the man dropped his sword and stumbled back, falling flat onto the ground. Roth jumped on top of him and resumed his thrashing. Fist after fist, he threw his knuckles into the man's blood-gushing face. Roth could feel the crowd of people circling to smother them, screaming for him to stop.

Ludwyn and two other men did all they could to drag Roth off the unconscious man. His hands were bloodied red, and his sight blurred. Roth stepped away slowly, realizing what he'd done. He dropped to his knees in a moment of regret and looked up at Ruth and Ludwyn, who themselves looked too panicked to know what to say or do. *It all happened so fast. The courts will have me*, he thought, staring at the puddle of blood. *All the cantons in Bovere will have me banned.*

The loud yells of worry around him soured to silence as the people began to disperse. Sentinels, dressed similarly to the man he had knocked unconscious, came over to herd the finely dressed patrons of the Applewood Tavern away from the scene on the floor. Three others drew their swords and kept their tips pointed down at Roth, constraining him to his knees. Moments passed for what felt like an eternity before Roth heard a lady's croaky voice shout near the door, "*What happened to Kean? Who did this?*"

A plump lady with round cheeks, coated heavily with rosy makeup, walked between the splitting crowd. Her dark, curled hair was pinned up in a poof like a nest of birchbees, and she wore a pine-green dress with long ruffles from her wide hips down. She covered her gasping mouth as soon as she saw the bloodied sentinel lying on the floor.

"I did," Roth admitted, looking up with a face full of guilt.

"Who are you?" the finely dressed lady asked.

"Roth Fendorse."

"I will have you charged for this in the highest of courts. Where do you work?" From her side, she motioned for a few sentinels to help the older man named Kean up off the ground. Roth watched them start to render aid as they dragged his limp body toward the tavern's corner.

At her opposite side was an even plumper man who stood no taller than Ruth's waist. He was balding and wore round spectacles wedged into the crest of his mushroomed nose. Before Roth could even answer, the short man stood on his toes and whispered into the woman's ear. Her face turned from anger to dismay as she widened her eyes up at the ceiling in desperate thought.

"I work in the Northwoods as a ranger," he said.

"Which canton?" she snapped to ask.

"Tergona."

"And you said you're a ranger? Which millhouse?"

"Multiple. Whichever one in the Northwoods needs my work at the time," he answered, then nodded to Ruth. "My sister is a bookkeeper for one of the Lomberg's millhouses."

The lady turned to Ruth, who stood beside Roth, trying to console him. "Do you realize what he's done? Do you know who I am?"

Ruth looked too scared to answer. "Yes," his twin sister uttered, nodding to the tiny pin of a silver pine she wore on the collar of her dress. "You are Lady Orean Lomberg, heiress to the Lomberg family and owner of its blockshared mills."

"*Correct.* And that means what, exactly?"

"That must mean the man my brother just knocked out worked for you as a sentinel."

"Not just my sentinel—my *bondsman*," Lady Lomberg looked down at Roth to say. "The first time in eighty solurns that my family had a bondsman make it to the final fight, and this happens. *Unbelievable.*"

That man was supposed to fight in the pit tomorrow? Roth questioned himself in disbelief.

Lady Lomberg glanced back and forth at the twins. "Now that you mention it, the two of you do look alike. Only, she seems to be a bushel of gold's worth smarter than you."

"She is," Ludwyn butted in out of nowhere.

Without acknowledging the comment, Lady Lomberg turned to her assistant as if to ask for advice. After a moment of whispering, she sent for more sentinels and ordered that they usher Roth away.

"*Wait,*" he pleaded, his eyes shifting in worry. "Instead of charging me with this crime in court, allow me to repay my debt to you directly. In a way, I already work for you. *Please.*" Roth clenched his hands together and shook them in front of his chest. The last thing he wanted was to face the courts of Bovere.

Caught aback, Lady Lomberg croaked a mocking laugh. "And how will you, *a ranger*, possibly be able to pay me back? Do you know how much tossing this fight will cost me? Where, in the Plane, would *you* be able to find the gold to repay *me?*"

Roth sulked his chin low in thought, looking down at the wood of the floor from where he knelt. He knew he didn't have the gold to repay the Lady, or even the gold to survive the courts. He and his family were poor. But what Roth knew he did have was grit—unlike the pampered people here in Bovere. And so, he said, "Allow me to fight for you tomorrow in the pit. I will be your bondsman."

Laughs erupted from the Lady and the sentinels that surrounded her. With a steadfast face, Roth stood up from his knees. The Lady's black eyes grew still and widened as soon as she witnessed how tall he towered above her and all her sentinels. After a long pause to gulp down her pride, Lady Lomberg asked, "What is your experience, then, Roth the Ranger?"

Roth looked over at the bloodied body in the corner of the room. He thought hard about telling her the truth—that he had no combat training with a sword like all her sentinels had. He'd never even held one before. All he ever needed in the Northwoods was his axe. And though he enjoyed fighting and tussling in waged matches with those scruffy men of the mills, who did their best to mimic the fights of a pit, those were very different.

No man of the northern cantons had the wealth to afford weapons or armor. Their fights were all fist-to-fist and done under the cover of night, hidden away from any spectacle. He was the best his side of the woods had to offer. But just that. The final pit fight in Bovere would be a contest of unimaginable proportion.

But Roth knew that if he faltered on his courage now, his future would be over. With all these witnesses here to see it, he'd broken the most important covenant of the Regent—the prohibition of violent instigation and provocation. Locking his eyes to Lady Lomberg's own, he swallowed loudly and said with confidence, "I've never lost a fight in my life. Look at what I did to your best sentinel. I could do the same to them all."

Lady Orean Lomberg glanced over at the Applewood Tavern's dimly lit corner, toward the bloodied and half-unconscious man, before returning her gaze up to Roth. Her face smirked as if she had no other choice but to become convinced. "Roth Fendorse, so be it. You will stand in for Kean and be my bondsman for the Regent's final pit fight tomorrow. Win this for me, and you will represent the Eastern Plane at the Isle of Azil."

Roth smiled broadly from ear to ear.

"Fail to win, and I will take you to court," she added with a croaking sneer. "Be at the spiraling tent west of the pit at sunrise. You'll know it by the Silver Pine. My assistant Frand will take care of your needs."

Roth gasped for relief, though none came. "Thank you."

CHAPTER 5

SUN

"*Why me? Why'd you do it?*" Cleo stood before his father, questioning him within the Consolate Chamber the morning after his celebratory dinner. "You heard what they were saying."

"Most of it was true, was it not?" Sepatus asked from behind the marble desk of his workstead. "Besides, their gossip and criticisms were a cause of my actions, not yours. They can be upset about it all they want, but it won't change my decision."

"But I'm just a cagerman, Father. *Surely*, you have time to reconsider. And of all the brigades, you chose the Sixth," Cleo rattled off quickly, trying to distract Sepatus from the stacks of scribbled-on parchment littering his desk. His father reached into a drawer and pulled out a small, folded letter. Behind him, he grabbed the Sunspear, lifted it slightly, and then peered at the silver bowl on the corner of his desk, watching a flame ignite below it.

"Actually, I don't. And you're not a cagerman anymore. The Sixth Brigade is renowned across the Plane for its skill, yes. But it's also the only rotary brigade of the Guard. And it falls under my jurisdiction alone, not dictated by some entangling magistrate and the needs of their partition." His father reached for the sealing stamp, dipped it into the small silver bowl, and then indented the melted red wax onto the fold of the letter. "Here are your orders. Give them to the Sixth's clerk when you reach Fort Rastrum."

Unbelievable. Cleo grabbed the folded parchment and glanced at the royal red wax seal embolded by crossed swords. Encircling it was a shield shaped like the sun. By the time he looked up, his father had returned to writing with his quill in hand. "Can you at least answer my question?"

Sepatus sighed as he lowered the feather and rubbed the shadows under his eyes. "I need commanders I can trust. And you have the capability to be a fine leader for Sacrim. You weren't just any cagerman, Cleo. Kladden was one of the finest commanders in the Guard during his day, and you've trained under him for more than half a decade. And I've done my best to teach you all I know."

Cleo's thoughts sprang to refute his father's words. *By spending all your time here in the chamber or traveling to the other brigades?*

"Worrying won't change this. When Clyus stepped down from his position as Consolar Vizar, he nominated his son. That Calegri boy had the support of everyone in the chamber. This should be no different."

"But there is a difference. You're still the general. And Cayen was voted in by the chambermen. Where was my vote?"

"A vote? Cleo, you've been in Sazara long enough to know better."

Cleo looked away from his father's stern stare.

"Don't be so naive." Sepatus bent his neck to peer out of the open door to his workstead. He took a deep breath and reset the collar of his white undergarment. "Only a fool would believe Clyus had stepped down from anything. The pockets of those magistrates and chambermen are deep because of him."

Cleo knew his father was right. The Temple of Sciron had five shrines in Sacrim, one in each partition, which held and distributed the gold, silver, and copper coins for most people throughout the Southern Plane. But if there was any man who had more influence than those deacons on the temple and its wealth, it would be Clyus Calegri.

"If it makes you feel any better, I'm conscripting Kladden into the Guard's service again. He will serve as your commandant and will travel with you to Fort Rastrum. Also, now that you're one of the six commanders in the Guard, you're required to be at the Isle of Azil for the Descindation. It's in a little more than a moon's time, so you'll do well to get settled at the fort quickly, then make your way north."

Cleo breathed a sigh of relief, knowing that Kladden would be there alongside him to rely on. "*Understood.*" He placed the open palm of his right hand on his heart. Sepatus did the same. Cleo quickly struck his hand down to his side to return the Guard's peace-time salute to a superior officer.

Just as Cleo turned sharply to leave his father's workstead, Sepatus said, "Wait...*Commander Scordisci*, you might need this." His father stood up and unlatched his belt, slid his sheath off, and held it out over his desk.

The sword. Cleo's broad face sparked into a smile; his eyes became drawn to its shiny, black pearl pommel.

"This has been in our family for quite a few generations. I've made my own alterations to it over the solurns, but now, it should be yours. Not that I've had much use for it lately." With a smile that mirrored Cleo's own, he lifted the Sunspear and nodded wittingly toward it.

The fraying gray around Cleo's green eyes widened as he took the shortsword by its leather-wrapped hilt, unsheathed it, and then pointed its thin-sloped tip to the tall ceiling. Twirling its edge, he admired the silver shimmer that reflected from its recessed fuller down to its short and rounded guard, past the hilt, and onto its pommel. Again, he stared into the shiny black pearl fastened to the bottom handle of the sword, one just smaller than his fist. "This is all…just too nice, Father. Thank you."

"The blade may still be a tad longer than your spine's length, but you'll grow into it. Just be sure you put it to good use. And *remember*, the swing of a commander carries a heavy burden."

"*Understood,*" Cleo said again, this time with a beaming grin. He sheathed his new shortsword and laced it through his belt. "Thank you again, Father."

"Next time I see you will be at the isle. Be good, Cleo."

"Same to you, *General.*" Cleo shook his father's hand with a grip around each other's wrists before turning sharply to depart.

The smell of incense dissipated throughout the Consolate Chamber as Cleo shuffled down the marble stairs and exited through the tall double doors. From under its overhanging pediment, he took a left and found his horse, which he had tied to the stable's post at the corner of the square. "*Good Dahlia,*" he whispered to it while mounting the saddle of his stallion.

Through the streets of Sazara, he went, his left hand gripped firmly to the hilt of his new sword. Cleo navigated his way through the sharp turns and side streets of the mangled alleys before he finally broke past the dense buildings of limestone and red granite. He breathed a sigh of fresh air and drove Dahlia into full stride up the hill's winding path.

The outskirts between the city and Sazara's wall were where most of the wealthy lived. Some villas were granted by Sacrim's chamber, while others were paid for by personal gold. But most, in private, at least, referred to the expansive plot of villas as a refuge away from the depravity of Sazara's streets. The general's villa stood three stories tall in the middle of the sloping hill overlooking the harbor. Like the others nearby, it was erected with clay bricks of varying shades and had an expanse of thin-leaved olive trees around its exterior. The courtyard in the villa's rear contained a rare patch of grass, which, to Cleo, always looked more like a field of stray hay.

Cleo rode to the stable behind the courtyard, connected by an arched portico. He dismounted Dahlia, led his horse to its stall, and then moved under the shade to walk inside. "Where do you think you're going?" a familiar voice shouted to ask from the portico's far end.

"*Kladden!* Man, am I glad to see you." Cleo rushed over to shake his wrist. "I could have used you there last night. It was brutal."

"So I heard. I do what I can to avoid those things."

Cleo broke their long shake with a short laugh. "Now I see why."

"I don't know how your father does it. Or why, for that matter. He's always been special in that way." Kladden turned Cleo around and began walking him back toward the stable. "I had the maids pack you a mule. We've got a full day's ride ahead of us, so check to make sure it's all there."

Leaving already, Cleo thought to himself as he rummaged through the packs. "What's this?" He took out and lifted a long royal-red silken cloak.

"My old commander's cloak. I had Eileen cut it down this morning, so hopefully, it won't be too long. Throw it on, will ya."

Cleo wrapped the cloak around his neck and pinned its corners to the strap of his bronze vest, under the golden insignia of Sacrim at his shoulder. Stretching his arms wide, he flared out its bottom, which hung below the leather spades of his skirt. "This is great, Kladden…it fits perfectly. Thank you."

"Looks better on you than it did on me," Kladden said. "Actually, you look more like your father did when he first became commander of the Fourth Brigade. I still remember that day. I was his young commandant, then. And I'll never forget the pride on that bastard's face. Little did the other guardsmen know, he was trembling beneath his spades. I'd never seen him so nervous. And he was much older than you are now," Kladden rambled on, unsuspecting of Cleo's sensitivity to the situation. "Man, that cloak…just brings it all back."

"You sure it isn't this?" Cleo asked, flashing the pearly black pommel of the new sword at his waist.

"Even got his sword too. Well, aren't the two of you just twins? If only you could hang that big pearl from between your legs, you might finally catch yourself a woman like he did," Kladden said, laughing before he could finish his sentence.

"Sounds like something only an ugly brute like yourself would need to do."

"Think you can just say whatever you want now that you've got that pretty sword? I'm the one with a wife." Kladden's laugh drifted. "And I've managed to keep her around."

Cleo gave Kladden a soft shove on his shoulder, thinking of his mother. "But, if there was one good thing that came out of last night, it's this."

"So you might think. It's one thing to wear a pretty sword. It's another to use it." Kladden pulled his horse and mule out from the stable and tied the two together. "By the rays of the Benevolent Sun, have you got a ways to go before you can keep up with me. And I'm only getting younger. Speaking of which." He nodded toward the back door of the villa.

"*You weren't going to tell me goodbye?*" Clara shouted at them.

Cleo turned and saw his sister walking their way. "I tried to tell you this morning, but you were asleep. Blame the wine from last night, not me."

"Fair enough," she said, still dressed in her silken morning robe. Clara walked over and gave him a passive hug. Her auburn hair was knotted in conjoined loops, and the powder on her face was still smeared from her eyebrows down.

Cleo took another look at her, scanning her from head to toe. "No, really, *blame the wine.*"

"Oh, hush. Last night was all a blur. If Sazara's good for anything, it's a party. But at least one of us had fun."

"I can tell," Kladden butted in to say with a deep laugh.

"Congratulations, by the way," Clara told him, ignoring the comment from their father's closest friend.

Cleo could see her eyes screaming with jealousy. "Thank you."

"Well, you two should be off." His older sister finally turned to the stocky man, who was much taller than them both. She reached out to pat him on his exposed shoulder. "Kladden, take care of him, just like you always have."

"*Always*," Kladden replied, bowing his head politely to her before mounting the saddle of his gray stallion. For as old as he was, Kladden had always kept himself in the most martial of sculpted states. He was nimble but strong, as anyone could tell by counting the number of veins protruding from his legs and arms.

Cleo accompanied his new commandant, tying his mule to Dahlia, and then mounting the saddle. He waved one last time to Clara as she walked back to the villa. The two of them rode off up the dirt path. The dead grass below their horses' hooves crunched like summer beetles as they trotted slowly toward the wall that surrounded Sazara. From the First Brigade's central fort, which stood at its southernmost point, the curving wall's limestone bricks stood three stories tall and connected to each end of the harbor's breakwaters. At its top was a patrol path protected by battlements, which led from the fort to Sazara's eastern and western gates.

"The central gate should be open. At least, it usually is. Let's see if they recognize your new cloak," Kladden told him as they rode toward the First Brigade's fort. On both sides of its tall iron gate were two large towers mimicking the shape of the harbor's lighthouses. Guardsmen scattered above and below the wall's path, dressed in bronze armor, padded vests, and spaded skirts. A few of them scurried down to each side of its arched opening and formed lines, saluting them as passing officers. "*I guess they did*—a privilege of your new position."

"You sure it wasn't your big head they recognized?" Cleo asked as they rode through to the other side.

"*Big head?* At least mine isn't inflated with all that nonsense the vident rammed into yours," Kladden said back with a laugh.

"Knowledge isn't nonsense. It keeps my mind sharp."

Kladden reached for the shortsword sheathed at his waist. "But I have something sharper. In fact, I'd bet a thousand golds you don't have a clue where to go from here. What's that sharp mind telling you?"

"South, then east," Cleo said as he unfolded the parchment map from the side of his saddle.

"*Sure.* But what would you do without that map of yours? How would you know which way to point that brick of a chin?"

Cleo thought for a moment before answering, "That's a stupid question. I would need the map to know where I am and where I need to go. Everything in this partition is just dirt and dead shrubs."

"*Wrong.* I've got something better than a map. It's all up here because I've lived it." Kladden pointed his finger to the side of his head. "Don't need one of those, just like I don't need those ghastly books you spend days stuffing your head inside. The Benevolent Sun will always light the way."

"My map still works at night."

Kladden rolled his eyes. "All it'd take is my sharp blade to cut up that map of yours, and then what would you do? You'd be lost."

"You know, Kladden, you're lucky you're big and good with a sword. Just being weak, ugly, and dumb would have made for an awful commander," Cleo said, laughing across the short span of red-shaded dirt between them.

"*No.* You're just lucky I'm best friends with your father."

They carried on cracking jokes at one another as they headed south, then east across the barren land, passing the few wagon-backed travelers who brought food and cargo into Sazara from the surrounding partitions. Every so often, Kladden would stop them to ask if they carried anything good. However, nothing seemed to meet Cleo's specific interests.

As the daylight began to fade, they stopped under a small tree for shade and ate a quick meal, which the villa's maids had packed for them earlier. When they resumed their route, Cleo passed the time by counting the brown-scaled lizards he spotted soaking in the heat, making irrelevant notes in his mind about the different species of beetles they hunted.

Before nightfall, they rode until they reached the wall of wooden logs that encased Fort Rastrum. Cleo took Kladden's lead as they trotted slowly to the watchtower near the fort's only gate. At its top were posts waving the flag of Sacrim's insignia—royal red with crossed swords embossed onto a bronze shield with ten curving rays emitting from its sides.

"*Who arrives?*" a voice shouted from the top of the tower. Several guardsmen had their bows knocked but not drawn at the sight of them on horseback.

"*Cleo Scordisci, commander of the Sixth Brigade,*" Cleo shouted in an unusually deep tone.

Kladden looked over at Cleo as if he wanted to laugh. Instead, he held his composure and turned his gaze up to the tower. "Kladden Sordin, commandant of the Sixth Brigade."

"*Enter.*"

At the gate below the tower, two wooden doors swung open to reveal a shallow and shadowed tunnel. Kladden led them in as Cleo's horse had to be startled to enter. "Now's not the time to pretend," he whispered to Cleo as soon as he caught up. "You're a commander now—act like it."

Cleo gulped the dryness down and nodded back. At the edge of the tunnel, a frail man stood wearing a guardsman's vest atop a long-sleeved, golden undergarment.

"You must be the Sixth's clerk?" Kladden asked.

"Yes, sir. Orders, if you will." Cleo reached into his small side satchel and pulled out the sealed parchment Sepatus had given him earlier that morning. "*Very well.*" He slowly swung his legs off Dhalia to be sure not to let a sole slip. "The cavalry's attendants will take your horses. I'll have your belongings brought up to the commander's tower. If you will, please follow me."

Cleo and Kladden kicked up dry dirt between their high-strapped sandals as they walked toward the tall, wooden-framed building in the dark of night. Five arched buildings were aligned uniformly in the center of the fort, providing barracks for each one-thousand-guardsman battalion of the Sixth Brigade. Split between each were fields of red dirt, typically used for training. However, as Cleo walked past, he noticed them littered with wagons and open crates.

The first battalion of every brigade within the Guard was the cavalry, which comprised the most skilled of guardsmen trained to fight with spears and swords on horseback. The next two battalions were the brigade's main force of spearmen and swordsmen, disciplined in tactical formations with shields. The fourth battalion was armed with bows, and the fifth battalion was an amalgamation of the brigade's supply and craftsmen, who spent their efforts in the keep or as builders or cooks.

"Here are the commander's quarters to house you both," the Sixth Brigade's clerk said as he opened the door. "Up the stairs, the commandant's and assistant's berths are to the right and left. Commander's is at the end of the hall. A steward from the fifth battalion will be assigned to attend to you in the morning. Is there anything you may need now?" the clerk asked.

"A name," Kladden replied rudely.

"Sorry…sir?"

"What's your name?"

"Oh, sorry, sir. It's Arwin."

"Arwin, thank you. That will be all."

A few younger guardsmen hurried in through the door, holding the packs that once rested on the sides of their mules. "Perfect timing. Up the stairs," Arwin said, pointing to direct them. "If that's all, I shall meet with you both tomorrow."

Cleo nodded. When all the guardsmen had finally left, Kladden shut the door behind them and told Cleo, "Never trust a clerk. They've got their eyes on every post and an ear in every rank."

"He seemed like a nice man."

"They all seem nice. That's their job. They're nice to anyone who'll keep them around."

"So, like Eileen?"

Kladden rolled his eyes. "You're lucky I came here with you. Don't make me leave."

"Don't make me use my rank," Cleo said with a laugh.

Kladden lowered his chin and tightened his chest, flexing Cleo's way. "Rank means nothing when the swinging starts."

"You're the last person on the Plane I'd want to fight, Kladden."

"At least I've taught you something." Kladden grinned proudly. "But as for that clerk, you've got a squirmy one."

"*We've* got," Cleo corrected him.

"What's this about rank, again? You're the commander, not me. I've already served my time."

"Our duty to Sacrim must always endure," Cleo said, his voice swaying with sarcasm.

"Well, I'm going to get some rest. And you should, too. We've endured enough on that ride in, and tomorrow will be a full one."

"That, it will be." Cleo began to walk up the creaky staircase. After a few steps, he paused, turned around, and then asked, "Any advice for the morrow?"

"*Don't pretend*," Kladden said from the depths of his heavy chest as if to mock how Cleo had sounded earlier. "If you know it and I can see it, then they'll sniff it. Just be yourself. I've known you since you were a boy, Cleo. If anyone's been bred to be a great leader, it's you. You've got the skills. Use them."

A great leader, Cleo thought, nodding his head slowly. "Thanks, Kladden." He walked up the stairs and down the hall toward his new berth.

His belongings were spread across the floor of a room much larger than he had expected. A candlelit desk was situated near the room's corner, under a glass window that overlooked the fort's five barracks. Behind them, Cleo saw a large brick building with two tall chimneys.

He held a deep breath and took it all in, his gaze unwavering from the two stacks that rose tall above the horizon. Cleo's memory brought him back to the study within the general's villa. The chimneys reminded him of the harbor's twin lighthouses, which had often distracted him from his studies with Vident Lement. As he continued staring their way, Cleo realized that Kladden was right. He was bred for this role. For most of Cleo's life, Vident Lement and Kladden were devoted to his instruction, teaching and training him to be proficient in each of their skills and trades.

And despite the enmity he held toward Sepatus's aptitude as a father, Cleo wished he could one day be a great leader like he was. Sepatus was a man admired by most within the Guard, the best at what he did. His guidance was inspirational, and his decisions were reflective and deliberate. However Cleo felt about his father's choice at the party, he knew it carried meaning. His fate was where his feet were now, whether it came as an old man later in life or as the cagerman he recently was. Now, there was no time for distractions or fakery. This was his moment to make a name for himself as a commander of Sacrim's Guard. And it was his moment to be great at it, like his father was. Cleo tucked himself in for the night, negating any nerves or anxious feelings about what the morrow would bring.

Heavy knocks came from behind the door of his berth. "*Commander*," a soft voice crept between the crack of its slow opening. "Commandant Kladden sent me to wake you."

Cleo sat up and looked out of his window. "Daylight hasn't yet broken... *Who are you?*"

"Your steward, sir. Can I get you anything?"

"Tea. Black. Tell Kladden I'll be down shortly," Cleo said, rubbing his eyes.

"The tea is ready. And he's waiting for you, sir."

"I heard you the first time." Cleo scrunched his nose, taking his time to stand up. The scruffy-haired man nodded a few times before scurrying away. Cleo readied himself back into his commander's uniform, then made his way down the creaky stairs.

"Finally awake," Kladden said.

"Not yet. I need my tea."

"It's there."

Cleo waddled toward the table with his eyes half closed and poured his cup of tea from the steaming clay pot. "I did some thinking last night."

"And?"

"I'd like to see the brigade. To see where we stand. And assess our options."

"Smart," Kladden said, sipping from his cup. "Better to do that before the clerk gets here. And talk to the men without any of the captains' influence."

"Even smarter," Cleo noted. He looked out of the window and saw the earliest hue of the new day's sun rising in the west. "Well, now is as good a time as any."

"After you, *Commander*."

Cleo finished his tea, then led Kladden to rove the first battalion's barracks. Guardsmen on watch at each side of the door saluted, then turned sharply to open it. Cleo entered first and saw the corridor bare and its ceiling shallow. Its supporting beams and posts were diseased with rot. Old reins and saddles were flung across the floor, tangled and distorted.

Cleo leaned toward his commandant and whispered, "Fort Rastrum isn't how I remembered it."

"How so?" Kladden asked.

"I was young when I last came here with my father. But the decay is noticeable."

Kladden nodded in agreement. The captain's door was shut, so Cleo walked along the dimly lit corridor, into the bunkroom. Double bunks lined the walls, providing racks for the first battalion to rest. Those up and dressing stood sharp to salute when they saw their new commander walk by.

"You, there, what's your name?" Cleo asked an older guardsman, one who looked seasoned in more ways than just his age.

"Tomas Sadius, sir."

"Tomas, what do you find to be most important to the Sixth?"

"Most important—sir?" the older guardsman stuttered slightly. "My brothers, sir. And their trust."

"And you?" Cleo asked another guardsman whom he had just called over.

"Yes, sir."

"What do you find to be most important to the Sixth?"

"Our training, sir, and the well-keeping of our warhorses…and probably the weapons, sir," the man barely dressed in his uniform answered.

"And you? What do you feel we need?" Cleo asked another guardsman.

"*Need?* Sir, we could always do with better living quarters. And food—better food would do us well, sir."

"*Understood.* Carry on," Cleo commanded with a nod.

From the first battalion, they strolled from barracks to barracks to monitor the men's morning routine and their interwoven schedules of training. Occasionally, Cleo would stop to ask the same questions of some of the older guardsmen, and he received many similar answers. It wasn't until he, Kladden, and his straggling steward had finished their walk through the fifth battalion's barracks that they saw Arwin hurrying his way through the courtyard, practically galloping his twigs for legs.

"Isn't it a little early for a clerk to be up?" Kladden shouted to ask him.

"*Commander.* Commandant. The captains and vice-captains await you in the mess for your meeting."

"*Meeting?*" Cleo scrunched his face in confusion. "I never called for a meeting."

"Yes, a meeting, sir. One has been called by Captain Ostin of the first battalion. I'm sure it's to introduce themselves to you."

"You couldn't have told me this yesterday or earlier this morning?"

"I apologize, sir. It must have slipped from my memory."

"Very well. Take me to them." Cleo looked at Kladden and watched him roll his eyes.

They followed Arwin down the length of the courtyard, toward the two-chimneyed mess hall, and into its open and expansive central room. He led them toward a door in the far corner, behind and between the evenly spaced tables, then up a lone flight of stairs. Arwin opened the door at the edge of the unlit hallway and gestured for them to enter.

Cleo walked into the modestly sized room first, which contained a crescent-shaped table with candles lit at each end. A smaller, more common, rectangular table faced the crescent's curve. *This is a bloody interrogation, not a meeting,* Cleo thought. *I definitely need to shake things up.*

Most of the captains, wearing gold cloaks pinned to their padded vests, stood to salute Cleo as he walked to the center of the crescent table. It wasn't until Kladden entered from behind Cleo that the balding man and his vice-captain stood to render their salutes.

"Which one of you is Captain Ostin?" Cleo asked.

"*I*," the balding man at the center said.

Cleo wanted to admonish the man—first for calling the meeting without his approval, then for deferring his salute. But Cleo needed to be smart and not fall prey to the old captain's obvious bait. *How would my father handle this?* he asked himself. But his thoughts drifted back to Kladden's advice. *Just be yourself. I can do this.*

"Thank you for calling this meeting," Cleo announced with a bouncing cough to clear his throat. "This morning, I walked Fort Rastrum and talked to the guardsmen. I would first like to commend all your hard work and the effort you have all contributed to the Guard's fine standing. I hope to follow in Commander Cresdan's footsteps and continue to carry on the Sixth Brigade's outstanding reputation across Sacrim and the Plane."

Cleo paused and looked around the room, locking his eyes onto each of their faces. He didn't want to give them a moment to speak. "At the same time, I am not unaware of the situation I find myself in—barely removed from being a cagerman, son of the Consolar General, and now your commander. I know the difficulties I face in earning your support and trust. And I plan to achieve that and more. But as I walked the barracks today, I asked the men what they thought was most important to the Sixth." Cleo could tell certain eyes paid him the fullest attention while others still gave him their neglect. "And what I found was that not a single guardsman answered that it was their commander who was the most important. Many, though, mentioned things that involved *you*, their captains. Things that each of you affect every day. *You* are what's important to the guardsmen of this brigade, not me. And so, you—captains of this Sixth Brigade—I must ask that your actions be for those under you and not out of spite for those above. Lead not for me, but for them."

The balding man's face softened, and his firm, bushy eyebrows relaxed. Cleo continued, "With that said, the Sixth Brigade is Sacrim's only rotary unit, elite among the other five and not tied to any one partition.

My first action will be to hold true to our Guard's creed and sharpen our most important skill—marching. With these men having been here at Fort Rastrum for many solurns, it is far time for this brigade to find a new fort to station. On the morrow, each of you will receive marching orders. We head east, then north, to an old fort near Cignus. We will work hard to build it up. There will be enough time, then, and during our march, for me to meet with each of you individually."

Most of the captains, and even Kladden, shared a stunned look at Cleo's poise and directive. With his chest stuck out in pride, Cleo stopped at the center of the table and added, "There is one other thing. It is my duty, as a commander, to travel to the Isle of Azil for the Descindation. Upon our arrival at the new fort, I shall entrust my full command to Kladden for a short period of time."

Cleo turned to Kladden, the strongest and fiercest-looking man in the room. His commandant nodded aggressively in return. Cleo spun back around to face his new captains. He could tell they seemed intimidated, uncertain over what would come next. "That will be all. You're dismissed."

CHAPTER 6

SEA

"Get up, you wretched slug," a hefty man gnarled through iron bars, then tossed a dirty rag into Dane's cell. "Clean yourself—we're almost pier side."

"Pier side? Where am I?"

It all hurts.

Dane's bony cheek was molded against the wet floorboard. He opened his eyes and felt the soggy splinters lift from the deck as he raised his head. His arms, which were shackled together at his frail wrists, struggled to stretch across his narrow cell to grab the rag thrown in its corner.

A deep pounding sound shook the deck when Dane tried to crawl. He thought for a moment that his heart had fallen from his chest or maybe that he'd been pounded to the ground again. The more he tried to drag himself toward the blurry blob of a rag, the more Dane realized that the thumping formed a rhythm. Little by little, he moved forward until he was close enough to grab the rusted iron bars and lift his shoulders off the ground. With his less-tender arm, he reached for the rag and tried to poke his head between the bars, turning his chin in the direction of the noise. There, ahead of him, Dane saw a shimmer of light sprouting through the dark blur.

My eye. Dane brushed the tips of his fingers over his left eye and pushed in gently. The skin surrounding it was as solid as a rock, swollen shut by a taut lump that blocked his sight.

"You're on the *Marcer*, son. And you look like shit," a voice lofted from across the narrow passageway. "I don't know what you did, but it must have been pretty bad."

Marcer? I must be on that tribute galley, Dane realized. He shuddered to move his back against the bars of the cell with a depleted groan. "It was a fight. With some officers of the King's Navy. In a dispute over tribute."

"*Tribute*," the cold, sour voice scoffed. "Spineless bastards. All of them. How bad?"

Dane thought for a moment, trying to recall what had happened from his lapse of memory. "I got a few hits in. On one of them, at least. I think. After that, I'm not sure." He could tell the voice came from a cell opposite his own. "What about you?"

"A fight similar to yours, I guess. Except I made sure to remember it all."

Dane waited in silence for the man hidden in the darkness to continue. But when he didn't, Dane figured it would be best not to prod. "What's that noise?" he asked instead.

"The drums."

"Drums? For what?"

"For the oarsmen…to keep the ship rowing in rhythm," the man replied, his raspy voice drifting closer to the passageway. Dane rubbed his good eye and barely made out the man's face—a pale figure with long, gray hair.

Dane grabbed the iron bars again and lifted his bony body to stand upright. He looked out past the open doorway at the end of the passageway and saw shades of deep blue. The familiar scent of the salty ocean drifted his way. Dane tilted his head farther out, between the bars of his cell, trying to get a view over the ship's bow. The shaded blur began to form into distinct lines of gray landforms, which were covered by blankets of white snow. *Land…* "Wherever we're going, we're almost there."

"Well, you should be on your knees, then, praying to whatever god you believe in that this ship turns around." The man hurled a wad of spit onto the deck. "For both our sakes."

Turn back… The girls. Mother. Maven. The thought of Dane's family came back to him in a panic. *I hope they're okay.* His face grew grim as his mind wandered, contemplating how and where they might be or what the officers and tributars might do now that he was gone. *They could have been taken, too. If so, where? Maybe they're on this ship with me.* His mind became strangled with thoughts, pondering the possibilities as he looked around in frantic spurts. But the galley's cells held only him and the other man. Being there to provide for his family had been a responsibility he'd borne since his father had gone.

And now he was gone, too.

Before Dane could sit back down, the drumming below deck stopped. "*Ready to dock*," a deep voice screamed from above. Sounds of wooden planks bending broke between the bars of the iron cell that stood in their support. Dane could feel the movement of the ship slow and begin to drift with the waves.

Though tribute galleys frequented Niven often, Dane never really thought them to be big, at least compared to the war galleys he'd seen moored in Minoska. He had also never been inside one before. But from what he could gather, Dane knew he was being held at the aft end of the ship, in the aftcastle that was easily accessible to the open main deck. Below was the hold, where they stored the collected tribute. And the deck under that, he knew, was for the oarsmen.

Dane groaned as he moved to glance at the stirring commotion. Through the open door to the main deck, he continued to look out with his good eye before the light became shut by a shadow.

"*Ah*, look who's finally awake. Had a comfy nap, did ya?" the hefty man from before asked. Iron jangled at his waist as he waddled to enter the narrow passageway. A rotten smell wafted with each breath Dane took, brushing under his bruised and clogged nose. "Off you go." The hefty tributar went to the old man in the cell across from Dane first, picking him up by the scraps of his torn garment.

The sound of iron shackles clanking like rattles filled the darkened room as the old man was pushed down the passageway toward the main deck. In the split of light, the raspy-voiced man glanced back briefly, allowing Dane to glimpse his face. His lifeless eyes were frozen with an empty stare, and his skin was pale, covered by a mangled beard and stringy hair.

"*You*, now…out," the tributar growled, stumbling toward him.

Dane could barely distinguish the symbol stitched at the top corner of his black coat—a star of faded gold. *A marshal*, he realized. *Not a tributar.* Dane grunted as he tried to lift his legs, but neither would budge. Looking down, he saw a chain stretched taut between his feet, attached by shackles around his ankles.

"*Move*," the marshal demanded. He grabbed Dane by the shoulder and yanked him out of the cell.

With a shove, Dane was thrust toward the light. His heavy feet could barely keep up with his bruised body. He glanced behind him and saw a short chain hooked to a metal ball that rolled behind him and between each cell of the passageway. Another shove came, and Dane was sent tumbling forward. The ball and chain bounced and rolled across the deck as Dane's balance went wayward, causing him to trip over the chain and plunge his shoulder into one of the cell's iron bars.

"Forgot how to walk, now, did we?" The stank-ridden marshal picked him back up and shoved him again. Dane stumbled through the open doorway and onto the main deck, shivering as he entered the cold wind.

Marines and officers alike, dressed in thick black coats of wool and silver helmets rounded like a bowl, stood along the deck, commanding the frail men around them who wore rags like Dane. He watched as they threw bundles of frayed lines onto the pier to his left. Others carried buckets or barrels back and forth. But none made eye contact with him, as if he were the ghost of a life they'd left behind long ago.

To his right, a long bank of piers stretched along the curving coast farther than his good eye would let him see. But even through the blur, Dane couldn't miss the White Tower. *We're in Minoska,* he knew. At the farthest point of land, past the last pier of Minoska's port, the watchtower stood tall, mortared by graystone from the square of its base to the top of its rectangular battlements. It was a historic relic from the days when the Kingdom of Marredom was first united in 441, before the descent. But like most else in the Northern Plane, it now stood feeble, its graystone weathered.

"*Down you go,*" the marshal said as he pushed Dane down the gangway and off the tribute galley. His feet moved quickly, much quicker than before, as the ball rolled down to the pier faster than his feet would move. It didn't take much for Dane to fall again. This time, however, he had a pillow of snow to catch his shoulder. "*Get up,* you pathetic twat."

I can barely move, Dane thought as the marshal lifted him again.

"See that wagon at the end of the pier? We've gotten you your own chariot since you've forgotten how to walk." On the wagon ahead was the same gray-haired man from the cell, sitting in the back of its bed, smirking his way. With each step Dane took up the pier, he watched his cold agony release from every cloud of breath.

"*Pphhh.*" Dane let out a coughing heave and covered his nose. A row of small barrel buckets was strapped together in the back of the wagon, filled with what must have been rancid feces. The odor was heavy and pungent but light enough to float through the cold air and engulf Dane's weak gasps. Against his will, Dane climbed in.

The marshal slapped the back end of the donkey that pulled the wagon. "They're your problem now, Erv."

"It's only going to get worse," the old man murmured to Dane, his smirk gone.

"Do you know what they plan to do to us?" Dane asked, trying to talk above the smell.

"There's no us, kid. There's me, and then there's you. And we've both done different stuff."

"I thought you were in a fight like me?"

"I said *similar*. And you should be happy about that. If you're lucky, they'll go easy on you."

"Hush, back there. No chatter," the man named Erv at the donkey's reins croaked.

Erv was bundled in a thick coat the color of midnight and wore a muffed hat that covered his ears. Dane could tell he was too old to be an officer or a marine. And he knew it would have been difficult for him to turn around and enforce his demands on the two of them. But marines in plenty strolled beside the wagon as they traveled down the island's muddied path, which led to and from Minoska and its port. They escorted lines of men dressed in rags, frailer than Dane was, moving like ice ants as they carried buckets of supplies from the city back to the ships.

Their wagon passed farther inland until the White Tower, which once protected the Plane's largest port, faded into the distance. Though the sun was in spring, it never really showed itself in Marredom. Jagged rocks with divots of puddled snow still seemed to have their place, scattering to surround most of Minoska. Dane stared at them as they passed with nervous anticipation, until they rode above the peak of a hill, where the full span of the city came into view. The buildings were as he remembered them—low to the ground to keep the heat within, with steeple-pitched roofs to funnel the snow. Minoska's streets were unorganized, as if erected at random, most standing as square structures of graystone.

As they rode toward it, the wagon entered Norkatis Street, named after Marredom's first King, Hansthilen Norkatis, and the vision in Dane's eye slowly began to return. The city's central street was wide and long and led straight from the muddy road of the port to the King's castle. Eight unequally spaced towers of graystone with a connecting curtain wall between them stood tall to surround King Mordin the Fourth's lusterless home. A wooden gate, where Norkatis Street met the front-facing wall, was stiffened by flattened iron bars and kept closed to shield the King and his family behind its shadows.

Rattle came from the slow-turning wheels as the wagon rolled down its uneven stones. Dane looked around and saw most of the buildings empty, void of any people. Halfway to the King's castle, the street widened. Along both sides were rows of tall wooden pillars, shaved of their bark, with two long chains dangling from their tops. Dane saw a group of marines standing at the street's center, halfway between them and the King's castle, as if they were awaiting their arrival.

"That should do it," Erv said, tugging at the reins.

"*Off,*" one of the marines walked toward them to shout.

Dane let the old man across from him exit before he struggled to jump out of the wagon's bed. The stockiest marine led them to the side of the street and pointed each of them to a wooden pillar. Marines in black coats of a lower rank unlocked the old man's shackles at both his hands and feet, then ordered him to sit and hug the base of a pillar. His shoulders and hips were pulled taut to the shaved wood, and his shackles were reapplied. The stocky marine grabbed both ends of the long chain that dangled from its top and locked his shackles to it. Dane stood still, watching with an empty pit in his stomach, knowing that he was next.

"You, here," the large marine said, pointing to the following pillar. With each slow step Dane took, he could feel the cold stone numb his toes. He wished it would cover the rest of his sore body, or even his other eye, to blind him from what he was about to feel and see.

The marines in black coats unlatched his shackles and forced him to sit at the pillar's base. His arms were pulled taut, and his shoulders yanked, driving his empty stomach flat against the round of the trunk. The same was done to his feet at the bottom, pressing his thighs against the wood until his numb toes pointed right at the old man at the pillar in front of him. He twisted his neck to find relief, burying his chin into the pillar's wood.

"*Why me?*" Dane finally opened his mouth to whisper. But without anyone there to answer, he closed his eyes. *I've forsaken my life…and for what? I don't even know what's become of my family.*

As the day's last light dwindled, Dane sat motionless on the cold stones of Norkatis Street, left only with his thoughts. Other than the marines on watch to patrol the city, he counted just four people walking alone—a far cry from what he had witnessed the last time he was in Minoska.

Before the day his father was taken, tradition in Marredom required that a pilgrimage be made to Minoska by the head of every family each solurn to pay tribute and fealty to the King and receive his distribution. The few times Dane had traveled here with his father, he'd found Norkatis Street to be bustling, packed like tinfish with the fair-skinned and blond-haired people of Marredom. But as King Mordin the Fourth aged, he grew suspicious that his people weren't truthful in what they gave. He presumed that most were hiding more than they needed within their homes. And so, the King of Marredom had the tradition changed. Nearly a decade ago, he deployed a new fleet of tribute galleys, which came to the homes and towns to collect his tribute, abating the traditional pilgrimage to Minoska. What was once a center for trade between the islands had become a desolate city, filled only with marines and officers who came to and from the port between their time at sea.

To Dane's fading content, he managed to tuck his narrow chin into his neck and ease the soreness that pierced his shoulders. Pressing his left ear against the wood, he closed his eyes and listened. His thoughts echoed inside its grains, bouncing back and forth with worry over what was to come. But the pillar never spoke back, as if it didn't want to be there any more than Dane did.

Without relief, Dane opened his eyes and turned his neck. Inside the building beside the street, a woman and her young daughter were staring at him through a small, open window. Succumbing to embarrassment or rage, or both, he lashed out as silently as his anger would allow. "*What are you looking at?*"

They continued to stare at him, shifting their glare from him to the old man, before they scurried back into the building's darkness. Dane turned to the wooden trunk and smashed his forehead against it. The despair he felt inside rose higher than the pillar itself. Within its running grains, he saw layers of stained blood smushed in painful shades, left by those who had once sat where he now did.

"Kid, don't fight it," the old man insisted.

"*What should we do?*" Dane asked back, whispering to the man he couldn't see.

"There's no *we*. All you can do is hope that sun doesn't rise in the morning."

"*Psst…psst,*" came a sound from the building to his right. Dane closed his eyes again, afraid that a marine might have been listening and was there to scold him. "*Psst.*" The sound grew louder. Dane looked over and saw the same little girl from the window, her head covered by a gray cloth, crouching behind their half-open door. She put a finger over her mouth and looked at him as if she wanted a response.

Dane did what he could to nod.

The little girl scurried over to him quickly, crouching behind Dane's back to hide from the officers and marines. "*Here.*" She lifted a leather waterskin to his mouth, and he drank, gulping to quench his bottomless thirst. She reached into her small bag and leaned close enough for Dane to glimpse her face.

Ellian? Alva? Is that you?

Her hand lifted to his mouth, holding a molded lump of mash. Dane bit into what tasted like bitter groundfish and pickled onion, which may have been a few days too old. To wash out the taste, he nodded again at the waterskin. She held it up, and he took another long sip. "*I'm so sorry,*" he told her. The young girl scooted to the side of Dane's shoulder, crouching enough to reveal her face in the moonlight.

It isn't them, he realized.

"*It's okay,*" the girl whispered. She left Dane and scurried up the street toward the old man.

"*Wait!*" Dane whimpered. But the girl had already gone. "*Thank you.*"

His body was weak, and his throat was still thirsty. But the little girl he had thought once shamed him had been the only one there to help him. *Bitter. Life is already too bitter,* he pondered as his eyes closed.

"*UP!*" a deep voice commanded.

Dane awoke as the northern sun began to shine over his shoulder. The same large marine from the day before reached down and unlocked the chain at his feet, then placed his hands under Dane's armpits, sliding his body up the blood-stained pillar. Dane's hips were stiff and his legs unmoving, as if they'd been pricked full of needles. Like a boulder rolling down a hill, his knees crumbled under the weight of his heavy chest.

"*Stand*," the marine commanded.

Dane masked his unease behind the gaunt hollows of his cheeks as he struggled to stand back up. He squinted his eyes to open and saw a small crowd of people encircling the two pillars. They dressed in long, black overcoats and rags of gray, which blended in with the buildings behind them. Dane scanned the crowd, looking for anyone who could help—his mother, Maven, or maybe even the little girl from the night before. But all he saw of those who stood to surround him were the cold smirks of older women, their scant children, and the King's officers and marines.

A shiver shot down Dane's spine as he turned to look away. Stretching from his shoulder to the top of his feet, his body became drenched by a splash of freezing seawater. Behind him, two marines stood with buckets in their hands, chuckling at his misery.

"That should wake him," the hefty marine said.

Dane shivered as his head was jerked backward, gripped from under his sharp chin. He could see the black coat of another marine walking closer. One of them yanked his blond hair, tilting his head farther back. The slicing sound of steel shears came from behind his ears. Dane winced, expecting more pain.

"We're just chopping your hair, *idiot*," one of the marines told him.

When the slicing sound stopped, another bucket of freezing seawater was poured onto his head. He could feel the coldness streaming from the top of his bare scalp to his knees, sliding to his feet, which were braced against the stone ground. Again, his knees collapsed beside his blond locks.

"No one told you to rest. *UP!*" the marine commanded, picking Dane back up.

"*Silence*," a lighter voice shouted above the chattering crowd.

Dane looked toward the center of the street and saw a man standing upon a makeshift platform—a simple wagon they had just rolled in. Like the others, he wore a silver helmet and black coat, but with three silver stars stitched above his chest.

"I, Chief Marshal Marskov Dagrain, have come today to prosecute justice on the King of Marredom's behalf. Hutchinsen of Kovick—by order of King Mordin the Fourth, you are sentenced to hang for your offense of murder against his own. Daneus of Niven—by order of King Mordin the Fourth, you are herewith sentenced to fifteen lashings for your offense of fifteen counts of theft. Adjunctly, you are hereby sentenced to a lifetime of service to the King for your offense of striking his own."

Lifetime of service?

Dane's thoughts muddled as the crowd's attention panned to the old man named Hutchinsen. The stocky marine walked from beside the platform to his pillar carrying a long rope. He tied one of its ends to the free chain that dangled from the top of the pillar and grabbed the other side, attaching it to the shackles at the old man's feet. Dane could hear the stocky marine shouting commands to four or five others.

The men in black coats and silver helmets moved to form a line, then began pulling at the rope, sequencing their grips one hand over the other. Shouts came from the crowd as Hutchinsen was lifted feet first up the tall pillar with his arms hanging below his head. Once his feet were pulled to the pillar's peak, half the marines left to grab the rope at his wrists and pulled his overturned body taut, tying it off at the base. Dane struggled to watch as Hutchinsen's body became stretched. He could hear his bones disjointing, breaking as he dangled upside down, high above the crowd and their homes.

"*IT WAS WORTH IT, YOU SCUM!*" Hutchinsen struggled to empty his lungs, wincing in pain. "*I'D DO IT AGAIN. EVERY DAY.*"

The crowd croaked lowly at the old man's comments. At the behest of the chief marshal, the marines lowered his limp body closer to the ground. One of them shoved a wet rag in his mouth, and then hoisted him back to the top, tying it off again and leaving his body outstretched, upside down, to die.

Dane clenched his eyes shut when he saw the marines begin to walk his way. He could hear the clattering footsteps of the crowd moving from Hutchinsen's pillar to his own. Within moments, a loud crack had split the air, slashing right behind his ear and onto his exposed, shirt-torn back. A sharp pain fluttered throughout his body as if the burning of a thousand fires had been lit under his skin. His arms hugged the pillar tightly in the hope that he could sink his pain into the grains of his only friend. Dane turned his chin to the side and pressed his ear against it, listening for help. But again, all he heard was his own echoing cry.

"*One*," the marine behind him counted aloud.

Another lash came by the crack from a long whip. This time, Dane could feel his skin break, and his blood began to trickle down to the cold stone.

"*Two.*"

After the third lash, his knees collapsed, and he shuddered to the ground in pain. The whips continued without pause or remorse. Dane's back and knees were bloodied; his fingers were numb from grappling the chain around the pillar. It was his only escape. With each strike, he'd pull harder. But just like his father would have, Dane refused to cry or shout aloud in horror.

"*...Eight.*"

Make it stop. Please. Make it stop, he thought, repeating those words over and over in his mind. *Be strong. I did nothing wrong.* Dane fought to open his eyes.

Father? The figure of a man who looked identical to his father stood at the fore of the crowd. As Dane stared into his eyes with a glimmer of hope, another lash came. He buried his head into the pillar once more, grasping tightly at the chains of his shackles. Dane opened them again, hoping to see his father still there, rushing over to save him. But the figure of the man had vanished. *Why did you leave us? Why did you leave me? I should never have run... I'll never run again.*

"*...Fifteen.*"

Finally.

"Daneus of Niven," the chief marshal said from atop the platform. "For your adjunct sentence, you shall serve your life to King Mordin the Fourth as an oarsman aboard the *Fereclis*—galley of war."

Oarsman? Fereclis?

As soon as Dane's left arm was unshackled, his shoulder collapsed coldly below his knees into the bloodied pool, numb and silent. The only thing he could hear was the sharp crack of the whip repeating in his mind. His pain was finally over—or so he thought.

The large marine grabbed his unshackled left wrist and held it straight out, forcing the bottom of his forearm to face the sky. Dane could barely lift his head. Marines began to huddle beside him. On one side, a man held what looked like a clay vase with a thin iron rod sticking out from its top. On the other stood the chief marshal with the three silver stars stitched at his chest. Finger by finger, he slid black gloves onto his hands. He reached for the handle of the iron rod and lifted it out of the vase. Its bottom end glowed like the sun with the darkness of unending lashes.

With a look of determined death, the chief marshal moved the glowing bottom of the rod above Dane's exposed forearm. A scream of agony tore through the air as Dane's arm was melted by its piercing fire. Out of instinct, Dane pressed his ear against the pillar and squeezed it tight, hoping for a quench of salvation. Through his screaming peril, he heard the pillar's echo. It was his father's voice, saying softly through the grains, "*I'm sorry, my son.*"

Dane opened his eyes when the source of the scorching had finally lifted. Fading in and out, he looked down at the inside of his left forearm and saw the branding mark of crossed oars emboldened by blood.

"Bring him to the *Fereclis*," the chief marshal ordered.

CHAPTER 7

SKY

M y own mother.

Vanna sat awake in her grot, staring into the winding ripples that were etched into the low ceiling. The day prior, she had achieved her highest of all aims by becoming a Sister of the Silo. And yet, she couldn't escape the means by which it had come.

Were they my siblings? My real siblings?

The entrance door at the floor below opened, and the screech from its hinges broke her night-long ponder. Vanna quickly donned her half-cape and followed Alice and Elaine down the steps to form a standing line.

"Each of you has a new assignment," one of the Sisters Vanna had never seen before told them, handing them each a folded parchment. "In these are the directions to your new silos. You are to leave now. Open them only in the sky."

An anxious temptation to open the wax-sealed parchment crossed Vanna's mind as soon as the Sister exited their cavern. Written within it was the culmination of all her days of training, all she had endured, and all she had worked so hard to achieve. Her temptation didn't just cease with her own; she wanted to see what Alice's and Elaine's read, too. They were the only companions Vanna had—familiar faces from her earliest memories. And now, she knew, they were about to depart their separate ways.

As Children of the Silo, they were told little about what it meant to live as a Sister. The Grand Dame had led their instruction by the rule of a silent fist, keeping their order and its doings in the shadows of Astria, where it belonged. And the Sisters who assisted her had always kept their tongues twisted tight, so their dealings and locations never had the chance to reach the Astrian people or those from a foreign region of the Plane.

But from her days of training, Vanna knew that each order of the Sisters operated in a group of three, with an overseer charged to lead. The older Vanna grew as a Child, the more her training in this grouping of three intensified. Combat with the telson and other weapons of the Plane was no longer conducted alone but in combination with two other Children. And when they took to the sky on their rooks, they learned to fly in formations of three. Their training in these groups was Vanna's only opportunity to connect with the other Children and, more specifically, to connect with Alice and Elaine.

The Grand Dame had forbidden most communal conversation, especially while they were young. In their long days of training and rigorous studies, or while eating their daily ration of bland greens and grains, the three were together gripped by the same hand that squeezed their lives void of any pleasure. When to wake and speak, what to dress like, and how to behave were all carefully controlled by the Grand Dame and her assisting Sisters. The only feeling of pleasure Vanna was allowed to experience was that of tasks completed. And by becoming Sisters together, Vanna trusted Alice and Elaine. The three of them shared an unbreakable bond born through silence, understood by the looks they gave each other, alone. But now, she had been given a new assignment, one to join an order of seasoned Sisters she'd never met before.

Vanna returned to her grot and stuffed her few possessions and clothes into a modestly sized linen sack. She took one final look around the dim walls and then carried her belongings back to the entrance door.

"This is it," Alice said as soon as Vanna reached the bottom steps.

"So, it is."

"Elaine is still packing. I'll see her off. You should go." Alice dropped her sack and hugged Vanna tightly around her neck. Vanna jumped aback, startled. "I know. I shouldn't have done that. But if I didn't, who would?" When she released her arms, Vanna saw the corners of her eyes begin to puddle with the faintest hint of tears. The misshapen brown mole on her forehead strained as she held back her emotions. "You've been a true sister to me."

"You shouldn't have. We're all Sisters, now, *remember*," Vanna said against her own surge of emotion. She wanted to say so much more—to thank Alice one last time for always being there. Even in their silence and days of separation, she was someone Vanna considered a friend, someone who had experienced the same life she had. With the feelings Alice revealed now, Vanna was sure the past day's events had affected her in a similar way.

Our own birth mothers, she thought as she stared into Alice's soggy eyes. They were eyes that spoke more words than her mouth ever could. Vanna's memory flashed with the vision she had witnessed from the oil. She didn't know whether Alice had seen the same thing she had or felt the same fear. And she was too afraid to ask. Vanna had done all she could to push her thoughts of that experience into the recesses of her mind.

"I've got to go," Vanna said before she said too much. For as clever as the Sisters were, she never knew who could be listening.

Vanna held her breath as she walked out of the wrought iron door, down the short winding path, and into the rooks' resting nook. She opened the recessed cage where Little Wing slept and blew softly into her flute. Her rook opened its eyes and stood. Vanna grabbed the chain linked to its neck and led it to the bottom of the Silo. Little Wing spread her wings wide as soon as they reached the light that columned in from above, stretching to soak the fresh air between her feathers.

Vanna mounted from the smaller wing, strapped herself into the saddle, and tightened her sack tightly to its rear. She blew once into her flute again—this time, with a screech—and Little Wing took flight. Her rook flapped its wings violently to climb up, out from the Silo, until they broke into the open blue of the morning sky. When they were alone with the clouds, Vanna reached for her side pocket and read the note she had been given moments ago.

Vanna—Order of the Brazen Talons.

South. Follow the Mirador River until the foothills at the fork. Break east until you see the branchless tree.

Arutam.

Vanna yanked at the leather reins, and Little Wing turned her stubby-hooked beak south. Three quick and smooth notes from her flute sent her rook speedily through the air, gliding between the lowest crests of the Plane's western range of mountains.

Brazen Talons? Vanna pondered. Her thoughts grew like the clouds that hung above her head. The river she searched for ran from Astria's highest peaks south, stretching between the middle of its two foothills.

Wide with white rapids, the Mirador River was easy for Vanna to spot and follow. What was hard to find, though, was its splitting fork. Vanna blew once, and Little Wing flapped her broad wings to gain altitude.

There.

Vanna saw the height of the peaks beyond the point where the river broke into two, continuing until the fork was just below. The lower she and Little Wing flew, the smaller the separation between the river and its rocky slope became. Its curving banks were filled with grassy shrubs that sprouted in bushels from the mountain's rough, rocky sides. Pulling to her left, she turned Little Wing away from the southern valley to follow the curve of the river that hooked east. *A branchless tree... That could be anywhere,* Vanna thought.

Just as she began to question her instructions, Vanna saw a tall mountain nub littered with cracks that stood out from the rest. They flew toward it, and she spotted the bare branches of a leafless tree standing as broken as the cliffs it grew from. She guided Little Wing to hover slowly above it, searching for the Silo's opening. *There it is.* Vanna took a deep breath before dropping into its shadowed hole.

An off-putting smell stuck to its narrow walls as Little Wing curled her wings to glide them down into the Silo's bottom. Two doors and a nook, smaller than the Children's Silo, stood at the base of the wall behind them. Vanna sent Little Wing to rest, then walked toward the middle of the two doors.

"*Arutam,*" she said the varukian word for autumn loudly.

A Sister of the Silo opened the door. She was an older woman with short brown hair that bobbed back and forth when she turned. "*It's about time.* I'm Arazell, but you can call me Zell. This is Lora." She pointed at the other Sister sitting at a desk with her back to Vanna within their tiny cavern.

Lora stood up and moved to greet her with a broad smile and bubbly eyes. She was shorter than Vanna and Zell but shared her long black braids. "Welcome," she said, grabbing Vanna's hand to drag her inside. "I know how hard the first days as a Sister can be. But you should know, you've joined the absolute best."

"I'm still shocked the Grand Dame allowed a Child to join the Talons," Zell said. "You better be special."

"*Special?*" Vanna questioned. "I'm not sure what you mean."

"It's okay. We know you don't have a choice about which order you're placed in," Lora interjected, rolling her eyes as soon as Zell looked away.

"What I *mean* is that the Brazen Talons haven't had a Child join their ranks in quite some time," Zell said. "Our third, Julia, was promoted recently, and they filled her spot with you—*a Child.*"

"Hmm, there were only three of us who made it through. Maybe there just weren't many options," Vanna said.

"That still doesn't explain why they would replace *her* with *you.* Send you elsewhere and promote the Sister you replace," Zell said. She reminded Vanna a great deal of the Grand Dame. They were both tall with broad shoulders and had stern, bushy eyebrows. And they both spoke in a deep, demeaning tone. "Anyway, I'm your overseer. You should get ready. We'll be leaving soon."

"*Leaving?*"

"I apologize that there isn't enough time to get you acclimated," Lora responded.

Zell's dark eyes shifted sharply her way. "We're a half-moon behind schedule."

"I'll show you to your new grot," Lora told her, waving her hands for Vanna to follow. The entrance room was cornered with tables and chairs that led to a short hallway. "To the left is our hold," she explained, pointing to the closed door they walked past. "And here it is. I think Zell would like you to be ready as soon as possible. I'm sorry you won't have the time to settle in."

Ready for what? Vanna questioned, listening more to Lora's reassuring smile than the words she spoke. But instead of asking, she just watched Lora leave and return to the Silo's entrance room.

Her new grot was similar in size to her old one but much more private, with an enclosed wall and door that separated it from the hallway. She no longer needed strings to hang her clothes, as a large wooden chest sat opposite her hay-padded bed. There, she placed what little belongings she had, untied her black half-cape, and then sat on her bed to take it all in.

Everything is changing so quickly.

Still sitting, she closed her eyes and leaned back. *This is nice—my own space. I could sink right through this bed*, she thought, until indistinguishable shouts rumbled from the entrance room. Vanna opened her eyes and saw the patterns of winding ripples etched into the ceiling, the same as her old grot. *Of course. Some things never change.*

"*We don't have time to waste. We need to be leaving,*" Zell's voice rang again through the walls. Vanna readied herself without needing another warning, then followed the two of them out of the cavern, toward the base of the Silo.

"You haven't trained with us yet, so you'll have to pick things up quickly," Zell told Vanna as they walked to grab their rooks from the nook. "As Lora said, we're the best. So I expect you to be the best, too."

It seems like I'll have to be, Vanna thought.

Little Wing was easily the smallest of the three rooks, making her timid and erratic around the larger birds. Zell's rook, Felix, was shades darker and had a heavy chest with broad wings. Lora's rook, Assira, stood the tallest and had a distinguishably proud and boxy head.

"We fly in a sharp angle. Zell is the overseer, so she'll lead. And I'm to her left. Just follow her wing and you'll be okay," Lora reassured her.

"Here." Zell handed the two of them a small rucksack. "I'll explain our task in detail when we arrive. We'll be flying high into Sacrim until we reach Sazara to relieve the order of Sisters currently there. There's no room for error. Vanna, your rook knows the commands, correct?" Vanna nodded, then took two steps to climb onto her saddle and strap herself in, tying the rucksack behind her. "*Good.* Let's fly."

Zell played a long, screeching note from her polished flute and then took off through the high opening of the Silo. Lora and Assira lifted second, flinging gusts of air down, forcing Vanna to shield her eyes from the swirling debris. Little Wing clenched her head to the side, and her eye met Vanna's. She patted her rook twice on its feathered neck and whispered, "*We can do it.*"

Flying above the Silo, Zell and Lora slowly gained altitude until Vanna managed to catch up. It wasn't until they were well above the clouds that they formed their sharp-angled formation. As the Brazen Talons flew south with the wind, Little Wing struggled to match the speed and formation of the larger rooks. When they turned east and flew above a field of white crashing waves, the wind shifted to thrash into Vanna's face. She tucked her chin against Little Wing's feathers and focused on the tip of Felix's wing. *We can do it,* she thought, trying to muster confidence.

Long and far, high above the water, the Brazen Talons flew until two screeching whistles finally came from Zell's flute. Felix bobbed its head down, then disappeared below a rift of clouds. Vanna looked to her left and saw the tailfeather of Lora's rook track downward to follow. She quickly grabbed her flute, blew twice, and then yanked at Little Wing's reins so they, too, could fly below the white clouds.

The rays from the sun cast a long, reflecting glimmer onto the Barren Sea below. To their right was a tall, jagged cliff, which looked as if the land had sheared and dropped its missing half into the water. Zell stuck her right arm high in the air. A moment later, her rook darted toward the jagged coast. Vanna followed in a much more rounded and wide turn, forcing Lora to turn wide, too. As they flew low to mask their arrival, spray from the sea's waves began to splash across Vanna's face. The three of them headed for the lone dip in the cliff's ledge, covered by a shadow from the midday sun, where they slowed to gain altitude before landing.

Vanna unsaddled and walked toward Zell and Lora, who were already rummaging through their rucksacks. "Put yours on," Zell commanded. Vanna reached inside and pulled out a short, sun-yellow robe that tied at one shoulder. She undressed from her undergarments, hose, and half-cape, then donned her new outfit and tucked her telson into the waist strap behind her spine. "Find the jar and run it through your hair. And this one on your skin. We need to blend in." Vanna followed her overseer's orders, undoing her braids and running the oily red paste through her long, frumpy hair. With the other jar, she tanned her exposed, pale skin.

"You look perfect," Lora told her with a soft smile.

"Vanna, you're familiar with the Southern Plane and Sazara from your studies, yes?" Zell asked.

"Yes."

"Good. Our first converge is a second-story room to the left of their harbor's first pier. That's where we'll sleep for the duration of our stay. You'll know it by its red-framed window. Our rooks stay here, at the secondary converge, until we leave, which may be a while."

Vanna patted Little Wing gently goodbye and commanded with her flute that she stay. They climbed up the jagged coastline, then walked along its cliff-side ledge. Sweat from the southern sun soaked her pale skin, making Vanna worry that it might ruin the oil that kept her disguised. After a long trek east, a curving wall shaded pale by weathered limestone appeared above the horizon.

"There. By the skeleton trees—underground exit ducts from Sazara," Zell pointed out. Four trees, bare of any leaves, grew from the side of the cliff. The closer they walked toward them, the louder Vanna heard a stream flowing out from it like a waterfall into the sea. She followed behind Zell and Lora as they plunged themselves off the side of the cliff and into the duct's limestone tunnel.

Water trickled through Vanna's toes, which stuck out from her flat-bottomed sandals. She followed them farther into the darkness, passing multiple drainage points until they spotted an engraved signal common to the Sisters. Zell forced the iron grating above them open, then peeked her bob-topped head up through its hole. "*Clear.*"

On her signal, they climbed out from the underground water ducts and into the eastern extent of Sazara's streets. As they moved to walk along the city's harbor, Vanna was surprised to see the people here wandering around as freely as they did, running and riding in all directions, up and down its winding and uneven streets. She panned between the alleys, watching Sazarans enter and exit the buildings, which seemed to all have their sidewalls smushed tightly together. They found the first converge and walked up to the second floor, stowing their rucksacks away and reaffixing their disguises.

Zell left them to meet with the overseer of the order they were relieving. Vanna sat staring out of the first converge's window, gazing out at Sazara's harbor and the twin lighthouses that stood tall at its entrance. By the time she returned, the day had turned to dusk. "We have our first task," Zell told them, seeming more flustered than before.

"Already?" Lora asked, striking up from her seat. "We've only just arrived."

Vanna looked on in silence.

"Alyv said this was urgent. The brief is simple—I'll be attending an important meeting near the Temple of Sciron. Lora, you'll be my lookout. Vanna, you'll be my support—stay close in case I need you. And don't break character. This is the real deal," Zell commanded. "I'll give you the details you need to know once we're there."

Zell didn't take long to rush them back out the door. Into and through the narrow streets of Sazara, they traveled, cutting from left to right in a path Vanna couldn't remember. Her new overseer ensured they stayed close enough to follow each other without becoming lost. But crossing Arcus Street was a challenge. Crowds of Sazarans packed its wide curve, flowing into and out of its busy markets and bathhouses. Vanna struggled to keep up, lifting her head above the people with prying eyes.

She managed to follow Zell and Lora down a skinny alley. "This is your point of access, Vanna. Enter through the back door and find the last room on the right. There should be a lady named Raelan directing the services. Listen to what she says, and don't speak—no matter what. Remember, blend in and lie low. I just need you inside the building to help if anything goes wrong. And if that's the case, I'll be the one to find you," Zell told her.

Vanna only nodded.

"This meeting shouldn't be long. If I don't find you before then, return to the first converge," her overseer added.

"*Got it,*" Vanna uttered in a confident lie. Though she didn't know why or what it was she was doing, Vanna was now a Sister of the Silo and needed to act like one. All her days of training in the art of combat and secretive surveillance had brought her to this day—this moment. This time, it was real.

"Good luck," Lora told her.

Vanna straightened out the wrinkles in her robe, then walked through the raggedy wooden door. Various smells of smoldering meats and wood-burning fires wafted from the rooms as she walked down the narrow passageway. A whirlwind of commotion came from the last door on the right. Vanna took a moment to calm herself before walking toward it. When she turned the corner, she only wished that Zell had given her more details.

Men and women dressed in white and black garments and aprons walked around frantically, carrying trays, pots, and pans filled with food and drink. *Raelan?* As Vanna looked around, she noticed a woman with wrinkled skin and curly red hair. Vanna walked over to the lady who turned in circles, pointing and directing the chaos. "Raelan?"

"*Excuse me?*"

"Are you Raelan?"

"It's *Miss* Raelan… And who are you?"

I shouldn't have spoken, Vanna knew. She paused for a moment, trying to think of an answer. "Julia."

"Well, Julia, you look like you need work." Miss Raelen glanced around the room frantically, then returned her gaze to Vanna, scanning her from top to bottom. "*Mm-hmm.*" She hummed as she twirled Vanna's hair and squeezed the bottoms below her waist. Vanna jumped but caught herself. "With those round eyes and even rounder bottoms, you're far too pretty to help cook or greet. *Follow me.*"

This isn't good, Vanna thought. *This is the opposite of lying low.*

She followed Miss Raelan between the rush of servants to reach a double set of swinging doors. "Wait here for the cooks to bring a cart. When it comes, roll it through that door there and then wait against the wall. Servers will plate the trays of food, so all you need to do is stand there and look pretty. It's all you're good for, so be good at it," Miss Raelan instructed her before rushing back off the same way she came.

Vanna waited for a while, watching as people passed back and forth. Some dressed like her, while others had their white aprons stained in spots of brown or orange. She debated abandoning her overseer's orders and returning to the converge. But Vanna knew that was never something a Sister should do, especially for someone as new as she was. One of the cooks finally rolled a cart down the long hallway and left it for her to grab. Vanna pushed it cautiously into the vestibule, then past a man, who held the doors open as she rolled it through the tall, arched entrance.

Zell's meeting, Vanna realized as soon as she entered. *She won't be pleased about this.*

The ceiling of the long room stretched high, past the point of distinguishing any of the gold-leafed engravings and murals shrouding it above. A long and smooth marble table extended the length of the room, with rows of embroidered chairs tucked into its sides. Just five people sat in the middle. Vanna rolled the cart down half the table's length and stopped to place it beside the wall. Two servants uncovered the silver platter and took its plates to the table. Vanna turned her back to the wall like Miss Raelan had instructed and saw Zell in one of the chairs across the table, facing her. In the brief moment when their eyes met, she could see them flash with concern and roll with ridicule.

"What is the status?" The man with white hair and his back to Vanna asked with a deep, grumbling voice.

"Partial." Next to Zell sat a man in a blue overcoat. His skin was pale, like her own, but his eyes were blue, and his hair was light and scraggly. To Vanna, his demeanor matched his appearance—rugged, unlike anyone she had seen in the city.

"Partial? I expected more for the price I am paying, Galobaron."

"We have five completed galleons and six more on the island in work," the man in the blue overcoat named Galobaron said. "All five have a full crew trained by yours truly. Though, recruiting good men from Corlis has been hard, as you might imagine."

The man with his back to Vanna looked up at the tall ceiling in thought.

"We've been hard at work with the plans and materials you have provided, Clyus. Timber for the masts is the hardest to come by."

The one with his back to me must be Clyus Calegri, Vanna realized, recognizing the man and his reputation from her studies.

"That will have to do for now," Clyus told him. "Take what vessels you have ready and leave the rifts. Bring them into the Barren Sea."

Galobaron paused his eating. His face remained still, and his eyes lifted, locking onto Clyus. "Surely, more time would be of use."

"Each day we spend building instead of transporting costs me gold," Clyus stated. "Though the time may be nigh, it has not yet arrived. Your fleet is to remain unseen until I call upon you."

"That will be a challenge."

"If the tales I've heard about you are true, Noreas Galobaron, you can handle it."

The man in the blue overcoat, named Noreas Galobaron, withered a smirk, then looked at Zell in the chair beside him. "What is she doing here?"

Can he tell Zell is from Astria? Vanna stood as still as possible next to the cart, worrying about her own disguise. Her thoughts clung to what she would say or do if she, too, were called out.

"This venture of ours includes the Astrians. Without them, you wouldn't have the plans for those ships. But she is here on behalf of her Queen at my request."

Noreas Galobaron turned to look at Zell with an enticing stare, licking his cracked lips. "You know, I've always appreciated the beauty of those Astrian women. Their silky hair and those tight hose they always wear. It's a shame they all hide away in that secluded city. Even with all that on to conceal you, you still manage to look good. What are you doing after this, miss?"

"Must I also remind you, Noreas, that entanglement between the four regions of the Plane is still forbidden," the frail man dressed in crimson to Clyus's right stated.

"The Vice-deacon is right," Clyus added. "You, more than anyone, should know better."

"What about *her*?" Noreas asked, pointing his stubby finger at Vanna. "She's the prettiest I've seen down here in a while." Vanna's eyes widened as she flattened herself against the wall. Her breathing paused, not knowing if she would need to speak.

"*Noreas Galobaron*, we are in the back hall of the Temple of Sciron. Show some decorum for once," the Vice-deacon demanded.

Clyus turned his head around to stare at Vanna, looking her up and down. His hazel eyes were captivating and his sharp, freckled face was clean-shaven. The man had few wrinkles for how old she had assumed him to be and gazed at her as if he could tell she was Astrian. "The Vice-deacon is right," he finally said, returning his attention to the table. "The temple is no place to chase your lusts."

Vanna exhaled. She continued to listen to their conversation, pretending she wasn't.

"Now, back to the matter at hand," Clyus said. "Our building operations on the islands must still continue. Do you have a trusted hand you are willing to hand them to?"

"I do."

"Good. I will be in contact. And as for our contact, the pier at my summer house will do."

"I am still unsure of this, Clyus," the Vice-deacon said, almost nervously. "What if he is spotted or seen by the norks? It would ruin our advantage."

"Forgive him," Clyus stated, looking up from his plate to wipe his mouth. "That nork King doesn't worry me. Time has passed that old tripe by, just as our new fleet of sailed ships will. But if trouble does come, we have reliable friends in the west."

"What if it comes before I can reach that summer home?" Noreas asked.

"We'll get help to you from the air, by means of those western birds," Clyus answered.

Noreas nodded in agreement, taking larger and faster bites than the others. "What about the General? I'm sure Sepatus won't take kindly to upsetting the Plane's current peace. He's a man of tradition, surely, you know."

"The Sunspear in Sepatus's hands is no more than a scepter. But like I mentioned, if difficulty arises, we have friends in the west," Clyus replied.

"And what of the hens?" Noreas asked more bluntly than before. "They worry everyone."

"Those hens in the east are smart, yes. But they'll chase after gold just like they always have. We'll begin by undercutting the cost those norks levy to transport their goods, so they'll oblige…*hopefully*."

"*Hopefully*," Noreas scoffed as he finished his meal. He tossed his silverware onto the table. "Well, then, if there is nothing left to discuss, I'll be off."

"Are we boring you, Noreas?"

"Not yet. I'm just a busy man, as you might imagine."

"Well, now you'll be even busier. *Here*." Clyus stood up and handed him a folded parchment, sealed by the wax insignia of Sacrim's crossed swords. "This is your letter of marque, officially commissioning you as the captain of Sacrim's newest fleet of privateers, signed by the Consolar Vizar himself. You'll need that when we begin negotiating with those *hens*."

When Noreas stood and reached for the letter, Clyus snapped it away. "But your subjugation to me remains. I paid for them…those ships are still my assets. *Be ready* when I call upon you."

Noreas, who was taller than Vanna had expected, took the letter and nodded.

After he left the room, Clyus turned back to Zell and slid another folded note across the table. "And you as well. That is for Queen Helera. Please deliver it to her, unadulterated."

"*Understood.*"

Clyus and his salutor left the table, cautiously staring Vanna down as they exited the long room. But of all the glares, none were as distressing to Vanna as Zell's. With her eyes alone, Vanna knew she had witnessed a meeting she wasn't supposed to.

Chapter 8

Stone

"I can't believe this is happening," Ludwyn said with his eyes fixated below on Bovere's fighting pit.

"It's midday. Roth should be out any time now." Ruth clenched her sweat-soaked palms to the splintering edge of the bench seat. Men and women from all over the Regent sat in the stands around them, shouting bets as they tossed coins of copper and silver over and under each other's outstretched arms. Most of the crowd, which by Ruth's estimation must have numbered north of twenty thousand, seemed more than happy to trade their coins for wagers against her brother. The only thing she saw change hands more were the mugs of burnt-stout and amber ale that flowed from barrels to mugs in celebration of one of the Regent's largest events—its champion-deciding bondfight.

She and Ludwyn sat near the top of the stands, sober and coinless, as they watched the loose sand of the empty pit rise off the ground with each impending breeze. Along the pit's barrier was a wooden-planked oval wall, shaped like the inner belly of a half-cut cask, to keep the rowdy crowd aback. The man Roth was to fight was named Eaton, the bondsman and commanding sentinel of Duram Lavant—head of his royal family and owner of the most harvestable blockshares in the Regent. This morning, Ruth learned that Eaton was the same champion who had represented the Regent at the Isle of Azil during the last Descindation, five solurns ago.

Ruth sat silently in her seat, praying to the Divine One for Roth's protection. It was all she could do to drown out Eaton's name being sung and shouted from most of the stands' sections. The seat she occupied was meant for Roth, while she was supposed to be sitting on one of the benches inside the Cathedral. Instead, she was only able to witness its beauty from a distance, as the two of them had to tussle through the dense crowd outside to make it to Roth's fight on time.

For the entirety of the night before, Ruth had lain awake, staring up at the ceiling of her room in the Motley Inn, uttering those same words of prayer over and over again. She felt a deep sense of regret for having dragged them both to the Applewood Tavern. And she couldn't help but feel that she was the reason why Roth was in danger today. Ruth, though, had made sure her brother couldn't escape her berating tantrum the moment they returned to their rooms. Instead of a costly trial in a Boverian court or possible expulsion from most of the wealthy cantons in the Regent, he now faced a bloody beating for everyone to witness—or worse, death.

Toward the center of the pit walked a line of men holding the hollowed longhorns of an elkan ram. All seven of them bellowed a deep and melodic sound to quiet the crowd. From the tunnel to her right, a man dressed in segmented plates of silver armor walked out, holding an indigo-colored flag with a golden bushel of wheat at its center.

"That must be Eaton," Ludwyn explained, pointing down to the man as if she couldn't see.

Eaton raised his flag into the air and turned in a circle to face the relentless roars from the stands. With a thump, he planted the flag deep into the sand in front of the tunnel. He donned his shimmering helmet and drew the longsword at his waist. With his shield in one hand, he thrust the sword into the air, riling the crowd to cheer louder.

"Where's Roth?" she asked nervously after moments passed without his entry.

"He's coming. He'll be okay," Ludwyn tried to reassure her while the stands grew restless.

"I don't think *I'll* be okay." From the left tunnel of the pit, Roth finally walked out after having to duck under its rounded arch to enter from its shadow. "*Where's his armor? Or his sword?*" Ruth asked, though her questions were drowned by boos and hollering. Out of worry, she looked over at Ludwyn, who just sat beside her, clapping louder than anyone in their section.

"He's never used one," Ludwyn answered with a teasing laugh. "All Roth knows is that forest axe of his. And his *fists*."

"You two have always been so dumb," she mumbled to herself, turning her gaze back to Roth below. "Mother and father would kill you if they saw you here today, *pulling this*."

"If they only saw half of what we did in the Northwoods, this wouldn't worry them."

Ruth could faintly see her twin brother's raggedy brown hair tucked behind the crest of his large ears. In one hand, he held a moss-colored flag with the insignia of a pine tree stitched in silver at its center—the same Lomberg coat that Kean had worn across his tabard. In his other hand, he held only a felling axe. Dressed in his clover shawl, Roth took his time to lean the flag against the pit's sidewall, causing the crowd to erupt into another chorus of boos. As their echoes continued to fill the tense air, those in the stands close to him tossed their ale or stouts at Roth before he finally caught on and moved toward the pit's center.

"He'll be okay. He looks calm," Ludwyn said with his eyes unmoved on the pit below.

"Calmness won't keep him alive."

"No, but that axe will. Roth's the best fighter in the Northwoods. And you haven't seen some of those bears he's taken on with that thing like I have."

"Bears don't have armor or swords and haven't been trained to fight like a knight in combat."

"Eaton doesn't have claws or jaws or weigh three times the size he does. He doesn't even stand to Roth's shoulders. I think if I were Roth, I'd rather be fighting this guy."

"*I'd rather he not be fighting at all*," she whispered, shaking her head in a fit of disagreement. But Ludwyn was right. Her twin brother did look calm, especially for the moment he now found himself in.

As the primary doctrine of its covenant, the Regent had no man or woman reign as king, queen, or ruler of its land. No, it was a free land where the Divine One was declared Supreme King, and every man and woman was sovereign under it, which brought contention when it came time for the Plane's Descindation. The winner of the final bondfight today would go on to represent the Regent at the Isle of Azil, and their accompanying bondsman would become the Eastern Plane's official emissary. Many heads of the royal families, and even those of the lesser, competed every half-decade for this honor. And there, of all people, was Roth, her twin brother from the small town of Tergona, fighting to become the Regent's next champion.

Ruth could only look down at the pit and tremble with worry. Those drunk in the stands around her were persistent with their screams and chants, singing songs about her brother losing. Some spoke in vulgar shouts of violence she wished she hadn't heard. But from what Ruth could gather, it wasn't so much that they hated her brother—it was just that they knew and loved Eaton. Roth was the clear underdog, an unknown, taken from the depths of the woods to be fodder for the man who was the Regent's best chance at victory against the other three champions of the Plane.

But Ruth knew her brother. And she knew it was never going to be that easy. Roth had always been stubborn and bold. He was born with an axe in his hand and loved to fight, which made watching this contest a worrisome ordeal.

The horns blew again in three bellowing spurts. Eaton took long strides toward Roth at the center of the pit, slowing to see how he might move or react. With a rush from the impatient roar of the crowd, Eaton began to glide above the sandy dirt, moving to charge at Roth and take the first swing. Roth was forced to backpedal away from his longsword's reach and duck around each of his side-winding sweeps.

"*He's got too much armor on! He's slow!*" Ludwyn shouted into the mix of the crowd.

Lud's right, Ruth thought. *Be quick, Roth.* Her hands moved from the wooden edge of the bench to clasp together under her nose. Roth continued to sweep away from Eaton's one-handed blows until his back was closing in on the pit's sidewall.

A swing from Eaton's sword caught Roth on his left shoulder, slicing through his shawl to draw first blood. In a terrified fit, Ruth closed her eyes and whispered a prayer. "*May the Divine One protect you, Roth. May its spirit give you the strength to win this fight. May divine justice rule in your favor.*"

When the crowd's shouts peaked again, Ruth opened her eyes. Roth's shoulders were pressed against the curving sidewall as he struggled to weave away from Eaton's slow thrusts. "*SWING, ROTH! SWING!*" she stood up and clamored.

Roth jolted himself back into the fight as if he'd heard his twin's supporting cry. With one hand on his axe's handle, he thrust the blunt top of its head straight into Eaton's armored chest, forcing him to stumble back.

"*Now!*" Ludwyn yelled.

Roth raised his axe head high in the air with both hands gripping its handle. In a single swing, he struck its blade straight through Eaton's rising shield. He yanked his axe back with a slick swipe, stripping it from Eaton's grip, then tossed the pierced shield off to the side. The crowd in the stands around her groaned into shallow silence as Roth charged forward, forcing Eaton to backstep faster. Ruth could only watch in horror as Roth slashed his axe from side to side, scraping Eaton's shining shoulder and breastplate armor until he became too slow to evade.

Ruth, along with everyone else in the stands, could tell that the tide of the bondfight had changed. Eaton was too slow to keep up with Roth's quick movements, especially with his heavy armor. And with his smaller stature, it was clear that he was too weak for Roth's brutish strength.

Roth stepped forward to plant his left foot hard into the sandy dirt, then swiveled his right. With a heavy-handed swing, he drove his axe straight through the blade of Eaton's longsword, shattering it into pieces. Its shards scattered into the air and landed like hail near Eaton's indigo flag.

Eaton began to flail and swing with whatever sharp splinter remained attached to his sword's hilt. Roth shifted away from his erratic moves, then lifted the head of his axe again, high into the sky. With all his might, he drove its sharp edge straight through Eaton's elbow, just between the space of his armor left exposed. The crowd burst aloud into a single gasp of disbelief as Eaton's arm was severed to the ground. Ruth whipped her head away and covered her hands over her eyes, throwing herself down to sit on the bench.

To her left, Ludwyn continued to clap and scream louder than anyone, taunting those around them. He finally turned back to Ruth, who still couldn't bear to look, and hugged her tightly, jumping up and down with childlike excitement. "*He did it! Roth did it! I told you he could do it! Roth is the champion!*"

I'm just glad he survived, she thought.

Ruth slowly uncovered her eyes and looked up to see Ludwyn's bush of a beard squinching his face to smile down at her. In the rashness of the moment, his eyes caught a peculiar glare, and his feet stopped jumping. Before she could think of what to say or do, he leaned his head in as if he wanted to kiss her.

Out of nervousness, Ruth threw herself to stand back up and turned toward the pit, joining the growing number who clapped in applause. Down below, Eaton was being carried out of the pit. Roth stood in the center with a proud smile, shoveling his axe into the air. Ruth looked up to the sky with a smile of relief that began to mirror his own. *You really did it…*

† † †

"Do you smell that?" Roth tucked his big-eared head back into their luxurious double carriage and kicked his legs up onto the cushioned bench, letting out a sigh. "The scent of *success*."

"It's been nearly a quarter-moon already. You can give it a break," Ruth told him with her back against the coachman's wall.

Beside her sat Frand, Lady Lomberg's assistant, who was assigned the most difficult task of ensuring Roth stayed out of trouble and was everywhere she needed him to be. "Actually, he isn't wrong," he turned to tell Ruth, pushing up his follicles that rested on the hump of his mushroom-shaped nose. "We've just made the last turn and are now riding along the Regent's western coastline. You can smell the ocean from here."

Ruth leaned her head in and peeked over his plump body to view the rocky coast. Other than their quick stop at the Grand Forks, she hadn't had much of a view that wasn't either fields of wheat, meadows of green grass with endless herds of sheep, or the rivers and forestry that stretched between them. It made her smile to feel the coast's breeze and see the waves crash against the boulders and pebbles of the beach.

Across from her and next to Roth sat Ludwyn, who, too, was struggling to see the coast over Roth's broad shoulders. Since Roth had won his bondfight at the pit, Ruth had rarely spoken to, or even seen, either of them. Though they all still stayed in Bovere for days after the fight, Ludwyn had followed Roth around as he was paraded through every major canton of the city as the Regent's newest champion. Ruth, instead, had decided to fulfill her earlier wishes and spent her time in the Cathedral, attending its daily Divine Services and praying within its grand walls of historic beauty. Each day, she'd visit with the Cathedral's novices and juniors who studied in the college on the campus behind it, then walk through the central plaza to view the grand monuments and all its displays of art. In the evenings, she'd take long strolls through Bovere's gardens and explore the small-market shops along its many cobblestone-paved creeks.

In those few days Ruth spent alone, she had almost forgotten what Ludwyn had tried to do the day Roth had won, when he leaned in to kiss her. And what she couldn't. She was so caught up with emotion after Roth had survived and with her own travels throughout Bovere that she had pushed that weird memory to the recesses of her mind.

But as they rode in the carriage across from one another for the past few days, that feeling of unsettled awkwardness had returned to the surface of her mind. Ruth had never kissed a boy before. In all her nineteen solurns of life, she had been coddled away in Tergona—a small town near the Northwoods where everyone still knew her as Edmon and Roseanna's little girl. And there, Ludwyn was still just the boy from the two-roomed shack up its lone path.

But that was before Roth had become the Regent's champion. Her twin brother was now a figure the crowd in the streets revered, one who couldn't stroll anywhere without being stopped and encouraged to bring the Eastern Plane back to its rightful glory. And both he and Ludwyn always seemed to have a bounty of young Boverian women straddling their sides everywhere they went.

In that quarter-moon's pass, though, Ruth was still just Ruth. She turned her attention back to the inside of the carriage and reopened her book. Every so often, she would glance across the carriage at Ludwyn. He had mostly kept his eyes closed in a slumber like Roth, trying to recover from the series of drunken nights they had just enjoyed. Ludwyn was shorter than Roth and not nearly as stocky. He kept his short hair combed cleanly over, sweeping its oily curls across the square corners of his broad forehead. From his bushy eyebrows down, dark hairs covered his body like a wool blanket. Ruth's mother would often joke about how much he belonged in the Northwoods, and that the day would soon come when Roth would mistake him for one of those bears they always told tales of.

Ludwyn was a nice young man and a good friend of their family. He had grown up with only his aging mother and had become like a second brother to Ruth and even a third child to the Fendorses. But Ruth couldn't, and never had, thought of him in any romantic way. And she had always just assumed he shared that feeling. That was, until moments after Roth had won his fight in the pit.

"It shouldn't be too long until we pass Roverra," Frand said as he cracked open a fresh jar of pickled cheese. After drying the oil off two curdled balls, he popped them into his mouth and mumbled, "One of my favorite places…and the most fun to be after the Descindation."

"Why is that?"

"It's where everyone who is anyone goes, for a moon or two even, after the Descindation. Most royals have their third or fourth estates out this way, along the beach. It's a little less formal than our gala at the Court of Champions. But still, only a few coatless people are wealthy enough to traverse its streets."

"*Coatless people?*" she asked.

"Oh, right. I've forgotten you aren't from Bovere. Men, or women, I might add, without a family coat of arms."

Ruth's eyebrows tightened. "A *slur*, you mean. For the poor."

"No, not really. There are many historic coats today that are not wealthy. Some of the old royals, like the Ockmans, or the Furths, that once had grand estates across the lands a thousand solurns ago, are now struggling today to get by."

"Just like the rest of us. What happened to them? Do you have a coat?"

"Today's market isn't like the old. Land for estates is harder to come by, and most of our goods now get shipped to the Southern Plane for profit—even from Lady Lomberg's own mills. The norks set the price of transport, but the gold they pay down there makes the trade worth it," Frand explained as he scoffed down a few more curdled balls of pickled cheese. "And I wear the Lomberg's, of course—the silver pine. Generations of my father's fathers have worked in various positions for their heads. Our family extends beyond blood."

Ruth looked down with a hint of despair, thinking about her own family. They were simple and small. Their heirlooms were iron pans and pots or relics found and scavenged in the fields from the Age of Knights. They had no castles or estates and no grand stories or tales written in the books of history. And they had no coat of arms to brandish their grand herald on a flag or as a pin on their collars like the royals did today.

"Don't look too down, dear," Frand said, trying to cheer her up. "Most in the Regent are coatless. The crowd that will fill the isle and the Tessereum, like they had the streets of Bovere, will almost all be coatless. And if Roth wins, there's no doubt that Lady Lomberg will make him one of her own."

But that's Roth. What about me? Ruth looked back at Frand and smiled through her affliction.

"Oh, look, you can see the wharf that leads up the Fleming River just ahead. Only a little way to go now."

Ruth gazed out at the four long piers that stretched out from the rocky coast. "Where are all the boats?"

"Taking people to the isle, of course. Sometimes I forget none of you have been to the Descindation before. It's quite the spectacle. Our allotment on the eastern side of the Tessereum will be packed with tents and festivities, like always—the most fun of times."

"How many of these have you been to?"

"This one will be my sixth—well, maybe seventh. But I was too young to remember the first. And it was before I was in the High Stands, so I choose not to count it."

"That's so many," Ruth said with a gasp that leaned toward sarcasm. "You're a lot older than I expected."

Frand grunted in response, clearly hoping she'd be impressed by how often he had traveled to the isle. "Roverra should be just ahead."

Beyond their view from the carriage's window, Ruth saw an assortment of tall buildings that were brightly colored in various shades of blue, yellow, and white, lined along the coast. She could faintly see blobs of people in white and green garbs festively walking up and down its main street, which followed a length of the beach. Distanced from them all was Roverra's sceptory, which Ruth looked upon with fondness. "The water there looks so pretty. From here, we cross the Tannen Bridge, right?"

"Yes. It's just a little farther. Roverra is the last city and canton before we officially leave the Regent."

Ruth carried a smile of genuine excitement as their carriage traveled south along the dirt path to reach the Tannen Bridge. Frand had woken the two boys up and tried to explain the historical significance of the bridge that connected the Eastern Plane to the Isle of Azil, though they cared little. Held by columns of mortared stone that stretched tall above the water, the bridge's arches spanned far to support its wide lanes. Down below, and far north of the Grand Channel, Ruth recognized three ships of the norks' navy blazing along the coast with speed from their oars as they traveled west.

"Haven't seen those before either, huh?" Frand asked.

"No…I can't say I have."

"They tend to stick to Roark's River, to go to and from Bovere. And they usually run one or two cargo galleys to one galley of war. Around this time, though, their cargo is people. And they make the most from transporting those from Astria. Which is why I'm surprised to see them this far east. Maybe that northern port on the isle is already full."

"Have we made it yet?" Roth asked. He rubbed his eyes and drank from his waterskin.

"Almost," Frand replied. "Up ahead of our caravan, you might be able to see the allotment. We'll have to pass through it to reach the Court of Champions at the foot of the Tessereum."

Ruth released a deep breath and took it all in. It was her first time out of the Regent and her first time witnessing the Isle of Azil. The land was broader and taller than she presumed it to be. From coast to coast, the sea straddled its rocky shore, indistinguishable from one end of the bridge to the other. The green of its grass lifted the isle to life, though it grew far fewer trees than the meadows of the Eastern Plane. Ruth imagined it like a painting, capturing the colors in her mind as if each thought was a stroke from her brush. And the image painted was one she would never forget.

Her brother stuck his head out the window and ran his hands across his tired face, cracking a smile. Farther down the isle's dirt road, the carriage traveled toward its center, rolling along in the middle of Lady Lomberg's long caravan. The people of the Regent began to swarm to their windows from all directions as they passed tents sprouted by spikes and colorful sheets of canvas. Behind them, Ruth saw campfires lift the smells of smoked meat into the cloudless air. The sounds of music and laughter wafted toward them like the breeze off the coast. She waved politely at everyone who cheered them on, feeling overwhelmed at the never-ending parade of new but familiar faces of adoration.

After a long journey through the fanatical crowd, the carriage finally came to a stop when it entered a cool shadow. Ruth exited with her back to the masses, being held back by a gate and a conglomeration of sentinels who guarded it. In silent awe, she looked up at the white-bricked eastern wall of the Tessereum. Vines of ivy wrapped around the arena's marble pillars that stood tall to support its square outer edge. Directly ahead, at the bottom, was the Court of Champions—a four-story block-shaped building with a wrap-around balcony that bordered its highest floor. At its center was a tall but thin pillar that rose to spiral halfway up the Tessereum's outer wall.

"This is *incredible*," she said with her mouth hanging open.

"Each of the four allotments has one identical," Frand sputtered, hurrying away from the crowd.

While Ruth and Ludwyn were struck still by its size, Roth walked calmly toward the court. When they didn't follow, he turned back and asked, "Just like Tergona, *right?*"

"*Right.*" Ruth could only smile as Lady Lomberg's sentinels escorted them inside the first floor and showed them each to their guest rooms. But before Ruth could even settle down from her exhilaration, Frand had returned from the floor above to inform her and Ludwyn that they were both invited to join Roth and the rest of Lady Lomberg's distinguished guests at the court's gala on the third floor, at evening's end.

And so, Ruth took her time to change into the only gown she owned—a dress stitched by her mother when she became a lady. It was a shade lighter than shale, and its bottom crest fluffed out like a bell-bottomed pear. She struggled to fit its ruffles of white lace over her broad shoulders and had to wrap her larger chest tightly to slip it up. Using the lone mirror in her small guest room, she brushed out her long chestnut-colored hair, then took a deep breath to settle her nerves.

Ludwyn stood waiting for her outside of their rooms. "Ruth, you look great," he complimented her, to which she politely thanked him.

When they reached the grand door to the third floor's open gala, they found Roth. Both boys were dressed in bland gray coats, which looked as if they didn't quite fit and hadn't ever been worn before. "Roth and I look like we've just been dragged in from the allotment," Ludwyn sneered.

"We may as well have been," Roth said with a laugh, clearly not as nervous as either of them.

Dark drapes hung from the windows of the Court of Champions' grand room, set against white marble walls and a tracery of tiled floors. Older men and women, dressed in the most magnificent coats and gowns, filled the room, chatting in whispers from one group to another, just above the duet of harps in the background. Near the room's center was a half-columned pedestal, and atop it was a glass-enclosed vase. Before she could even see inside it, Roth and Ludwyn shouted to each other in excitement, "*The Stonehammer!*"

The two boys darted right at it without stopping to talk or introduce themselves to anyone. To her recognition, a handful of Tohenic knights stood in protection of the Stonehammer, wearing a thin layer of chainmail under their pure-white surcoats. At each of their chests was the symbol of the Divine Crest—three interlocking circles stitched black, with the bottom two hanging from the single loop above. Ruth knew it immediately as the same crest all thirteen of the divine sages wore in metal, locked to a chain around their neck.

Three of the Tohenic knights rushed forward, bracing the handles of their longswords to stop the two of them from getting any closer to the amulon. Ruth peeked around to get a better view inside the vase and saw the petrified hand, cut at its wrist, holding the Stonehammer's short handle. At its head was a dull but shimmering stone, one the color of an emerald.

For quite some time, Ruth wandered around the gala alone. It was obvious that none of them belonged. She tried to remember each face that passed, admiring their fine dresses and outfits, doing her best to fit in. Every so often, Ludwyn would return to her side and ask if she needed a drink. But it wasn't until a calm voice came from behind her shoulder that Ruth had anyone to converse with. "First time?"

An older man, who was nearly the same height as her, being taller than most, walked closer to Ruth in a silken black tunic. To the left of his chest, near his collar, was the small pin of a white dove flower with seven petals. *A frocked knight,* Ruth recognized. On the other collar was a pin with crossed hammers. "Yes."

"Quite a spectacle, isn't it?"

"The Stonehammer? Or the Court of Champions?"

"Both. I'm Favian Gravelot, by the way." He stuck his hand out to shake her own.

"Pleasure. Ruth Fendorse."

"Ah, you must be related to our champion."

"His twin sister, yes." Ruth looked across the dimly lit room and saw Roth and Ludwyn at the bar with chalices of wine in both of their hands.

"I can see the resemblance," he said, looking her up and down. "Well, I wish him the best of luck. This will be the Plane's thirty-fourth Descindation, and it may yet be the best."

The man she chatted with was what Ruth had always aspired to be— an honorary knight of the Cathedral. And so, she tried hard to restrain herself and say only what was formal and appropriate in such a setting. "I can only pray to the Divine One for Roth's safety," Ruth said calmly.

"Ah, a praying young woman. That's a good sight to see in today's age. Most of the fights I've been to have been won by Sacrim or Astria. But you should feel confident to know that none that I have witnessed resulted in the death of our own."

"That's *comforting*," Ruth lied. The older man had a soft and gentle face, one that rounded to shape his perfectly cut silver hair.

"But by the looks of it, he'll be okay," Favian said with a laugh, pointing across the room.

There, Roth stood shouting near the room's far corner, toe to toe and a head's length taller than a group of sentinels struggling to hold him back. *Of all times...Roth. Why must you always embarrass us?* "I should go. It was a pleasure to meet you, sir," Ruth said in a panic before she hurried across the room. She wove through the commotion and sudden silence to try to corral and untangle Roth away.

"It's okay—it's okay," she heard Ludwyn say, trying to calm him down.

"What's happened now?" Frand scampered over to ask, his voice whining with disappointment.

"One of the men, I think maybe a sentinel of Duram Lavant, insulted him. Well, more than insulted him," Ludwyn explained as a few of the other sentinels still held Roth back. "Something about a coatless hen...and that he was a bastard son of a mangy bear...well, they said it in a phrase I won't repeat—about your mother, Ruth."

"This is the gala in the Court of Champions, not some backwoods hut! *And he's our champion, for the Gate's sake!* He needs to save all of that fighting—regardless of what those scoundrels tell him," Frand plundered out fast, spitting between his words as he spoke.

"He's probably just nervous. I'll get him out of here," Ruth told them.

Ludwyn gave her a guilty look, then said, "No. I'll do it, Ruth. You enjoy the night. If you can, find Lady Lomberg and tell her I have Roth. And maybe ask her when I need to have him awake for tomorrow."

Ruth nodded and watched as Ludwyn and a few other sentinels escorted the red-faced Roth away. She searched around the room for the short and plump Lady Lomberg but couldn't spot her anywhere. "Frand," Ruth finally said, tugging at his busy sleeve as he tried to get the people's attention back to the party. "Where is Lady Lomberg?"

"Does it look like I know? Check the next floor, if I had a guess. She's probably up there drinking."

Ruth walked out of the gala, feeling every eye from the wealthy members of the royal families judging her as she headed toward the door. She walked up the stairs to the top floor. At its far edge was a shadowed figure leaning against the rail of the balcony, just as Frand had guessed.

"Lady Lomberg?" Ruth walked closer to ask cautiously.

"*Yes?* Can I help you?" Lady Lomberg turned around slowly in her tight green dress, holding a chalice of wine in her hand. "Oh, it's just you."

Ruth joined her beside the railing and looked out at the isle's eastern allotment. Columns of smoke rose between the tents scattered throughout the isle's eastern field. Off in the distance, tunes from lutes and barrel drums played loudly above the laughs and chatter from the drunken dances, filling the air as far back as the night would allow her to see.

"What do you want?" Lady Lomberg asked with a drunken slur.

"To let you know that Roth had a scuffle with some sentinels and left the party. And to ask where he needs to be tomorrow."

"Do I look like his mother? If anything, you should know—you're smart."

Ruth looked back out at the tents in silence, realizing that if anyone knew, it would have been Frand.

"That was mean of me. I apologize." Lady Lomberg relaxed her shoulders, then joined her to gaze out at the allotment. "You're luckier than you know. Not just to be here, but to have a family that actually cares about you back home. At least, that's what Frand tells me. Sometimes, when I used to come to these things, I would wish that I could be down there, with them, away from all of this and these people."

Ruth didn't know what to say. She could tell that Lady Lomberg was drunk.

"But here I am—*today*—the hosting emissary."

"Is that why you're up here?"

"*No.*" She laughed with a drunken croak. "The fourth floor is reserved for the bondsman and the emissary. I'm up here now because Lucas Clovin is down there. And the rest of them. The Orlaiths...the Bangors...even the damned Ockmans paid for seats in the High Stands. *One hundred* gold coins to sit on their flat tushes, and I'm the dumb one who's given you and your other friend seats up there for free."

"Thank you," Ruth said, her eyes pinned back in disbelief. Other than the scarce times at the mill, it was rare for Ruth to see a single gold coin in Tergona, let alone a hundred of them.

"Don't thank me, thank your brother. He had it added to our bonding contract before he ever fought back in Bovere."

Ruth smiled as she turned to look at Lady Lomberg. "I will. I just hope I'll have the chance to do so after his fight."

"You will. The Descindation can get reckless, yes, but deaths tend to be a rare occurrence. At least between the good fighters. Though that changes here and there." She smirked. "It's all just a rouse to keep the people of the Plane at ease—to fill their lust for blood and war without needing actual blood and war. The following morning, the four leaders of the regions have to meet in the Convault—*the real war*. And who gets to go this time? *Me*."

That's the real reason why she's so nervous, Ruth realized. "That sounds like a great honor."

"*Honor*," Lady Lomberg sneered. "I sure hope so. At least, that's what I'm owed."

"Is that why they've brought the Stonehammer up from the crypts of the Cathedral?"

"For pageantry's sake, yes. But I don't even get to touch the damned thing. The last person who did still has their hand wrapped around it. Something about some damned covenant."

"I saw."

"As if it isn't already hard enough being a woman in a Plane run by mad men. They could at least let me hold it like they get to with their pricks every day." Ruth laughed as Lady Lomberg lifted her chalice, motioning for her to take a sip. "Drink. It helps with the nerves. I have a lot riding on this fight."

I hope Roth won't disappoint you, Ruth thought as she sipped the wine. She looked out at the allotment that was filled to the brim with drunken travelers from all over the Regent. While watching them from high above, Ruth slowly remembered where she came from and where she always wanted to be. Standing there, high in the Court of Champions, surrounded by people of class and those who carried respect from the Cathedral, Ruth felt like she belonged. And she couldn't understand why Lady Lomberg felt otherwise. "I do, too."

"Wine is how we women will survive."

Ruth just smiled and took another sip. "*I pray that to be true.*"

CHAPTER 9

SUN

"**B**loody barbarians, those headless hens. Just look at them," Commander Kastas hissed.

Cleo looked to his right, shaded from the cloudless sun by the brim of his bronze helmet. Frivolous singing from a bouncing wall of green and brown filled every seat of the Tessereum's east stands as the champions from each region of the four Planes readied their weapons and armor to fight. Cleo had reached his seat in the southernmost high stands just in time to witness the Descindation's opening ceremony. After leaving Kladden in charge of the Sixth Brigade at Fort Corlach near Cignus, he rode for three days straight with an accompanying escort to arrive at the Isle of Azil on time.

Four double-horse chariots led in from each tunnel of the Tessereum's lower pit, pulling black-and-white-robed figures beating on large, leather tumble drums with a restless rhythm. They traveled in a rounding circle, passing between each sharp-sided division of the Tessereum's square-shaped marble stands. As they wound their way toward the pit's center, their path dwindled, slowing their chariots to stop behind each of the four champions that faced their respective regions.

Cleo watched in eager anticipation, still trying to catch his breath from climbing the Court of Champions' spiraling stairs. In a lapsing pause, he scanned the other three stands of the Tessereum. The Astrians in the stands to his left sat with quiet and calm women who dressed in shades of black and purple. Straight across from his own, Marredom's stands were practically empty. Their lower seats were filled only a few rows deep, despite their high stands in the middle being crowded from shoulder to shoulder. Cleo was too far away to discern any of their faces, but it was clear that neither of those two crowds matched the fervent intensity of the

Regent's or their own. And for as much as he didn't want to admit it, the hens of the east were certainly the loudest.

The oldest of the men, dressed in a white sleeveless robe with a long beard and hair to match, walked from his chariot holding a satin black sack. From the middle of the Tessereum's pit, he waited for the four crowds of the Plane to come to silence before proclaiming aloud, "*We welcome all of you to the Isle of Azil for the Plane's thirty-fourth Descindation, in our seven hundred and forty-first solar season's turn since the descent. With great honor, I must remind you all why we are gathered here today. For peace. For cooperation. For resolve. Since the end of the Amulonic War, we have established this tournament within the Descindation Treaty as a continuation of our shared ideals. Each of our four regions' champions shall fight for their home Plane in reverence, with respect for the lives of our forefathers lost and the lives of our future children we shall save. May our treaty continue forevermore... Now, we shall cast the die!*"

The Tessereum and its thousands of onlookers all erupted from their seats with thunderous applause. Cleo could feel the hair on his bare arms rise like leaves to the sun as he stood with the crowd to clap for the four champions below. There, each of them selected a black or white stone from the man's sack to match their first opponent.

Cleo nervously shifted his royal-red cloak to the side when the crowd finally settled. He took the changing moment to look around. On the right side of their high stands, where he sat, were many members of Sacrim's Guard, along with their family members and distinguished guests. Sepatus and his assistants sat at the forefront, while the six commanders had a row reserved for them near the top—a place where Cleo felt he didn't yet belong. Besides his passing conversation with Commander Giganti when he first took his seat, Cleo received only glares and near-silent scoffs from the others.

To worsen his situation, the Fifth Brigade's commander, Jep Kastas, sat beside Cleo on his left. He was an old, sun-beaten brute from the Fifth Partition—home to the Sineaqe desert, which connected Sacrim to the Regent and was known for its dismal conditions. And Commander Kastas certainly had the personality to match. He and the Fifth Brigade were the only guardsmen allowed to deviate from their standard uniform. His exposed, weathered skin was wrapped tightly in cloth, the same as his neck and head, which covered everything except the dark spots and boils that speckled across his hairless face.

On the left side of Sacrim's high stands sat the Consolar Vizar and his accompanying magistrates and chambermen, as well as their families and guests. In all of Cleo's discomfort, there was one sight—other than the pit below—that helped to better his mood. Scarlett Calegri sat just above a row of chambermen, laughing and clapping with a group of young women similar in age.

Cleo caught a glimpse of her smile after he delayed taking his seat. She wore a crimson dress stitched with emblems of golden roses patterned on its sleeved but strapless brims. Her orange hair curled perfectly and was knotted into a bundle, pinned high by fresh-cut roses. Despite his obstructed view, Cleo couldn't help but look her way, peering over to glimpse her peachy lips that sculpted her contagious smile. Scarlett's face had a warm and soft allure, far more welcoming than that of the commanders Cleo sat beside.

As the chariots left to exit back through the tunnels, a deep horn, hidden from the Tessereum, bellowed in echoes to ready the first fight. The crowd's roar grew, and Cleo glanced over at Scarlett once more. With a nervous startle, he saw her glancing back. Her blue eyes had caught Cleo's own and widened with enthusiasm. Before he could break his glare back to the pit, Scarlett stood up from her group of sitting friends and began to sidestep toward him.

"Can I sit here?" she asked an older woman in the row before Cleo. Scarlett squeezed into the space she left, giving the older lady in the pink gown a thankful smile. "How are you, *Commander?*"

"You can still call me Cleo, Scarlett," he replied in a tone that matched her sarcasm. "I'm glad to see you here."

"It *was* Cleo the last time I saw you. Now, I'm not so sure. *Look at you.* Cloak, helmet, sword, and everything. You fit right in," she said with her freckled shoulders turned away from the pit, toward him.

Cleo was captivated by the graceful curve between her shoulders and neck. "I don't know if *fit in* are the right words. I might just be a little too young for that," he responded lowly so the other commanders couldn't hear him.

Cleo was glad to hear the horn bellow once more. The first fight had officially begun, and the people around him had no choice but to move their attention down to the pit below, away from their friendly conversation. Even Scarlett had turned toward the square-walled arena that bounced with loose sand from the occasional breeze. Near the eastern tunnel stood a giant man with his back to the boisterous crowd, dressed without armor and wielding only an axe. Opposite him was a much smaller woman who wore tight black leather from boot to neck. She had overlapping segments of black armor, and her double braids hung loosely to her waist. The pale woman patted the bottom of the long-handled weapon she held, and its blade fell to dangle from its connecting chain. Cleo recognized it as a telson from his teachings with Vident Lement—the weapon of choice for those old rook riders from the west.

"My gold is on the woman," Scarlett turned back to tell Cleo.

"*No way…* Do you see how big that man is?"

"Cleo, you should know your history as well as anyone. Those Astrian women know how to fight."

She has a point. Cleo just bobbed his head in agreement.

"Should we bet on it?" Scarlett asked with an enticing smirk.

"I don't think commanders should be engaging in that sort of thing."

"*Oh*, come on. Just a friendly wager."

"Okay, fine." Cleo's smile grew as if he couldn't deny her request. The two fighting champions began to move closer. "What'll it be?"

"Let's see…if I win, you join me at Jade's father's camp tonight out in the allotment. He's throwing a party, and everyone in Sazara will be there."

Cleo couldn't prevent his green eyes from glinting as he smiled at the possibility of spending the night with Scarlett and her friends. From what he knew of the young women in Sazara, they loved their wine and their dancing, and it was sure to be a night filled with fun. "And if I win?"

"Well, what would you want?"

He thought hard to answer her question as the fight finally rang aloud with its first clashes. After Scarlett's suggestion, he just wanted her to win so that he could join her at the party. But Cleo knew he couldn't be too honest and tell her how he really felt. And so, he thought of something similar. "If I win, you join me at the after-party in the Court of Champions."

"*Oh*, come on…that sounds miserable. Another night with all those boring chambermen. Spare me from that, *please*, Cleo."

"You were so confident earlier that the woman from Astria would win, so you shouldn't worry," Cleo said with a soft laugh.

Scarlett released a sarcastic sigh. "*Fine*. Deal." Her soft lips curled into a smile as she stuck out her wrist for the two of them to shake. "Now that we've bet on it, I should probably tell you that the Regent's champion isn't even a fighter. He's just a forest ranger. It was a last-moment switch for the man who was supposed to fight."

"You and your secrets, huh," Cleo said with a smirk. But Cleo was glad to learn that the Astrian woman would likely win. "You haven't changed a bit."

Scarlett smiled, then turned back to the pit with the rest of the high stands, watching the first fight as it began to grow interesting. The Astrian woman charged forward, fast and light-footed, forcing the tall man to backstep in frantic spurts. His large frame, covered only by a plain shawl, struggled to evade any of her quick strikes. In his hand was only an axe, which he swung slowly and moved to block her swinging slashes.

"You sure you still want to keep this bet?" Scarlett turned again to ask with a smirk of her own.

Cleo rolled his eyes, watching intensely as the eastern stands grew quieter with each passing moment. Their champion already had several small cuts on his arms and legs from the telson's swinging blade. He struggled to keep up with the woman's swift speed. Scarlett cheered and clapped as the Astrian woman kept pushing him backward, far enough until his broad shoulders became pinned against their southern wall of the pit. Cleo looked down eagerly in excitement, almost forgetting what it was like to see a real fight in person—especially now that the action was so close.

Those seated in the lowest rows of the southern stands hurled insults at the fight. The Regent's champion had taken another deep cut on the side of his arm. But when she slung her blade down from the sky again, he lifted his axe. This time, the telson's chain had caught the handle, wrapping around it like the threads of a spool. Gasps filled the air. The giant champion tugged her close, then threw his clenched fist into the woman's chest. The eastern stands burst into cheers, much louder than earlier, forming a chant that clamored the words "*BEAR! BEAR! BEAR!*" over and over again.

The Astrian champion had been flung back and landed harshly on her shoulder. With her telson now thrown far away, the man rushed in with his axe, delivering blow after two-handed blow into the thick sand. The woman in black wiggled away like a slug, trying to escape the heat of summer's sun.

"*Are you sure he hasn't fought before?*" Cleo leaned in to tease Scarlett.

With each dig of his axe, the stands to their right cheered in waves of hopeful crows. But the braided woman managed to squirm away and avoid his deathly thumps. Weaponless, she fought hard to evade his strikes and crawled back onto her feet to throw a few flailing punches of her own.

Just as Scarlett turned around to respond, the Regent's crowd rang aloud in cheer. The giant man had grabbed the Astrian woman by her wrist and broken her arm with a swing from the blunt end of his axe. He dangled her in the air and threw his axe to the ground, driving his stone of a fist straight into the woman's stomach. She rolled around on the sand, unable to stand back up.

"That's no man...that's a beast," Commander Kastas snarled after watching the entire fight in silence.

"No. That's a *bear*," Cleo said with a smile, before realizing that he had won the wager with Scarlett. His smile quickly simmered as he stood to join the stands in applause.

The man in the white robe reentered through the tunnel and raised the tired and bloody arm of the Regent's champion. "*Roth Fendorse of Tergona, champion of the Regent, advances!*"

"Looks as if I'll be seeing you tonight at the court," Cleo said beneath the stand-shaking stomps of the drunken, eastern crowd.

"Unfortunately, so." Scarlett let out a disappointed sigh. "Guess I'll just have to wear one of my longer gowns tonight and not my short, fun one."

Cleo sneered under his breath. "We'll make fun of it, just like we used to when we were kids, back in the square."

"I'm sure we will. That's the only way I'll survive the night. But I guess I won't be needing this." Scarlett reached for her fire-orange hair and pulled out a blood rose. "Here, you take it. You can hand it back to me tonight—on our date."

Date? Beneath his vest, Cleo's chest began to beat with nervous thumps, matching the loud claps and deep stomps of the Tessereum's stands. He took the rose and said, "*Gladly.*"

"I'm going back to sit with Jade and Leanne. But this was fun, *Commander.* I shall see you tonight."

Cleo couldn't hide the grin that shone from the deepest trough of his knotted stomach. What he did hide, though, was her rose. At least before the other commanders could notice. As Scarlett shuffled her way through the shoulders of the standing crowd, the younger commander to the left of Kastas leaned over to tell Cleo, "Stare any longer, and she won't come back."

Cleo caught himself and chuckled to sway away the younger man's comment. "Wouldn't want that now, would we?"

"Commander Salvitore Galiano," he said, squeezing to move between Kastas and Cleo. "But you can call me Sal." The commander of the Third Brigade was significantly taller than Cleo and appeared to be half a decade older. The cheeks of his face were as wide as Kladden's, and unlike Scarlett's soft and conforming profile. He had unusually long brown hair tied back like a horse's tail, hidden under his bronze helmet.

"Commander Cleo Scordisci." Cleo reached out and shook his fellow commander's wrist.

"*Ah*, so I finally meet the new blood everyone's been chatting about. You should know better than anyone to be careful with that one. If it weren't her father, it'd be your own."

"I'm aware," Cleo stated with the warm air taken out of him. His flat-chinned smile turned sour as he pictured the conflict that would arise if he placed his father in that situation.

Clyus Calegri and Sepatus already had enough contention, after having shared the dual seats of Sacrim's consol for more than a decade before his son had taken over as Sacrim's vizar. Cleo didn't need anyone to tell him he'd be better off avoiding Scarlett. Her father was a man who commanded respect—someone who would have a line of people ready to kiss his signet if he found himself outside Sazara's streets long enough. He was a man who meant as much to the people of Sacrim as its founders, Claros included. And he was the wealthiest among the wealthy and the most powerful of all in the Southern Plane. All besides Sepatus, that is, who wielded the only thing capable of keeping Clyus's ambitions corralled.

The election of Cleo's father to the rank of consolar general had ended a long lineage of Calegri blood wielding the Sunspear. And Clyus, along with his many cousins and distant relatives, resented Sepatus for it. When he was young, Cleo learned quickly that if he saw Scarlett more often than just their occasional passings, his father would have him sent back to Cignus the next day. But the more he pictured the curls of her hair, her soft lips, and enchanting freckles, the more he felt his desire to be beside her too enticing.

Cleo continued to talk with Sal about the Guard while the Tessereum's south stands cheered on their champion, Kroton, as he readied to take the pit. Kroton was sun-weathered, like most southerners, and reminded Cleo of Kladden by the way his stocky body filled out his tall frame. Kroton drew his shortsword from its sheath and lifted its tip toward the sun. With his shield hand, he unclasped his gold cloak and stomped powerfully toward the center of the pit.

"He's one of the Calegris' salutors," Sal explained.

"He certainly looks the part."

At the opposite end, Marredom's champion walked out of their tunnel to much quieter applause. Tall and lengthy, the pale man wore a silver helmet and a black tunic under a full suit of chainmail.

"Who does he think he is, some sort of knight?" Commander Kastas mocked. "That age is long gone."

"I wouldn't be so sure about that," Sal noted. "There are still a few in the east, guarding that bloody Cathedral."

"The Tohenic knights?" Cleo asked, remembering their name from Vident Lement's teachings.

"That's it. I think."

"They are as much knights as those royals are royal," Kastas scoffed. "But this fool is just a nork. Embarrassing is what it is."

"Come on, Kroton," Sal cheered.

"Sacrim has won the last few, and after seeing the field, this has the makings to be no different. At least, if I were a betting man," Cleo said.

"You were a betting man just a few moments ago," Sal stated with a light chuckle.

Cleo looked the other way, realizing that Sal, and likely Kastas, must have overheard some of his conversation with Scarlett.

"But this is different. It would be stealing if someone dared to wager on that nork."

"At least he's got a sword," Cleo said.

"He'd be better off fighting with one of those paddles."

Cleo laughed at the northern champion's expense as the row of commanders sat with the rest of the crowd, awaiting the horn's deep bellow. Sure enough, the fight began just as they had described. Kroton was practically toying with the frail champion from Marredom, chasing him left and right without even attempting to deliver any swings with his shortsword. To the north's growing anger, Kroton cornered their champion against the northern wall, then looked up at them to laugh. The blond-haired champion unleashed his own retaliatory attempts with his curved saber, but none were meaningful against Kroton's broad shield of bronze.

I could have fought this one, Cleo thought, glancing over at Scarlett, who was enjoying Sacrim's dominance. He followed some of the commanders as they turned toward the eastern crowd to measure their reactions. It seemed as if everyone in the Tessereum knew that the winner would be decided between the two of them.

Kroton delivered a heavy one-handed strike that punctured the loose chainmail of Marredom's champion, drawing first blood at his shoulder. From then on, the toying stopped. Each of his quick slashes caused flying figures of blood to paint both of their armor red. Kroton's smooth and controlling moves led to the final thrust of his narrow shortsword being driven straight through the stomach of the Northern Plane's champion. The southern stands all stood to cheer as Kroton slowly withdrew his sword, forcing the pale man to collapse impishly onto the sand.

"That was too easy," Cleo said.

Through the loud lauding of the crowd, the white-robed man returned to the pit and directed his assistants to carry Marredom's champion away. He lifted the arm of Sacrim's champion and announced, *"Kroton Sarnesi of Sazara, champion of Sacrim, advances!"*

Cleo looked down at the front row of the high stands and saw his father and Cayen standing side by side. Both clapped without smiling, wearing matching robes and inverted cloaks. Cleo glanced over at Scarlett and watched her and her friends all fawning over the much older Kroton as he readied himself near their tunnel for the final fight. Eventually, the Regent's bear of a champion reentered the pit to stir the eastern stands of the Tessereum into a frenzy. His left shoulder was now wrapped by a blood-stained bandage under his arm and around his chest, half-hidden by a fresh green garment.

"Should make quick work of this injured bear," Kastas scoffed.

"Forget a fight. He'd be smart not to die," Sal added. Cleo agreed, but the Regent's champion looked focused, unamused by the crowds' glorifying chants that sang his name, as loud as those chants were.

"Die, he might."

Cleo scrunched his nose and looked at the corner between the stands to his right, watching the southern and eastern crowds yell fiercely at each other. Sal noticed Cleo's gaze and said, "That's how you can tell the Descindation Treaty works. Better they fight and yell here than back out in the Plane."

"Wouldn't it be better if they didn't fight or yell at all?" Cleo asked.

"Everyone knows that would be impossible. War is in our nature."

Cleo reaffixed his bronze-brimmed helmet to shade his eyes from the sun as the horn blew for the final time. Kroton charged forward from their side of the pit, the spades of his skirt flittering in the air. The intense cheers were loud enough to shake the white stone under Cleo's sandals, empowering their champion on. He was quick. Much quicker than before, especially without any of his taunting and toying. The champion from the east, named Roth Fendorse, struggled to keep up, still using his wood-splitting axe to block or maneuver around Kroton's powerful swings.

"Just land one already, dammit," Sal said impatiently. "I put thirty golds on us winning it."

Cleo was impressed by how Roth moved for such a large man. It was as if he could read what Kroton would do before he did it. But even then, the Regent's champion was yet to throw a single swing of his own.

Just as Cleo had that thought, the man they called *bear* began to stumble back with clumsy feet, left and right, without intention, until they became cornered between the east and south stands, shadowed by both. With a hand on each opposite end of his axe, Roth lifted it to block one of Kroton's strong, downward strikes. The wooden handle of his axe splintered in half, drawing groans from the eastern stands. Weaponless, the large champion seemed confused. He weaved around two of Kroton's swings, then reached down to scoop a handful of sand, throwing it like a plume of smoke into Kroton's face.

The Southern Plane's champion backstepped away, struggling to see. Roth used the opening to shove his thick boot straight into Kroton's chest, flinging him backward into the air. Everyone surrounding Cleo gasped aloud in unison as the large champion lunged on top of the now swordless Kroton. On the ground, he wailed. Roth finally gripped Kroton's shield and slung it aside.

Punch after punch, Cleo heard the crunch of Kroton's bronze helmet begin to crack against his skull. Some of the women who stood in the rows in front of Cleo turned around and shielded their eyes. Others broke from their gasps to plead for the Regent's champion to stop. It took all four of the robed men of the isle to rush onto the pit and throw Roth off the mashed man.

"*Well*, there goes my gold," Sal said with a sigh.

"Those hens always fight dirty," Kastas scoffed.

Cleo was left wordless, like most, filled with disappointment that a hen of a forest ranger had defeated one of Sacrim's most well-trained warriors. "It was trickery," he tried to say, unsure if the words had come out. To make matters worse, the crowd from the east had erupted into the loudest of roars, stomping to shake the marble Tessereum and taunting those in the south with vindicated fervor.

He glanced over at Scarlett, who stood huddled with her two friends, Jade and Leanne, covering their eyes in horror. Sections of the southern stands had already begun to descend from their seats, down to the Tessereum's bottom stairs, with faces that ranged from disgust to disappointment.

Cleo's was neither. He stood like the other five commanders, with their bronze chest plates stuck out in pride. Part of Cleo wished he could have fought instead. He would have spent solurns training with Kladden for that moment to bring Sacrim to their rightful glory. Maybe then, the crowd would be singing his name, and Scarlett wouldn't be able to resist him, regardless of who her father was. But it wasn't. And instead, his home region had lost to a bear of a barbarian.

Cleo followed the rest of the saddened high stands out from the setting sun, through the tunnel, and down the tall set of spiraling stairs. Once he entered the Court of Champions, Cleo walked down an empty corridor when he felt a hand reach for his elbow. He turned around, half startled. "*Fa-ather*."

"Cleo, I wanted to talk to you away from the crowd," Sepatus said. His voice was less stern than usual. He removed his bronze helmet, which had two high-profile, sleek running spikes. He held it under his arm beside the Sunspear. Cleo could feel its heat emanating toward him like waves crashing against the breakwaters of Sazara's harbor. "I hope the command of your new brigade has found you well. I received your post that you've moved from Rastrum to Corlach."

"Yes." Cleo removed his own bronze helmet, which had just a single running spike.

"Smart of you…keep those captains on their toes. Some in the chamber think that was my doing, to weaken Sazara," Sepatus said with an incredulous grin. "It's probably good to keep them on their toes, too."

Cleo's face squinched as he smiled at his father's comment.

"But there's more I must ask of you, son."

"What is it?"

"Kroton's father is a high chamberman to the Third Magistrate. He was supposed to join Cayen, myself, and two others at the Convault tomorrow morning."

Cleo knew immediately where this was headed. *Vident Lement was right. I can't fight in the pit, but here I am, being thrown into the politics of the Plane—no sword, but a quill…great.*

Sepatus continued, "As you can tell, the fight didn't go as planned, and Sarnesi dropped out of the meeting."

"And you want me to take his spot?" Cleo asked.

"Yes. I know it's a lot to ask of you. And you're still fresh in your command. But it's my decision to appoint someone to fill his open seat, and there isn't anyone else here I trust more than you."

"I understand," Cleo said, pretending to ponder his position.

"You won't be asked to contribute. Cayen and I will handle any arbitrations on behalf of Sacrim as dual consols. But it would be good for you to witness. Not many get this opportunity."

"And what of the party tonight at the court?"

"Given what happened at the pit today, I doubt it will be too eventful. You should forgo it and get some rest. We'll meet by the fountain at the break of morning."

"*Very well.*"

Instead of heeding his father's advice, Cleo went to his guest room and dressed out of his commander's armor and cloak. He washed in the basin and donned his ceremonial robe, fitted with golden patterns of swans and swords crossed at his chest. As the evening passed into night, Cleo made his way to the third floor of the court and found it filled with men, bare of youth, discussing their quiet conversations over chalices of wine.

Cleo held Scarlett's rose in his hand. He scanned the room from corner to corner but found no sight of his supposed date. Figuring she was still readying, Cleo wandered toward a window that overlooked the

Southern Plane's allotment. He gazed out at the organized gallery of tents in all their sizes and colors. Below was the entrance gate, where he watched all who were allowed to enter and exit the Court of Champions. Cleo stood there, sipping the same smooth wine, chalice after chalice, waiting for Scarlett to arrive. His eyes scanned back and forth, from the window to the court's doors, in anticipation of his date to join him. But as night passed, all Cleo saw was the beaming moon traverse the night sky.

Scarlett never came. Cleo outlasted the older men and women of the party, who dwindled in number until he was the last left. The pit of his stomach, which was once tied in a nervous knot, was now left empty to swash only with wine. Cleo contemplated whether he should toss her rose into the wind, hoping it might find its way back to whatever party she was enjoying with her friends. But instead, he tucked it away and retired for the night with the loneliest feeling of regret.

"Thanks for showing up," Sepatus said to Cleo as he met him near the fountain on the bottom floor of the court the following morning.

As if I had a choice.

Across the pool of water stood Cayen Calegri, beside his salutor, dressed in a white robe and a gold-colored cloak stitched along its collar with the mane of a lion. "*Good.* You finally made it. I thought I'd have to send him to wake you up." The young Consolar Vizar nodded to his salutor.

"Commander Scordisci." A man much shorter than Cayen, dressed in a golden robe, scurried toward him and stuck out his hand. His yellow-tinted teeth shone as he reached to shake Cleo's wrist. "First Magistrate, Simon Crudeli."

"Pleasure."

"First time?" he asked while rubbing the oiled curls of his short hair. "It is for me. I can't wait a moment longer."

"Yes. Yes, it is," Cleo responded with far less enthusiasm.

"The host is here," Cayen said sternly.

Cleo was the last in their group of five to follow the host toward the court's farthest corridor, toward the Tessereum. A thick, iron-clad door reinforced by black metal arches stood at its end. In his airy white robe and long gray beard, the host fumbled his ring of keys until he found the one that unlocked the heavy door. He mumbled something Cleo couldn't hear as they followed him down the stairs of the dark tunnel. Its blackstone side walls matched the arch of the narrow door and looked as if it had decades of dust draped between every crevice of stone. Cleo stepped down steadily with his hands gripped to his commander's cloak, holding it tight so it wouldn't sweep the dust across his sandals.

The staircase led to another locked iron-clad door, which opened to reveal a room, crossed at its low ceiling by a groined vault with the same grim blackstones as the tunnel. Oil lanterns hung from the columns supporting the vault's shallow arches, bright enough to reach the bottom crests of the surrounding walls.

"*Welcome to the Convault*," Sepatus turned around to tell him with an unusual smile.

"Are we underneath the Tessereum?" Cleo asked.

"That we are," Sepatus answered, taking the center chair of five tucked beneath the table, which was shaped like a hollow, square-sided ring. Cleo grabbed the iron-backed chair to his father's right, and the First Magistrate took the chair at the end. Cleo didn't bother to check Cayen's dismay on the opposite side, knowing that his father, especially with the Sunspear, was Sacrim's true spokesman and should rightfully take the commanding middle seat.

Across the table, a gray-haired old man emerged from the shadows, holding a large spear similar to his father's but with three larger prongs at its top, dulled by silver-azilian. On his head was a silver crown, revolved by several hooks shaped like the prongs of his spear. *The King of Marredom …with the Seatrident*, Cleo recognized. The pale King was tall and had an awkward arch to his broad back, which he covered with a long, black coat edged at its seams with white fur. Marredom's King was followed in by four similarly dressed men who shared his tall height and older age.

Two groups entered from each of the table's other ends. To Cleo's right, moving to stand beside the central chair, was a poofy-haired woman with puffy cheeks, dressed in a sparkling green-and-gold gown, which, to Cleo's observation, didn't seem to flatter her curvy sides. To his left, near Cayen's salutor, was a taller woman with straight black hair and a strong jaw. *The Queen of Astria,* he recognized, as the woman wielding the Skybow took the middle chair. In each of the four seats beside her sat four identical, burly-looking women in tight black hoses, half-capes, and braided hair.

Before the plump woman to his right sat down, a man in chainmail and a white surcoat helped her lift a glass-enclosed vase onto the table. *The Stonehammer.* For the entirety of his life, Cleo had heard only tales from

Vident Lement and his books about the four amulons. And before today, he had only ever seen his father's Sunspear. At that moment, Cleo knew his father was right. *Not many will ever get this opportunity.*

The same bearded, white-robed man from the fight the day prior lifted a cut-out corner of the table and walked toward its center. The middle was open in all ways but for a perfectly sided black cube that stood to the man's waist, which looked to Cleo as if it had been carved from the floor.

"Thank you all for gathering here this morning in the Convault, in continuation of the Descindation Treaty's thirty-fourth meeting, in our seven hundred and forty-first turn of the solar season since the descent," the man said in a harsh, scratchy voice. He turned slowly around the table as he spoke. "For those unaware, the Convault was established after the Amulonic War to continue our pact of peace between the Plane's four great regions. It is a time to further our cooperation and resolve diplomatically through discord as opposed to war outside of the Tessereum's walls. If there are no leading questions, you are all welcome to read the Descindation Treaty for yourself, which I will now place here on the sanctum. At the conclusion of our meeting and prior to your exit from the Convault, I ask that each amulon-wielding emissary sign or seal at the treaty's end to re-pledge your region's commitment to our shared peace. All discussions shall take place in the common tongue."

In the man's hand was a tall scroll, which he unrolled and placed atop the black cube. Cleo watched nervously, waiting to see who would speak first. He could feel the vitality move in circles around the table from each of the four amulons and their wielders. A familiar voice finally broke the tense air. "I believe we have a new emissary. Introductions might be in order," his father said, lifting his open palm to the right of the table.

"I'm Lady Orean Lomberg of Bovere. To my right is Talam Franclare and my escort. To my left, Favian Gravelot and Lucas Clovin."

"Queen Helera. *Pleasure.*"

"Consolar General, Sepatus Scordisci. To my left is Consolar Vizar, Cayen Calegri."

"King of Marredom, Mordin the Fourth," the old man across from them grumbled coldly. "*So,* the Lomberg family, *is that right?*"

"Yes."

117

The man turned his saggy cheeks away from her. "*Figures*. Orlan leaves his forests to a woman, and the price of my wood doubles."

"*Ahem*," Queen Helera hissed, her broad shoulders pinned to the back of her chair.

"Sorry. *An ugly woman*," King Mordin corrected.

"The Convault is no place to levy insults," Sepatus reminded him sternly.

Before the King of Marredom could respond, the man to Lady Lomberg's right said, "If I'm not mistaken, King Mordin, you began charging more for your transport of the Regent's export directly after our last meeting."

"They're my ships. I charge what I must to feed my people. But my fleet hasn't changed. It seems to be your people causing this—from all your desires and indulgences." He turned his face to the Eastern and Southern Plane's emissaries.

Cayen, ignoring their bickering comments, stated aloud, "I have a resolution to bring forth for a vote—that an amendment to the treaty be made, releasing the restriction of intermarrying between the four regions of the Plane."

Cleo's father looked to his left with a face of unsettled bewilderment. Cayen's resolution seemed odd to everyone at the table, causing stirs of whispers and side talk for quite a while after he'd spoken.

"All must agree. You may cast your hands to vote," the white-robed man said from the darkened corner. Around the table, Cleo scanned and saw Cayen raise his hand but not his father, rendering Sacrim's vote moot. The only other emissary to raise their hand, as a shock to the Northern and Eastern Planes, was Queen Helera. "Very well. The resolution shall be voided."

Sepatus broke the awkward silence by asking the Franclare gentleman, "What is the Regent's forecast of ore?"

"We should see an increase in supply over the coming solurns. Kilgore's mines in Garsenden will continue to be fruitful."

"Do you not already have enough steel for that army of yours down there, General?" King Mordin asked.

Sepatus ignored his question, calm and collected as Cleo always knew his father to be. He turned to their left to ask Queen Helera, "And yours?"

"Astrian mines will continue to provide what they can."

King Mordin, who looked aggravated by being ignored, laughed aloud, saying, "I guess not, then. That sun in the south sure has gotten to you,

General. What good is all that ore without my ships and their transport to bring them to you? Have you forgotten that your men in bronze can't float?"

"And your ships cannot fly," Queen Helera interjected with a wry snarl, before his father could respond.

"As if your birds could ever compete with my fleet," he scoffed. "You'd all be starving and poor if it weren't for my galleys bringing your food and cargo across the Plane."

"You may have a fleet, King Mordin. But tell me, whose people are starving and poor?" Cayen asked him, his voice bellowing boldly.

A long string of silence hung between the emissaries of the table as King Mordin's frosted blue eyes wandered around like a cornered cat. He lifted a grimacing smile, then stared deep into Cayen's eyes. Cleo had never felt tension like this before. His own palms were moist with sweat, and he hadn't spoken a single word. *This is true power,* he thought, realizing that his father's life's work was for moments like these, in contention with people like this. They were all killers—true killers. The kind that ruled. With a single choice, they could alter the course of hundreds of thousands of people's lives. Or end them. And with their amulons, no one across the Plane stood to contest the decisions they made.

But Cleo felt proud to be sitting there with them at the table. It was a place where he felt he was beginning to belong. Especially beside his father—the man he knew, deep down, everyone in the Convault feared as much as they respected. *A rightful ruler…if only Cayen weren't such a fool.*

The King of Marredom finally turned his glaring smirk to Queen Helera and said, "Fortune can change like the *wind.* You lot should know all about that."

CHAPTER 10

SEA

"Make way," an officer ordered as he barreled across the main deck of the *Fereclis*.

The scabs on Dane's knees were planted into the planks of the deck, scoring through the holes of his ripped trousers. Steady, he kept them, until the officer's boot plunged into Dane's hovering chest. He dropped his cleaning stone, and his elbow collapsed, knocking over the bucket of sandy water he shared with the other oarsmen. Dane's back, still stiff from his fifteen lashes, ached in pain as his chest fell flat to the wet deck.

"Clean that up," the silver-capped officer commanded.

Dane struggled to lift himself and grab his empty bucket. It'd been nearly a moon's pass since he'd boarded the war galley and was taken from Niven. One moon down, but a lifetime's more, he knew, still to go. Dane gripped the bucket tightly, yanking at it to release his frustration. He looked down into its empty puddle and saw his dying reflection. Eyes once blue now looked desolate and gray, like storm clouds covering a once-perfect sky. He could see his sharp chin and cheekbones protruding, round and bare like his shaven scalp. His face was indistinguishable from the other oarsmen, all masked with doom.

Dane carried the empty bucket across the *Fereclis*'s main deck, toward the opposite bulwark's railing. For a moment, he could feel the cooling breeze and see the sun begin to set in the east. There, halfway to the horizon, was land. Dane had heard whispers from his benchmates about where their galley of war was now anchored. But, to him, it didn't matter. The water here was clean and crystal blue, the air was warm, and the green blur of the coast was filled with more life than he had ever seen before. He could smell the freshness that lifted where the three met, breezing past him slowly as the waves reached the shore. In that brief moment, all Dane knew was that he wasn't in Marredom anymore.

His mind clung to a single thought as he stood beside the railing—he should jump in and escape this living death. *To swim to life.* But his ankles and wrists were latched by iron shackles, cutting deep into his skin. Any attempt to escape by course of the sea, and he would simply sink to the bottom without the need for an officer or marine to chase after him.

Maybe it was possible to swim with these chains, being so close to shore, he questioned. *I wouldn't have to go far. If I become food for the fish, then so be it. They deserve my life more than these officers and marines do.*

"Do you hear that?" Nathan asked from behind his shoulder. Nathan was a fellow oarsman assigned to the bench in front of Dane on the oar deck down below, and the two of them shared the same rotation. Whether it be at the oars, scrubbing the decks, or even the rare chance they had to rest and eat, Nathan was never far from Dane's side.

"I do, but barely," Dane replied. He could faintly hear roaring coming from the land, of what sounded like fading cheers. "Any clue what it is?"

"It's the Descindation. Probably a good fight if I had to guess."

Descindation? Dane wasn't sure what that was. *Must be important,* he thought. *Important enough to have every pier here filled with galleys while the rest of us are anchored out.* "Like a party?" Dane looked back across the main deck and saw the two dozen or so oarsmen still scrubbing the salt off the planks. A few officers stood chatting in small groups. The closer Dane looked, the more he realized that they all shared the same pout of jealousy. *They must be the few left on board while the rest went ashore.* Dane noticed, too, that the *Fereclis's* skiffs were missing. *It's no wonder they've been so cruel.*

"I guess you could call it that. Never been, so I'm not sure. I've only heard its tales," Nathan replied.

"Never been? You're here now," Dane joked back, trying to cheer him up.

But Nathan didn't laugh. Instead, he tied his bucket to the line and lowered it into the water. When he hoisted it back up, he poured in a handful of sand, then responded, "*No*...now, I'll likely never go."

With his own pout of misery, Nathan returned to his spot on the deck and resumed his scrubbing, leaving Dane alone to look down at the water. The tempting allure of jumping in was all he could picture. No one would stop him. Night would soon fall and smother the land and sea with darkness. *No one would even know I was gone.* But the bell near the galley's aftcastle rang five times, breaking his thought and signaling for the oarsmen's change of rotation.

"Get a move below deck, all of you," an officer shouted at the slow-moving group of oarsmen. The sound of chains clanking as they were dragged and bounced across the wooden-planked deck stung Dane deeper than his scabs ever could. That sound, moving in a single line, had become a reminder of where he was—trapped aboard this floating prison. It was a sound he wished would vanish forever.

Despite his disdain, Dane followed in line with the other oarsmen toward the officer with his hand resting on the curved saber sheathed at his waist. Dane's eyes gleamed at the saber's handle as he passed. He glanced up and down, then side to side, searching the main deck for the other officers. His mind rang like the ship's bell with phantasmal thoughts of how he could snatch it and fight to escape.

"Heads forward," the officer stated, staring the oarsmen down.

Why sink when you could fight?

But that moment had passed him just as quickly as the one to jump. Dane walked past the officer in line with the other oarsmen, headed for the stairs near the bow. He couldn't tell whether his feelings were of regret or missed relief. If there was any time to try to escape, Dane knew that now, with most of the officers and marines gone ashore, would certainly be it.

But that wasn't who Dane was. He wasn't a fool or a revolutionary. Dane was a nork—a people from the cold, northern islands known to endure suffering quietly. As a child, he had been instilled with the perseverance of his father and the docility of his mother. Hard work was all he was raised to know, the only way to survive the north's long winters. However, something inside Dane had awoken that day, back in Niven, when he'd attacked the officer who toiled with his mother. And again, the day he was lashed against the pillar in Minoska. He was no longer an innocent boy, afraid to upset the stable contentment of life. No. Dane's disposition had been changed forever.

The *Fereclis* was a flagship of the King's Navy from its largest class of war galleys. She was comparable in size to many of the cargo galleys Dane would often see beside them at sea, with their deeper and more rounded hulls, but was longer and carried more oars. One of his two benchmates, Piney, had mentioned before that she had a hundred and twenty oars in total, while most other war galleys had around ninety. And some had even fewer.

Dane creaked his way down the wooden stairs at the forwardmost end of the war galley on which he was to serve his lifetime's sentence. Below the main deck was the kitchen's mess and the officers' quarters, shielded by a locked bulkhead. Dane passed by it like he usually did, his mouth salivating from the smell that leaked between the seams of its wood. The two oar decks below were identical but had their benches offset so the oars could row in unison. Both decks were open from forward to aft and had thirty bench seats on each side of the central passageway. Dane passed by the massive leather-hide barrel drum at the bow, then continued down another set of stairs to the lower oar deck.

Dane's bench was by far the worst of any. It was the last on the port side, typically reserved for the newest oarsmen or, sometimes, the worst-behaved. Directly behind their bench seat was the corner passage that led to their deck's only two heads. The small cupboard room had just two seats with buckets below, which emitted its horrific smell behind him every waking moment of the day and all throughout the night. To make matters worse, his bench's hammock, which they had only one to split between the three benchmates, hung in the center of the passageway, around the corner from the deck's only shit buckets. It was Dane's turn to sleep, but, as usual, with a change in rotation, there was a line of oarsmen waiting to relieve themselves.

An officer monitored their line as they continued aft, down the middle of the oar deck. Even at his young age, Dane was taller than most of the oarsmen. He was one of the few who had to duck his head as they passed around the chimney chute, which ran from the main deck down to the bottom-most hold below. From the edge of his bench, he sometimes saw crates of food and barrels of wine and water being pulled up and down, dangled from a line like a string teasing an alley cat. And every time he walked past it, he would peek down into the hold's darkness to see what he was missing out on, trying to get a whiff of its enchanting smell.

"Did you see it?" Piney asked as Dane scuttled past the line of stench-ridden oarsmen. His benchmate, Piney, was much older than Nathan and himself, but didn't hold the same dreary look as either of them. Or any of the other oarsmen, for that matter. Piney always had a smile draped across his frog-like face and spoke with an emphasis filled with the pleasantries of life. At first, Dane had found his benchmate to be annoying. But as time passed, Piney had become one of the few things that made sitting at the aftmost bench somewhat bearable.

"See what?"

"The Tessereum, of course. I was on cleaning duty last night and came back down before sunrise, so I missed it. All I saw was black. No stars. No moon. No nothing. Might as well have just stuck my face between Elwer's legs and stared into his rear."

Dane laughed like he usually did when Piney spoke. "No, I couldn't see anything but land in the distance. We did hear some cheers from far out, though." He looked over at Nathan, who had just walked over. "This man might know." Dane patted his shackled hand against Nathan's chest.

"Nathan wouldn't know shit," Piney said in his typical high-pitched hew. He was much shorter than Dane and Nathan but had the confidence of a colossus without the voice to match. Dane had assumed Piney's inflated pride came from the shackles everyone wore and the officers who kept everyone in line. The other oarsmen had been in them for so long that he figured that Piney had forgotten what it was like to talk to a man who could throw a punch and fight back. But for anyone here, doing so would bring about a sentence of death.

"I've been before," Piney said. "To the Descindation."

Nathan blurted without hesitation, "*Horseshit*, you have."

"Why would I lie to a fellow oarsman?"

"You? Lie? Oh, Piney, please. You speak more lies than the King himself." Nathan squeezed between the line for the head, moving to sit on the bench in front of them. "I'd believe whales could fly before I ever believed you."

"Whales can fly." Piney paused, squinting his wide and bulging eyes together. "At least they did the last time I threw your mother off me."

Nathan reached to grab Piney's throat, but Dane yanked at his shoulders and held him back. "Maybe a little too far, Piney."

"Eh, he'll be okay." Some of the guys in line beside their bench were still laughing as Nathan pretended to cool off. "Anyway, you wouldn't have missed it."

"The Tessereum, or Nathan's mother?" Dane replied with a crackling laugh of his own. Nathan, who was sterner than most, just gave Dane a hard shove in the arm.

As they should have expected, an officer charged back aft, pushing the oarsmen in line aside and yelling at them to quit their foolery. Dane's bench was two decks below the marines' and officers' sleeping quarters, and they were often scolded to keep quiet because of it. The last thing any of them wanted was to wake those resting above.

Piney waited for the officer to return forward, near the drum, before he leaned over to Dane and whispered above the silence, "*Nathan's mother, by the way.*" The men around them cackled like a pack of wild dogs, trying to hide their laughs. "It's a shame you couldn't see it though. Everyone should see it at least once, I reckon."

"You included," Nathan barked back. He turned his scrawny legs over to face Dane, Piney, and their third benchmate, Elwer, who was asleep against their oar's porthole. "Well, then, since you claim to have been there before, tell us what it was like."

"White stone, it was, with four columned walls and pretty arches between them. Sorta like a tall brick, but open in the middle, where the fighting happens. Then, there's the court, you see, right outside each end. It's just a building, white brick too, but it's for fancy people and those like that. Never seen prettier ladies than I have when I was at the isle, though, that's for certain," Piney said, using his shackled hands to describe the figures. Dane listened intently. "It's just a big party, you see. After the Amulonic War ended, all those kings and queens made peace. They decided to make war a festival…a tournament between the four great regions of the Plane, to see who the best of them was. And, of all places, they put it at the Isle of Azil where Rondor found his descended star."

"Descended star?" Dane asked.

"Crikes, Dane, you haven't *heard* of Rondor's star before?" Piney asked him, drawing his voice out at the peak of his question.

Dane only shook his head. He was proud of where he was from, in Niven, along the western edge of Marredom's largest island. But after being on board the *Fereclis*, even if it were only for a moon's pass, it felt like he, himself, was a descended star, far removed from the reality of the Plane, and dropped from the sky onto this ship. Even Nathan had heard of Rondor and mocked Dane for not knowing what it was.

Piney continued in the grimy darkness of the oar deck, "Rondor was a royal knight…one of the last in the Age of Knights, that is. From a big, strong, and wealthy family of the Eastern Plane. The Regent, we call it today. You've heard of that now, *haven't you?*"

Dane had, but just faintly. He nodded so Piney would continue.

"Rondor saw the star descend from the sky and followed it across the Grand Channel, until he found it buried like a crater into the isle. But the isle had gone astray. *You see*, a storm, one like we've never seen, followed the star down to the Plane. With it came the winds and rain and lightning that brought death by the thousands to those who were outcasts of the Plane—those people forced to live there on the isle at the time. Like none other had seen. The people who hadn't died left to save themselves from its torment. All but Rondor. A knight, as brave as he was, marched right into the storm to find its source. You see, the star was dull and shiny at the same time, with colors and light not from this Plane. And when Rondor reached it, he found it had a pulse."

"*A pulse?*" Nathan asked.

"Yeah, a pulse. Like a heartbeat," Piney replied bluntly. "A living rock."

Nathan lifted the side of his face along with his eyebrows in a tell of disbelief. "That's not the tale I heard."

Elwer, of all people, lifted his gray-haired head from where it leaned against the oar's porthole to say, "A pulse is right. It's why the amulons today always need to be near a person or held by one. If they don't have a body to channel that pulse through, they become erratic and lash out…like Piney's mythical storm."

"Thank you, Elwer," Piney said sarcastically, half whispering now that the sun had fully set. "Which is why when Rondor touched the fallen rock of a star, the storm ceased, and normality was brought back to the isle." Dane nodded along, listening to Piney's tale, believing it more now that he'd heard Elwer talk for the first time in days. "From there, Rondor scoured across the Plane in search of a way he could mold the star, to better channel its pulse—one he named Azil, after the namesake of the isle." Piney paused to check the officers who huddled near the drums before continuing, "Rondor traveled south with it, down near the volcanoes of the Vyporean Range. From there, the tale says, he used the smoldering heat from whatever lava he could find to forge the star into what we know as the Staff of Azil. With it, he commanded the storm and all the elements of the Plane. But the Vypores claimed some of that star for itself. Storms today still ravage that place, making it impossible to travel south of the Plane. Even by ship."

"Then what of the amulons, like Elwer mentioned? How did we go from the staff to the amulons?" Dane asked, looking over at Nathan, who had his eyes closed, shaking his head. Dane knew what the amulons were—that they gave their wielder a commanding power over one of the four primal elements of the Plane. But he never thought to question where they had come from or how they came to be. Seemingly, neither had Nathan.

"That's a story in itself...but if you must know, Rondor passed the staff down to his family for seven generations, or something like that, until it was in the hands of a true tyrant. His great-great-great-great-grand-nephew. One they called Rexam. *You see*, my mother always counted the greats on each finger of her hand," Piney explained as he stretched out his fingers to count them. "Wait, five, not four greats," he corrected. "But if you think the croaks on this ship are bad, you should hear the stories she'd tell about this fella. Rexam swept across the Plane, wiping out entire civilizations with the power of the staff. It was out of vengeance, they say." Piney looked forward again, near the drums, to make sure the officers couldn't hear him. "*Well*, no one really knows the truth of it. And it was his own brother who killed him. A man by the name of Regnam...I think that's what it was. Regnam's Revolt is what the bookmen call it. After he'd fought him, he searched the Plane for a smith who could split the Staff of Azil and divide its power, until he did just that. And now we have the four amulons." Piney looked around, proud that he still had the attention of Dane, Nathan, and even the last few oarsmen still in line to use the head.

"It's called *azilian*," Elwer opened his eyes again to say. "When the Staff of Azil became molten, they used crucibles to separate it by weight and then reforge it. Thus, we have the Sunspear, with its tip of gold-azilian...the Seatrident, pronged by silver-azilian...the Skybow, with its limbs of amethyst-azilian...and the Stonehammer, with its head of emerald-azilian. Each named after what it most resembled. The regular azilian was used for all its other handles and such."

Even Piney looked surprised, not just that Elwer had spoken for as long as he did, but also at what he had said. He turned to the frail man on his left. "How does a man like you, with all that knowledge, just sit there in silence for all this time, sleeping away?"

"Because I, a *bookman*, don't like any of you," he answered, leaning his thick head back against the ship's planks.

"That's fair enough," Piney replied. "I mean, no one really likes Nathan."

Dane laughed, looking over at Nathan to ensure Piney hadn't upset him again. Nathan just rolled his eyes and asked, "How was it that you knew all of that, about the staff? My family always told me that the Staff of Azil was only a tale and that it was the amulons that had been found buried in chests under the ground on the isle. As if they were left from a time long past and never meant to be found. And that it was Rondor who killed all those people on the isle to hide his secret. At least, that's what my mother always said."

Elwer waited a long moment to reply. "Everything has a tale, son. Whether you believe it or not, I couldn't care. Your beliefs won't make it any more or less true."

"Right, but how did you come to know it as true?" Dane asked.

"Who said I thought it was true?"

"Everyone's got a reason to hate those royals in the east," Piney added.

Dane looked over at Nathan and shrugged his frail shoulders. "Fair enough." The line next to his hammock had dwindled, so Dane quickly got up and hopped inside, swinging from side to side as it hung from the frame of the ceiling. "Well, I'm hitting the sack."

"Me too," Nathan said, following him into his own.

Piney reared a quirky smirk. "Elwer finally speaks to us, and you two go to bed. No wonder he doesn't like any of you."

Dane waved his hand out from the hammock's white cloth, shooing Piney's comment away. He took a dirty rag from his pocket and tied it around his head, closing his eyes to fall asleep.

"GET UP! EVERYBODY UP! TO YOUR STATIONS!"

Dane's eyes shot open to the sound of beating barrel drums rumbling their loud pounds between his ears. *What's going on?*

He lifted his head out of his hammock's nestled cocoon and looked forward. Oarsmen scattered from left to right in their dirty and torn gray garments. Some, still half-naked, carried their daily allowance of stew and bread, angered by their only bites of peace being broken, forcing them back onto their bench.

"What's happening?" Dane asked, looking over at Nathan, who was as confused as he was. Dane got up and fixed his garment, adjusted his shackles, and slipped his boots back on.

The lower oar deck was dimly lit by lanterns near the drum, forcing him to squint out of the oar's porthole to ensure it was still night outside. Before he could reach the bench beside him, Piney rushed down the central passageway, shouldering him and the others out of the way.

"Hurry, grab the extension," he told Dane.

Dane cracked his knuckles, lifted the thick lumber from under their bench, and slid it past Elwer, who still sat beside the porthole. Elwer hinged the extension lever to the end of their oar and lifted it so Piney and Dane could take their seats. The drummers switched their beating from erratic slams to a fast and flowing rhythm, alternating the deepening pounds between their deck and the one above them. Dane's bench was the last to join the fray, after having to follow the pattern of all the benches ahead. *Pull...down circle. Pull...down circle,* he repeated in his head, pushing the thin but solid handle of the oar with each row.

The hardened skin over the busted blisters on his hand stung with agony, as if he were gripping steel stripped straight from a fire. His legs were locked with his feet lodged against the bottom ledge of the bench before him. Typically, the oarsman rowed alone or in pairs. But this was the fourth time in his short period on board that their entire bench was sent to row together. With them all working in unison, Dane noticed the difference in speed that the *Fereclis* would travel, even as far below the main deck as he was.

But after rowing for long periods all at once, everyone became tired together. And none so much or as quickly as Piney, who wasn't nearly as strong as Dane or able to match the endurance of the sea-weathered Elwer. Dane was hopeful that this would only be a quick sprint; otherwise, he'd have to row twice as hard to make up for his weaker benchmate. But for whatever eerie reason, this time, the call to their stations seemed different. None of the three times prior had he seen Piney move as motivated as he was now.

"*What's going on?*" Dane shouted above the drumming to ask.

"I saw him," Piney said between rows.

"Saw who?"

"Maris, King Mordin's son," Piney answered as they rowed again. "*Our captain.*"

"And?" Dane asked, still confused. He'd never seen Maris before, who typically stayed locked away in the aftcastle. But Dane knew he was the son of the King, so he never really questioned it. Some of the other oarsmen talked fondly of King Mordin's youngest son. Or, at least, more fondly than his other five children.

"And," Piney said, taking a deep breath. "He was with a woman."

"A woman?" Dane asked. "I thought they couldn't bring women on board."

"I guess you can do what you want when you're the captain."

Nathan turned his head around to ask above the beating of the drums, "How'd you see that?"

"I was hanging over the side of the ship, scrubbing the hull like I usually did, when his skiff rowed up. I was all the way aft, but I saw them pull her up."

"Was she pretty?" Nathan's benchmate asked with a maniacal laugh.

"I couldn't tell, the fog was growing…but if I were a betting man, I'd say she probably wasn't as good-looking as Nathan's mother," Piney replied, heaving a raspy chuckle. "No, she had a black bag over her head. I couldn't see a thing. But she did have on a nice dress, though. Red, by the looks of it. With flowers on it."

A bag? Dane was confused. *Why would he put a bag over her head?*

"I couldn't hear a word they were saying, but I don't think she came on board by choice. Either way, we might be rowing for a while." As soon as Piney had said those words, the entire aft corner of the oar deck let out a groaning hiss.

Dane's shoulders dropped as low as his confidence. Being at anchor near such a beautiful coast, in a land he'd never seen before, was a treat compared to what he was being forced to do now. And for what he would likely be doing for a while. For as often as he thought about jumping overboard, Dane knew it would be hard to leave his benchmates behind. Their struggle was his own, even now, when the beating of the drums felt as if it would never end.

Dane glanced to his left, out of the oar's tiny porthole, trying to get a glimpse of the sea. The morning sun slowly began to shine onto it, reflecting the salty glimmer that would occasionally spray their way. He welcomed its cleansing wash when the waves would crash into the *Fereclis*'s broadside. For those brief moments, it swept away the stench of death that scoured everywhere around him—the odor, the puke from sea sickness, and the wafting from the head behind their bench soaked every breath he took.

But worse than the smells was the pain. The lashes on his back were sore, and the blisters on his hands burned by everlasting fire. His shoulders and hands were exhausted. And every time he'd lifted his oar to row, Dane saw the branding on his forearm flash in front of him, reminding him of his new life. It had healed enough to show the paddles of the two crossed oars in a reddened, bumpy outline. *Worse than death,* he thought with each push and pull.

The only thing Dane had to keep him going was the figure of his mother and sisters' faces, and his brother, Maven's, too… *How careless he was.* For as much as he appreciated his new friends, his family back home was where Dane found comfort and support. And love. Providing for them gave him purpose. And now he had none—other than at the oar. But Dane knew that was a past life. His life was now a nightmare of perpetual misery, stuck inside a floating prison that drifted above the sea's darkness of death.

If only I could wake from this… I should have just jumped.

CHAPTER 11

SKY

"It feels *different*, doesn't it?" Lora asked Vanna as they walked near Sazara's harbor.

"It does." Vanna watched the bristling blue water wash its waves against the seawall, splashing back and forth between the empty piers, caught within its own whirling pool. The two of them had spent the day walking around its crescent-shaped path, commenting on all the luxurious limestone and red granite homes that stood stories tall opposite the water.

Since their meeting in the back of the Temple of Sciron, the Brazen Talons had been under orders to remain in Sazara and await their next task. During that time, Vanna and Lora would leave Zell each afternoon to walk the city and explore its interwoven alleys and streets. Lora justified it by claiming they were collecting information, though they both knew Zell saw through their intentions.

"I wonder where they've all gone," Lora said curiously. "This place was a racket just a few days ago."

"Hmm, it's almost as if the Sazarans are too afraid to come out of their homes. Spring is coming to an end, so maybe it's the summer's heat that scared them all inside," Vanna said, peering up at the blazing sun in jest.

"Sazarans would be the last people of the Plane scared of the heat."

"Maybe it's just one of their days of worship," Vanna mentioned as they passed by more empty alleys.

"What kind of people would worship the sun by staying inside?"

"*The Astrians*," Vanna replied, causing Lora to snort a sly laugh.

During their walks, the two often shared mocking remarks about the differences between the southern and western regions of the Plane. Most revolved around the Sazarans' clothing, or lack of clothing, for that matter. That, or how often they would yell out of windows and down the streets at one another. Most Sacrimians had a rapid manner of speech. They slurred their words together and mingled their sentences without stopping to take a breath. She and Lora would often laugh by trying to talk the way they did, so full of emotion, while they waved their fingers and hands in the air and ended each statement in an exhaustive drawl.

In her training as a Child of the Sisters, Vanna was taught each of the four regions' languages, despite most of the Plane today speaking and writing in roalish. But it wasn't until she heard the scipyrian dialect in person that she realized how different their way of speaking actually was. Undisciplined and erratic was how Lora liked to describe them, which, to Vanna, certainly seemed fitting.

The two Sisters did their best to blend in while they walked the foreign city. Each morning, they applied the colored paste to their hair and tanning oil to their skin. And they would dress in scampish tops and skirts, or loose robes, before they would leave their hideaway by the harbor. Their overseer, Zell, found disdain in the openness of dress that was common among the women here. But neither Vanna nor Lora seemed to mind, even with the lustful stares. Though they mocked the Sazarans for it, Vanna was just happy to feel the cooling whisk of air flow across her skin, making their walks in the southern heat somewhat bearable. And she was glad to watch her skin grow as tan as the people here, helping her evade any wary attention.

Vanna's favorite thing to do in the city was visit its countless shops and markets, which were erected inside and out of nearly every street. From the window-filled walkways to the pop-up wooden carts, she loved seeing the crafts and curated dishes the Sazarans would make and how they would shout at her for a sale. Assortments of flavored oils with thin and crispy bread, peppered eggs, smoked fowl, or her favorite, seared shuttlefish with creamy rice, never failed to make Vanna happy. Sazara was a far cry from resembling anything Vanna knew of Mount Matron. But she enjoyed it.

Though she grew up separated from her home Plane's people, Vanna knew them to be much colder and far more reserved. Most Astrians stuck to themselves and dressed in their long-hooded and dark-covered clothing as they worked or studied alone, there and back, from home to work, only to repeat their days again. Their dishes were mundane, and their conversations were often banal. It was a cultural awakening when Vanna saw the parents here allow their kids to roam freely outside by themselves, running wild throughout Sazara's buildings and alleys. Though, in the depths of her thoughts, this rare glimpse of youthful freedom was one she found to be intriguing or, at the very least, envious of.

On the other hand, Lora thought Sazara was dirty, and its people were like rats, scurrying for scraps up and down its grassless streets. In truth, though, Sazara was cluttered with smelly and sweaty people, and most of its streets were littered with decaying food or heaps of long-standing trash. And any rat Lora did spot, of which there were always a few, she made sure to point it out to Vanna and compare Sazara's lack of cleanliness to Mount Matron's. Even in the outer district, where the people were comparably poor, Astria's only city had never been this filthy.

But Vanna came to like the Sazarans and know them as active people who enjoyed being outdoors in the sun, running through the streets with their games of tossed rocks, clean or dirty, whether they be young or old, or even rich or poor. Most seemed to congregate in the large, open space close to the harbor, which she knew from her time of studies to be Sazara's square.

In the Silo as a Child, she had been forced to read and understand what the different regions, cities, and cultures across the Plane were like. She spent many solurns in the depths of candlelit books, hovering over the words that spilled their written history. But Vanna had learned very quickly, even after their first walk, that no amount of reading about a city could ever compare to living within it. Eating their food, hearing their dialect and slang, or even breathing their air, all made Vanna feel like a normal person in a life she'd never had. Even if, like today, or like most of her childhood, it had all seemingly vanished.

"I wonder where they all went," Vanna said, her voice laced with concern. They had turned the corner to see the square barren. Only a few carts and stragglers passed through it. Most of whom Vanna recognized as chambermen walking to and from the surrounding buildings for work.

"Looks as if that vizar finally released the cats."

"Maybe we're the cats," Vanna replied in jest. This time, though, Lora didn't laugh. They walked down a path outside the square, noticing that most of the windows of the narrow buildings had their sunshades closed. "*Odd.*"

"Finally," a voice said from behind them. Vanna whipped herself around like the stalking cat she thought they were and saw Zell walking their way. "I've been looking for you two everywhere. We need to go back. *Now*," she said lowly so no one could hear. "You two head back to the converge first. I'll wait to follow."

Vanna and Lora walked the rest of the way back in silence. They needed a moment's break to sharpen their minds back to their training. With a single instruction, Zell had thrust Vanna back into the only thing she was raised to know—her obligation to the Queen of Astria and to the Sisters of Silo. It was more than an instinct. It was in her blood, embedded deep within every action she made. Though, with the days of freedom Vanna had enjoyed for the past half-moon, a small part of her wished she had been born with southern blood instead.

The red-framed second-story window that overlooked the harbor came up on their right as they walked down the crescent-shaped path. Vanna followed Lora into the building and up the staircase to the floor they shared. Not a word stretched between them as they sat at the table in the corner of the room, waiting for Zell to return. Vanna heard her footsteps coming up the stairs and looked out of the window to ensure she wasn't followed.

"What's going on?" Lora asked as Zell hurried to their table. "The city's desolate."

"This." She threw a small, folded parchment onto the table. "Read it." Zell grabbed the nearest candle from the shelf in the opposite corner and lit it. After they read their new orders, she held the note above the flame and burned its message.

Vanna sat motionless. The last word had stung and kept her still in her seat. Instead of the weary alley cat, she had become a withered worm, caught between the limestone streets and Sazara's scorching sun.

Execute a word that still haunted her sleepless nights.

It took her a moment to recall the prior phrasings of the message, but from what Vanna had gathered, their new orders would take them undercover inside the Consolate Chamber within Sazara's square. Zell gave them the brief, then distributed their disguises. Their plan was simple and similar to the one before. Vanna was to support Zell, and Lora was to be their lookout until their target was confirmed, followed, and then executed.

According to Lora, Zell was a woman of devotion and discipline, a high achiever within the ranks of Sisters. She had studied the chambermen's movements intensely over the past half-moon. In her brief, Zell explained that each partition of Sacrim had a magistrate elected as their leader, distinguished by their fanciful golden robes and gold-colored cord that they tied at their shoulder. Under each magistrate were ten high chambermen in charge of administering political matters, such as justice, trade, or building, who wore a single golden robe without the cord. Each high chamberman appointed however many lower chambermen they needed to execute their duties, known by their more common and simple red robes and golden cords.

The chambermen in Sazara ranged in rank from high to low, denoted by how they dressed. Those who wore the outfit Zell disguised in acted as assistants in the chamber or as scribes in their meetings. Such a rank was low enough that there were many, with new members constantly being let go and reappointed regularly. The white robe and golden sash Vanna donned were common for the chambermen's accompanying servants, who usually flooded the square in plenty.

Wearing her disguise made Vanna half-forget the time of freedom she had just enjoyed. During the nights throughout their stay, and in the darkness of their converge, the three Sisters did train, however. Zell ensured that their combat skills with their telsons hadn't grown dull. Which, for times like the one Vanna now found herself in, made her appreciate her overseer's strict propensity a little more.

When all three were ready, Vanna followed Zell and Lora down the stairs and onto the city's streets, heading for the opposite end of the square. The chamber and its tall limestone columns and shallow-pediment roofs enticed a feeling of grandeur, projecting the power of Sacrim onto its people. Vanna followed Zell past the front entrance and around the chamber's side stable, toward its back corner, until they reached an unguarded arched lintel. Zell used her hairpin to unlock its bronze handle, then led the two of them down a short staircase and through a narrow hallway.

"This is the servant's entrance. Looks like most of them are already on station for the day," Zell turned to tell her as they walked quietly. "Stay close."

Vanna nodded, then followed her up the stairs. The main floor of the chamber was filled with moving shades of white and red that flowed left and right down the central hallway in a frantic fashion. The smell of incense lifted throughout. Seeing everyone inside confirmed Vanna's earlier notion that there were more people here than outside in the streets and alleys of Sazara. She followed Zell down the hallway toward the front of the chamber, trying not to bump or run into anything that might bring them unwanted attention.

Zell turned left, then entered a giant room with a marble and gold placard above its frame that read: *Assembly.* In its center was a large wooden table complex in its running grains. A broad iron bowl hung from the ceiling above it. Two men and a woman dressed as magistrates sat at the table's far end. Chairs, some empty and others occupied by people in various robes, were arranged against the outer wall with standing space between each. Zell found an empty seat close to the door and readied her parchment, quill, and thin tablet. Vanna followed in from behind and stood against the wall in the open space beside her, the same as the other servants.

Sweat began to trickle down Vanna's chest into her robe. The air in the room was tense. She didn't know what would happen or why things were happening. Yet she could feel the tautness in each of their breaths and see the nerves strangling their shifting eyes. Even those who sat at the table were quiet and rarely looked at one another, like children waiting to be scolded or rewarded. Vanna couldn't tell. And it seemed as if neither could they.

Thundering footsteps clapped from the outside hallway, increasing their sandal-slapping sound as they grew closer to the assembly room. The people inside became distinctly fluttered. The chambermen adjusted their robes and hair and waited for those pounding footsteps to march through the open door. A thinner man who wore a gold cloak stormed in through its opening. Following him were five massive men in chest plates of bronze armor and flowing cloaks of red and gold. *Salutors,* Vanna recognized.

She looked around, moving only her eyes, waiting to see the man turn around so she could catch his face. He paced back and forth, stomping his way toward the far end of the table before he finally turned her way.

It's just a boy, Vanna thought. *An angry one, at that.* She wondered how these grown adults could be so nervous or scared around someone who was just a child—especially one with such pasty skin and narrow shoulders. His hair was short but full and colored a pungent orange, like a log's ember breathing its last signs of life. His face, though, was familiar to Vanna, almost as if she'd seen his eyes before and felt their gripping stare.

"Where's the general?" the boy asked in a deeper tone than she had expected. Three of his salutors helped themselves to open chairs at the table, while two remained standing behind his shoulders.

"He should be arriving soon," the lady magistrate at the table replied, her voice lingering with concern.

"We left the isle at the same time. He should be here by now," the boy said, walking out of the assembly room to look down the hallway. Vanna grew worried, witnessing his irrationality—one of a young man who seemed to hold an important role, so easily angered. She watched him pace in stomps back and forth along the table's length.

A long and awkward moment passed before the clanking of metal against the floor came, echoing from the chamber's hallway. Vanna looked to her right and saw a man with long, peppered hair and a royal-red cloak walk through the open door. He held the tall Sunspear in his right hand, topped at its spearhead by gold-azilian. *The Consolar General of Sacrim,* Vanna recognized. He raised the Sunspear off the ground, and the iron bowl that hung from the ceiling caught flame.

"*Well?*" the boy asked with a tone of expectation.

"I have deployed the Sixth Brigade in search of her," the general responded.

"That's it? Where are they headed?"

The general stayed close to the door, near the opposite end of the long table. "Through the Sineaqe Gorge, up into the Regent."

"That's my *little sister*. You need to be doing more...and quicker. And of all things, you chose to send the brigade led by a boy—*your boy*," he scowled without looking the much older general in the eyes. "And you sent him the long way? It might be a quarter-solurn before he even reaches Bovere."

"I'm doing all I am allowed to do under our law."

"What of the other brigades? Why not send them too? And why not go back through the isle where she was *taken* from?" the boy asked, frustration fuming behind his eyes.

"Cayen, as Sacrim's Consolar Vizar, you, of all people, should know and understand our law. And that of the Plane's Descindation Treaty. No one marches anyone or anything onto the isle," the general reminded him. "I only have the authority to deploy the Sixth Brigade outside of Sacrim. The others require full votes from all five magistrates." Now, it was the general who seemed to be growing frustrated. "We haven't yet uncovered the details of this circumstance. We don't even know if she was taken. Or by whom. For all we know, it's still possible she fled of her own volition."

That must be why the streets of Sazara were so bare, Vanna thought. *The Consolar Vizar's sister, taken from the Isle of Azil.*

"Don't you dare make such a claim again," the boy named Cayen demanded. "You and I both know who took her."

"Do *we?*"

"Don't play the fool, General Sepatus. We both sat at the table with that sea scum the following morning."

"King Mordin, you mean to say?"

"Who *else* could it be? You saw the way he talked down to everyone there. He's worse than scum, and more than anything, he hates Sacrim and despises my family."

"We can't be certain of this accusation without proof," the general said calmly after a moment's pause in thought.

"*I am.*" Cayen placed his hands on the table, staring into its dark grains in search of an answer. Vanna scanned his outfit of white-patterned silk, tracing out the image of what appeared to be the paw of a lion at the top of his chest and a mane at its seams. Footsteps came from the hallway again, this time much slower. Cayen looked up, and the rest of the room followed, watching as three men entered the assembly room. "*Father.*"

"The Consolar General is right," said the man dressed in a robe with its garb lathered by fine lace. Vanna had seen him once before, as well as the man to his left, who wore long crimson drapes. *Clyus...and the Vice-deacon.* She hadn't seen the other man's face until now, but his thin white hair and outfit matched what she saw in their meeting behind the temple. On Clyus's right was a single salutor who looked seasoned and stern.

Vanna became concerned, hoping that Clyus wouldn't recognize her.

They, too, walked toward the opposite side of the room, allowing her to release the air she held tight within her chest. Vanna looked down at Zell, who sat undisturbed, scribing away. Eventually, she looked up and gave a nod—one of confident assurance.

"There would be war if General Sepatus marched Sacrim's Guard onto the isle," Clyus said from beside Cayen. "A war we would do best to avoid."

"But *Scarlett.* What about *Scarlett?*"

"Cayen, you are correct as well," his father said in a calm, deep voice. "By your instincts, you believe the King of Marredom has committed this travesty. I am inclined to think you are correct. But I am also confident that the general is doing all he can within his own realm of action. Both can be true."

"We don't have the votes currently at the table," Sepatus stated. "The Fourth and Fifth Magistrates traveled home after the Descindation. I sent couriers to recall them here, but their return might take a quarter-moon."

"We don't have time to wait for them," Cayen said impatiently.

"And there's no telling whether we'd all agree to send our guardsmen out of Sacrim," one of the male magistrates at the table blurted aloud.

"Seldan is right," Sepatus said. "I know this is of the highest importance to you, Consolar Vizar, but it would be a question of war should we deploy all our guardsmen outside of Sacrim, through the isle—just after the Descindation, as well."

Cayen's face flushed as red as the Consolar General's cloak. "So, the plan is to do *nothing*?"

"We haven't done *nothing*. I've sent the Sixth Brigade in search of Scarlett—five thousand of our finest guardsmen. They'll march into Bovere with a flag of peace. And if needed, we'll fund their transport to Marredom in search of the girl," Sepatus replied.

"That'll be the day," the lady magistrate said. "The Regent might be understanding, even with some of the other partitions' brigades, but Marredom won't take kindly to any guardsmen on their island. That hasn't happened since the Amulonic War."

"King Mordin shouldn't have taken my sister, then."

"We don't yet have proof he took her," Seldan responded.

"We don't need proof. We have the greatest fighting force across the entire Plane, and we should use all of it to find her," one of the other magistrates said.

"Magistrate Crudeli," Sepatus said sternly. "Must I remind you who the general is? I will not enter into war unwarranted and without proof. And I will not deploy our Guard outside of Sacrim without the approval of all five of Sacrim's magistrates. That is final."

"Forgive him and my son. We are all dealing with the current situation in our own way," Clyus said, walking closer to Cayen to pat him on the shoulder. "We should all take a moment to think. From what I have heard, your son Cleo is fond of Scarlett. Is that correct?"

"They are friends…you could say that," Sepatus replied, sitting down to cool off.

"Maybe that might be motivation enough for him to get her back."

"It just may."

"If he and his brigade manage to do so, I think it would be necessary to reward him with the privilege of my daughter's hand in marriage. They could be joined here, in the Temple of Sciron, with all of you as witnesses to my offer." Clyus turned around the room with the palms of his hands held high. Vanna tucked her chin down quickly, hoping he hadn't seen her.

Sepatus's face became puzzled. Vanna, too, thought it odd that such an offer would be made at a time like this. *His own daughter is missing, and he offers her hand in marriage?*

"*Very well*," Sepatus said, almost as if he were asking a question.

Cayen continued his pacing, clearly disgusted by the suggestion his father had made. Clyus looked at him to make sure he caught his attention. "And if you must know, I, too, am exhausting all avenues in search of my daughter. I have assets in places around the Plane, some new and others old, and will stop at nothing to have my daughter returned to my arms."

To Vanna, the general seemed like a simple man. He was more honest than the others, at least, by the expressions he wore on the brim of his cloak. After Clyus had spoken, Vanna could see the genuine concern and inklings of intrigue draped across his face, one not hidden by gold and jewels or occupied by power like the others.

But instead of pursuing the answer to his bewilderment, the Consolar General just nodded, tucking his strong chin low for a moment, then saying, "*Good.* We'll reconvene when the Fourth and Fifth Magistrates arrive to cast their votes. In the meantime, I'll ensure that all our brigades are readily available for when the decision is made."

Cayen nodded aggressively, then stood up from the table and stormed out. The magistrates silently followed behind. Vanna and Zell were the last to exit the assembly room, following far behind the flowing crowd who walked out of the Consolate Chamber between its tall pillars and under its overhanging pediment. The sun was already half set in the east when they reached the opposite end of the square, where Lora sat, watching from beside a barren, stained wall.

"Do we have confirmation?" Zell asked her as they moved down a side alley, hidden between two buildings.

"We do," Lora answered. Vanna and Zell threw off their robes, dressing in new garments from the sacks Lora held.

"Did you get his direction? I missed him leaving the chamber."

"He got into a carriage bound south, up the hill. But we'll need to hurry, though. It's getting dark," Lora replied, helping the two of them change under the cover of the growing shade.

"*Dark is good*," Zell whispered under her breath.

Vanna followed them as they left toward the outskirts of the city. Their target was a few blocks ahead of them in a horse-pulled carriage, moving slowly enough that they could follow it on foot. As long as they stayed close and were covered by the tall buildings' walls, Zell was sure they wouldn't be spotted, even with the empty streets.

The three Sisters watched from a distance once the carriage exited the dense center of Sazara. Near the outskirts, they waited under the cover of night for the carriage to travel farther uphill, toward the bare villas, with nothing but red-shaded dirt and scarce trees surrounding them. On Zell's signal, they jumped from tree to tree, crawling through the rough and dry dirt when the distances between the plots of land became too far. Zell led them to a thick-trunked olive tree they could all huddle behind. Vanna saw the carriage they followed pull in front of a large home.

"That's our target," Zell confirmed again, pulling her head in from around the thick bark. "We'll wait for the carriage to depart before we go in. Lora and I will take care of the two guards at the front. Vanna, I'll meet you at the rear."

"Same plan as before?" Lora asked.

"Yes. Lora, you check the stable and make sure the horses are still there. We'll need to use them to exit Sazara through the gate. Vanna, you stay on my shoulder. Lora will enter from above as cover. Let's make this clean," her overseer commanded.

The three of them watched for quite some time, waiting for the carriage to return onto the curving path from which it came. In a single line, they crawled between and around the narrow patches of unkempt brush that grew scarcely above their prone bodies. When they were close enough to stand, Vanna hurried to the rear of the villa, while Zell and Lora straddled around the building's side. She waited under the stone covering near the back door until Zell rejoined her, unmarked.

Zell used her hairpin again, wiggling it into the door's lock. She pulled at its handle in silence, though Vanna's heart thumped heavily, making Zell turn around and gesture for her to calm down. They both drew their telsons and crouched to walk through the dark rooms, lit only by moonlight that crept in from the surrounding windows.

Empty again, Vanna thought as they swept from room to room throughout the first floor. She followed Zell up the central marble staircase, moving slowly from step to step. Before they reached the top floor, commotion came from a closed room on their left. Vanna waited for Zell's signal, but even she seemed to struggle to decide their next move. *Rush in too quickly, and you risk blowing your cover…wait it out, and any surprise you might have had may no longer be in your favor.*

"We're going in," Zell whispered to her. Vanna swallowed her spit as if it were her own fear. It went down her throat slowly, sliding past her thumping heart. Beating, if nothing else, but to push her fear right back up. Vanna nodded back, pretending she was ready.

This is no test.

Remember your training, Vanna.

Zell crouched over the handle of the closed door and gripped its knob with her fingers. Vanna watched eagerly from her shoulder, waiting for the inevitable click of bronze against bronze that would bring about uncertainty. In a single swoop, Zell sprang the door open and rushed in. Vanna turned the corner, trying to follow her overseer, panning the darkened room from left to right.

There.

The man she could barely see had his back to them. He quickly turned around and gasped for air. From the lone window's light, Vanna saw the whites of his eyes gaping wide, shifting in panic as if they were stars falling across a black sky. She paused momentarily, unsure of how Zell would attack the man, who seemed to have been caught readying himself for bed.

Zell brazenly slashed twice with the blade-end of her telson, catching him the second time across his forearm, which he held out in defense. In his nightly robe, he scurried a few steps to their right, away from the doorway they had rushed in through. She heard Zell grunt with each of her swift swings, which he had managed to weave and avoid.

Vanna's body felt dense as she hurried toward them near the darkest corner of the large room, disappointed that she hadn't yet gotten close enough to help her overseer. She wanted to jump in and throw a stab or two of her own, but Zell had left no opening between her skillful combinations. From the depths of the dark, Vanna heard the clash of steel against steel.

That isn't good.

In his hand, the darkened man now held a small dagger, which he had interlocked with Zell's telson, between each of their faces. The man groaned, forcing Zell to backstep with far more strength than she could match.

"*Vanna, now!*" Zell yelled in desperation as they began to tussle toward her.

Vanna swept in from Zell's left side and shoved her telson's blade into the man's stomach. She pulled it out, readying to attack again, when the man slid his blade to her side, forcing Vanna to jump back. At that moment, just before Vanna could lunge to thrust again, the man pushed Zell away with his free hand and slung the blade of his dagger straight into her chest.

"*NOOO!*" Fury filled Vanna as she screamed aloud. The rapids of unease that once rushed through her now moved like a tidal wave, flowing down to each finger that gripped her telson. Zell's body fell to the floor with both hands grasping at her chest. The man tumbled backward into the darkness, toward his bed, trying to stop his stomach from oozing blood.

From the open window on the opposite side, Vanna heard the sound of sandals smashing loudly onto the floor. She turned and saw Lora. The man looked to his right, near the window where Lora now stood, with a dying gaze of disbelief. In the darkness, she could see him turn to glance once at Vanna, then back again at Lora, who was much closer. She could tell he was debating on what to do, estimating his options. With a grunt, he finally jolted to the corner split between them both.

Vanna leaped to catch him as soon as he turned to run. With her telson gripped in one hand, she spun and lunged onto his back. Releasing her own grunt and heave, she stabbed its blade between his falling shoulders. The man collapsed onto his stomach; his head hit the floor hard as Vanna's weight now straddled him. His right arm was stretched out, reaching motionless toward the room's corner.

Vanna looked up from atop the dying man. There, in the lone glimmer of moonlight from the window, stood the Sunspear, leaning against the recessed crest of the room's wall. As the Consolar General of Sacrim took his final breath, Vanna closed her eyes.

But in the darkness of her mind, she saw her mother's eyes staring back.

CHAPTER 12

STONE

The sun lightened into the color of a blood peach to welcome the early tide of dusk. Roth sat at a corner table with his lap full, staring out of a window inside the Willowdale Tavern. On each leg of his black wool trousers sat a young woman of dark hair and tan skin—one named Tabitha and the other, Joleah. "Pass some of that redleaf this way, will ya, Lud."

Ludwyn packed the end bowl of his wooden shortpipe with some fresh redleaf, then lit it to an ember. He patted it down, lit it once more, then handed it behind the back of Joleah. "Here."

"You're a lifesaver." Roth puffed on its curved stem and blew the nut-scented smoke between the two girls. "Hard to do with your hands this full," he said with a laugh.

"Agreed."

Roth took a sip of burnt-stout between his draws of smoke, then shook the mug's remaining foam in the air for the barkeeper to see. "You could get some too, you know. Not the stout, but the women. Take your pick—Roverra is full of beautiful broads. And most come from wealth. They'd all be happy to flock to our corner," Roth said proudly as he took another draw from Ludwyn's pipe. "Just not either of these two."

"I'm okay for now, thanks."

The keeper from the bar came with a fresh tray of mugs, and Roth threw down four silver coins in payment. When they both reached for a drink, their eyes met, and Ludwyn fidgeted away in a bout of uncertainty. "Something wrong, Lud? You seem off."

"Just need some time to recover, is all. It's been a busy moon."

"Oh, come on. Tell me."

"I think, just maybe, the woods back home have been calling me," Ludwyn said, running his fingers through his beard.

"*Ah*, don't give me that. We've been in those woods our whole lives. *This is exciting.* The drinks pour themselves, and the women don't want to leave our laps. I'd take this over those bark ticks every single day." Roth reached for Joleah's chest with a drunken chuckle. "After my fight, there wasn't a moment that went by on that isle I will probably remember. But also, none that I'll forget. Too many people and too many parades—the drinks and the women. What's not to like?"

"That's what I'm worried about," Ludwyn said. He grabbed a mug from the table and took a long sip. "Think I might just need something a little more permanent."

"*Ah*, don't get soft on me now, Lud. Especially after all that nonsense you used to talk back in the woods. It was our dream to be out here, in the cities—where the pretty women are, surrounded by pockets deep with gold. And now you get the pick of the litter. Just take a look."

"*Your dream*," Roth heard his best friend say under his breath. But Ludwyn still turned his flat, hairy chin away from the largest table in the corner of the tavern to look across the dimly lit room. Young women with long, brown hair, dressed similarly to Tabitha and Joleah, in shades of green and white summer dresses, danced with young men to the sounds of wooden pipes, barrel drums, and lutes. In silence, Ludwyn turned his head back to the table, lifted his mug, and took another long sip.

"Oh, come on, Lud. If the perfect girl for you isn't here in this room with us, then she doesn't exist," Roth said. "She definitely isn't back in Tergona." He took another hit from the shortpipe, then handed it back to Ludwyn, who sat unmoved in his loosely tied white garment. "You see these two? It doesn't get any better—*wait...*" Roth leaned his head behind the girls to get a better look at Ludwyn, his bushy eyebrows curling in question. "You—you don't mean to tell me... Not my sister—no way. Ruth?" He lunged to shove Ludwyn in the shoulder.

"No." Ludwyn drank from his mug again.

"Oh, come on. You can do better than Ruth, Lud." Roth watched his best friend's round eyes spurning to look anywhere but his own.

"That isn't what I meant." In a nervous spout, Ludwyn tried to change the subject by saying, "But Ruth did mention something about catching one of the last boats out of here tomorrow. To go home."

"Lud, you're not really thinking about leaving me, now, are you? I go through all of that—first at the pit in Bovere, then at the Tessereum on the isle—with my life at stake, to be sitting right here with these beautiful women and a fat sack of gold…and you're more worried about Ruth and Tergona."

"No—no, it isn't like that," he stammered, trying to explain.

"I can tell you're lying. You know that, right? I've known you my whole life. You think I can't tell?" Roth let out a mocking laugh and then shoved him again. "That's my sister, you little tosh."

"I can promise—" Ludwyn tried to say before the music cut abruptly quiet.

Roth looked out across the tavern's dance floor and saw the dense crowd begin to ripple out of the way. "*What now?*" Just as soon as they had spoken her name, he saw his tall twin sister, dressed in her long plaid skirt and buttoned garment, barreling her way toward their table in the darkened corner.

"What are you doing?" she asked Roth, glaring into the eyes of the girls on his lap. "*Leave us.*"

After Tabitha and Joleah stood to leave, Roth responded, "I'm just having fun. I would ask what you're doing, but I already know—you've come to ruin it."

Ruth turned her chin away from them both. The music and commotion began to pick back up behind her. "You know, I've come here to help you. But now that I think about it, I don't think you deserve it."

"All you ever do is try to help me. Maybe it would be a good idea if you tried helping yourself for once. Have some fun. Loosen up."

"No, you definitely don't deserve it."

Just as Ruth began to turn and walk away, Roth looked across the round table at Ludwyn and saw him angle his face and bushy eyebrows his way in judgment. "Okay…*okay*…you're right," Roth let out against his will. "What is it?"

But instead of giving in to his sanctimonious plea, Ruth just continued to berate him. "You know, you've been given the perfect opportunity, and all you've managed to do is piss it away. For more than a quarter-moon now, you've drowned yourself in stout, wasted more gold than either of us has ever seen in our lives—*and probably ever will*—and sunken yourself into the shallowest of women."

"Oh, *please*," Roth said, grabbing the shortpipe back from Ludwyn to take another draw.

"That stinks, by the way. It's disgusting."

"Give me a break, Ruth. We're just having fun. I could have died in that pit and at the Tessereum. I earned this…and I deserve it. Jealousy isn't a good look on you."

"*Jealousy?* You think I want parades of people drooling over me? You think I want all this adoration? You can't go anywhere without someone noticing you. Roth, you really think I, of all people, want that?"

Roth slumped his shoulders and looked over at Ludwyn again for an answer, only to see him roll his eyes toward the window, away from them both. "Well, what do you want, Ruth? Gold? I've already given you a sack from my winnings."

"No, you idiot. I just want you to be okay. You're ruining yourself and throwing this perfect opportunity away. You're the champion of the Plane, for the Gate's sake. Have some dignity," she said, fighting the tears that looked ready to ripple down her angered face.

"What opportunity? I've made it this far myself, haven't I?"

"Roth, you really are such an idiot. The dinner tonight? At the Colchester Estate? The one in your bond with Lady Lomberg for you to attend?"

His stomach rolled like Ludwyn's eyes. "*Shit.* That's tonight?"

"Yes. Frand has been looking for you everywhere. He was a mess when he found me in the sceptory and interrupted my reading."

"When is it?" Roth asked, shifting himself to sit up in a panic. He turned back toward the window and saw the day's light barely hanging onto the horizon.

"Probably soon. Frand told me that Lady Lomberg has a tunic and overcoat waiting for you back at the inn," Ruth responded, turning away from his thanks. "Oh, and by the way, I'm leaving to go home tomorrow. Lud's coming, too. You know, back to the family you haven't written to once since we've left. I would say you can come, but it looks like you've already made your choice."

Out of shame, Roth looked down at the stout-stained grains of the wooden floor. By the time he looked back up, his twin sister was gone.

"Well, that didn't go well," Ludwyn said.

But Roth didn't respond. For as much as he didn't want to admit it, Ruth was right. And he could tell that his best friend was beginning to feel the same way. But for as much fun as he'd had on the isle and in Roverra, the last thing he wanted to do was sober up, dress fancy, and be surrounded by a pretentious crowd of royals.

"So, are you going to go?" Lud asked him.

"I don't have a choice if it's in my bond. Lady Lomberg would take me to those courts and probably make me forfeit most of my winnings."

"I would do anything for you, Roth. You know that. And by anything, I would even go as far as to tell you that you should listen to your sister. These people have endless gold and real work. You should take advantage of that. You can earn so much more than just your bond's winnings."

"*Gold*," Roth snarled under his breath. *That's all anyone here cares about.*

"And if you need to, go back home with Ruth—with us, on the morrow. Take some time to visit your family and be back in the Northwoods, where you belong. Even if it's only for a little while. It would be good for you to remember that person you once were, and how proud your parents would be to see you now."

Home, Roth pondered for a moment in silence. "You're probably right. When I fought back in the pit, my mind would go blank. I would close my eyes and see myself in the forest with nothing but trees around me. Even with the roaring crowd and their rush of emotion, all I could feel and hear were the howling owls, the songs of the birds, and the breaking of twigs. And all I could smell was the pine and morning dew. I would smile, seeing the campfires we would light and all the creatures we would find and chase after. It calmed me and brought me back down to who I was—who I am. The Northwoods was my cage, not the pit."

"Then just do what you did in the pit with these people here. Instead of warriors with armor and steel, you're fighting old men and women with their pockets and fancy words," Ludwyn said, taking a long draw from his pipe. "We've done enough to enjoy our time, especially at the isle. But that won't last forever."

"Thanks, Lud," Roth said as he stood up. "I should go get dressed before Ruth comes back again and kills me." Ludwyn laughed and joined him to stand. Roth lifted an arm around his best friend's shoulder and rustled him tight in a warm, brotherly moment. "I'll do my best to be on that boat with you two tomorrow," he told him.

"*You better.*"

Roth tightened the white ruffles of his neckband, tucked in his boots, and straightened his black overcoat before skipping down the stairs to the entrance hall of the Longfin Inn.

"You're late," Lady Lomberg said from the table beside the door. In her silken-moss gown, she took a hefty sip of wine from her chalice and adjusted the loose straps that hugged the sides of her arms.

"You look nice," Roth replied with a hollow smile.

"*As always.*"

When she turned away, Roth rolled his eyes. He followed her out the door, toward the carriage waiting for them in the center of the road. She shrugged off two sentinels before entering, mumbling something incoherent about their not being allowed in anyway. Nestled between the carriage's seats was a fresh bottle of aged wine, to which Lady Lomberg poured two fresh glasses and offered one to Roth.

"No, thank you," he said, recalling what Ruth and Ludwyn had told him earlier.

"Really? *You? The drunken bear?*" she slurred to ask him.

"Yes. I'm fine."

Lady Lomberg patted her poofy hair and checked the powder that covered her cheeks. "More for myself, then."

The carriage traveled down Roverra's rock-leveled road with homes and shops on each side that were taller than they were wide and had lightly painted ash bricks and dark shutters to outline every window. White fences enclosed their plots of land, and most had broad coastal oaks, whose limbs wound wide to support their heavy age, in abundance. Most of the royal families operated their work steads out of Bovere but had grand castles and luxurious estates scattered across the Eastern Plane. Unbeknownst to most, Roverra was a city of class, a beachside dwelling with the finest weather, making it an old destination for any royal who could afford it.

When the carriage finally reached the street closest to the shore, they turned left and continued south for a long, smoother stretch. "There's something I've been meaning to ask you," Lady Lomberg said while pouring herself another glass.

"What is it?"

"With you having won the Descindation." She paused, almost forcing herself to continue, "I thought it might be fitting, and be in both our interests, that we continue our bond."

"What would that mean?" Roth asked.

"After this, you would continue to work for me in Bovere. I'd offer you the position of honorary sentinel, and you would wear my family's coat—the silver pine of the Lombergs."

Roth was taken aback by her proposal. Before he had arrived in Bovere, he could barely distinguish one royal family of the Regent apart from another. And now, there he sat, being given the opportunity to join one.

This is my chance to be something…to grow up and mature. Through the window, he turned away from Lady Lomberg and looked out at the starlit beach the carriage strolled beside. In the distance, he pictured a thicket of wet pines as if they stretched tall, out from the beach's sand. *The Northwoods. Home.* He thought back to everything Ruth had told him, and everything he and Ludwyn had shared. Between the tall trunks of pine, he could see the faces of his family and friends all laughing, singing, and dancing like they used to when they were younger. His mother and father were there, smiling at him through the shimmering waves that formed between the needles and leaves of his imaginary forest. Below, he and Ruth were together, there with Ludwyn, exploring the woods without a care about the Plane or its politics. Ludwyn was right. It was the only place Roth really knew, and it was the place he was the most himself. The Northwoods was his home.

Roth turned back to Lady Lomberg. "Thank you for the offer. I think I'll need some time to think it over."

"*Time?* You need *time?*" she asked, her voice curling with contempt. "This is a rare opportunity."

"Yes. I'm going home after tonight. My family is there, and I haven't seen them in a while."

"That—that can be arranged," she drunkenly stuttered as their carriage came to an abrupt stop. "I guess we've made it. We will discuss this more at a later time." Roth nodded, then followed Lady Lomberg out of the carriage. After fixing her lengthy gown, she instructed him, "*Here,* take my arm. With or without my family's coat, you are still my date, so you should act in good behavior."

Date?

With the taste of revulsion in his mouth, he led the much shorter and plumper Lady Lomberg to the stairs, mumbling to himself in a sarcastic snicker, "*You should expect nothing less from me.*" Roth found the position they were in ironic. Just earlier, he was being told to quit his foolishness and overindulgent drinking, yet Lady Lomberg showed up to the dinner drunk herself. *To be like this,* he thought, *she must be nervous.*

The Colchester Estate was a simpler home than he had expected. Like the others, it was tall with white shingle siding and dark-painted shutters. Together, they walked up the stairs to the front door, which had a wraparound porch that led to a balcony overlooking the beach. The doorman let them in, and Lady Lomberg directed Roth to escort her to the estate's highest floor.

Through a pair of red doors on the third floor, they entered, welcomed by claps of applause from older men and women who dressed in similar black overcoats and illustrious gowns draped by the finest fur stoles. Roth waved to them, then held up Lady Lomberg's grasped hand in his own nervous bout of recognition. "*Welcome, welcome! Glad you could make it, congratulations!*" the voices shouted as they glided toward the center of the room. Once the music from the harp and brass began to play again, Lady Lomberg shoved her hand down and whispered into Roth's ear, "*Don't do that again.*"

Roth simply smiled and looked around. The room's length extended from its front wall to the back, where the doors opened to another balcony, allowing a cool breeze to flow in from the shore. In that direction, Lady Lomberg pointed and dragged Roth away from the attention. "There— someone you might want to talk to."

Next to the balcony's glass door was a younger couple. As they walked closer, Roth noticed that the man, who had a sharp jaw and proud face, wore two painted iron pins on each collar of his overcoat. One was a shield, colored light like oak, with crossed axes in black at its center. The other was a white dove flower with seven petals. Lady Lomberg introduced them: "Owen and Alice, this is Roth Fendorse. Roth, the Orlaiths."

"Pleasure," he said, shaking each of their hands.

"Congratulations on your victory. You made the Regent very proud," Owen told him. "I couldn't help but notice what axe you used during the fight. It was one of our own."

"Ahh," Roth said, his voice trailing with intrigue. "That must have been what that brandishing on its head meant. That axe is a beauty."

"Only the best from the Orlaiths," the man said with a delighted smile. Roth stood nearly a head-length taller than them both, as he did with most at the estate. But unlike the taverns he'd visited, no one here seemed intimidated by his presence. Most stuck to their small gatherings and chatted among themselves, pompously drifting from one party to the next with chalices of wine in their hands.

"I'm going to the bar. *You two have fun*," Lady Lomberg slurred as she sputtered away. Roth continued to chat with Owen about the axes he'd used back in the Northwoods, even giving his recommendations on the size and features of the heads and handles he'd like to see.

They talked for quite a while until the sound of metal ringing against glass broke the air, slowing the music and bringing the chatter to a halt. The crowd of people, who didn't number more than a hundred, all looked toward the room's center, where an older man with silver hair and the finest black overcoat stood.

"I'd like first to welcome you all to the Colchester Estate and give you my thanks—"

"That's Talam Franclare…from the Grand Forks," Owen leaned to tell Roth.

"Another great Descindation has been sealed in our Regent's history, and so we continue to celebrate," the older man named Talam Franclare said with a drifting but loud voice. "This one, of course, will be remembered in our history more than most. It is the first time in many solurns that we have had our champion reign victorious over the Plane. In that honor, I would like to recognize a new member here today, as a toast to a face that I hope will be more common in the coming solurns… *Roth Fendorse of Tergona!*"

Unsure of what to do, Roth raised his hand and thanked the clapping crowd. "Come up here, now, if you please." From the door by the balcony, Roth walked to the center of the room. Without the drinks to calm him, his nerves became tangled, leaving his face pale. "This isn't something we do regularly, but I think it's fitting for a champion, such as yourself—for restoring our rightful place at the top of the Plane. In the tradition of the royal families of the Regent, and on behalf of myself, the most noble, Moscah Mantis and Vittoria Bovere, and the many others who could not make it here tonight, we request that the Royal Order hereby recognize the *Coat of Fendorse*," Talam Franclare proclaimed, waving in two elderly gentlemen from the crowd.

Roth couldn't help but broaden his smile as a proud glimmer shimmered in his eyes, despite not fully understanding what was happening. He heard the man mention a Coat of Fendorse, but it didn't make much sense until one of the older gentlemen grabbed the collar of his overcoat and shoved a small iron pin onto it. Roth looked down and saw it shaped like a flag painted olive green. At its center was the brown paw of a bear with four claws.

Talam Franclare shook his hand, then handed him a piece of parchment that was rolled up and sealed. "Here is your family's official royal deed of recognition."

Gratitude filled Roth's tall body. He couldn't help but give his thanks to everyone who surrounded him, despite not knowing anyone's names. All he could think about was how badly he wanted to tell Ludwyn, his family, and even Ruth. And how proud of him they would all be.

"Thank you, sir," Roth said, still trying to hold back his nerves. He looked out at the fanciful crowd, then began shaking hands, one by one. In the very back, beside the bar, was Lady Lomberg, who didn't bother to clap or cheer or even come over to give her congratulations. Instead, she stood guzzling down her wine with a disturbed look on her face. But Roth didn't bother to console her. This was his moment, and he was proud of what he had to show for it.

As the smooth music picked back up, Roth became smothered by people walking over to give their praise. Names he could barely remember from people and couples introducing themselves sped quickly by him. *The Bardons*, with their coat of a sky-colored rooster on a maroon shield...*the Furths*, with their red fox...*cousins of the Ockmans*, with the flag of a buffalo atop an overturned barrel...*the Bangors*, with the curling horns of a ram, all came and went. But none were ever so enticing as a lady who introduced herself as Elvina Damas.

She was younger, like himself, tan and tiny, and had long sun-kissed hair. At the trim near her steep chest was a pin of gold with the blood-colored horns of a bull at its center. Roth followed her captivating gaze long after she'd introduced herself until Owen Orlaith came back over and asked for a word. "Thought it'd be a good idea to get you out of that mess," he said as soon as he pulled him away.

Roth laughed. "It was, until I met her."

"Ah, that's definitely one you should stay away from. Her father may be old and have passed his heir onto her, but don't think for a moment that that bastard wouldn't extort you and ruin your life. He's one of the wealthiest men in the Regent for a reason."

"Am I right to assume the man who introduced me is the wealthiest?"

"No, no. Not by a long shot. The Boveres have been at the top for quite a few centuries now. Talam's just the eldest descendant of Tohen the Second, or so they claim. The Franclares still have their connections to the Cathedral, though, that's for sure. Talam's older brother is a divine sage, and I think he might have an older cousin there as well."

"So, it's the Cathedral that decided this?"

"No one really knows. All we know is that the most powerful of the historic royal families in the east never really show their faces. And most heads of the families you see here answer directly to them."

"Who could the Franclares possibly answer to?"

"The Mantis in Florington," Owen Orlaith answered with a smirk.

Loud yells began to erupt from the room's far end before Roth could respond. Through the commotion, Roth heard Lady Lomberg's raspy voice yelling at the keeper behind the bar, ordering him to give her another chalice of wine. "Maybe I should go help," Roth excused himself as he walked over, trying to ease the situation.

Lady Lomberg's hair was a tangled mess, and she refused to stop berating the keeper to pour her more wine. A finely dressed man hurried over to help, to which she cried even louder, *"Favian, don't you dare touch me!"*

"Orean, you've had enough. Let's go downstairs," the old man with a gentle face told her.

"Favian, you know this was supposed to be my night. They only did this to embarrass me. Where are my congratulations? Where are my thanks?"

As the music halted, Roth walked closer and said, "Come on, let's go." Lady Lomberg's plump face softened when she looked into his eyes—as if he were still the prize she wanted to show off. Without acknowledging her wailing, Roth picked her up and threw her over his shoulder. He quickly followed the man named Favian out of the door and down the grand stairs.

"There should be a room here, to the right, at the end of this hall," Favian said as he led them through the second floor of the estate.

"She's just had a lot of wine to drink, that's all." They entered the dark room with a padded bed at its center, which Roth placed her on, and lit a candle at one of its two side tables. Before she could rush back after him with her drunken cries, Roth slipped out of the door and back into the red-carpeted hallway, holding it shut.

Favian stood beside him with his head sunken into the palm of his hand. "I'm sorry about that. It's not just the wine. She thought she was going to get one of these," he said, pointing his finger to the pin of a seven-petaled white dove flower at his chest.

Roth was unsure of what that meant but nodded in agreement anyway.

"*To become frocked—an honorary knight,*" the man whispered. "Furlak's Royal Order of Cathedral Knighthood," he added after glancing at Roth's confused face. "She knew better than anyone that would be harder to come by. Orean still owes her fortune and debt to the Colvin family." Again, Roth just nodded. "Now, with that embarrassment, she'll never become one. The Cathedral doesn't take kindly to the unrestrained. But, at least, now, she should sleep the night off well."

"She should," Roth said, unsure what to make of the kind man.

"I'm going back up to the party. Roth, be sure to tell your sister Ruth I said hello."

"*Sure,*" Roth replied, more confused now than before. "I'll check on Lady Lomberg and will rejoin everyone after." When Favian walked back up the steps, Roth turned to open the door quietly, trying not to let out what he thought would be more crying wails.

Instead, what he saw was much worse. On her knees, in the middle of the bed, was Lady Lomberg stripped naked. With her hands on her hips, she said, "I've seen how you look at me…not like you do with those younger girls."

"*What? No*…Lady Lomberg," Roth rattled in a panic. "You're just my boss…*my bondsman.*"

Without listening to anything Roth said, she lifted her breasts that sagged like unripe melons, trying to entice him. "Just think of the team we would be, Roth. This could be yours for the night…and every night. *Come work for me.*"

"Lady—Lomberg, *what are you doing?* You've—you've had way too much to drink," Roth stuttered nervously. "*Here*, put these back on." He hurried to grab her dress and undergarments that were thrown beside the bed.

But when he moved closer, Lady Lomberg threw herself onto him. She stood up on the bed and began to kiss his neck. The grossness of her sweaty perfume snuffed any polite thought out of his head. "Stop, please, stop," he told her repeatedly. Roth's unease grew as the moments passed slowly. He didn't know what to say or do to get her to listen. The last thing he wanted was for this to continue despite the wailing she would cause.

"Oh, Roth...*you know you want this.*"

"*STOP!*" In a snap, Roth pushed her shoulders away from him. The top of her plump body flailed in the air. Her legs were unable to stop her from tumbling off the bed. Her arms whirled in circles, and then Roth heard a loud smack—one like a stone snapping through a tree after being rolled off a tall cliff.

He rushed over to the opposite side of the bed and saw blood begin to puddle under her head. Lady Lomberg's naked body sat limp and motionless, sprawled out on the floor under the sharp corner of the bedside table. His hand shook as he checked her neck for a pulse. But none came.

What have I done? Roth's heart beat too fast for him to move. His mind became scattered with a thousand questions he didn't have a single answer to. *My life is done—they've all witnessed me here with her.*

What are they going to do to me?

I've killed Lady Lomberg... I need to leave... I can't be here...

Amid his panic, Roth covered her body with her dress, then rushed quickly back out of the door. Sprinting down the stairs as fast as he could, he hopped into the closest carriage and told the man to take him back to the Longfin Inn.

For the entire ride, a replay of what had happened revolved repeatedly in his mind. Images of the people he'd just met—Owen, Favian, and the rest, who had all congratulated him—were now like shadows that stood tall, looking down on him in judgment.

What have I done? I need to leave...

He rushed inside his room when he reached the inn, stuffed everything into his sack, grabbed his axe, and then dressed back in his clover-colored shawl. Across the hall from his upstairs room, he knocked to wake Ludwyn and Ruth. "We need to go. *Now,*" he told them between the doors of their split rooms.

Ruth opened her own, rubbing her eyes. "*Roth—what?* I'm going back to bed. I told you we'd leave in the morning."

"*No,* you don't understand. We need to leave now. Something's happened."

"What is it?" Ludwyn asked when he opened his door, adjusting his undergarments.

"*Lady Lomberg is dead.*"

"What do you mean, *dead?*" Ruth asked, her voice stern. "*What did you do?*"

"It wasn't my fault. It was an accident. She was really drunk and came onto me...and—look, I don't have time to explain. We need to leave. Now. They'll hold you both here until they have me. It was an accident—*I promise.*"

"*Roth...you...*" For the first time ever, Roth heard his sister swear, albeit under her breath. She stormed back inside her room, hurrying to pack her sack. "Can't you ever do anything right?"

"Don't worry, Roth, I believe you," Ludwyn said with blind confidence as he bent down to tie his boots.

"We need to hurry," Roth told them both, pacing back and forth in the hallway, unable to stand still. Once their belongings were gathered, they rushed downstairs and out of the inn, hurrying toward the rock-laid road beside the shore.

"I hope that boat we're supposed to take up Fleming's River in the morning is at the wharf. It was the last one unbooked," Ruth said with scorn.

"Can't we catch a carriage there?" Ludwyn asked as they began to follow Ruth, who turned north in the direction of the wharf.

"*No,*" she growled without turning around. "We need to avoid anyone witnessing us—witnessing *Roth.*"

Roth followed them both, too scared to speak about what he'd done. The royal families had just given him an official coat, and he hadn't even bothered to tell them. Now, it was all for naught. They walked on in silence, guided only by the light from the full moon that followed them north. Long into the night, they went far up Roverra's coastline. Both Ludwyn and Ruth were half asleep by the time they could see the near empty piers of the wharf.

"That one, there," Ruth said, pointing to the only boat tied to the closest pier, a small wooden dory. "It was the only option left. It's a two-seater, so we'll have to squeeze in."

"Two-seater? Roth takes up two seats himself," Ludwyn groaned to complain.

"Well, I didn't think Roth would come when I booked it. But like I said, we're going to have to squeeze in," Ruth reiterated. "Unless you want to walk to Bovere."

"Roth, you're rowing the whole way. I hope you know that," Ludwyn said with a delirious laugh as they walked down the pier. While at its very edge, Roth threw their sacks onto the small boat before lurching in. He stretched out his hand to Ruth for her to join him.

"*Um—guys—look*," she stuttered, staring out across the ocean. Ruth moved her shaking hand to point its way. "What is *that?*"

Roth turned from inside the small boat and looked to his right, out into the ocean's horizon. Where the sky's darkness met the sea, he saw a large bolt, lit by a flame at its spearhead, being hurled with a whistle through the air. Ahead of it and farther to his right, the flaming bolt landed to plunder itself into an oared ship.

A scouring sound began to resonate toward them as soon as the front end of the ship ignited in flame. Roth veered his gaze and saw the ship, one with large sheets strung flat above its hull, stalking the oared vessel like prey. From its bow, another large flame ignited.

Speechless, the three of them dropped everything and watched as a second bolt was flung into the air, striking the oared ship once more. Far out, across the waves of the Salic Ocean, cries of painful agony came in echoing screams as the ship on fire began to sink. Roth's eyes were enamored. His jaw hung open without a belief in what he was witnessing.

"*Norks*...and their galleys," his sister stated aloud in awe. "*We have to help them.*"

"Help them? What about helping me?" he asked, though Ruth was already heading back toward land. Roth stood still in the tiny boat and shook his head, feeling that he, too, was on fire, sinking just the same.

I'm the one who needs help.

CHAPTER 13

SUN

"It's bloody big, isn't it?"

"Yes, Captain Sovano. Yes, it is," Kladden said while staring up in awe at the towering canyon walls of the Sineaqe Gorge.

More than half a moon had passed since Cleo departed from the Isle of Azil. Late into his second day of travels back to Fort Corlach, he was met by a courier relaying to him the most urgent of posts—orders from his father. The Consolar General of Sacrim had officially ordered the deployment of the Sixth Brigade into the Regent, by way of the Sineaqe Gorge, in search of the missing Scarlett Calegri.

Upon reading his father's message, Cleo wanted nothing more than to storm back to the isle and search every tent and camp across all four allotments surrounding the Tessereum. He wanted to turn the days back to that night in the Court of Champions, where he stood near the window, waiting for Scarlett to show up. He wanted to take back whatever harsh feelings he had embedded inside the pit of his stomach, of loneliness and resentment. If only he had lost their wager, he could have been there for Scarlett and stopped this from ever happening.

For as much as Cleo had rejected being given this command, he couldn't help but feel that his father's decision was now vindicated. Leading the search for Scarlett was where Cleo knew he was supposed to be—where he needed to be. With his father's orders, he felt now, more than ever before, that his duty had a purpose. A purpose that he, more than any other, deserved to fulfill.

Cleo held his father's orders, reading the parchment repeatedly as he led the Sixth Brigade south, then east, to the rim of the Southern Plane. His assignment was personal, though Cleo knew he needed to hold true to the duties of a commander. In his fits of silent fury, he would look down

161

at the sack strapped to Dahlia's saddle and see the petals of the blood rose Scarlett had given him. As the days passed with the brigade's march, its life and color had slowly begun to fade and wither from its bud.

But Cleo's promise hadn't.

"Ready your men, Captains. Kladden and I will ride to meet the guides. Have them pack up their tents. We march through at daybreak," Cleo commanded, turning his stallion back toward the three horse-ridden captains.

"The first battalion will be ready," Captain Ostin told him.

"And the second," Captain Sovano added. Captain Jostell of the third battalion nodded in agreement.

"*Good*." As Cleo turned back toward the gorge, he became silenced by its enormity. He clicked the heel of his strapped sandal against Dahlia's side, forcing its hooves to kick up sand as he and Kladden trotted off toward its single slit of an opening.

"It was a good idea to leave behind most of the fifth battalion in Fort Corlach. Don't think they would have made it, dragging those wagons through this. Especially in this heat," Kladden commented when he caught up to Cleo.

"No. They would have only slowed us down. They're better served rebuilding that old fort for our return."

"They have their work cut out for them, that's for sure. That place was scattered with rotted wood, and its buildings stood by crumbled bricks. And it smelled of feral hog."

"Hopefully, by the time we find Scarlett and bring her home, it'll be done."

"The Regent is a big land, Cleo. That fort might be done before we ever get to Bovere, let alone find her. *If we even do*," Kladden said with a drifting sigh.

Cleo whipped his head around rashly and looked right at him. "*We will*."

"Cleo, I know how close you used to be to that girl when you were young, and even what you may think of her now, but she could be anywhere. The Eastern Plane is endless. And those hens are scattered all over it. There's no telling where she is, or if she's even there."

"We're going to find her."

Kladden rolled his eyes and nodded along silently as they continued their stride.

"Have you been out this way before?" Cleo asked once his impudence had settled.

"To the gorge? *No.* I've only heard of its tales, like everyone else. Tales of horror, that is. And of its creatures. Anything that could survive this desert heat, especially now at the beginning of summer, isn't something I'm very fond of meeting. The people included."

"Vident Lement always mentioned that the gorge was an oasis for all things horrid. A maze of misery, with skeletons of the dead spread throughout its shadows."

"Which is why I'm glad we'll have guides. Otherwise, I think I'd try my odds with the Sineaqe Desert," Kladden said.

"You'd really be begging for death, then."

"I'd rather die at the hands of the Benevolent Sun than those venomous bats and slithering scorpions. But the Fifth Partition is a dreadful place no matter where you find yourself in it. The people here don't even consider themselves part of Sacrim. And I don't claim them either."

"It's been less than three hundred solurns since they joined Sacrim, and we practically invaded them to make that happen," Cleo commented as they rode.

"Oh, we invaded them alright…and it was for control of this passage right here." Kladden pointed up to the tall walls of the gorge, which were split at its opening like a log chopped from an axe driven down by the sun itself.

"If only crossing our brigade through the Isle of Azil weren't still forbidden," Cleo growled. "It's a full day's march to make it through this maze."

"If these guides manage to get us through before nightfall, I will gladly pay an extra sack of gold from my own pockets."

"Why nightfall?"

"*The venomous bats?*"

"That's only a myth, Kladden," Cleo said with a light laugh.

"Well, I won't be the one to find out."

"Maybe we should ask them."

Three figures stood at the edge of the gorge's narrow path, in the shadows between its mammoth, jagged walls. As they rode closer, Cleo noticed that two of them were much taller than the third. But all three were dressed in long-sleeved garments and trousers, wrapped tightly with tan cloth from their ankles to the top of their heads, like a cocoon that revealed only their eyes.

Cleo dismounted his horse and walked over. Without a word of welcome, the taller one in the middle stuck out his hand with his palm held up. Cleo dropped the satin sack he had grabbed from Dahlia's saddle into the man's hand. He nodded, then handed the sack to his shorter partner, who lifted it next to their ear and jingled the clanking gold.

Scarlett? Cleo couldn't help but let his mind wander in thought about her. Even with their heads wrapped in tan cloth, he could tell from the tiny open slivers that the shorter one was a woman—one with beaming blue eyes and seemingly pale skin, similar to Scarlett. Cleo stared into the woman's eyes, waiting for her to look at him as she counted their payment for passage.

"It's all there," the woman said in a raspy, crackling voice.

No…this was never going to be that easy.

"Good," the guide in the middle said. The taller man stuck out his arm to shake Cleo's wrist. His eyes were dark, smothered by gloom, the same as the other man's. "Gareb. This is Joshua and Sorah."

"Commander Cleo Scordisci. Pleasure."

After Kladden introduced himself, Gareb asked, "How many?"

"Four thousand, give or take. Nearly a thousand on horseback and close to a hundred wagons. Each with a mule." Cleo could see the pit of the man's eyes shifting past his shoulders.

"That shouldn't be an issue. I had the gorge shut down today for any other traffic, by your general's message. We'll have to move along quickly so the last of your group makes it out before nightfall."

"*See,*" Kladden turned to whisper to Cleo, curling one of his stubby eyebrows.

Cleo mounted back onto his horse and turned around to wave in his marching brigade. Half of the cavalry from the first battalion led at the fore, with the other half at the rear. The captains ensured each battalion was split into two tight columns, with the second battalion's spearmen leading the swordsmen, as usual. Behind them were the wagons carrying supplies for their journey. At the forefront of the two columns were two horse-ridden guardsmen waving the royal red flag of Sacrim high in the air.

"So, no horses for you lot?" Kladden asked as he mounted his own.

"Horses frighten easily," Gareb replied bluntly.

"And they don't climb well," Joshua added.

Kladden sighed and shook his head in disbelief, dragging his knuckled chin up and down the sides of the sand-ridden cliffs they were readying to enter. "*Why would we need to climb?*" he looked at Cleo to ask sarcastically, with a told-you-so grin.

"We need to be moving. Daybreak has risen," Gareb instructed them.

It didn't take long for the Sixth Brigade to meet them at the front of the path, where the three guides began to lead them through. The sandstone cliffs of the gorge widened once they passed through its entry. But its jagged walls still towered tall enough to shade the early-morning sun from the pathway. Despite the gorge's ominous turns and tight crevices, their horses didn't seem to mind the stable footing, which was packed solidly with sand and cushioned by the soft dust that floated in from the desert.

Cleo rode ahead in silence, trying to peek past every turn the guides led them around. Though he wasn't nearly as worried as Kladden, Cleo could tell why the tales of those creatures he had mentioned existed. Every glance at the darkened shadows that burrowed between the gorge's many caves made him question what lurked inside. Whenever he felt his mind and its irrationality drifting into fanaticism, he would think of his teachings with Vident Lement and ground himself back to reality. And if that didn't work, he would think of Scarlett, the reason why they needed to push through.

As they marched along, it became obvious to Cleo just how necessary the guides were. The Sixth Brigade had taken turn after winding turn through its maze without any hope of remembering which way they went or where they even were, let alone where they needed to be going. Every jagged cliff looked the same as the one they passed and blocked much of the sun's course. And every cave stood like a black mirror, waiting for them to give up hope. The guides, though, weren't troubled by the gorge's confusion, having crossed through, back and forth, countless times, day after day. On their backs, they carried just a single leather sack and a simple waterskin, fit for only a day's trek. Cleo looked down at his own flask attached to Dahlia's saddle and noticed it was half empty.

Water was like gold in Sineaqe. He knew it to be treasured more than steel was to the east, or lumber to the north, or even those precious gems to the west. Cleo checked his map consistently during their days leading in, which detailed every spring and fresh creek they would come across before their journey. The last one they had crossed was now a two-day ride away. If hope became lost, Cleo knew those two days would be two too many.

Cleo looked back to check on his brigade every so often as they traversed the gorge. Captain Ostin had assured him that the men were still in high spirits, though the look below the brim of their bronze helmets said otherwise. For as strong-willed as the guardsmen of the Sixth Brigade were, the gorge and its lamenting heat were the worst of challenges. When he could, Cleo rode ahead to ask the guides about their travel and the path's condition, looking for points of rest. The two men, though, spoke very little. And when they did, they gave only shallow answers, proclaiming they must keep moving forward to reach the end before nightfall. Of the guides, only the girl named Sorah was willing to engage in conversation with Cleo.

"What's the reason for your travel east?" she asked him.

Cleo looked down at her from atop his horse. "We're in search of a missing woman."

Sorah seemed to ponder a bit before replying, "She must be quite important to be sending this many guardsmen outside of Sacrim."

"She is important, yes." Cleo pictured Scarlett's gentle face. *She's important to me,* he wanted to say. "But we're on a peacetime expedition. We aren't traveling for war." Cleo reached into the sack on the side of his saddle and pulled out a green flag patterned with white stripes, which the Regent's covenant recognized as a symbol of peace. He showed it to her and explained that carrying their colors represented their submission to the Eastern Plane's covenants.

Their plan, at least the one given to him by his father, was for the Sixth Brigade to travel north between Decanan and Tammon, across the Regent's rolling meadows, then follow the Fleming River east until they reached Bovere. From there, he was to meet with the royal families and ask for their permission to search the cantons. If their answer wasn't to his liking, his father had given him a wagon filled with sacks of gold so they could pay the royal families to search the Regent with their own men.

Everyone in the east has a price, as Vident Lement would say. But in Cleo's mind, it would never come to that. He would be the one to find Scarlett, whether the royal families allowed him to or not.

"You look quite young to be leading this many men," she commented, her voice still raspy.

"Age is only a number. Besides, you're the one currently leading us." Despite the rags that covered her head, Cleo saw her cheekbones rise, which he assumed was from a smile.

"A wise child," she said, her voice lingering with sarcasm. "No wonder they put you in charge. Did you know the girl you're after? Or are you just following orders?"

"Both. She was once a good friend."

"Then, I'm sorry she's missing, and I hope you're able to find her."

"*Me too.*"

"Just a little way left before the first stop," she broke her calm demeanor to say.

Cleo sighed in relief. "Finally."

The guides led Cleo and the Sixth Brigade to reach a buckle, where a tall, wind-swept sandstone column stood between two equally wide paths. Above them, the midday sun now scorched, causing Cleo and most of the brigade behind him to drench their bronze armor and underclothes with sweat. The Southern Plane was renowned for its intense heat. But, as Cleo quickly realized, Sineaqe's heat was different, especially while trapped within the breezeless, tall walls of its narrow gorge.

"We'll stop here for a moment," Gareb turned around to say. "The Finger marks more than a third of the way through. Drink up and rest while you can. The sun will be at its brightest for the next third."

Cleo scrunched his nose and let out a short sigh as he dismounted his horse, dragging it into a crevice for what little shade was available. "I never knew what heat was until today," he told Kladden, who followed him with his own horse into the shade.

"I don't think we're in Sacrim anymore," he replied, pouring water for both of their horses. "I think I'll take back what I said earlier about crossing that desert."

Cleo laughed but with reserve. "It's hard to imagine what the first Scipyrians had to go through when they were forced to cross through here over two thousand solurns ago."

"Without a guide either. Other than the Benevolent Sun, that is."

Cleo looked up into the sky and stared into the sun's blinding light. "They were the toughest of people. Scyrus the Sacred…and the Arukians and Atholians. We complain about those knights and their pompousness, but without our ancestors' exile, we might have ended up just like them."

"I'd rather burn to death in this forsaken rim than live my life running around like one of those headless hens, bowing down to some ghost and its tree."

"Or kneeling to those old kings and queens and their greedy families. I don't think any of the other five brigades could have made it this far," Cleo said with a smirk, looking back at his guardsmen, who, too, were taking advantage of their rest in the crowded shade.

"It's been a few centuries since the Guard came out this way. I wouldn't blame them."

Cleo watched the guides wait for their timeglass of sand to run empty. He looked up at the sun again and saw a single small cloud, offering half its whiteness as cover. Within its haze, a sliver of shining light reflected back to the entrance from where they started. It was just enough to split the sun into pillars of noticeable rays, spread directly above the tall walls of the gorge. Still gazing back at where it landed, Cleo began to notice an odd commotion coming from the cavalry at the rear. He stood to look and wondered what his men might have seen.

"Must be one of those damn scorpions. Better be a giant one for all of this," Kladden said. He let out a miserable grunt and got up to follow Cleo toward the center of the path.

Even the guides grew concerned, watching as the guardsmen began to split down the middle, as if they were the wake of a boat traveling downriver. Cleo stared cautiously, using his hand to cover the glare from the sun, so he could see what or who it was.

To his surprise, a familiar face rode forward between the middle of the brigade. *Vident Lement.* He could barely make out the face of the old man on horseback as he trotted in, draped by the burnt-orange vestment that flowed behind him in all its folds and loosened threads. *What are you doing all the way out here?* Cleo questioned, looking on in confusion.

"Is that really Vident Lement? He looks like shit," Kladden blurted aloud.

"*It is.* And he does." Cleo rushed over to meet him as soon as he passed by Captain Ostin near the head of the first battalion. "Vident Lement, *what are you doing here?* Why not send a courier? You're in no shape to ride this far—especially here in this heat," Cleo stated rapidly while helping his panting preceptor off his horse.

Cleo could tell something wasn't right. Vident Lement looked rough, worse than he had ever seen him before. His silken vestment was unkempt and frayed, and the hairs that encircled his balding head were unbrushed, as if he hadn't slept in days. Worst of all, his calmness and stoic sense had vanished.

"It's your father... *Cleo,*" he replied, trying to catch his breath. "General Sepatus has been *murdered.*"

Cleo stood still under the sun. The words his preceptor had uttered echoed back and forth within his empty mind. "*Murdered...*" He broke his endless gaze to repeat it to himself slowly in disbelief.

That can't be... Who could kill my father?

The sun's heat was nothing compared to the fury that began to rage within Cleo's heart. His face flushed blood red, and his body couldn't move. *It can't be.* If it had come from anyone else, he never would have believed them. Cleo's chest rattled, daring him to speak. "*What happened?*"

From their reactions alone, neither Kladden nor Vident Lement had ever seen Cleo this angry. Both looked at each other, almost too scared to respond.

"We still don't know. Just—just that he'd been murdered," Vident Lement stuttered.

Kladden grabbed Cleo by the arm, pulling him away from his brigade so they couldn't see the wrath of his unfolding emotions. "Cleo, *breathe...breathe.* You're going to be okay."

But he wasn't. And he felt like he would never be.

The mountain of anger he now felt, along with the guilt from Scarlett before, plummeted any rational thought far from his mind. Cleo wanted nothing more than to bury himself within one of those caves along the gorge's walls like the skeleton he was, never to see the sun again. And like those bats that lurked within them, Cleo felt venomous.

Vident Lement walked slowly to where Cleo and Kladden stood, far enough away so that no one could hear them. "I heard the news a quarter-moon ago. I packed up everything immediately and left that very day. With your father gone, Sazara isn't safe."

"What of his burning?" Cleo asked, trying to gather himself.

"I'm sorry, Cleo. I don't think they've found his body."

Cleo clenched his fists. "What do you mean, *they haven't found his body*? How do you know he's even dead?"

"The villa burned to the ground."

Cleo lifted his gaze to the sky. His jaw gnashed and his eyes strained.

Kladden tried his best to calm Cleo before turning to Vident Lement to ask, "What of the Sunspear?"

"That, they did find. But I presume there would be a vote in the chamber for the next Consolar General. Kladden, you might be a strong candidate."

"I'm not interested."

"*How do they not know who did it?* Who could even kill my father?" Cleo threw his hands into the air as he spoke, trying to hold back the oncoming tears.

Vident Lement paused before acknowledging any of Cleo's questions. "I have my guesses, but I dare not speak them…"

"No, *do*."

"Those deacons of the temple have always used their hordes of gold to their advantage by controlling the issuance and collection within their large following. And you know well about their connections to the Calegri family and the others in relation—"

"Excuse yourself, Lement. There's no need to bring the Temple of Sciron into this," Kladden interjected. "Have your feud with the Calegri clan, but the temple is revered across Sacrim with thousands of worshipers, myself included."

Vident Lement rolled his eyes in response, refusing to continue what he was going to say.

"The Benevolent Sun is the source of all light on the Plane, and all life moves to point its way. Us included. Without it, and the deacons who profess our faith, we would all be living in darkness—in death."

"Those deacons are the embodiment of darkness," Vident Lement snarled back.

"Refute yourself from their disrespect," Kladden told him, his temper growing.

"You *really* would make a great candidate."

Kladden grabbed the thin, old man by the collar of his vestment and lifted him into the air. "*Kladden, enough!*" Cleo yelled as two of the captains rushed over to stop the fighting. "Both of you need to stop... My father is *dead.*"

"Ahem, Commander," Captain Sovano said, tapping him on the shoulder. Cleo turned around and saw all three of the guides beside him.

"We need to move. We don't have daylight to waste, especially with this many travelers," Gareb told him.

"I need a moment." Cleo sulked, lowering his shoulders in despair. *I need more than a moment,* he thought, wiping away the puddling tears.

"Make it quick," Gareb said.

He scoffed the rag-wearing man away. His father had just been murdered, and there he stood, trapped within the forsaken rim of the Southern Plane. *I need to make a decision...but which way do I go?* Cleo pondered while pacing in circles. It felt as if he were walking in quicksand. Each step of his sandals sank him deeper into its swallow. *Continue on with my father's orders to find and rescue Scarlett,* who was so dear to him, *or turn back to Sazara and find the people who murdered my father...and avenge his death.*

As a commander, Cleo knew he had a duty to the Guard and to follow its orders. But for as long as Cleo had been alive to know it, the Guard was his father.

What of the duty to myself? To my family?

I don't have a choice, Cleo knew. "*We're going back,*" he stated boldly.

"*What?*" Vident Lement rushed over to him to question him. "You—can't. There's no telling what these people will do...or what they will turn Sacrim into without your father around."

"We're heading back to Sazara. I'm not going to let my father die alone without finding out who or what did this to him. No. *He would do the same for any of us.*"

"The boy is right," Kladden said. "He'd be following the orders of a general no longer in command. And we can't wait here. Cleo commands his own men now."

"Your father would honor his commitment and his duty. And what of Scarlett? Finding her could be the key to your survival," Vident Lement pleaded.

Scarlett. For as much as Cleo wanted to find and save her, deep down, he knew the truth—the same truth Kladden had told him earlier. *It was never going to be that easy.*

"Scarlett isn't some pawn. And I want to save her more than anyone here. But there's no telling if we'd even find her or how long it would take to do so. And there's certainly no telling what would become of Sacrim in that time," Cleo said sternly. "You claim the Temple of Sciron to be at fault. If you really felt that way, you'd support my decision to turn back and seek justice. The odds of finding my father's killer back home are far greater than our wanderings across the Eastern Plane to find Scarlett," he added, almost against his will. "What kind of *man* would I be if I ran away from my own *father's* death?"

"Cleo...*son*, please listen to me, I beg of you. *Be calm.* Only from calmness can you discern strength," Vident Lement continued to plead, resting his hand on Cleo's shoulder. "If your father was their target, then you will be too. The Eastern Plane could be a place of refuge."

"I'm a Scordisci, Vident Lement. And a commander of the Sixth Brigade. Not some refugee. Thank you for your counsel, but I've already made my decision. My duty is to justice. *I'm going to tell the men.*"

Vident Lement looked defeated, sulking his nimble shoulders low as he watched Cleo and Kladden mount their horses. Kladden looked back at the frail man with a face as stern as steel as Cleo rode off down the center of the gorge, where his guardsmen were still split between each of its tall walls. Halfway down their broken formation, Cleo stopped and trotted Dahlia in circles, gazing into the eyes of his brigade as they waited to hear what had happened.

"*There's been a change of order,*" Cleo yelled so everyone could hear him. "*Our general has been murdered by forces still at large in Sazara.*" Murmurs from the guardsmen's chatter echoed against the jagged walls, loud enough for Cleo to hear some of what they were saying.

Cleo waited for the men to quiet before continuing, "*Some of you may have never met the man, but as you are all aware, General Sepatus was my father. He was an honorable man who wanted the best for each of you and for Sacrim. He was a true warrior. The kind that creates peace and brings order to his home. His life was no different from your own...he once stood where each of you does today. From a lowly cagerman, he worked hard to earn your trust. And he worked hard to earn the rightful seat as your Consolar General.*"

As Cleo looked around, a single tear shoveled down from the crest of his eye. His rage was resurfacing. "*He was not just my father, but a father to any man who calls himself a guardsman of Sacrim. If you trusted him, trust me now. I do not command that you follow me but that you continue to follow him and his rightful justice. And I plan to march back to Sazara and seek it! Join me if you dare to do the same!*"

Cleo grabbed at his waist with his right hand, just under the black pearl pommel, and unsheathed his father's sword. He could feel the men's raw emotion as they yelled aloud in unison, stomping their sandals and spears into the packed sand. Startled by their echoes, Dahlia reared its front legs into the air, and Cleo pointed the tip of his sword to the sky. Like kindling to a fire, their encouragement fanned the flames of his venom and warmed the cold that had once sunken into the depths of his skeletal bones. Cleo looked up at his sword, pointing to the sun, and traced the light that fluttered between the lone cloud as it drifted back toward Sacrim.

I'm coming, Father.

CHAPTER 14

SEA

Flying free, gliding above the spray of salt that splashed up from the sea,
From the sun it dashed, that bright orange beak, swooping down before the knee.
Fear of hunger, for a fish it flew, the breaking waves became its haven,
Fast, it carried its catch to the coast, landing its callous claws without craven.
Feathers of clouds lofted white and wide, stretching to gather the water's praise,
Free it flew, the snow pelican, a beautiful memory from Niven's last days.

*F*inally," a feathery voice breached through the blackness.
Dane opened his eyes and gasped loudly for air, spitting out the seawater that was lodged in the depths of his chest. The blurred figure in front of him grew small as he felt the hands that had once grabbed his nose and chin rise to turn the bones of his body over on his side.

"*Dane*, you're safe… *Dane*, wake up," a familiar voice said, coming from one of the figures surrounding him.

Piney? "Where am I? What happened?" Dane panted frantically, patting the pebble-laden sand he lay upon. "Am I dead? Wait, why are *you* here?"

"These two, right here, saved us," Piney tried to explain, pointing to the two figures beside him. Dane rubbed his eyes to get rid of the blur. Even with the bright light from the full moon, it was difficult to make out what was in front of him.

"Actually, that saved you," a hairy young man said, pointing to two buckets that were enclosed by seats and wrapped together by twine. "We just swam out to pull it ashore. We thought you were gone."

Dane grunted as he rolled over, using all his strength to lift his back off the ground and sit up. He rubbed his eyes once more and saw a greenish-brown blur crouch down in front of him. "*Thank you.*"

The figure slowly shaped itself into clarity until he could make out what he was seeing. There, crouched in front of him, was a girl. One with a soft chin, thin lips, and round, light-brown eyes, which matched the color of her long hair. She reached out her hand to help him stand up. "I'm Ruth."

"*Dane,*" he said, grabbing hold of her hand that was as big as his own. Every part of his body throbbed in harsh jabs of pain as he stood. He reached for his shoulders and back but felt only the bones under his skin and the scars from the lashes, which were too stiff to stretch away his aching pain. "We must have been rowing for three days straight… I can't move a thing."

The hairy man from behind the tall girl moved closer. "Sounds about as miserable as you look. I'm Ludwyn, by the way."

"Who would have thought it?" Piney walked between them. "I mean…a bucket of shit. Those same buckets I hated with every breath I took and every smell they stuffed me with. That will be a story to tell, huh? The shit buckets that saved my scrawny ass. People are gonna think I had one of those moon-old ventral stews when I tell 'em."

Dane glanced over at the two buckets strapped together on the ground. "That can't be? *Can it?* Where's everyone else? *Where are we?*"

Nathan. Dane looked out at the moonlit ocean but saw only the wreckage from their ship washing ashore. The more he scanned past the breaking waves, the more his memory started to come back to him. *The exhaustion*—he would never have been able to swim anywhere, even without his shackles. *And the fire*—above and in front of him, and all around, it surrounded everything and everywhere he looked, smoldering the planks of the *Fereclis* into chaos. The screams of burning pain he heard rang like the ship's bell inside his mind as it all started to come back. Without those shit buckets to save him, he would have surely sunk to the bottom. *Down with the ship I hated, in a nightmare I would never have awoken from.*

"There were a few others. Some ran inland. Two men walked that way as soon as they came ashore," Ruth said, pointing south. "And a girl that my brother took north."

The girl. That must have been it.

"Well, that explains it, then," Piney said, rubbing the crest between his knuckled chin. "No wonder we sank. Girls on ships are shit luck. Should have known better than to bring one aboard."

"*Actually*," Ruth said from deep within her lofty chest. "Your ship was attacked. That's why it sank."

"You didn't have girls on your ship?" Ludwyn asked with a sneer of cynicism. "That sounds like torture."

"*What do you know of torture?*" Dane sneered under his breath. He shifted his gaze back to the wreckage that was still floating in, of things that looked like planks of the hull cracked in half, with lines of rope draped around them. Dane limped closer to the water with his shackles dangling across the pebbles and found a broken oar lodged in the sand. He picked it up and held it against the glimmer of light from the sky. At that moment, he couldn't help but splinter a smile himself—to still be alive and finally off that ship, despite barely being able to distinguish his nightmare from reality.

Sunken to the bottom of the sea…where it belongs.

"We're just a way north of Roverra, by the way," Ruth said. She walked to join him by the pulling tide.

"No clue where that is. I'm from the Marredom—an island in the north."

"I know where Marredom is… You think I couldn't tell you two were *norks*? A skeleton on one of those oared galleys with blond hair and pale skin. Where else would you be from?"

Dane just tucked his chin into his chest, despondent. It was the first time he'd heard that word used as an insult, and he wasn't sure how to take it. A nork had always just been the common word for the people of Marredom, one named after their ancestral founder and their old language, norkatis. Dane knew it was a language as harsh and as cold as they were, spoken directly and with meaning, especially when compared to the flowing roalish everyone spoke today. But he had never heard that word used in a derogatory manner, at least until then.

"We're on the western coast of the Regent, north of the Grand Channel. Roverra is the last canton before the Isle of Azil," Ruth explained in a softer voice than before. "Here, have some of this. You look like you need it." She handed Dane the waterskin strapped around her shoulder and a cloth from her sack that unraveled to reveal a few thin crisps.

"I'm allowed to have this?"

Ruth looked at him in disbelief, as if she thought his question was more of a joke than it was a truthful inquiry. "Yes...*of course.*"

"Thank you."

"Are all the women here as tall as you?" Piney asked, walking over as soon as he saw her hand Dane food and water. In his share of munching, he circled around Ruth and inspected her from head to toe. "Dane, she's just about as tall as you."

"No. But I'm not from here. The Regent is a big place," she said, half ignoring Piney.

"We're from Tergona. A small town far east and farther north," Ludwyn said after he left the wreckage he was sifting through.

"That explains it—got nork blood in you," Piney replied between sips. "Me, I'm just a runt. I never got that northern growth like my brothers did. But I blame my mother for that. You see, they said I cried too much when I was little, and my mother had to feed me on her bad tit just to shut me up. Rotten milk will do it."

"Of course you norks drink rotten milk," Ludwyn said with a mocking smirk. "But you do look like you'd make for a great rider. Maybe we should take you back to those horse tracks in Bovere. We could make a fortune betting on you," he added with a chuckle.

"Be nice, Ludwyn. They've been through a lot," the tall girl named Ruth said, giving her hairy friend an ominous stare. "But speaking of which, we should be leaving too. Roverra and the wharf are just south, that way." She pointed down the shoreline. "Ludwyn and I can't go back to Roverra, but from the wharf, you might be able to catch a ride back to Marredom."

Piney shot the water out of his mouth and broke into laughter with what little strength his weak body had. "You think I'm going back *there?*" he practically yelled. "Woman...I would rather have drowned than ever step foot back on one of those galleys. *Can you see the bones on that boy's body?*" Piney stopped his fussing to point at Dane.

"Go where you want, then," Ludwyn said bluntly. "Roth took the last boat from there anyway."

"There should still be a few new arrivals within the next couple of days that could take them somewhere safe," Ruth said, turning to her friend. "We can at least show them back to the wharf. From there, they can go wherever they please."

"Ruth, that's the opposite way from home. We need to be on our way. Have you forgotten what Roth has done? All of Roverra will be looking for him—for us."

"What Roth did and what we have done are two different things. We're innocent, Lud. I think you forget that."

"But why even go through the trouble of having to prove it? You heard Roth. They will just hold us until they find him. We're accomplices to his escape."

"No one knows that, and they don't have any proof. They couldn't hold us."

"But they would. When we let Roth leave upriver with that crying girl, he made me swear to him that I'd protect you and bring you home. Walking back toward that den of royals would be a mistake."

"I don't need your protection," Ruth said sternly, her soft complexion beginning to glow red.

"Going back to that wharf sounds good to me. Anywhere is better than the *Fereclis*," Dane cut between them to say.

"Look at them, Ludwyn. They need our help. It's not even daybreak yet. By the time those royals wake and find Lady Lomberg, we'll be way out ahead of them, headed home."

"They have horses and carriages, Ruth...and hounds for our trail."

"Lud, we haven't done anything wrong."

The hairy young man just turned the other way and ran his finger through the bush of his black hair, realizing that she wouldn't budge.

"What about *these*?" Piney asked, dangling his bony hands out in front of the birdcage of his chest, shaking his shackles. "They're going to think I'm some sort of criminal."

"Wait," Ludwyn said, pausing with a glare of precaution. "How do we know you two aren't?"

Piney just looked at the hairy young man stupidly and raised his shackles higher. "Because the real criminals are the people who would torture us like this."

"Piney's right," Dane added. "I'm no criminal."

"Someone on one of those boats should have a shear or an axe," Ruth told them, before glancing over at Ludwyn. "They need our help, Lud. I'm bringing them back to the wharf whether you come to *protect* me or not."

Dane and Piney struggled to follow Ruth and Ludwyn down the shoreline, toward the wharf. With each shackle-clanking step he took across the beach, his forgotten sense of freedom grew like a promise that felt perpetually fulfilled. From the worst three days he'd ever had as an oarsman to miraculously escaping his assured death, Dane was just happy to feel the free land under his feet and breathe the fresh air of its breeze. He wasn't sure where he and Piney would go, or what would come of them, or whether he should even trust the two foreigners they had just met, but none of that bothered him.

What did bother him, though, was knowing that the rest of the oarsmen deserved to be there on the beach beside him. There were many who had served their time in multitudes more than he had. And those, like his friend Nathan, who deserved to escape just as much, if not more, than he did. Every so often, he would think back to what Ruth had mentioned and glance inland with the hope of seeing Nathan, or any of the other oarsmen, rushing over to join them. Instead, all Dane saw were the occasional bloated and pale bodies floating off in the distance, the opposite way.

A different kind of freedom, he thought.

Just as the sun was beginning to rise from the ocean's horizon, Ruth stopped sharply in front of them. She grabbed Ludwyn's sleeve and turned around slowly. "*That wasn't there before.*"

Dane looked over her shoulder and could barely make out a ship with three posts, like the tall trunks of a tree, sticking out from its hull.

"And it's tied up to the pier at the wharf," Ludwyn said, trying his best to whisper.

"That must be the same ship from before—the one that sank them," Ruth stammered over her words.

"Maybe they didn't see us," Dane said, looking back the way they had come to see if they could still turn around.

"Oh, *they did.*" Ludwyn lifted his hand slowly to point at the shadowed figures that were now rushing onto the beach from the pier. "What do we do? We can't fight them. Do we run?"

"If they were the ones who sank a galley from Marredom, then maybe they aren't that bad after all," Piney said from behind, calmer than them all.

"The short one might have a point," Ruth acknowledged through her shaking voice. "We don't know what they want. But they're docked in the Regent, so they have to respect our covenants."

"They just sank a ship, Ruth… They don't have to respect anything," Ludwyn responded. "And I think we know what they want—these two, *dead*."

Dane could see the four or five figures begin to move more swiftly down the coast, headed in their direction. He didn't have an answer to any of their bickering, but the last thing he wanted was to be thrown back onto a ship again like a ragged prisoner. His body wouldn't make it. "Maybe we should run inland."

Ruth looked him up and down, running her fingers through the thick of her hair. "You can't run anywhere with those things on, *dummy*. They'll catch you both instantly. Besides, the two of you are too weak and can barely stand. Even without those on, you wouldn't make it."

She's right. Pretentious, but right, Dane thought.

"Maybe we can treat them like we would a bear in the Northwoods …run right at them and scream," Ludwyn suggested.

Ruth rolled her eyes and adjusted the strap of her sack. "Didn't you just say that they sank a ship? How are we supposed to scare them?"

"I tried to tell you this was a bad idea, Ruth," Ludwyn said.

"Oh, hush."

Between their quarreling, Piney butted in to say, "I don't think we have much of a choice. I'll just play it cool like I usually do." He trotted out in front of their group without allowing any of them to respond, walking toward the shadowed men with his chest stuck out. They were too far away for Dane to make out their faces, but he could see that they wore sleeved garments, long-cut trousers, and boots similar to the officers and marines of the King's Navy. They all seemed to match, except the man in the middle, who wore a long blue overcoat. The man in the middle lifted his arm into the air and waved some sort of signal, and the two figures on his left began running toward them.

"*Hold it,*" one of them commanded when Piney got too close. Both of their hands rested on the handles of their curved swords, sheathed at their waist in caution. "*We've got the girl,*" the other one shouted back toward the man in the blue coat.

"Tie them up and bring them in." The man in blue turned and began walking back to the wharf.

Closer, the two men moved slowly toward them, until Dane could make out their harsh and brutish faces. They had wrinkled, sun-splotched skin, tanned darker than he'd ever seen before, with stringy bits of loose hair that looked as if it hadn't been washed in many moons.

To his surprise, however, the two men didn't act as harshly as the officers and marines back on the *Fereclis* had. As Dane and the other three were being corralled, the men acted avoidant, especially in the way they handled Ruth, which they seemed almost too afraid to touch. For Piney and himself, they didn't even bother to tie their wrists, as one of them mentioned that their shackles were enough. Even then, the two shorter men still pushed Dane and the other three toward their ship tied at the pier.

Dread and terror crept back up from beneath Dane's feet with each rattle of his shackles. He had only a moment's breath of freedom before being cast back to do the bidding of another ship and its captain. The closer they were pushed toward it, the larger that ship grew in size, looming to match his impending doom.

"*Hurry up*, we need to be underway before dawn breaks," one of the voices ahead shouted. They moved to drag them along faster until they reached the first pier. Dane moved his gaze just enough to see a short line of men already on their knees, halfway down the planks. That same tangy voice ordered the three of them to join the line, and Ruth was escorted to the tall man in the blue overcoat.

"Who is this?" the man asked.

"The woman. You said we were after a woman. She was by the wreckage the same as them," the short and stocky man mumbled, pointing at Dane, Piney, and Ludwyn.

"She doesn't have red hair, you idiot. She's a hen. Cowen, move her to the line with the rest of them," the man commanded.

One of the brutish-looking men brought Ruth next to Dane and shoved her down by her shoulders until she knelt. Dane turned to look at her, crumpling his face with sadness. He had been in her position before, but nothing matched the sorrow of experiencing it for the first time. The kind girl who had saved him now faced the possibility of a fate far worse than his own, and he was in no place to return the favor.

"We need to make this quick," the man in blue said. "*Girl*." Ruth looked up as he stomped closer. His forehead was thick and intimidating, and he had light, stringy hair that hung to the sides of his high cheekbones. "What are you doing all the way out here?" he asked.

Dane could feel her knees tremble against the planks as she broke her silence to say, "I'm from the Regent... I came when I saw the wreckage— to help save anyone that may have needed it."

"Did you happen to see a girl with red hair?"

Ruth held a long pause, making Dane question what her answer would be. He knew she had mentioned earlier that her brother had taken the girl from his ship upriver. But admitting so might just put her and her brother in danger. "*No*," Ruth lied.

"*You*." The man walked down the line. "What's your name?"

"Dane," he said, not nearly as frightened as Ruth had.

"Why were you on that beach?"

"I'm an oarsman in the King's Navy. She saved me and him from drowning." He nodded sideways to Piney on his left.

"Take these two norks' shackles off," the man commanded.

One of the men who had corralled them onto the pier walked toward a chest to grab what looked to Dane like a shearing lever. He moved in front of each of them and slid the cold metal under their wrists, then sliced their iron shackles off. Dane felt an instant release of relief. Those wrought-iron shackles, which had become inseparable from his bones, were finally gone, freeing his arms and shoulders to stretch out from each of his sides like a bird finally flung from its nest.

"*Show me*," the man in the blue overcoat commanded, staring Dane in the eyes. One of the stocky men grabbed Dane's left arm and slid back the half sleeve of his torn gray garment, revealing his branding of crossed oars. "And you." The man did the same for Piney. "*Very well*. Galen, cut their ankles free and grab them something to eat and drink."

Dane's relief shifted from his wrists to his ankles like a cloud lifted high in the sky, free to move with the wind where it pleased. *Maybe I am finally free,* he thought, daring to smile.

The man in the blue coat, who seemed to Dane to be their captain, continued to question the rest of those they had captured down the line.

Ludwyn gave the same answer as Ruth, which the man found odd. But it wasn't until he reached the line's opposite end that the captain's temper began to flare.

"So, boys, I guess we have here two marines and now, by the looks of it, two officers of that nork King's fleet. *You.* What's your name?"

The man Dane couldn't see stayed silent.

"*You,*" he said, moving to the one at the far end. "That's a nice coat you have on. What's your name?"

In a tremble, Dane heard the man respond, "Hallem."

"Tell me, Hallem, were you an officer on the *Fereclis,* the galley we sank?"

"*Yes.*"

"And was there a girl on that ship?"

"I can't say—*I just follow orders.*"

Dane bent over to look down the line and saw the officer trembling. He was a younger man compared to the rest—one he'd seen the face of maybe once or twice while scrubbing the decks. The captain in the blue overcoat waited, watching until the young officer turned his head to the other one beside him. Noticing it, the captain asked, "So, you follow his orders?"

The young officer nodded.

"I will only ask you one more time. What's your name?"

The other officer at the end of the line stayed silent long enough to make the captain draw the curved sword from his waist. He pointed its tip back to Hallem, pressing it against his neck. "*What's his name?* If you have anything to say, say it now. Or the last thing you'll speak is whatever froth floats out of you from the sea's bottom."

"It's *Maris*—his name is Maris."

Without even a moment's hesitation, Piney jumped up, screaming, "*That's him*—that's the bastard that took the girl in red. *I saw it.* He snatched her that night...at the Isle of Azil."

Maris tried to move, jumping up from his knees before the mate named Cowen tackled him back onto the planks of the pier. "Noreas, what should we do with him?"

"I know just the thing," Captain Noreas responded. "*Maris,* you say. That name sounds faintly familiar. You wouldn't happen to have an older brother named Malis, would you? Or a *father*—one named Mordin? The *King of Marredom*, that Mordin?"

"*Oh*, that's him, alright," Piney blurted out again.

Noreas looked back, almost annoyed at Piney for interrupting what Maris might say. He placed his sword back into his sheath and took his long overcoat off, handing it to one of the men beside him. With his right hand, he curled back the long sleeve of his gray garment. "Do you see these crossed oars?" Captain Noreas asked, pointing to his own forearm.

A smile branched across Dane's gaunt face. *He's one of us*, he realized.

Maris nodded without saying a word. "I served as an oarsman for seven and a half solurns before I jumped ship. I was one of the lucky ones, like these two here are now."

"A former oarsman killing oarsmen…how fitting for a man such as yourself to sink a galley *full* of them," Maris said, finally breaking his silence. His platinum hair and perfectly sculpted pale face glittered in the early light of the rising sun.

Noreas stood still in thought, then twisted his chest around and threw his fist straight into Maris's jaw. Blood spewed into the water between the pier and their ship. Noreas stretched his hand and cracked his knuckles. "I consider them freed now." He threw another fist into Maris's stomach, forcing his knees to collapse as he gasped for air. Cowen grabbed him from under his shoulders, thrusting him to stand back up. Noreas looked at him with disgust, then turned to Hallem. "*You*. Where's the girl? This is your last chance."

Hallem leaned back on his knees, pleading, "Please… I really don't know. She could have drowned."

"*Very well*. Galen, bring him aboard, we'll post him to the mast until we find our answer." When Galen grabbed Hallem, Captain Noreas corrected, "*No*, not him—Maris."

Dane watched as Maris looked up in horror at the large ship tied to the pier. Before he could say another word, one of Noreas's men stuffed a rag into his mouth and dragged him up the gangway.

"Take Hallem and the other two marines up there, too. We'll show them why they call it a seabed. You three," Captain Noreas said, turning to point to Dane, Piney, and Ludwyn. "You are welcome to join our crew. We could always use more mates."

Without hesitation, Piney jumped up again and said, "*I'm in!*"

"Cowen, send that one to the kitchens."

Piney's shoulders stooped low, his scrawny arms falling to his side. "But I'm good with a sword, sir."

"The kitchens need the men, and you talk too much. But you'll be able to carry a saber down there too, as is all our right."

"What about me?" Dane heard the feathery voice ask from his right.

To his left, Ludwyn whispered across his chest, "*Ruth…what are you doing? We can't go with them.*"

"We don't let women serve in our new fleet," Captain Noreas responded. "It goes against tradition."

"How come? I'm headed north, too. And I've been on a boat before," Ruth exclaimed.

"This isn't a boat. She's a ship—*a galleon*. And a unique one at that." The captain walked toward the gangway, then paused momentarily and turned back around. "What makes you think we're headed north?"

Ruth became quiet once more, as if she didn't know what to say or how to respond. Piney, who was gathering himself to walk down the pier, turned back to her and asked, "Didn't you say earlier that your brother took a girl north on the last boat from here?"

Piney… Dane thought, letting out a gasp of disbelief. *That girl saved us.*

"She was a girl—I think—but I didn't get a good look at her," Ruth stammered to explain. "It was dark, and I couldn't really see her, so I wasn't sure. My brother was the one who swam out to rescue her…and she was begging to leave, like she'd been tortured, or worse. And she looked badly bruised—but we only had one tiny boat. And I didn't want to be wrong earlier."

"*MEN, AT YOUR STATIONS!*" Captain Noreas commanded up at the ship's main deck, deeper than before. "See, I knew that little one liked to talk. Where did that girl go? Which way did he take her?"

Ruth stood silently in thought. "I'll tell you, but you are going to have to take me with you," she stated, her stammer gone.

"*Fine,*" Noreas said, turning to stomp his way back toward the ship. "Come along, then."

"*Ruth,* what are you doing? Are you mad? We can't go with them," her hairy friend pleaded.

"I can and I will. They'll bring us back home, up north, and we'll be hidden away from any of the royals who might be searching for us. It's okay, Ludwyn. Like Roth always said, I could use the adventure."

Dane stood up and left the two of them to bicker. Without needing to speak the words, his choice was already made. He followed Piney down the pier, looking up in awe at the ship he was about to board. Whatever fear he'd once held had now vanished, replaced with the hope that he could one day be as free and as fearless as his new captain—the former oarsman who had just released him from his shackles. He wanted to be as free as that man was—free like the royal-red flag that waved at the ship's stern, lofted high in the air with a spiraling seashell of gold stitched at its center.

Finally free, Dane thought to himself with a smile.

He took one step from the pier onto the bending gangway and looked along the ship's leafed planks. All the way forward was a single word painted in white near the bow.

In old norkatis, it read, *Widow.*

CHAPTER 15

SKY

"*H*urry," Vanna whispered.

The night sky spoke in silence, without any stars to light their way. Each dig of the stable horse's hooves shook Zell's lifeless body, which was strapped to the saddle behind her. It took Lora and herself half the night to wrap the two bodies in separate bed sheets and clean up their bloodied mess, wiping the villa clean of any evidence.

Vanna was glad it was dark. It eased with their escape and hid her from herself. The Consolar General of Sacrim was her second kill. Though it was far less personal than the first, the loss of her overseer left Vanna knowing that she had failed. Zell's death may as well have been her third. She couldn't bring herself to look back at her body that lay limp, strapped on the horse behind her.

Vanna had been trained to ignore her emotions—to be without remorse for what needed to be done, all to fulfill a duty the Children were raised from birth to deliver. She had survived the harshest tests of torture and witnessed some of the other Children disappear, or even die, due to mishaps in training. Her own pain was a feeling she easily repressed. But Vanna had come to learn that, when bringing that pain and death onto others, she had no control.

Mishaps, she pondered as she galloped behind Lora, escaping west out of Sazara. Vanna couldn't help but feel that if it weren't for her inaction, Zell might still be alive. And she could only wonder why Lora was placed on lookout and not herself. Lora was a seasoned Sister. She was stronger and more skilled in combat than Vanna and would have acted sooner to save their overseer.

At least this time, it was from the back, she thought. *I didn't have to look into his eyes.*

187

Despite Zell no longer leading them, she and Lora still followed their overseer's plan. They had each taken a horse from the stable behind the villa and rode south, then west, toward Sazara's outer wall. The western gate was one of three that stayed open day and night, with wagons and travelers passing through it from Sacrim's surrounding partitions. But all three, along with the pathway that connected them above, were readily stationed with guardsmen from Sacrim's First Brigade.

"How should we handle this?" Vanna asked Lora as they rode within sight of the wall's iron-clad gate. At each side of its haunch were guardsmen doused in bronze, holding spears in their hands and wearing shields at their backs.

"Just cover your face and act normal. There are only a few of them. We can take them if we need to," Lora responded as if Vanna should have already known.

"*Act normal?* We have dead bodies strapped to our horses."

Lora tugged at her own darkened bed sheet to make sure the general's body was still secured. "They don't know that."

Vanna trotted slowly behind Lora and followed her orders, covering her face and hair with loose cloth. She slid her telson under Zell's body and kept her hand grasped tightly to its long handle. *Don't do it,* she thought anxiously, reluctant to make another kill.

Luckily enough, the guardsmen who stood the night's watch were half asleep with their eyes fading closed. The two Sisters passed through without questioning under the sharp flatbars of the gate's crowned arch. Vanna didn't bother to turn her gaze back and check if any other guardsmen were on the opposite side. Instead, she sighed in relief and moved her telson back behind her spine, bringing her horse to a gallop to catch up to Lora in the open field of red-shaded dirt.

"We'll ride out to the nearest tree, then call our rooks," Lora told Vanna, her double braids bobbing with every gallop.

With one hand on the horse's reins and the other on Zell's shaking body behind her, Vanna did her best to keep up. For the Children of the Silo, riding a horse was a skill taught at a very young age, one long before flying, as the Sisters deemed it an inferior method of travel. And for good reason. Rooks were faster and could cover longer distances. Their ride was smooth, and their obedience, once bonded, never wavered. They weren't beholden to the rough terrains below and could be hidden high in the sky, forgotten like a distant star, to avoid any and every interaction with the common people below.

Rooks were the largest birds of prey across the Plane—the last descendants of the ancient king birds—and preferred to live alone, high in the mountains. When Vanna and the other Children reached the age of eleven, they were given an egg the size of their heads. They were commanded to care for it as if it were their own and to play it notes and melodies provided by the Sisters from their hand-carved flutes. Once hatched, the rooks were taken away to be meekened and tamed by a Sister before they were returned to the Children a solurn later.

By that time, Little Wing had grown large enough to ride. Each rook was bonded to the pitch from their flutes, and the Children were taught the Sisters' commands. It was then that Vanna's training had evolved. She was no longer kept isolated from the other Children to train with the telson, or read her histories, but had been placed in groupings of three. They flew day and night over Astria's western range of mountains, training with the Grand Dame and her assisting Sisters to complete perilous tasks that proved their worth.

On the back of Little Wing, the two today were one, flying free, ungrounded, and unhindered by the paths laid out by man. The stars provided their bearings, giving the Sisters of the Silo a living map of the Plane. That sight from the sky was their learned advantage, but Vanna appreciated Little Wing for more than just the tool she was trained to be. The two had a connection. It was a special bond, one of friendship and trust—more than she had ever felt from the Grand Dame or any of the other Sisters.

"*There*," Lora shouted, pointing off in the distance.

Vanna left the grassless path to follow her. They rode toward a field of olive trees, which had thick trunks and broad-leafed branches that grew like fingers out from the blinding dark. She slowed her horse once they reached the cover of the largest tree. From around her neck, Vanna pulled out her flute. With a deep breath, she and Lora blew to play their long and high-pitched calling sounds.

"And now we wait." Lora dismounted her horse and moved to lean against one of the trees, breathing an exhausted pass of relief.

"Do you think they heard that? It's been more than a moon's pass since we left them. There's no telling where they are now."

"They heard it alright. And they shouldn't have gone too far."

Vanna whipped her legs off her horse and joined Lora near the base of the tree. "What do we do now?"

"What do you mean? We wait."

"I meant the Brazen Talons. Zell was our overseer. What is the plan without her?"

"We go back to the Silo, inform the Grand Dame of what happened, and then wait for her replacement."

"So, that's it… She gets replaced that easily?"

"What do you want us to do, throw a parade for her?" Lora asked, her voice drawing with contempt.

"An honorable rest is all."

"The last thing Zell would have wanted was for her body to be put out on display. As Sisters, we live and die in the shadows of the Plane's charade. She knew this and lived it better than most."

"Hmm, you're right," Vanna admitted, looking up into the blackness of the sky. "Our Sister Stars still have their shadows whether we see them or not."

"*Here*," Lora said as she returned to the stable horses. "Change back into your half-cape and help me with her body."

Vanna changed out of her robe, then grabbed a section of sheet wrapped around Zell's shoulders, helping Lora lift it off her horse and move it near the tree. "Should we bury her here?"

"No. The Sisters will take care of it. We can't leave any evidence behind, especially after who we just executed," Lora explained as she unraveled the sheets.

Zell's body was pale but didn't yet smell. Lifeless, it lay with both arms dangling at her side, hanging like broken branches from her shoulders. Vanna looked at her eyes for a while, waiting to see if they'd open again. She bent down and snagged the flute around Zell's neck. "Should we call her rook, too?"

"No. We could call Felix in and give it the commands, but I don't think her rook would follow us back to the Silo without Zell. Especially if it saw her body like this. They had a strong bond," Lora said. "It'd be better to leave Felix free. It'll find its way back to the mountains in time."

Vanna tucked Zell's flute between her waistline and continued searching through the rest of her belongings. Across her back, she had a small leather sack filled with items they shared between themselves during their stay in Sazara. Vanna grabbed her telson and placed it with her own belongings, then continued to pat her body down. In Zell's right pocket, she felt a tiny lump. She reached into it and pulled out a small, folded piece of parchment. *The note from the meeting behind the Temple,* Vanna recognized.

She glanced back toward their horses and saw Lora searching the hazy sky, waiting for their rooks to arrive. Vanna hesitated, then tucked the note into her waist next to the flute and pretended to keep searching.

"There they are," Lora said.

Vanna looked up and saw Little Wing tail Lora's rook, gliding high, just under the black of the sky. They both blew another long, high-pitched note from their flutes, then waited for the large birds to land. As Little Wing slowed to brace its talons into the dirt, Vanna rushed to caress the feathers that smoothed the rounded top of her head.

"That isn't healthy, you know," Lora reminded her.

But Vanna didn't care. They weren't in the Silo, and she wasn't a Child anymore.

"*Here*, you take her, and I'll take the general's body. It's heavier," Lora said, helping to lift Zell's body onto Little Wing. "I'll lead the way and try to guide us back. Just stay on my wing."

Vanna strapped Zell's body to Little Wing's back, then helped lift the general's body onto Assira. The two Sisters mounted their saddles and took off. Older rooks, like Lora's, could carry two, or even three, riders with ease—a common practice for those Sisters who rode in tandem. Little Wing, though, was still small and seemed to struggle carrying the extra weight. But, high into the sky, she managed to follow Assira. They kept climbing higher in search of the stars, but it came to no avail. Instead, with three smooth whistles from her flute, Lora commanded them to speed up, gliding faster and forward, straight into the darkness.

Eventually, Lora looked back and saw Vanna trailing too far away. She yanked on the reins of Assira to bring them side by side. "*I think this is the way,*" Lora shouted.

Vanna only nodded. She, herself, was unsure of their route, especially without any light from the stars to guide them. She hunched down, resting her cheek on Little Wing's neck, and continued to fly through the haze of black. Her ability to see Lora was dwindling, but she caught her hand rising to the side as her rook tailed off to turn right. Vanna blew hard into her flute, trying to follow.

North. We should be back over the Barren Sea soon, where, hopefully, this haze will clear.

Just as Vanna had that thought, she heard a whirling sound growing straight ahead. Out of instinct, she tucked her cheek back against Little Wing's neck. Flung swiftly past her head was an arrow. Vanna threw her head back up in confusion and looked in all directions, trying to find where it had come from. Through the haze, she saw two wings split broad and wide, flapping heavily in front of her. Without even giving the command, Little Wing darted below it, gliding under the dark-feathered chest of the large rook hovering in the air. Vanna's only thought was to escape. She blew into her flute with two screeching sounds, followed by three smooth whistles to force Little Wing to glide farther below and pick up speed.

An arrow from another rook? Why would a Sister attack me?

Was it Lora?

Urgency pulsated throughout her body as she scanned the dazed sky in confusion. All around her, Vanna felt surrounded and smothered by the unexpected. An arrow she was lucky to have survived from might come again. *But from where?* Vanna hoped that it wasn't Lora who had turned on her. *No…she could have done that by the olive trees…or anywhere,* she thought.

Vanna knew she couldn't keep flying through the black as a soft target, waiting to be preyed upon. With a single sound, she commanded Little Wing to lift them higher into the sky and, hopefully, out of the haze.

There. Vanna spotted the rim of its barrier.

They tumbled fast toward it, flying at the dim stars until they breached through the light. Off in the distance, she saw Lora and her rook flying sideways, weaving through the sky. Following her were two rooks of similar size, both dark like the one she had seen before.

So, it's both of us they want.

She rushed Little Wing to chase after them, patting Zell's body behind her to make sure it was still there. With her right hand, she reached behind her waist for her telson. *Those two haven't seen me yet.* Vanna flew high above them, gaining altitude for a trained advantage. She could see the three rooks below her, circling in a rounded chase as she waited for a gap between them to open.

Now.

Vanna sent her rook soaring down like a falling arrow, fast through the sky. Little Wing tucked its wings in at her side and gained speed, letting out a daring screech as they darted at one of the darker rooks trailing Lora. She could see a pale Sister dressed in all black, scathing in surprise when she looked up and noticed Vanna's attack from above.

Vanna raised the telson's blade above her head. With her own fierce growl, she slashed it into the darker rook's neck just as they hurled past them.

Hit.

From above, Vanna heard the rook she sliced open screech aloud in the worst cries of pain—one that even made Little Wing's feathers shudder. Vanna looked up and saw it withering with one wing flapping uncontrollably as it fell into the daunting blackness. Before she could even process what she'd done, the saddle Vanna was strapped into lunged her body to the left with a roaring thrust, which should have easily flung her off.

What the...

To her right, the largest rook of them all flew past them with a fleeting gust from its wide-winding wings. She and Little Wing were shaken but tried their best to regain stability. Vanna looked up and saw it looping back around. She could barely make out the single black-haired loop behind the Sister who rode it. There, the Sister sat, hunched in her saddle, riding a rook bigger than any Vanna had ever seen before.

The Grand Dame, she recognized. Her rattled mind had gone from confusion to despair, and from anger to anguish. She was being hunted by the Sister who was in command of them all, on the back of the fiercest predator in the sky. *This is no test.*

Vanna flung Little Wing's saddle to fly low, trying to catch up with Lora. Only together, Vanna knew, did they have any chance of survival. Left and right, she scanned her head back and forth, frantically searching for Lora and her rook. Behind her, she felt the growing presence of the Grand Dame, gaining speed.

Shit, she thought as soon as she heard another whistling noise fly right past her head. *We need to turn fast, something quicker than its broad wings can handle.*

With sharp and gliding turns, they flew on, in and around the chase, as Little Wing constantly changed speeds and height until they had entered back into the smothering darkness. *Maybe with this haze, she might lose us.* With every deepening screech it gave, Vanna could feel the large rook's heated breath grow. And every chance Vanna got, she would turn her head back to check the gap between them. She knew she couldn't survive, being chased by the Grand Dame. But to turn and weave, Little Wing would lose her speed. Vanna's choices were narrowing.

In and out, they twisted, flying as far and as fast as Vanna had ever seen Little Wing go. With nowhere else to maneuver, she had no option but to take the chase low, down to the ground.

A dense blanket of fog smothered Vanna's face, coating her sweat. The lower they went, the denser its blanket grew, until she could barely distinguish Little Wing's beak from in front of her. Little Wing threw out her wings, trying to halt their flight in midair and break their descent into a hovering flap. Gusts of wind battered its floating body as a flash of lightning struck beside them. Bright and loud, its deepening echo shook them both, as if the air beside her had been split in half.

Vanna gave a quick command to reset Little Wing and descend, breaching below the storm clouds they now found themselves within. Pelted by flinging raindrops, she scanned the sky, looking for the Grand Dame who had disappeared behind her. Far off and covered by clouds flashing with the heat of lightning, she saw movement. With a short tug, they chased after it.

Vanna could feel Little Wing's heart thumping with pure exhaustion under her. She'd never seen her rook fly this fast before or for so great a distance. And Little Wing had done it all with an extra body tied at her back. But Vanna knew she needed more from her rook if they were to survive.

With speed, they flew right at the movement Vanna spotted. Through the rain, she saw that it, too, was a chase—Lora's chase. *They must have been a team of three,* Vanna realized after stabbing one of the rooks now missing from the sky. She tried her best to maneuver Little Wing so Lora could see her. With a wide turn, the two chasing rooks began to head directly at her.

"*Pass her to me,*" Vanna whispered to herself for confidence. "*I'll take her.*"

Instead, the Sister in chase saw the trap and tailed off, flying high into the sky to evade Vanna's attack. Lora's rook slowed to hover right beside them.

"*What's going on?*" Vanna screamed through the rain.

"*They're cleaning their loose ends,*" she yelled back. Lora's rook, too, was soaked and struggling to breathe. "*They want us dead.*"

"*Why would they do that to us?*"

"*I don't have time to explain. That way is farther south. I know where we can lose them… Follow me!*" Lora shouted, then commanded her rook to fly in the direction she had pointed.

"*South? Why south?*" Vanna questioned, hesitating to give her own command to follow.

But as soon as she tugged at Little Wing's reins to move, Vanna saw an arrow sling straight through Lora's chest. Shivers filled her body as if lightning from the storm had struck them both. Vanna sat helplessly, watching Lora's body hang off the side of her rook's saddle with her legs still strapped to it. From the depths of the sky above, two more arrows struck Assira. As it bellowed a dying screech into the sky, Little Wing reacted without command, thrusting them both out of the way.

Sorrow flowed from Vanna's heart, outpouring anger into every hair that stood up from her exposed skin. Lora was as kind a Sister as she could have known and had become a friend to her during their stay in Sazara. But now Vanna was alone—truly alone. She was no longer a Sister but one now hunted by them. The only family Vanna ever had was now either dead or wanted her dead.

"*Sisters…*" she decried. *I'll be faster without her.* Vanna untied the straps that held Zell's body to the saddle, then tugged on Little Wing's feathers hard enough to rip them out.

"*South.*"

They flew in the direction Lora had pointed, leaving Zell's body to fall freely with the rain from the storm. Lifeless through the sky, it descended. Vanna looked back, expecting to be trailed closely by two large rooks. Instead, there was only one. *The Grand Dame's.* From the corner of her eye, she saw the tail end of the other, darting down toward her fallen Sisters to collect their bodies.

"Good. *Let's even up the sky.*"

With a rush of angered confidence, she directed Little Wing higher, rising above the lightning-filled clouds. From side to side, they turned and wove as they continued south faster than before. Vanna tried to catch glimpses of the Grand Dame's trail whenever she could, hanging on tightly as Little Wing dodged the arrows being slung their way.

"*Woahhhh*," Vanna screeched, pulling up on her saddle with a harsh gasp. Out of nowhere, through the downpouring rain that fell before them, came a jagged wall staring her in the face like a dam to a river. Little Wing panicked, flaunting her wings wide to try to push them aside. Her sharp talons scraped along the cliff's black wall to scale its round extent.

At that moment, Vanna glanced back, hoping to see that the Grand Dame had flown straight into it. But there was nothing—no rook or their wreckage. Once she and Little Wing had cleared around its other side, Vanna looked down below and saw hundreds of the same sharpened rock formations sticking up from the ground like a jagged field of black shears. *The Vypores,* Vanna recognized from her studies. *The southern volcanic range of Sacrim.*

"*AGGGGHHHH*," Vanna thrashed and screamed aloud in agony. She immediately grabbed her thigh and looked down. Lodged in her leg was the feathered half of an arrow that struck her with a piercing pain. *I've been hit.*

Little Wing tried to scurry away, but the arrow had come from directly above. Her hesitation had left them sitting still, open and vulnerable above a valley of bladed rock funnels. In her throbbing pain, Vanna looked up and saw the Grand Dame hovering above them. When their eyes met, the leader of the Sisters plummeted down from the sky.

Before Vanna could even move, another arrow had pierced her left shoulder, dousing her numb and wet body with more agony. Her vision began to drain as the rain pounded onto her face. Each drop felt like an arrow, leaking out her life like the ghost of a star she would become. Little Wing did her best to escape, but there was nowhere left to fly, or even land, to escape the Grand Dame's onslaught from above. Feeling only the wind as it passed, Vanna held her eyes open long enough to see another arrow lunge right past her face to strike Little Wing's side.

"*NOOOOOOOOO!*" Vanna tried to scream. But whatever words had come out, she couldn't hear. Her rook opened its beak to join her in screeching, flooding the air with the most harrowing sound. In the night's fading light, all she could see was Little Wing whipping her head back and forth, fighting to keep them both alive.

Vanna heard only the whistling of air follow them as they descended, playing its sorrowful notes that flapped between Little Wing's lifeless feathers. She looked up with one last blink and watched as the sky swallowed them into its dismal slumber.

Falling isn't flying, Vanna thought before facing the dark.

CHAPTER 16

STONE

"May the Divine One guide our travels, keep the *Widow* afloat, and protect us on our journey. May we find comfort in your sagacious spirit—"

"Do you hens ever shut up?"

Ruth opened her eyes at the bow of the *Widow* and looked out at the morning sea. The thumping sound of boots across the deck came to a squeaky stop behind her. From her gaze out at the calm waves, she turned around. There stood Cowen, the *Widow*'s first mate, holding a bucket out in front of his half-buttoned, hair-grazed chest.

"Here you are." Cowen shoved the bucket filled with sandy water toward her, motioning for her to grab it. "No free rides. Now that that storm has passed, you can help the mates get the rest of this salt off my deck."

Ruth took the bucket and snarled back, "I don't appreciate my prayer being interrupted."

"And I don't appreciate salt on my deck. That god can't hear you out here anyway," Cowen said, then turned around sharply before she could reply.

For all she knew, Cowen could very well have been right. The *Widow* was far from any land, and Ruth was the farthest from her home she'd ever been. She had only seen the Salic Ocean once before, from Roverra's beach. And now that same blend of gray and blue was the only sight to be seen, from one horizon to the other.

Ruth's first two days on board were rough. While the *Widow* traveled through a rolling storm, she had hidden away in her cabin with her head stuffed into a bucket similar to the one she now held. Captain Noreas had made it a priority to separate her from the rest of the mates, granting her a room on the deck near the aft end of the mess. It was a small cupboard room beside a busy stairwell, just long enough to fit a hammock lengthwise. But to Ruth's displeasure, the room's confining planks carried a pungent stench of old mash and sour wine. And her frequent but quick trips to dump her privy bucket's fill had become an amusing sight to the mates who witnessed her as they passed between the decks.

The crew of the *Widow* was unlike any people Ruth had ever come across before. Most had long, unkempt hair and leathery, sun-splotched skin—some exhibiting strange art and obscure lettering marked by black and red ink on their arms, chests, and necks. Their odor smelled worse than her cupboard room, and nearly all carried a mangled look across their faces whenever they looked her way. Ruth knew that ship work was grimy work by their outfits alone, as their loose-fitting white garments were continually stained, and their trousers were patterned with rips and tears. But, for whatever reason, she hadn't expected the character of the mates to be so grimy, too.

Ruth wanted to avoid it all at any cost—the storm, the stenches, and the scorn. When the weather had finally calmed, she forged the courage to walk out onto the *Widow*'s main deck. At the foredeck, she escaped the smells and bottomless retch to feel the slow breeze before sunrise, praying to calm her potent nerves. But as daylight broke, the mates flowed up from below, and the waving looks of revulsion poured back her way.

Ruth looked down below to watch the waves crash into the ship's bow one last time before she joined their work. Behind her stood one of the ship's two mounted ballistas. She walked around it purposefully, trying to avoid its complexities despite it being unloaded and resting with its thick wooden arch pointed at the sky. *An instrument of death,* she thought.

"This is no place for a skirt," a voice shouted across the main deck as she walked aft along the side railing. Across the bending planks came Dane, dressed in the same garments as the mates, with his trousers tucked into his black-leather boots and a saber sheathed at his waist.

"This plaid skirt is all I have."

"Talk to Rigel in the hold down below. He can help you out with some fresh clothes." Ruth just nodded politely, not knowing who or where that was. And she knew she would never dress like them anyway. Dane looked down at her bucket. "Scrubbing duty, huh?"

"I think so."

"I've had my share... You definitely won't want to be wearing that, though. It'll be difficult on your knees."

"I'm not even sure what I'm supposed to be doing."

"Scrubbing? It's easy. All you need—"

"*No*," Ruth said, cutting him off. "On this ship."

Dane looked around at the other mates who kept busy, either cleaning the deck or mending the rigging lines of the sails near the forward masts and up along their cross-yards. "You'll pick it up," he told her confidently. "But your friend, the hairy one who was with you, mentioned that you weren't feeling well. It'll take some time to get situated."

"*Situated*," Ruth grumbled. "Everyone and everything here is either rude or smelly. And most of the time, it's both." Her fluster grew. She looked up to calm herself, thinking of the Divine Gates. "All the mates stare at me and give me weird and mean looks."

Dane sighed. "I know why." Ruth just stared at him intently, waiting to hear the answer. "It's what Piney mentioned—women on ships are shit luck."

"You don't actually believe that, do you?"

"Me? No. But that storm we just sailed through probably didn't help to convince the mates," Dane answered.

Ruth shook her head and looked out at the morning sun. "That's nonsense."

"I agree. Just give it time. They'll come around."

But I could use a friend now, she thought. "Where's Ludwyn?"

"He's down below, sleeping. He had the night watch."

Ruth nodded and glanced over to the stairwell before turning her attention back to the scrawny young nork. "You look much better than you did two days ago."

"I've never been better. Captain Noreas let me sleep and recover the first day, and they fed me well. That meal the next morning was probably the most I've ever eaten in a single sitting. And they don't even yell at me when I stop working to have a look out at the sea or chat with the other mates. I've just been trying to learn as much as possible," Dane said with a smile. Ruth could see the genuine joy behind the blue of his eyes. Unlike her own, they shone in a way that showed his curing better than any meat on his bones could have. "I should thank you again for saving me back on that beach."

"Thank my brother. He's the reason we were out there."

"When I meet him, I will," Dane said with a stern face as if he meant it. "Being here on this ship has changed everything for me. Even the breeze off the waves feels so much better when you're free."

A mocking smirk rose from the corner of Ruth's lips as she looked down at the wooden bucket in her hands. "You call this free? We're floating on a wooden box in the middle of the ocean. I can't go anywhere. And now, they're putting me to work."

"I wouldn't take any work Cowen gives you too seriously. I heard him in the mess just yesterday mention how fun it would be to toy with you. Besides, Galen runs the deck anyway." Dane moved to lean over the bulwark, looking down at the sea that ran smoothly along the belly of the *Widow*'s hull. "You may not be able to go anywhere, but she sure can. This is the finest ship I've ever seen. The mates have shown me how the rigging works for the sails." He turned and pointed at the taller two masts near the *Widow*'s center. Ruth followed his gaze. "There are the cross-yards where the two main sails of the mast unfurl. The foremast is the same, with its lines leading here." Dane skipped down the side of the deck to show her the notch where the lines were tied off. "There's another mast near the aftcastle, just forward of the quarterdeck where the helm is. But that one's only half the size."

Ruth struggled to keep up as she watched Dane point to and explain most of the rigging and tangled lines that were fastened throughout the deck. With cautious steps, she followed him as they drifted aft, weaving in and around the working mates. Ruth was glad she had someone knowledgeable to rely on—someone who was as new to the *Widow* as she was. Though she only retained a little of the information he provided, Dane's jovial smile made her forget those unpleasant nights sick at sea and the discomforting nerves from being around the disgruntled crew.

Stairs on each side of the main deck led up to a raised level, where he showed her the watchstanders who stood beside the ship's helm at the quarterdeck. Behind it and the aftmost mast stood the enclosed aftcastle Dane had spoken of. As they returned to the center of the main deck, Ruth asked, "So, sails?"

"Like sheets, yes. The wind carries us and pushes the ship across the sea, so there's no need for oars unless we're coming upon a harbor or pier. Even then, Galen told me they don't really use them. The ship has to be much bigger to support—"

"*And if there's no wind?*" Ruth asked.

Dane looked at Ruth with his own face now squished in confusion, without an answer to the question he seemingly hadn't pondered. Behind them came a deep, growling voice, one Ruth had heard before.

"That's my job." Ruth turned and saw Captain Noreas, who stood as tall as she and Dane. "To find the wind."

How can someone find the wind? Ruth wondered but was too intimidated to ask.

"I saw you two strolling by the quarterdeck, so I figured I'd check on you. Those sails are what set the *Widow* apart. *Distance and speed.* The norks' war galleys have to get close to ram anything they want to board. So, as long as we can keep a distance, we can pick them apart with those," Captain Noreas explained, pointing to the forward ballista.

"So, you just sink them, then?" Ruth asked.

The captain strolled between the masts, where two small boats were secured to their cradles. "Not always. We can board them with these."

"Two small boats? That's it?"

"*Options* are what they give us, *girl*. But we managed to sink his galley without them."

"*Sink*," Ruth grumbled. "I was there. I heard their screams and the pain you brought to all those people just like him." She pointed to Dane, who looked like he wanted no part in their discussion.

"Aren't you just so innocent. One day, when you grow up, young miss, you'll learn that there are things much worse than war."

"*War?*" Ruth's tone was unsettled, taken aback by the way Captain Noreas had spoken to her. "You sink a single ship and think you can sail your one galley into a war?"

"*Galleon*," Noreas corrected. "The Plane is changing, and change makes war inevitable. It's the cycle of life, *dear*. But we aren't alone. Although there are only a few of us, I do have a fleet—five in total, each a sight distance away from the other." He reached within his blue coat and pulled out a copper-tube spyglass. Lengthening it, he held its smaller end against his eye and pointed it past the *Widow*'s stern. "See, the *Bessie* is still there. And the *Morsbrum*, *Rithron*, and *Baroness* aren't too far behind. Take a look for yourself."

Ruth took the spyglass and looked out at the sea. Near the edge of the horizon was a flapping white sail. "*I see it.*" She handed the spyglass back to Noreas and scanned the deck. Tied at the bottom of the central mast was the *Widow's* prisoner, Maris. His mouth was stuffed with rags, and his knees were buckled in exhaustion. "I see him too. Is that also one of your cruel realities of war? To treat a man like that?"

"*Darling*, if you think that's bad, you should ask your friend here what those officers in that King's Navy do to people like him."

"*He's right*," Dane admitted, almost against his will.

"Speaking of which, you don't look so well yourself," Captain Noreas told her.

Ruth shook her head frenziedly and patted her hair, realizing she had no idea what she looked like. The last time she had seen a mirror was three days ago when they'd left the Longfin Inn. "I was seasick."

Captain Noreas let out an eye-rolling chuckle. "And you still look seasick. Go to the mess and get yourself something to eat. *Oh*, and when you get the chance, wake that friend of yours and meet me in my quarters. You can come too, *oarsman*."

Ruth lifted her chin and shifted her eyes away from his mockery, then followed Dane aft toward the stairwell and down into the deck below. A bulkhead blocked off the crew's main sleeping quarters to keep the light out. Dane left Ruth and entered through its only door to wake Ludwyn. From between its cracks, like rows of crops, she could see their white hammocks hanging like linen bags from the crossbeams of the shallow ceiling. And within it, she could smell its horrible odor of salt-dried sweat.

Mates funneled up and down the stairs as Ruth waited, carrying deck hammers, spikes, and girdled lines. Some made haughty jokes as they passed, while others taunted her silently with stares from their lusterless eyes. *May the Divine One help me, please,* she thought repeatedly, waiting for the only friends she had to rejoin her.

"He's coming," Dane said when he finally exited the mate's sleeping quarters. Out from behind the door walked the square-headed Ludwyn, whose short and curly brown hair was perfectly combed over and oiled flat.

"Lud, you just had to do your hair, didn't you?" Ruth sniveled to ask.

"And beard," he replied with a soft smirk, looking her up and down. "At least one of us takes care of ourselves."

Ruth rolled her eyes, patting her head again.

"Perks of having your head shaved," Dane said as he ran his pale fingers across his blond stubs.

"I'd kill to be as hairless as you," Ludwyn told him.

"You know, I had some long golden locks before being taken in as an oarsman. Sort of like what Captain Noreas has," Dane turned to tell them as he walked down the stairs. "I'll grow it back out again; you'll see."

After hearing Dane's comment, Ruth realized that Captain Noreas didn't look like the other mates. He was tall and had pale skin similar to Dane's, and his hair was a shade darker than blond but still much lighter than everyone else's on board. Noreas was once an oarsman, after all. But Ruth still questioned where the rest of the crew had come from.

Down below, the mess deck had two passageways that ran lengthwise along each side of the ship's extent, separated by the kitchen at its center. "I'll be just one moment." Ruth turned aft and opened the door to her measly cupboard room, searching for the small mirror within her sack.

"It smells awful back here," Dane said, squeezing the long bridge of his nose and turning the opposite way. The two boys stood at the doorstep and watched Ruth brush out her frizzled hair.

"I think this was a food storage cabinet before."

"It smells more like puke than food," Ludwyn told her.

"Like I said, I'd rather not talk about it…*okay*. I'm ready."

"She's a lot quicker than you are," Dane joked to Ludwyn, who seemed displeased at the comment. They passed the kitchen's windows as they walked down the port-side passageway. Five mates in waist-tied aprons were hard at work, stirring iron pots or chopping greens with hatchet cleavers. "*Piney!*"

As they turned the corner into the mess hall, which had half-empty tables pinned to the floor, Piney came out from around the corner to greet them. "*I love this ship*," he said, reaching high to wrap his arm around Dane's shoulder. Piney turned to Ruth and Ludwyn and thanked them again for saving him.

"Each time I come down here, you look like you've gained another belly roll," Dane said.

"So, do you like the kitchens?" Ruth asked as she peeked back at the mates at work, wondering if that might be something she'd be interested in.

"I couldn't ask for better. I get fresh biscuits straight from the ovens and seared fillets whenever I please. Speaking of which…you three go take a seat. I'll bring you out something we've made for ourselves—don't think you'd like that onion stew much, anyway." Piney rushed away from their thanks, back down the opposite passageway, while they found an open table.

Ruth could feel stares coming from the table in the mess's corner, where three older men sat, rubbing their grizzly gray beards. "Don't worry about them," Dane told her.

"They're probably scared of you like most men are," Ludwyn joked. When Ruth didn't laugh, he paused before clarifying, "I just meant that you're much taller than most of them."

"They may not be from Marredom, but they definitely share our cold hearts," Dane said.

"Where would they be from, then?" Ludwyn asked as Piney began to walk over to their table with three plates.

"They all speak so fast, and that flag at the top mast…I think I've seen it before—the red one with a golden shell. I believe it's an insignia of Sacrim from one of their five partitions," Ruth said.

Piney placed the plates down on the table in front of them. "Here you are."

"Well, Ruth, if they didn't hate us before, they sure will now." Ludwyn laughed at his own joke, looking down at their plates. On each was a seared slice of aged meat atop flatbread with a simmering green glaze.

"Salted mutton us cooks made for later, flatbread dotted with butter-mashed peas. Don't expect something this good—"

"Piney, you seem to know everything, so maybe you might know this too—where did Captain Noreas get his crew from?" Ruth asked.

Piney's bulging lips smirked with displeasure. "Not even a thanks, first, *mm-hmm*." Just as they opened their mouths to thank him, he continued, "I would happen to know, as you've rightly guessed. Most come from a city called Corlis, in what they've told me is western Sacrim."

"That explains it—I knew I was right! The Silver Sea is out that way, too, and its rifts of islands."

"I told you she was smart," Ludwyn said, almost too proudly.

"*Edgy bunch*, if you ask me. But I haven't talked to anyone who would rather be there than here on this boat. I wouldn't take their spite to heart too much. You two are outsiders and not mates like me and Dane are here." Piney rested his hand on the handle of his curved saber and lowered his eyebrows down its way.

Dane chuckled. "Maybe they are like us norks after all."

"Scoundrels more so, by the looks of it," Ludwyn said more seriously. Ruth could tell he didn't take too kindly to the mate's mannerisms either.

"They wouldn't dare do a thing, though, that's for sure…*not even a finger*," Piney mumbled to reassure them. "Captain Noreas has marshals on every deck, night and day. And none of us knows which ones they are. He brings people into his captain's quarters every so often, but no one knows who he keeps close to his chest. Other than Cowen, of course."

"We're headed there after our meal, too."

"Well, then, the three of you better eat up. Don't want to keep him waiting, that's for sure. First thing I was told when I got to the kitchens— the man can be a rightful crank. But I guess you'd have to be to corral all these men out at sea."

"Thank you, Piney," Dane said. Ruth and Ludwyn repeated their thanks as he drifted his way back toward the kitchen.

As they ate their delicious meal, Ruth felt at ease now that she knew more about the crew and where they were from. *Understanding*, she thought. *That's all I need. And them.* They licked their plates clean, then walked back up the stairs to the main deck. The sails were at full span as the *Widow* traveled faster with the wind and the waves. Ruth held on tight to the railing of the bulwark as they sifted through the mates mending the sails.

"It's like a symphony," Ludwyn shouted from behind.

"A chaotic one." Ruth could see Dane ahead turn to laugh at their confusion. "At least you look at home," she told him.

"Like Piney said, *I love this ship*," he shouted back. They followed Dane up a short flight of stairs to the quarterdeck. "That's the officer of the watch," Dane explained from a distance, pointing to the man who wore a sharply curved black hat. "And the helmsman at the wheel…and the navigator behind them."

They entered the aftcastle—a shallow two-story wooden structure with its outer walls flush to both sides of the hull. Inside were two closed doors to their right and left and a central passageway that led to the aft ballista mounted on the stern deck. A short set of stairs was indented into the side of the passageway's bulkhead. Dane led them up and knocked on the door, standing at the edge of its last step.

"*Come in*," Captain Noreas's deep voice shouted.

When they entered, Ruth looked around with her jaw dropped in awe at how much space the captain's quarters had compared to the rest of the ship. Though still bland, with wooden planking and timber frames throughout, his quarters had a finely crafted desk pinned to the center of the floor. Large windows lined each of its three bulkheads, providing a wide view of the sunlit sea.

"Oh, good. I thought maybe you three might have gotten lost or something," Captain Noreas said from the cushioned seat of his desk. On the wall behind each of his shoulders were two oil paintings—one of the *Widow* with her sails strong at sea and the other, a calm coastal city featuring a black-towered castle that stood tall over a harbor.

"Those are nice paintings," Ruth broke the quiet awkwardness to say.

"That they are. Corlis and her *Widow*. You seem to have an eye for good art."

To her right, she could barely see Ludwyn rolling his eyes. He was one of the few people who knew that painting was one of her favorite things to do and how easily she could go on and on when talking about it. But instead, she just replied, "I like to think so."

"Well, I take it your first few days have been an adjustment. But you'll learn to float even with the sea eventually." Captain Noreas took a long sip from his shiny steel mug. "I brought the two of you up here for a reason. I wouldn't take our fleet up the Fleming River, even if we could fit, so we're making the long passage north. Take a look at this chart. I need you to point me to where that brother of yours is taking the girl."

Ruth's nerves rose as if her seasickness had returned to siphon the pit of her stomach once more. She didn't yet know whether she could trust her new captain. And for all she knew, he could be bringing his fleet and its supposed war to her hometown. With him was a crew that had already sunk a ship and killed dozens, if not hundreds, of people. And she didn't know what they would do to Tergona or what they might do to that poor girl if they found her.

In her mind again, she uttered a short prayer. Her thoughts drifted easily back to her readings from the Cathedral. *Honesty and the truth,* she thought. *It's the right way—the way of the Divine One.* After all, Captain Noreas had welcomed them in, fed them, and helped them escape any repercussions from those courts in the Regent's wealthiest cantons.

Ruth walked up to the edge of the desk and looked down at his chart. She'd never seen anything like it. Shades of green and blue mapped out every parcel of land and every speck of sea throughout the Plane, with numbers and fine roalish lettering to describe each, all drawn on a thinly lined and perfectly spaced grid. "This is fine work, too," Ruth said calmly. "There. Tergona is where he'll be headed. Our *home*."

"And you're sure of it?"

"*Absolutely*. Cubby Cove is only a short trek east from Tergona." She pointed again to a small blue inlet shaped like the curve of a cub's tiny claw near the northeastern coast of the Regent.

"That settles it, then. We'll bring the fleet there and hopefully find our girl." Ruth turned to walk away before Captain Noreas cleared his throat and added, "There's one other thing. I know you both think you're only here for the ride home, but I expect you to follow the rules on my ship. We are all free mates here. And if you're going to be with us, you might as well be one of us." Captain Noreas stood up from his leather cushioned chair and opened the large chest behind him. From it, he took out two sheathed sabers, each thin and curved with a rounded guard to protect their shell-like pommels. He held them both out across the desk. "The crew will respect you more if you wear one of these."

Ludwyn gladly reached for one of the sabers and quickly strapped it around his waist. Ruth knew she needed to gain the respect and confidence of the *Widow*'s crew. But, at the same time, she had never held a sword before and was strongly opposed to violence of any kind. It was everything she and the divine sages of the Cathedral stood against. "*I can't,*" she let out.

"*Oh, Ruth*—" Ludwyn tried to say before Captain Noreas interrupted.

"You can and you will. You're on a warship, so *take* it. That's an order."

Ruth shook her head and looked away.

"I get you have your convictions, but the sea doesn't care. And neither do those ships of the King's Navy."

Deep inside, Ruth felt intimidated—not just because she was on a ship floating in the middle of the ocean, destined to be a target of those norks that lurked beyond the horizon. But by Captain Noreas, whose presence alone carried a fearsome aura. "Life is too precious to me," Ruth told him softly.

"What is life worth if you can't protect it?" Captain Noreas asked her, shoving the saber farther across his desk.

He's right, Ruth realized. Against her earlier will, she walked slowly back to the desk, reached across it, and took the saber. "Just don't expect me to use it."

Captain Noreas smiled. "*Welcome aboard.*"

CHAPTER 17

SUN

"What's the count?"

"Sixteen barrels of water, nine chests of salted beef, thirteen of grains, and a few wagons left of pickled fruits and greens," Kladden listed to Cleo. "Oh, and two barrels of sour wine."

"Is that enough for us to reach Sazara?" Cleo asked from his saddle, following behind Gareb and the two other guides.

"The sour wine?" Kladden asked, making light of their situation. "No."

"Should we travel back to Fort Corlach instead? We could send a courier ahead to inform Arwin of our return. We have the rest of our stores and guardsmen there."

"I don't think that'll be necessary. By the captains' count, we have forty-two hundred men. What we have should be enough to reach the nearest markets and springs. I don't see a need to go northeast, toward Cignus. It would only slow our march to Sazara. Besides, Andar is closer."

"Very well." Cleo heeded his commandant's advice as they continued to travel out of the Sineaqe Gorge. "And what of the forty-two hundred men?"

"As motivated as ever. If it wasn't your speech, then it might very well be that they expect a quick return to their families."

"Likely the latter. But I can't make them any promises. There's no telling how those in Sazara will take to our return."

"You have a skill for that sort of thing. First at Fort Rastrum with the captains, then back there with the brigade. Your father would be proud of you. And I'm sure that his spirit, more than anyone else's, has rejoined the Benevolent Sun to see it. His will be of the first to return."

"I'm sure of that too," Cleo lied. "Thank you for the kind words, Kladden, but it all just comes from the heart."

Kladden turned around to check the distance between them and the flags that were waving the insignia of Sacrim at the forefront of the first battalion. "At least we know they trust you now. Even that washed-up captain, Ostin, is now following you without contention. Also, I think that vident needed to hear those words just as much as the guardsmen did."

Straggling next to Captain Ostin and the first battalion was Vident Lement. On his horse, he slumped with his shoulders slacked in defeat. His eyes were half closed, drowned in sorrow. Even with Cleo turning to scan back at him, he still just stared blankly ahead.

I wish I could show my sorrow that way, too, Cleo thought to himself with a sigh. Since the days of his youth in Cignus, when his mother and father were still together, and before he was even a cagerman, Cleo had known Vident Lement. His father had employed him as his personal advisor and as a preceptor to both him and his older sister, Clara. When Sepatus was voted in as Sacrim's Consolar General, Vident Lement was dragged from his station in Cignus to Sazara. Cleo's father had always mentioned in passing that Vident Lement was the smartest man he knew. And Cleo certainly agreed with that sentiment. *If my father trusted him for so long, maybe I should have too,* he thought in a moment of doubt.

Drooping to look down at his saddle, Cleo saw both of his earlier options staring back at him. To his left, sheathed around his waist, was the black pearl pommel of his father's sword. To his right, in the side pouch strapped to Dahlia's saddle, were the last few petals of the withering blood rose Scarlett had given him. *I haven't forgotten about you, Scarlett.* Cleo closed his eyes in thought as his horse trotted along, hoping that the decision he had made was the correct one.

"He'll be fine," Kladden blurted aloud. "Those vidents just aren't outside enough."

And you guardsmen aren't inside enough, Cleo thought to himself.

However, Kladden, too, was trusted by Sepatus within his realm of work in Sacrim's Guard—a realm Cleo now found himself thrust to the forefront of. At one point, Kladden had served as Sepatus's commandant in the Fourth Brigade before commanding the Third himself. He was also the man his father considered his best friend, trusting him enough to train Cleo as a cagerman. And his father had even gone as far as to send Kladden back into the Guard to serve as Cleo's commandant.

Despite his doubt, Cleo had already settled on his decision. And it was his own, not Vident Lement's or Kladden's. All Cleo could do now was look up at the lone cloud that still meandered high in the sky and hope that he was following it in the right direction. Though its strands of white no longer covered the sun, it now drifted the same way he did, back west, toward Sazara.

For the entirety of his young life, Cleo had never believed in those signs of the sky, despite the vast majority of Sacrim being filled with those who did. He took after his father in that manner, who raised him and his sister outside the teachings of the Temple of Sciron, even against his mother Corianne's wishes. His father, as well as Vident Lement, believed that those ceremonial practices of the temple were for one of only two types of people—fanatics who were easily controlled and fanatics who desired nothing but control. But even in this lifelong reservation, Cleo couldn't help but gaze up at the single cloud in the sky. And by following it, he rationalized his decision to turn back home.

Cleo led his guardsmen back through the sharp turning path and jagged walls of the Sineaqe Gorge. As they neared the path's beginning, one of the taller guides, presumably Gareb, threw his tan-wrapped fist into the air. Cleo ordered his brigade's march to a halt and watched as Gareb crept around the wall's edge, past where he could see him. In his ragged sleeves, Gareb quickly trotted back to Cleo's side, staring at him atop his horse. Hesitating, he whispered, "There are men dressed like you all waiting at the entrance."

Cleo's broad face crimped in confusion. *"Men dressed like us?"*

Kladden immediately threw the reins of his horse around and commanded, *"FIRST BATTALION TO THE REAR, SECOND BATTALION TO YOUR MARKS. SHIELDS DOWN, SPEARS UP!"*

Cleo sat still on his saddle, hearing only the rumbling scratch of bronze against steel behind him as the hooves of the first battalion's cavalry scattered toward the back of their formation.

Why would another brigade be here? His mind wandered with endless questions as he adjusted the rounding rim and cheek plates of his bronze helmet. Cleo patted the black pearl pommel of his father's sword to ensure it was still there. He took one gulp to swallow his nerves and turned to check on his brigade. Kladden rode back and forth between the narrow walls beside Captain Sovano, yelling with haste at the guardsmen from the second battalion to straighten out their columns and tighten their rounded shields. As he scanned their formation, Cleo noticed Vident Lement still at the forefront. There, he sat, staring at him, unmoved by the rumbling commotion.

Kladden finally stopped his corralling, locking his eyes with Cleo's. Without knowing what to say, Cleo yielded a fierce nod of readiness. He turned back ahead and tapped Dahlia into a slow stride. Pounding followed him from behind, foot by sandaled foot, all in unison as they marched toward the gorge's entrance.

Cleo was the first to turn the jagged corner and made a concerning effort to ensure his face was kept stern, regardless of what he was leading his brigade toward. Inside, he tried to bury his fear, thinking only of how his father would act in this situation. But mantled upon his father's face was Vident Lement's penetrating eyes, staring back at him.

Maybe he was right.

Cleo turned around the corner's edge and saw a tall man dressed in the same royal-red cloak as his own, encircled by three horses. Behind them was a wall of bronze, as far back as Cleo could see and broader than the gorge's entrance.

The closer the Sixth Brigade marched, the clearer Cleo saw the face of the tall guardsman in the middle. Commander Jep Kastas of the Fifth Brigade stood still, wearing the same tan cloth as the guides wrapped around his sun-beaten neck and exposed arms and legs. Behind their wall of shields, Cleo noticed that all his guardsmen dressed similarly. They were men of Sineaqe, those brutes of the Fifth Partition. Like all other brigades besides the Sixth, they lived everyday lives and held work outside of the Guard. But at that moment, Cleo didn't care that they weren't occupational warriors. Kastas's guardsmen at the forefront were as tall as he was, sun-beaten and broad-muscled, and carried swords, spears, and shields like his own.

Cleo marched his brigade forward, then raised his fist into the air, bringing them to a halt. He glanced back once more. Their wall of shields had become squeezed between the narrow entry walls of the gorge. Commander Kastas stood a few broad steps away from its opening. Kladden followed Cleo as they dismounted their horses and walked slowly toward the encircling wall of the Fifth Brigade. With only his eyes, Cleo scanned from left to right. *No escape,* he realized, as Kastas's guardsmen were locked shield to shield, rounding from one corner of the tall cliff to the other.

"*What is the meaning of this?*" Kladden demanded.

"Cleo Scordisci," Commander Kastas spoke loudly. He reached for his waist to pull out a scroll of rolled parchment. He unwound it and read, "*Your presence is formally requested in Sazara to relinquish your title as commander of Sacrim's Sixth Brigade. In your place, I name Jep Kastas of Sineaqe as acting commander of the joint Fifth and Sixth Brigade, with orders to facilitate your escort. Signed,* Consolar General Cayen Calegri."

"*Consolar general? Cayen Calegri?*" Cleo asked angrily.

"This must be some sort of joke," Kladden berated. "The consolar general is dead… *Sepatus is dead.* Who gave that child his command—this authority?"

Cleo stood still, infuriated by what he'd just heard. He knew his reaction couldn't be too rash. He and his guardsmen were trapped within the gorge's tall walls. Any wrongful flinch and it could cost them their lives. At that moment, out of desperation, Cleo looked up at the lone cloud and saw it still drifting west. *Don't fail me.* "Is it not against the chamber's law for Cayen Calegri to hold both seats of the consol? How can you, a fellow commander of Sacrim's Guard, allow for such an abuse of power to go unreprimanded?"

"Cayen Calegri no longer holds the seat of consolar vizar," Commander Kastas responded.

"Then who does?"

"Sacrim's chamber held a dual vote the day after Sepatus Scordisci's death. Cayen stepped down as consolar vizar before he was elected general. In his place, the chamber voted Clyus Calegri to become Sacrim's consolar vizar."

"*Ahh,* that explains it," Kladden let out in the deepest bouts of scorn. "Your general is murdered, and you allow his murderer to re-assume power. Clyus may as well sit in both seats of the consol—forget his boy."

"Watch it, Kladden. *That boy* is now your general. Sepatus's death is still under investigation by the chamber. Any wrongful allegations against the consol will be treated as treason against Sacrim."

Treason, Cleo thought, laughing to himself in misery. *Those hiding behind their chamber desks crying treason are the very committers themselves —only the wrongful and weak project their faults like this.*

Kladden cocked back and spit, landing his soggy grievance right at Commander Kastas's feet. Cleo turned and saw Kladden's thick, black-stubbled skin turn redder than their cloaks. From the side of his eye, he saw a horseman riding forward to join their discussion. Beside him came Vident Lement. As a vident, he was forbidden to speak aloud in public, so he whispered into Cleo's ear, "*There's still time to turn back.*"

"*There's no going back,*" Cleo responded. "My father would never stand for this."

"Your father is dead," Commander Kastas stated boldly, overhearing him speak.

"*Cleo, please listen,*" Vident Lement continued, his whisper growing louder. "*War isn't the answer. We can still turn back to the Regent and fulfill your father's orders.*"

"No," Cleo said sternly.

"Listen to that old man if you like," Commander Kastas said. "But half of my brigade is waiting for you on the other side of the gorge. We weren't expecting you to turn around so soon, but I sent them ahead just a few days before you arrived. You're trapped, *boy.*"

Cleo looked at Kladden for an answer, but all he could see were his bulging eyes fixated on ripping Kastas's head from his body. *How did I let myself fall for this? What can I do?*

As he tried thinking of an answer, Vident Lement leaned in again and whispered lowly, "*A man who stands upon one leg struggles to walk.*"

Cleo scrunched his nose, his green-tinted eyes narrowed as he scanned the Fifth Brigade's formation. Vident Lement was right. In front of him was only half of Kastas's guardsmen, making Cleo's outnumber the Fifth Brigade's by nearly half. The longer Cleo thought, the more he realized that his guardsmen, too, had the advantage. Though they were trapped between the gorge's narrow walls and faced a bronze wall of brutal-looking men, no brigade was as well-trained and skilled as the Sixth. War was their vocation.

"You should be ashamed to call yourself a commander, *Jep,*" Cleo said loudly. "There you stand, so full of pride, all the while forgetting the very first rule of war."

"And that would be what, *boy?*"

"*Numbers dictate control.*"

Commander Kastas looked around, slightly bemused by Cleo's statement, before laughing aloud. "You're the one with your numbers trapped between the walls of Sineaqe's gorge, you insolent chump. Who here holds control? Orders are orders."

To his side, Cleo could tell that Kladden had caught on to what Vident Lement had noticed and to what choice Cleo had already made. "*And gold is gold,*" Kladden said.

Sliding steel broke the air as Commander Kastas drew the shortsword from his hip. In a clanking response, Cleo's guardsmen slung the tips of their spears down, resting the edge of their sharp spikes atop the crouching man in front of them. Cleo's and Kladden's horses broke into crying neighs, rearing wildly as they cantered off behind their splitting men.

"My duty is to Sacrim and the consolar general. I will not have my honor questioned by some boy and his drooling hound. You're coming with me, *dead or alive.*"

Just as Cleo reached for his sword, he felt an odd coldness slide across the front of his neck. He looked down, as little as his knuckled chin would allow, and saw a single blade held by a pale hand no bigger than it was.

"Not quick enough," the raspy voice said from behind him.

Without turning his shoulders, Cleo moved his head just enough to see Sorah's beaming blue eyes staring back at him. *Really? Of all people?*

Kladden drew his double-edged shortsword in response. "Even the guide's bitch is in on the Calegri cut." The other two guides, Gareb and Josh, sprinted out of the gorge, cutting between the moving shields of Kastas's guardsmen. "I guess not all of them got paid."

Sorah unraveled the cloth that was wrapped around her face and head. She shook out her long, curly red hair, which Cleo could just barely see swaying to his left.

"*Fair enough,*" Cleo struggled to say. He released the grip around his sword.

"*The Rosenari send their regards,*" Sorah whispered into his ear.

Cousins to the Calegris, Cleo recognized, trying to make sense of what was happening. His mind raced to grasp the situation he now found himself in. Scarlett was missing, his father was murdered, and now he, too, was just a slash away from facing a similar fate. *But what can I do? Kladden is too far. If he moves, this wrench will end me.*

"I will give you and your brigade one last chance to come peacefully to Sazara. *Drop your swords and surrender*," Commander Kastas ordered.

Cleo wiggled his head, trying to respond. Out from where the cloud's shade moved to his left, he saw a wave of orange flutter through the sky. Following it came a loud and blunt sound. Cleo felt the cold blade release from his neck and turned behind him to see Vident Lement gripping the bounds of a large leather book in both of his hands.

Sorah stumbled back, patting her head in pain, clearly surprised. Cleo could only smile after realizing that it was Vident Lement who had saved him by swinging his only weapon—a book.

Kladden had seized the opening to charge toward Sorah, rushing in with his shortsword to slice it straight through her arm that had once held her blade. Sorah spun around in shock, holding her blood-squirting shoulder by the ragged cloth that was drenched in red. Before he could even thank Vident Lement, his preceptor had already scurried away on his horse, headed for the back of the Sixth Brigade's formation.

"*Cleo, now!*" Kladden didn't hesitate to scream.

Cleo turned to his brigade and waved them ahead. The bronze wall marched swiftly to the edge of the gorge's entrance, surrounding Kladden and Cleo as they tucked behind them for safety. Cleo's heart pounded as he drew his sword. He saw the white around Kastas's eyes widen in the fading sight ahead. Sorah managed to scamper off, chased away by the enclosing shields as she screamed aloud in pain. When she breached their line, Kastas pointed the tip of his sword to the sky.

"*SHIELDS UP!*" Cleo ordered after recognizing Kastas's command. The sound of bronze against bronze shuddered above as his guardsmen pointed the round of their shields to the sky. Within moments, a torrent of arrows was flung, whistling from behind the Fifth Brigade's wall, only to clank their tips loudly against the Sixth Brigade's upturned defense. "*Drops from a tiny shower*," Cleo whispered to himself.

He waited for the clashing sound of arrows to dwindle before commanding again, "*And this is lightning... OSTIN, FLASH, NOW!*" The galloping hooves of the first battalion's cavalry rode fast from the rear. Cleo looked back and waited for them to reach the second battalion's last man. "*SPLIT! NOW!*"

The battalions of spearmen and swordsmen heeded his command, splitting themselves in half. Their shields scattered toward each side of the narrow walls as the warhorses of Captain Ostin's cavalry kicked up sand with speed. Cleo moved to the right, turning to see Ostin's ugly face grin past him with a fearless smile. Each pound of their hooves dug deeper into the sandy dirt, leaving cratered divots as they passed out of the gorge's entrance. The cloakless guardsmen on horseback all held their sharpened spears pointed forward, with shields at their backs, yelling the cries of war.

Cleo's first battalion charged ahead with intensity, breaching the Fifth Brigade's line of shields with their spears as they rammed their horses through. Nearly a thousand in total stormed through the front line, dispersing themselves within Kastas's formation to disband his rag-wearing guardsmen into chaos. Cleo smiled as he watched Kastas's wall break with shouts of panic and horror. *They are no match for the Sixth,* he knew. "*CHARGE!*" Cleo pointed his father's shortsword forward.

His battalions of spearmen and swordsmen rushed ahead at full speed, straight at Kastas's broken brigade. Cleo led them on, searching for any man with a dirty cloth wrapped around their neck or arms. Using the rumbling of moving shields in front of him, he glided in and around, striking his blade wherever he could. His heart pulsated with each swing, thinking of nothing but his next move and driven only by the instincts of his training with Kladden. Cleo gained confidence with each thrust and cry from the men he killed. From it, he poured out the anger of his father's death and all the regret he still felt for not being there to protect Scarlett.

There he was, caught in his first real battle, causing death and bloodshed like he'd never seen before. And within it, he was skilled; no one he crossed was a match for him with his father's blade. His training with one of the fiercest warriors across the Plane had left him without a spare skill or lost ability. Cleo could only wonder what damage Kladden must have been causing. In that thought, he paused his thrusts and slashes to scan the fray, almost frantically, trying to gather where he was. He could see the first battalion's cavalry breaking far behind the last line of the Fifth Brigade. Now, it was Kastas who was trapped.

There, Cleo thought, breaking a bloodied smile.

Alone, Kladden was fighting off scores of cloth-draped guardsmen. Screaming with each of his tall swings, he counted aloud a number, one that Cleo could barely make out but sounded somewhere in the thirties. *Must be his kills,* Cleo knew, himself being nowhere near that tally.

Kladden moved fluidly, sweeping between the barrages of guardsmen to do what he did best. Cleo paused and watched him work, happy that he was on his side. In the short break of battle, their eyes met. Kladden continued to swing with purpose, moving closer and closer to where Cleo fought. When he came just a short distance away, Cleo heard him scream aloud, "*You've got a ways to go!*"

"*No way I'm catching up to you,*" Cleo screamed back, before noticing that he really couldn't. Not because of his skill, but because there were now so few guardsmen left fighting from the Fifth Brigade. He paused and scanned the desert filled with blood and bodies, struck with a thought. "*HALT!*" Cleo commanded above the sound of battle. At that moment, he noticed his brigade outnumbered Kastas's by ten to one. It was a bloodbath and an unpleasant one at that. "*HALT!*" he bellowed again, before all his guardsmen finally listened.

Kladden looked confused, as if he couldn't stop, and appeared almost angry or upset that Cleo would call off their fighting when they had all the momentum. Cleo waited until the silence simmered. "*We're killing our own.* These men are just as much a part of Sacrim's Guard as we are. *Where is Kastas?*"

"Right here," Captain Sovano's voice shouted from afar.

"Bring him to me," Cleo ordered, waiting for his bloodied and sweat-soaked guardsmen to disperse. Captain Sovano escorted the swordless Kastas to stand before Cleo. With a kick from behind his knee, Sovano shoved Kastas's shoulder down to kneel.

"*Kastas,* you are no commander," Cleo stated. The guardsmen of the Sixth Brigade circled to surround them. Those alive from the Fifth all dropped their swords and were moved to the center, behind where Kastas kneeled.

Kladden walked up slowly, clearly the bloodiest. He stopped beside Cleo and stared straight into Commander Kastas's cloudy eyes. "Bronze and steel beat gold every time, *Jep.*"

Commander Kastas couldn't look either of them in the eye. Cleo walked closer to him and lifted his shortsword, placing its blade beside Kastas's neck. "This sword was my father's," Cleo told him sternly. "My father—*the rightful general of Sacrim*—was an honorable man, one driven by duty and respect. One who believed in justice. Without these, a man is not a man. *And without him, Sacrim is not Sacrim.*" Cleo looked down at

Commander Kastas with ferocity, waiting for him to turn his head and face him. "I believe you have led your men astray, Commander Kastas. The loss of their blood is your fault." He scanned the few hundred men left from the Fifth Brigade. Those not dead or partially dismembered were trembling for mercy. "*Any of you who wish to rebuke Commander Kastas and his corrupted orders from the consol may join us—the Sixth Brigade!*"

More than half of the men, wrapped with bloodied cloth around their exposed arms and legs, walked slowly into a separate group, looking for refuge. Cleo waited as more joined, until they far outnumbered those kept still, stubbornly stuck in their place, surrounded by the Sixth's swords and spears.

Kastas looked around frantically, sneering with disgust and watching as his own men rebuked him. "*TRAITORS, ALL OF YOU. TRAITORS TO SACRIM!*"

"*Jep Kastas*," Cleo said once the movement had settled. Kastas looked back at him and spit at Cleo, landing his dry and bloody droplets onto Cleo's bronze chest plate. "No, Kastas. *You are the traitor.* I, Commander Cleo Justinian Scordisci of Sacrim's Sixth Brigade, sentence you to die."

With a single swipe, Cleo shifted his right arm back and swung his father's blade straight through Kastas's neck. Like a geyser unleashed from cracked stone, blood squirted out from the hole left between Kastas's shoulders as his body fell impishly forward.

Cleo walked toward his head, which had rolled just a few steps away. He grabbed it by its thinning hair and lifted it into the air. Spinning it around for all to see, he commanded, "*Bring me a courier to take his head to Sazara!*"

CHAPTER 18

SEA

"*Bring the bottom foresail afold,*" the *Widow's* deck chief, Galen, shouted to the mates near the bow. Dane scampered toward the central mast and loosened the rigging at its base. He and Ludwyn took turns pulling at the loose end of the line until the bottom sail was furled in and tied to the cross-yard.

The *Widow* had been traveling north at sea for more than a quarter-moon's pass. Dane's days on board had sped by quickly in comparison to those he had spent on the *Fereclis.* It gave him joy to stand the morning and evening watches on the main deck, handling the lines with the other mates, some of whom he now called his friends. Between hoisting and lowering the sails with the changing wind, he would gladly scrub the *Widow's* decks and clean the sails and hull, all of his own volition.

Dane took pride in his newfound freedom. He stood the same deck watches as Ludwyn, who had his switched to join him, while Ruth had begun to help in the kitchens with Piney. Learning to sail the open sea on a galleon the size of the *Widow* had become easier to Dane with each passing day. While the wind was smooth, he would wander onto the quarterdeck to watch the captain and first mate at work. With every order they'd shout, he'd check the wind gauge above the aftcastle and try to sneak a gaze at the navigator's chart.

Most of all, though, Dane loved the view. Each morning at sunrise and every night at sunset, he'd catch the golden sun shimmering to and from the horizon. He loved watching the way its rays would reflect and glisten across the water as it rose and set with the passing waves. But when the beauty of the sun had gone, and he still sat alone, the sea always reminded him of his family back home. Like a mirror, he could see the memories of his sisters when they were younger and his mother and brother, too, outlined by the crests of the waves as they drifted away or crashed under their own growing weight.

To Dane, the sea was just a collection of tears poured out by those who cried the hardest for help—the same help he was no longer there to provide. Whether it be the weeping from his family, or those oarsmen lost at sea, or even from some mourning god of Marredom, the sea's pool of tears was what Dane promised himself would lead him back home. They were tears that needed answering, and his hand to help wipe away. Before he'd return to the deck to start his watch or strike below to eat or rest for the night, he'd look out at this pool of tears one last time with the faintest glimmer of hope. He hoped that his family was safe and provided for. And he hoped that they, too, were witnessing the same beautiful sun that he did.

This morning's view, however, was different. As the *Widow* traveled north, a dense fog grew to encase most of the ship's surroundings, blocking almost any sight out at the water, let alone the sun. The mates on deck all seemed to share an eerie sense of suspense and moved around cautiously to try to get a glimpse of what lurked behind the shadowed veil.

"*There*, look—just there!" Dane heard his friend Caji shout from the bow. He and Ludwyn hurried over to the ship's starboard side, toward the mates bent over the side rail.

"They look like skimmers," Dane pointed out. Three birds with white feathers and black underbodies glided just above the spray at the curve of the *Widow*'s stem. "We must be close to shore."

"Shore? Like land? Do you think we'll get to set foot?" Ludwyn rattled off his questions without taking a breath.

"*I doubt it*," Flyde replied, slurring his speech. "We've been at sea for moons now. We couldn't even get off when we were pier side at that damned beach for a night!"

"Look!" Caji said again, this time pointing farther out over the railing. "Dane, you were right!"

Dane squinted his eyes and could barely make out the rock-riddled ridge emerging behind the curtain of dense fog.

"No way we're docking there," Flyde said. "That cliff looks like it goes halfway up our mast."

"But we can still anchor, right?" Caji asked just as the older deck chief, Galen, walked over.

"Not happening. We're under strict orders from Cowen and the captain to continue north around Geldring's Ledge, then turn east," Galen said.

"*Geldring's Ledge?* That's the northwestern tip of the Regent." Ludwyn quickly scurried away from their group. "I'm going to get Ruth…she'd love to see this!"

"I can feel the change in the air," one of the oldest and groggiest mates, Cal, said from behind Dane.

"We all can. It's called fog," Caji chirped back.

"*No.* It isn't that," Cal replied.

Aft, near the stairs, Dane spotted Ludwyn bringing Ruth up to the main deck. "Nice, isn't it? To see land?" he asked her as soon as she joined their pausing gaze.

"Even nicer knowing it's the Regent," Ludwyn replied.

Ruth let out a long sigh. "One step closer to home."

"Your homes must be nice. You both seem to miss it so much," Dane said.

"Not quite. Neither of us is wealthy by any stretch of the meaning," Ruth told him, staring out at the tall ridge along the coastline. Below the cliff's ledge, a few of the mates pointed out the patterning stacks of mounded rocks that sprouted up from the sea, where waves were caught sloshing between. "The Regent has its flaws, but it's home. It's the people and our covenant freedoms that make it great. And our faith in the Divine One that holds it all together."

"*The people,*" Dane agreed, not knowing what the rest of it really meant. He missed his family, too, regardless of how terrible the conditions of his home were. "I don't think you two know what flaws are."

"After meeting you and Captain Noreas, I don't think I'd want to see what flaws Marredom has. Or what the people there are like," Ludwyn said.

Ruth gave Ludwyn a shove on his shoulder. "Is it really that bad?"

"I grew up in a one-room shack with my mother, my two sisters, and my brother. Anything we gathered, caught, or hunted had to be brought as tribute to the King, and then the rations were distributed back to us later. And if you could guess how much he kept and then how much he gave back, you'd probably be right."

Ludwyn's smirk receded. "That sounds like a rightful pit. He lines his pockets while his own people starve."

"Why is Marredom like that?" Ruth asked, her face frowning with concern.

"Growing up, we were always told it was because of the winter storms. Most of the water north would freeze, and some of the birds would migrate west. Most of Marredom is just a ruck of snow and stone, so it's hard to grow any crops. Even back home in Niven, the winter's ice slosh would be too much for my little boat."

"At least that King let you have a boat," Ludwyn said light-heartedly.

"They let my father keep it. It was his. He built it himself. But that was before the King made his decree and recalled everyone to the city. Before he was taken. My father taught me how to fish with it when I was young. Even then, as I said, anything I'd catch would go straight back to the tributars. Or, at least, it was supposed to."

"*Taken?*" Ruth asked curiously. Dane could see her thin lips and broader forehead turn at the thought.

"By the King's officers and marines. Who knows where he is today or if he's even alive."

"Ruth, maybe you should take back what you said about flaws. You're making Tergona sound like the Divine Gates," Ludwyn said with a chuckle, paying more attention to the land behind the fog than their conversation.

"Don't joke about that, Lud."

"The Cathedral, or Dane's misery?"

"*Both*," she replied sternly.

"It's okay. I'm just glad to be here now, and I have you two to thank for that." Dane looked at them both and smiled. "And them, up there." He turned to nod his brow up at the quarterdeck. "I'm going to see if I can take a better look at this ledge from up above."

Dane left the two of them and the other mates to chat as he made his way aft, up the stairs to the quarterdeck. There, he saw Cowen standing at the port side of the ship, staring out with his spyglass into the fog-smothered sea. "You're looking the wrong way. Land is that way," Dane told the *Widow*'s first mate.

"I'm not looking for land. I have charts for that. I'm looking for what isn't on them."

"*Galleys?*"

"Boy, you're a bright one. We're just about to turn east off the ledge, and we'll be right in the thick of it. The North Sea connects to Roark's River."

"And?" Dane asked, feeding his annoyance as he shouted orders to the helmsman at the wheel.

"Roark's River is the widest river to Bovere, one that those oared galleys can fit within. It's the route they take to transport those goods in and out of the Regent."

Dane stayed silent, observing the commands from the quarterdeck as the *Widow* turned east through the fog.

As their time sailing along Geldring's Ledge continued to pass, the lookout in the crow's nest, atop the aft mast in front of the quarterdeck, stuttered to shout below, "*Sir—spotting. Two—port side.*"

Cowen whipped his spyglass back open and scanned the sea for any sign of movement. "There you are. *Knew we'd catch at least a few.*" He hurried his short legs and grimy body to the quarterdeck's ledge, leaning over to shout, "*All hands at your stations! To your quarters!*"

Just as Dane tried to leave the quarterdeck, Cowen grabbed his arm. "*Not you.* Go wake Captain Noreas and tell him two ships were spotted off the port bow."

Dane hurried into the aftcastle, bounding his way up its short stairs. He knocked on the captain's door for quite some time before it finally opened. Captain Noreas's face and hair looked disheveled, but he still wore his sharp and clean blue overcoat. With a tug on the curling brim of his cap, one Dane had never seen him wear before, his captain skipped down to the quarterdeck, shoveling him out of the way.

"Lookouts, lift the lantern to the crow's nest," Noreas commanded calmly as he stomped his boots in circles around the helm. "*Where are these two ships?*" He pulled out his spyglass and scanned its round cone through the fog's veil. "I only see the one war galley. Let's just hope they haven't seen us. *BOWMEN, AT THE BALLISTAS!*" he commanded down to the main deck.

"Should we tack, sir?" Cowen asked.

"No, stay the course along the ledge. We'll bring the *Rithron* and *Baroness* around their broadside. Cowen, are you sure you saw two?"

"Yes, sir."

"Then we'll hit the one we can see first. Looks to me like this one is the cargo's escort. *Perfect.*"

"Aye."

"*LANTERNS, SIGNAL TWO BY FOUR-ONE, THEN TWO BY ONE.*"

"*Very well,*" relayed the lookouts from above.

Dane tried his best to avoid the commotion on the quarterdeck. He asked one of the mates who stood watch nearby what that meant and was told that it was a signal to the other ships of the fleet—two boats spotted, four-one was their location off the port bow, two was to split their fleet in half, and one was to fire at will.

"Cowen, bring us to the wind on my signal," Noreas commanded. "I just hope the others can see the lanterns through this fog."

Cowen hurried to the central railing. "*ALL HANDS AT THEIR RIGGING! FULL SAILS AHEAD!*" As he went back beside the wheel, he saw Dane standing still on the quarterdeck, just watching. "What do you think you're doing? *Get down to the deck and help the men.*"

Dane quickly sprinted down the stairs, where he saw Ruth ducking beside the last step, clinging to its post, away from the *Widow*'s frantic crew. "What's happening?" she asked, clearly worried.

"Two of the King's galleys were spotted off the port side," Dane answered in passing, trying to get to his rigging station.

"They don't mean to sink them, *do they?*"

"They do." Dane moved near the central mast and helped the mates heave on the line to drop the sails lower. With each grab and pull, his shoulders ached and the lashed scars on his back strained. *I can't let Captain Noreas down,* he thought to himself. As his hands reached again to grab the line, he stared at the blood-pulsing scabs where his shackles once lined his wrists.

"*Tie it off,*" he heard Galen shout.

Dane looked up to make sure the two sails were tight at full span. He grabbed the taut line and braced it around the metal hooks at the bottom of the mast. The *Widow* began veering to port. He rushed to the side railing and looked aft. Two of the galleons that once followed them had turned with speed to surround the war galley on its opposite side.

We're squeezing it, he thought, the closer the *Widow* sailed toward the ship with winding oars. Dane could faintly hear the drums beating below deck. He glanced down at the inside of his left forearm, to the crossed oars branded boldly on his pale skin. All the memories he had once blocked to the back of his mind flashed to the forefront. He could see himself sitting there on the oar deck of the *Fereclis*, next to Piney and Elwer, right behind Nathan. *The smells…the pain…and the agony.*

"*Bolt loaded and lit, sir,*" the bowmen at the foredeck shouted to break his thought. The older mate stood with his chest lodged behind the ballista's long cavity, aiming its curved arms at the war galley they were closing in on. At its far edge was a flaming four-pronged tip, lit by a bundle of soaked rags tied behind its sharp blades.

Again, his memory flashed back to that night—the night his life had changed forever. At the time, and with everything that had happened to him since, Dane had been too exhausted to remember it in full. It was a night of pure darkness, one of enervation that had forced his eyes shut. His back coddled like sour cheese under the hottest of flames, one lit by the scoring pain at his shoulders and the blisters at his hands, rear, and feet. All he could hear were the barrel drums beating at the forward end of the oar deck—until they didn't.

The drumming had erupted into terrifying screams. His shut-eyed darkness opened to see nothing but flames. There beside him was Piney. In his eyes, Dane only saw the glaring reflection of death and felt the heat cook whatever life he had left. The full memory of that night was starting to come back to him. It was Piney who had yanked Dane off their bench and away from the blaze. And it was Piney who had made him grab the shit buckets behind them. As he thought back now with more clarity, he was at a loss for words as to how he could ever thank his friend.

I'll never be able to settle my gratitude, Piney.

Dane's icy-blue eyes were still, captivated by the bolt's flame at the foredeck of the *Widow.* Within it, he could see his fellow oarsmen caught ablaze and hear their dying screams. There, that same fire was waiting to launch itself again into the broadside of a war galley—a war galley filled with oarsmen just as he once was.

Death, Dane thought. *Fire is death.*

"*FIRE!*" Noreas commanded from the depths of his chest. Dane quickly turned his way as soon as he heard the ropes of the ballista slapping against their arms. He heard the forward and aft bolts strung loose, whirling through the air. Behind Captain Noreas on the quarterdeck was Ruth, being pulled back with her finger pointed at his face. Dane couldn't hear what she was screaming, but her eyes were watery red, and the veins across her forehead were as strained as the lines for the sails stretched to full speed.

"Boy, does she have courage," one of the mates to Dane's left said.

Shit, Ruth. Dane rushed up the stairs as fast as he could, stomping his boots onto the quarterdeck to help the mates pull her back.

"*Why did you do it? You murderer, look at what you've done!*"

Once he had his arms under her shoulders, Dane glanced out at the sea and saw the war galley they surrounded, lit ablaze. The two other galleons on its opposite side had struck their target just the same. The war galley's deck had been set on fire, and its hull was pierced below, flooding with water from the North Sea. As its bow began to tilt forward, Dane could faintly hear the screams below deck ring like the ship's bells, calling out for salvation.

"*FIRE!*" Captain Noreas commanded again.

This time, Dane saw it in its entirety. The second battery of bolts flew flamingly through the foggy air to strike the back-end of the war galley's lower hull.

That's where I would have been... Dane thought with a feeling of tangled misery. At that very moment, he let Ruth go. She ran right up to Captain Noreas, who stood near the port railing, and thrashed her fists into his blue coat, begging him to stop.

"Look, *girl*," he told her sternly as he grabbed her wrists, forcing her wailing to stop. "I'm the captain of this fleet—"

"You didn't have to kill them—*you murderer!* They didn't do anything to you!"

Captain Noreas let go, took a deep breath, and then walked calmly back to the helm at the center of the quarterdeck. She followed closely behind him, her plaid green skirt swirling with each angered step, before he turned to her again, this time placing both of his hands behind his back. "Like I tried to tell you, I'm the captain. Therefore, I alone bear that burden. Not you."

"There are other ways," she tried to plead.

Dane saw Captain Noreas's bushy eyebrows lower to hide what he really wanted to say. Instead, he just asked, "Like what?"

Ruth looked over at Dane, then back at Captain Noreas. "You could board them and save those who are helpless. *Look at Dane...and look at yourself.* They need our help. They deserve it."

A look of intrigue crossed Captain Noreas's muscled chin as he twisted his lips into a crooked smirk. Against Dane's expectation, he turned to his first mate and ordered, "Find me that cargo galley, Cowen. It shouldn't have drifted too far. The girl makes a good point."

Ruth's wailing finger, which she once had pointed in his face, fell to her side in surprise. "*Thank—you*," she stuttered, almost as if she were asking a question.

Captain Noreas drifted closer to the main deck. "*READY TO LOWER THE BOATS. LANTERNS...SIGNAL FIVE BY TWO!*" He turned back to Ruth and continued, "I'm not doing this for you, *girl*. The cargo galley that slipped away will have something I want. Treasures...and *gold*."

"That's all you care about?" Ruth asked.

"Don't worry, dear, we won't lay a hand on your precious oarsmen. But I can't claim the same for those officers. They deserve death," Captain Noreas scolded back.

"That sounds more than fair," Ludwyn said.

"Who asked you?" Cowen snarled at him, whipping his shoulders around from the helm. "*Get your ass down to the main deck.* You too, Dane. Both of you will be on those boats."

Captain Noreas stood beside the open railing. "This is your last chance to join us, *darling*."

Up above, past where Dane could see, Ruth answered with silence. He sat beside Ludwyn in the middle of the boat lowered into the water below, watching Captain Noreas climb down the rope-tied ladder. The captain boarded at the bow, then pushed off from the *Widow*'s hull. Jorgi, from behind Dane, released the line, and the ten of them on his side began to row.

"We have the fog to our advantage," Noreas told them. "They won't see us coming. Have your hooks ready."

"You should be pretty good at this, huh, Dane?" Ludwyn asked, trying to ease his nerves. Dane just held his short oar by its knobbed end and continued to help thrust their small boat through the eerie fog. He didn't bother to answer Ludwyn or try to joke back.

Dane's thoughts, though, weren't of his time on the *Fereclis* with an oar in his hand. Instead, they were drawn back to his home in Niven with his brother, Maven. The last time he was with him, they were rowing their own tiny boat into a storm. Now, he found himself sitting alongside his new brothers, doing the same.

The dense fog soon blanketed the *Widow* as they drifted farther out of its sight. Just ahead, Captain Noreas spotted the two small boats from the *Bessie*, which followed them through the stagnating waves. He lifted the tiny glass lantern at the bow and flashed its light twice, to which they returned just one.

"*Men, ready your hooks,*" Captain Noreas turned to whisper to them. Bundles of line with three-pronged hooks attached at their ends littered the floorboard between the benches. Flyde sat in front of Dane and grabbed their own, unraveling its knots to have their hook ready.

Out from the fog came the lapped planks of the cargo galley's hull. A single row of oars, one row less than his war galley had, was resting gently out of the water. Beside Flyde, Caji turned to ask Dane why they weren't rowing. Just behind them, the older mate, Cal, answered in a cotton-mouthed whisper, "*Their captain thinks they can hide in the fog.*"

But to Dane, his answer didn't make sense. The cargo galley was outnumbered five to one, and instead of trying to escape, they now sat as an easy target. Dane couldn't help but wonder if they were riding into a trap.

"*Can't be hit with fire if you can't be seen,*" the old man added.

On Captain Noreas's signal, the mates pulled the oars out from the water to silence their wake. They drifted their broadside close to the cargo galley's bow and waited for the three boats behind them to follow. Noreas turned around and waited, then whispered his command, "*Toss 'em.*"

This is it, a chance to bring justice for myself and my family, Dane thought, wiping his palms of their sweat. Flyde and the other mates on his side all threw their hooks into the fog, catching its prongs onto the cargo galley's side railing. Without a word, Captain Noreas led their climb, scaling between the outstretched oars and up the hull's side. He drew his saber from its sheath as soon as he disappeared into the haze.

Ludwyn gulped loudly beside him while they waited for Caji to clear the line. Dane stood, cracked his knuckles, and then followed the mates to scale the galley's hull. He heard boots clattering across the main deck as he passed between the oar's portholes. The stomping soon turned to shouts, then the clashing of steel against steel. Dane breached his head above the railing and saw Caji and Flyde with their sabers in hand, fighting a silver-capped officer through the dense fog.

Dane lifted his chest above the deck and swung his legs over its sides to join their assault. Surrounded by wailing grunts, he slung his saber out from his waist and swung low at the officer, slicing at his legs to free Caji and Flyde's stabs. As the faceless man in black fell to the deck, Dane drove his saber into his chest and let out a gasp of relief.

For all my days of struggle…you bastards.

But before he could even look up, an obscure figure ran right past him, screaming foolishly. It was one of the mates charging across the deck, into the fog.

"*Ludwyn?*" Caji asked.

"That isn't good." Dane rushed after him, passing by groups of fighting mates and officers until he found Ludwyn near the galley's stairs, surrounded by several black coats with silver caps. Ludwyn wailed his saber with worry, clanking its tip around the four or five blades that now encircled him. Again, Dane rushed in and went for their legs, piercing his curved sword through the closest one's thigh, then swiping at the other's chest.

"Seems like you've found the party," Captain Noreas's deep voice grumbled from behind Dane's shoulder. Together, they swung through the officers' defenses, fighting each two on one, swing for swing. "*Lud, down!*" Captain Noreas bellowed to make Ludwyn duck in distress. With brash skill, Captain Noreas spun and stabbed his saber straight through the officer between them.

"*Thank you,*" Ludwyn clamored.

"Don't thank me…get your ass up and fight!"

On the opposite side of the deck, Dane spotted mates from the other two galleons climbing up to join the fight. Side by side with Captain Noreas, the two made quick work of the officers as the boarding mates soon began to overwhelm the battle. The *Bessie's* captain led the rear of their assault as they encircled the few officers still alive. Most had thrown their sabers down and surrendered.

"*Take no prisoners!*" Captain Noreas shouted. Dane stood still, rushing with vengeance, as he watched his captain stab his bloody saber through the stomach of an officer with his hands in the air. One by one, bodies, dead or just barely alive, were launched into the foggy sea. Noreas commanded that those hiding below be hunted and killed. As he kicked in the door to the stairs, the captain shouted back to the mates' cheer, "*Let's go find that damned gold!*"

Dane's heartbeat finally began to slow. "*And the oarsmen...*" he whispered to himself.

"Open her up," Captain Noreas commanded, back aboard the main deck of the *Widow*.

Dane labored to pull at the line tied to the last cargo chest, lifting it from their small boat over the side railing.

"What do you think it'll be, boys?"

Shouts rang out from the mates as Cowen wedged the iron lock open. Dane rushed to join the crowd that huddled around the chests. Shoveling his way to get a better view, he saw one of their hinges cracked ajar. Inside were ingots of gold wrapped in purple velvet, dishware made of silver, purple jewels, and a few fine, golden-framed portraits of past queens and dignitaries.

"Looks like we've struck Astrian treasure!" Captain Noreas shouted. Cheers of victory continued to ring across the *Widow*'s deck. He lifted each item into the air with a rich and jolly laugh before Cowen had it moved to unlock the next one.

Five chests in total were taken from the soon-to-be-scuttled cargo galley, filled with an abundance of amethyst-tinted rugs and drapes and various clothing made of silk. Several crates of fresh greens and barrels of wine and water stores were split between the four captains under Noreas's command—Markas, Simion, Jalek, and Sonny. Dane and his fellow mates had spent half the day struggling to bring their spoils on board, only to be interrupted by Ruth, who had fluttered her way up from the kitchens to join them on the main deck.

"I hope you all are happy with yourselves," she said, quieting the crowd.

"As you could probably tell, *we are*." Captain Noreas dangled the silver chain around his neck. "You've made us rich, *darling*. You should be happy, too."

"You had all those men killed...*and I'm the one who should be happy?*"

Ludwyn moved beside her and attempted to calm her down. Captain Noreas looked at them both, then responded, "*No*, your friend Ludwyn, here, should be the happy one. Dane and I had to save his ass a few times, by my reckoning. Maybe next time you should come along and show him how it's done. You sure have the shoulders for it."

Dane watched Ruth's eyebrows wither and her face redden. "But not the stomach…*or the brains*," she snarled back.

Captain Noreas ignored her comment and strutted to the open railing on the deck's opposite end. He looked down at the sea, then turned back to Ruth, who stood encircled by the crowd of mates. "Well, Ruth, *darling*, it looks like your treasure has finally arrived."

Up from the rope ladder that hung off the *Widow*'s side climbed dozens of men dressed in rags, smelling of vomit and death. *The oarsmen,* Dane recognized with a smile as they passed by him in line.

Captain Noreas lifted a burgeoning smirk. "Ruth, be a dear and help the *Widow*'s newest shipmates find some food and a place to rest their heads."

"*It would be my pleasure*," she responded with a smirk of her own.

Mine too, Dane thought in agreement. *Thank you, Ruth.*

CHAPTER 19

SKY

A pounding pain reverberated throughout Vanna's body as she lay motionless on a smooth stone floor. Behind the blackness of her eyes was a flashing memory of bright lightning that continued to strike her with each stab of pain. Her eyes struggled to open as much as her arms struggled to move. With a grunt and a wince, Vanna lifted her back off the ground and tried to open her eyes. Blurred in the graying distance, she heard the pouring of rain.

Am I dead?

Vanna patted the warm ground around her, searching for her bearings. Between her and the stone floor was a flattened bundle of straw. The more she moved, the worse the pain struck her stiff shoulder and leg. As her vision slowly started to clarify, Vanna began to realize that she hadn't died. At least, she didn't think so. Above her head, she looked and saw torrents of black teeth plummeting from the sharp ridges of the shallow ceiling.

"*A cave*," she murmured to herself.

"You're awake," a calming voice said from behind her.

Vanna whipped her head around as fast as her body would allow, ignoring the anguish that came with it. Sitting beside the curving wall of the cave was an elderly couple, both of whom had graying hair and copper-tinted skin. The man stood up and walked toward the cave's entrance, stopping at the carved-out table etched smooth from the otherwise jagged stone wall. Out of caution, Vanna crunched her elbows in a hurry and tried to lift her body off the floor.

"Don't bother, you'll hurt yourself," the woman told Vanna, who was struggling to get up herself.

"Am I dead?"

"Oh, no, dear. But I can see why you might think that. I still wonder how you survived that fall. You must be a fighter." The old, hunched-back man stirred and squished a mortar and pestle. "Just like her." With a smirk, he nodded to the lady.

"So, you know the old tongue?" the lady asked.

Vanna caught herself. The couple had been speaking in sacred scipyrian, and she hadn't realized it. And in her prior question, she had spoken it back to them. Vanna silently nodded.

"Good. That's all we know out here."

Vanna continued to scan the cave, looking behind her and into its endless dark shadow. It reminded her of a Silo, or one of its many caverns kept hidden away. In that thought, her memory stirred, starting to return. *The Sisters. Little Wing.* "Where's my rook?"

"The bird? It didn't make it. I'm sorry to say," the old woman replied.

Vanna turned back to the cave's opening in quiet despair. *Little Wing, gone...* The one bond she could rely on was now broken, just like everything else.

"I watched you fall. *Well*, from our own town, not from here. That bird saved your life by gliding down the way it did, with its good wing," the man said, trying his best to cheer her up.

The tiny lady walked toward the rain, where Vanna could see her clearly. "I didn't believe it when Arzak told me to come take a look. I mean, I've heard tales about those rook riders, but never did I think I'd see one. And there you were, falling from the sky in the middle of a storm. Who would have thought?"

"Not me," Vanna whispered to herself. Shivers slithered down her spine as she pictured the two of them falling once more. *It should have been me who saved Little Wing. She'd be better off being free with these strange people. "Wait,* who are you? Where am I?"

"You're in the Vyporean Range, dear. Within one of the many caves of an extinct volcano. Vyllini, to be exact," the woman said as she wandered slowly toward Vanna on the floor. "I'm Juni, and this is Arzak. We picked you up and brought you here as soon as you landed—to one of the closest caves unused by our people."

Vanna sat silent in thought.

"What's your name, dear?"

"Vanna…" *If that's even my name anymore.* "Where is my rook?"

Arzak stood up from his chair near the table and walked toward them. "Just outside the other wall, in a smaller cave a little lower than our own. It took the both of us, a sack and a rope, to drag it out of the rain. It was a struggle to bring it all the way up here, as you might imagine."

"A struggle, yes, but not impossible," Juni added with a smirk, as if she were disappointed in his slothfulness.

"I'd like to see her," Vanna said, still speaking in sacred scipyrian.

"If you wish—actually, I know just the thing. But first, eat this." Arzak moved closer to hand Vanna a thin crisp with what looked like curdled honey spread across its top.

Vanna peeked around the gray garments that covered his frail body. In a jar on the table were three flowers with orange petals and yellow buds. *Vilova,* she recognized. "I can't take that. The vilova flower is banned in Astria." Vanna shook her head and retracted her twitching hand away from his reach.

"So, you're an Astrian woman. We thought so."

The worry within Vanna grew.

"But this isn't vilova, dear. It's vilovian nectar," the man explained more calmly than she had expected. "Here in the Vypores, the vilova flower grows naturally. In fact, it was here before it was taken to those mountains in the west. But here, we have something you don't," he said, extending it to her once more.

Vanna looked at it grossly. "And what is that?"

"A type of butterfly called the selephanta, native only here, in the Vypores," Juni responded. "They fly all over and are just the prettiest little things. Their wings are the color of the sun, just like the flower."

"And they love the vilova. In whatever way they do, they nibble at its core and leave this nectar there, stuck to it." Arzak grabbed his chair and moved it next to where Vanna sat atop the straw padding.

"What will it do?" Vanna asked, now more curious than afraid. Her instincts were as numb as her body, but she realized that if they had saved her before, they weren't likely to try to kill her now.

"*It will heal ya,*" Juni replied. She moved her chair to sit by Arzak so that all three were now facing the downpour.

"And by the looks of it, you need a lot of healing," Arzak added with a lighthearted laugh.

"I might need healing in more places than just my body…odd as that might look," Vanna said. She threw off the wool blanket that covered her legs. Her black hose had been ripped open, and her left leg was wrapped in bandages of bloodied cloth. She glanced at her shoulder and realized that it, too, was wrapped.

"We stitched you up good," Juni said. "Well, he stitched you up. His hands are much steadier than mine."

"That's right. You were a bloody mess. After I fixed you up, I rubbed some of that nectar over your wounds to numb the pain. So, either way, you're feeling it."

"Thank you." Vanna held her hand over the bandage and gently pressed on it to feel the pain. Surprisingly, her wounds hadn't stung as much as she thought they would. She smiled with gratitude and looked up to ask, "Do you two really live all the way out here? I've read about this place and understood it to be barren."

"No. Well, *yes*, in the Vypores, that is," Arzak replied. "But not here in this cave. Our town is about a half-day's hike away. There are caves just the same as this, scattered all across our range of extinct and dormant volcanoes."

"There's more of you?"

"We're doing our best to keep our people alive, but I wouldn't say there are *more*. My sisters and our daughter Sapharo are there too. And there are just a few other towns scattered about. We're the last of what's left of old Scipyria," Juni said, smudging with confidence. "The others don't take as kindly to outsiders as we do. They say it's to protect our heritage, but if they had it their way, there would be no heritage to protect. Not that there are many outsiders anyway. We might see just a brave traveler or two every few solurns."

Vanna listened intently. The old couple spoke quickly like the Sazarans but with a different dialect, one that was more formal and less emotional in its articulation. The two of them also didn't look like any Sacrimians Vanna had seen before. Their cheeks were strong and their chins proud, both with flat hair that came to a peak farther back along their rounded heads. Like most others in the Southern Plane, though, they shared the same hawkish nose and sun-darkened skin.

Feeling more trusting of the kind couple now than earlier, Vanna took the nectar crisp and bit into it. It tasted just as it looked—sticky honey, like gooey sap, as if it had trickled from the inside of a tree. After a few bites to finish the crisp, she took a few sips of tea they offered her and looked out past the entry of the cave, where the rain began to drift into a drizzle. Vanna could feel the stiffness of her body beginning to soften and her soreness starting to wane. "*I think I can feel it.*"

"Good, but the best is yet to come. Though it might take a little while to soak in," Arzak told her. "If I might ask, what is a young Astrian woman, such as yourself, doing all the way down here in the Vypores?"

"Not sure I could tell you. And even if I did, I'm not sure you'd believe it."

"Well, go ahead, give it your best."

"I was a part of a special group and did everything I was told. It was all I was raised to know," Vanna uttered, trying to remember it all. "And within just a single day, the person who raised me, and the person I revered the most, tried to kill me to clean up our mess...*her mess.*"

Juni stood from her chair and walked towards the edge of the cave, looking up at the sky through the drizzle to see if there was anyone in the air who might still be looking for her. She turned back, shaking her head. "Whoever it was has to think you're dead by now. No one survives that fall. Especially in the field of shears. If not the fall, then it'd be the creatures that lurk out here, which would surely have done you in. It's been a few days. If they haven't found you by now, I doubt they ever will."

"*A few days?*" Vanna asked.

"Why, yes, dear. You were out cold."

Vanna sat up straighter, without a belief in what they had said. "She would find me. *Like a family would.* She taught me everything I know."

"Anyone who would do that to you isn't your family, dear," Juni responded above Arzak's stirring.

"I know that now," Vanna thought aloud. Those words hurt to hear, but inside, she knew they were true. "Now I have no one. Not my Sisters, not my mother, and now not even my rook."

"You have us," the man butted in with a chuckle, trying to cheer her up. "I can tell by your look that you might actually be one of us. *Family.* We're no different. Our people's history dates back a long way. *Here,* take this. I want to show you something." Arzak walked over holding a walking stick. With Juni's help, they raised her to her feet.

Vanna winced in pain, though her body felt numb. In truth, she felt good, despite her soreness and limping steps. It was as if her skin and strength were soft, and the air around her calm and lifting. She could smell it all as if it were a feeling itself—the last trickling raindrops, the tea near their fire, and even the unwashed odor under their arms.

"We took to cleaning you up." Juni shifted her hair to the side.

Maybe you two should clean up too, Vanna thought, but knew it would be too rude to say. Arzak reached over and handed her the smoothly carved walking stick. "Use this."

Vanna grabbed the stick and hobbled over to the table while Arzak and Juni walked out of the cave and out of sight, down the sloped path to their right. On the table, she reached for one of the vilova flowers in the jar and brought it up to her nose to sniff it. It had a sweeter smell than she'd expected, as if sugar fruit from the ripest of vines had blossomed into a flower.

Outside the cave's entrance, Vanna heard grunting. She looked out and saw the couple dragging two sides of a burlap sack by a rope-tied handle. "Here's your bird," Arzak struggled to say as they dragged the broad sack into the cave. "We had to remove some of its insides to drag the sack around, but it's here. If you'd like, we can give her a proper ceremony—*a sacred Scipyrian sacrifice.*"

Vanna took a moment to question what that even meant before her mind was taken back to the last conversation she'd had with Lora, overlooking Zell's dead body. *A ceremony is what Little Wing deserved.* "Sure. That would be nice." After a long pause to regain their breath, the couple continued to drag the sack deeper into the cave and its rounding darkness. "Where are we going?" Vanna asked, limping to follow them.

Juni stopped to grab a smaller stick, wrapped it in cloth, and then dipped it into a bucket of black oil. She lit it to fire with a scrape of stone, then turned to look at Vanna and replied, "We're entering one of the true temples."

"The original ones...not those scattered bastardly across Sacrim," Arzak added.

Juni handed the torch to Vanna and said, "Here, you lead the way."

"*Me?* I don't know where I'm going."

"That's why you need the fire," Arzak said with a laugh.

"And you can't drag the sack, now, can you?" Juni asked, jeering a white-teethed smile. "Don't worry, the path isn't too long."

Vanna hobbled ahead with the walking stick in one hand and the torch in the other, her body and bones loosening more with each step she took. The jagged black walls she lit to guide the way had an uneasy sense of eeriness about them, as if she should be questioning the unknown. Or maybe even questioning the couple that now followed her. She had just met the two of them, and there they were, taking her to a temple of sacrifice.

Arzak and Juni were friendly, though, and had taken good care to keep her alive. But after what had happened with the Grand Dame, Vanna couldn't trust anyone. Not anymore. Especially such elderly people who lived within the dangers of the Vyporean Range and claimed to be the last remnants of the Scipyrians—a people she had learned from her studies as a Child to be extinct.

Despite her concern, Vanna continued on. The rounded walls had gone from jagged and sharp to smooth, chiseled surfaces, narrowing the farther they traveled through it. She began to see engravings and symbols etched along the walls. The closer she looked, the more Vanna saw that its letters and phrasings were familiar. "Are these what I think they are?"

"Aruks, yes. An older version of them, at least," Arzak said as he tugged the massive sack along from behind. "I told you our people had a shared history."

From an early age, the Sisters taught Vanna to read, write, and speak all the old languages of the Plane. Chief among those was Astria's own, varukian. It was a fluid language to speak, but one that was written harshly, with jagged symbols and letters like glyphs that used congruent and straightforward shapes.

Vanna hurried to the wall as fast as her leg would let her. She ran her fingers through its etching and traced the words, trying to understand its meaning. "Is this a poem?"

"Close," Juni replied, letting go of the sack to watch Vanna. "A chant. One about the people who built this temple a long time ago—around two millennia ago, if I had a guess."

"I thought you said we were in a cave of an extinct volcano?"

"*We are*," Arzak responded, still grunting to drag the sack along. "These are the true temples of the Sacred Scipyrians. The sister people to

240

the Arukians and those Atholians who had followed them out of the Eastern Plane."

"Driven out," Juni corrected.

"Yes, driven out. First by the royals and their knights. Then again by Rexam the Rageful."

"I've read the history," Vanna said as she stared intensely at the aruks, still trying to read them in full. The Astrial Academy within the inner district of Mount Matron was filled with ancient texts and scrolls that documented the movements of the stars, numbers in nature, and the language and dogmas of those who had passed. Though Vanna had never been inside the academy before, the Sisters had access to all its texts. Most important in their studies as Children were those of the Plane's history, of which they were forced to learn about the origins, culture, and language of all its distinct people.

Two thousand solurns before the descent, the Eastern Plane, inhabited by the vast majority of the Plane's people at that time, put an end to the horse-ridden raids that swept across their land like a plague. Clans of families used to war with one another, looting each other's tribes, collecting their women and gold as a prize, and oppressing men for their labor. At that time, the people had been landlocked within the vast river meadows of the east, too afraid to cross through Torrent's Sleeve or trek through the Sineaqe Desert.

As the clans grew in numbers and wealth, so too did their willingness to withhold and protect their valued possessions and power. Castles were built in their grandeur to guard the families' treasures; men were forced to swear fealty to their protection, and blood lineages were given titles of royalty.

In the solurn 1523 B.D., seven of the wealthiest families enshrined their alliance in a pact known to the Eastern Plane as the Royal Order. Knights of the families were paid well in gold, clad in scales of silver and steel, and wielded armies of lancers and troopers with their warhorses and longswords. They gave them the authority to hunt down and kill those horse-ridden riders who chose to still roam free. For over three decades, the Royal War raged until the last of the surviving clans in the south were driven out of the Eastern Plane and forced, with no other choice, through the Sineaqe Gorge to settle in modern-day Sacrim.

By 1410 B.D., the three sister clans—the Scipyrians, Arukians, and Atholians—had made the Southern Plane their home, establishing themselves among the pale, red-haired natives as a joint people in the city they called Scipyria. There, they grew in number, marrying and intermarrying between the clans for more than two hundred solurns. In 1227 B.D., the head of the Scipyrian family, known to the people as the vizar, left his Arukian wife to join hands with the most beautiful of all fire-haired women. This act was viewed as a treacherous breach of loyalty to the Arukians. Out of vengeance and filled with fury, his wife left the Southern Plane with her clan and trekked across Vantham's Throat, which earned its namesake from her crossing. Irissa Vantham led her people to the empty mountains of the Western Plane and established the settlement that would later become Mount Matron.

As an Astrian woman herself, Vanna took immense pride in knowing her people's history and the surrounding Plane's cultures. As she traced her pale fingers along the warm black wall, she could feel the history she had read for so long under candlelight come to life. Only, the glyphs here didn't exactly match the history she'd been told. "I just don't understand why it's written in our aruks and not in scipyrian."

Arzak walked over to join her. "History is muddied by inconveniences. This varukian text predates that of Scipyria. And this—the Vyllini temple—was their first of seven creations. Back then, the Arukians were known as the tribe of virgins for their beauty and pontific nature. They were also the most knowledgeable in the arts and with words. And, *of course*, their sacrifices. It wasn't until Scyrus the Third's wife, Irissa Vantham, left him that the Scipyrian's own language emerged across the Southern Plane. As evidenced here."

"You mean *he left her*, right?" Vanna asked.

"Oh, *no*, dear. The man had his obsessions with fire and hers with ruling, but as these walls will tell…she was never interested in men. She found them to be like wild animals who found joy in battling one another but didn't have the slightest inclination to turn their eyes toward the sky and strive for anything more. To Irissa, it was women who held the true power, as vassals for life—to create as the moon had from above. While men, instead, worshiped the prideful *fire* below."

"That isn't the history I know."

"Like I had said, history is full of inconveniences. But, here, within the temple, you can read it for yourself."

Vanna held the torchlight to the text. The aruks written were from an age long ago, with words and sequences she couldn't really understand. Their jagged strikes and dotted lettering were harsher than she'd ever seen before, with their phrasing in passages written with missing end letters and emphasis unlike the common, or even ancient, varukian.

"Come along. There's more to see," Juni told her.

With her walking stick in hand, Vanna limped to lead them farther into the cave. Her skin felt melted, and her left leg was like a stream of water, walking as if it weren't even there. *The vilovian nectar,* Vanna realized. She noticed that her mind, too, had been wiped clean of any anger that had once stung her so deeply. As they walked around the curve of the cave's wall, Vanna saw a light breach through the darkness. Her lips, which felt swollen like the sting from a wormwasp, drew a smile from cheek to cheek.

The light continued to pour in from above. Vanna limped closer and saw the conical hole left at the volcano's open top. Inside, the ground was smooth and flat. Mosaics of varukian art and text were faintly painted and etched into the ring-shaped outer wall. At the center was a bowl carved deep into the ground, similar in size to the gaping hole of the volcano's peak directly above it. Vanna could barely see the tip of a flame raging through the drizzling rain that fell in the bowl's center. She walked beside its rim and saw black sand filled within its rounded bottom, fueling the ever-burning fire.

"This is one of the *true* temples of Scipyria," Juni said.

"It reminds me of the Silos back home."

Arzak left Little Wing by the entrance and joined the two of them. "Where do you think those Astrian women got the idea?"

In Vanna's mind, it all began to make sense—the history of her people taught by the Sisters and her Queen wasn't their true history. No, those words could very well have been a fabrication, written to sway the people and their beliefs, meekening them like a rook to the pitch of their own desired notes. Many Astrians still held resentment for the warlike men of the south, in part because of the tales of their origin. But it could have been a lie, just like the life she had lived. Vanna understood that it was in the relics of history where the truth survived. And it was in the light of fire where they were revealed. "You said there are seven of these?"

"Yes. Most of the others have the more common sacred scipyrian written along their walls. As you might imagine, it took hundreds of solurns to excavate these insides and smooth them out. Our people would trek daily from Scipyria—or what they call today *Andar*—to the Vyporean Range. Not to mention all the creatures that lurk here, which they had to endure. But yes, *seven*. One temple for each royal family."

"That's quite dark."

"These are temples of sacrifice, after all. To the Scipyrians, the royals were a proud and haughty people who coveted a land they considered sacred for their own greed. More than anything else, though, they knew the royals to be murderers. They tried to hide behind their gold and steel, but there's no castle big enough to conceal the depravity of their hearts. First in the Royal War, and then again with Rexam and his rage. Our people's history is one of passion and purpose. But it's also one littered by slaughter and exile. It couldn't be better signified by this—the ever-lit black sand flame of *Solvros Somar*, which has been burning since the temple's inception." Juni circled the rounding wall of Vyllini's temple as she continued to speak, "This is where they came, all those solurns ago, to worship the true fire—the same immortal spirit that lives within us all. The one whose will we each share behind the blackness of our eyes and in the warmth of our hearts. It is our own piece of that grand star in the sky, but only just that—*a piece*. It is in Solvros Somar where the true spirit lives. And one day, Solvros Somar will return to incarnate himself again as man, just as the sovereign smoke foretold. The Scipyrians acknowledged the sun and its power, but were wise not to worship it…like those fools today do now."

Vanna disparaged her illusory statement about a flame incarnating itself as man and asked instead, "The Temple of Sciron?"

"Yes. *Bastards*, those. Instead of the true fire within us all, they bend their knees to deacons…and to their gold, above anything. Our temples had no supposed truth-teller they must bow to or man they must worship. *No*, we all share one common purpose—*keeping the fire alive*."

Arzak walked back to the sack where Little Wing rested and asked Juni for her help. Together, they dragged the burlap sack to the edge of the bowl carved into the ground. Juni turned back to Vanna and asked, "May I?"

"Please."

As they untied the sack, Vanna saw Little Wing for what she knew would be the final time. Its beak, which once shimmered black, was now dulled in death. Vanna plucked a single, brown-speckled feather from its tinier wing on the ground beside her. The elderly couple then crouched to push the large bird into the black sand fire.

They stood back up, watching Vanna's rook slide down to catch flame. They spoke in unison, deeper than before, to say, "*In the Chalice of Vyllini, we sacrifice thee—*"

Chalice… Vanna pondered, remembering when she was anointed as a Sister in Mudin Spring. *It's all connected.* Next to her, Arzak gave her a slight nudge with his elbow. "Sorry—*Little Wing.*"

"*To the everlasting primordial fire, Solvros Somar, the true light of the Plane and ever-dwelling immortal spirit of life and death. It is in thee our spirit originated, and from thee our spirit shall return. May this body be consumed to nourish your everlasting light.*"

Vanna stared deep into the fire, watching Little Wing's body burn. She listened as its feathers and bones cracked with the growing pillows of smoke. In the chalice below, she could smell the withering of life and see the true light absorbing its source. The fire pranced with its own story, burning her rook to feed its sacrificial dance.

"Typically, the Scipyrians would join their hands together and chant as they rounded in circles between the chalice and the temple's ring," Juni explained. "But as you could probably tell, we no longer have the people for that."

Black smoke continued to rise high, out through the volcanic opening of the temple. Within it, Vanna watched as the smoke told its tale. She could see herself as a Child in the Silo, comforting the egg the Sisters had given her as she played it her songs. In its blackness, she saw the memory of her rook hatching and the day she first rode it, giving Little Wing her name. Vanna had smiled that day more than any other. As she saw herself grow older, around her came the other Children with their rooks, flying through the sky—faster and stronger with each passing moon. Vanna even saw that fateful day she was chased by the Grand Dame, the day she and Little Wing were betrayed and left to die. *The bravery,* Vanna thought of her rook as she watched its body burn. "*The smoke speaks and reveals it all.*"

"That it does," Arzak said, placing his hand on her good shoulder.

Vanna looked around the ring of the temple and saw the invisible figures of Scipyria's past, dancing in circles as they sang their silent songs. With broad smiles, those ancient people celebrated a life born by the warmth of fire—joined together in festive joy as one people. *A family, keeping the light.* Together, they all came back to life, vivid enough to make Vanna smile as she watched, wishing only that she could join them.

"So does that vilovian nectar," Juni added with a crackling laugh.

That's right… Vanna thought. She forced her mind to snap back to reality. The figures who once danced were now gone. And the smoke that once ascended from Little Wing's body had begun to dwindle. Vanna knew that what she saw wasn't real. But she also knew what she felt was. She was no longer alone. Her inner fire was now fanned with a flame from the true source—one she knew she needed to keep alive with the breath of her own air.

At that moment, Vanna understood that her past life was one surrounded by people who had never loved her, or ever cared for her, the way she knew she needed. The Sisters of the Silo were never her family, but a foreign people from a place she knew she couldn't return.

CHAPTER 20

STONE

"Here, take my hand," Roth said from beside the dock. "Where are we?"

Roth stretched out his arm and lifted Scarlett out of their tiny boat. "Lansdale. Should be, at least. An outer canton of Bovere."

The two of them had spent the last five days together, rowing up the Fleming River in near silence. Roth was desperate to return to the Northwoods and escape what tragedy had befallen him back in Roverra. He wanted to forget that night at the Colchester Estate as if it were just a nightmare and the days ahead were what was real. But any time his mind would wander, or his eyes would shut to try to sleep, the image of Lady Lomberg's plump face, lying there naked in the corner of the candlelit room, came back alive to haunt him.

For the last moon and a half's pass, Roth had been a hero—someone the people of Regent looked up to and admired, and one many others feared. The royal families had paved his future for glory and wealth. He was supposed to be their champion, a man they could parade around the Eastern Plane as a sign of strength and victory. His fate would be inked in their history books, lauded as a tale for all the young boys who were poor and coatless, like he once was. But now, he was alone. And his name was destined only for the warrant the sentinels would be hunting him for. Roth had gone from being the Regent's hero to a man destined for a life of labor in the mines of Garsenden. By his foolish actions that night, he had thrown it all away, just as Ruth had foretold.

However, Roth wasn't actually alone. There, in front of him, and on the bench seat of their tiny dory, had been Scarlett, a girl whose terrors seemed to somehow trump his own. Anytime Roth became caught in his swirling cascade of misery, he'd think back to the moment when Scarlett first awoke.

Half a day after he'd taken her upriver, she vaulted herself up and let out the most deafening cry for help. Her tiny, freckled body shook like the loose pin of a rattling wheel as she twirled around in her torn-up crimson dress, threatening to kill him and jump overboard into the river's current.

Roth never thought of himself as having the friendliest of faces. His size alone caused most to view him as intimidating, and his face, he knew, wasn't the most graceful of sights. He had a slanted crook for a chin and wings-for-ears that rivaled only his forehead in scale. Despite this, he never thought of himself as looking threatening or dangerous or even ugly enough to cause the reaction that Scarlett had given. But the more he sat in silence next to the trembling young girl, trying only to calm her down, the more Roth realized that her shrieking cries were not of the present but of the past, just like his own.

He did his best to comfort and console her back to sleep and gave her his spare clover-colored shawl, which draped like a tunic past her knees. On the first day, Roth had asked for her name and let her sleep to recover. For most of the days to follow, Scarlett still looked almost too traumatized to speak. Roth didn't mind, though. He had his own horror to keep hidden, one he dared not share with her. And he had his work set out for him, rowing their tiny boat upriver until they reached as far inland as it would take them.

The Fleming River wasn't nearly as wide or populated as Roark's, which made their journey east one of ease in concealment and evasion. During the daylight, they'd find a covered tree, not too far from the river, to rest since Roth's shoulders would grow tired and sore from rowing throughout the night. But as they lay under the broad groves and oaks, neither of them found their desired rest. The two didn't know a thing about each other, but Roth could tell from the second he looked into her sky-colored eyes that they shared the same sight—one of lost hope.

Scarlett was tiny, especially in comparison to Roth, and had soft skin marred by bruised splotches like the hide of cattle. Her hair was as orange as the fruit and had been frizzled in a mess since the day he'd swum out and pulled her ashore. Despite her current state, Roth found Scarlett, the girl he presumed to be from the Southern Plane, to be far prettier than any woman he'd ever seen back in Roverra or Bovere—more so even than Elvina Damas.

"Are you hungry?" Roth broke the dense air beside the dock to ask her. She answered with an obvious nod. "We'll find some food first, then a bed to stay in. From the morrow on, we'll be on horseback." Roth instructed Scarlett to lift the hood of the shawl over her head, the same as he did, so that her noticeably distinct hair would be hidden.

Onto the cobblestone roads of Lansdale, they went. The evening grew dim with a drizzle of rain as they walked beside a row of tiny cottages with thatched roofs, much like most homes outside the populated cantons of Bovere. Packs of dogs roamed freely between the buildings, sniffing the empty barrels that lined the side streets and alleyways. The people he saw here seemed to be older and more conservative in their dress. Most of the men looked of the laboring sort, whose generations of families worked in the surrounding fields of grain and greens. And the women, for as much as Roth could tell, kept inside to manage their markets and coin.

A perfect place to lay low, Roth thought the farther they walked down the street's side path. He scanned every sign that hung out from under their roofs by wooden posts, which dangled their painted pictures into the narrow road. Scarlett followed Roth from close behind, hiding herself under his tall shadow until he spotted a sign with an image of a bed that read, *The Stonebroke Inn.*

"*Perfect,*" Roth whispered back to her. "We should be able to get a meal here, too."

He led Scarlett through the dust-ridden door of the inn. Inside was a short and shallow room, lit by lanterns hung from each corner of its decaying bar. They took a seat at the booth against the sidewall, leaving space between themselves and the tables clustered in the center, which two groups of drinking men occupied.

"Could you go up to the bar and ask the lady for food and stout?" Roth asked Scarlett. "We'll need a room upstairs, too."

"*Me?* No—*why?*" she stuttered nervously in response.

"Because…I can't. You're hungry, aren't you? Here's a silver and some coppers."

"Why can't you do it?"

Roth hadn't yet thought of an excuse but knew he needed to hold back from revealing the truth. "I don't want them to recognize me."

Instead of asking why, Scarlett just scoffed at him with her eyes. Her stomach let out a gurgling growl. She stood up, though her bitter stare remained. "We need *two* rooms."

"Here," he said, handing her another silver. "Two stews and two stouts."

"I don't want a drink," she told him, keeping her scowl of disdain.

"Then they're both for me."

As Scarlett walked to the bar, Roth scanned the room. Of the tables beside them, one looked harmless, crowded with men late in their age who sat with mugs full of stout playing Roth's favorite game of Cornerstones. At the other table sat men as young as he was, dirtied and rowdy, who looked as if they had just finished a long day of smithing work.

Scarlett returned with two fists of stout in clay mugs, nearly too big for her to hold. Beside the table, she paused. Holding them tight to her lean chest, she said, "*Tell me.*"

"Tell you what?"

"Or no stout. I'll have them both for myself."

"What am I supposed to be telling you, exactly?" Part of him was still dazed by hearing her talk more now than she had for their entire journey upriver. The other part just wanted this conversation to end.

"Why they might recognize you...and why you don't want them to," she stated with the same wary blue gaze as before, taking her seat across from him.

Roth looked at her in puzzlement, debating within his mind over what to say. "I'm the champion of the Regent. At the Descindation. The one who won."

"*Ahhh*, I knew you looked familiar!" Scarlett struggled not to shout.

"You were there?"

"Unfortunately."

"From the south?"

"How could you tell?" Scarlett asked sarcastically, moving her hood just enough to flash the color of her hair. Roth took a sip from the mug she'd slid across the table. The other, to his surprise, she had kept for herself. Scarlett sipped on her own and then immediately coughed it back up. "*What is this? Pig's piss?*"

"Shhh," he reminded her as one of the younger men looked their way. "Only the Regent's finest—burnt-stout."

"It's awful."

"Not as awful as being spotted. I'm sure you wouldn't want that either."

"No, not here, at least." She looked around the room with just her eyes. "I grew up hearing how pretty Bovere was. I'm not sure why."

"You aren't yet in the heart of Bovere. We're far away from the central plaza," he explained after taking a hefty sip. "If you don't mind me asking, how does a southern girl such as yourself end up on one of those nork galleys, then wash onto the shores of the Eastern Plane?"

"Actually, I *do* mind you asking." Scarlett took the lengthiest of sips, then held her face flat. "It was all against my will. And I'd rather not talk about it."

"Understandable."

"You didn't finish that last part," she said.

"What *last part?*"

"Why wouldn't you want them to recognize you? Shouldn't they be celebrating you?"

"Like you said…I'd rather not talk about it."

"Embarrassed by the attention?" Scarlett asked as if she already knew.

"No, that isn't it. I've had more than my fill of that for the past quarter-moon, that's for sure. Let's just say I had an accident. Something happened. I didn't mean for it to happen, and it wasn't exactly my fault. But it happened when I was at a party with many royals—the most powerful people in the Plane. And I'm sure, by now, they've seen it."

"So, you are *embarrassed,*" Scarlett said. For the first time in five days, Roth saw a smirk grow across her freckled face.

"No, not that kind of accident."

"I've heard of them before—those royals. I sort of come from a family like that myself, back in Sacrim," she admitted.

"That doesn't really come as a surprise to me."

Scarlett scoffed with her eyes again. "It's not all you think it is, you know. All the wealth in the Plane, and they always seem to want more."

"It must be difficult being born into such a privileged family. I can only imagine how tough your life must have been," Roth snarled.

Scarlett's face blushed red as if he had stricken her sternest of nerves. "I've come to learn that there's a price to privilege. My family's name is the reason I just went through what I did. And it isn't something I can control or something I even wanted or asked for."

Roth sipped his stout, considering whether he should continue to share his disdain with her. But instead, he just looked around the barroom and avoided rousing her to bring them any unwanted attention. "Seems like everyone has it rough these days."

"It's hard to grow up without a real family. It was always just me, my mother, and my two baby sisters. My father, I rarely saw, and my brother, I don't even recognize anymore. I had friends. Girls with families of similar status and wealth, but none who really cared about me. Anyone who tried just wanted to use me to get to my father."

"To your father or his gold?"

"*His power*," Scarlett corrected. "One thing I had to learn early is that wealth attracts attention. And attention attracts jealousy, which then leads to conflict. And with that conflict comes pain and death and misery. What is the common saying? That every blade has two sides? Well, my father's blade is the longest."

"Not every blade. My axe is only sharp at one end."

"Your axe is meant for wood, not for men."

"You should have warned those champions of that back on the isle."

"There's a lot I should have done on that isle. And so much more that I would change. If I could go back, I would have never even gone."

"*Me too*," Roth admitted under his breath, though he wasn't sure if he truly believed it. "When I was young, my parents would tell me all the stories of the Regent's old knights—*Timothy the Regnant...Beglan the Brave...Farum and Fanor, the Twins...*and, of course, *Tohen the First.* They were who I always aspired to be. Not those kings of the Regent's past. The knights were noble, brave, and strong warriors who defended the innocent and protected our land from *evil*."

Scarlett's lips grimaced. "*Evil.*"

"But as I grew older, I gave that aspiration up and just settled with being a ranger in the Northwoods. It was all I ever knew. Becoming the champion is the closest thing anyone could ever get to having tales of your name sung across the Plane like those knights still do. Don't get me wrong, I loved every moment of it. But that status, and all the attention from those wealthy men and women that came with it, brought out the worst in me. And those commanding sentinels, whom we today might consider to be knights, as I learned, were all just the scum of the Plane. If I could take it all back, I would...and if there are any tales that should be sung, it should be about me as a ranger in the woods."

Scarlett lifted a soft smile in agreement. "Well put."

"Stew for two," said the short barmaid with white hair dressed in a dirty apron. She walked over to their table and placed a bowl before them both. Roth thanked her without looking up and watched as Scarlett dug in. "Here's your keys. Up the stairs, last two rooms on the left," the barmaid told them before drifting away.

"This is awful, but I can't stop eating it."

Roth ate quickly through his own, ripping the finger bread apart and smearing it around the rim of the bowl. "Might need seconds, by the look of it."

"Or thirds."

"You'll have to pay for those yourself," he said with a laugh. "You're the one with daddy's gold."

But Scarlett didn't laugh at his joke. Instead, she listened to the voices of the younger men at the table beside them, which grew louder as they continued to eat. With empty mugs littered across their table, the four dirtied men spoke first of work and women, before they began to talk of rumors and tales.

"*There will be war on the Plane, I'll tell ya,*" one of them said in a growling voice.

"*Always the south, too,*" another added. "*Those bastards can't ever just live in peace.*"

"*If not the south, then those norks. And they'll bring it this way, put it on our plate to fix, just like they always do, leaving us to clean up their mess.*"

Roth peeked over and saw one of the larger men say, "*With that general murdered, who knows who they'll blame it on.*"

General murdered? he questioned to himself. He glanced over at Scarlett and saw her pale face begin to crumple as she paused her eating.

"*Oh, come on, Greggor, we all know who it was.*"

"*That damned temple, that's who.*"

"*Word around town is that the daughter of one of them was kidnapped at the isle after the fight. Caused a ruckus in that place. Probably why he was murdered.*"

253

Scarlett turned to stare at the darkened wall beside their booth. Out from the corner of her eye fell a thread-like tear. Roth was unsure of how to console her. For the word of her missing to stretch this far east, he knew her family wasn't just wealthy. No, she was right about what she had said before. Her father must be powerful.

"*The bear's fight, you mean,*" one of the quieter ones corrected, making some of the men applaud with flatter.

"*Certainly was. Say, Jarrow, you think it was the General who took that girl? Maybe that's why they offed him.*"

"*I doubt it. My friend Carl, whose cousin was a sentinel, told me once that that General was no southern general. At least in usual relations. But now, with him out of the way, there's no telling what will happen.*"

"*Oh, yes, there is,*" the drunken one with a growling voice said. "*War.*" Roth looked over and saw the young man named Greggor wave his empty mug in the air to signal the barmaid back over.

"*I certainly won't be fighting a foreign war for some southern girl.*"

Roth turned back to Scarlett and saw her face turning red with tears. He wanted to reach out his hand, to comfort her and take back what he had said earlier. Roth realized that Scarlett was right. Her position wasn't one of privilege—it was of plight.

"*We haven't escaped from the talk of the Plane either,*" the old barmaid said to the men at the table while she refilled their drinks from a vase.

"*What have you heard, Miss Bell?*"

"*It's only gossip. But apparently, the Regent's champion—that bear you lot love to sing about—murdered his own bondsman.*"

Roth's eyes slung open. He fluttered his head away in the same direction Scarlett had, hoping that no one had spotted him or recognized him for his size. There was, however, already someone there in the inn who knew who he was. And she was sitting right across from him.

Scarlett turned her teary face to look at him. Her blue eyes, riddled with veins of red, were now gaping larger than his own. She looked just as frightened as the day he'd swum out and pulled her ashore, as if she feared for her life to be there, sitting across from him, the man who had murdered his own bondsman. Her fingers fluttered around the rim of her empty bowl, almost unsure of what to do.

"It's not what you think it is," Roth pleaded to her. "I promise... It wasn't my fault—it was only an accident."

"I need to leave," she stated bluntly. "To bed, then home. *I can't do this.*"

"You don't believe them over me, *do you?* I'm the one who rescued you on that beach, the one who brought you all this way, safely here."

Scarlett slung herself out from their booth, took one of the keys, and left in a hurry for the stairs. As he sat alone, Roth tucked his chin low, staring into the grains of the table, trying to think of what he could have done differently. *Maybe I should have told her the truth sooner…from my own mouth.* His mind tempered with the hope that Scarlett herself wouldn't say or do anything. *No, she won't. I could give her away just the same,* he reasoned.

In their short time together, since the day he swam out to save her on the beach near Roverra, Roth had felt obliged to protect her. Scarlett shared a similar innocence to his sister, Ruth, and reminded him of the young fawn and babes of the Northwoods he would find straggling alone, lost without their mothers. If these men knew of her situation, then there were likely to be many others. And Roth knew there was no telling what lengths the men of the Regent would go to for a simple sack of gold.

In the streaming grains of the inn's table, his mind returned to the Northwoods. *Cheap wood,* he thought as he ran his bulging finger along its winding path. *Not like ours, back home.* By its trace, Roth knew Tergona was still his destination, whether Scarlett came or not. Across the table, he took her mug and finished the drink she'd left half full.

Back to where I started, he thought. *Alone with my stout and my sorrow.* The barmaid drifted over to his table to take the empty bowls and refill both mugs. He could tell she thought him to be some rude outside traveler from a distant canton. And she'd be right.

Alone, he drank with his drifting thoughts, refill after refill. Each sip of stout brought the urge to have another. Part of him was too worried to go upstairs and try to sleep, unsure of what would come now that Scarlett knew his secret. *Nice and numb,* he thought to himself as he drowned out the drunken chatter from the table beside him. Or, more importantly, the chatter within his own mind.

It wasn't until Roth had to fight to keep his eyes open that he took his sack and axe, which he had hidden under the table, up the stairs to find his room. Without undressing, he plopped his outstretched body onto the stiff featherbed and dangled his feet off its side. There, he lay, numb as can be, drifting off into a drunken slumber.

A loud crack broke through the darkness, forcing Roth to wake up in a sweat. From the room's lone window, he could hear rain pouring against its tiny glass. Even with his eyes crusted shut, the continual flashes of light from the dark sky were enough to brighten his room, keeping him from sleeping.

Roth turned over from side to side and covered his sweaty face with the wool blanket, trying to wish the storm away. But every effort to find comfort only made things worse. Whether it be the rain or his thoughts, he continued to toss and turn until he could close his eyes no longer. There, in the darkness of the shallow ceiling, Roth opened them and saw Lady Lomberg's face outlined within the wooden beams. He hurled himself up out of bed and patted around frantically, trying to remember where he was. *Lansdale… Scarlett…*

Roth stood up and left his room to enter the hallway, lit by two lanterns at each end. The last door on the left was slivered open. "*Scarlett?*" He tiptoed to squeeze his body inside with the lantern's light held out. *Empty,* he realized after scanning the room. The sheets and blanket on the bed had been crumpled up and folded aside. *But where could she have gone?*

Roth returned to his own room to think through an answer. *She could be on her way back south, alone…or*—as his clouded mind tended to turn back to the same conclusion—*spotted by one of those drunken men downstairs.* Either way, Roth felt obliged to find out.

He wiped his sweaty hair, grabbed his axe and sack, then headed down the stairs. Lifting the hood of his clover-colored shawl back over his head, he left through the dark and empty barroom. Into the black of night, he went, crossing through the cobblestone roads, trying to stay under the brimmed roofs to shield himself from the pouring rain. He wandered from building to building, looking for any sign of light or a stable around their corners.

There. Roth crossed into an alley and peered around the door of a covered stable. "*It's okay—it's okay,*" he tried to calm the few horses who reared and trembled from his startle. "*It's just a storm,*" he whispered, patting them on the head. *So, she didn't take one of these.* After the crack of a close bout of lightning, a faint scream broke the air behind him.

Roth ran out into the middle of the road and twirled in search of any light. Near the far edge of the building opposite the stable, a window up the stairs reflected the dim yellow gleam of a lit lantern. He checked its locked front door once, then reared back and kicked it in with the heel of his boot.

"*Scarlett…*" he uttered into the dark and empty room. Roth rushed up the stairs with his axe in hand until he spotted the same light creeping out from under a closed door. He kicked it in and pointed its head out in the air.

In the center of the room, tied to a chair, was Scarlett, mumbling through a rag wrapped around her mouth. When he grabbed it and yanked it off, Scarlett yelled, "*Behind—behind you!*"

Roth swung his wide shoulders around and saw an elderly man limp briskly through the doorway with the large kitchen cleaver held blade-side out. The old man lifted the cleaver, and Roth tried to sway out of its way, spinning and turning to lunge aside. With an angered growl, the old man threw his fists into the air, clipping the sharp blade into the side of Roth's arm.

Roth felt no pain. He looked down in the dimly lit room and saw the old man's blade lying on the floor, below the blood that trickled from the side of his arm, just below his shoulder. "*You missed…*" he hissed back at the old man, who was now backing away slowly without a weapon, until his shoulders became caught against the wall.

"It's you—*the bear*—the champion. I'm sorry, I saw her at the bar—*I just wanted to earn myself some gold.*"

"Save your sorry for the Gates." With his right hand, Roth swung the blunt end of his axe into the side of the man's head, heaving his elderly body down to the ground. "Tell no one we've been here, or I'll be sure to send you to them," Roth demanded, though the man remained silent.

Roth used the cleaver to cut Scarlett free from the chair. Her pale face was full of tears, trembling in speechless fright. He couldn't hear what she mumbled, but it sounded like an apology. Or, at the very least, a mournful cry of regret.

"Did he hurt you?"

Scarlett just looked at him with a flat, blank stare as if her pain was still one of remembrance—flashings from what could have been rather than from what was.

Something much deeper, Roth realized. "Here I was, worried about that table of younger men."

Scarlett just continued to shake her head from side to side.

"I'm just glad I found you. What were you thinking, running off like that?"

"I wasn't. I was just scared by what those men had said. About you—but also about everything else. About me and about war," she stuttered. "*I never asked for any of this.*"

But I did, Roth thought to himself.

"You're bleeding." Scarlett ripped a piece of cloth from her old crimson dress in Roth's sack and tied it around his oozing arm.

"It's nothing. But thank you."

"*No,* thank you. That's the second time now—that you've saved me."

Roth looked down at the bandage. "We'll help keep each other safe from now on…how about that?"

"*Deal.*"

"Now, let's get out of here. There are some horses in a stable around the corner. And I'm sure this old man has some food we can pack, too. It'll be a long ride east."

"East?"

"*Home,*" Roth corrected.

CHAPTER 21

SUN

"Captain Thorp, it's a pleasure for you to join us," Kladden said to the broad-necked, short man as he walked around the campfire to sit across from Cleo.

"Sorry I'm late. I was getting your new guardsmen situated in their tents. They aren't yet accustomed to the traveling camp, as you might imagine. Even after five nights."

"Not a worry." Cleo kept his stare into the fire encircled by stones. "Captain Sovano, can you pass the stew?"

Sovano handed Cleo the iron pot that he had just taken off the spit. "Here you are."

Cleo poured his bowl of iguana stew, made by the stewards who had trapped their catch during the brigade's march out of the Fifth Partition as they headed west. Cleo passed the pot around the circle of captains, pointing to Thorp to say, "Eat up. There's no telling what tomorrow morning will bring."

"Oh, I had my fill earlier with the men back there. Thank you."

"The food around these tents beats anything you had with them," Kladden stated. "Besides, you should heed your new commander's order. He's right. Who knows, this might just be your last."

Captain Thorp obliged, as anyone would when Kladden gave them a smiling suggestion. He took the pot and filled his own, wafting the steam away from his face. After a few bites, he asked, "Commandant Kladden, you're from Andar, right?"

Kladden took a sip from his steel chalice. "I am. As were the fathers of my father."

"And you were the commander of the Third Brigade for over a decade and a half, correct?"

"Yes."

Captain Sovano cut the Fifth Brigade's old commandant off before he could continue, asking, "So, tell us, then. What do you think we'll see?"

"Andar is filled with tough but honorable men. Men with backbone. Our history, in alliance with Cignus, dates back centuries. But it seems as though, today, things may have changed," Kladden replied. He ripped off a piece of sourloaf and scooped it into his stew. "It was once the fertile land that fed all our ancestors of Sacrim. We took pride in that. But now, those days are gone, thanks to those half-wits in Sazara."

From his studies with Vident Lement, Cleo knew that Kladden was right. The Sacrimian War, which began in 409 A.D., brought the forgotten Andar and Cignus to revolt against Sazara and its ally, Corlis. From Claros Sciron to Vizar Sisenno, the wielder of the Sunspear had entrenched their rule in Sazara, expanding the reach of their flourishing city to enrich themselves at the expense of their brothers and sisters to the south.

At the time, however, General Crimus of Andar stood firm against their growing rule. Though they were outnumbered nearly five to one and lost most of their warriors in battle, the general's use of subterfuge brought an end to the four-solurn war. General Crimus had snuck a company of his best warriors into Sazara, hidden under the cargo of waggoneers, and slit the throat of the Vizar in the dead of night. The Vizar's death brought an end to the war and, thus, peace to the Southern Plane, uniting it as one with four equal partitions to balance Sazara's might. The chamber had separated the once-singular, judicial and military authority of the Vizar to create Sacrim's dual-seated consol, and elected magistrates were given executive power over each partition. But as Cleo had come to learn, Sazara's might and influence had never truly diminished.

"We need the supplies and men," Cleo stated, still staring into the flames. "Kastas's head will reach Sazara soon, and there's no telling how Cayen might respond."

"Right. But what do we do if Andar doesn't comply?" Captain Ostin asked. "You heard Kastas. Even the Third Magistrate, Emeth Seldan, must have voted to confirm the Calegris."

"The Third Brigade's fort is still a few days' ride north of Andar. I don't want a fight or to lose any more men than we already have. The few hundred we lost back at the gorge were a few hundred too many," Cleo responded.

He looked at his newest captain, who sat eating across their campfire. "We welcome all the help we can get and are thankful for those who came from the Fifth. But we'll need many more if we want to find justice."

"That ploy the Calegris pulled at the gorge has escalated things," Captain Sovano stated.

"Very much so," Cleo acknowledged. "And as Kladden said, Andar has always been Cignus's ally. Their help in this fight would give us a big advantage. It's a move I hope the Calegris won't expect."

"Cleo's right," Kladden said. "The Calegris failed with their surprise. There's no telling how they'll respond now. Marching what we have straight into Sazara would be a mistake. Cignus and the Fourth Brigade will always side with Cleo and will help us when called upon. But we will need Andar's support if we're going to have a chance."

"We don't want a fight at Andar, but what happens if they do?" Captain Ostin asked.

"We'll lay siege and hoard out their incoming supplies from a distance. Or we'll sneak in to recruit anyone who would be loyal to the Guard and hopefully leave before the Third Brigade arrives," Cleo replied.

"What, are you afraid of some farm boys?" Kladden asked with a deepening chuckle.

Captain Ostin was pleased with Cleo's direct answer until Kladden had butted in. He looked around the fire's circle and took a long sip of his sour wine. "What do any of you know of the Third Brigade?"

"Nervous much, Ostin?" Captain Sovano joined in to laugh at him, along with the others. Ostin just shook his head and rolled his eyes, waiting to hear if anyone had anything practical to say.

But Cleo didn't laugh. He'd grown to respect Captain Ostin's stern disposition and the way he led the first battalion. "Galiano Salvitore is their commander. I sat by him, along with Kastas, at the Isle of Azil during the Descindation. He was friendlier than Kastas was, at least. He's older than me but still young, at least younger than the other commanders. But he seemed sharp."

"When I knew him, he was just a quiet young fella. He was only a cagerman then, right when I was leaving the Guard. His father's got wealth and connections to their magistrate, but all I've really heard is that he loves two things—wine and women," Kladden said.

"*Don't we all?*" Captain Jostell asked from his stump beside Sovano.

The men mostly laughed, their taut bellies shaking under their loosened garments. Cleo could tell that their joy was a reminiscence of a time passed, memories of women they had slept with, and the long nights of drinking with their brothers. They were memories Cleo didn't yet have and would likely never share due to his rank. The thought brought him back to picture Scarlett and her warm, freckled smile and what could have been had he been there to save her on the isle.

But again, Cleo wasn't the only one not to laugh. Off in the corner, away from their campfire, was Vident Lement, leaning against a broad acacia tree. He sat next to his own tiny, twig fire, lit with just enough light for him to see the pages of his book.

"If you'll excuse me, men," Cleo said politely. He stood up and walked between two canvas tents toward the tree. "What are you reading?"

Without looking up from his leatherbound book, the same one he had used back at the gorge, Vident Lement simply replied, "*Phicantics.*"

"That one is massive. I should thank you and that book again for saving me back at the gorge."

Vident Lement just sat silently and continued to read.

"How is it that I've never seen this one until now?"

His preceptor looked up at him, closed the cover of his book, and replied, "Same reason you've never been to the vident's library."

Cleo sat down next to him and leaned his back against the round of the tree. "You've never shown it to me."

"You aren't a vident. You'd have to take our vows if you want to view its pages. Looking at it now would do you more harm than good."

"So, it's some sort of secret?"

"One could call it that."

"A book so important you dare not show it to me. Sounds like a dangerous secret, indeed. Only, now, it makes me want to know what's inside it even more."

"You probably wouldn't find it too interesting," Vident Lement said as he rubbed the top of his balding gray head.

"Try me."

"This one book encompasses the entire doctrine of the vidents. It's one of history and nature and our philosophies—of logic, mostly."

"Logic, you say?"

"Yes, logic—the sharpening tool of reason. Before one can know what to think, one must understand how to think. And in order to understand how to think, one must ask themself why they think."

Cleo smiled. "That does sound quite boring. But what isn't is seeing you all the way out here, away from the comforts of your desk."

Vident Lement let out a long sigh and then glanced up into the moonlit sky. "It reminds me of a time back when I was your age, before I became an honorable vident."

"In Seith?" Cleo asked, trying to remember where he was from.

"Yes… That small river town, east of Cignus."

"What was that like?"

Vident Lement rubbed the frizzled chin hairs that were starting to grow between the crevice of his chin. "The coastal plains were beautiful. I came from a large family of seven, and all we had was just a tiny little hut, a day's hike away from Torrent's Sleeve. My father, brothers, and I would roam those plains and camp out under the stars to trap for food. Thinking back to it all brings me so much joy."

"Is your family still around? You've never talked about them before."

"Probably so. My parents are long gone, but that's to be expected at my age. My siblings are probably still out there…*somewhere*. But the vidents are my family now. Just as you are, too, Cleo."

Cleo's grin grew. "You don't know? You haven't spoken to them?"

"Not since I took my vidential vows, no. We live a life of solitude, away from the commotion of the Plane. We even take on a new name to leave our old life behind."

"*Wait*," Cleo said as he shuffled the dirt and grass off his palms. "Lement isn't even your real name? What is it, then? And how am I just now finding this out?"

"Oh, I couldn't tell you. Even if I wanted to, I've lived my life longer as a vident than I did as my past self."

"You're making me rethink everything I know," Cleo said with a disconcerting laugh.

"Cleo, I've been beside you since you were born. And your father and sister before that. If anyone knows me best, besides your father, it's you. By the way, I had a courier sent to Cignus to inform your mother and sister of your father's passing before I left. I felt your need may have been more urgent, so I rode here personally."

"*Thank you*. I probably should have heeded your advice back there, at the gorge. For that, I apologize. But I would have had my throat shredded if you hadn't been there."

"Duty calls us all," Vident Lement stated as he moved his book off his burnt-orange vestment and gazed back up at Cleo. "I have questions of the Plane that need answering anyway."

"In what way?"

"In a way that takes me out of Sazara," he responded with a smile. "Most won't be answered, but it is our duty as a vident to try. We've only been in Sacrim for a hundred and twenty-three solurns, so finding them might be a challenge."

Cleo thought deeply about what sort of answers the vident might not already have. From his perspective, Vident Lement had an answer for nearly everything.

"*Contributing*," his scrawny preceptor thought aloud.

Contributing... Cleo pondered. "Contributing to what?"

"This book, here," he replied, lifting it back up. Cleo inspected the engraved shape on its cover, one with inner shavings of overlapped circles that formed a flower with four petals at its center. "And to life, its nature and its order, in its history, explanations, and governing laws. From arithmetic and shapes, to species and dogmas, and even medicinal art. Phicantics is a study of it all...*of life*."

"So, what you're saying is that book is the reason why you're so smart...and that I'm still not allowed to read it." Cleo snickered.

Vident Lement just rolled his eyes and smirked. "Smart men wrote the pages of this book, and it is our duty as vidents to publish our own contributions to it. I have made only a few but hope to make many more."

"Well, if you decide to stay with me on the brigade's path, you might see more than you'd want."

Vident Lement let out a light laugh. "It seems I now have nowhere else to go. All the Plane's greatest thinkers were hermits. But even a hermit must, at times, shed its shell. The first vident, Kron Videli, was himself a traveler. Maybe one day I'll bring home a library just like he did."

"A library no one but the vidents gets to see."

"*Correct*," Vident Lement said with an elderly groan. "Knowledge should be shared, but it must remain protected to survive. The vident couldn't contribute to the Plane without it."

"If you're so worried about protecting that book, then this might not be the best journey for you," Cleo noted. "Even tomorrow, there's no telling what we will face at Andar."

"If anything, this book will be protecting me. *And you.*" Vident Lement paused to look at its leather cover once more. "Just a moon's pass ago, I never would have thought your father would be gone. And I, beside you now, traveling toward the grounds of old Scipyria."

"You and me both. Even just a half-solurn ago. Our lives have changed so quickly."

"And the Plane is changing with it. It's in the air. And not just here. The others will feel it, too."

"I'm thankful I still have you and Kladden. But I just wish my father could be here to show me the way. I've thought about him every day."

"Wherever he may be now, I'm sure he's thinking of you, too, Cleo."

"For most of my life, I held a grudge against him. And he never knew it," Cleo said, tilting his chin to look up at the night sky. "I spent far more time in Sazara with you and Kladden than I ever did with him. He was always a general first and foremost. And then he was a father before he was ever a friend. For being my blood, sometimes I felt like I barely knew him, which is why I don't like talking about him. I never have."

"*May the dead enjoy their peace*," Vident Lement said, nodding in agreement. "Your father was a man of honor and duty. And the guardsmen all loved him for it. There's good to see in that."

"*Our duty to Sacrim must always endure*," Cleo whispered under his breath, mocking an article of the cagerman's creed.

"And his duty was to be a father to many. That's an unfortunate burden you bore, Cleo, I know."

"I just wish I could go back and apologize to him for being so critical. He was the best at what he did. And whether I agreed with him or not, he always knew what was right and what needed to be done before anyone else."

"That he did," Vident Lement remarked with a smirk. "But you were right too—to turn back. There was no correct choice, Cleo. You carried out your decision with true leadership, just like your father would have.

That's what's important. It's what made your decision the right one. And in the end, Sacrim will be better for it."

As he always did, Cleo listened to the wisdom Vident Lement provided. But even with his help and assurance, Cleo still felt trapped—second-guessing what needed to be or should be done. "With everything that's happened lately, I just feel dull. As if whatever it was that used to make me sharp is now gone."

"What do you think that was, then, that made you sharp?"

Again, Cleo thought in silence, hearing only his captains jostle back by the fire. "I guess it was eagerness to impress my father. Or, of late, to impress Scarlett. And now, the only two things that really pushed me are no longer in my life. What's supposed to sharpen me now?"

Vident Lement pondered Cleo's question, turning once more to look up at the stars in the sky. "The way you acted back in the gorge and the way you led your men, you're as sharp as I've ever seen you, Cleo. *Right now*. Why do you think that is?"

"*Anger*. From trying to impress ghosts," Cleo replied.

"Why try to impress a ghost when you can impress yourself? There is plenty of you to be impressed by without anyone else's appeal. You have my trust, Cleo, for who you are and who you've always been. Not for what others think of you."

Trust, Cleo thought. "Thank you. And you have mine as well, Vident Lement," he said, turning to look at the frail man in his dirty burnt-orange drapes. "Or whatever your real name is." Cleo laughed as he stood and glanced up at the sky and its shimmering stars. "If we make it out alive tomorrow, I'll take you on a trip to see those ruins of old Scipyria that you would always talk about."

"I would like that very much. Be careful, Cleo. *Always*."

Sunrise broke the Sixth Brigade's nightly rest. The morning was spent packing up their stakes, posts, and canvas tents as they collected their belongings and readied themselves to finish their march west toward Andar. Just a few days prior, Cleo had officially led them out of the Fifth Partition, from the hot desert sand, into the Third Partition's foxtail valleys, where the fields of harvest grew in plenty.

With most of the crops grown tall to the guardsmen's hips, Cleo was forced to lead them down the dirt path frequented by Sacrim's waggoneers, who transported the Southern Plane's cargo from one partition to another. Every so often, a pack would stop along the path to try to sell whatever goods they could muster from their wagons. Most, or at least the ones that carried food, would turn empty by the time the last of the brigade marched by. Cleo ordered the wagons aft so that everyone could take part and made the waggoneers swear they wouldn't divulge his brigade's movements to anyone.

They were only half a day's march away from Andar, and the distance left would be a far easier one than any of the days prior. To his left, off in the distance, Cleo could barely see the Vyporean Range that stretched from Sacrim's southern coast all the way west, to Corlis and the Silver Sea. To Cleo, it was precisely how Vident Lement's studies had described—dark clouds sparked with the heat of lightning that sat incessantly above its seven tallest extinct volcanoes.

Cleo had read many tales about the worry the old Scipyrians had while living near the Vypores. Most were legends and stories he thought to be made up at the time—to scare the children of Sacrim from ever wandering too far south. But now, after witnessing it for the very first time, he understood their veracity.

The mixing of ash, along with the hot draft from the Vypore's tall peaks, as well as the rain from the constant storms nearby, gave this southern land the most fertile soil of any across all five partitions. For much of Sacrim's past, Andar had provided nearly all the wheat and produce for the Southern Plane. It wasn't until Sazara grew so large in its population that Andar's importance as an agricultural source was overtaken by those imports from the east, which arrived on the norks' merchant galleys. Since that day, Andar hadn't been the same.

"Wouldn't want to be caught in that," Kladden stated, riding his horse next to Cleo ahead of the brigade.

Cleo looked to his left at the storm that raged above the Vypores and then behind him once more. His guardsmen no longer waved the royal red flag of Sacrim. "No. *No, I wouldn't.* The breeze from this distance is nice enough."

"*Ah,* how I've missed it."

"I just hope Andar feels the same about you."

"I can think of a handful of women who just might," Kladden said with a laugh that gargled from his thick neck.

"That's if they still recognize that ugly, aging face of yours."

"My face isn't what I hope they'll recognize."

Cleo laughed, continuing their banter back and forth, in which they brought up everything but Eileen, Kladden's wife, who was still back in Sazara. He knew it was a difficult topic. One Kladden was accustomed to avoiding after serving his entire life in the Guard, surrounded by men who knew nothing but their brotherhood, which was shared in wine, women, and war. Of which, they bragged about them all.

Together, the two continued to lead the brigade along the loosened dirt path, up and down the hills that stretched far from the base of the Vyporean Range. They passed by heaping rows of crops in groups, separated only by plots of tall grass between the tilled soil. Kladden commented that they must be getting close, and Cleo was forced to command his men not to pick at the crops along their way.

"*Shit*," Cleo said as soon as he broke his riding gaze, just atop the hill that overlooked Andar. "*What are they doing here?*"

"Should have sent a scout ahead...*dammit*," Kladden blurted out in frustration. He quickly turned and rode back to Captain Ostin near the first battalion.

In front of the gateless city of Andar was the entirety of the Third Brigade, stretched wide in their typical formation, awaiting Cleo's arrival. There, they stood still, in heaps of bronze, with their cavalry at the forefront. The battalions at the rear were in decks—formations of one hundred— lined by ten columns and led by their second battalion's spearmen.

"*Kladden!*" Cleo shouted without turning around. "*When ready.*"

Cleo could only wait, watching alone from atop the hill as he stared down at the city from Dahlia's saddle. It was wider than he had expected but much shorter in height, at least compared to Sazara or Cignus. The buildings were connected in single and double-story rows that traced the sharp and rounded streets throughout the city like a maze. Much of it was built of beige travertine, just as Vident Lement's books had described it. At its center, Cleo could see one building stretched taller than the rest, supported by its marble pillars, which he recognized to be the Temple of Sciron's shrine in Andar.

"*READY!*" Kladden relayed back to him after a long delay.

Cleo motioned with his arm forward, the other resting on the black pearl pommel of the sword at his waist. With one kick, Dahlia began her trot, striding down the hill, followed by a narrow formation of the Sixth Brigade's cavalry. When the back row of the Sixth Brigade's swordsmen crossed over the peak of the hill, Cleo saw five horses from the Third Brigade's front line begin to ride forward.

What are they doing? Why aren't they all marching?

Cleo ordered his brigade to slow, then halted them altogether, watching as the five warhorses rode on toward him. He looked back at Kladden and asked, "Should we ride to meet them?"

Kladden nodded in response, shaking the brim of his bronze helmet up and down. He turned back to point at Captain Ostin and Captain Thorp, motioning for them to follow. Cleo sat up and panned from left to right behind his cavalry, asking for Vident Lement to come forward as well. Within a few short moments, he saw his old preceptor ride between his brigade's formation, toward the front of their line.

"Vident Lement, you're coming with us," Cleo told him. Without another word, the four of them followed Cleo down the hill.

Though the breeze was soft and quiet, the silence of their standoff was loud, screaming with tension at the unease and wonderings of what might come next. The foxtail grass was short in the valley that split the two brigades, which were still far enough away for Cleo to feel confident that they wouldn't be ambushed. Salvitore Galiano rode at the center of their five, with flags raised at each end, waving Sacrim's colors—royal red with golden crossed swords emboldened by the bronze shield of the sun.

Cleo stopped Dahlia and dismounted as soon as he could see their faces. The other four followed his lead, walking to meet them in Andar's outer valley. When they came close enough, Cleo removed his helmet and nodded confidently. "*Commander Salvitore.*"

"Commander Cleo," Sal responded, matching his stern tone. Sal's hair was long, just like it was back at the isle, and of a darker brown than Cleo's, like the bark of cedar. The Third Brigade's commander was as tall as Kladden, but not nearly as broad or muscled. Both did, however, share the traits of a man from Andar, with a broad olive forehead and lean cheekbones that creased the curve of their lips. "Where are your flags, Commander? Does the Sixth Brigade not still fly the insignia of Sacrim?"

"That's why I have come to Andar," Cleo responded. He paused and looked at each of Sal's men. "To commission my own."

Sal smirked and stared into Cleo's eyes, then turned back to his captains with his royal-red cloak flowing behind him with the breeze. One of the men off to the side, who was dressed in the same burnt-orange vestment as Vident Lement, handed Sal a scroll with its seal already broken. Cleo didn't break eye contact with Sal, not even to look back at Vident Lement to see if he recognized the man.

Sal switched his helmet from one hand to the other, took the scroll, and then unwound it. Loudly, he read, "*Commander Salvitore Galiano of the Third Brigade.*" He paused for a brief moment, looking up at Cleo to make sure he was listening. "*By the command of Sacrim's Consolar General, you are hereby ordered to Andar, city of the Third Partition, in its defense with preeminent authorization to facilitate its protection and escort of the now joint Fifth and Sixth Brigades. Upon the arrival of Commander Jep Kastas, you shall relinquish your authority to assist in his escort, the former Commander Cleo Scordisci, in all needs provided... Signed,* Consolar General Cayen Calegri."

He definitely wasn't expecting us. At least, no more than we were expecting him, Cleo thought, still staring at Sal in silence.

"Where is Commander Kastas?" Sal asked in a snobbish tone.

"I can't speak for the afterlife, but his head is currently off to Sazara," Cleo replied.

Sal waited with a puzzled look on his face, pondering how a brute of a man such as Kastas could have been killed by what he seemed to think was just a boy. He carried his gaze off into the sky, up toward the midday sun, then turned to hand his helmet to the captain behind him. "If what you say is true, then we won't be needing this." In one motion, he lifted the parchment out in front of his chest and ripped it in half.

Cleo couldn't help but release a smile of relief, enthused that he and his men wouldn't have to face another battle. The outcome this time could have gone very differently. Though they weren't all warriors like Cleo's in the Sixth, Andar's guardsmen were generational farmers and had historical ties to the bravery of old Scipyria. From a young age, they were raised to be tough and resilient. And Cleo's men, besides being outnumbered, were tired and hungry from their travels and still recovering from their battle at the gorge. They needed the rest. And now, hopefully, they would find it.

Sal, who stood nearly a head taller than Cleo, walked up to him and stuck out his hand. Cleo grabbed him by his thin wrist and shook, tightening his grip while staring him in the eyes. He then moved over to Cleo's right and shook Kladden's wrist. "It's an honor to see you again, *sir.*"

"You as well."

"Well, then." Sal sighed, walking back toward his captains in their gold cloaks. "Your men can feed and rest for three nights' time, but I can't offer you any more."

"Thank you," Cleo said with gratitude, placing his fist over his heart and then striking it to his side.

"I heard the news of your father, and I render my condolences. I hope you find the justice you seek."

"Thank you, Sal."

"But with that said, I can only allow you access to recruit from the cagermen of Andar, not anyone from my brigade."

"Understood."

"Andar and Cignus have historic ties as brothers in one. With our magistrate off in Sazara, I see no problem with this. You and your captains are welcome to stay in his palace. Vident Linus and Captain Clodis will show you the way."

Sal turned back to mount his horse. Before he could ride off, Cleo asked, "Will I see you there, in the city?"

"Who but I should be the one to share with you our wine and women?"

Cleo smiled.

Chapter 22

Sea

"Do the depths ever frighten you?"

"Not at this time of night, no," Captain Noreas said from the quarterdeck of the *Widow*. "*Helmsman*, bring us around—port tack."

"*Aye*, sir." Dane spun the spoked wheel that stood from his knees to his shoulders. Captain Noreas shouted commands down at the deck chief to shift the rigging of the sails, then returned to Dane's side.

For the past two days, the fleet had been making passage east, sailing across the North Sea, where the waves grew treacherous and the wind blew cold. The most significant threat of all, though, was what lurked in between. The span of sea they were crossing was one of the most heavily trafficked waters of the King's Navy, a frequent route that fed into Roark's River, then down into Bovere. Out of caution, Captain Noreas had ordered each mate of the *Widow* to stand an extra watch until they turned south on their final stretch to Cubby Cove.

And so, Dane took to the helm. His two-a-day watches on the deck were combined, so he had time to sleep in the evening before waking after night's mid to stand his third. For nearly a moon's pass, he had loitered on the quarterdeck, observing the officer of the watch's and helmsman's commands to learn everything they did or said. When one of the extra helm watches became open, Dane eagerly asked to fill the position.

The night prior was his first time taking orders at the ship's wheel. Dane had assumed that Captain Noreas stuck him on his own watch due to his lack of experience and the likelihood that he would need guidance. He took to his captain's commands that night with dedication and focus to impress him and prove that he belonged. Repeating each command, he kept a stern watch on the moonlit sea for any movement past the waves and stayed conscious of the wind's direction and the sails' response.

Most of all, though, Dane took to his new watch at the helm with a smile. He took pride in being the mate to steer their galleon and guide it along on their journey. And he felt a sense of honor in being beside Captain Noreas—a man Dane admired—as the helmsman to his captain's watch.

"I don't get scared of what I can't see," Captain Noreas said from behind his shoulder.

"Is that not what frightens most—the unknown that lurks below?"

"When you've been at sea for as long as I have, you learn to take what the water gives you. People have their superstitions, but most of those are useless out here."

"So, you aren't superstitious, Captain?" Dane asked, making light of the passing time.

"I'm not some fool, no. People in every corner of the Plane have their beliefs. The south has the sun and their smoke. In the east, it's some invisible ghost. The west has the moon and her sister stars in the sky. And what have we norks got? Forced to worship some cruel king and the gray hairs that fall from his ass every morning."

Dane bent a smile in agreement as he held the wheel's spoke with a single hand to keep the *Widow*'s course. "Everybody's got to have something, especially while alone out here. The sea itself can be quite mystical, don't you think?" he asked his captain.

"I don't think anyone would want what I have. With all the bodies I've sunk to the bottom, one of them will eventually come back up to haunt me," Noreas said, rolling his eyes. "Though, we norks do have some old tales and myths about the sea. And of them all, the Jaws of Myrph is my least favorite."

"I've never heard that one before."

"You must not be from Minoska."

"*Niven*," Dane proclaimed proudly.

"Never heard of it," Captain Noreas said, dismissing Dane's smile. "Minoska is full of tales that come in and out of that port, and the Jaws of Myrph is one of the oldest. It's the story of Myrph, a sea serpent that slithers along the ocean floor, one with jaws wide enough to clasp an entire ship between its teeth and a length long enough to coil itself around Marredom's main island. As Myrph grew older, it became wise. It stopped taunting men at the surface and began lurking at the bottom-most depths, coming up only to swallow sinking ships and drowning men. Where it went, storms of rain and wind followed. They even say the waves themselves are a result of its rippling slither."

"People don't actually believe that, do they?" Dane asked.

"I'm sure there are some, but I haven't yet finished. With each man devoured, the sea serpent Myrph digested them into eggs—in due time, of course. Out of these eggs hatched the beasts of the sea in their thousands, with fins and jaws of their own, to hunt man from the murky depths and to defend the sea alongside their master serpent. It wasn't until man wielded the Seatrident that Myrph was forced to recognize an equal master. With it came the power to tame the sea, and thus, dominate the serpent and its spawn."

"Drowning is already harsh enough. I don't see why they needed to make it any scarier," Dane said.

"Which is why those tales don't frighten me. I'm destined for the noose, not the depths. But myths are only myths, Dane. The real sea serpent that lives today, if you listened to the story, is that King of Marredom."

Dane thought about the myth and the power the Seatrident had in King Mordin's hands. He had never seen Marredom's old King before but knew him to be no different than the serpent Captain Noreas had spoken of. And with the Seatrident, he was, indeed, the master of the sea and King of the north, which to Dane was just as frightening as the depths themselves. "Do you think he'll want revenge for the two galleys we've sunk?"

"Not yet, at least," Captain Noreas said bluntly as he rounded the railing of the quarterdeck. "Pirating has existed for as long as those galleys have. It's why every cargo galley has its escort. But it might be a few moons before he realizes that those two ships haven't made it to their destination."

"So, that makes us pirates, then?"

"*Privateers*," Captain Noreas corrected him. From the inside pocket of his blue coat, which had ruffles of fur along its seams, he pulled out a folded piece of parchment and shook it in the air. "Officially commissioned by the Consolar Vizar of Sacrim, himself."

"*Sacrim?*"

"We were supposed to have a company of guardsmen on board each ship. And some of those women from Astria, too. They were the ones who conceived the idea of combining the sky and sea. Brilliant bunch, them.

And pleasant to the eye. But women on ships are shit luck, and we were in a hurry, so we left Corlis without them. Probably best for the mates."

"But Sacrim, sir?"

"Someone had to pay for these galleons and their crew. And, as it just so happens, that man is the father of the red-haired girl we're searching for."

Dane didn't say anything back. Instead, he looked forward and down at the deck below, at the mates who were on watch, working to rig the lines and scrub the decks or just standing around, chatting. The letter Captain Noreas had mentioned was a sharp reminder that their fleet wasn't on some noble campaign against the serpent King of Marredom. They had a purpose, one from a foreign land and some wealthy man, to do the bidding for which they were paid. With that humbling thought, Dane turned and looked out at the blackness above the sea.

Captain Noreas shouted down commands to navigate them away from the broadside waves. "If it makes you feel any better, I take orders from no man. But I will happily take their gold."

"A true nork of Minoska," Dane replied with a softer smile than before.

The night had been cold, chilled by northern winds that made his knees buckle as he stood his watch on the exposed deck. Captain Noreas took his rove below, inspecting the rigging at the masts and their cross-yards and talking to the mates who mended their sails. Dane could see him scan the sea for the other galleons of their fleet, looking for their lanterns to ensure they still followed the *Widow*'s lead. He returned to the quarterdeck and chatted with the navigator in the back corner, who held his charts up to the lantern's light. Dane could hear them whisper of knotted speed from the growing whirl of wind and discuss the date on which they expected to arrive.

"*That girl.*" Captain Noreas's boots stomped back toward the helm. "Has your friend Ruth mentioned anything more?"

"No, not that I've heard."

"I guess we can only trust that she's right."

"*Captain,*" Dane said after a long pause to look down at the main mast, where Maris was still tied at its base. "Why do you think he took her?"

Captain Noreas stopped where he stood as if he had to be cautious about what he would say. "You're standing on it."

Dane was more confused now than before. "The *Widow*?"

"King Mordin is an old man. Callous and malevolent as he may be, he isn't a fool. Corlis is a port city full of thieves and lowly scoundrels—the worst across Sacrim—with loose lips that would parrot for pay. There's no doubt in my mind that he heard whispers of the creation of this fleet…one that would bring competition to his stranglehold on the transport of goods across the Plane. But like I mentioned earlier, he shouldn't yet have proof over who to blame."

Dane released his firm grip from the wheel and pondered his captain's words.

"To better answer your question from before, he will want revenge, yes. And more than likely, it would be for what he may think is the death of his son," Captain Noreas said, nodding toward the base of the mast. "We were in a long chase with that bastard. But time is of the essence to know when and where. Our fleet was supposed to be solurns away from being ready. And where we're headed now, we'll be far out from under his nose."

"East?"

"East, yes. If Maris took that girl under his orders, then it's possible King Mordin may presume it to be us who recovered her. And if that's so, we'd be sailing south to bring her home. Not east, like we are now."

"And he'd deploy his galleys south, too, in response, right? To try to find his son?"

"Yes, that's the idea."

Dane's mind rolled with questions. "But what about our return? Wouldn't we have to bring her back this way to go south again?"

"Eventually. Crossing the North Sea again may be a challenge. Which is why those galleys being south should help our cause. And the Salic Ocean is massive. I'm sure we'll have a few run-ins, but—"

"*As long as we keep our distance*," Dane interjected, repeating his captain's prior words.

"Exactly," Captain Noreas said.

"I've been listening."

"Smart of you."

Dane just smiled at his captain's praise, keeping hold of the helm to steady the ship.

"But the path of collision we are on may be inevitable. Our fleet is a threat to that King. And they are a threat to us. Which will make it either us or them who triumphs."

"Why couldn't we both exist?"

Captain Noreas chuckled. When it faded, he took a deep breath and shook his head. "Because power is the only resource of the Plane. Dare to threaten those who hold it, and you'll face the wrath of war."

In Dane's mind, the motives began to make sense. *King Mordin would rather start a war than face a trading competition on the seas—seas he thinks he owns.* His smile vanished as his thoughts lingered on the terror that war would bring across the Plane. Shivers strung through his frigid legs as he stood still in the cold night's breeze, steering the very ship he now realized would become a target for the King of Marredom and whatever serpents lurked below.

Captain Noreas placed his bulging hand on Dane's shoulder. "I wouldn't fret too much, though. This is a mighty ship."

"But we'll need more," Dane said bluntly, turning to squint at the fleet that sailed behind them off in the moonlit distance. "Since it's likely there will be war."

Captain Noreas paused for a while, rubbing his wiry beard in thought. "They may have the numbers, but we dictate the timing." When Dane didn't respond, Captain Noreas continued, "We do have more galleons being built back in the Silver Sea. But building them takes time and labor, and then we'd have to fill the crew to sail it—none of which we can do without our pay. The fleet we have out here is only a third, or even a quarter, of what it was meant to be. The King of Marredom may soon be at war with us, but that doesn't mean our fleet has to be with him."

"*Captain*, you have his son, a prince of Marredom, tied at your mast."

Captain Noreas made light of his comment by barreling a laugh and commending Dane's astuteness. "Prince Maris is important leverage to have, to be able to trade with in the future should a bad situation arise. His life might one day secure our own."

Dane nodded in understanding, though his questions continued to swirl. "Sir, might I ask why we need to build new ships when there are already so many around us? Those cargo galleys of the King's Navy have wide enough hulls. Why not seize them for ourselves? They don't have many marines like on the war galleys, and we've already squandered one of them for their goods. We'd just need trees large and long enough for the masts and cloth for the sails. That'd be quicker than building them from nothing, right?"

Captain Noreas walked in circles around Dane at the helm, looking down at the planks of the deck in thought. "You make a good point, Dane. If, or when, war does come, we will certainly need more ships...but towing them all the way back to the Silver Sea for a refit would be a challenge. And we'd eventually need the pay to crew them."

"Ruth is from the Northwoods. She mentioned before that there's a millhouse there that processes wood from their forest. We're already headed that way, sir."

"Need I remind you again as to why we are on course that way? My mission comes first—to return that girl, Scarlett Calegri, to her father. Without his gold, we wouldn't be here."

Dane silenced himself for a long moment, then gathered the courage to respond, "Sir, those cargo galleys have chests of gold and treasure. Would that not be enough to rival whatever it is that man would pay?"

"You are still too green to understand what I said earlier about the Plane's resources," Captain Noreas responded. His brawny, intimidating smirk returned. "Power doesn't always rest with wealth. Regardless, I am a man of my word."

"Commendable, sir," Dane said, showing his captain respect.

"But your suggestions aren't lost on me. You make good sense," Captain Noreas said. "And there is quite a large shipyard at Nordheim that may be of use."

"Nordheim?"

"Third island from Marredom, to its east," Captain Noreas clarified. He walked to Dane's side and saw his face still muddled in confusion. "Dane...you make for a fine helmsman, but it would do you well to study the charts. Especially if you claim to be nork," he added with a chuckle. "I might just have Cowen put you on a few navigation understudy watches."

"I would like that."

"And I'll convene with the other captains in the morning to discuss your suggestions."

A smile curved like the moon's crescent across Dane's face, one brighter than the lantern that hung from the wheel's post in front of him. With the crashing of the waves below, he could feel his contributions helping to carry the *Widow* along in more ways than just its course through the sea. His boots were planted heavy and strong on the quarterdeck, a place where he felt he belonged.

Captain Noreas handed the watch to his navigator, then left for his cabin within the aftcastle. Dane took to the helm with pride, picturing himself in dreaming images as if he were a captain, just like Noreas. However, as Captain Noreas had mentioned, Dane knew he was still too green to dare make any commands of the mates down below. He knew them as his equals and didn't have the courage or muscle to order any of them around. But the more Dane smiled and pictured himself in fanciful images, the more he was reminded that Captain Noreas, too, had once been a simple oarsman.

His captain returned to the quarterdeck with a face that bared the look of fierce determination, as if he weren't to be bothered. He ordered the topsails to be half-hoisted and the bow to be brought southeast. Dane repeated his command and spun the spoked wheel three times over. The wooden planks below creaked as the rudder turned to move the ship away from the waves that slapped against its port side. The *Widow* turned to smooth itself with the wind, traveling along to surf with the waves in a manner much faster than before. The mate near the large lantern at the crow's nest was given a note, one long in its flashes, to pass as a message to the ships behind them.

Dane waited a while for Captain Noreas to ease himself back into his watch before he thought to resume their conversation. "Sir, might I ask how an oarsman such as yourself came to captain an entire fleet?"

"Do you ask how I came to be an oarsman or a captain?"

"*Both*—I guess," Dane stammered as he fought to keep the *Widow* on its new course.

"You might find this quite unbelievable or even amusing, but I joined the King's Navy of my own accord."

"*What*? Why would you do that?"

"I grew up in Minoska with nothing—no family or gold or even a home. My own mother left me on a doorstep when I was just a child with nothing but this," Captain Noreas said. He pulled a chain out from around his neck, which was once hidden under his garment. Attached to it was a silver leaf, just smaller than his fist. It hung by its thick stem, where tinier veins branched out. As Dane looked at it closer under the lantern's light, he noticed that only the veins themselves were there, and what looked to be a leaf was actually leafless.

"Would wearing that count as one of your superstitions?" Dane asked with a youthful smirk.

"The most *super*...yes," Captain Noreas responded, his chuckle drifting into a sigh. "I spent most of my younger days stealing to survive, and I was damn good at it. But as I sat and slept on the cold stones of those streets in Minoska, I would see those officers of the King's Navy and all those marines walking in and out of that port in their tight, black-coated uniforms and shiny silver caps. They drank for pleasure and were always fed. And they had coats to keep them warm and a place to lay their heads. In their groupings of friends, they just laughed at everyone else's misery—especially my own." Captain Noreas moved to lean over the rail in front of the helm, looking down at the deck below. "I was young and dumb. I didn't know anything about oarsmen, or what those ships did, or how they really ran. And so, when I was growing into a man, I got caught stealing bread on purpose. Back then, there were no pillars on Norkatis Street. My lashes were in the presence of the King's brother, an admiral now named Morven, where I proclaimed my desire to join his fleet."

"That's tragic," Dane thought aloud.

"The real tragedy was not knowing how good I had it on those streets. They stuck me on the admiral's war galley, a ship of true might named the *Klitan*. For seven and a half hard solurns, I had an oar in my hands."

"I spent only a moon or two as one... I couldn't imagine seven solurns."

"That's still two moons too many. When I was moved to the first bench, I knew I needed to leave. Each night, for seven or eight passes of the moon, I stayed awake to shave away at my shackles with a rock I had pocketed above deck. The cargo galley we escorted at that time did a run in Sazara, then west toward Vantham's Throat. One night, when we dropped anchor, I could see the land in all its beauty. I swapped the midnight watch with another oarsman, one too green to know any better, to scrub the outer hull...and then I was gone. I had finally broken my shackles and gone over the side, swimming as silently as I could until I hit land. I ran like I never had before until I stumbled my way into Corlis."

"That's incredible," Dane said, thinking back to the time when he had thoughts of doing the same.

"But, of course, I was right back where I had started—sleeping on the streets, having to beg for food and work."

"Seems like a far cry from becoming a captain."

"*It was*. I took to what I knew and began stealing again until a man by the name of Casari caught me. To this day, I'm still thankful he took me in and taught me to turn my skill as a thief into a profession—*their profession*. Night and day, we made our smuggling runs. From the rim of the Vypores to Vantham's Throat, we snuck it all into and out of Corlis and then Sazara, helping Casari make his fortune," Captain Noreas explained as he looked out at the sea.

"But a *captain*, sir?"

"That wasn't my only skill. As an oarsman, I listened to everything those officers and marines said on the deck of the *Klitan*. From routes to procedures to sea states and how to read the stars and their sun compasses. When Casari passed from illness, I organized my own team of smugglers…*my own family*. But I was smart, you see. I took the smuggling to the sea—the Silver Sea, to be exact. We hopped from island to island along those that scattered between the rifts of Sacrim's western coast, where no ship of the King's Navy or guardsmen from Sacrim could find us. I guess you could say that I became the reason why no cargo galleys today cross Vantham's Throat or make port in Corlis anymore, like they used to do so often."

"You didn't have ships like this, though, right?"

"No, not in the slightest. We had thirty or so smaller boats that we rowed ourselves to ambush our targets and move the goods we were being paid to transport."

"So, you were a pirate after all." Dane laughed.

"*A smuggler*," his captain corrected. "And a damn good one at that."

"When you say family, sir, do you mean actual family?"

"They are more than kin—Cowen, Markas, Simion…all of them. They have the trust of my life, and I, theirs. You seem quite interested in my past, Dane. What of your own?"

"I have a younger brother who's the reason I was forced into becoming an oarsman. And two younger sisters, and—"

"Any lady friend back home that you miss?"

"My mother, if that counts," Dane said.

His captain chuckled. "Every man at sea secretly misses his mother. It's probably good I never knew mine."

Dane knew that to be true, at least for himself. "My mother's heart was too soft for Marredom. She was a comforter, not a fighter—a gardener stuck in a place that grew nothing."

"Which is why you and I must fight, Dane. Fight to make the Plane better for people like her."

"And for my younger sisters, too. I just hope they're surviving without me." Dane stared blankly ahead. His mind was taken back to his family. He wondered where they were and how they were doing. The urge to turn the ship over and head north, back home, loomed heavy in his heart. "My mother spoke often of Marredom's past. Or, at least, the past her ancestors had lived. There were good days, once, she'd say, when every island was like its own family and their neighbors, like their own blood. They took care of one another. They would share their stores of food and sour milk during the long winters, dance around the fire they always kept warm, and tell tales of those trolls hidden in the forests."

"And that King has turned it all backward. But your mother was right—Marredom was once a lively place from the stories I've heard. Especially the dancing bit. And the trolls. *Ah*, to live in the north of old, where the beauty of the blue-eyed women, themselves, was enough to warm your shivers. At least, before they opened their mouths."

Dane laughed.

"Your friend Ruth is quite pretty, don't you think?"

He made light of his captain's question, trying his best to laugh it off as a joke. "She's strange blood, sir. And besides, Ruth can be quite pompous. I think she's only interested in those books of hers and that Cathedral. And she's way too smart for anyone. Especially for a nork like me."

"That strange blood nonsense is all bullshit, Dane. People are all different in their own way. And Ruth may be strong-willed in that regard, but her blood bleeds the same color as your own."

"Sir, you don't believe that the regions of the Plane should be kept separate?"

"The regions, sure. But the people forced to be? *No*. I don't just believe it. I lived it. I'm a nork living in Corlis. And my wife was Sacrimian. Which makes my son mixed blood."

Dane looked out at the ocean's waves in fear of saying the wrong thing. This was the most he'd heard about Captain Noreas's life, and it was coming straight from him, unlike those rumors Piney and the other mates often spread. The last thing Dane wanted was to insult the man he looked up to so highly, especially in such a rare conversation.

"We could never officially marry, for obvious reasons, but she was my wife nonetheless."

Hearing Captain Noreas talk about his past and open up, in comparison to the stern clam he usually was, was in itself a reason to view the Plane in a different light. He was a man who had lived his life to the fullest and had been successful in escaping the misery they had both known. Dane trusted every word his captain spoke and listened to any and every lesson he gave, soaking it all in like the sponge on the deck he once was.

Out in the blackness of the night, Dane pictured Ruth standing like she usually did, with her long hair dangling in threads between the open pages of her book. And how she'd talk, always to the point, as if she knew exactly what she wanted and would defend what she knew was right. He had always thought of Ruth as his friend, the gentle girl who had saved him on the Regent's beachside. The girl with a feathery voice who was pretty, yes. But one, also, who knew a life much different from his own— one of suffering.

For the first time in his life, Dane had the freedom to choose. But he had learned very quickly that determining what he liked or disliked was a difficult task. Back home, he had only known a life of toil and duty, necessary for survival: who to talk to, what to say, where to be, and when and what to eat every single day had already been decided for him. But here, on this ship, he had freedom.

Dane had never kissed a girl before and never had the luxury of thinking of women in that way. And in Niven and its surrounding towns, there weren't very many young women anyway. But the more he thought about what Captain Noreas had said, the more he realized that he probably wouldn't favor a girl from the Northern Plane, as callous and cold as they usually were. No, Captain Noreas was right. Ruth was pretty and gentle and cared for anyone and everyone around her, something Dane realized he would prefer. Like his mother, she was a gardener.

"I only tell you this because you remind me of my son. The two of you are quite close in age," Captain Noreas said after he paced around the quarterdeck, scanning the gauge for the wind. "Both of you have that same inner drive to learn from listening and watching. And the will to lead your peers by example and show them how it's done, as you have with the oarsmen—our newest mates. You may not see it, but I do. The two of you would be friends."

"I hope to have the honor of meeting him one day," Dane responded as his watch at the helm was coming to an end. His relief, a mate named Callan, had walked up to the deck and asked for Dane's leave.

"*Me too*," Captain Noreas told him.

Dane left the quarterdeck and made his way below with a smile, headed for his sleeping quarters to turn in for the night. Instead of stopping, his curiosity led him to wander one deck below. In the faint corner of the kitchen's side passageway, he saw Ruth sitting at a table in the mess with her head stuffed inside her book. For a long moment, Dane stopped and stood still, watching her as she read alone, in peace. He thought about what Captain Noreas had said and even considered going over to talk to her. But rather than test a good night's fortune, Dane just lifted a silent smile and admired her from a distance.

Maybe she isn't so strange after all.

CHAPTER 23

SKY

V anna unraveled the braids of her hair and let it flow with the wind in freedom. Like the branches of the willow tree she sat under, their tangled threads danced, and her smile grew as green as their leaves in full blossom. Unlike the broad willow tree, however, Vanna was finally without roots.

For nearly a half-moon, she had stayed near and slept within Vyllini's cave to recover. Arzak and Juni had gone back and forth from their tiny commune to bring her food and supplies while she rested and healed. During that time, Vanna explored the nearby temples and their surrounding terrain. She had taken on the task of learning the ancient aruks and their meaning, keeping her mind active by continuing to discover the true history of her people.

However, Vanna knew she couldn't stay there forever. Arzak and Juni were incredibly kind, helping her to heal and giving her the freedom to wander. But the people of the Vypores would never take her in as one of their own, and it would be impossible to live a life out there alone. Once Vanna had healed enough to walk without any support, she knew it was time to leave.

Arzak and Juni had said their goodbyes the day prior, packing her a sack for the journey and showing her the path that led to the closest city— Andar. There, they told her, was a man who could help her find work and a place to rest her head, one of the few who had stayed in contact with the remnant Scipyrian people. Occasionally, this man had supplies and food sent to them from the city to help support their lineage's survival. The man she needed to find in Andar was named Vident Linus.

Juni had gifted her a two-piece skirt and top, colored like the shell of a tree nut, which she had mentioned once belonged to her daughter.

During the rare window in which the storms had cleared, Vanna hiked for a day down the only trail that led out from the Vypores. The staggered and tall cliffs, sharp rock formations, and snaking paths made it hard for her healing leg to handle. And she did her best to avoid the crawling critters and burrows of the beasts. But Vanna powered through the day and night, determined to reach a new life with only her sack and a torch in hand.

At first light the following morning, she stopped and plopped under the shade of a willow tree to break her fast and rest. A near-endless valley of foxtail grass grew in the distance. It wound through the hilly plains, shimmering in shades of green and gold as they waved with the cloud-covered breeze. The rim of Vypores stood just behind her. Vanna glanced up in awe at its seven tallest peaks, admiring its peril from below. For as horrid and dismal as the Vypores appeared on the outside, she knew the beauty it held within.

Vanna had avoided going through her newly packed sack since the night she was stricken from the sky. But after her long hike, she had grown hungry. Vanna broke her worry and reached in to find what food Arzak and Juni had packed for her. At the very bottom, her fingers felt a cold touch—one like glass—which she grabbed and pulled out. In her hand, she held the long hilt of her telson with its blade still sheathed. Embedded at the bottom of its knob was a small stone of amethyst. In her mind, her worry worsened, realizing that if anyone were to discover her telson, it would give away her hiding intentions.

Her first instinct was to bury it, along with Zell's, under the willow tree she rested beside. Vanna wanted to leave it there, not just so that she couldn't be ousted as a Sister, but so that she could forget everything she had once used it for. Her telson was a reminder of it all, of a life Vanna had now shed. She unsheathed its blade and stared into its shimmer. In its reflection, she saw her eyes. Round and gray, they had a different gleam now than when she would stare into them in the mirror of her grot. Eyes once filled with fear and contempt now looked light and lively, like a star that had grown to outshine its constellation.

Instead of burying it, she wrapped both telsons in a rag and shoved them back into the very bottom of her sack. Vanna continued to pat around inside until she felt its tiny side pocket. Opening it, she saw a small, velvet black pouch tightened by strings woven around its top. She dumped it out onto the patches of dried grass around her. Out fell a jar and two wooden palm-size flutes. Vanna's eyes lit up with temptation.

To call Felix back? Zell's rook might come, and we could fly anywhere, she contemplated.

A small part of her even hoped that Little Wing would spring back to life from its ashes. All she needed to do was play the notes the Sisters had taught her. But deep inside, Vanna knew those hopes were futile. Little Wing was dead. And calling for Felix would only bring her right back to where she had started. Zell's rook was likely far west by now, near Mount Matron, and might be followed by the Sisters should it leave. Vanna knew it would be easy for them to hunt her down in the air. And that's if the rook would even obey her commands.

Little Wing, Vanna pondered intimately. She reached into her sack again and found the feather she had plucked back in Vyllini's temple. *You deserve to be free, like I am now.* Vanna tossed Little Wing's feather into the air and watched as it flew high into the sky with the breeze.

After a short shut of her eyes in reminiscent thought, she shoved the two flutes back into the pouch. In the same tiny pocket, she felt something a little less rigid. Again confused, she pulled out the note she had taken from Zell's pocket the night she had died—the same note that Clyus Calegri had given her during their meeting the first day they arrived in Sazara. Without hesitation, Vanna peeled open the wax seal of Sacrim's insignia and read:

Our new proposal must now move more swiftly. After autumn's end, travel to Sazara so we may join our hands and land as one. You will receive what was promised to you. CC.

Vanna read the short message over and over again, trying to make sense of its meaning. Zell was supposed to pass this note to the Grand Dame, and then, Vanna remembered, to the Queen.

Marriage? Clyus Calegri and Queen Helera?

But what Vanna had pondered on the longest was the claim to join their lands as one. For as far back as she knew, and across all the ages of history, intermarriage between the four regions of the Plane and outside of one's own kindred had always been forbidden. Vanna was taught that this mutual agreement was out of respect for one another's territory, rules, and culture. But most of all, it was for their own survival.

The people of the Plane had always clung to their heritage, holding outsiders in contempt and feuding with each other in conflicts over land, methods of rule, or even bloodlines, as Vanna had learned in Vyllini's temple. The strength of one's family, and later clan, was the strength of their existence. It was understood by all that the borders between the regions of the Plane today were firm and that any sort of assimilation was impossible.

Vanna thought long and hard about the prospect of Astria and Sacrim joining together as one. The Queen today and those of the past had always kept to themselves, hidden away within the inner district of Mount Matron. And Vanna knew the Astrians were far too reserved of a people to ever live a shared life among southerners.

"*Hmm, it would never work*," she whispered to herself, shaking her head. However, when Vanna looked down to read it again, she realized that her concern was senseless. Vanna, after all, held Clyus Calegri's message in her hands, not the Queen. And with her intervention, the chance of their hands and land joining as one might never come to fruition.

Vanna stuffed the note back into the velvet pouch alongside her flutes and picked up the tiny jar beside it. She opened it and saw the gooey resin of vilovian nectar filled within, which Arzak and Juni must have packed for her travels. Despite the distressing note Vanna had just read, a smile softened between her cheeks.

Throughout her stay, Juni and Arzak helped to apply the nectar to her wounds and re-bandage her shoulder and leg until her scars had sealed shut. But Vanna didn't smile because she now had more nectar for her wounds. She smiled because she had more to consume—more to feel its love and euphoric comfort, which had lifted her to bliss the first day she was in the temple. Vanna felt the strong urge to take more, even now, so that she could feel its embrace once more.

But Vanna knew her hike to Andar would be long, and she'd only been a day into it. She needed to keep her mind clear, to be watchful of the sky for any Sisters that might be lurking above. And when she finally reached the city, Vanna knew she needed to be sharp and remain focused. The Sisters could be undercover anywhere in Andar, and she needed to find Vident Linus. So, Vanna ate the dried meat Arzi and Juni had packed, then stuffed all her belongings back into her sack. She left the willow tree to walk through the foxtail grass, looking for the path that would lead her to her new life.

† † †

From afar, Vanna saw the gateless city of Andar erected from the surrounding hills of Sacrim's vast southern valley. She had hiked beside its fields of tilled soil for three days, laden with wheat and tall stalks of bean, ready for autumn's early harvest. There she stood, staring down at Andar under the heat of the blistering sun. Although she had enjoyed her time hiking alone, Vanna was delighted to finally see people and walk within their bustling city.

"OUT OF THE WAY, GIRL...MOVE!"

Vanna leaped off the dirt path and whipped her shoulders around just as a carriage led by two horses flung past her. Fading curses and incoherent slurs were lofted from the coachman as it sped toward Andar. Vanna watched as bushels of radish peppers and bundles of sliced chard flew out from its back. That moment had snapped her back to reality. Though she may now be free, Vanna knew that life among southerners was never going to be easy.

"Could be worse," she whispered, trying not to remind herself of the life she'd lived before. Vanna reawakened her smile and headed down the trail, picking up some of the fallen food to have as a snack and stuffing the rest in her sack to save for later.

Below, the city stood out from the ground like a maze, as if it were the largest field of all those that surrounded it. Its streets split like a labyrinth, with winding rows of rectangular buildings connected in erratic heights and varying depths. Each row of sun-weathered buildings had shallow-tiled roofs offset in their sun-orange color and assorted circular windows left open to the air. The eclectic design of Andar was more unusual than Vanna had ever seen before, and, to her, the city looked like a chaotic mess. Large, timber-built stables encircled the outermost buildings. Hundreds of horses, mules, and cattle rested under its shade, while hundreds more were left aloof to bathe in the sun, be washed, or fed by the men and boys who worked the surrounding fields.

Vanna waved to those who smiled and whistled at her as she walked by, taking her first steps onto the shale-tiled streets of Andar. The children she strolled past all shared her happy smile, and the women, who grouped into gossiping bunches, waved in polite recognition. Without a clue of where to go, Vanna wandered her way down its winding streets, gazing into the open homes and shops that were far more orderly than she had expected them to be.

The quaint aroma of roasted meat, one she had only smelled before in Sazara, floated into the street from a nearby building. Its entrance was left open, so Vanna wandered inside. The tables and chairs under the shade were half-filled by women dressed similarly to those she had seen earlier, wearing patterned tops braced by thin straps over their shoulders and long, flowing skirts that fell below their knees. With them were children who laughed and played in bright-flowing garments, exposing their sun-soaked skin.

Vanna followed the smell to reach the counter, where a man stained with oil and ash stared blankly back at her. "*Can I help you?*" he asked rudely. "We have pitted lamb…that's it."

"I'll take the lamb."

The man turned and sliced a few reddened pieces of meat off the roast over a fire and dashed it with chopped greens. He handed her the plate and said, "That'll be five coppers."

In an abrupt panic, Vanna froze. *I don't have any coins.* She rummaged through her sack, hoping that maybe Arzak or Juni had left her some, before realizing that they likely had none either. As the man began to pull the plate away, a woman from the group at the table beside her reached her hand out and dropped a few copper coins onto the counter. Vanna turned to the mature mother and said, "*Thank you.*"

"Don't thank me, thank my husband. They're his coins," the tall, tanned, and thin woman replied. Vanna took the plate of lamb and followed her away from the counter. "You don't look like you're from here."

Again, Vanna panicked. The last thing she wanted was to be noticed as an outcast and have it be revealed that she was Astrian or even a Sister. In her frantic thoughts, she smiled politely back and asked, "What gave it away?"

"Your outfit. Women around here like their fashion," the woman replied, looking her up and down.

Vanna sighed with a gasp of relief. It wasn't her skin, hair, or rounded waist that gave it away. It was something that she could change. "I'm a traveler," Vanna said. "Without the coins to afford such nice things."

"Well, then, I hope you enjoy Andar and that lamb." The mother turned and walked back to her seat at the table.

"*Wait.*" Vanna hurried over, following the nice lady to her table. "Would you happen to know where I might find a man by the name of Vident Linus?"

"No. The vidents aren't familiar to me. But I would ask around the courtyard near the temple. Or the palace. They're both near the city's center. You can't miss it."

"Thank you." Vanna walked out of the building and scarfed her lamb down under the shade of a lesser-traversed street. There, she leaned against a curving wall and watched the people of Andar pass, studying what they wore and their mannerisms in conversation. In that time alone, Vanna came to realize that everyone inside the city traveled on foot and, when needed, wheeled their own smaller wagons up and down its winding streets. In her recollection, she couldn't spot a single horse. *Must be why these streets are so clean,* she figured.

She found a trash heap to dump her remains, then continued her walk toward Andar's central courtyard. The buildings she strolled by began to crowd with growing groups of people who huddled in and around the shops that sold more items than just food. Handmade clay bowls and vases, crafted with smooth kindling, filled the shelves. Paintings, swathed in vibrant colors, hung from the walls, and rugs, threaded with bright patterns, were draped in between. Vanna looked around in a daze, stopping only to run her fingers through the thin jewelry, until she spotted what she was looking for—clothes fit for a woman of Andar.

Inside the shop, she scanned the racks hung by a string from aisle to aisle, looking for a skirt and top that would fit her size. Vanna was modest in height and in her chest, but had broader hips and stronger shoulders than most of the women she'd seen in Sacrim. One of the aisles she passed had clothes that would likely fit, but each piece had bright colors and floral patterns, making her sneer. For most of Vanna's life, the only color she'd worn was black.

But Vanna knew she needed to make concessions if she wanted to fit in. When the corner aisle was clear of people, she grabbed a peach-colored top, a robe stitched with roses, and a long, ruffled white skirt. Vanna hurried to throw both on, slipping out of the bland outfit Juni had given her. She hoped she could sneak out of the shop without paying. Stuffing the old outfit into her sack, Vanna turned back around the aisle's corner and darted for the door. But just as she had looked up, a group of men in bronze armor and spaded skirts walked in with shortswords sheathed at their waists.

Guardsmen, Vanna recognized in fright, quickly spinning away from them. *They're here for me... Is it because I've stolen? Or did that woman from the lamb shop give me away? Or maybe the Grand Dame told them to look for me...*

With slow, flat-bottomed steps, she paced back down the outer aisle, watching the group of five guardsmen as they split to have a look around the shop. Her heart began to beat heavily, the same as it had in the general's villa. One of the guardsmen finally broke their silence, shouting to another, "*Do you think Mara would like this?*"

Mara? Vanna peeked over the string hanging between the racks and saw the guardsmen holding up a strapless top. The other man shouted back, "I don't know if Mara will like it, but I sure do."

Maybe they aren't looking for me, she wondered. Like a rook hunting its prey from the sky, Vanna stalked patiently. Her eyes glanced between the spacing of clothes until she saw another guardsman walk toward their group and say, "I don't think you'd look very good in this."

Vanna used their abrupt roar of laughter to rush out of the shop as fast as she could. The farther she traveled down the streets toward the city's center, the more Sacrimian guardsmen she began to notice—far more than she had ever seen back in Sazara, most of whom looked down at her with lustful stares. Though alert, Vanna kept her cool until a winding street led her under an archway and into Andar's central courtyard.

The tiled ground was clean and encircled by arched columns rather than buildings, where children ran and played around the central pool of spring water at its center. Guardsmen in groupings of three or four paraded about, staring eagerly at the gossiping women, who seemed to always be without their husbands. *Most of the men must work out in the fields,* Vanna realized, finding an open bench.

It wasn't until an older guardsman, bald with wrinkled skin and crooked eyes, came close enough by himself that Vanna had the courage to ask, "Excuse me, *sir,* do you know where I might find a man named Vident Linus?"

"Vident *Lement?*" the guardsman asked back, almost startled that she was asking him for help.

"Linus," Vanna repeated.

"I don't know a Linus, but I know a Vident Lement. He's in that building, just there—the magistrate's palace," the ugly guardsman said, pointing toward a tall building beside the domed temple.

As soon as the man had turned to point, Vanna saw a gold cloak hanging from the back of his shoulders. She knew this needed to end quickly. "Thank you."

Vanna could feel the eyes of the off-putting captain follow her as she stood up from the bench and walked across the courtyard. And she could feel most of the other guardsmen doing the same. Vanna left under the arches and found herself along a street much wider than any of the others. The Temple of Sciron at Andar wasn't nearly as grand as the largest in Sazara, but it was still circular in its construction and had tall marble columns supporting its domed roof. At its very top, though, was the same sun-stained glass ornament shaped round like an orb.

Passing by it, Vanna strolled until she reached the palace's luxurious steps. On both engraved red oak doors hung a golden ring doorknocker in the shape of a snake, curling to eat its tail. Before she could finish her last knock, the door to her right opened. Behind it was a guardsman, one without a cloak, helmet, or weapon. And without a word, he looked at her as if he expected her to speak.

"I'm looking for—Vident Linus," Vanna stuttered.

"Who are you?" the guardsman asked sternly.

Vanna froze again, realizing that she should have thought this through more. "Vanna."

"Vanna, *who?* What is it you need of Vident Linus?"

"Vanna—*Sapharo*," she stuttered again, thinking only of Arzak and Juni's daughter. "I was sent to find him by a man named Arzak of the Vypores."

The guardsman nodded, then opened the door to let her in. But as she strode to step inside, he stopped her and grabbed her sack.

The telsons…of all things. Please…no.

The stern-faced guardsman opened her sack and looked around, then stuck his hands in and fumbled to pull out some of the greens she had picked up earlier. Vanna's heart skipped worse than her stutter, and all she could feel were the droplets of sweat beginning to form on her face. She looked around nervously, thinking only of what she would do when he pulled them out—*when they discover that I'm a Sister of the Silo from Astria.*

Doubt and misery crept under her skin. She turned away from the door, looking for any path to run, but saw only men in bronze with shields, shortswords, and spears crowding to fill the wide street. *Back to the Vypores*, she thought. *Maybe I should have called Zell's rook…maybe I still can.*

"Okay, this way," the guardsman said, handing the sack back to her.

Vanna released her gasp, hiding the calamity that came before those words. *He didn't see them.*

She followed the guardsman through a dark and bare hallway, turning right, then left, and down another hallway lit only by torches between the paintings along the wall. The guardsman opened one of the palace's many doors and commanded her to take a seat, telling her that Vident Linus would be with her shortly.

The tiny room was empty, except for the unbalanced wooden table at its center and a set of chairs tucked into its sides. A single window let in the room's only light. Vanna placed her sack next to the chair facing the door and took a seat as instructed. For a lengthy period of time, she waited. Long enough to watch the light dim as the sun slowly set in the east. Out of boredom, she brushed through her hair and reorganized her sack to make sure her telsons were still hidden.

Without a knock, the door opened. A man wearing a burnt-orange vestment that draped like a tablecloth to cover everything but his bald head and thin neck walked in. In a calm, delaying voice, the man said, "I was told you asked for me."

Vanna was taken aback by how old the man sounded, given the lack of wrinkles on his face. "Vident Linus, yes."

Vident Linus moved to sit in the chair opposite her. "*Well.*"

"I was told to find you—that you might have work for me. And a place for me to stay."

"And who was it that told you this?"

"Arzak and Juni. From the Vypores," she answered with confidence.

"The Vypores, *huh?* What did you say your name was, again?"

"Vanna Sapharo."

Vident Linus nodded gently, then looked out of the window above her head. "It's been quite some time since I've been in contact with the dwindling folk that live out that way. To be honest, I thought they'd be dead by now. Fascinating people, though, they seemed. But I never managed to make that journey, personally. You see, my work has kept me busy…and, to be quite frank, the stories I hear about that place, *which* I'm sure you are well aware of, haven't pulled at me hard enough to make me want to risk my life." He stared piercingly into Vanna's eyes as if he meant to question her by them alone. "If not the storms, then that jagged trail. And if not the trail, then the dozen or so venomous creatures that call the Vypores home. And if not any of those, then it'd surely be the folk. I apologize for any disrespect or *rashness*, but from what I've heard, they are quite fond of their ancient practices. Isn't that so?"

Practices? Does he mean sacrifices?

It was as if he could see through her lies. All Vanna could do was stare back blankly into his eyes. As a Child, Vanna had endured intensive days of torture, prevailing through the many interrogations conducted by the Sisters for training. But with each of those painful days, Vanna had an understanding that it was all spurious—that by knowing the ends, she could withstand the means. Only now, without the guidance of the Sisters, Vanna no longer knew what end awaited her.

"*We are,*" she answered with confidence to hide her naivety.

"You don't strike me as someone who would partake in that sort of thing. You seem *far* too gentle. But, in any case, I think I may be of help to you. As the seasons change, so too does luck. We currently have a few distinguished guests here at the palace, and I know just the thing you can help us with. *Follow me.*"

Vanna grabbed her sack and went with him down the hall. At its end was an enclosed staircase behind a wall, where they walked up its four flights. They circled another hallway around the outskirts of the palace, and then Vident Linus opened a smaller door that led toward the center.

They entered a larger room than the one she was held in, filled with shelves on both ends and a table with glasses and a tray in the middle. "*Here.* You can leave your bag in there," he told her, opening an empty shelf. He showed her a few more, above and around it, then added, "These are the assortments of wine, glasses, and trays, which you can fill. The only men you are to serve are the guests dressed like me in our vestments of orange. There are three of them sitting at a table in the far-left corner of the grand room, with chairs along the wall's edge for you to sit in while you wait on them. All you need to do is pour them some wine when their glasses run dry. *Can you do that?*"

"*Yes,*" Vanna answered. *I'm an expert at that, actually.*

"*Good.* I'll be there to join them later in the evening. *Remember*, just the men in orange. If anyone else gives you trouble, come straight to me."

"Understood."

Vident Linus trudged his thin body back out the door. As soon as he had left, Vanna searched the rest of the drawers and found nothing but more bottles of wine and shelves filled with other bags. She grabbed the chalices and carried the tray with a few bottles on it out through the opposite door.

The dimly lit room was three stories tall and left open to the palace's far end. Various levels of square floors were interconnected by steps, going up and down, then up or down some more. Four inner columns at each corner mimicked those on the outside, which held up the palace's fanciful glass ceiling. Each square was carpeted in red velvet and lined with gold lace—some featuring multiple marble tables, while others featured couches with large palm leaves decorated at their corners. Through the dim torchlight smothered by clouds of smoke, Vanna saw the table in the back left corner of the room.

As she stepped out with the tray in her hands, the smell of incense and sour wine filled the air, and she heard nothing but the dangling clank of gold that lofted between the laughs of burly guardsmen. The room was filled with filth, as far as she could tell. Vanna tried her best not to look at the many squares with couches as she walked past. From the corner of her eye, she could tell they were crammed with guardsmen who had bare-skinned women draped across their laps. And all the women she saw had the most perfect of tanned bodies and wore only thin chains of golden links at their waists, ears, and necks, which dangled like chimes in the wind as they walked from square to square and from couch to couch. Most, she realized, were there to dance, while others carried trays similar to her own.

Vanna ignored the shouts for her to join them and carried her tray straight to the tiny table in the back left corner. There, a balding man sat alongside two much younger men. All three of them dressed in orange robes and faced the wall, turned away from the indecency. "*Wine?*"

"Yes, please," the older man said kindly. To Vanna, he didn't sound as old as Vident Linus, though he certainly looked it. His knuckled chin and high cheekbones were wrinkly but strong compared to the two younger men at the table, who shared round faces and the same full set of bronze hair. Vanna poured them each a glass, then looked for the nearest chair to sit.

As she sat facing the room, Vanna witnessed the filth that filled it, which she found to be disgusting and demoralizing. In the west, Astrian women led their households and would never disgrace or degrade themselves by dancing naked for men, the way southern women did here. But Vanna knew she was a far cry from the Western Plane. Her only other option was to stare at the ceiling and occasionally glance over to the table where the men in orange sat. She was glad Vident Linus had her serve these men rather than the guardsmen huddled between the squares of smoke and seduction, as she would most assuredly have left.

Vanna peeked again at the table and saw the men talking. She sat close enough to hear what they were saying. "What do you think he will do?" one of the younger men asked.

The older one responded, "What can he do? He's cast his stones already with what he did at the gorge. But in all honesty, it was a better outcome than what we could have hoped for."

"*Sir*, I know as a chief vident you aren't allowed to opine, but what do you think will happen to Sacrim? Everything seems to be in chaos."

The older man turned to look across the room at the guardsmen who indulged themselves in wine and women, then looked back at the round table, down at his drink. "*Somel*," he said, the sacred scipyrian word for war.

Vanna's body shivered as she turned back slowly, pretending to look on at the guardsmen's filth. The older chief vident continued to speak in sacred scipyrian, with words that were unintelligible under the din of shouting men and the clanking chains of the dancing women. Vanna listened intently, hearing only the last words of his sentence: "*Bloody it will be, but worth it if the temple falls. It's about time someone took a bite at that painted apple. Nice and red on the outside, only to hide its rotted core.*"

She didn't turn to look at them again but felt the two younger men's silence as a response itself. The one closest to her broke through the background noise, still speaking in sacred scipyrian, to ask, "*And what of the boy?*"

"*He's our only hope. The Sunspear dictates our future, as well as his own. Sacrim needs it in his hands.*"

One of the bronze-haired men turned to look at Vanna, then motioned her over for more wine. Vanna walked toward them with her tray and began to refill their glasses. As she did so, they continued to talk in what they thought was a language hidden from her, and likely from everyone else. The younger one to her left commented, "*This poor girl. How did she find herself here?*"

The one on the opposite end added, "*She's far too pretty to be dancing naked like the rest of them.*"

"*I certainly agree.*"

Without thinking, Vanna responded in sacred scipyrian to say, "*Thank you.*"

The younger man instantly flinched and knocked over his wine. To her right, the older man grabbed her wrist and asked in the common roalish tongue, "*Excuse me*, where did you learn to speak sacred scipyrian?"

Vanna hesitated, then tried to move to find a rag to clean up the man's mess. "I—learned it in Vypores—where I grew up," she stuttered to lie.

The old vident let go of her wrist and looked up at her in confusion. "People still live there? I had heard that was only a myth."

"It's no myth, sir."

"Exotic, yes. Those Scipyrians fled to the Vypores more than seven hundred solurns ago. Any people who can survive there for that long must be a special breed."

"Yes," Vanna said, scanning the other two vidents, who looked everywhere but at her, clearly embarrassed by what they had said.

The older one remained still. "You didn't hear anything earlier, correct?"

Vanna nodded with the bottle of wine still in her hand. "Correct," she lied again.

"Good," the older vident said. "Well, I, like most of the vidents, am fascinated by your people's history and culture. And I would love to learn more. As a matter of fact, I happen to be traveling to the ruins of old Scipyria, near the outskirts of the city, on the morrow. Maybe you should join us. I would be fascinated to hear your people's stories from the source."

"I'm not sure if I'd be of much help."

"*Oh*, there's no need for your help. I only wish to inquire. I have endless questions to ask, and I'm sure you have plenty of answers to give. *Here*." The chief vident stood up from the table. He was taller than she had expected him to be, but old and oily, nonetheless. "Come with me. I'll introduce you to the man who'll be taking us."

Vanna didn't want to go, but he insisted. He walked slowly across the grand room, turning only to introduce himself, saying, "I'm Vident Lement, by the way."

"Vanna... *Sapharo*."

"What a beautiful name." Vident Lement turned the corner toward one of the central squares, where a long couch sat in the middle, cushioned by red velvet to match the carpet below. Vanna walked up the steps behind Vident Lement, who struggled to ensure that he didn't look at or touch any of the dancing women who surrounded them. She wanted to laugh at his reactions as he sneered and swatted them away. Only, it seemed as if he were more scared of them than disgusted like she was. "Vanna, here we are."

Reluctantly, Vanna followed him closer to the couch.

Vident Lement stepped to the side and turned her way, lifting his palm toward a young man sitting in the middle. "I'd like you to meet Cleo Scordisci, who will be taking us to the ruins on the morrow." The young man had copper-colored hair and a chiseled jaw, which broke into a broad smile at her sight. On his lap was the prettiest woman of them all, with bronze skin and the largest of bare chests, holding his chalice of wine in her hand.

Disgusting, Vanna thought. *Painted apples, everywhere.*

Cleo swung himself up from the couch when Vanna's scowl became noticeable, brushing the woman off his lap and disregarding the chalice she tried to hand him. His green eyes continued to gaze upon her own with an unwavering attachment. He stretched out his hand. In a dramatically deep tone, he said, "*I'm Cleo*. Nice to meet you."

Out of disgust, Vanna withheld her hand from touching his own. Instead, she simply sneered, "*Vanna*. Pleasure."

CHAPTER 24

STONE

The *Widow*'s hull creaked in bending hisses as waves from the North Sea barreled into its broadside. Ruth sat awake in her tiny cupboard, swaying from side to side in her hammock as she rocked with the ship's roll. She'd been on board long enough to learn that most weather at sea would pass if you just gave it patience. But for Ruth, patience was a virtue beginning to become stretched thin.

Alone in her cupboard room, she dangled with her thoughts, pondering what life was like outside of this floating wooden box. Most of her free time at sea was occupied by either reading or praying. And quite often, during both, she would catch her mind dwelling on where her twin brother, Roth, might be. Anytime her mind lingered on the thought too long, she would catch herself grinning, wondering how Roth could possibly be getting by without her. For as much as the two annoyed each other, she missed her twin brother and prayed, more than anything, that he'd be safe back in Tergona when she finally arrived home.

Ruth's parents, Edmon and Roseanna, too, dwelt heavily in her thoughts. Ruth had no way to contact her parents and knew they must be worried. She could picture her mother pacing back and forth on their porch, contemplating whether they should leave Tergona to search for the two of them or not. And by now, they would likely have heard what Roth had done. The more Ruth pondered, though, the more she knew that all she could do was pray. Their lives, just like her own, were in the hands of the Divine One.

In her lap, under the light of the lone candle, was the one thing Ruth had to keep her sane—her book, *Emanations*. It was the middle volume of three in the Covenant of the Divine Tomes. The others, being *Inception* and *Procession*, together comprised one of the Three Monuments. In its words and in its story, Ruth found a fragment of home. Reading was a refuge that took her back to Tergona, where, in her mind, she could return to her rocking chair and gaze out of the lone window in the nook of her room. Or to the sceptory in Prestown, where she would read with those of the Sacred College and help around their grounds, to clean and cook. And if it wasn't a book in her hand, it was a brush and a tiny tin of paint. Ruth knew her boredom and regret came because she hadn't brought more of either with her when they first departed for Bovere.

If only I'd known then how much my life would change, she thought, staring at the black leather-bound cover. Her life was now an emanation of an adventure itself. Turn after unexpected turn, it had been altered due to the success and ineptitude of her twin brother. Not once did she imagine that that boy from the Northwoods would become the Plane's champion and bring her to dine with the royal families. And not once did she imagine that she'd be trapped on this floating warship of an island, a fugitive from his crime, surrounded by these foreign men and their grimy work.

Ruth did, however, learn to trust the creaking hull of the *Widow.* Enough to feel comfortable that it and Captain Noreas were capable of guiding her safely home. Their fleet had just a few run-ins with those galleys of the norks' navy, which, to Ruth's satisfaction, brought the arrival of new mates for their fleet. The oarsmen Captain Noreas had freed gave her purpose on board, in helping to care for and comfort those who needed it most. Nearly all the newest mates had arrived in the worst of conditions, which inspired Ruth to make sure that all were cleaned and fed, had their bandages wrapped, and were rested. But after just a few days, those same oarsmen had been put to work with the other mates on deck to rig the sails, clean, and cook. And all were given sabers that they strapped to their sides with pride.

And so, Ruth found herself right back where she had been, helping out in the mess and the kitchens where she could and walking the main deck when the day's work had calmed. All of which had become quite boring and routine. Though the mates now took to her kindness, each day was a repeat of the one past—the same as the one before. After her third read of the massive volume, Ruth found herself needing a change— *something different.*

The morning's mess had the kitchens at full arms to prepare the mates' meal for their change of watch. Ruth readied herself in her cabin, then left to find Piney and ask what it was they needed her to do. Every seat at every table was filled with mates, young and old, who chowed on their fish stew and morning ration of sliced biscuits. At the corner window of the side passageway, Ruth waited for Piney to look up and notice her prying eyes.

"How's the morning treating you?" she asked as soon as he walked over.

"Could be better." Piney threw his stain-splattered rag over his uneven shoulder. "Running low on the usual. The mates just yap and yap and expect me and the boys to cook up something new…like I'm supposed to be some sort of sorcerer that can pull a rabbit to roast out of my magic ass."

Ruth laughed like she usually did when the two of them talked. "If there is a rabbit on the menu tomorrow, I, for one, won't be eating it."

"Speaking of which, you could use some food, child…no matter whose ass it came out of. Look at you." Piney grabbed the back of her arm, just above her elbow, and gave it a solid shake. "You get any thinner and they're gonna put an oar in your hand and send you below deck."

With less of a laugh than before, Ruth blushed, then glanced out at the mess to avoid her embarrassment. But Piney was right. She rarely ate on board, and when she did, she risked the chance that it'd be scoffed back up at the most untimely of occasions. The sea and its conditions, especially in the north, were not her friend.

"Do me a favor, will ya. Here's the key. Go down to the stores and grab that bucket of brined bird. It's supposed to be saved for the captain, but I don't think he'll notice if one is missing."

"Oh, Piney…you don't have to do that. I'll just have a biscuit, like the rest of the mates."

"Well, if you don't eat it, I will. Difference is, if they catch me bringing that bird up from the stores, they might tie me to the mast like they did that prince fella." Ruth giggled only a little and took the key from Piney at his pestering demand, turning to walk back down the passageway.

But Piney's comment had festered in her mind. The more she thought about the nork King's son being tied to the mast, the more she realized just how terrible that punishment truly was. He was given food and time for the bucket and was even tied up at night while seated, so his legs could rest. But the man had become bare to his bones, more so even than the oarsmen they had saved, and was gagged all alone, constrained with nothing but the wind of the deck for nearly a moon's pass.

To Ruth, Captain Noreas was a principled man. He was a captain who listened to the advice of those under him and could make compromises with his decisions. He was strict but understanding and always held true to his maxims in the fairest of ways. But, to Ruth, his punishment for Maris was almost too extreme. For someone like Captain Noreas to torture him the way he had been, Ruth realized that those officers of the King's Navy must be truly evil.

Ruth made her way with the key for the storeroom back down the mess deck's side passageway. But before she could reach the aft stairs, she heard a rumbling sound break the air—one much worse than the creaking of the hull or the whirling of the wind. Stomps began to plunder and bend the planks above as commands erupted in shouting yells from the quarterdeck. Ruth recognized the sounds as those of an imminent storm, but one not of weather.

"*TO QUARTERS! MEN, AT YOUR STATIONS!*" one of the mates relayed down the stairway toward the mess.

Mates by the multitude rushed in a line down the same passageway she had come from, jostling her out of the way to skip their boots up to the main deck. There, Ruth stood with the key for the stores in her hand, watching them hurry past her to get to their rigging stations. For a moment's pause, Ruth debated what she should do.

Part of her knew that what she had always done was right and safe. She should just go down below and grab what Piney had asked her to. And then she should just stay where she belonged, simmering away from the danger in the mess while the mates above deck faced down whatever galleys they must have spotted at sea. But the more Ruth thought, the more she recognized that this was an opportunity. And inside, her instincts were telling her that this moment could bring her something different— an excitement away from the drudgery of life on board. Ruth felt compelled to see firsthand how evil those officers were and why Captain Noreas had treated Maris the way he did.

And as long as she was on board, she was a mate too.

Ruth trickled her way aft into her tiny cabin. She placed the key in her sack and curled her long hair into a knotted bun, tied tightly at the back. With her saber, she cut her plaid skirt so that it frayed at her knees and loosened the string that wrapped around the top collar of her undergarment. Around her waist, she tightened the buckle of her sheathed saber, which she hadn't worn since Captain Noreas had handed it to her back in his captain's quarters. Ruth stared long into her mirror to gain a wink of confidence, then stomped her way up to the main deck.

She found it littered with curling lines and bolts being carried forward and aft, two men at a time. Most of the mates rushed around in frantic chaos, like birds scattering at the breaking of a branch, following whatever commands were shouted left and right of the main mast. Ruth searched under the cloudless sky as best she could but saw only the crashing of white-capped waves far out in the distance.

"What are you doing up here?" Ludwyn asked as soon as he spotted her. "And why do you have that saber at your waist?"

"*What's going on?*"

"You tell me," Ludwyn said back, looking her up and down. "The lookout spotted four nork galleys."

"*BOWMEN, MAN YOUR BALLISTAS!*" Captain Noreas commanded from the railing of the quarterdeck just above them. "*WE FIRE AT THE WAR GALLEYS ONLY!*"

Ruth followed Ludwyn to the starboard railing and looked in the direction the forward ballista moved to point. Just two tiny specks, as far out as she could see, sat above the breaking waves. "We aren't nearly close enough," she stated.

"They're running away," one of the mates noted.

Ruth glanced up at the sails and saw them flapping wildly like the wings of an injured bird from each corner of the cross-yards. "But we don't have the wind." At the base of the central mast was Dane, winding his dirty elbows back and forth to lead two of the newer mates in tightening their line.

"I'm going to help," Ludwyn told her.

"*Helmsman, bring us a quarter to starboard,*" Captain Noreas shouted above the deck's clamor. "*Cowen, starboard tack!*"

Near the side railing where Ruth stood, several mates rushed to loosen the lines, heaving to spin the cross-yards around. As the *Widow* turned, Ruth spotted the two other galleys trailing far behind the pair from earlier. *The war galleys are leaving the cargo galleys behind,* she realized.

"*Prepare the boats!*"

The bow of the *Widow* and the fleet behind them were now moving in line with the wind to intercept the space left between the two pairs of galleys. Ruth scampered out of the way as the mates all worked to release and lift the two small boats from their central cradles.

"What are you doing up here, *girl?*" a deep voice asked, startling her from behind. Walking down the steps onto the main deck was Captain Noreas in his black boots and blue coat. "And what is that you have on?"

"*My saber.*"

The captain barreled a deep laugh, rolling his eyes and nodding at the mates beside him. "And why would you be needing that?"

"Because I'm coming."

"*Coming where?*"

"On one of those boats."

Before Ruth could even finish, Cowen and the rest of the mates all burst out into mocking fits of laughter.

"All of that holier-than-thou nonsense you talk about the Divine Gates, yet here you are… What's changed, *darling?*" Ruth lifted the handle of her saber out from the sheath at her waist, which made Noreas laugh even harder. "Now you want to join us killers, is that right?"

"I'm wearing it for my own protection."

"Maybe giving you that thing wasn't such a good idea after all," Captain Noreas said as he wandered to check the rigging of one of the small boats being lifted by the boom. "You'll do more harm than good swinging that thing around."

Ruth's face flushed red, and her broad forehead creased with anger. She followed the captain, sticking to his side. "I'm a mate just like the rest of the men—*I'm coming.* I need to see it. Those oarsmen…I want to help them."

"*BOARDING PARTY…PREPARE TO LOWER!*" he commanded the mates. They used the long boom to lift the boat and swivel it out over the side. "Fine. Have it your way. Just don't get in mine. *Cowen,* you have the ship."

"*Aye,* sir." Cowen stared into Ruth's eyes with a gaze of disdain.

Something different indeed, Ruth thought. An uneven smirk lifted across her face as she stared back at him.

The mates worked to lower each of the boats into the rolling sea and began to climb down the knotted-rope ladder over the ship's side. Captain

Noreas scanned the horizon with his spyglass to ensure the other two war galleys were far gone from the two that their fleet was approaching. "Not you, *Lud*," he turned back from the railing to say. "You're switching places with your friend here."

"*But*—sir," Ludwyn struggled to utter. His eyes widened, and his hands reached to scrum the tangling hairs of his bushy beard. Ruth could tell exactly what he was thinking—that he needed to be there if she was there, to protect her like he had promised to Roth.

"That's an order. You're staying with Cowen and the other mates to man the *Widow*. You're someone she might be more useful with a saber than, after all."

Ludwyn drifted away from the boarding group with a look of embarrassment. Ruth followed after him. "I'm sorry, Lud."

"Why are you doing this? You don't need to go," he tried to plead, his shoulders slumped.

"I need to see it."

"No, you don't." Ruth watched Ludwyn's eyes spin away, as if he knew any effort to convince her otherwise would be futile. He let out a long sigh, refusing to look her way. "Just promise me you'll be safe. Roth and your parents would kill me if anything happened to you."

"I know. And I will," Ruth told him. When his gaze finally shifted back to her, she could tell he wanted to say so much more. Or do so much more.

But before he could, Ruth left him to rejoin the boarding party. With shaking hands, she lowered herself down the side of the *Widow*'s hull, doing her best to keep her shredded skirt from flapping up with the breeze. The tiny boat rolled from side to side when she entered. Her saber's sheath clanked against the other mates and their oars as she made her way to the bench where Ludwyn last sat, right beside Dane. Captain Noreas pushed their boat off from the *Widow*'s hull, and the mates soon let go of the lines that kept them still. Dane handed her an oar, then turned his narrow chin to point in any direction but her own. Ruth found it unsettling that he seemed just as nervous as she did. For as long as she'd known Dane, he was always confident in himself and his abilities and kept a cool demeanor regardless of the situation. But in seeing him like this, unable to look her in the eyes, Ruth could feel that something was different.

To both sides came the small boats from the other four galleons of the fleet—ten in all, bearing straight toward the two slow-moving cargo galleys. Sitting to her left, Dane continued to stare forward, pushing his long, pale arms faster the closer they came to the galley's side. Its oars stuck out like the needles of a plump pincushion, moving ever so slightly in a maze of turns. Ruth's choice was no longer a thought or a whimsical decision but had become a reality—one that grew more vivid the larger the cargo galley loomed ahead.

Out of regret, Ruth began to question herself, asking why she'd even come. This wasn't her. That morning, on Roverra's beach, also wasn't her. She was a homebody like her parents, a faithful servant of the Divine One, and a woman of peace. But there she was, willfully rowing her way toward an oncoming battle in the middle of the North Sea.

She thought about asking Captain Noreas to turn back, to crumble that confidence she once had while she was alone in her tiny cupboard cabin. She could even swim back. It would be humiliating to reveal that self to the other mates, but Ruth knew she was no warrior and no breaker of shackles. No, she'd always been a comforter, and that was where she was the most comfortable. But instead of giving in to her regret, Ruth sat in solace and whispered a prayer of protection to the Divine One.

As their tiny boat drifted closer, Dane finally turned her way and said, "*You're staying.*"

"*What?*"

"I'm not letting you on that galley," he said above the sloshing waves. "We don't have the fog to hide us this time. It might get ugly."

Ruth didn't know what to say. She wanted to thank him, but at the same time, she didn't want to divulge her doubts. Instead, within her thoughts, she thanked the Divine One and nodded in agreement, swallowing whatever pride she thought she once had.

"They're just cargo galleys, but they'll still have a few officers on board. They will fight us at the railings and on their decks. We'll outnumber their two ships, but you aren't going up. At least not until the fighting has cleared. It's too dangerous."

She looked into Dane's icy eyes with a silent thanks. His face soured to sternness with a look she'd never seen from him before. Dane, himself, appeared dangerous, as if he were fighting for something he couldn't lose.

"I'll give you the signal when the deck's clear."

Their small boat, along with five of the others, slowed its way to the cargo galley on the right. It was a blocky vessel with wide lines that dipped into the swell of the sea like a bulging belly. Captain Noreas broke the silence by commanding the mates to throw their hooks. He led their charge, scaling the side of the hull with his saber in hand, weaving in and around the oars that began to tuck themselves inside.

Ruth's hands no longer shook but were now soaked from finger to palm in a pulsating sweat. Dane joined the mates after forcing the others not to question her staying. One by one, their boots stormed onto the main deck of the cargo galley. Between the break of the wooden planks and the cloudless sky, she heard men shout with anger, filling the air with the clashes of steel and blood drawn. *The sounds of battle,* Ruth knew.

In the tiny boat, she waited alone, rocking from side to side with every thump of her heart. Ruth closed her eyes and repeated her prayer over and over again, wanting nothing more than to drown out the death scouring above. "*May the Divine One protect the mates of the Widow. May those suffering find peace…and your justice. May your sagacious spirit engulf these men and cleanse them of their ignorance. Please, be with them. Please, be with me.*"

"*Ruth!*" Dane broke her endless prayer to shout below. "It's clear."

Up the side of the galley, she climbed, scaling around the oared portholes by the fraying twine of line that she grasped tightly. When Dane helped her over the railing, she saw what she dreaded the most. Puddles of trickling blood stained the sand-swashed deck that was scattered wayward with silver caps and loose sabers. Toward the galley's center, a mound of dead bodies in a blur of black and gray began to form a pile. With another thankful prayer, Ruth was glad to see Dane alive and less bloody than most. She followed him aft, watching as the mates tied up those who'd surrendered. The few officers still alive were gagged like Maris to await Captain Noreas's trial.

"*We lost ten of our own,*" Dane whispered back to her.

"I will pray for them."

"You might want to save those prayers until we go down below."

Ruth swallowed the dry air in her throat and timidly waited for Dane, who wandered off toward the grouping of mates huddled near Captain Noreas. In shouting commands, he ordered that the two cargo galleys be nested beside one another and the plundered cargo below be brought up to the main decks. Dane walked over to a small chest and returned with Caji and a pair of long iron shears. "Are you ready?"

No, she thought to herself, but nodded anyway, following the two of them toward the aftcastle. With his saber in hand, Dane led them through a door down below deck, where Ruth saw the mates of the *Widow* and the other galleons gleefully carrying chests up from the cargo hold. With smiles and cheerful laughter, they wore their treasured jewelry, donned their newfound clothes, ate whatever food they could find stuffed in the galley's burlap sacks, and drank from its barrels.

Ruth shifted to cover her nose as soon as Dane opened the lower door of the stairwell that led to the deck below. The smell of skin-soaked feces and rancid puke wafted throughout the dense air like a raging kettle soaking its steam into the grains of the galley's wood. She lifted the collar of her garment over her nose and continued down.

Dane stopped before she could see what lay ahead. "*Oarsmen of the galley, we come in peace,*" he announced, sheathing his saber. "*I was once an oarsman just like all of you. We come to free you from your shackles… So, please, do not attack us. We have food and rest for each of you. And a life worth living.*" In a show of support, Dane lifted his left arm and curled the sleeve of his garment to show the branding of crossed oars on the inside of his forearm. "*See…*"

Ruth entered behind him cautiously, lowering the squeeze around her nose to free her hands. Whether they were for defense, she couldn't yet tell. On the benches split down the middle of the aisle, she saw the faces of men, both young and old, staring at her with a glimmer of hope in their eyes. Each one, drenched in sweat and starved bare to their bones, looked at her as if she were some savior spirit sent from the Divine Gates.

She may as well have been.

Their stench alone, though, was enough to make her puke. She could tell that these oarsmen hadn't showered in many solurns or eaten a real meal in many moons. Dane and Caji began to snip them from their shackles, while Ruth stood by the stairs. She and two other mates helped wave the decrepit oarsmen along, funneling them up to the main deck. Most who passed thanked her with grating smiles and comments of gratitude. Others looked at her for the woman she was, with lustful eyes, as if they'd never seen one before, making her lay a resting hand of claim on her saber's handle.

When Dane had finally made it to the last row, and Caji and the other mates went back above deck, Ruth gained enough confidence to walk down the central aisle and meet him. The benches on both sides were scraped raw like the wreckage she'd seen wash ashore on Roverra's beach, darkened by the stains of things she'd rather not imagine. "So…this is what we're fighting."

"This is what I'm fighting, yes," Dane replied as he snipped the ankle shackles off the last oarsman. "But our fight isn't everyone's."

Ruth followed Dane's chin as he looked up at the decks above. "This is worse than I imagined. I don't know how you survived it… It's torture. They all looked so beaten. How can those officers do this to *people*?"

"We *were* beaten." Dane turned his back to her and lifted the bottom tail of his white garment to his shoulders. Red lines of healed lashes scoured his back, sticking out of his pale skin like a range of mountains traced onto a map.

Ruth disregarded the unease she had earlier and moved closer to him. Gripped by sadness, she ran her fingers along the imprint of his lash marks. Her eyes grew blurred, watering with a vivid image of what Dane and all the other oarsmen had suffered. "*This is so much worse than I could have imagined.*"

Dane lowered his shirt and turned to stare into her eyes. "All because I didn't want my family to starve."

"How could anyone do this to another person? It's cruel and evil."

"It's greed, is what it is. To the King and those officers, we're just cattle—a means of labor for their use."

"We need to change this—all of this," Ruth stuttered, spinning to scan the oar deck. Her eyes jumped from bench to bloodied bench. Though they were empty, their stains remained.

"*I will,*" Dane said sternly. His cold eyes sharpened with a look of determined confidence. He took a step forward and reached out to grab her hand. Dane lifted it, rubbing his hardened fingers against her own, and leaned in.

But before Dane could come any closer, a storm of stomping boots had erupted on the deck above, shuffling their way down the stairs to break the two of them apart.

"*ON DECK…EVERYONE ON THE MAIN DECK!*" Flyde bade, skipping down to enter the oar deck. "*Those two war galleys are back, and they're headed straight for us!*"

CHAPTER 25

SUN

For the first time in a moon's pass, Cleo shaved the peach fuzz that sprouted across his face. *Like weeds,* he thought of them as he dabbed his sharpened blade into the bowl of water resting below his washroom's mirror. With each fine slice, splotchy patches of his thin copper hairs fell onto the tiled floor beside his feet.

Sacrim's Guard held a longstanding rule that its guardsmen should be kept clean-shaven, among many others, so that they maintain a uniform appearance. From his earliest days as a cagerman, Cleo was taught the importance of conformity, which was exemplified by each's outward appearance. *Tight hair, smooth face, and a sharp sword,* as the captains would say—they needed to dress as one to act as one if they wanted to fight as one.

Only, the Guard was no longer one. It was now split and shaven into frays like his hair that sprawled across the floor. After the Calegris had turned the Fifth Brigade against him back in the Sineaqe Gorge, Cleo thought very little of the Guard and its rules or uniformity—rules his father once lived by and instilled in him every day, some of which he created. But now, with his father gone, Cleo felt no qualms about casting them aside. In his brigade's travels and stay in Andar, he commanded that his captains and officers only enforce those rules that would keep their guardsmen satisfied and loyal to their cause. Which, of course, meant beards for every man and extended rations to fill their lustful appetite.

Cleo, though, never really liked the look of his patchy face. His hair grew long but thin, in splotches near the top of his cheeks rather than under his knuckled chin. Despite all the side remarks about how much older his facial hair made him look, Cleo hadn't decided to shave until the night before. There, at the magistrate's palace, he was introduced to a young woman who would be joining their morning excursion to the ruins of Scipyria. Vident Lement, a man whose vows prohibited him from engaging in conjugal or promiscuous relationships, was, of all people, the one to introduce him. Cleo was caught by the younger woman's captivating gray eyes and found her complexion to be quite mysterious. Upon his asking, Vident Lement explained that she was from the Vypores, which Cleo thought to be peculiar, but fitting. Though he regretted the circumstance of their meeting, Cleo was just glad that there would be another. And so, he shaved.

With a slick brush through his copper hair, he patted his comb against the side of the wooden bowl and dressed in his commander's uniform, which Cleo had cleaned by his new steward, Jones. The boy was a quiet and tall cagerman from Andar and a distant third nephew to Kladden. After one final look in the foggy mirror, Cleo left for the palace's hallway on the first floor and wrapped his way around the building's square turns. He departed through its grand red-oak doors and skipped down its steep steps. Where the last step met the wide street stood Jones, dressed in his cagerman's leather vest, holding the reins to his horse, Dahlia. Cleo mounted his saddle and swept his royal-red cloak aside to glance ahead.

Up the street, and between the grazing of people, were Vident Lement and the young, paler woman from the night before, both saddled on stable horses. Cleo trotted ahead of the six or seven escorting guardsmen, who were still mounting their own. The two of them drifted closer to the walkway on the side of the street, where they found shade near the chalky beige wall. Cleo rode up to them slowly and said, "Good afternoon."

"Cleo...*ah*, finally. Well, should we be off now? I haven't been this giddy in quite a while," Vident Lement said, already teetering his horse back toward the middle of the street.

Instead of following his preceptor, Cleo turned to the girl, who wore a long and ruffled, flower-patterned skirt and a one-sleeved garment that strapped around her shoulder. After an awkward pause, he said, "*I'm Cleo. Nice to meet you.*"

"We met already...just last night," she replied coldly.

"I just thought re-introductions might be in order."

"*What for?* Did you forget my name already?" The young woman with strong cheeks turned her horse around and followed Vident Lement.

Cleo was baffled trying to find the right words to say. As much as he didn't want to admit it, he couldn't remember what her name was. That night in the palace, and most of the nights in Andar before it, he had let himself go to sulk in a daze of drinks and the wilderness of women. And as the son of the general, and now a commander, he wasn't used to being shunned by any common woman he took an interest in. But it pained him that for as much as he remembered the girl's face throughout his sleepless night, he had forgotten her name.

"We're all here now, I think. We should be ready to set off," Vident Lement noted, clapping proudly to himself as the two other vidents rode up the street to meet them.

Behind their caravan was a company of Cleo's guardsmen, who trailed their group in a staggered pattern to each of their sides for protection. When they exited the central courtyard, one of the younger vidents took the lead, guiding their excursion to the ruins. Cleo rode on in silence as they passed the many shaded shops and fountains of Andar's winding streets, which were clean, but crowded by women and children in droves. After a few turns, when they finally cleared the crowd, Cleo hurried Dahlia to catch up to the girl who rode behind the three chatting vidents. "I should apologize," he told her, his tone soft.

"Apologize for what?" she asked coldly again.

"For forgetting your name…and the circumstances under which we met."

The girl trotted slowly along in silence before finally turning his way. "I thought horses weren't allowed on the streets of Andar."

"They aren't," Cleo responded, confused by the nature of what she was saying. "But being the commander of a brigade has its privileges." He stuck his chest out proudly, trying to impress her.

Instead, she just continued to stare forward, unamused. "Do those privileges include the naked woman you had on your lap last night?"

"Like I tried to tell you, I apologize for the circumstance. That wasn't typical of me," Cleo told her. In the past, he would have found a girl with this disposition to be quite repulsive. She was cold and rude and uninterested in even trying to be cordial with him. But each time Cleo glanced over at her, he couldn't help but feel a pulse of attraction. It was as if her rejection only amplified his desire. "But yes, to answer your question. I was only being kind and respectful as a guest of Andar should."

"*Very noble of you.*" She turned the curve of her chin away from him to glance into the shops they passed. "And what about the respect for Andar's traditions? This is the first time I've seen horses on the city's streets."

"Are you, yourself, not riding? I am trying to be nice to you, but if my presence offends you, you're welcome to get right off your horse," Cleo let out, upset by how their conversation was going. But still, he stayed by her side, looking back only to make sure his guardsmen followed.

After they traveled quite a distance in silence, the young woman finally said, "Vanna—*Vanna Sapharo.*"

"It's a pleasure to meet you, Vanna," Cleo replied with a smile, sticking out his arm. Vanna took him by his bare wrist and shook, their eyes meeting only for a brief, warmer moment. "As a token of my apology, I'd like to extend to you an invitation for dinner on the rooftop of the magistrate's palace. We usually eat by nightfall, and it would be nice if you joined me— *us,*" Cleo stuttered to reaffix his proposition.

"Sure."

Cleo pinched his broad cheekbones to the crest of his eyes with a smile, one she could clearly see. But he didn't care. Their grouping of horses sprang into a gallop once they rode along the dirt path beside the fields of foxtail grass. Cleo was surprised to see how well Vanna rode, especially in her long and loose skirt. He took his time, enjoying the view of the grassy plains and watching her from behind, as her long, shiny hair flowed with the wind. Eventually, she sped up to ride alongside Vident Lement, who himself was struggling to maintain his reins on the blotchy dirt path.

After a lengthy ride west, they peeled off to the left, in the direction of the distant Vypores. Far off, Cleo noticed notions of the ruins poking out from the plains in what appeared to be broken circles of rubble. The closer they rode toward it, the clearer he could see three marble columns standing high above the rest. To his left and right, fragments of slate and marble casts of buildings were scattered in pieces across the ground. Most seemed to be carved smoothly on one end, while the other was rough and coarse like that of black sand. Tall, hay-like weeds grew between the cracks of the remains in the rare areas where smog from the Vypores hadn't left its stain. At the ruin's center, Vident Lement was the first to hop off his horse. The other two honorable vidents followed after him as he moved through the ruins, gliding his wrinkly hands along the countless broken stones.

"So, what do you think?" Cleo asked after walking over to join them.

"It's *fascinating*." Vident Lement hadn't turned around to look at him. "The sheer account of history here. I can smell it just as easily as I can see it. The scorch is permanent."

"Just don't taste it," Cleo said in jest. "It's larger than I expected."

"Oh, Scipyria was grand, alright. At its height, it'd make a mockery of the largest cities across the Plane today—Bovere included. Some accounts even state that it took an entire day's light to cross from one end to another."

"*Quite unbelievable*," Cleo said, gasping as he gazed across the ruins. In his mind, he tried to picture what the city might have looked like were it still standing. "And these buildings must have been, what, two thousand solurns old?"

"Give or take," Vident Lement replied. He was too fixated on the words he found carved into a stone to look up. "Scipyria was founded by Scyrus the Sacred in 1410, before the descent, and lasted until Rexam scoured his way across the Plane. They call it ruins, but really, it's a graveyard. Hundreds of thousands, if not millions, of people were slaughtered on this very dirt."

Cleo looked around again, over and across the flat plains, trying to grasp how that could have happened. In his teachings with Vident Lement, he had read the old stories of Rexam and his rage when he wielded the Staff of Azil. Trying to imagine those dark tales of history had always been a challenge for him. But to stand where they once stood and breathe the air they once had made the worst of their images come to life in front of him.

"Men, women, and children alike." Vident Lement stood up to gaze at its enormity. "Had it not been for the man's own brother, Regnam, who knows what the Plane would look like today."

"So, you think those old tales are accurate?"

"*It's all we have*. But yes, the vidents have our hands on multiple accounts that might prove its veracity. Rexam was the seventh in his lineage to rule with the staff, and he did so from one of the mightiest castles in the Eastern Plane. He came from a powerful family, one of the strongest during the Age of Knights, fit to wield its power."

"It's all so hard to imagine." When Vident Lement paused his speaking, Cleo looked across the ruins at Vanna, who was wandering along a path, talking to the two younger vidents.

"But there was contention, even in those days. Scipyria itself was a strong city at the time, with a warring force large enough to rival those royal kings and queens that reigned in the east. The first to wield the staff, Rondor, was wise and just with his newfound power. He made frequent journeys to visit Scipyria and thought of the vizars in those days to be his friends. Some tales even proclaim that he needed their help to forge the descended remains of the fallen star in order to make the staff."

"Do you believe that?"

"It isn't for a vident to hold beliefs, Cleo. But if I had to choose, I think I would say there is some truth in it."

"Then what changed?"

"*Ah*, you see, Rexam didn't take too kindly to the Southern Plane like his ancestor Rondor had. He held his reservations for us, as people, in the same way the old royals did. Rexam thought of us as unsophisticated—barbarians, even. It was an old prejudice from a time long past that the Scipyrians still rode in hordes on horseback without a true home, raiding their collections of castle-protected gold. But Scipyria had evolved since the time of Scyrus, when he and his sister-families were driven from the Eastern Plane. And his lineage branched wide. As you might recall, your own family originates from his rather well-known relatives—the Scorinis."

Cleo rubbed his chin in thought. He had read at length on the heraldry of families and their history across the Plane, of things they had accomplished, built, or squandered. But the truth of the relationships they had with one another, especially across the regions, was still shrouded in mystery to Cleo. "But what exactly was the cause?"

"The vizar back then was a haughty man named Clovis. At that time, until the solurn 107, after the descent, the Staff of Azil was in the hands of Rexam and Regnam's mother, Evelise. Who, by all accounts, was one of the most beautiful women to ever grace the Plane. Clovis extended his hands to her favor, as any powerful man would, and sought to join the two regions of the Planes in trade and in peace."

"That would never happen," Cleo scoffed.

"Oh, but it almost did. Her eldest son, Rexam, was the one who foiled the proposal. He thought that the Vizar of Scipyria had malicious intentions, and claimed to have discovered a plot by Clovis to murder Evelise and steal the staff from her after their wedding."

"Is there any proof of that?"

"The plot? No, none that I have seen. But either way, Rexam couldn't stop his mother and her will to wed a man as charming and as strong as Clovis was. But this is where the tale becomes muddled. On the night they eloped—or, as some might say, the night before they were to elope—Rexam claimed to have found his mother lying dead in her castle's bedroom chambers. His account states that he fought Clovis in a bloody fit for the staff and killed him out of revenge for the murder of his mother."

"There's no way people really believe that," Cleo scoffed again.

"Some still do, even the most powerful in the east. From that day, Rexam became paranoid and enraged, blaming his mother's death on us Scipyrians and our envy of the staff and its power. For twenty-four solurns, he ruled in terror, scouring mightily across the Plane to eliminate anyone who might oppose his control. An entire generation was decimated. And if it weren't for him, all of the Plane today wouldn't be speaking and writing in roalish—the language of those old royals, which the people once called *royalish*."

Cleo looked out over the ruins, pondering the circumstances of his father's death and the vengeance he felt within his own heart, back in the gorge. Attempting to grasp the sheer power the Staff of Azil must have possessed in that age was impossible. But, to Cleo, the ruins painted its clearest picture. It was one of fury and of death, with control over all four of the Plane's originating elements, enough to wipe out an entire city of people at the hands of a single man. Cleo knew that power could drive anyone into paranoia.

Power and vengeance, he pondered, trying to think of where the power of the Plane was concentrated today. *In Sazara...with the Sunspear,* he understood, *in the hands of a man where it doesn't belong.*

"But this calamity was six hundred and twenty-seven solurns ago," Vident Lement said as he wandered in the direction of the two vident pupils.

"It doesn't seem like much has changed here since."

"You'd do best to learn from this history, Cleo, so it may change. Death and time will pass, but the nature of man's heart has always remained the same. Power is persuasive, you know... Like man, it always seeks to grow."

"Persuasive, *yes*. Which is why so many chase after it," Cleo said.

"That's right. But it can only grow inside of you if you feed it desire. Your father knew well how to starve it." Vident Lement glanced up at the sun in the sky. "It's easy to spot if you have the eyes to see."

"How so?" Cleo asked.

"Power consumes people. And by its consumption, it takes after our nature. We, as people, have three: our physical body, the intellect and reason of our mind, and the invisible passion of our heart. Thus, power also manifests itself in three ways. But to most, only one of those is visible in our Plane today."

"The amulons?"

"Correct," Vident Lement replied. "Brute force, as we vidents proclaim."

"Then what are the other two?" Cleo asked.

"Bribery and belief—the trickery of the mind and the zeal of the heart. Those in the east are masters in their manipulation. Like foxes, if you may. And it seems as if the Calegris have been trying to emulate their success. But the men who manifest these powers tend not to like the purifying light. And it takes a wiser man among the commons to notice them."

Cleo took heed of Vident Lement's advice and glanced across the ruins again at Vanna, who crouched near a broken marble block. Vident Lement's wisdom had struck him deeply, but probably not in the manner he had hoped. Cleo's desire and thoughts were drawn not to power but to protection. Not of vengeance but of justice. And not of the past but of the future. He had no means of bribery or belief, and he didn't wield the Sunspear—the strongest means of brute force in the Southern Plane. But what Cleo did have was determination—the will to stop them all, to save the lives and the things he cared for.

From this rationalization, Cleo surveyed the wasteland he stood over, glancing at the broken bits with shivers shaking down the length of his spine. *They just wanted peace. Where was their justice? Where was their protection? Their future had been taken from them just as mine is being taken from me now.* To Cleo, these broken fragments were just shards of past lives, telling the story of a people who were too weak and had suffered death and decimation as a consequence. He shivered, thinking of the torture they must have endured.

While walking alone in the ruins, Cleo vowed quietly to himself that he would never be weak enough to allow something this terrible to happen again to him or his people. He needed to stand strong against those who wielded power. *And to protect those who are innocent,* he thought, his eyes locking again with Vanna's. She stood and walked toward the two of them, meeting in the center of the ruin's largest standing columns.

"Were you reading something?" Vident Lement asked.

"A poem," she responded. "Well, more like a chant, similar to those in the temples."

"A chant…in the temples?" His question was more of disbelief than of intrigue.

"The true temples," she said, pointing to the Vypores in the far distance. Vident Lement turned to gaze at the tall peaks of extinct volcanoes that stood in the backdrop below a darkened sky.

"You don't mean to say that those are *temples*, do you?"

"*I do.* The largest seven have their insides hollowed. Scripts of sacred scipyrian and varukian line their inner walls—"

"*Sir,*" a growling voice said from one of the guardsmen rushing their way. "A rider."

Cleo spun back around and saw Jones riding fast toward them in front of a cloud of kicked-up dirt, whipping his reins with each hurling gallop. Immediately, he thought that his steward was bringing news of another battle, or death, or even the possibility that one of Cayen's brigades had attacked Andar. But whatever the circumstances, Cleo knew this couldn't be good.

"*Commander,*" Jones said. He jumped down from his horse, panting. "A man named Arwin, sir—he's ridden to Andar and said he needs to see you."

"*Arwin?* What about?"

"I dunno, sir, but it's urgent. Said he rode here in a quarter-moon's time."

Without pause, Cleo ran to mount Dahlia. Jones hopped back onto his horse and followed behind. Cleo circled back to Vanna, who had already begun drifting away. "We may need to reschedule our dinner," he told her.

Like the ruins they stood upon, Vanna's face remained unmoved.

Cleo quickly galloped Dahlia into stride, leaping back onto the dirt path that led to Andar. His mind wandered with growing questions the

319

longer they rode. Once they were within the city's walkways, he shouted at the people who traversed the shops in the evening shade, telling them to move out of the way as he forced his way past them. Arwin sat at the bottom step of the magistrate's palace with his scrawny hands between his face and his elbows dug deep into his lap.

"*Arwin.*" Cleo hopped off his horse and rushed to his old clerk. "What's going on?"

"Sir—it's the Fourth Brigade. I got your message in Corlach and rode straight to Cignus to hand your letter to Commander Giganti."

"*And?*" Cleo asked, lifting Arwin by a grip around his scrawny shoulders. "Come, let's move inside, away from these people."

Cleo took Arwin by the arm and led him up the stairs, turning to avoid the crowd that had gathered around their commotion. Once the guardsmen had shut the door, Arwin began to shout between his gasping pants, "Commander Giganti is *dead*... The First Brigade *stormed* Cignus... I rode here as quickly as I could, Commander."

A sharp pain wrenched itself deep into the pit of Cleo's stomach as if another knife had stabbed him straight in his heart. *My home.* He had taken Kladden's advice to ride west to Andar instead of Cignus, as it was closer and their support more prudent. But in doing so, he'd left Cignus vulnerable, and the First Brigade of the Calegris must have pounced. Cleo couldn't help but paint the images of Scipyria's ruins over the streets of his own home—the city where he was born, where he knew his earliest memories as a boy, and where his mother, Corianne, and his sister, Clara, still were. "*What of my family?*" he insisted, gripping Arwin again by both of his shoulders.

"They cleared the city out—I don't know. The Fourth Brigade put up a fight. But—I heard from one of Giganti's captains that they took your mother. Your sister, no one knows," Arwin uttered, his face flushed with fear.

The wound that was once in Cleo's heart now consumed the bounds of his body as if the knife had been pulled out and slashed across every segment of his skin. He was a failure, the one too weak to protect what was most important—his family. First his father, and now his mother. And there he stood, weak and powerless, no different than those Scipyrians of old.

"*How many?*"

"*Dead?*" Arwin waited for Cleo to nod before he continued, "The estimates weren't final."

Cleo strengthened his grip.

"About two-thirds of their brigade, sir. Some in the city scattered and fled, if they could."

Cleo let go out of despair.

"I sent what was left of them in the direction of Fort Corlach, where some of our fifth battalion still are."

"What else did you see?"

"They *destroyed* it…like wildfire. They stormed the temple in Cignus and took all its gold—your family's gold, too—sir. They were gone by the time I reached it. The destruction and the death…it's unlike anything I've ever seen. Against our own people, sir. Even the most innocent among us. *They burned so much.*"

"*Enough,*" Cleo ordered him to stop out of disgust. He wanted nothing more than to drop to his knees and crumble like the weak man he was. The vow he had just made to himself among the ruins of Scipyria was already worthless. *I am worthless.*

Cleo closed his eyes to think. But in the blackness, he saw his father's face staring back at him—a face that beamed with disappointment. *What can I do, Father? I need to act—like you would. I need to think steps ahead… I need help,* Cleo thought. His mind bounced frantically from thought to thought, trying to think of an answer.

Help—that's it. He opened his eyes and turned to one of the palace's guardsmen near the door. "Call the captains for counsel. Find Commander Sal and his men. Summon them all to the grand room. I need them here, *now.*"

Both Arwin and the guardsmen darted off quickly. Cleo walked to the fourth floor of the palace and ordered that a table be arranged in the center of the grand room. One by one, each of the captains from Cleo's brigade and those from the Third stormed in, asking various questions as to the meaning of the meeting. But Cleo sat still, breathing heaves of enraged silence until Kladden walked through the door.

"Cleo, what happened?"

"The Calegris hit Cignus. *Hard.*"

Without a word, and as if he already knew, Kladden's face sharpened into a fierce form of anger, pounding his sandals toward the end of the table to take his seat to the right of Cleo. Moments passed in silence until Commander Sal walked through the door, forcing his guests and captains to stand and salute. Cleo, though, didn't flinch.

"I've heard the news," Sal said solemnly as he walked to the opposite end of the long table, waving for his men to be seated.

"They expected me to be there," Cleo said. "Cayen Calegri had his First Brigade murder men who were not in this fight. Men of the Fourth, Commander Giganti included. And even some of the innocent people of Cignus. They were ambushed. And they burned much of it to the ground. I tried to have a message sent to him by my clerk, Arwin." Cleo lifted his hand and pointed to him in the corner of the room. "Upon Arwin's arrival, he saw what remained, the death and the thievery—*from the hands of the Calegris.*" In anger, Cleo slung himself up out of his chair and began pacing back and forth. "My own home set ablaze, my mother captured, and my father dead," he continued to rage, looking up only to meet Commander Sal's eyes. "*Will you not now join our cause?*"

The grand room descended into silence. All the captains at the table turned their heads to Sal, whose sweaty forehead was layered with concern. He took his seat and stated, "Cleo, I think of you and of Cignus as our friends. You and your men have been guests of Andar for more than a quarter-moon's time now, far past our initial offering. We have given you our supplies, our cagermen, and our women, all to take as your own. And we have shared in drinks, laughs, and brotherhood. But what you are asking from me now isn't mine to give."

"That's your answer? What are you scared of, *Salvitore?* Do you not think Andar will be next? After they ransacked Cignus, where do you think they'll turn once they know I'm here?"

Commander Sal stood up from his seat. "That is exactly what I am fearful of. The people of Andar are already questioning why your brigade has been garrisoning itself here for so long. Once they hear the news about Cignus, this city will erupt into chaos. Which is why my men must stay *here*, and yours must *leave*. Before the sun sets tomorrow, you must all be gone."

Internally, Cleo panicked. That wasn't the response he wanted. Or the answer he needed. "Where have your ethics gone, *Commander?* What would my father have done if he were in your position…or Kladden, the man who held your command before? They both stand by me."

"Your father is *dead*, Cleo. You're fighting a war you can't win against a man who stands atop mountains of gold and an amassment of arms four times the size of your own—"

"We have warriors—*true Scipyrian warriors*, unlike whatever you call yourself," Cleo thundered aloud. He turned to his steward Jones, waving as if he wanted something. Jones rushed forward to the table and reached into his sack to hand Cleo a folded cloth. Cleo grabbed both of its corners and waved it out from behind his chair.

"What is this? Some sort of flag?" Commander Sal asked, as if to mock him.

"Yes." The flag Cleo held was as orange as sunrise, with a white shortsword pointing to the sky in the middle. At the bottom of its pommel was a blood rose and, from it, spread the white wings of a swan. Its wings stretched wide to encircle the sword, touching its last feathers to the tip of the blade.

"I have one for you, Commander Sal, if you'd accept it."

"Is this some sort of joke? You're asking me to commit treason against Sacrim—against the security of my people…all without our magistrate's approval."

"*Correct.*"

Commander Sal looked sharply into Cleo's eyes. After a dry gulp, he said, "By sunset tomorrow, you must all be gone." With a sharp turn, he stormed out of the palace's grand room; his captains followed closely behind.

As soon as the doors had closed, Cleo slammed his clenched fists hard against the table.

"Well." Kladden sighed in desperate relief. "I don't think that could have gone any worse."

Cleo sat back down and slumped low in his chair, wiping his face and tracing back his raggedy copper hair. "What do we do now?"

"For a start, insulting a fellow commander when you need his support probably isn't the smartest of moves."

"If the roles were reversed, I think he'd be just as upset."

"But they aren't," Kladden responded. "You need him more than he needs you."

"I think our new insignia will work. It'll give the men something to rally behind," Captain Thorp said, trying to cheer Cleo up.

Cleo just turned away and continued sulking. "What do we do next? We have to leave, but we need to be steps ahead of Sazara."

"You're the commander of this *new Scipyrian* Guard. What do you think?" Kladden asked him.

Think, Cleo. Think.

"*New Scipyria…*" Cleo whispered to himself. *That's it.* "Jones, parchment and quill, please." His steward rushed over and handed Cleo his supplies. He threw the parchment down onto the table and began to write. "Captain Ostin, how many cagermen have we recruited?"

"A few hundred—three, maybe four, in total."

"Good," Cleo responded. "Arwin, when you rode here from Cignus, did you see any guardsmen of the First Brigade marching this way?"

All the way from the back corner, Cleo heard Arwin shout, "*No.*"

"So, there's a third left of the Fourth Brigade near Cignus and nearly a full battalion of our own at Fort Corlach. *Kladden*," Cleo said abruptly, looking up from the parchment with a conniving smirk. "Cayen's brigade isn't marching to invade Andar—"

"They're marching back to protect Sazara from us and Andar," Kladden said, finishing his statement.

"But they don't know that Sal won't budge," Captain Ostin stated.

"*Correct*," Cleo said. "Since we weren't in Cignus, the Calegris might be expecting Sal's escort in compliance with Cayen's order. Or, like Kladden just mentioned, our combined forces, the Sixth Brigade and Sal's Third, to march north on Sazara sometime soon."

"But neither of those is happening," Captain Sovano noted.

"And without Sal's help, we can't take Sazara," Kladden added.

"We need more men, and we won't find the help here," Cleo thought aloud, rubbing his broad, knuckled chin.

"So?" Kladden asked, raising a brow in confusion.

"So, *instead*, I'm sending you, Captain Thorp, and Captain Jostell east to Fort Corlach with a thousand of our guardsmen and half the cagermen we've just recruited. Take those from our battalion there and recruit more from what's left of Cignus. Those who survived will want revenge."

"And where will you go, Cleo?" Kladden asked.

"West—to Corlis."

"The Second Brigade at Fort Saxoram is the weakest of us all. I like our odds," Captain Sovano said, nodding to Cleo.

"That's if they're still there," Kladden noted. "If the Calegris were smart, they would have them recalled to defend Sazara."

"The people of Corlis are a mangy bunch. They'll do anything for pay," Captain Ostin noted.

"Both of which would make our task of recruiting easier," Cleo said. "Kladden, you'll command our new East Brigade. I'll command the West Brigade. Stay near Cignus until you receive a courier. When the date is decided upon, we'll strike Sazara together."

"From the east and west at the same time... I like it. Consider it done," Kladden said with an enticing grin. He pointed to the parchment and asked, "Are those my orders?"

"No. Nothing written should travel between us. The Calegris could have their men anywhere."

"Then what is it?"

"A message to Sazara—a proclamation, establishing New Scipyria as sovereign in rule over the Southern Plane," Cleo said, picking up the parchment and holding it to the ceiling's light. "The old order of Sacrim shall be *no more*."

CHAPTER 26

SEA

D ane breached the main deck of the cargo galley and shuffled his way to look across its bow. Bearing toward them across the North Sea were the two returning war galleys of the King's Navy. Between the mess of oarsmen, mates, and the mangled bodies scattered across the deck, Dane moved to find Captain Noreas huddled with his most trusted men.

"I knew I should have chased down those damned galleys when we had the chance," Captain Noreas growled. "We don't have any lanterns to signal or flags to mark."

"Cowen has raised the *Widow*'s sails, sir. He must have spotted them too," the captain of the *Bessie*, Markas, said.

"Sonny, can you see his gauge?"

The other captain hurried to the side railing and scanned the sea with his spyglass. "Wind is bare. Northwest, but against them."

"Those galleys have already circled back around to us. They're too fast. Cowen and the others won't reach us in time," Captain Noreas grumbled.

To Dane's right, Ruth barged her broad shoulders through the mates to join the huddling captains. "Where are those small boats? Shouldn't we be getting everyone off?"

"If you used your eyes, *girl*, you would see they've already left to bring those chests of cargo back to the galleons," Captain Noreas replied without bothering to give her any attention.

"So, we're *stranded?*" Ruth asked, her last words tailing off with worry. Dane could see the panic set in as she ran to the railing to check the distance between them and the two war galleys.

"Sir," Dane moved closer to Captain Noreas to get his attention.

"What is it, Dane?"

"We still have the oarsmen, sir."

Captain Noreas circled in his black-leather boots. His eyes jumped to count the oarsmen who stood between the decks of the two galleys nested together. "That, we do…"

"We can give sabers to them—the ones from the officers on board, and they'll fight for you," Dane told him.

"They're going to have to. *And more.*" Captain Noreas wasted no time hurrying toward the center of the two decks. He climbed atop one of the cargo chests and bellowed aloud, *"All hands, listen here."* The deck turned silent, and all eyes pointed his way. *"Every oarsman on this galley is a free man. But free men must still fight. Headed our way now are those same officers and marines who put you in the very chains we have broken. As the captain who freed you all, I must ask you one last time to man your oars. Not as a prisoner or a slave, but as one of us—a free mate of my fleet!"* The growing crowd of oarsmen, who stood to surround Captain Noreas, clung to every word he said, their faces dawning with hope. *"Oarsmen…grab a saber and find your oars. We're going to split these two galleys to the sea!"*

In a whirlwind of gleeful shouts, the oarsmen, still clothed in gray rags that hung loose from their bone-stretched skin, bounded across the two decks. One by one, the mates of the fleet gave those who looked fit enough to fight a saber, then directed them back down to the oar deck for one final sitting at their bench.

"Markas and Simion," Captain Noreas said, hurrying back to them. "You're with me. Dane, Sonny, and Jalek, you're in command of this galley."

Command? "Sir—me?" Dane asked, his face befuddled.

"You heard what I said, right?"

"But, sir, I've never been in command before."

"What better time than now? These men will follow you." With a thousand questions ringing through Dane's mind, Captain Noreas answered them all with a single statement: "No other captain knows these oars like you and I do. You have command, that's an order."

Dane cracked his knuckles and clenched his hands into fists, souring his icy blue eyes with conviction. Captain Noreas crossed the plank between the two tied-together galleys and ordered half the mates and oarsmen on deck to follow him. Once the lines between them were loosened and let off, Dane turned to Sonny, the scruffy-haired captain of smaller stature and strong shoulders, for direction.

"Dane, right? You take the helm. Jalek, you set the speed below," Sonny ordered.

"Aye…we'll have to relay our commands to you," Dane told Jalek, before he saw Ruth moving to join them.

"I'm in. What do you need me to do?" she asked.

While the other two captains rolled their eyes, Dane remained steadfast and said, "Good. We could use your help. Caji, follow Jalek, and stand between the stairs. Find an oarsman to take the drums. Ruth, stay on the deck close to me. I need you to be my extra set of eyes and to relay my commands down below."

"*Aye.*"

Dane nodded, then made his way toward the quarterdeck. When he reached the top of the stairs, he turned to look forward across the open sea and saw the two war galleys clearly. Both had long ramming spikes protruding from their bows and moved in unison as they grew in size, rowing with speed to close the distance.

"*GET A MOVE BELOW!*" Sonny commanded, rushing those who still lingered on the deck.

Dane grabbed the spokes of the wheel and yelled down to Ruth near the stairs: "*Port forward, Starboard aft!*"

Ruth repeated the command to Caji in the stairwell, who then relayed it to Jalek below. Drumming began to beat on the oar deck, two decks below the main. Dane's fingers pulsated with every pound they slammed as he spun the wheel for a starboard turn. The beating rhythm rang throughout his body, jogging back his memory. He could see himself, once more, on the bench with an oar in his hand, rowing through the most gruesome inflictions of pain.

But Dane knew that now wasn't the time to recall his nightmares. No, he had been given command and now had the mates and the oarsmen's lives in his hands. This wasn't about his lust for vengeance, or even his will to prove himself to Captain Noreas. It was about their survival, especially now, with Ruth on board beside him. To Dane, that was all that mattered.

As the cargo galley turned, waves from the sea broke over its side railing. The mates from the *Widow* and the *Rithron* cleared the deck, throwing some of the dead bodies overboard on Sonny's orders. Dane looked back to his left and saw Captain Noreas's galley struggling to gain any momentum.

Come on...

Behind them, he searched for Cowen and the *Widow*, hoping to see their sails at full breadth, breezing past them to cut the two war galleys off. Instead, he saw only the sea and the gaping spew of waves clattering in between. *The wind is too soft for them,* he realized.

"*FASTER! FASTER!*" Sonny commanded Ruth from the main deck, who then shouted below.

"*Full forward!*" Dane yelled to correct him.

From behind, Dane heard the unleashing of bolts stream into the air. He looked up and saw their flaming tips spiraling toward the war galleys, only to plunge straight into the sea, far too short.

"*We're not going to make it,*" Ruth cried, swiveling her gaze back and forth.

Just ahead, Dane saw the long spoke from the bow of one of the war galleys speeding to close their path of collision. *She's right,* he thought. *We're going to need an opening.* Dane stood unmoved behind the helm for longer than Sonny liked, waiting patiently through the commotion on deck and watching the oars of the war galley as it pushed through the sea, headed toward them. *Wait for it... Wait... Now.* "*RUTH, REVERSE... STARBOARD FORWARD, PORT AFT!*"

As she repeated his command, Dane spun the wheel to shift the galley's lone rudder in the opposite direction. He could hear the rhythm of the drumming below the deck change as the oars slapped their long paddles against their own wake. The stern end of their cargo galley began to swing to the side, its bow dipping into the trough of the waves as its back end drifted around in a sweeping circle.

"*IT'S WORKING!*" Sonny was elated in surprise. "*THEY'RE GOING TO MISS US!*"

Dane let out a long sigh of relief and smiled. His last-moment turn had worked.

Just past their starboard railing, the war galley brandished its oars at full speed, barreling its way with just enough distance to miss ramming its bow into their own. The two galleys passed side by side across the narrow split of the sea, their oars close enough to clap one another as they drifted away. Above its long and sleek dark-planked sides were countless officers and marines dressed in black overcoats and silver helmets, all with sabers in hand, ready for war. Dane spotted their captain near the helm. The old, graying man wore a wide-curving hat and stared into his eyes with the palest gaze of death.

Sonny led the mates on their own deck to raise their sabers and bellow intimidating shouts over their crossing oars. Dane's eyes followed the war galley's path as it struggled to reverse its course and turn back around. But just after it had quickly passed them, a flaming bolt from one of their fleet's galleons had soared through the air and struck the war galley's deck, setting it ablaze. Bolt after bolt began to shower it with fire. Dane looked on and watched as those same officers and marines they had just missed colliding with now cried out in burning anguish.

"*Justice...*" he whispered under his breath.

"*Dane! Look!*" Ruth yelled aloud, pointing the opposite way.

"No...no..."

Across the sea, the cargo galley Captain Noreas commanded was struggling to turn. Its starboard broadside was open to the other war galley, which was on a similar path, headed straight at them. Dane couldn't remove his eyes from watching. Within moments, the planks of his captain's hull shattered into splinters from the long spoke of the war galley's bow that rammed into their side.

"*BRING US AROUND TO THEM! FULL FORWARD!*" Dane quickly told Ruth, who again relayed his command below.

The two clashed galleys were too far away for their own fleet's bolts to reach. Dane's ship began to pick up speed, racing faster and farther away from the burning cries behind them. "*Port halt!*" he yelled below, changing the rhythm of the drums again. The cargo galley they commandeered began to turn with the help of his helm, before he ordered the oars slowed to half speed.

War rang out on the two collided ships. Dane brought them closer and saw the mates under Captain Noreas brawling with their sabers in hand against the marines' own. The colors above the chaos blended in fits of white, black, and silver that spurned with gasps of life taken and bodies splashed as they were tossed overboard.

"*Mates...*" Dane shouted. "*Prepare to board!*"

One by one, they threw their hooked lines across to catch them on the port railing of Captain Noreas's cargo galley. The mates heaved at the lines to pull them close and began tossing their planks across. In lines of shouts and clanking sabers, Sonny led them to board the two clashed galleys.

"*BRING THE OARSMEN OUT TO BOARD!*" Dane ordered below. He left the helm to join Ruth beside the stairs. With faces of fury, the rescued oarsmen charged up to the main deck and joined those who had already crossed into battle.

"You're staying here," Dane told Ruth, who looked almost too scared, or even dazed, to argue with him. With his saber in hand, he pressed forward, crossing one of the five planks braced over the sliver of sea. He jumped into the chaos and began fighting alongside Caji. They slashed their sabers in unison, taking on the King's marines and their warring assault of stabs and jabs amid the terror of grunts and wails.

"*They're sharp,*" Dane said, his heart thumping with every swing he took.

"*And tall,*" Caji added through the death-rattle of screams that surrounded them.

Bodies of mates and marines and their congealed blood littered the main deck in every direction Dane tried to move. But he was glad that Caji was by his side. Dane had never been taught how to fight, but he was tall, like the marines, and clever, like the oarsmen. Caji, though, was just as sharp as both of them and had his skills of dueling with a sword drilled to near perfection. With every misstep Dane took, Caji was there to right his movement.

But as they hugged the port side railing, the oarsmen from Dane's cargo galley still flooded across the planks to join them. "*We need to move,*" Caji told him through the chaos, after stabbing his saber through the gut of a marine.

"*There...I see Captain Noreas,*" Dane said between swings. Moving toward the quarterdeck, he and Caji slashed and chopped to help the mates wherever they could. The two of them made their way up a short flight of stairs, where Dane saw Captain Noreas fighting off two marines and an officer by himself.

"*Glad you finally decided to join me,*" their captain said while skipping away from a wayward lunge.

Dane thrust his own into the mix, ducking below one of the marine's swings to swipe at his waist. "*YOU SWINE... YOU BARBARIANS!*" the officer cried aloud as he moved to swing his saber at Dane's arm.

But before he could even turn to move, Caji stabbed his curved blade straight into the man's shoulder. With his arms flailing to the side, Captain Noreas swung his saber around and sliced it clean through the officer's neck. *"Just like a barbarian would,"* he shouted with a blood-quenching laugh.

Dane got up quickly and held the back of his left arm where he'd been cut. The three of them closed in on the two marines until their tall legs became trapped against the railing's side. Caji swung broadly and missed, then Dane shoved the tip of his saber straight into the ugly man's heart. With a look of righteousness, he stared deep into the marine's desperate blue eyes, then shoved his flailing body overboard.

"Nice one, Dane!" Captain Noreas commended, before overpowering the other to do the same.

Dane glanced back toward the main deck. Bodies and blood were scattered across the decks of the clashed galleys, painting their planks the color of perpetual death. The mates and oarsmen had chopped their way through most of the officers and marines.

Captain Noreas turned to look at him and said, "You made all the difference today, Dane… *Thank you.*"

He accepted his captain's praise with an emboldened nod, then followed him below to kill whatever dwindling evil remained.

† † †

Songs of brotherhood and fellowship swept in unison to head below deck as the mates of the *Widow* followed the ringing clang of the evening meal's bell. It had been well over a quarter-moon since Dane had been raised to second mate, after their clashing battle in the North Sea. Since then, Captain Noreas's fleet had managed to capture and free another cargo galley of the King's Navy and faced far less of a contest in doing so. A few days prior, the fleet had finally turned south around the eastern coast of the Regent, out from the torrential winds and away from any further clashes in the North Sea.

Dane took relief from his understudy watch as deck chief and looked out over the eastern horizon, watching the sun begin to set over the glassy sea. The mates around him were full of joy and ditty, singing their way to feast on flat cakes and fried eggs as they awaited the morning's final passage to their anchorage in Cubby Cove.

Instead of following them below or singing their songs, Dane wandered to the foredeck of the ship and looked down into the water. There, in its glimmering reflection, he saw the face of a young man he no longer recognized. His dangling blond hair had grown past his ears, and the stubble on his sharp-cheeked face had formed into darker patches. It was the face of a man changed, having grown from a boy in such a short time since the days he would gaze into the creek behind his home in Niven.

But here, in the sea that split itself to let the *Widow* pass, Dane found his real home. It was on the water with his new friends and mentors where he was forced to grow and learn the lessons of brotherhood. *The sea does that*, Dane thought to himself. *It carries you and raises you to float above itself, with the freedom to go anywhere.* He thought deeply about the paradox that once was. How he'd once been enslaved on the same seas that were so obviously meant for freedom.

Like life, it flows.

"You didn't want to join them?" a feathery voice asked from behind his shoulder. Dane looked back and saw Ruth walking by herself across the deck to meet him near the bow. "I figured you'd be up here. I saw Caji and Flyde with their drinks below. But you weren't with them."

"I wanted to catch one last sunset before we hit land tomorrow," Dane tried to explain.

Ruth moved to sit beside him, dangling her feet off the deck edge. She looked out to share his view of the peach-lit luster that mellowed between the sky and sea. "Maybe they're the ones missing out."

Ruth was right. But Dane was glad it was only her up here to talk to him. On a ship now filled with well over a hundred mates, with the addition of the freed oarsmen, he rarely had a moment to himself. And if it had been any of the other mates who had tried to join him, Dane would have found it annoying. But not Ruth.

"The eastern coast here is so beautiful. Do you always get sunsets like this?"

"No. Tergona is shrouded in the Northwoods. We get rain and dreary skies more than anything."

"Niven was similar. Except with snow for most of the solurn."

"Now that I could do without," Ruth said with a soft giggle. "But I'm so happy, I can just smell the wet pines from here."

"Must be nice—going home," Dane said with a hint of jealousy.

"It's the greatest feeling ever."

I can only imagine, he thought. "What's it like? Your home?"

"Small…but vast. Tergona is just one of many tiny cantons that surround the Northwoods. And we're also one of the smallest. You could count the number of families on both your hands."

"And with Niven, it would be just one hand," Dane said with a laugh. He leaned his pale arms over the railing in thought. "What's a canton?"

"Like property markers. To divide who owns what and where."

"You get to own the land?"

"Well, *of course*. I mean, we don't own the canton itself, but parcels of the land within it, sure. At least where our home is and where we might work and toil."

"And anyone can have this?"

Ruth looked back at him in a puzzled way as if she had forgotten how isolated Marredom was from the rest of the Plane. "Yes, we have that right because of the Regent's covenant. It's all accounted for by deeds and made to chart. But they're all different. In Tergona, the land is divided by our family's plots. We have a shared pact that goes back hundreds of solurns, when we united our lands under a single canton. But in the bigger cities, like Bovere and Tammon, or Florington, or even Partha and Decanan, there are many, many wealthy families whose lineage goes back for several millennia. For those, a single family might own a large canton, or multiple, at that."

"And the people of the Regent just let them have it? So, there's no king or queen who decides?"

"*No.*" Ruth laughed a little. She looked back at him from her gaze at the sunset. "We have our founding covenants to protect us. They've changed over time, from the Age of Knights to Furlak—the first man to wield the Stonehammer—and then again with the Cathedral. But we don't just let them have the land. They have a right to own it so long as they are using it," Ruth explained. "Something you clearly aren't familiar with."

"Not in the slightest," Dane admitted with a disparaging smirk. In his mind, he pictured what Marredom might look like if its people were allowed to be as free as those in the Regent. Everything they had back home had been given to them by the King, and any of it, including their own lives, was just as easily taken back by him. To Dane, the Eastern Plane sounded like paradise.

"It still has its shortfalls, like anything else. The wealthy do well to maintain their wealth, which puts pressure on us lowly people. Especially those who live and work within their cantons. But here—*at home*—there isn't anyone commanding us on how to live."

Dane looked out at the sunset. His expression shifted into a smile of hope. This was the happiest he'd ever seen Ruth, and he now knew why. In the morning, he'd be joining her to set foot on this free land that she loved so dearly. And he couldn't wait to find out more about it. "What about that book of yours? Doesn't that command you how to live?"

"I wouldn't say *command*. *Emanations* is more of a teaching—a story, in a way."

"Well, maybe if I stay in the Regent long enough, you can teach me to read it."

Ruth laughed at his comment before realizing what he'd said. "*You don't know how to read?*"

"Not in roalish, at least…no. My mother never learned, so we only spoke it. Before you begin to laugh at me, I do know norkatis. At least, most of its words, I can read and write."

"*Deal*," Ruth said, sticking her hand out. "You teach me norkatis, and I'll teach you to read the Tomes."

Dane moved to sit beside her and shook her soft hand with a broader smile than before. "Just to warn you, norkatis is harsh."

"I'll be fine…and *Emantions* is deep, just to warn *you*," she bantered back.

Dane laughed a little again, then realized that Ruth was serious. "*How deep?* For as much as you read that book, you never really talk much about it."

"I guess it's sort of personal to me. But *deep* is right. It's the second volume in the story of our beginnings, written by Tohen the Second."

"Not that I know who that is, but please, continue."

"Tohen the Second, a man priorly known as Fredrick, changed his name in 195 A.D. after he discovered the writings of the philosopher-knight Tohen, who lived amid the harshest days of conflict during the Age of Knights. In his translations and interpretations, he, along with his son Tavhen and their followers, founded our Three Monuments. First to be established was the Council of the Divine Sages. Then came the Covenant of the Divine Tomes—the middle volume is what I have with me here. And last was the building and enshrinement of the Cathedral of the Divine One."

"And everyone in the Regent follows the teachings of this Tohen guy?"

"No, not everyone. But most do. At least, they claim to. The divine sages have built many sceptories across the Eastern Plane, where most of us get our formal teachings. And when I was in Bovere, I got to visit the Cathedral and worship with some of them, as well as those in the Sacred College. It's all so magnificent," Ruth explained as she stared out across the sea once more.

"Sounds intriguing," Dane said. "And that book teaches you all of this?"

"Not quite. *Emanations* is a little different than the others. It teaches of the battle between love and strife."

"Love and strife? How so?"

"It's the story of the Plane's first family, Theris and his sister-wife Lerosa, and the four children she bore, Lassara, Heoria, Baromon, and Tannen. With each child she brought into the Plane, the two parents saw the remnants of their children's spirit following their bodies."

"Following?"

"Yes." Ruth giggled. "Like a shadow. It's what we in the Cathedral call the Divine Split—when the Divine One first passed through the Divine Gates to manifest life here on the Plane, which is explained in the first volume, *Inception*. As the divine sages so eloquently put it, it's the inquisition between revelation and reason."

"But how does that even happen?"

"You'd have to read the first volume to find out!" Ruth replied with elation.

Dane crossed his arms. "*Oh*, come on...just tell me. I'll read it anyway—once you teach me."

"Okay, okay. Out of loneliness, the originating spirit of the Divine One, the creator of us all, split itself into two, one male and one female—Theris and Lerosa. And for any new life to be created, two spirits must learn to reunite together again through love, as one, in a ritual of imitation. But it's a paradox, as you'll see. For every new life created, it takes half the spirit from one parent and half from the other. So, by unifying into one, life and the Divine One's original spirit fractures and splits further into more, creating strife. In the studies of the sages, they call it the Schismatic Paradox."

"So…sort of like a mule, then, right? What was once a horse and once a donkey is no longer a horse or a donkey?"

"*Exactly*," Ruth commended him. "See, you're going to do just fine in the Regent."

"Tell me more about this father, though. You said he could see the split spirits?"

"Yes. He could, and the mother could, as well. The original fractures were so fresh that the spirits themselves still soared alongside us in the Plane. Only, the two parents saw them in very different ways. Theris thought they brought danger to his children and the Plane, while Lerosa thought they brought blessings."

"What kind? How could they be so different?"

"For their first child, Lassara, there was the spirit they named Ophia, which taught the beauty of love and its opposite—the temptation for lust. For Heoria, there was the spirit Veraphen, which taught strength through might and the passions of pride. For Baromon, the spirit Fulstham taught of supreme knowledge and that of secrets. And then, for Tannen, there was the spirit Grevalus, which taught of wealth and of envy. Their father, Theris, scoured across the Plane to hunt these spirits and kill what strife he thought they caused. To find them, he went after his own children, whom he saw to be dangerous—or, even now, evil, as the spirits taught them their ways. At the same time, his wife sought to protect her children and their spirits with her motherly love, embracing the good in their teachings."

"So, what happened to them?"

"You'd have to read the Tomes to find out," Ruth said with a smirk. "I can't ruin it all for you!"

"Oh, come on."

Ruth's smirk grew. "Nope. Not happening. You'll have to read it one day."

"You really are brilliant, you know," Dane said. He looked at her with a sideways smile, trying to get her to divulge its end. When she held silent, he added, "It's impressive. And maybe even a little intimidating."

"Only a little? The Tomes—"

"I meant *you*, not the book."

Ruth's smile grew to match his own, her rounded eyes blinking to hide the clouds of blush that painted her cheeks. "I'm the only girl on this ship. I need to have something! But I didn't create the teachings; I only follow them."

"If someone as smart as you follows them, then maybe everyone else should, too," Dane said, looking into her brown eyes. Inside them, he caught sight of her own spirit—the emanation of her true self. Ruth was the gentlest person he'd ever met and embodied the pure bliss of innocence within her soft gaze. Her face was lavished with emotion as she smiled, talked, and yearned for understanding. And her long hair always dangled perfectly as she read or was deep in thought or careful conversation.

At that moment, Dane felt the tingling urge to lean in and kiss her. But he wasn't sure if Ruth reciprocated his feelings. From his perspective, she never showed an interest in that way. Dane's mind lingered with doubt. Below, his gut crunched in a nervous knot, as if the Jaws of Myrph had leaped out of the sea and bitten a hole inside his chest. With it came a sinking feeling, as if his confidence had been stolen down to the depths.

Part of Dane thought that it was wrong for him to feel this way. Ruth was strong-willed and independent, and the two had become good friends. He cared about her in the same way he knew she cared about him. She was genuine and herself—no longer strange but unique. And the two of them shared the same goal. Dane felt that his adulation for Ruth was like a treasure he needed to hide—to bury deep beside his doubt in the depths so it could never be discovered. The last thing he wanted was to risk ruining the trust of their friendship.

But just as he turned his gaze from her to the sea, they both became startled by footsteps creaking along the deck behind them. "Having fun, are we?" Ludwyn's voice asked.

"Hey, Lud," Ruth said in a lighter, surprised tone.

Dane noticed the look on Ludwyn's bushy face, one that drooped with sadness as if he'd been left out. Or rather, just that Ruth had left him out. "We were just catching the last sunset at sea for a while," he tried to explain.

Ruth stood and began moving away from the railing. "I guess we should head down below."

"With everyone else...*yeah*. Let's do that," Ludwyn replied.

As the two of them left to join the feast below, Dane looked out at the sea one last time and saw the sun's final few rays hit the calm water with warm, open arms. But as he looked down at his reflection, he saw his young face, the same as it was back home in Niven. Despite reaching the rank of second mate, learning to become a deck chief, and gaining the confidence of his captain, Dane knew he hadn't yet taken the one step to become a man. Deep within the depths of his doubt, he knew he was still just a boy.

"Bring her around," Captain Noreas commanded. "This looks like a lovely spot, wouldn't you say so, mates?"

Shouts of joy streamed from the deck's chatter as Dane helped to carry the last few stakes and chests of canvas tarps up from the hold. Their fleet of five, as well as the two cargo galleys they towed, had arrived in the morning to be welcomed by the tree-lined inlet of Cubby Cove, right where Ruth said they should be.

"I've never been anywhere this beautiful," Caji said with his brawny jaw lodged open. They placed the last chest near the growing pile of equipment used to set up camp, then rushed over to the side railing to get a better view beside the mates.

"Home...we finally made it," Ludwyn said.

Dane gasped. "It's *glorious*." Layers of wet pines, tall and thick, grew from the cove's steep and sloping side to embed themselves within the rock-laden shore. Their roots found a foothold in the most precarious of spots, hidden behind the summer blooms of the short and shaggy shrubs. "I've never seen this much green in my life."

"This is a whole lot better than all that dull blue, isn't it?" Ruth's soft voice asked from behind.

Caji turned around to view the other side of the protected cove. "I wasn't expecting much, but this surpasses anything I could have imagined."

"I'm just surprised at how tall all of these trees climb," Dane added, turning his narrow chin up to the cloudy sky.

"Cubby Cove, along with most of the eastern coastline, is a lot steeper than the rest of the Northwoods," Ruth explained. "But once you break through the tree line, it all becomes quite flat."

"*PREPARE TO LAY ANCHOR!*" Galen relayed Captain Noreas's command forward.

"Then how far is Tergona from here?" Dane asked her as he faded away from the foredeck.

"Not far at all, actually. A quarter-day hike. If that."

A team of mates, old and new, heaved at the line that passed through the *Widow*'s forwardmost porthole. Captain Noreas sifted through the crowded deck to make his way beside the forward ballista. "On my mark." With his saber in hand, he hung over the side of the hull and sliced at the line that tied the iron anchor to its side shell. He waved at the deck chief to drop the sails before commanding them to release the line. Dane rushed over to the port railing and watched as the anchor splashed into the deep blue water below.

"*Mates*," Captain Noreas turned to say above the cheers on deck. As they struggled to quiet down, excited to finally touch land, he continued, "Every one of you has earned this time to rest. We'll set up camp for a few days, just there, on the coast." He pointed at the center of the cove's curve, where a flat stretch of land was padded with grass behind the pebbled shore. "Cowen, have the boats lowered to bring the camp posts and tents in first. *Piney*, where are you at?"

From the back of the crowd, Dane heard Piney's distinct and squeaky voice shout his name aloud. While the crew all laughed, Captain Noreas said, "Piney, bring those barrels of Sacrimian wine up from the hold, will ya." Even Dane, who had never had this wine before, joined in to clap with the crew. "*Let's feast tonight, boys!*"

"This might just be the best day of my life," Ruth said, her voice giddy. "I can't wait to see my family."

Captain Noreas quickly shoveled his way over to them. "Now…rest won't be for us all. Where is that brother of yours?"

Ruth's face fell into a frown. "He should be in Tergona."

"*Should?*" Captain Noreas asked sternly.

"Yes. It's only a short distance from here. South, then west, along the pebbled trail."

"Good. While they drink their wine, we'll head that way." Captain Noreas turned to look at the mast, where Maris was still tied and gagged. "And he's coming too. He's going to verify that we have the right girl."

Dane and Ruth drifted to follow him over to the central mast, where Captain Noreas yanked away the dirty rag stuffed in the prince's mouth. "*You ready to take a trip?*" he asked, mocking the disheveled young man.

Maris, whose face was once perfectly sculpted, now looked ill and diseased, his face a field of bruises. The wiry hair on his head hung long and platinum-blond, and his eyes looked faded of any light. He spat a dry heave on the deck and then coughed, struggling to breathe whatever fresh air he could through his slender neck.

"*You're coming with us.* We need to make sure that girl is the one you took...*you bastard.*"

But Maris didn't respond. Instead, he looked deeply into Captain Noreas's eyes with a deadly expression. It was a look Dane had seen before, one most of those officers and marines shared, as if behind their eyes was just a black pit left lifeless and empty. *Pure strife*, Dane recognized.

Captain Noreas pointed at two of the mates who stood beside them and commanded, "Ready him to be taken ashore. And clean him up while you're at it—the man stinks of mold and manure."

The mates bumped past him, following Captain Noreas's orders, and Dane turned around to scan the campsite. As he was admiring the beautiful view, he heard a splash of grunts and gasps fountaining behind him. Dane spun back around as quickly as he could and saw Maris with his fist now free, shoved against Captain Noreas's chest.

No...no...no. Dane's feet were anchored to the deck. His eyes were stuck still as if layers of winter's ice had frozen over him.

This can't be...

Mates in droves piled past him, rushing to pull Maris off Captain Noreas by the bones of his frail body. As Maris was being thrown back, Dane saw the bloodied tip of a sharp, wooden shank lift itself out of Captain Noreas's chest in a slowed motion. Noreas held his hands between the opening of his blue overcoat. His shoulders bowed as he pressed hard against his chest, trying to stop the gushing of blood. His pale face swelled in disbelief. Smothering shouts from all around grew as he gasped for air, one knee collapsing under the other until his body fell to the side.

Dane ran over to Captain Noreas as fast as he could and turned his back against the wood. Without knowing what else to do, Dane moved his hand over his captain's slowing heart, trying to stop the bleeding. A single tear pierced through the frost of his pale face.

In his last, dying breath, Captain Noreas said, "*Take care of my fleet... Mal—please.*"

341

CHAPTER 27

SKY

Clouds, plump and soft, shifted across the sky like fraying balls sheared off a lamb's hind to follow Vanna west as she rode at the tail end of the brigade's march. Under her saddle was a calm stable horse named Paisley, provided to her by the guardsmen back in Andar, with small black spots scattered along her short and stocky legs. She was a runt compared to the rest of the warhorses and was even mocked as a mule by the guardsmen who rode in front of her. But Vanna didn't mind. She didn't need the fastest or brawniest horse to carry her along in her journey. She was no longer a Sister or even a warrior like they were. No, Vanna was now just a common girl from the uncommon region of the Vypores and a guest of Vident Lement.

Two nights prior, she had awoken to knocks at the door of her tiny guest room in the magistrate's palace. At the opposite end of her panic was Vident Lement, who, himself, looked more concerned than she was. He spent his urgent time pleading for Vanna to join him and the traveling guardsmen as they were readying to march west to Corlis, within Sacrim's Second Partition.

Earlier that day, she and the three vidents had explored the ruins of Scipyria until long past sunset. Even after Cleo had left, Vanna stayed with the balding old man at his request, tracing the fragments of history and doing her best to answer his endless stream of questions, most of which dealt with the Vyporean temples and the people's migration to Astria.

At first, it felt to Vanna like an interrogation of her past, as if he might discover her real roots. But to the Sisters' credit, with the knowledge she was taught under their tutelage, the answers to his questions of history came to her quite easily. Vanna was relieved to see him take notes as he listened to every word she said, realizing that they came not from a place of interrogation but from personal inquiry. To her, the old man seemed authentic in nature and genuine in his curiosity.

And so, Vanna struggled through the night, contemplating whether she should leave with him and the traveling guardsmen—or not. Andar was a beautiful city, rich in culture and filled with kind people. It had delicious food that filled her with delight, as well as shops with colorful crafts and the most creative clothing. The streets abounded with women, families, and happy children who welcomed her without the indecency she had encountered in Sazara or even the cold dereliction she had known in Mount Matron.

Since the day she arrived in Sazara with Zell and Lora, Vanna had always looked at the men of Sacrim's Guard with apprehension or even aversion. For the entirety of her life, they had been the enemy. And she was the one who had murdered their general. Those men in bronze—with their spears, shields, and spaded skirts—were a reminder of the repercussions she might one day have to face for what she'd done, and everything that she still needed to hide from.

But in contrast to those thoughts, Vanna knew no one in Andar. She had no family to come home to, or work to take on, and she'd only seen Vident Linus once more after their first meeting when he'd led her to her small guest room in the palace. Instead, it was Vident Lement who had been asking her all those questions and chatting with her about the Plane's history and languages, with intrigue and interesting conversation. And it was Vident Lement who was imploring her to join him as they planned to leave the city without an opposing voice to say otherwise. He was an open and friendly old man, full of knowledge and eager to explore the Plane, just like she was.

Above all her apprehension, however, Vanna's concern loomed largest regarding the Sisters. They were proficient in embedding themselves across the Plane, under the noses of the people and their rulers. She knew from Lora that the orders were often sent to cities to gather information, disrupt rival intentions, and strike when necessary. Vanna was worried that she might be recognized should she stay too long in Andar, where women brimmed in the streets. The Sisters could be easily hidden anywhere among them. But she also knew that the one place the Sisters could never be hidden within was a brigade full of guardsmen.

And so, Vanna chose to leave, to join the travelers on their journey west across Sacrim.

"I need rest," Vident Lement said as he slowed from the head of the march to greet her and Vident Evander near the rear. Riding beside Vanna was the younger, honorable vident, dressed in his burnt-orange vestment and single silver cord, who had also chosen to leave Andar behind to further his training.

"Those old bones aren't getting any stronger," Evander told him.

"You should have seen me riding to the Sineaqe Gorge; this is nothing compared to that. Slow and steady…just how I like it."

"How does it look up ahead?" Vanna asked.

"Same as it does back here. Only, less smelly."

Vanna lifted a smile in agreement. The cavalry's horses up ahead often left trails of dung along their path, and the unpleasant stench of body odor from the men she rode behind frequently wafted her way. Occasionally, she found herself veering outside of the brigade's five columns to avoid heaving—or worse, puking.

"Vanna, how are you coming along?" Vident Lement asked.

"Hm, tired, the same. I'm just glad I have Evander back here to keep me amused."

"Don't listen to her," Evander said. "She hasn't laughed at a single one of my jokes for the past two days."

"Then it probably isn't your jokes that are keeping her amused," Vident Lement said with a light chuckle.

Vanna joined in with his laugh. "It definitely isn't."

"Maybe it's the hair," Vident Lement noted.

Evander threw his hand out from his drooping drapes and ran his fingers through his dark hair, which was cut like a bowl atop his quirky, egg-shaped head. "*Oh*, it isn't that bad."

Vident Lement, who had only thinned gray strands himself, reinforced his claim by saying, "When we stop tonight, I'll have one of the guardsmen clean it up."

"*Tonight?*" Vanna asked, sighing in relief.

"Yes. I was just told that we'd set up camp before nightfall, a short ride from here, so the brigade can regain its strength. *And morale.*"

Vanna turned around to check on the pack mule they shared, tied to her saddle. Just over the grassy plains, she could faintly see a few peaks of the Vypores, which were now mere specks across the horizon compared to their actual grandeur. "Good."

"I'm just looking forward to a fully cooked meal," Vident Evander said.

"Evander, you do know we don't eat with the guardsmen, right?" Vident Lement asked.

"What do you mean?"

"As a vident, such as yourself, we aren't members of the Guard, so we don't share their meals at camp. Did you not pack any of your own food to cook?"

Vanna chuckled again as Evander frantically patted and opened the side packs on his horse. "For a vident, you sure are clumsy."

"You can always beg for a hot plate from one of those guardsmen when they're chopping at your hair tonight," Vident Lement said, joining the amusement. "But in all seriousness, I packed plenty for all three of us to share."

Evander's cheeks turned rosy. "Where would I be without my chief vident?"

"Hungry and ugly," Vanna responded. Just as Vident Lement broke out into laughter again, Vanna asked more seriously, "Chief vident, as in *the* chief?"

"No, there are a few chief vidents," Evander replied, glad that the attention was being diverted away from his mockery. "It's a position they hold."

"What makes that position different from your own?"

"You'd have to become a vident to find out," Evander replied.

"*Oh*, he's only kidding," Lement said. "She's been helpful with our questions, so I suppose we should be helpful with hers. As a chief vident, we are more concerned with the future of the Plane—its direction and our contributions to it through counsel and our publications. For the few of us as there are, most are assigned as top advisers to influential men and women across Sacrim—by those, at least, who are willing to learn from us."

"Or those who can afford it," Evander added.

Gold, Vanna thought. *Sacrim always revolves around gold.* "What of the other younger vidents, then? How does he become like you?"

"Time, really. And patience from those above you who grant your ascendance. Let me remember… Evander, is it thirty-six full moons that pass as an honorable vident before you are capable of ascending?"

"Correct."

"Right. Then, as a grand vident, you receive your second cord. Another thirty-six moons to become a noble vident. That's when the fun begins. You see, as an honorable vident, your only duty is to follow a chief around, to assist him as a pupil. And as a grand vident, you never leave our library. But as a noble vident…that's when you begin to teach as a preceptor. Though, for the most part, you guide only the indigent across our five partitions. I found my time here to be the most rewarding."

"I have fifteen moons left before I'm eligible," Evander said. "Think I'd be better off in the library if I'm being honest."

"Most are. Which is why the ascension past a noble vident is rare. Many just enjoy returning to teach in our library."

"How long, then, does it take to go from a noble to chief vident?" Vanna asked.

"One hundred and eight moons. *Well,* just at a minimum. For most, it's much longer. We chiefs hold a selection process that questions each vident on more than just their knowledge. It's a filter of ethics and integrity, one that challenges the vows we each take—a true test of their will."

"What test is that?"

"If I told you, I'd be compromising my vows now, wouldn't I? Though, I'm sure Evander, here, would like to know."

Vanna looked over at Evander, who just smiled precariously and said, *"I would."*

She turned back to Lement and asked, "Telling me your vows wouldn't, though, right?"

Vident Lement smirked. "Evander certainly could. It's the first thing he should have remembered from his beginning days."

With a look of near torture, Evander asked, "Do I have to?"

"What, have you forgotten them already?"

Evander steadied his face. "They go something like this: 'I, Vident Evander, pledge myself to purity in my thoughts, humility in my actions, and integrity in my speech. I pledge to have courage in my beliefs and adoration in my surroundings—to nurture the weak, enhance the poor, and carry empathy for my brothers, all in servitude to the Plane. For the virtue of the *vident* is the virtue of us *all*.'"

"*Very good*," Vident Lement applauded with a slow, sarcastic clap. "Now, each of those has its own meaning that we are sworn to uphold. For example, in pledging to have integrity in our speech, we, as vidents, are not to opine, to admit only the truth, and are not to speak in public or to the public."

"Why is that?" Vanna asked. "Wouldn't you want most people to hear what it was you had to say?"

"You'd think so, wouldn't you? Except that most people aren't always the right people. As a chief vident, I've come to understand the truth in this. You see, people, as individuals, levy a personal wall of defense. When they are together in a large group, however, they rely on each other's walls."

"Not a physical wall, right?" Evander asked, sounding slightly confused.

"No, not a physical one. A mental wall of reason. Suppose I were to walk into Sazara with a speech aimed at the nastiness of the Calegris, one that called for an uprising to overthrow the Consolar Vizar. Now, with that speech, if I went from person to person, reading it to only one at a time, exactly as I had it written, who would listen to me?"

"Maybe a few, but probably not enough to actually overthrow them," Evander replied.

"Right. Now, gather all those people in a hall together, give them the same exact speech, and you'd find that most might gladly rise up in anger."

Vanna understood exactly what Vident Lement was saying. *People feed off each other's flames.* "Like fire."

"What was that?" Vident Lement asked.

"A wall of reason is needed to protect our internal fire. Otherwise, it spreads to consume whatever is closest."

"*Ah*, she gets it," Vident Lement said proudly. "And true fire is just as invisible as our thoughts. It's the flames that we see...the passion, like the outcome of an infuriated mob that has the capability to set an entire forest ablaze—or even a city. Fire typically burns slowly away at its source. But when fed and enraged with undue air, it ignites into a harsh, uncontrollable blaze. We'd all do best to guard our own."

Vanna, herself, felt burned away. Her source was now different from the one she had known when she was a Child of the Silo. She appreciated the time she had in the Vypores and, more recently, with the vidents, where she was surrounded by people who cared about knowledge and the truth, regardless of the isolation it brought. "We should focus instead on feeding our own fires and fanning our own flames," Vanna said, the memory of her first time in Vyllini's temple passing through her mind.

"And it is with a wall of reason that we protect it." Vident Lement reiterated, staring forward at the West Brigade. "Vanna, you know, maybe we could make an exception for you and allow a woman to enter our ranks."

"I'm not sure I'd want to restrict myself as much as you all do," she responded. *I've had enough of that in my life.*

"I find my restrictions to be good. They keep me honest."

"Women can be honest without them."

"Another truth," Vident Lement said with a lighter laugh.

They carried on their back-and-forth discussions, mostly with those that rattled Evander, until the guardsmen marching at the fore began to slow. Near the front of the brigade, Vanna saw them turn left, circling out into the flat grassy plains toward a lone patch of trees to set up camp. She followed Vident Lement toward their separate plot, then helped them unpack their belongings and pitch their tents for the night.

As the sun began to set in the eastern sky, Evander left to gather twigs for their fire. Sitting with his back against the trunk of the closest tree was Vident Lement, who kept his head stuffed inside a large leather-bound book, reading with the help of whatever dwindling light remained.

Vanna sat upon a log, staring into the flames in thought, when she saw a figure from the darkening shade approach slowly through the smoke. "Still want to have that dinner I owe you?"

Cleo's face breached the blackness. "I thought you'd forgotten about me like you had my name."

"*Vanna Sapharo,*" he said proudly. Almost too proudly.

"Simple enough. Is dinner all you want?"

"No."

"At least you're honest. But dinner is all you're going to—"

"I'm aware," Cleo interjected. "Let me guess; you were going to lecture me about how you aren't like those women I was with back in Andar."

"Well, no—not exactly," she stuttered, glancing back into the fire. "Good."

Vanna turned to the tree, a short distance away, where Vident Lement sat, staring into his book. "Would he like to join us?"

Cleo's tanned face turned brash as he peered over at the broad beech tree. "He'll be okay. I've been sharing meals with him since I was a child. I'm sure he wouldn't mind missing one."

Vident Lement simply waved and shouted, "*You two go on*. Just bring back two hot plates, if you can."

"Will do." Cleo held out his hand to help Vanna up.

With a timid look, she grabbed his calloused hand and stood. He was taller than her, but just barely, and had stocky shoulders and legs that didn't seem to match the thinness of his chest and gut. His face was quite handsome, though, as much as Vanna didn't want to admit it. He had eyes a shade of green she'd never seen before and broad, firm cheeks, unlike any commoner in Sazara or Andar. But what enticed Vanna most about Cleo was the way he carried himself—with a native charisma, as if his courage came without a care.

He turned back, almost catching her stare, to say, "Thanks for coming."

"Sure. It was just going to be me and the stars for the night."

"I meant with the brigade...and me, to Corlis."

"You can thank Vident Lement for that. He's the one who convinced me to come."

"I know. I asked him to," Cleo said bluntly.

Of course. Vanna rolled her eyes, and her pale cheeks turned sour. Part of her wanted to turn around, to go back to her tent and rest so she could ride back to Andar in the morning. Inside, she thought of herself the way the Grand Dame might have—a fool for falling for such a simple trap. But instead, Vanna fought her temptation to leave and followed him in disquieting silence.

When she'd first met Cleo in the magistrate's palace, Vanna knew exactly the sort of person he was. Cleo was a young man who sat drinking with naked women and much older men, all of whom seemed to be at his command. And in their first conversation, as they rode to the ruins, Vanna found him to be haughty and arrogant. He was full of pride and spoke with assuredness, rash in his reactions. It was as if he didn't respect the people of Andar and their traditions—or even Vanna, the person.

As a Sister, Vanna was taught the superior skill of reading people—to find what motivated them and follow it through as leverage with action. They understood that the root of power was leverage. Cleo was someone who'd had his whole life of wealth and status handed to him and would use every bit of it to his advantage to gain more. His type held no quandary in stomping on the poor or weak to gain it. And there he was, leveraging the innocence of Vident Lement to justify his personal desire.

"I'm sorry if that offends you, but I didn't mean it in that way. To be fair, Vident Lement does like you and enjoys your company. He tells me you're brilliant and quite witty."

If I were actually brilliant, I would never have fallen for this, Vanna thought to herself.

"I know I haven't been the best of hosts either. It's been difficult as of late, leading this many men, especially when most of them are older than me. It's been a challenge."

Vanna responded with silence.

"It's one thing to command from orders, but it's a whole other to be the one giving them. Being at the top, making every decision, can be isolating."

"You seem to be doing fine," Vanna admitted, trying to avoid his conversation.

"Fine isn't the word for what's happened to me as of late. It might only seem that way because of the people I have around me. Or *had* around me."

"Had?"

"Yes. All those I've lost and those I've now sent east. We had to leave Andar in a hurry because of what happened to my home, Cignus," Cleo said as they continued to walk along the outskirts of the brigade's encampment.

Vanna followed him to a fire near a tree, isolated from the other canvas tents, where they would be alone. "I heard. That must be hard."

"It is." Cleo reached into a sack next to one of the logs and asked, "Fresh fruit? We also have a few boiled eggs and some legs of smothered rabbit."

Vanna nodded and took the fruit. "Vident Lement was right about that, too. The guardsmen here do eat well."

"We have our stores. And the men do well to trap along the way," Cleo told her, removing his bronze breastplate and untying the cord of his undergarment. "But as commanders and captains, we typically get the pick of the share."

"*Fitting.*"

Cleo looked at her with an expression as if he knew he should tread carefully. "But we have my stewards to thank for that, not me. They do all the preparation and cooking."

So, he does have some humility…but is it genuine? Vanna questioned. She watched as he made her a plate and offered her a chalice of wine, which she took to sip gently on.

"Sacrimian wine is the best."

Vanna could tell he seemed nervous, as if the words he spoke were siphoned through his mind a few times before they were let out. To settle the awkwardness, she took a few bites from her plate. "It's quite good. And the rabbit is tasty."

Cleo, though, took no time to square down his meal, finishing most of it before Vanna had enjoyed half of her own. "How was it, back where you're from? I know we didn't get to chat much at the ruins, but Vident Lement mentioned that you were from the Vypores. Is that right?"

"Yes," Vanna lied. "Stormy…and threatening."

"It's the most dangerous place of them all, from what I've read. A girl like you must be quite strong to survive that."

A girl like me, she snarled inside. "It wasn't all that bad. Even you look like you could probably survive."

Cleo laughed her comment off as if it were a joke. "I'm tougher than I look, you know."

"Or is it just this guard of yours that makes you look tough?"

"Probably both," he said, laughing again. "I'd say those two are one and the same now. I spent most of my childhood surrounded by it. Every solurn since I was the age of twelve was spent in training and preparation, just so I could be here, doing this, today."

What Cleo had said brought Vanna back to a time when she was young, as a Child of the Sisters. "I know that feeling."

"How so?"

"I…just meant…we had to watch our backs, is all. Like you said, the Vypores are dangerous." Cleo looked at her in a confused way, as if, just maybe, he were starting to see through her lie. But instead of prodding, he just took a sip of wine. "What was that like? Training all those days?"

"My father was really tough on me. But it was my commandant, Kladden, who was the most brutal. At least when I was a cagerman. For those who meet the standards, Sacrim's Guard places us in a fort far east of Sazara, along the coast. It was a training school, almost, to learn with shortswords and drill as future guardsmen."

Vanna listened as Cleo spoke, though she already knew about the cagermen from her time studying in the Silo. "All the guardsmen have to go through this?"

"Not all, but most. For the Sixth Brigade, it's required. Being a guardsman is the only field of work for every man here. Each of them was selected from the five partitions as the strongest and most disciplined of warriors. The formations and tactics, and, above everything, their skill, all come quite naturally."

"Seems to be quite the advantage."

"That school makes the advantage. It made me into a man, that's for sure. Fight after fight, morning, day, and night. It was the worst thing I'd ever been through—at the time, at least. The captains there were harsh and fed us little. In the second solurn, we drilled in formations to learn how to fight and defend the boy beside you with a shield and spear. There wasn't a day that went by that I didn't draw a bruise or blood."

Vanna nodded and sipped her wine.

"There was this one vice-captain, too—a man named Cleven Sciarra—that wanted me dead. When I said earlier that they fed us little, I meant *he* fed me little. Or, at least, he ensured that was my condition. Every bowl of porridge had half missing, and every guardsman he led swung at me with their full might—even when I wasn't yet ready. Making it out of that fort may very well have been a miracle."

"Brutal." *If only I could tell you what the Sisters did to us,* Vanna thought. *But maybe you would survive.*

"Brutal enough for boys to die. The one friend I had there, a boy named Silvano from Sazara, suffered such a fate. We were close. Silvano and I slept under the same sheets and protected each other's shoulders with our shields in formation. When we weren't sparring, we were having laughs. And when we weren't having laughs, we were sharing stories of our past. And when I starved, he was the only one who risked sharing his bread with me."

"What happened to him?"

Cleo looked like he didn't want to answer. "A nasty injury…one that grew nastier by the day. Cut after cut, we endured, but all it took was one. It made him sick. And then, one day, he was gone. I still have vivid memories of that night the officers informed us of his fate. I should have been there, closer beside him, to stop it—to protect him like the shield I was supposed to be."

As Cleo's head turned away from her own, Vanna said, "You shouldn't be so harsh on yourself."

"*Harsh*," Cleo scoffed, turning to stare into the fire. "Each one lost hurts more than I could describe. Especially now, as a commander. If harshness is what keeps them alive, then *harsh* is what I need to be. They are all my brothers."

And mine were not my sisters. Her mind raced with the memories of her own childhood, raised alone in the darkness of the Silos. The more she thought about it, the more she realized that maybe Cleo wasn't who she made him out to be. Maybe it was just a role he filled or a face he needed to wear to be the man the Guard required, just like she had with the Sisters.

"They're all I have now. My mother and sister were there, in Cignus. And from what I was told, the Calegris burned most of it to the ground."

Vanna watched as his eyes scorched with pain, trying to fight the flame of emotion that roared inside. "Why not march this brigade into Cignus, then?"

"That would be *too* harsh," Cleo admitted, almost regretfully. "To be honest with you, I couldn't bring myself to see it. I wasn't the closest with my mother, though. Or my sister, for that matter. My parents separated before I even became a cagerman. That's when they moved away. And I was young, then. But they're still my family. And they were all I had left. It would be too tough on me to return and see what I let happen to them."

A single tear looked as if it wanted to shed down Cleo's cheek. Vanna's heart opened to his show of emotion. She moved closer beside him and patted her hand on his knee in support. The person she'd met before was different than the one she now sat beside. He was hurt, just like she was. Deeply. But Cleo was still stuck in a position that required him to act and feel the pain of its consequences. *This is the real him,* she knew, joining him to stare into the fire.

"Cignus was a beautiful place," he continued, wiping his face to hide his shame. "Filled with streams that ran within its valleys, the greenest anywhere in Sacrim, and nestled between the rolling hills of the coasts. Being in Andar sort of reminded me of it, and of my early childhood—a place where the people are all family and care for one another."

"It sounds beautiful."

"It is—*or it was*. This is a personal war for me now. Those who rule in the Consolate Chamber have stripped my family from me and are doing all they can to take away my future—*Sacrim's future*," he corrected.

Vanna was well aware of what Cleo spoke of. She had been there, in Sazara, and seen the power those men in the chamber and the temple had. And she had lived a similar life herself, stripped of her family and her future by the Sisters of the Silo, who held all the power in Astria. She related to Cleo and felt for his war—the personal vengeance they both shared, one of misery and pain. For as many guardsmen as he had at his command, Vanna realized that Cleo was just as alone as she was.

She looked deep into his eyes and could see the innocent aspiration that carried him to continue on. Innocently green, like the valleys he claimed to be from. As if, within them, were a field of flowers that sprang out of the ground, fighting through the dirt and into the air to grow a life of its own. *Green, like a warm garden. Maybe I was wrong to be so cold.* "I believe in your future," she told him.

Cleo turned and reached his arm around her, hugging her in thanks for her support. He pulled back to break the awkwardness and looked up into the starlit sky. "I haven't ever talked to anyone like this, the way I have with you tonight. I'm sorry. It all just sort of came out. But thank you, *Vanna*, for listening."

"It's okay," she said back with a glimmering smile. "You're a lot easier to talk to now than before, too."

Cleo just laughed a little and continued to apologize, keeping his gaze up at the sky. "I won't forget your name again, I promise. All I'll need to do is look up at the sky, and the stars up there will spell it out." With his finger pointed high, he traced the figure of her name as if it were a constellation.

And in the image the stars displayed, Vanna smiled.

CHAPTER 28

STONE

"*There, up ahead,*" Roth whispered behind the fraying trunk of a broad wet pine.

"*There are hundreds of them,*" Scarlett said softly from around the other side. "*Any clue why they're here? Do you think they followed us? Are they looking for me?*"

"*I doubt it. There's no way,*" Roth said confidently. "*Unless... No, that can't be.*"

"*Unless what?*"

"Unless my sister and Lud are on one of those ships."

Roth and Scarlett had trekked their way east, then north, along the Regent's dirt-laid path to the Northwoods for nearly a moon's pass. Since leaving Bovere, Roth had been cautious and ensured they stayed hidden from any travelers along the trail. He'd purchased canvas hides to erect their campsites, rather than risk staying a night in any tavern or lodge. And to Scarlett's dismay, Roth had reverted to his skills as a ranger to hunt or scavenge for every meal, avoiding any markets for food.

Their expedition to Tergona, though, had still been one of silence. While not nearly as mute as their first few days up the Fleming River, Roth and Scarlett had learned to trust each other's company. She had grown fond of the Regent's vast meadows of green countryside, with streams and rivers and towns scattered seemingly everywhere. Roth, however, begrudged her frequent desires to wander and was cautious not to let her slip out of his sight again.

Despite their prolonged journey, he was elated to have finally arrived at the easternmost canton of the Northwoods. In the brisk breeze of autumn, the two had spent the day prior watching his hometown from afar, waiting to see if his mom or pop, or even Ruth or Ludwyn, would ever leave their tiny little cabin. The next morning, when he'd planned to sneak in to see them, he found Tergona's only road flushed with chattering folk over a supposed arrival near Cubby Cove.

And so, Roth led Scarlett around the brim of the Northwoods to discover a fleet of seven vessels anchored within its curved protection. They watched carefully from atop a ridge as small boats began to row ashore and the amassment of foreigners once aboard marched inland. Roth followed their passage from a distance and found them to be heading toward one of the few bare plots beside Tergona—the Aledan Burial Mounds.

Scarlett tagged behind Roth as they swept between the tall barks of the wet pines he knew all too well, doing his best to avoid crunching the fallen twigs between the mulch and their feet. They went around the mound's outskirts, watching as, one by one, the same men from the boats queued to pass a plotted hole.

"*It looks like some sort of ceremony,*" Scarlett whispered between the bushes.

"*It's a funeral.*"

"Who for?"

"How would I know? But whoever it is, they must be important," Roth answered, continuing to scan the men. In his strong hand, he gripped the handle of his axe tightly, ready to pounce at the prospect of foreigners invading his home canton. He thought about running back to warn his mom and pop and maybe try to move the rest of Tergona to the nearby canton of Havenhill, or even Prestown, for safety.

That was until Scarlett spotted an all-too-familiar face. "There's a girl, just there, past that short one to the left. The one walking up now."

Roth's crooked face brimmed with a smile. "That's Ruth, alright…in the plaid-cut skirt." A thousand questions rolled through his head, wondering how or why she was with these men and how it was that she, of all people, had come to arrive here on their ships. The Ruth he knew would never have done such a thing.

"*Sheesh.* You weren't joking when you said she looked like you. She's taller than most of the men."

"By the looks of it, they've turned her into one," Roth said with a quiet chuckle. "But she doesn't look like their prisoner."

"No, she has a sword at her waist, the same as them all."

"I see Lud too. There, the only one covered like a bear with hair."

"That's your friend, right?" Scarlett asked, her concern now smoldering.

"Yes. When he goes to leave, we'll follow him." Roth crept his way closer to the line of men who were walking toward the coast, leaving the burial mounds. The closer he observed them, the clearer he saw their foreign features, unfamiliar to the Eastern Plane. Most had unkempt, stringy, reddish hair or shades of blond and were dressed in ragged clothes to hide their sun-splotched or pale skin. However, as the line continued to pass on the pebble trail back to the cove, he could see that their faces all shared the same solemn look of despair.

In the distance, Roth finally spotted Ludwyn between the green foliage. He let out the call of a ranger—a sound, deep like the hoot of an owl, which he made three times with one of his hands covering the space between his thin lips and stubby nose.

Ludwyn's square-jawed face lit up as he scanned the tree line. Behind him, he tugged on Ruth's arm to get her attention, listening as Roth made the call of a ranger once more. With an abrupt smile, the two of them left the line of men and dashed into the woods, heading in their direction.

"*Roth!*" Ludwyn said with elation as soon as he emerged from cover. "Boy, am I glad to see you!"

"More than ever," Roth replied as he gave his best friend a big bear hug. "And you too, Ruth… *Look at you.*"

Ruth rushed over and wrapped her arms tightly around him. "No, look at you!" She gleamed, refusing to let go. "*I prayed so long for this day to come.*"

"Both of you were on those boats?"

"Sailed up from Roverra's coast on 'em," Ludwyn replied with a proud smile.

"That's *unbelievable.* Guys, this is Scarlett," Roth said, turning to introduce her. She was much shorter than the three of them and still wore his shawl's hood to cover her fire-orange hair. "Scarlett, Ruth and Ludwyn."

"So, this is the girl who has caused us so much trouble," Ruth said as she stuck out her hand.

"My goodness, you are beautiful," Ludwyn commented.

"Caused probably isn't the right word," Scarlett replied. "All Roth talks about is you two. And this place. It's a pleasure to finally meet you."

"Beautiful...and smelly," Ludwyn said after he shook her hand. "You should probably keep that hood of yours up. Don't want these savages to get a look at you."

"*Savages?* They aren't here to plunder Tergona, *right?*" Roth questioned, raising his axe.

Ruth laughed to dismiss his concern. "No. They wouldn't do that...but they do want her. At least they did before Maris murdered Captain Noreas."

"*Maris?*" Scarlett asked, her blue eyes broadening with unease. "He's here?"

"Is that the man who took you?" Ruth asked. When Scarlett gave a squeamish nod, she continued, "Don't worry, he's our prisoner—still on the *Widow* as we speak."

"Your *prisoner* managed to kill your *captain?*" Roth asked.

"It's a hard one to explain," Ludwyn responded, almost unamused.

"We'll have to tell you about it later, when we have more time," Ruth said. "Have you seen Mom and Pop yet? How long have you been in Tergona?"

"Just a day or two. But no, not yet. We had a long journey in, and I just figured if people were still looking for me, our home might be the first place they'd come."

"That's smart of you—for once. I'm just surprised you managed to find your way up here all alone," Ruth told him.

"I wasn't alone." Roth looked over at Scarlett, who still seemed somewhat traumatized after hearing Maris's name.

"Needed a woman's help again, I see," Ruth said, attempting to cheer her up. "Well, I'm headed to the house after this. I'll tell them you're here and safe, too. I've been dying to see them."

"Why don't we all meet up later, at our spot?" Roth suggested, looking over at Ludwyn.

"In the brush?"

"Yeah. Ruth, can you bring Mom and Pop so I don't have to worry about sneaking in?"

"Yes, that'd be perfect," Ruth replied.

"We'll make a campfire, just like we used to," Ludwyn added.

Roth couldn't hold his smile back. "*Great.*" He hugged them both tightly again and watched as the pair headed back onto the trail.

As the evening unfolded, Roth and Scarlett sat in the brush of the Northwoods, waiting for their friends to arrive. Their spot was a small, cleared patch, hidden away in the Northwoods, with a stone-encircled firepit at its center, surrounded by overturned logs for seating. Roth gathered a few twigs and chopped whatever dried wood he could find to start the fire.

"Look who it is! *My boy!*" his mother's growling voice said from a distance.

Roth turned to look down at the narrow trail and saw his mother, Roseanna, leading a line of familiar faces. "*Mom!*" He rushed over to embrace his tall but portly mother, picking her up by the scruff of her long skirt to give her a sweeping hug.

"*Ohhh,* put me down…put me down. My goodness, you reek. Have you forgotten how to wash yourself… I just know I taught you better," she clamored, puffing her short, shaggy brown hair back into place. "I ought to be giving you a whipping or two if what I heard is true."

As he let her go and ignored her affable tone, he noticed his father, Edmon, right behind her, carrying a burlap sack over his brawny shoulder. "Glad you're home, son."

"Me too." Roth shook his pop's hand, then grabbed the sack to carry it himself. Behind them, at a distance, was Ruth, who led his old ranger friends, Trey and Leland, out into the woods. Trey was older than Roth, and Leland was much younger than both of them. He waited to greet his scruffy-haired friends with a slick smile before they all trailed their chattering way back to the brush's fire.

"Where's Lud?" Roth asked.

"He's coming. He and Dane are carrying in a cask of wine from the cove," Ruth replied.

"Dane?"

"My friend from Marredom."

"I, for one, can't wait to try this Sacrimian wine Ruth has been telling me so much about," their mother said. "I brought some food in that sack there, too. Salted stag, some sprouts, and a few fresh wheaten loaves—your favorite."

"Great. We've been starving." Roth glanced over to where Scarlett sat to make sure she was okay.

Just as he was about to introduce her, Ludwyn and Dane crackled their way through the thick brush, carrying between them the half-cask of wine.

"The party has arrived!" His mother rejoiced, taking her mug out first and high-stepping toward the wooden barrel. Dane placed it gently down on top of a stump, then turned it over and removed the plug to fill her cup.

Roth could tell that the lengthy blond-haired boy found his mother to be quite rude or even obnoxious. To break their awkwardness, he said aloud, "Mom, come over here. I'd like to introduce you to Scarlett."

"*My*, isn't she beautiful," his mother said, stepping around the fire to shake Scarlett's hand. "And you didn't even tell me you had a girlfriend…"

"She isn't my girl—"

Scarlett pulled the hood of her shawl down out of respect. "That hair you have, my goodness… *Now*, Roth, you know how I feel about these foreigners. But for this beauty, I think I can make an exception."

"Mom, we aren't together."

"Oh, well, excuse me, then," she stated rudely, moving to sit next to Edmon.

While Roth filled mugs for Scarlett and himself, Ruth announced, "This is Dane, too, everyone."

"*Another foreigner*…and a nork at that." Their mother gasped long enough to shake the blubber off her belly. "*My*, you two really have had quite the journey."

"And we're glad to be back home," Ruth reminded her. "Safe and intact."

After Roth handed Scarlett a mug of wine, he moved to help his quieter father unload the sack of food and place their iron-spoked stand above the fire. Edmond loaded the pot with broth, sprouts, and cubed meat, then placed it on the hook to cook as they all found their seats.

"So, tell us, Roth," Trey said to his left, from between Ludwyn and Leland. "What was it like in that pit? We've been dying to know since we heard the news."

"It was all a dream, really. Or a nightmare. It sort of all sprang from nowhere," Roth tried to explain. He began to tell the stories of his fights on the isle, and how he came to be the Regent's champion. Leland and

Trey hung onto his every word as Roth stood swinging his axe by the fire, replaying every moment of action he could remember.

Nothing made Roth happier than seeing his old friends and sharing drinks by the fire, just like they used to. But across from them sat Ruth, who didn't look nearly as enthused. She spent her time chatting with Dane, to her right, before finally looking up at him with a smirk to say, "You're making all of this violence sound so much more glorious than it should be."

"*Forgive me*. I'm doing my best to remove all the dreadful parts of my own story," Roth said sarcastically. "I'm allowed to have fun, Ruth…is that okay?"

"So, what happened in Roverra, was that fun too?"

In a much more serious tone, Roth replied, "That was an accident, Ruth. I've explained that endlessly, and I'm sorry for what happened."

"No, tell us too. What happened there?" his mother asked between sips. "From what we've heard, there's no way my Rothy boy could have done such a thing."

Roth glanced back to his left and saw all his friends laughing at his expense. "*It's complicated*. My bondsman was Lady Orean Lomberg—"

"Of the Lomberg coat?" his mother asked with a surprised look. "You didn't murder this woman, now, did you? You really are in a whirlwind of trouble… Her family—"

"I know, I know. She's a royal. If they hand me over to the courts, every canton will have me barred from entry. Well, almost every canton. Besides Garsenden."

"They'd turn you into a labor mule down there, in their mines," Trey said.

"I don't know, Ruth, the best fighters of the Plane come from Garsenden. They're all stone-cold killers and train day and night in the old art of fighting. They'd be happy to take you in," Leland said with a grin.

"Good point. They fight dirty down there. Not like those knights of Florington or Decanan," Ludwyn added.

Leland's grin grew larger. "I even heard the men down there still fight with the horns of rams bludgeoned to their helmets."

"Thanks, guys. But my plan right now is not to be banished to some mine down there."

"There is another way," Ruth told him.

"That isn't happening," Roth responded sternly, thinking of the Cathedral.

"Roth, forget the cantons. If any member of those royal families wanted you dead, there'd be nothing you could do to stop it. And, if anything, those judges they keep on their payroll would be the same ones to cover it up," Roseanna stammered quickly.

"I know. I've met my share of royals. Speaking of which." Roth bent down and rummaged through his sack. "Before it all happened, I was at a fancy dinner in Roverra, and they gave me this." He pulled out a tiny pin and a rolled piece of parchment. "My Royal Deed, establishing the *Coat of Fendorse*, officially commissioned by the Royal Order."

His friends and parents all gasped, then stood to surround him and inspect the tiny iron pin. They took turns holding it and pivoting its olive-colored, four-fingered bear claw up against the fire as the light from the sky began to dwindle.

"So, what does that mean?" Ruth asked in disbelief. "We're a *royal family* now? How can that be?"

"I don't get a seat at their table or anything—especially not now, since I'm probably a warranted man. But I guess that's right—our family is now officially recognized as a royal family. *Here*." Roth tossed the pin across the fire, landing it in Ruth's lap.

"The Coat of Fendorse, huh," their mother stated aloud. "Maybe they can't kill you now after all."

Ruth picked it up and held its shiny side to the light. "So, the claw of a bear?"

"*Keep it*," he said to his twin sister, startling everyone into surprise.

"*No*, I can't. You earned this, not me."

"You represent the Fendorse family better than I ever could."

"You got that right," their mother commented.

"*Thank you*." Ruth smiled like he hadn't seen her do in many solurns. She clasped the pin tightly in her fist and took the rolled parchment with the other hand.

"What happened to that lady?" Leland asked bluntly to interrupt their warm moment.

"Before this was even given to me, she asked me to join her family and to work for her in Bovere. I think she had some lofty ambitions for herself.

And then, that night, the Royal Order sort of rejected her. Anyway, she got really drunk at the dinner, and I had to pull her away from the party and bring her downstairs. Then, out of nowhere, she came onto me and wouldn't stop, so I shoved her off."

"That can't be it, surely," Ludwyn said. "Came on to you? That hag?"

"I wish it wasn't so... But like I said—"

"She was a drunk," Ruth interjected to acknowledge her brother's perspective.

"And not the prettiest sight when naked," Roth added to make his friends laugh. Beside him, he looked down and saw Scarlett sitting silently, staring into the fire. "But I didn't mean for it to happen, I promise. I shoved her off me, and her head hit the corner of the nightstand... And I didn't know what to do, so I panicked."

"Just after that was when we saw that ship sink, and these two wash ashore," Ruth added, pointing at Dane and Scarlett.

Roth looked at them both and could tell that neither wanted to share their tale. Instead, Ruth and Ludwyn told the account of their journey on board the fleet of sailed ships and how they had managed to survive the passage home. Their father, Edmon, spoke only to announce that their food was ready, then proceeded to scoop bowls for them all.

Deep into the night, they ate and drank around the campfire in warm company, telling stories of their time apart. The more Dane and Scarlett sipped the fine Sacrimian wine, the more they began to open up to Roth and Ruth's family and friends and share their own stories of what it was like to grow up in a foreign region of the Plane.

"Being somewhat close to those islands up north, we always heard stories of what it was like, but I never imagined the conditions were that bad," Roseanna said.

"And he didn't even tell you the worst of it," Ruth added.

"What can be worse than that King?"

"Being an oarsman," Dane answered solemnly. "I was just the lucky one to wash ashore, into the hands of Captain Noreas."

"He was a good leader. Lud, here, though, didn't care for him much," Ruth said. "But we did manage to free a few hundred of those oarsmen that nork King had in bondage—those he forced to row his galleys, just like Dane."

"Was that the man you buried earlier? Your captain?" Roth asked.

"*Yep*," Ruth replied in a saddened tone. "Cowen wanted to bury him at sea, but Dane brought up some myth of Marredom and convinced them that wasn't what he would have wanted."

"Boy, did he go berserk," Ludwyn said between his puffs of redleaf from Trey's shortpipe.

"Cowen?" Roth asked.

"The *Widow*'s first mate," Ruth explained. "He wanted Maris dead for murdering Captain Noreas."

"He didn't just want him dead—he wanted to kill him himself. Or torture him, really," Ludwyn clarified. "I've never seen him that angry. Most of the mates wanted the same, though, to be fair."

"*Scarlett*," Dane spoke over the fire. "Was this the same man who took you?"

"*Yes*," she admitted again, reluctantly.

Dane rubbed his scruffy blond chin. "Since Captain Noreas's passing, we haven't decided what to do with him. What do you think should be done?"

"I just want to go home, that's all," Scarlett replied.

"But what of Maris—what should his justice be?" Ruth asked her.

Scarlett stared into the flames, pausing for a while in thought. "He should *rot* on a spike and *burn* under the hottest of flames for what he did to me." Everyone around the fire simmered to silence. Roth took a heavy sip from his mug. He had never asked Scarlett about the details of what happened to her after she was taken from the isle. And now, after that, he was glad he hadn't. No part of him wanted to imagine what she had endured.

"That settles it, then," Dane said. "I'll bring that up to Cowen in the morning. Then we can take you back to Sazara on the *Widow*."

"*I'm not getting on another boat*," Scarlett said back sternly.

"I thought you said you wanted to go home?" Ruth asked.

"I do. But not on another boat... *No way.*"

"Cowen won't like that," Dane sneered under his breath.

Roth could see his twin sister across the fire trying to think of a possible solution. Before she could speak, their mother drunkenly butted in and said, "If the pretty girl doesn't want to be on a boat, then she won't go on the boat."

"But how else would she get back home?" Ruth asked.

"She can stay with us if she wants, here in Tergona. We now have both of your empty rooms," Roseanna answered with a slight roll of her eyes.

"It wouldn't be safe," Roth added. "Half the Regent and all the royals would be looking for her."

"*That's it!*" Ruth yelled aloud. "Who better to bring her to than the royals?"

"Are you insane? I'm not just going to hand her over to them. They'd take me to those gallows they call a court and have Roverra's judge ban me from every canton in the Regent," Roth pleaded.

"You don't have to bring her... *I will.*" Ruth lifted the rolled parchment and pin from her lap and waved them in the air. "They're looking for you, not me. And it isn't like the royals will mistreat her. From what you said about her family and their wealth, Scarlett would probably live like a queen in Bovere. They have sentinels there to protect her and the gold to contrive her exchange back to Sazara."

"And you'd be the one there to defend her along the way? She's a *target*. What if there's trouble, like what we had on our travels?"

"I can join them," Ludwyn proclaimed with a grin.

Roth let out a mocking laugh. "No offense, Lud, but they'd probably be safer without you."

"No. We could use him," Ruth stated. "I still have my saber, but he'd be a help. Just in case."

"I've never known the royals to be malicious," Scarlett admitted. "My father held trade talks with some of them quite often, actually. I think that could work."

"*See.* It'd be good for both of them. The royals get their gold, and Scarlett gets to return home."

Roth's face soured as he looked into the fire. He didn't want to part with Scarlett. Throughout their travels, and even in their silence, the two of them shared a unique trust and mutual understanding. Roth felt obliged to stay by Scarlett's side and protect her. And as he looked up, Roth found that he wasn't alone in that thought. Dane sat shaking his head from his seat beside Ruth, turning away. *At least Lud looks somewhat happy,* he thought after scanning to his left to see his best friend still grinning.

"What about Cowen?" Dane asked. "He won't allow that."

"Cowen isn't the captain," Ludwyn was quick to reply.

"Then who is?" Dane asked.

"No one yet, at least," Ruth said. "Captain Noreas centered his fleet around their mission to find Scarlett and bring her back to Sazara. But now he's gone, and Scarlett will soon be gone too."

"There's still Markas and the other captains—Sonny and Simion. I know Jalek is young, but he could do it too," Dane said.

"That fleet would sink if any of them were left in charge," Ludwyn said with a smoke-ridden laugh. "Cowen is the only real option."

"Other than yourself, *Dane*," Ruth said. "I was there—we all saw what you did in the North Sea. And everyone knows how fondly Captain Noreas thought of you, especially the other captains. And those oarsmen all look up to you. They practically outnumber the mates now, anyway. Who but yourself has been where they once were?"

Roth looked over at Ludwyn and saw his face turn distraught. Dane seemed like a friendly young man. He was quiet and reserved with his words. And he was thin but had solid bones. From what Ruth had just said, he could tell that those people she listed weren't the only ones who looked fondly on Dane. To Roth, it was clear that his sister did too. And he could tell just how much that might have hurt Ludwyn on their journey.

"*I can't*," Dane let out. "I don't want that power."

Around the circle, to everyone's surprise, the twins' father, Edmon, said, "Then it sounds like you'd be perfect for it."

"Listen to the man, will ya. Don't be such a wimp." Roseanna gave her husband an encouraging hug. "I just want those boats gone and out of here anyway."

"You sound just like my old captain, sir." Dane laughed a bit before admitting, "I haven't told anyone this yet, but Captain Noreas, in his last breath, asked me to take care of the fleet."

"See!" Ruth said. "Now you have to!"

"I just don't think I could get all the old mates on board."

"Oh, screw them," Ludwyn said. "They're all southern scoundrels anyway."

"*Ahem*," Roth coughed, leaning his head to his side where Scarlett sat.

"*Sorry*, miss… I just meant—"

"It's okay," Scarlett said. "No offense taken."

"What do you think the fleet should do now that they'll no longer be chasing after Scarlett?" Ruth asked Dane.

The scrawny young nork paused for a long moment and looked around the forest, then up at the starlit sky. "I want to make things right in the north—to free every oarsman and help my family back home and make sure they are all taken care of. Them and the rest of Marredom. It'd be a challenge to get the mates from the south to join this cause. Some might even want to return home. But it's the right thing to do."

Ruth moved to put her hand on Dane's shoulder, which Roth again could tell bothered Ludwyn to no end. With confidence, she said, "I believe you can make that happen."

Dane smiled. "From everything Ruth has told me, the Regent seems like a wonderful place. The people of the north deserve to live free like you all do here in the east."

"The Regent's about as wonderful as a mule's ass," their mother retorted.

"*Oh*, hush," Ruth said, trying to quiet their laughter. "I think that's very noble of you, Dane. Whatever we can do, we'll try to help."

"But I don't want war. I just want to compete with the King on the seas and earn our people's trust. To do that, we'll need more ships. We'd need to convert and refit those galleys first and foremost. Which means lumber for the masts—"

"My father, here, knows his way around nearly every mill in the area. These lot do, too," Roth said, glancing over at his friends.

"We can make that happen," Trent said after Edmon nodded.

"But you're gonna need some gold for payment," Leland added.

"We have that, and better, to trade with—if the mates will allow it," Dane said. "Captain Noreas mentioned once that there's a shipyard on an island out east named Nordheim. If we can get the lumber, we can bring the cargo galleys there to get their masts, cross-yards, and lifts refit."

"You'll need more crew to man them," Ludwyn stated.

"*I'll join you*," Roth said. "I'd miss the Northwoods, but it's not like I can really stay here anyway. I'd have to look over my shoulder every waking day and sleep out here alone every night."

"Good luck with those seas," Ruth told her brother with a snobby chuckle.

"You've managed them—shouldn't be too difficult for a bear to handle."

"We could use a man like you," Dane broke a faint smile to say. "Ludwyn's right, though. We'll need all the help we can get to man this fleet of free men."

"*A free fleet...*" Ruth spoke aloud. "I like it."

"All of my babies have finally come home, only to tell me they plan to leave again," Roseanna said, her voice creaking with guilt.

"We'll be back again," Ruth told her confidently. "*I promise.*"

With a deep breath and a long sip of wine, Dane said, "I'll convene with Cowen and the mates in the morning. And if everything goes right, we'll be back too."

"Good luck, *Captain*," Roth told him.

Dane took a long sip of wine. "Thanks. *I'm going to need it.*"

Chapter 29

Sun

"Captain Jove, how does it look ahead?"

"Of the five scouts I sent out, all returned the same. Fort Saxoram is empty."

"As expected," Cleo mumbled, guiding Dahlia's strong neck back toward the grove where his guardsmen were halted.

After having split the Sixth Brigade into two, giving command of the East Brigade to Kladden, Cleo reorganized his own into three battalions. Captain Ostin remained in command of the first, leading the cavalry that now rode more than half a thousand strong. In the second battalion, Cleo promoted a younger guardsman from Cignus named Kenrick Jove to lead the swordsmen and spearmen, which had become an assorted mix of the Sixth's guardsmen and cagermen from Andar. Captain Sovano was reassigned to the West Brigade's third battalion to host its archers and supply wagons from the rear.

Just down the hill, at the edge of the grove's shadow, Cleo saw his men sitting still, awaiting his next command. At the fore of each column were the orange flags of New Scipyria rippling in the air, hoisted tall above the sea of bronze. Cleo scanned their wide formation, stopping his gaze at its center to lift a telling smile. There, on horseback beside Vident Lement, was Vanna, who had ridden at the lead beside him for the last quarter-moon.

Even from atop the hill, out from the hidden green of the grove, he could see her long hair swaying with the breeze. Her defined legs straddled a saddle, and one of her fair shoulders stuck out from her single-strapped cherry top. As Cleo sat watching her chat with Vident Lement, part of him wished their march west would continue for a few more days, if not for another quarter-moon, or even longer. He looked forward to stopping the West Brigade's march to set up camp for their alternating nights of rest.

Dinner with her, away from the rest of the brigade, always came with deep talks and spouts of playful banter.

After his past moons' whirlwind of misery, Vanna had become Cleo's reason to smile. She was a happy distraction from his sufferings as of late, from his father's death to the First Brigade's assault on Cignus. And his feelings for Scarlett had practically vanished since the day they first shared a meal together.

Cleo's time with Vanna was a peaceful moment away from his captains, who were always asking him to make difficult decisions or discussing the men's menial chatter and needs. And his time with her was even a moment away from Vident Lement, who kept his mind sharp in the evenings by issuing questions to him regarding the historic commanding patterns of Sacrim's past heroes. Most of his questioning dealt with those bloody conflicts of the Amulonic War—of Commander Sylvian, who led Sacrim's Guard through the Sineaqe Gorge to defeat Torent Stoneface at Garsenden and Oxgurd, and even his victories at Furth and the Heights of Leith, before he was finally defeated by Timothy the Regnant. But all of it had become like the buzzing of flies that swarmed annoyingly around a meal he long awaited. Other than vengeance for the destruction of his family and homeland, time with Vanna was what Cleo hungered for the most.

He rode Dahlia down toward the front line of the first battalion. Two of his captains trotted up to meet him, their stained-gold cloaks surfing above their horses' rears. "Jove's scouts gave the clear," Cleo told them.

"Good. It's like Kladden had said—the Calegris must have recalled the Second Brigade to Sazara," Captain Ostin replied, his voice stern. "My men could use the rest."

"Mine as well."

"That settles it, then," Cleo said, glancing back at the grove's tree line. "Corlis is only a day and a half's ride from the fort. We'll rest in its shade and grab whatever supplies the Second Brigade left, then leave on the morrow for Corlis."

"We'll need to be on our toes for that one. Dodgy place, Corlis is," Captain Sovano told Cleo.

"Sovano's right, Commander. Corlis is known for being a haven for criminals and smugglers," Captain Ostin added.

"Then we should fit right in," Cleo told his two captains. "Have your men ready to march again in the morning. We'll need to be fully fit when we reach Corlis. The Second may not be here, but that doesn't guarantee they're in Sazara."

The captains nodded, then whipped the reins of their horses back toward the West Brigade. Cleo sat tight to his saddle, looking at the grove, which grew sparingly with cedars that offered little cover. With most of his guardsmen still halted within it, he was thankful the Second Brigade wasn't still stationed at Fort Saxoram. To Cleo, there was no doubt that his three-thousand-man march would have been spotted while transiting the open plains of western Sacrim. And the open hillside, between the grove and the fort, would have given any attack on them a large buffer—all with the advantage of having the high ground. Cleo couldn't help but ponder how ugly things could have gotten.

Instead, Cleo's West Brigade marched forward in peace, each column led by the spearmen with their shields strapped sharply at their back. To the sides and rear were the cavalry's warhorses of the first battalion, who gaffed around loosely to surround them. Thump after thump, their sandals marched in unison toward Cleo. Halfway up the open hill, he sat waiting for them, his royal-red cloak sifting with the breeze.

"The wagons at the rear might have to tussle to pass, but our columns should hold through the trees," Captain Sovano yelled out at him in passing.

"*Very well*," Cleo acknowledged. He rode farther down the front line to meet Vanna and the two vidents.

"Shall we?" Vident Lement said, lifting his palm out above the mane of his horse, motioning for Cleo to ride ahead of him. "I was just telling Vanna here how good the food is in Corlis. Best flamed fish across all Sacrim. That's for certain."

"Is that so?" Cleo asked.

"Vident Lement tells me you've always been a picky eater," Vanna said casually beside Evander.

"When I was younger, sure. But my time with the Guard has changed that."

"Even as a commander, with the meals I see you have?"

Cleo turned back to Vanna and chuckled. "Yes, even as a commander, rabbit and rice can grow tiresome. I'd kill for a well-roasted shoulder...or even the loin…fat and juicy, like we would have back in Sazara. To give up meat, you vidents must be mad."

Vident Lement simply smiled. "Why do you think I'm so excited for the fish in Corlis?"

"To be fair, we've been away from any sort of sea for far too long. I'll be sure that's first on the list."

"Excellent! We shall have my favorite, then—flamed fish, roasted saltnuts, some brined peaches, and maybe a loaf of shortbread," Vident Lement said.

Vident Evander, who was typically quiet around Cleo, broke his silence to add, "I could go for a nice frosted cake."

Cleo turned to look back at the plump young man and laughed. As the rest of his brigade emerged from the grove, the worded jabs at Evander continued, with Vanna being the only one to come to his defense. It didn't take long for Cleo to lead them over the hill and see the curving wall of Fort Saxoram off in the distance. He paused for a moment and looked out across the grassy plains, which were lit by the evening sun, to mumble, "We never had a fort like *this one* either."

"Well, yours were never as old as this one," Vident Lement said, riding up beside him. "This fort predates the Temple of Sciron at Sazara—by quite some time, in fact. It was originally built to shelter the people near Corlis from those torrential storms that would linger between the Vypores and the rifts of the Silver Sea."

"It's beautiful," Vanna said from behind as the West Brigade continued to march around them.

"*That it is*. It was commissioned by the eighth consolar vizar of Sacrim at the time, a great-great-grandnephew of Claros. A man by the name of Sadrian Ceravello, if I remember correctly. In a few solurns, Evander will be able to tell you all about it." Vident Lement looked back at Evander, who just nodded gracelessly. "You can't tell from here, but the stone bricks are laid with shards of seashells within their mortar. And its outer wall wraps within itself in the shape of a curling shell. Similar to the Second Partition's historic insignia."

"It's a beauty, alright," Cleo said. He began to ride forward again within the middle of the brigade, after letting the cavalry and spearmen march ahead. "—to withstand the weathering of time."

"*Time is only life's shadow,*" Vident Lement stated from behind.

The closer they rode, the clearer Cleo could see Fort Saxoram in all its magnificence. All four of them stared up in awe at its curving wall that stood stories tall. Wrapped around it, vines and fraying moss grew in all places besides the fort's windowed openings. At its very top, to match the windows below, were battlements for archers that spanned every other shoulder length.

"*Do any of you hear that?*" Vanna asked suddenly.

"Hear what?" Cleo heard nothing but the sandal steps of his brigade marching around him. He turned around and saw Vanna halted on her runt of a horse.

Vanna's hand covered the brim of her brows as she lifted her chin to look up at the sky. "It sounds like a *whistle*—"

Like a flash of lightning striking down from above, Cleo saw a faint flicker pass between him and Vanna. With it came the whistling sound she had spoken of, growing rapidly until it altogether stopped—*everything stopped.* Cleo looked around frantically, watching as his guardsmen burst into echoing shouts, dropping their spears and shields to dart in every direction.

There, between the chaos, sitting motionless within their harrowing howls, was Vident Lement on his saddle, staring blankly at Cleo with both his hands covering his chest. Their eyes met faintly before Vident Lement looked down at the drapes of his burnt-orange vestment. He slowly lifted his hands and gasped in despair. At the center of his chest was a bloodied hole.

Cleo sat still, frozen in an anguish of disbelief. He looked up to the sky and saw droves of large birds swooping in and out of the clouds.

Rook riders, he realized.

"*HELP HIM...CLEO!*" he heard Vanna's voice break through the havoc. From her cry alone, Cleo snapped back into action, looking around to witness his men falling left and right from arrows slung from the backs of the large birds. "*CLEO, NOW!*"

Cleo jumped from Dahlia, who immediately reared and then galloped off into the frantic mess of guardsmen. He rushed to help Vanna lift Vident Lement's body off his pale horse.

"*Cleo…*" Vident Lement struggled to say. "*Give my book to Evander.*"

With a doubtful nod, Cleo grabbed the back of Vident Lement's neck and pressed his other hand on his wound. "Vident Lement—you'll be okay…"

"*The truth…Cleo—always stick to the truth. My name isn't Lement… remember?*" Blood began to spew out of the old man's mouth as he did his best to smile.

Cleo's hand became swathed with warmth. He switched the two of them back and forth, hoping out of desperation that one of them might stop the bleeding.

"*Sable…Sellieve, Cleo.*" With his dwindling, final breath, he toiled to say, "*The key lies in the black stone…*"

Cleo felt nothing but cold tears dripping down his cheek. "*What black stone?*" With the whirlwind of death continuing to hurl from the sky and the cries of his men smothering the air around him, all Cleo could do was stare into the eyes of Vident Lement…of *Sable Sellieve*. His pupils were round like the sun but grew black and lifeless, as death shadowed over his gentle spirit.

"*Here*, Cleo, Vanna, lift him onto me," he heard a voice shout from above.

Cleo looked up slowly, breaking his stare, to see Vident Evander sitting atop his horse with his arm outstretched. Directly behind him, in the backdrop of the sky, were the giant birds still storming down from the clouds.

In a blink, he heard Vanna's voice again, snapping him out of his teary haze. "*Grab his shoulders. CLEO…grab—*"

Without a thought of what to do, he threw Vident Lement's limp body onto Evander's horse. As arrows continued to sling past him, Cleo stood still and watched him dash through the chaos toward the doors of Fort Saxoram.

"*Cleo, take this—we need to get there too,*" Vanna urged, handing him a bronze shield.

"*How did I let this happen?*" Cleo mumbled to himself, crying in despair. "*I've failed…again.*"

"*This isn't the time to sulk—we need cover.*" Vanna grabbed his bloodied hand and yanked him toward the fort where his guardsmen were running.

They zigged from left to right over bodies of bronze that lay lifeless on the field of grass, dodging the ambush from above. Some guardsmen were still trying to squirm away, pierced by arrows lodged in open slits between their armor. Most on the ground he passed were painted the same color as his cloak—the revealing redness of death. Cleo could hear their squeals, crying out for his help as he sprinted behind Vanna.

He slung the bronze shield over his back, then lunged toward the fort's broken-in door. *It'd been locked,* he realized in horror. Shame overcame him once again, pricking him from his feet to his face as he followed Vanna inside. His men had trusted their blood to him, and he had let them all down.

Inside the shade of the fort, the guardsmen who were lucky to have escaped were all gasping for air and fainting with sighs as they pulled at arrows lodged in them or the bodies of their brothers. Cleo scanned the bloodshed, hurting more with each shout of pain.

"*Commander,*" he heard a voice yell from down the curving corridor. Captain Jove came running toward him, his sandals clanking against the stone floor. His gold cloak was stained with blood. "*Commander,* what shall we do?"

Cleo just looked at him, distraught, without a footing on what needed to be done. Vanna moved between them and asked, "Where are your archers?"

"Captain Sovano… *Where is Captain Sovano and his men?*" Cleo asked.

"Sovano's *dead,* sir. The archers were at the tail of the columns. *Most are gone.*"

"*No.*" Cleo shook his head and looked left and right down the wide curve of the corridor. "Where did they come from? Those birds in the sky? *How did we let this happen?* How did *I* let this happen?"

Captain Jove followed them as they walked around the fort's outermost wall, looking for stairs as more and more guardsmen were pouring inside its doors. "They must be from Astria, sir."

"This is a bloodbath. Even inside—we're sitting targets in here. They have us boxed in," Cleo uttered. He rushed up the stone staircase embedded against the inner wall. Vanna followed him as he crept toward the first window, where he saw a tall opening meant for just a single archer. From beyond the cry of his guardsmen, he could hear the same whistling Vanna had mentioned before. Not just of arrows being slung through the air, but of a noise, like a shrieking tune being played in the sky.

Cleo peeked his head around another opening and saw a flock of large birds flying above the grove's trees. His shoulders shrank, and his brows tightened when he saw the black-feathered birds swooping low, allowing the riders to release their arrows into the dwindling men who still sprinted toward the fort's cover.

"It's Astrian women, alright—*rook riders*," Cleo blurted out in confirmation after seeing another swoop lower. "I'd only heard the tales of those Sisters and the king birds they flew on. But I never thought there were this many still around. Or that they'd ever leave the west again."

"*Me either*," Vanna mumbled.

"*They're frightening.*"

"Powerful—*yes*," Vanna said as she began drifting toward the stairs.

"Where are you going?"

"To find a sword or spear—to fight."

"*You can't fight?*"

"Watch me."

Cleo rushed over and grabbed her arm with a bloodied grip. "I know the Vypores are tough, but this is war—*this is different.*"

Vanna tugged away, forcing herself down the steps. "We need one of those birds shot down, that's it."

"What do you mean? What are you talking about?" Cleo asked rapidly.

"You didn't see them? *The women?* They're controlling those birds with a sound from a flute."

"*And?*"

"And if we have one of those flutes, we might be able to throw them off."

Cleo nodded, confused. "We can try, but—"

"But what? Do you have a better plan?" Vanna asked bluntly, her face as angry as his own.

"But I can't lose you."

"*You won't.*" With a sharp turn, Vanna hurried down the stone stairs.

Cleo turned and walked away from the window. "Captain Jove, gather any guardsmen that can still fight. Send our spearman and whatever archers we have to the top floor of the fort. Send the shields below. We'll turtle in groups."

"Commander, we can't send—"

"That's an order, *Captain*. We have to fight. With the shields below, we'll draw them in. From the top, we'll bring our own rain—*one of fire*." Captain Jove nodded, then sprinted off down the stairs.

Cleo was left alone with his thoughts and the agonizing cry of screeches, both in the air and on the ground below. He looked down at his hands and felt broken, smoldering in the worst defeats of pain. Covering them was the blood of the man who had taught him almost everything he knew—a man he was closer to than his father. And now both were gone. Only, this time, he had witnessed it firsthand, still stained in red across each shaking finger.

Cleo's face sharpened to anger, kindling an inner fire that yearned for vengeance. Instead of curling to sulk in dismay, Cleo reminded himself that he must fight. He needed to fight for justice, now that everything else had been taken—*to fight for those I've lost so they hadn't died in vain.*

Steaming with fury, he rushed back toward the stairs and saw his guardsmen with shields panicking as they formed themselves into groups. Others continued to straggle or crawl inside, with the shafts of arrows sticking out from their exposed arms and legs. Cleo's men were as bloody and broken as he was. As he walked farther down, they all began to quiet and stare at him, waiting to hear what words their commander would say. With their silence, they spoke loudly.

Captain Jove quickly rushed to his side. "Six formations of shields are ready, sir. We've lost a few men to bring in the bows—"

"*Good.* Captain Jove, all we need is one bird. When we down it, drag the bitch who rides it inside," Cleo commanded. He looked out into the groups of guardsmen who huddled in the dimly lit stone corridor. With a deep breath, he stated aloud, "*Men... our brothers outside have fallen at the hands of those cowards in the air, too afraid to face the blades of our swords, where we know they would surely die. We need to bring one of those women down here so we can bring the fight to them... Don't let these vultures take another life. Archers, to the top! Shields up!*"

"*ARCHERS, TO THE TOP! SHIELDS, WITH ME!*" Captain Jove relayed his command.

The clanking sound of bronze against stone filled the air as the guardsmen huddled tightly to one another. From inside out, they lifted their shields above their heads, crouching low to the ground as they began to march out of Fort Saxoram's large wooden doors. Cleo hurried back up the stairs, to the top floor of the fort, guiding pairs of his guardsmen to the wall beside each window. "*ON MY COMMAND, WE FIRE!*"

At his open window, he lurched around its edge. The air grew silent as the guardsmen below marched out; their bronze shields clustered together like the shells of turtles. Cleo gulped as they weaved over and around the pilings of dead bodies outside the fort. And then, he heard it— the same whistling as before. Cleo tilted his head up to the sky and saw three large birds flying down, side by side, flinging their arrows at his guardsmen. *They're falling for it,* he thought, hearing the strange tunes of pitches playing as they descended. *That must be those flutes Vanna mentioned.*

"Wait for it...wait..." Cleo said patiently as he watched and waited for an opening. After a long moment of silence, he bellowed aloud, echoing through the top floor, "*FIRE, NOW!*"

Just as the three birds had swooped low to hover above the groupings of bronze shields, Cleo's guardsmen moved between the open gaps of the windows and unleashed their own flaming arrows. From the depths of the birds' chests, he heard the most perilous of screeches, forcing most of the men around him to drop their weapons and cover their ears. But Cleo stood strong. With an unwavering gaze, he grew a smirk, watching as the black-and-brown-feathered birds wailed in the air. The one they managed to hit began to fall from the sky. The other two fluttered their wings just enough to flee toward the grove.

A group of shielded guardsmen quickly ran toward the downed bird and dragged the woman's fighting body back toward the door. High above, Cleo witnessed most of the birds still in the sky, flying in interloping circles like hawks straddling their prey. He continued to watch, waiting to see if any more dared to swoop low and face the fire from his archers.

When the woman was dragged indoors, Cleo rushed back down the stairs. Captain Jove stood with his shortsword held to the throat of the tall and wide-shouldered Astrian woman. Her deep black hair was curled into braids, and her pale skin contrasted with the birthmark that stuck out on her forehead. Captain Jove shoved her to her knees as soon as he saw Cleo. "You said you wanted a bitch," his young Captain stated with a blood-lusted laugh. "And so, I've brought you a bitch."

"*Who sent you?*" Cleo asked.

The woman answered only with silence. In a split moment, he saw the Astrian woman turn to look over his shoulder. Her rounded eyes widened as if she'd been caught once more, surprised by what she had seen. Just as the woman opened her mouth to speak, Cleo saw the flash of a sword lunging into her chest.

To his left, Vanna stood beside the woman, holding the shortsword's handle. She pulled the blade out and reached for the Astrian woman's neck. In her hand, Vanna yanked at the small wooden object she wore as a necklace. With hatred still steaming behind his eyes, Cleo stared at the Astrian woman as she collapsed motionless to the ground, her eyes fixated on Vanna. The rook rider reached for her chest, but all she let out was the screeching cry of gasping air.

Captain Jove groaned out of annoyance, then chopped his sword down to kill her instantly. "That should shut the bitch up."

"This is what we needed," Vanna said, holding out a small wooden pipe carved hollow with three holes on its side.

"Did you have to kill her? We needed answers."

"We need *justice*," Vanna replied. She turned to walk toward the door, unwilling to challenge his questions any further.

But Cleo knew she was right. Retrieving this woman was all the confirmation he needed. Only, part of him wished he could have killed her himself. "You aren't going out there alone, are you?" he asked.

"No," Vanna replied sternly. "Those birds were thrown into a frenzy when they heard the screeches of each other's pain. Maybe I can give it a shot with this to try to do the same."

"How do we know it will work? How do you know *any* of this?" Cleo asked.

"You saw what happened when you hit this one's bird."

Cleo only nodded.

"I'm used to handling animals much more terrifying in the Vypores," Vanna said, haughty enough to sound convincing.

Cleo had no choice but to trust Vanna's plan. "I'll take my men up top. If, or *when*, this works, try to force them low, and we'll take them out." He left her with a nod and rushed back up the steps.

379

At the top floor of the fort, he waited by an open window, looking anywhere other than the piles of dead bodies that blanketed the ground. Cleo's feeling of failure crept back up his spine with cold shivers. His brigade was still trapped like a rabbit in a hole being hunted by hawks, and all he could do was put his trust in Vanna—the archaic young woman from the Vypores.

A shrieking noise came from the door below, varying in tones of graceless hymns. His guardsmen, hidden behind the fort's wall, all closed their ears as they had before. The tune changed repeatedly while Cleo looked up at the sky. *It's working,* he noticed. "*KEEP IT UP!*"

Vanna's notes pitched high and low from the surrounding silence of the fort. Most of the giant birds above began to descend, their wings fluttering spastically without control. He fought the urge to cover his ears, watching as their shrieks spread from one bird to another. Within moments, nearly all let out their own cries as they tumbled around in the sky, just as Vanna had predicted they would.

As soon as some were low enough, Cleo gave the command. "*FIRE!*"

Hordes of flaming arrows and spears were unleashed into the air. Their screeches rang louder as the birds pierced by flame began to fall from the sky. Cleo glanced out again and saw the rest hovering erratically, struggling to fly away toward the grove. He grabbed a bow and took part in casting their assault of flaming arrows onto the uncontrolled flock. In heaps, some of the giant birds collapsed to the ground in torment. "*CAPTAIN JOVE, NOW!*" Cleo ordered below.

Out from the doors of Fort Saxoram rushed his brigade of bronze, yelling their shouts of vengeance as they took to slaughtering any Astrian woman found fallen from the sky. From his window, Cleo counted just a handful of wings fleeing over the grove. He looked down at his hands in relief and mumbled, "*Blood for blood.*"

CHAPTER 30

SEA

"He certainly looks eager," Ruth told Dane from the tree line's edge of the Northwoods. Roth stood a few ledges below them with his axe and sack in hand, looking out at the fleet of galleons anchored in the protected waters of Cubby Cove.

"I think he'll fit in with the mates. If he's anything like you, then I'm sure of it."

"Well, that's the thing...he isn't," Ruth said with a crooked smirk.

"Then I guess we'll just have to put him to work and see what he's made of."

"Work him hard—*he needs it.*"

"We'll see what he can handle," Dane replied in a light-hearted tone. "When you see your parents again, tell them that I said *thank you.* They were so kind for letting me stay at their home and for making us all those meals."

"I will. Just promise me that you two will be safe. It might be a full moon or two's pass before I'll be back here, in Tergona."

"I promise. Maybe then we'll finally have the time for you to teach me roalish so I can get started on those tomes of yours."

"*Deal,*" Ruth said, her smirk melting into a lofty grin. "Which means that you have to make it back to Tergona too."

"I'll make sure of it," Dane responded. He glanced back out at the trickling waves and took in the crisp, fresh air that glided in with it. Though he had only been away from the fleet for a few days, it was still long enough to make him miss being at sea with his brothers. The ocean had become his domain, and the *Widow* his home, despite the man who had taken him into it now being gone.

Each day he stayed with Ruth in her parents' cabin, Dane left to visit the mounds where Captain Noreas was buried. He didn't know much of the Divine One, or the spirits and their dogma, at least not until he'd met Ruth. But as he knelt beside his captain's grave, he could feel its essence. Like a blanket cast from the surrounding trees of the Northwoods, it moved with every wind's sway and floated up from the fields of grass to comfort him.

Dane came to understand its very feeling through his memories—that invisible longing to recall what had passed. To him, memories were just a cold reminder of how easily life could fade. They emerged in his mind the same way waves washed over land, forming images in their reflection of life, only to be swept back away into the collective vastitude. Just as easily as they came and went, so, too, did life from the living, and memories from the mind.

The man he respected the most and looked up to like a second father was now buried under that same swaying comfort of life. Captain Noreas was someone Dane had just assumed to be invincible, the man who'd rescued him from a life of torture and imprisonment. His captain had given him the gift of confidence as a man and a life of purpose as a mate.

Around his neck, Dane gripped Captain Noreas's silver-leafed necklace tightly to his chest. With it, Dane thought, maybe he wasn't really gone—maybe that spirit Ruth had spoken so much of, the one that lived within us all, could still be kept alive. If he weren't already headed through those Divine Gates, then he'd be there, gripped within the tiny leaf that Dane held so tight. In his hands, he was real—not just some memory to be washed away with the waves, but something he could touch. Something that still existed. And with it, Dane hoped to find that same strength to lead that his captain had. *One that always found the wind.*

"Please, be safe," Ruth told Dane again, forcing his gaze back her way. Her face reddened to match the color of her eyes, which showed the smallest inklings of a tear. With one hand, she curled the loose brown strand that fell from the side of her hair back behind her ear. With the other, she grabbed Dane behind his pale neck and kissed him on the cheek.

Dane couldn't help but smile. His heart pounded for more as he felt her soft lips graze against the side of his bony face. *Comforting…just like that blanketing spirit in the woods,* he thought. Deep within his doubt, though, he knew Ruth still thought of him as just a friend. "I will."

"I'll be praying for you and the rest of the mates," she said with more composure than before, shooing him away. "*Walk on, now.*"

Dane was filled to the brim with confidence. He rustled with his tangled hair that now grew past his ears and gave Ruth one last wave before heading down the ledge to meet up with Roth.

"Finally ready?" Roth asked him as Dane stepped sideways from rock to rock down to the curve of the coast.

"I just hope *they're* ready," he responded, still reaming with confidence.

Ruth's twin brother was a massive young man and shared her comforting face, round chin, and straight eyebrows. Dane had always considered himself to be tall—and even Ruth, too—especially when compared to those mates from the south. But it was clear from the way he filled out his shoulders that Roth was of a different sort. His presence was imposing, and his body was like a single muscle that moved in unison to glide tall and strong above the ground.

"Spoke to my father yesterday. Those cedar logs you picked out, he said he could have the mill's men carry seven or eight of them by."

"Perfect. By when, would you think?"

"They can begin tomorrow."

"Even better. I'll try and have the mates sort through the cargo to see what they'd be willing to exchange," Dane said as they walked closer to the fleet's encampment on the flat, grassy shore.

Most of the mates were still waking from their drunken slumber or cooking their morning meals by spits and roasts of small fires when Dane and Roth strolled through. They stopped between the mess of tents, searching for Cowen and the other captains. Dane told the mates to spread the word that there was something he needed to tell everyone.

Near the largest campfire of all was Piney. The short and scrawny man ran right up to Roth and made circles around him, thrusting his pale finger into the muscles of his forearms, thighs, and chest. "What happened to Ruth's tits?"

Even Dane couldn't help but laugh like the rest of the mates who all shared seats around the fire. "This is Roth, her twin brother."

"*Twin?*" Piney's crackling voice asked. "There are two of you bloody hens? Where'd the other one go?"

"Ruth's headed off."

"I dunno, Dane," Piney said as he continued to poke at Roth and size him up. "I think I'd need to see them both here to believe ya. That crooked nose looks too hard to duplicate."

"Piney, you don't even know what *duplicate* means," Caji shouted from across the fire.

"Well, I know it when it's right in front of me, you numbnut. Anyways, excuse him. Welcome aboard, Roth. We're glad to have ya."

Roth nodded disconcertingly and replied, "Thank you. Just need to get my feet wet."

"With this ship, I'm sure you will. Just don't expect anything else to," Piney said, making the mates laugh aloud again. "I was told the east was filled with broad-brimmed broads. Our first stop in forever, and all we get is the man mold of Ruth."

"If I were you, I'd hold your tongue," Roth replied sternly.

"Get a look at the big guy, huh," Piney said, clearly swiveling away from any actual confrontation.

"He's just battering your balls," one of the mates shouted from around the fire. "Get used to it."

"Now isn't the time, Piney…where's Cowen?" Dane blurted between them to ask.

"Back on the *Widow*. Sleeping, probably," Piney responded. The look on his face told Dane that he was glad the conversation had shifted. "He hasn't left that boat to come ashore since we buried the captain. He says he's keeping watch on Maris, but I wouldn't be surprised if he hasn't already killed him."

"I was hoping he'd be here," Dane said, shaking his head while looking out at the anchored *Widow*. "I need your help to gather the mates—him especially."

"For what?"

"You'll find out. Just get as many as you can awake for me, will ya."

"Sure thing. I'll send a boat out to fetch him."

"Thank you."

The mates began to gather on the flat shore, away from the waning coast. Dane moved one of the larger cargo chests to the back of the camp to stand on, looking out at the anchored fleet. The longer they waited for Cowen to arrive, the more the mates crowded in, anxious to hear what it was he had to say. It didn't take long for them to grow unsettled and impatient, pestering Dane to tell them what this was all about.

"Okay, okay," Dane said to quiet their rumbling groans. As he stood above them all, his nerves began to wrap around his throat like a moonsnake to its prey, stifling his breathing with quick pants. He felt his face flush. Dane tried to calm himself, but his nerves only worsened. At that moment, he thought of the last thing that had brought him peace—Ruth's face. He brushed his fingers across the spot on his cheek where she had kissed him. With her image in mind, his confident smile returned to lift his unease and release the grip that once rattled his nerves.

She was right to push me to do this. She's always right. I can do this, he reminded himself over and over again. *It's what Captain Noreas wanted me to do—to take care of his fleet.*

"*Tell us what it is,*" Markas, the Captain of the *Bessie*, yelled from the front.

"A plan—for the fleet," Dane stuttered to say. Shouts from the back came in pairs, telling him to speak up. "*A plan for the fleet,*" he shouted louder.

"What sort of plan?"

Questions flooded in, muddling the mates into chatter. Dane rang out his voice with a cough and cracked his knuckles. *This is it—this is my chance to convince them.* "*I know how difficult it has been for everyone after Captain Noreas's passing... And I know how much we all miss him and the leadership he bestowed each and every day. His vision for this fleet always came—came with a purpose and a plan... With his passing, I know many of you may feel like that might now be lost.*"

As Dane scanned the eyes of the mates, which must have totaled more than seven or eight hundred, he found that they all looked very different from one another. To his left, some were blondish-haired and pale, both young and old, who were once oarsmen like himself. To his right were those who had been with Captain Noreas from the beginning. They were from the far-foreign city of Corlis and had dark, reddish hair splotched to cover their tanned and leathery skin. But all, as Dane realized when he continued to look into their eyes from atop the chest, were mates of one fleet. And silently, they all looked up to him.

"*Each of us here today comes from a different home... Some—even— from a faraway city in a distant region of the Plane. But under Captain Noreas's leadership, we were united by his command...united by the single sea and this one fleet...and united by each other as mates. What I have come to share with you this morning is a plan... One that will require—require us to remain united.*"

"What sort of plan?" one of the mates shouted from the back, breaking the silence between his speech.

Dane wanted to wait for Cowen to gain his approval. But as he looked ashore, he still saw no sight of Captain Noreas's most trusted first mate. "*To make this a free fleet…so we can continue to free all our fellow brothers still in bondage,*" he proclaimed, to hear most of the former oarsmen throw their arms up in cheer. The more Dane scanned the crowd, however, the more he could see that some were not as easily amused—namely, those mates from the Southern Plane. "*I know—to some of you—this plan may seem like a risk…and maybe it sounds unwise. But with these galleons, we can grow our fleet in numbers…and we can dominate the sea—and its trade. And with that, everyone here will find their riches. And I, as your captain of captains, will find mine.*"

As soon as Dane had said the word *captain*, the mates all around began to tussle in shouts. Roth, who stood beside the large cargo chest, had to step between some of them to keep the chaos from spreading too close to reaching Dane. Piney, of all people, had crawled his way through the crowd to climb atop the chest he stood upon.

"*Quiet down and listen to the man,*" Piney pleaded to the mates. "*Quiet down…QUIET DOWN,*" he bellowed with a snarky voice, one Dane had never heard before. The grumbling soon stopped, and Piney continued, "All of you sound like feral chickens clamoring over who might make the best rooster…" Dane couldn't help but chuckle, hiding his grin as he stepped back. "I've known Dane since my time as an oarsman back on the Fereclis. He's young, yes…and he isn't always the brightest—"

"*Thanks*, Piney," Dane remarked sarcastically under his breath so only he could hear him.

"But there is one thing he does have—a good heart…and a strong will, too. And if there's anyone here who could unite the new oarsmen and the old mates together, it's him. So, I will stand fast by my friend."

Just as Piney had finished, the wave of chatter came again, until one of Captain Noreas's closest captains, Markas, moved to face the crowd. "*I see it too,*" he told them loudly. "You all have—back in the North Sea. If it wasn't for him and his handling of that cargo galley, most of you might not be here today."

From the crowd came another captain, Sonny, who added, "I was there on that galley with him. Dane has what it takes to be a uniting leader, whether you agree with his vision or not. Captain Noreas trusted him just as much as any of us. If there's any of you norks I like, it's him."

Dane's narrow face formed a smile as he listened to more of the mates come to his defense. He could tell that most of the oarsmen they saved were already convinced, and it seemed that a growing number of mates from the Southern Plane took to the words of their captains, enticed to follow their lead.

Each captain had given Dane their commendation except for the captain of the *Morsbrum*, Simion. He stood in the center of the crowd, staring Dane down. "What is it you plan to do, then, exactly? Are we just supposed to follow some nork boy to our death and fight a war against that King? None of us signed on for this. And he has a fleet of nearly a hundred... We'd be sailing in a coffin."

Dane gulped but knew that many shared Captain Simion's concern. "*Our plan is not to war with the King of Marredom—it's only to become his competition. Sacrim is far away. If we break the fleet up now, for those of you wishing to return home, you will then be outnumbered even worse. We are stronger together... We need to stay united.*" Simion looked on, still unconvinced. Dane continued, "*It's true...he has the numbers. For now, at least. Which is why we need more ships. Our new friends here in the Regent have pledged to supply us with lumber for masts...which—which will be on these shores in the morning.*"

"But what of sails or ballistas? What you speak of doing will bring about war. There are only five of us, maybe seven, if you count the others. That isn't nearly enough."

"Which is why I said we'll need to add to our numbers," Dane told Simion sternly.

Piney interjected to say, "Every galleon has extra sails down in the hold and up forward in the locker."

"Thank you, Piney. *And for the ballistas...yes, we'll need to make more. But, for now, we'll have to take the ones aft and mount them at the foredeck of each galley we refit. There's a shipyard in Marredom, north—north of here at Nordheim, where we will do just that—where we will build our free fleet!*"

"But what of their numbers?" one of the mates shouted from the back to ask. "You heard Captain Simion. We can't beat that."

"*No...but we won't need to. More than half of the King's Navy is scattered across the Plane, transporting cargo like they normally do. As for the others, our sails will give us the advantage of speed and distance."* If we can find the wind, Dane thought. The questions the mates asked were ones Dane had already pondered over himself, from his time by the campfire with Ruth and her family, or when he was in the Northwoods, searching through the mill with Roth. He had thought through most of these, just like Captain Noreas would have, in preparation to give the best answers he could. All, though, except for one.

"*What gives you the right to stand where he stood?*" a groaning voice asked above the chatter, coming from the center of the splitting crowd. Between them marched Cowen, strapped with his trousers tucked into his boots and his blood-stained white garment left loose around his lean shoulders.

"—Cowen," Dane stuttered. He stepped down from the chest and walked toward the short, brutish man near the middle of the open space between the mates. "I wanted you to be here before…so I could share with you my plan."

Some of the mates, including Simion, moved to have Cowen's back. "I heard you, alright, screaming it as I rowed in. It seems to me you've forgotten our fleet's purpose." Dane looked on silently, waiting to hear what Cowen would say next. "*The girl.*"

"We have the girl," Dane responded boldly.

"*We?* Then where is she?"

Dane looked to his left and right and could see that most of the mates had moved to his side of the split. Beside him was Roth, the biggest of them all, with a face that sharpened to anger the moment Cowen had mentioned Scarlett. "We're bringing her home, where she belongs."

Cowen raised his head above the mates to scan the Northwoods' tree line, mocking his answer. "I still don't see her anywhere."

"That's because she's already left. She's headed to meet with the royals in Bovere for a safer exchange."

As soon as the words had left his tongue, Cowen drew the saber from the sheath at his waist. "*Mutiny…*is what this is," he grumbled with a deranged look of death, pointing the tip of his curved blade right at Dane. "First, you trick me into keeping the captain of our fleet's killer alive…then you try to take his fleet and send the girl away. You norks are all the same."

Roth shuffled to lift his felling axe onto his shoulder and rubbed its long handle as if he were waiting to swing. He broke his silence to say, "A warship was no place for Scarlett. And you'd do best to keep her out of your mouth."

Cowen hissed at Roth's comment, knowing it'd be dumb to try him any further.

"This is the furthest thing from a mutiny, Cowen," Dane insisted. "We are fulfilling Captain Noreas's mission to bring Scarlett home and are expanding the planks he laid for us all. And it will make everyone here rich."

"*You stupid nork.* That gold from her father would come to *us* when *we* would be the ones to bring her back to Sazara. *We'd* be rich, *then.* Not those bloody royals...and you call yourself a captain."

"With our free fleet as small as it is now, it would be a great risk to sail back through the North Sea and then south again just to deliver the girl to Sazara. We need more ships."

"*We? Our?* Who made you the captain of this *free fleet?*"

Dane looked around at the mates who stood beside him. He could feel their every breath warm the tense air between him and the mangled Cowen, who looked as if he hadn't slept in days. He could see most of the mates' eyes shimmering with purpose. *His purpose.* It was as if they were all one, looking on in his support. "*They did,*" Dane proclaimed, raising his hands to praise the majority around him.

Cowen lowered his saber, scanned from left to right, then realized that he was vastly outnumbered. He watched, waiting for any of the mates to refute Dane's statement. But none came. His baggy, bulging eyes winced with anger, though his stare remained blank, without an answer.

Dane tried to ease the strain by saying, "*Cowen,* we all know how tough it's been on you with Captain Noreas's passing. It's been hard on us all. But you're still welcome to stay with us... We would need you. *I would need you.*"

Cowen took a few steps forward to close the gap between them. Dane moved his left hand and gripped the handle of his saber, worrying over what he might do. But there, still a distance away, Cowen stopped short and hurled a wad of spit right at Dane's boot. "*Who gave you the right to wear that necklace?*"

Dane's frosted eyebrows sharpened to a point as he looked down at his thin chest. *Of all things, the necklace?* His mind was tempted toward fury as he thought back on how closely he had held it every time he sat alone beside Captain Noreas's grave. "I wear this in reverence," Dane replied sternly, his eyebrows furrowing.

Cowen stood silent without response. He sheathed his saber and turned to stomp back toward the anchored fleet. When he reached the edge of the splitting mates, he turned back one final time and said, "I'm taking the *Widow* back with me to Sacrim—where it belongs. Those who wish to join me may."

Dane counted nearly seventy of the mates, Simion included, who left to follow Cowen's departure. Most of them were stragglers who followed their lead, collecting their belongings from the tents. They loaded the small boats and began rowing back toward the *Widow*.

The mates who remained on the shore of Cubby Cove all stood in unison, watching the *Widow* pull its anchor. Around him, Dane heard them chatting nervously among themselves over all that had just occurred. In his mind, he, too, wished it had gone differently. Cowen was the most seasoned mate of them all and was the closest of any to Captain Noreas. His original plan was to win him over first. With Cowen's support, there wouldn't have been a single mate to go against them, and he'd still have the most skilled seaman on his decks. And the *Widow*. But now, that was no longer reality. Dane had to live with the aftermath of that confrontation and live to lead the fleet without him.

To his side came Piney, who patted him on the back and said, "Well done, *Captain*. Cowen was always a rightful prick anyway."

"*True*, but we could have used him. And the *Widow*."

"Maris is going to need all the prayers he can get."

"Where is Ruth when you need her?" Dane asked under his breath.

"I wouldn't be surprised if the first sail to fly is Maris hanging from the *Widow*'s mast," Piney said with a snarky laugh.

"If Cowen didn't take him, then he'd be hanging from ours."

"Eh, knowing Cowen, he'll probably take his sweet time to enjoy torturing the man."

"You're right. But thanks for what you said back there, Piney," Dane commended him as he strolled closer to watch the *Widow* set its anchor to the hull. "It made all the difference."

"It came from the heart. I could tell you looked nervous and whatnot."

"That's the most frightening thing I've ever done. Speaking isn't my strongest skill."

"Oh, we could tell," Piney replied, reaching to pat him on the shoulder. "I used to think that nothing could be worse than being an oarsman, but then I heard you say you wanted to be a captain…and people think I'm the crazy one."

"You still are," Dane snarled back with a laugh.

"Now we need to get you one of those hats—curved and sharp like Captain Noreas had."

"*And a ship*," Markas said as he walked over to stand beside Dane. "Our new captain is going to need his own ship."

Dane shook Markas's hand and thanked him. He was older than Dane by many solurns and had copper strands of long hair, speckled gray, with a beard that hung down to the round of his gut.

"I'm keeping the *Bessie*. Sonny and Jalek won't give up the *Rithron* or the *Baroness*," Markas said, looking out at the crowd of mates to find the other two captains. "So that leaves the obvious one free."

"Simion's ship it is—the *Morsbrum*," Piney said.

"*Yes*." Dane looked out at the galley Simion had left behind without the crew to man it.

"You're going to need to give her a new name, then," Markas stated. "As a fresh captain should. What do we call her?"

"I don't know, Dane, renaming a ship is shit luck," Piney said.

"Oh, don't listen to that," Markas retorted.

"Markas is right. She needs a new name," Dane said.

Piney rolled his eyes as Dane thought long and hard about what his ship should be named. He thought first of his mother, then of his father and family. He thought again of naming it after his hometown, Niven. But none of those sounded like they would fit whatever journey it was they were about to embark on. And the last thing he wanted was to have one of their names painted on the side and back of a ship that was destined for war.

Instead, he thought back to the last time he was his old self. There, on the dock, waiting to fish with his brother, was where he saw that snow pelican sweeping its way across the sea. And in the wave of his memory, it returned, too, when Dane had washed ashore back in Roverra. While in the haze of blackness, he saw its white feathers still soaring through the air. *Flying free,* Dane remembered, just before he met Ruth and heard her comforting voice for the first time.

"I know what I'll name her," Dane said, turning back to Piney and Markas. "*Freebird*."

CHAPTER 31

SKY

F ar crashing waves from the Silver Sea trickled into the tiny puddle
where Vanna sank her toes beneath the coarse sand. Silent, she sat,
smelling the salty breeze as she stared past the horizon. That same soaked
stone of a seat was where she found herself most days over the past moon,
rain or shine, since Cleo's West Brigade had garrisoned itself in Sacrim's
westernmost city of Corlis. It was a quarter-day's hike from that grimy city,
along its coastline of broken black stones, which stretched farther than
Vanna had ventured to explore.

Off in the distance, gliding above the blur that blended the fog and
the waves, was Mersi, the only rook the West Brigade had managed to
capture during their ambush at Fort Saxoram. Cleo's guardsmen had kept
it shackled in chains while they recovered and regrouped at the fort, eager
only to torture it for what it and the Sisters had done to their fellow
guardsmen. Each day they stayed there, whenever she could, Vanna had
urged Cleo to release the rook or, at the very least, kill it to save it from
suffering at the hands of their torture. But instead, on the day they were
to leave for Corlis, to her surprise, Cleo told Vanna that he intended to
keep the rook and use it as a weapon in the same manner the Sisters had.
And so, he ordered the guardsmen to drag the beaten bird along at the
back of their march as they made the last of their way west across Sacrim.

Vanna did all she could to comfort the rook, staying beside it at the
rear and feeding it to survive. As long as she was next to it and pleading
with annoyance that they stop flogging the bird, the guardsmen tended to
leave it alone. Though Mersi was small, Vanna could tell that it had already
reached its full growth, making it much older than Little Wing had been.
And with its age, Mersi was clever. She took to Vanna's protective presence
fondly, especially since Vanna wore the flute to which its pitch had paired.

393

On the day they arrived in Corlis, Vanna met with Cleo in his tent within the brigade's encampment, just outside the city's streets. In a fit of pleading groans, she urged him to set the rook free. At first, Cleo's refusal was harsh. He was stern with his rejections and couldn't bring himself to look her in the eyes. But when her pleading had faded, Cleo informed Vanna of his plan. By his captains' counsel, he knew the rook obeyed only her. And so, he granted Vanna a compromise, allowing it to fly free so long as she was the one to train it.

Without hesitation, Vanna had agreed.

She kept the rook she named Mersi down Corlis's rigid, rocky coastline, a quarter-day's walk south of the city. Each night, she'd chain it to one of the trees and return there the next morning to release it, allowing it to fly freely over the Silver Sea. Mersi, however, didn't need the training, and neither did she. Vanna would simply sit and watch as it glided above the breaking waves, free, as it needed to be.

Free to heal.

Vanna found that her time alone by the water was needed, just the same. The very moment she began to grow comfortable with her new life, her past had rippled back into it with blood—the blood of the Sisters and Cleo's guardsmen spilled as one beside the grove in a single pool of death. And each day she sat along the coastal rocks and looked out at the fog-ridden clouds, Vanna remembered the moment Alice's eyes had met her own. She could feel the unveiling judgment pierce between their gaze when she and her old friend—*her old Sister*—had recognized each other. From their earliest days of silence and solace, the two had been close. Alice had lived the same life she had, one of pain and duty—the life of discipline necessary to become a Sister of the Silo. And there, at Fort Saxoram, Alice had died as one, still caged by their blind conviction.

Vanna knew then, when their eyes first met inside the fort, that it would either be Alice's life or her own. Alice was still beholden to the Sisters' will, a will Vanna now detested, and would have ousted her to Cleo and his brigade the first chance she got. That revelation would have brought her own demise. Vanna couldn't let that happen, so she acted.

Regretfully.

Most afternoons, Vanna pondered what her life might have been like had she never been assigned to the Brazen Talons. She could have been just like any other Sister, still doing the Queen and the Grand Dame's bidding in the shadows. She could have been like Alice, sent to Sacrim to ambush Cleo and his brigade, assisting in what would have been their total slaughter. But with any assignment other than the Brazen Talons, Vanna would still be obeying without question, like Alice had, believing the Sisters' lies she was taught only to know. And like Alice, she would have been sworn to die a double death, never to fly free, just like they and the rooks were meant to be.

Now, though, Vanna's life was very different. She answered to no one but herself and her own actions. And she was accountable only to her thoughts. It was a freeing feeling, but at times, it left her with a pang of longing. Not a day sat by the Silver Sea passed without the temptation to take to the back of Mersi and fly off with the wind. There, she could escape it all and find some foreign, blank portion of the Plane to start anew.

But only here, in Corlis, was where Cleo still was.

Any thought of being truly alone had become a desolate pit itself. Like Vanna, Cleo's West Brigade was left despondent after the Sisters' ambush. Although all his losses were heavy, none weighed as much on Cleo as the loss of Vident Lement. He was a man who truly cared for Cleo and everyone he encountered and was a genuine, kind-hearted spirit. On the day the brigade burned the bodies at Fort Saxoram, Vanna thought back to their first meeting in the palace. She was glad she had someone to converse deeply with while they traveled, and she was glad Vident Lement had introduced her to Cleo. To hear his discourses of wisdom and knowledge of the Plane and its history, which he seemed to parse easily with tales of recollection, always kept her mind spinning. Vident Lement was someone Vanna knew Cleo relied heavily on. And in his absence, Vanna could tell that Cleo was different.

As the sun began to find its way back east, behind the breeze of autumn, Vanna used her flute to call Mersi back to the shore. She slipped on her sandals, grabbed her sack, and then guided the rook toward the largest tree to shackle it up for the night. She gave Mersi a comforting pat, then rustled her sack open to tuck her flute away. Inside, Vanna bumped her hand against the side pocket. She reached in and pulled out the note that Clyus Calegri had handed to Zell—the same one she had read when she left the Vypores. Vanna's breath grew heavy as she reread it once more. Her body became stoned like a guilt-ridden rock, wanting only to sink herself into the mushy sand and be taken away by the tide.

I could have saved them. If only I were honest with Cleo and told him what I knew. The Queen's and Clyus's land as one... It's no wonder Cleo's Brigade was ambushed by the Sisters. It wasn't just a marriage—it was a strategic union. An alliance.

A sense of urgency blossomed over her regret. Vanna threw her sack over her covered shoulder and dusted the sand off her black trousers and long-sleeved gray garment, which lent both its colors and its smell from the stones and the sea. She hurried off down the coast toward Corlis until she reached its vine-smothered blackstone streets.

The evening's fog of mist had lifted, leaving her trek alone toward the city's center exposed. Vanna did her best to ignore the many vagrants of Corlis who hurled their harassments and enticements her way, often as they came. Corlis was a desolate place, laden with far more men than women, all of whom hung drunkenly out of their randomly erected and often broken homes, haggling for their next copper coin.

Down its central street, Vanna trudged until she saw the four spiraling towers that connected the enveloping wall of Sacrim's only castle. What was once a historic landmark of Sacrim and host seat for the Second Partition's magistrate had become a mere watchtower over Corlis's harbor. Since the conclusion of the Sacrimian War in 413 A.D., the castle had been abandoned, left to be occupied by kingpins and smugglers alike. Built from the same seashell mortar as Fort Saxoram, it stood tall as a singular tower, situated in the middle of its vine-shrouded courtyard. Its highest peak was often concealed by Corlis's heavy fog, making its use as of late one of territorial significance rather than as a practical watchtower over the Silver Sea. To the people of Sacrim's Second Partition, its occupation by revolving authorities brought only temporary control, a false facsimile from those who made the real decisions in Sacrim. Inside was where Cleo set up his command, after having taken the streets of Corlis without contention.

Vanna made her earnest way to the front wall's gated door, manned by Cleo's guardsmen, who had it opened at her sight. She passed through its inner courtyard and was let inside the castle, heading toward the spiraling, central staircase that led up through its tall tower. On the seventh floor was where Vanna knew Cleo worked. Since their arrival nearly a moon's pass ago, she had seen its meeting room only once before. It was bland in its blackstone and carried a haunting stench, littered with critters, bugs, and their webs in abundance. She went farther up the stairs until she heard the voices of men tussling back and forth. Vanna crept up and around its curved wall, spiraling her way closer to find its grimy door left cracked ajar. She leaned one ear against the cold stone and heard Cleo's voice say, "*What will it take to convince them?*"

One of the indistinguishable voices replied, "*Silver should do it. We've recruited all we can, from the cagerman to the pensioned guardsmen who just want to leave the city. The rest are just looking for pay.*"

"*We have silver and copper for most of them, at least upfront, but not enough for an extended campaign,*" she heard Cleo say. "*We need to act fast. We no longer have surprise on our side. Cayen knows where we are and our numbers. We can only hope he thinks this is all of us. Evander, what did your connection in Sazara say theirs were again?*"

Vident Evander in a meeting with Cleo? Vanna heard a mumbling cough, before his familiar, squeaky voice said, "*Nearly twenty thousand, sir. Again, I'm not sure if that's to be believed—*"

"*It's believable, alright. They've pulled every man of fighting age from the streets of that city,*" another voice butted in.

"*Untrained, if that's the case. Besides the First and Second Brigades,*" Cleo said. "*Captain Jove, what are ours at currently? And Kladden's?*"

"*We've barely been able to restore what we lost at Fort Saxoram. But most are untrained boys. Kladden's courier arrived this morning. He couldn't give an exact number, but he mentioned it being much more than a full brigade.*"

"*That's promising, but not enough. Have the courier fed and rested. Put him on standby to send back when ready.*"

"*Will do, Commander. Sir…there's someone I'd like to introduce you to. This, here, is the Black Baron. For the right price, he said he could help us.*"

Vanna heard the sound of sandals against stone clattering around, from what she assumed to be Cleo meeting the man introduced as the Black Baron. But their voices were too far away, at least far enough that she couldn't make out their chatter. She listened on anyway, constantly looking back and forth from the round, narrow hallway and up and down its spiraling stairs. Her concern lingered over how quickly she could bolt away when they finally decided to end their meeting.

That was until she heard one of them ask, "*When do we leave?*"

Vanna's ears perked back up, anxious to hear when it was that they were to leave this disgusting city. Cleo's pungent voice replied, *"When Vanna has that bird ready. Hopefully soon."*

Me? Her eyes snapped wide.

Their clatter of footsteps grew louder, just after Vanna heard what she thought was the word *dismissed*. In a panic, and with her mind still scattered in thought, she scurried away from the door and up the spiraling stairs, trying to seem calm as she passed the guardsmen above. It wasn't until she stopped to catch her breath that she realized she'd gone up the stairs and not down, in the opposite direction of her own room.

The sandal steps below grew, echoing along the curving sidewall of the staircase and turning with the torchlit shadows that traced toward her. Vanna collected her twitching nerves and continued up the steps until she reached the top, final floor. In front of the broad door stood two guardsmen, blocking her way like bronze statues.

"Vanna?" she heard Cleo's voice ask just moments later. "What are you doing up here?"

"Cleo—hmm—it's been a moment. But—I wanted to come see you," she stuttered and paused awkwardly. "And I needed to show you something."

"Did something happen? Are you okay?" Cleo asked back with the concern of a commander.

From the day Vanna began training Mersi down the coast, she had rarely seen Cleo despite living below in the same castle. Cleo had shut himself in and isolated himself from everyone. Whispers had spread around the brigade that they only saw him when the fog cleared, looking out from his high, open balcony at the peak of the castle's tower, searching the air for any sight of those birds, anxious that they might return to ambush his brigade again. Others stated that he had quit altogether. But Vanna knew the real Cleo. And she knew why he was hiding.

He was hurt.

The two guardsmen beside the door saluted Cleo with closed fists over their hearts, striking them down to their sides. In sync, they turned and opened the double doors, waving Vanna in first. "Yes...everything's fine. It's just been quite a while since I've seen you," she said.

Instead of answering her, Cleo turned to the steward behind him and commanded that he bring them two meals instead of just one. Once they were alone within his expansive room, Cleo said, "*It has.* I've been meaning to talk to you, too, anyway."

Vanna followed behind him and looked around. The room was as black and lifeless as the rest of the rundown castle, which matched most of the buildings scattered throughout Corlis. A long and smooth marble table stretched across the room's center, making it feel more pleasant than it actually was. Past the table's far end was an open doorway to the wrap-around balcony that overlooked the Silver Sea.

Cleo walked directly toward its edge, stopping only to unpin his cloak and place it on the table. Vanna followed him slowly, looking curiously left and right at the various burrows carved within the room's side walls, which held assortments of stray chairs and unopened chests of his belongings. Closer to the balcony's opening was a burrow for his bed, which itself was larger than the room she stayed in below.

Vanna strolled toward the balcony. "What did you want to talk to me about?"

"*A plan.*"

She placed her sack on the ground and moved to lean against the blackstone balustrades. The sun had already set, allowing the full moon and stars to light the cloudless sky. Vanna struggled to restrain her long hair from tangling with the gusts that blew in with the sea. "What sort of plan?"

"One with you and that bird you've been training every day." Cleo still didn't bother to turn and look at her. Instead, he joined her by the balcony's ledge and gazed out at the crashing waves on each side of Corlis's harbor. "I'm sending you to Sazara as soon as you're both ready. I did some thinking after what happened at the fort, and I need someone inside the city's walls. Evander has shared with us the names of the vidents Vident Lement trusted most in Sazara. Loyalists. That bird should be able to get you close and undetected. And you're a woman, so no one should suspect it. We need to get the vidents this message," Cleo said, handing her a sealed parchment. "Find a bald vident named Maedrick and deliver this to him. He works for one of the Calegris' high chambermen, so he shouldn't be hard to recognize. But no one else can see it. I need to trust you."

Vanna stood still and silent—her thoughts were too loud to speak. *We haven't talked in nearly a moon, and the first words you say are orders to send me away? I'm no longer a Sister... All this time, I should have just left.*

But if I leave with that rook alone, I'm not flying into war.

Before she could spit out a single thought, Cleo asked, "When do you think it will be ready?"

"*It?*" Vanna asked back rudely. "*Cleo*, I'm not one of your guardsmen. What makes you think you can order me around?" The crests of Cleo's tanned cheeks lifted with his eyebrows in concern. Vanna could tell he wasn't expecting her to push back. "What if I don't want to go? Why would you think you could just send me away? *Did you even think about that?*"

In a flurry of emotion, Vanna's memory as a Child of the Sisters flashed again. It was all she knew her life to be—a piece on the Sisters' grand board, a faceless girl who lived within the shadows of death. And she hated it. Cleo was the only person she had ever confided her emotions in, and he had done the same with her. Their talks together were always away and separate from his brigade. And their relationship and friendship were their own. But there Cleo stood, trying to drag her into his war and make her just another piece on his board, one no different than his guardsmen.

"*I'm sorry*," Cleo said, his words ringing with a hymn of regret. "I—I didn't think you'd be that opposed to it. You seemed excited to train that bird."

"It's a *rook*, Cleo."

"The *rook*."

"I was and am excited to train it and to ride it. I just thought I'd be riding it beside you."

Cleo sank his knuckled chin toward the stone floor. "*You're right*," he mumbled.

"I know it's been hard on you...since the ambush at the fort, but you don't need to keep pushing the people who care about you away."

After a long bout of silence, he finally looked up at her. The life behind his green eyes had vanished. "I can't protect you, Vanna. I can't protect anyone...not Vident Lement, not my family, not my home, and not you. The longer you stay with me, the more danger you'll be in—the more danger I'll put you in."

"I can take care of myself, Cleo."

"There are things I can't control. I'm on a warpath, Vanna. A path paved by blood. One you don't belong on. And there's no going back. It's my head or theirs. I just want to make things right." Cleo looked back out at the stars, watching as the Silver Sea rang its tide in and out. After a long pause, with only the sound of the waves crashing far below, Cleo asked, "What was it you wanted to show me?"

Right. Vanna reached for her sack, unbuckled its top, and went to grab the note. She wanted to inform Cleo of the Calegris' alliance with Queen Helera, should they battle again. But in the same pouch beside it was the jar of vilovian nectar that Arzak and Juni had packed for her travels. There, at her feet, were two choices: one of healing, the other of war.

Before she could decide on which to grab, a knock came at the door behind them. Cleo turned to look across the long room and ordered him in. His steward from before carried in a tray with two silver plates, which he placed on the table. "Anything else, sir?"

"That'll be all."

As his steward departed, Cleo grabbed the tray and carried it out to the balcony. He placed it on a small stone table and grabbed two chairs so they could eat facing the hue of the sky and the sparkling of the sea. Vanna removed the silver cover from her plate and saw a filet of flamed fish, an assortment of saltnuts, brined peaches, and a slice of shortbread.

Vident Lement's favorite meal, she recognized immediately.

"I've had this every night since we've been in Corlis," Cleo admitted. "I hope it's okay."

Vanna's sight began to cloud as she thought back to all the conversations she had with his late preceptor. Vident Lement was a soft spirit who did his best to spread that same softness to Cleo. He was a father figure to him, someone he trusted, and she could see why. Vanna couldn't help but feel guilty about what had happened back at Fort Saxoram. She was the one who had heard the whistling of their flutes and arrows before anyone else. And she was the one who had the note telling of their alliance all along. If only she had reacted sooner, then maybe she could have saved him.

And with him, saved Cleo.

"It's more than okay," Vanna said softly. *This is the real Cleo,* she knew.

They each took a few bites before Vanna reached again for her sack, this time knowing exactly which to grab. She placed the glass jar next to her plate and said, "This is what I wanted to show you."

"What is that?"

"Vilovian nectar. It's from a flower in the Vypores—well, from the selephanta that harvests it. It'll help you feel better," she said, trying to sound confident. "*Here*, give me your slice of bread."

With a worried look on his face, he asked, "I thought the vilova flower was banned in Sacrim… This won't kill me, right?"

Vanna grabbed the shortbread from his plate and spread a good portion of the nectar on each of their slices. "No," she said with a slight giggle. "At least not your body."

"I don't know about this."

"Do you trust me?"

"Do I have a choice?" he asked back.

"No," Vanna said with another giggle. "You'll be okay, Cleo."

Looking less confused now than before, Cleo cautiously took the slice she handed him. Together, they ate it and continued to pick at their meals. Since that night in the Vypores, Vanna had forgotten what the nectar made her feel like. Before she could even finish her plate, her body had calmed to a softening ease, and her gaze had rested to settle over the top of the balustrade. Euphoria was all she felt. Her arms and legs were left tingling and numb as if she were again being wrapped by its comforting, warm blanket—one fit just for her.

She looked over at Cleo, who, too, hadn't finished his meal. Instead, he stared out at the moonlit water, the same as her. Eventually, he turned her way and asked, "Is it supposed to feel like this?"

Vanna looked into his softening eyes, this time with a more blissful smile. The gaping hole that had once been buried within them had melted closed, as if candles from a fresh wick had been lit behind their green window. It was a similar smile to the one he had the first time they had eaten together. Though she could tell his confidence was still shattered, he remained broad-faced and bold, with a strong jaw that connected the curve of his cheeks to his hooked nose. It was a face that Vanna missed. "*Yes.*"

"*I like it*," he admitted.

"I can tell."

"How so?"

"Because you're smiling," she replied.

"Do I not typically smile?"

"No…but I haven't seen you in a while, so it's hard to remember."

Cleo's smile shortened as he turned back toward the moon.

"You should change that. I like you better when you're smiling," Vanna told him.

Cleo chuckled. "I'm surprised anyone likes me at all."

"Many people like you, *Cleo*. All of your guardsmen look up to you. I'm sure they like you. I mean, they wouldn't be following you into war if they didn't."

"They're following me because they believe in our cause. Or maybe because they're still being paid to. But they hate the Calegris more than they like me. They hate the corruption in Sazara and all the wealth that's been taken from them and isolated there. That's the real reason the men follow me. Hatred and envy. Not admiration."

"Is that how you feel? That you hate the Calegris more than you like yourself?" Vanna asked.

Cleo sat in thoughtful silence for a moment that brought his gaze to the blackstone floor. "*Probably*…just from the horrible things they've put me through. And all the horrible things I've had to put others through to get back at them."

"I don't see you that way. I've been with your men for a while now, even in the rear of your march. I listen to what they say and see what they do. They wouldn't be following you if they didn't believe in you. You're fighting for something much bigger than yourself or even the cause that you all share. You're fighting for justice and for the future, Cleo. *A real future*…to make your home and the Southern Plane better. To make things right, like you said. They see that, and they look up to you. And they admire you. The *future* will admire you, too." As he turned to her, Vanna peered into his eyes again. Below, his cheeks were firm and wet, like the stone by the sea she sat upon earlier. "I admire you, *Cleo*."

Without hesitation, he placed his warm hand on her thigh and leaned in to kiss her. For as coarse and tight as his hands and skin were, his lips were soft. Like the tide from the coast, their tongues tugged back and forth, passionately numb. Between each slow pound, Vanna felt their hearts resonate.

Cleo stood in front of her and moved both of his hardened hands around her wide hips. He lifted her and ripped off her long skirt, turning to press her bare bottom on the top of the railing. She could feel his passion with each kiss, deeper and deeper as they connected. To her surprise, she wasn't nervous, despite not knowing what would come next. The two of them together felt raw and real, enhanced in serenity from the numbing gloss of the vilovian nectar.

Vanna could see and feel the full moon behind her shed its light onto his tanned shoulder as she kissed the spots where it glowed. Floating high in the tower, like the stars in the sky, she melted with each crash from the Silver Sea. *Each crash from Cleo.* Inside, she felt the real him, the one behind his bruised and broken body—the soft one that needed to heal with their rush of love. *Her love.*

Together, they were no longer alone.

Back and forth, they tugged until Vanna felt the stars burst behind her, one by one. In the moonlight's passion, they danced together toward the bed, lying beside one another in smiles of exhilaration and laughs of panting exhaustion. Vanna wrapped her arms and legs around his bare body. As Cleo tried to recover his breath, he ran his finger along the back of her rocky spine until he traced its way to the burnt-red scar on her thigh. "When did you get this?"

"A while ago. Before I met you—in the Vypores. It's okay, it's nothing, really."

"Are you *sure?*" he asked as he rubbed it softly. "This doesn't look like *nothing*. It wasn't a man that gave this to you, was it?"

"No, definitely not a man," Vanna said, giggling to make light of it. "You're the only man I've known, Cleo." She looked up at the patterns carved into the ceiling, trying to steer the conversation away from her past. "*Have you ever loved another woman?*"

"Not like this…no," Cleo responded with a laugh of his own. "At one point, there was a girl I was fond of, though. But since the day I met you, she has drifted from my mind."

"What was her name?"

"Now might not be the best time to talk about her," Cleo said, his smile fading.

"Oh, come on."

"Her name was Scarlett."

"What about this, *Scarlett*, then?" Vanna asked with a witty smirk.

Cleo tilted his head away from her own. "She was my first friend when I moved to Sazara. The young boys in the city were a prideful bunch and mocked me as an outsider from Cignus. They didn't let me play their games or tussle with them in the square. But Scarlett did. She was the first to be kind to me. And she had a powerful father, which made the other boys scared of her—and thus, me. I guess it gave me protection, in a way. But as we grew older, things changed. She became a woman, and I, a cagerman."

"Did this *Scarlett* not love you back?"

"I'm not sure. But I know her family would never have. You might find this quite amusing, but she was the daughter of Clyus—Cayen's sister," Cleo said.

"*The Calegris?*" Vanna gasped in disbelief. "What do you mean, *was?* What happened to her?"

"I don't know. And I'm not sure if I'll ever know. In fact, she's the reason I'm in this mess today."

"What do you mean?"

"Scarlett was taken after the Descindation at the Isle of Azil. And if that never happened, my father might still be alive. He was the one who ordered me to leave Sacrim—to find her and rescue her. And this was just after he appointed me as commander of the Sixth Brigade."

"*Appointed?*" Vanna asked. Her heart paused. "What do you mean, *ordered?*"

"My father was the Consolar General of Sacrim. He was a great man and the rightful wielder of the Sunspear. The Calegris murdered him for it—for their own control. And if Scarlett were never taken, and I never ordered away, he might still be alive."

Vanna became stricken with the worst infliction of guilt. Petrified like the heaviest of stones, her heart sank below Cleo's bed, sulking in unrelenting shame. There she lay, hardened like the moon itself, falling from the sky to sink to the bottom of the Silver Sea. The same waves that had just carried her high up in elation, with healing and with love, now felt like they were ripping her apart, limb by naked limb, drowning her below. Vanna couldn't move. Her eyes were stuck wide and white, and her skin grew pale.

All this time, it's been me—my fault. I was the one. I was the one who murdered Cleo's father.

What have I done?

CHAPTER 32

STONE

"This looks like a good place to stop for the night," Scarlett said from atop her borrowed horse.

Through the spacing between the trees, Ruth saw an assortment of cabins whose color matched the lilies sprouting up around them. "I think we might be better off setting up camp in the woods that way," Ruth said. She rummaged through her saddle's side pouch and pulled out her map. "Just there, the Stamford Stream runs through these woods."

"Stamford?" Ludwyn asked, turning from atop his horse up ahead.

"Yes. It looks like it branches off from Roark's, just north of Bovere."

"I've heard of Stamford before," Ludwyn said. "Small village in a vast canton. I think Bean's family was from around here."

"Bean?" Scarlett asked.

"A guy from the mill."

"He's a lucky man," Scarlett commented. When they turned the corner of the dirt trail, the three of them caught full sight of the tiny village. Off in the distance was an assortment of cabin homes surrounding an old castle, which was broader than it was tall and built from mortared fieldstones, shaping its square tower.

"Yep. We're definitely staying here," Ludwyn said as they trotted closer.

"I vote the same. Sorry, Ruth," Scarlett added with a squeaky smile.

"*Fine*. I could use a good bed anyway," Ruth admitted, then reminded Scarlett to don her hood and hide her frizzled orange hair.

The cabins they rode past under the afternoon sun doubled as homes and markets, with a few older couples rocking peacefully on their porches, waving for them to come inside. Ludwyn and Scarlett straggled off in search of food and trinkets, while Ruth asked a kind old lady if she knew of a place to stay. The elderly woman named Jenn pointed her in the direction of the castle up the hill. She explained that the last descendants of the Stamford family still served as the canton's landowner. To Ruth's discontent, though, she went on for ages describing how the once-thriving town had now become a mere pass-by village for travelers on their way to and from Bovere, lamenting the family for its demise. Ruth bit her tongue and tucked her chin before she finally escaped the old lady's conversation to head uphill.

"*We can come back later*," Ruth shouted to Ludwyn and Scarlett as they left the cabin on the opposite side of Stamford's main road. They tied their three horses to the hitching post outside the castle's courtyard, then climbed the stairs to its door. Ruth wafted away the drooping greenery to knock its iron ring.

Many moments passed before Ludwyn grabbed the ring to knock again. This time, it was louder and done with aggression. "Maybe we should just stay in the woods," he said, lifting his chin to look up at the castle's short tower, which had most of its weathered and cracked stones covered by moss.

Ruth turned and gave him a sarcastic nod just before the large door finally creaked open. Its entrance room was bare of any furnishings or decor. Out from behind the door's shadow came an old man, limping with the support of a stick. Ludwyn's eyes shifted toward Ruth as if he wished to apologize, though he kept his mouth sealed.

"We've come in search of a place to stay," Ruth said.

The man's skin folded in wrinkles near his joints and knuckles. His eyes sat above drooping, dark pockets, refusing to blink. He pulled his free hand from behind the door's knob to reveal a long, curved pipe and took a draw from its stem, staring at them intensely.

"Just for one night," Ludwyn added, taking a step back.

The old man took two more draws, then broke a faint smile. "Just there." He pointed the lip-end of his pipe toward the yellow-painted cabin down the road. "Ten coppers." Ruth reached into her sack and placed the coppers into the pale that the old man held out. He limped his way out of the entrance room and returned with a single key. "You can leave your horses there if you'd like. I'll have my stableman feed them."

"Thank you, sir." Ruth led the three of them to the small, yellow-painted cabin. To her, it didn't seem as old as the others and appeared better kept than the Stamford family's castle. Inside was just a single room with two simple beds split across its middle. "Lud, you get that one by the door—Scarlett and I will take the one by the window."

"You two sharing a bed?" he asked, his face forming a frown.

"Well, you won't be sharing one with me," Ruth sneered. "It's either that or the floor."

"Or the woods," Scarlett added with a freckled smirk. "With the way you smell, maybe that would be best."

As they giggled at his expense, Ludwyn replied, "Fine. Since you both seem to feel that way, I'll wash off, then." He pointed to the sprawled-out barrel-bucket in the corner of the room, half-hidden behind a curtain. "You two go find some food and leave me at peace."

"See, Ruth, stopping at Stamford was a good idea," Scarlett said.

Ruth laughed, then led Scarlett back out of the cabin. Together, they roamed from porch to porch, smiling as they filled their sacks with oats, glazed fruits, and an assortment of dried and salted meats for sale.

"The Eastern Plane is just so beautiful, and everyone here is always so nice," Scarlett told her as they continued down the main road.

"I wouldn't say *everyone*, but it sure beats being on one of those ships. You get tired of seeing the same blue and gray every day. It doesn't take long for the sky and the sea to blend into one," Ruth said.

"I don't think any place can beat the colors here. When I rode up with Roth, we didn't stop at any of these villages. But in a way, it was sort of a blessing. Everywhere we camped was as gorgeous as this. The greenest meadows, the most wonderful wildflowers, and all the shades of blue in the sky. I mean, just look at these lilies." Scarlett picked one of the yellow flowers up from its root.

"Sacrim isn't like this?" Ruth asked. "I've seen some paintings, but like most of us here in the east, I've never been."

"You aren't missing much. The closest thing we have to these plains is in Cignus, out east, in our Fourth Partition. But there are only a few creeks that run close to Torrent's Sleeve. It's great for vineyards but not for crops. We don't have the forests and lakes as you all do, or rivers that run with clean water, and all the wild animals that roam free between them. Roth told me about the great elk up north and explained all the different kinds of stags. I wish I could have stayed up there longer to see some of them."

"Exploring the Northwoods can be dangerous," Ruth told her.

"Unless you have a ranger with you," Scarlett replied. "Or at least, that's what Roth had said."

"He would."

"You know, maybe we should go check out the woods you pointed to on your map. We could do our own bit of exploration."

"I'm not sure that's a good idea," Ruth responded, curling a chestnut-colored strand of hair behind her ear.

"Oh, *come on*. Lud will be just fine without us. Besides, Roth also told me that you needed to get out more."

Ruth shook her head and rolled her eyes down at Scarlett. "And Roth told me to look after you."

"It'll be fun! Come on," Scarlett pleaded, though she had already begun drifting off in its direction.

"*Fine*," Ruth said with a sigh. "But we can't stay too long." As they made their way down the lone path through the woods, Scarlett stopped to inspect every flower or twitch from the twigs that she could find within the expanse of elm trees. The same strands of moss from the castle covered their branches, which were all strewn out like fingers reaching for the sky. Ruth struggled to keep up behind her, clamoring to say, "You might make for a good ranger after all."

"Is that so?" Scarlett smiled. "All those days we spent together… Roth could have at least shared with me some of his tips."

"Lud could, too. You've got the curiosity for it, that's for sure."

"Just not the size," Scarlett said with a soft giggle. "Roth also mentioned those bears back in the Northwoods. He told me all about them—more details than I wanted to hear."

"They aren't just in the Northwoods. They're here in these woods, too. But bigger." Scarlett's eyes widened, scanning the tree line where she'd once been so peacefully frolicking. "I'm only kidding," Ruth finally told her.

"You almost had me." Scarlett sighed in relief. "Any more talk of bears, and I might have just followed you back to that cabin."

"Maybe that isn't such a bad idea."

"*Oh, look!*" Scarlett practically screamed as she ran to follow the sound of streaming water. Just over a humped hill was the Stamford Stream, and in the water was a romp of otters tussling playfully with each other. "*Look how cute they all are!*"

Even Ruth couldn't help but smile as she watched them wrestle over a tiny school of fish in the middle of the stream. Scarlett threw her boots off and stepped atop the smooth stones to get a closer look. "They don't have otters in Sacrim?" she asked, shouting down to Scarlett below.

With a smile as bright as the evening sun, Scarlett turned back and shook her head. "No, but I want to take one back with me!"

"They're wild for a reason," Ruth explained from atop the hill. "You should keep them that way."

"That's no fun." Scarlett crouched on a stone just above the stream's running path and reached to pet one. "Loosen up a bit, *will ya.*"

Maybe she's right, Ruth thought to herself. She'd been so surrounded lately by brutish men and violence, and by the change it all brought, that Ruth barely recognized herself anymore. The girl she once knew, the one who rarely left Tergona and had always kept her head stuffed into her books, had become as much of a foreigner as Scarlett was. But Scarlett was right. Ruth knew she needed a break—to loosen up and relax for a change. *I deserve it.*

And so, Ruth sat upon the hill and watched Scarlett and the otters play. She took in the scenery around her and began to sway with the leaves and flowers that danced in the cooling breeze of autumn. Above her, she heard the birds chirping songs as they chased each other from branch to branch through the trees.

Wait, she realized. Ruth reached inside her sack and rummaged to its bottom. She pulled out a rolled piece of blank parchment and three tiny tin cans filled with colored oil. "*I forgot I even packed this,*" she whispered to herself with a smile, taking the brush out from inside the roll. She did her best to flatten the parchment against her book, then began to paint.

For quite a while, Ruth painted, trying to capture the moment with the medley of colors she mixed inside the can's lid. Every flower and cloud, the birds and the otters, and even Scarlett, who sat on a stone in the stream, Ruth brought to life on her parchment with a gleaming smile. "*Scarlett,*" she shouted. "Take off your hood so I can see your hair."

"Really? What are you doing up there?"

"Painting you."

With a giddy smile, Scarlett obliged, letting her frizzled hair out to frolic in the sun. Ruth's brown eyes wandered with each stroke of her brush, watching as Scarlett chased the otters in the water. Eventually, when Ruth allowed, Scarlett made her way back up the hill to see her work.

"*Ruth*, this is incredible! You can even see all my little freckles!" Scarlett said, elated, as she snatched the painting from Ruth's hands.

"It's still wet, so be careful."

"When did you learn to paint like this?"

"I used to paint on my porch all the time," she explained. "It's been a while, but I think it came out pretty good. I guess it's one of those skills that's hard to lose."

"*Pretty good?* Ruth, this is fantastic! You could make a fortune selling these."

"You think so?"

"Especially in Sazara…absolutely. I know a couple of markets on Arcus Street that would be thrilled to have art this nice," Scarlett said.

"Arcus Street?"

"One of the *few* things I actually miss about Sazara," Scarlett replied. "It has the best meals and shops, with clothes and art, and wine and theaters—actually, how much for it? I'd like to buy this one from you."

"*Oh*, Scarlett, you don't have to."

"Well, I can't, really. Not until I get home, at least. But when I do, five golds, I'd pay you for it, I'd reckon."

"*Five?*" Ruth's face squashed in disbelief; her crooked chin curved to form a heartwarming smile. "It's yours, then."

Scarlett wrapped her hand around Ruth and gave her a warm and wet hug. "I always wished I had a skill like this. Sazara is filled with so much art and fashion and decor. Are you sure you wouldn't want to come back with me? My father could make you very wealthy."

Ruth laughed. She thought back to her own family and the aspirations she once had when she was younger. In the pocket of her skirt, she felt the pin that Roth had given her of their family's coat—the claw of a bear. "At one point, I wanted that. To be one of those royals in Bovere, rich with wealth and influence. And I wanted to help in every way I could to contribute to the Cathedral."

"One point? What happened?"

"*Life*, I guess—seeing the Plane, especially with Roth back in Roverra and the isle, and then with Dane and Lud on the *Widow*. It all seems so exciting. But the more powerful people you meet, the more you realize that they aren't very different. In fact, they're mostly the same."

"What do you mean?" Scarlett asked.

"They all just want things for themselves and have their own grand ambitions. And they will trample on anyone or anything in their way to get it. When all they really need is a home and to be like the child they once were when they had one."

"That's beautiful, Ruth. And very true. Your home is as good a proof of that as any."

"Thank you, Scarlett. It would be too hard on me to become that person."

"But my offer still stands," she said back with a giggle. "Even if you don't want to come back to Sazara with me. I'll just have to find another way to get these paintings of yours."

"*Deal*," Ruth said with a grin. She gathered her belongings and stuffed them back into her sack.

"Look, you already have another admirer!"

Ruth stood up and looked down. At her feet, as if it had been there watching her the entire time, was a tiny baby otter. "*Come on*," Ruth told it, her voice gentle. "Let's take you back to the stream."

"Aw, Ruth, we should keep it!" Scarlett pleaded.

"Not happening." Ruth picked the baby otter up and carried it over to the others. As she turned to walk away, it hopped out of the stream and followed her back up the hill.

"*Oh*, Ruth…*come on*, you should. Look how cute it is."

Two more times, Ruth carried it down to the stream, only for it to follow her back up from the bank. "*Fine…*" she said, almost out of exhaustion. "But I'm not taking it. It's choosing to come."

"Look how cute it is," Scarlett said as she wiggled the baby otter's whiskers in Ruth's hands. "You need to name it!"

"*Nope.*"

"Oh, loosen up a bit, *will ya*," Scarlett said again, trying to recall the same playful tone that had worked earlier. She gave Ruth a slight shove on the shoulder and started listing names for her to pick. As Ruth led Scarlett back toward the cabin, she let the baby otter down onto the ground a few times to see if it would make its way back to the stream. But her efforts came to no avail. In the same manner of exhaustion, Ruth finally turned around and asked, "I guess it is cute, isn't it? And as long as it's sticking with us, we should give it a name, right?"

"Yes!"

"*Ozzy,*" Ruth said. She picked the otter back up and let it climb onto her shoulders. "Ozzy the otter, it is."

† † †

Sheets of rain trickled in light waves as the three of them made their way past Lake Gileed and into the northeastern cantons of Bovere. Ruth's newest friend, Ozzy, seemed to be the only one who enjoyed soaking under the showers as it scrambled from puddle to puddle between the creeks within the city. For the past quarter-moon, though, it had been Scarlett who'd cared the most for the little otter and all its whimpers and whines for food and attention. Despite it still clinging to Ruth, Scarlett had taken it in as her own and spent every waking day comforting and coddling their tiny friend.

"Which way are we headed?" Ludwyn asked Ruth as they rode along a cobblestone road that traced beside one of Bovere's elaborate creeks.

"To the workplace of the only royal family I'm familiar with—the Lombergs."

Ludwyn's head tilted with a smirk. "This ought to be interesting."

Interesting, indeed, she thought.

Ruth led them down the swerving path to cross over three shallow-stone bridges as they made their way toward the central plaza. Carriages passed by them in plenty as they traveled closer, the horses' hooves clanking loudly atop each stone. In the far distance and half-hidden by the rain clouds, Ruth could just barely make out the three tall spires of the Cathedral. With that as her bearing, she went west, keeping north, until they came across the tallest four-story brick building on Odrun's Road within the Lombergs' shared canton.

"*This is it,*" Ruth said, pointing up to the painted sign that hung above the building's covered porch. On it, she recognized, was the Lomberg family's coat—the silver pine. Ozzy jumped onto Ruth's shoulders, then burrowed into her side sack while Ruth tied up her horse and went to knock on the door.

413

They did their best to shake the rainwater off their drenched garments. A young attendant opened the door and invited them into the slender lobby. Ruth placed the pin of her family's coat on the collar of her gray overcoat, then told the attendant that she had come to see Frand. The first floor was open to the room above but shadowed at its side walls by a wraparound mezzanine balcony. Four long columns of wooden desks were situated in the center, with parchments scattered in loose piles and flung haphazardly to cover the floor. Ruth was taken aback by the people in fine black trousers and silken jackets that seemed to be walking everywhere and nowhere all at once, moving aimlessly from desk to desk.

"Sorry to keep you waiting," a familiar, squeaky voice came from around the corner. "Things have been quite a mess since Lady Lomberg's passing."

"Seems so," Ludwyn remarked as the bulbous man turned the corner, though he still faced the desks at the center of the room.

"Business dealings have since been handed to her younger cousin, Trenton. Which, as you might be able to tell, has had quite the adventure of learning. So, what dealings have you—"

As Frand turned his neckless head around, his eyes met Ruth's. "We came to call a meeting with the royal families," she said.

"*By what Gates have you come here?*" Frand asked, his breath spitting out in a series of wheezes. "*Sentinels!*" he cried out before she could even respond. The short man slowly backed away toward the center-room's light as if he were scared of what she—or, really, Ludwyn—might do. "You're a fool for showing your face here after what your brother did!"

Before Ruth could even say a word to reply, nearly a dozen men dressed in padded undervests and silver-laced green tabards stormed down to the first floor. In each of their hands were drawn longswords, which they kept pointed at Roth, Ludwyn, and Scarlett. One of the older sentinels gave a command, and their hands were clasped together, tied, and their sabers removed from their sides.

"Take them to Odrun's Hold…we'll see what the courts have to say," Frand ordered, following them out the door.

As they were being dragged out into the rain, a younger voice shouted from the lobby: "*Wait!*" Out came a thin man with ruffled hair and an even scruffier beard, rebuttoning his vest as he followed them outside. "*What is all of this commotion about?*"

"Trenton, this is no time for play. This, here, is the sister of Roth, the man who murdered your dearest cousin," Frand explained.

"Why would she come here, then?" Trenton asked, his undergarments astray and wrinkled.

"*For a meeting with the royals*," Ruth stated as a sentinel reached to cover her mouth.

Trenton's head tilted in questioning. He commanded his sentinel to allow her to speak. "What would they possibly want with you?"

"I have something that they want…*something worth mountains of gold*," Ruth pleaded. "Take me to them, *please*… They've recognized my family. Look at the pin on my coat."

"What is it you have?" he asked, moving closer to inspect her pin.

"I'll—I'll show you when I show them," she stuttered, knowing that she needed to be the one to bring Scarlett there herself. Ruth looked deeply into his face and young eyes, a visage that couldn't have been any further from resembling Lady Lomberg. Trenton had an innocence to him, seeming more curious and kind than brash and drunk.

Trenton spun to Frand, who looked perturbed that Lady Lomberg's younger cousin was even considering Ruth's proposition. "You know, Frand, we could use their favor. It might be worth it."

"Not a chance. *She aided in the escape of your cousin's own murderer!*"

"Olan," Trenton said to the old sentinel. "Get us a carriage. If it turns out that she has nothing to offer, the courts can have her."

Ruth sat across from Scarlett and Ludwyn with their hands tied in the Lombergs' tiny-windowed carriage for what felt like more than half the day. They had ridden far past Bovere's central plaza before being left down a darkened side alley. Ozzy, who had burrowed inside Ruth's sack, had been their only form of enjoyment, as they watched the tiny otter jump from lap to lap and whine at them to play.

"You. *Come*," a stern voice commanded when the carriage's door finally swung open. A sentinel dressed the same as the others, but with a navy-and-red tabard, grabbed Ruth by her broad shoulders and pulled her out of the carriage. She peeked left and right but couldn't tell where she was. They dragged her through an arched door and up two flights of stairs. In the darkness, she saw only the shimmer of the black ring on the man's long finger, gripping her by the collar of her overcoat. Many sentinels, with their longswords still sheathed, lined the candlelit sidewall. The one closest opened a set of double doors to let her inside a narrow and windowless brick room, lit only by lanterns hung from an iron-chained chandelier.

At its center was a long, polished oak table, where Ruth saw a Divine Sage of the Cathedral sitting at its far opposite end. The figure in the candle's shadows was dressed in a pristine white habit with three interlocking circles, one above the other two, attached to a chain that hung around his neck. As she walked closer to the table, Ruth noticed he had strands of gray hair strung out from his rounded headpiece and wrinkled skin that dangled from his thinning neck. Behind him, she could barely make out a Tohenic knight, dressed in a long-sleeved undersuit of chainmail with the Cathedral's Divine Crest emboldened on his white surcoat.

In the chairs that were spaced evenly along each side, with a few empty places, were the heads of many families within the Royal Order. Behind each of them, with their backs to the narrow walls, stood their commanding sentinels. Ruth walked forward slowly and nervously scanned the room, recognizing some of their faces from the gala at the Court of Champions. *Favian Gravelot… Duram Lavant… Athelson Bangor.* Each of them, numbering nearly twenty or so, wore the seven-petaled white dove flower pinned near the collar of their coat or to the front of their dress.

The man at the far end to the left, with silver hair and a strong, bulging jaw, spoke first. "Ruth Fendorse—sister to the Regent's champion, and now, I guess, one might say fugitive of the covenant—I, Talam Franclare, cordially welcome you to our table at the behest of Trenton Lomberg. Any member of a family recognized by the Royal Order, such as your own, *as far as I can still see by your pin*, is welcome to petition here with open arms."

Ruth could tell just by the slimy way he looked at her that he already wanted this to be over. As the royals at the table sat silently, Ruth struggled to keep her thoughts under control, especially while standing in the presence of a divine sage. In her mind, she had rehearsed repeatedly what it was she wanted to tell them. But now that she was finally here, her prepared words had become overshadowed by clouds of doubt and panic. All their eyes stared her down while her own could only wander in escape, finding the back wall. Tracing its darkened bricks, she began to see a figure of promise and hope: the image of Dane's slim face smiling back at her.

This is it—the moment we traveled all this way for. I can't let Dane down. "Thank you. In the north, there is a fleet that travels by sail—"

Talam Franclare raised his palm into the air to cut her off. "We know of this already."

Beside him, one of the others looked at her, then added, "The Royal Order has its eyes and ears everywhere. Not a whisper passes an ear across the Plane with someone at this table knowing of it."

"As Sir Clovin has shared, we are well aware of this fleet and its captain and the disruption they have caused to the transportation of our goods," Talam Franclare stated.

"Will you two let the girl speak?" the tanned woman across the table from them asked.

Ruth sucked the dry air down her throat and continued: "What you may not have heard is that the fleet's captain has passed. I come at the behest of its new captain, a man from Marredom named Dane, to seek your assistance."

More whispers began to circulate around the long table, until one of the men to Ruth's right asked, "Should we really be listening to this girl? A girl whose own brother murdered the head of a family recognized by the Royal Order?"

The woman to her far right jumped in again to reply, "Sir Leary, Orean was not one of us and would never become one of us. She had no seat at this table." *A frocked knight,* Ruth realized. "*Besides,* not one of you here liked her anyway."

As the table broke out into petty bickering, Talam Franclare, at the very end, shouted aloud to say, "*Miss Elvina is correct.* Ruth's faults are not her brother's. Now, what is the assistance that you seek?"

"*Gold,*" Ruth said bluntly. "Ten thousand. To build a fleet that will usurp Marredom's own."

Deep laughter erupted from everyone at the table except the Divine Sage, who sat calmly at the far end. Ruth's confidence plummeted. She could feel her face redden as they mocked her proposal. She half expected them to show her the door right there. To the right of Talam, when the laughter died down, Lucas Clovin stated aloud, "The Royal Order takes no part in the funding of foreign wars, *girl.*"

That's such a lie, Ruth thought to herself, but didn't have the courage to reply. "It wouldn't be for war, sir. It would be for trade. *Free trade,* with a fleet that isn't controlled by that King in the Northern Plane."

"Mind you, haven't you just stated that this fleet's newest captain is, himself, from Marredom? At least the last one was from the Southern Plane."

Newest captain, I hope, Ruth thought. "*Dane* is his name, sir. I was once with him in this fleet and saw him in action. He is an honorable man who was, himself, once enslaved as an oarsman by King Mordin. Dane is the antithesis to everything that King stands for."

"Funding this oarsman's fleet would be a terrible investment and a potential disaster to the Plane. There is already war in the South. Clovin is right. I have no desire to start another in the north," one of the old men she had never seen before joined in to say.

"It has already begun, sir," Ruth stated boldly.

"That's all well and dandy, *girl*," Talam Franclare said as he moved his hands into a fist on the table. "But I was told that you had something that might bring us wealth, not sink us out of it."

"*I do…*but it would need to be a trade, sir," Ruth said, only for them to erupt into laughter again.

"*And, that is?* What could you possibly have that would be worth ten thousand in gold?" Talam asked coldly.

Ruth turned to the sentinel behind her, the same one who had dragged her in, wearing the ring of black glass around his long finger. She whispered to him words that the rest of the room couldn't hear, and he left the room. As they all sat and waited, Favian Gravelot, the one man there she had spoken to before, said, "From what I have heard, this fleet with sails has done quite well against the King's own."

"Done well to disrupt our trade, *yes*," the man closest to her responded.

"*Andermon*, it would be worthwhile for you to admit the trouble that King Mordin has caused us in the past. This might be a perfect opportunity for us to seize hold of the market for transportation across the Plane."

"And what if it fails?" Lucas Colvin asked him. "What do you think that King would do next if he were to find out what our intentions were?"

"He does hold an *amulon*," Talam added.

"It would simply be an investment," Favian replied.

Ruth broke her silence to correct, "Not just an investment, sir. *A trade.*"

Most of those at the table laughed again as if they thought very little of anything she might have to offer. As the doors opened, in walked Scarlett dressed in her oversized shawl and loose trousers, escorted by Trenton Lomberg and the sentinel from before. The royals at the table continued to laugh until she pulled down the hood of her shawl to reveal her fiery-orange hair. "*This is Scarlett Calegri,*" Ruth stated aloud, forcing them all into silence.

"Well, *this* is certainly a surprise," Talam said, rubbing his angled, clean-shaven chin. Chatter across and between the table broke out again, with back-and-forth comments in a clatter of words Ruth couldn't discern.

"Her father would pay well to have her home," Elvina Damas said above all their clamor.

"On the basis of another loan?" one asked.

"Her father is at war," Andermon commented, silencing the rest.

"From what I have gathered, the man her father is at war with—the Scordisci boy—would also pay well to have her back in Sacrim," Lucas Clovin admitted. "But ten thousand in gold? I'm still unconvinced."

"*War? Cleo?*" Scarlett asked under her breath.

"*Ruth,*" the Divine Sage spoke softly to quiet the entire table. "I feel as though I have seen that face of yours before… Tell me, please, of your faith."

"*Sir.*" Ruth bowed politely as she addressed him. "You may have. I was in the Cathedral of the Divine One for a few days after the Regent's bondfight, in prayer for my brother's safety. I have been a firm believer in the Tohenic teachings since I was a little girl, and—"

"*I believe you,*" the older Divine Sage struggled to speak. "That must have been what it was… I recall seeing you there one of those days. You could have been with everyone else, doing anything else. But these patriciates cannot offer you their gold. As Lucas here had stated, our covenant forbids the funding of wars we are not actively involved in."

Ruth nodded politely again. Her heart sank through her chest with the feeling of failure.

"*However,* there is no covenant that forbids one of our own's protection abroad. Should they choose to provide you with protection from their sentinels, being that you are from a family of the Regent, I cannot stop them…and should they choose to exchange their services for the girl's delivery back home, I cannot stop them. It is by the grace of the Divine One that you have helped her arrive safely into our hands."

Just as the Divine Sage had finished his groaning speech, Favian Gravelot stood. "By the grace of the Divine One, I offer you a hundred of my own coat's sentinels as protection. And I will do everything I can to help deliver the girl, Scarlett Calegri, back to her home."

"I shall offer one hundred of my own, as well," Elvina stated.

"I, too," Owen Orlaith added.

Though most held their silence, Ruth was elated to hear a few more royals offer her their support. Part of her was sad she wouldn't receive the gold she hoped would build Dane's fleet. But Ruth knew that having the arms to protect his current fleet was better than returning with nothing at all.

When the voices had settled to a standstill, Talam Franclare stood from his chair. "Moscah will not be pleased with the disruption to his agreement with King Mordin. I shall inform him promptly." To most of the royals' unease, he stormed out of the room.

From the edge of the long table, Ruth turned to look at Scarlett and gave her the warmest of smiles. Just as she reached her hand around to hug her, the skin surrounding Scarlett's freckles grew eerily red. Her hand moved to catch it, but not soon enough. Scarlett bent over the long table and heaved the nastiest hurl of puke across its garnished top.

"*I think I'm pregnant.*"

CHAPTER 33

SUN

Cleo,

By the time you wake and read this note, I'll be flying to Sazara. I'm sorry for not telling you goodbye. I couldn't stay in Corlis any longer. You have my confidence that your message will reach the right hands. Please forgive me.

With love,

Vanna

"*With love,*" Cleo scoffed under his breath.

For the past six days, Cleo had reread Vanna's note whenever he found himself alone within the blackstone walls of Corlis's castle. After one of the best nights of his life, Vanna had left him without explanation.

Cleo wanted to crumple the note up and light it aflame the morning he found it on his desk, folded next to the wet tip of his quill. A small part of him knew something was wrong when he had awoken alone. He tried to convince himself that Vanna had just gone downstairs to her room, or into the city to break her fast, or even down the coast to see that bird. But after sending his guardsmen to search every street and back alley of Corlis, they all returned with the same answer—that both Vanna and the bird were gone. But what perplexed Cleo more than her absence was how, just before, she had seemed so adamantly opposed to delivering his message.

For the entirety of that next day, Cleo tormented himself over the possibilities of what he might have done wrong. *Had I been too forward? Said something? Did she even like me?* In his rambling of questions, Cleo became drawn to a single answer—that he was deluded by the possibility of happiness in a life full of misery. No matter how long Cleo pondered over his thoughts, each question's end led him to the same place: standing in that exact spot where he had given his love to Vanna. There, he stared out at Corlis's breaking waves, looking down on the harbor from behind the balustrades of his balcony, watching the sun as it chased the moon in the sky.

To Cleo, Vanna was a young, mysterious woman from a time long past—someone who didn't belong in present-day Sacrim. She lived outside of anything he'd known or was taught and came from a place that was just as intriguing to him as she was. Cleo knew that her prowess alone—one she seemed to carry above the rest with confidence and grace—was enough to make most men fall for her. If not for that, then it would have surely been her captivating hips and piercing gray eyes. Cleo knew just how lucky he was to have known her.

But now she was gone. And all he had was his path of war and death, in the company of those ghosts of his past. Cleo had done his best to push the mourning of them all to the back of his mind—even during the burning of Vident Lement's body outside of Fort Saxoram, which had kept him sleepless since. Cleo trusted Vident Lement more than anyone else. And when he had spoken fondly of Vanna, Cleo listened.

Considering the way Vanna had left, she had proven herself to be as mysterious to Cleo as he had originally thought. And as those six days had come and gone, Cleo became settled with the understanding that she was just another ghost to be added to his tally. Though his heart hung heavy with doubt, all Cleo could do was hope that her note was truthful—that she was now off, flying toward Sazara to deliver his message.

Since Vanna had left, it hadn't stopped raining in Corlis. Or so Cleo presumed. Most of his days were spent inside the worn-down castle walls, walking to and from his meeting room a few flights of stairs below. Day and night, he strained over decisions concerning his brigade and its dwindling supply of gold, waiting for any positive news that his captains might bring. He used the dreary weather as an excuse not to walk the city's streets and their encampment outside, to check on his guardsmen or meet those cagerman from Corlis who had just joined the West Brigade.

Truthfully, Cleo despised this city and its people. They reminded him of the crowds back in Sazara, but far worse. Most were poor and dirty, both in their lifestyle and their ethics. They spent their time wandering the streets and haggling for work, only to gamble it away or sink their earnings into bottomless barrels of wine. Even the richest were transparent about the corrupt way in which they made their gold. And with the few sacks of his own he had remaining, Cleo hoped he could still convince some of them to join his cause. He needed the men, or at least more men, if he wanted a chance against the amassment the Calegris had formed in Sazara. And so, day and night, Cleo pressured his captains to grow their forces.

With what little time he had in between, he pondered the last words of Vident Lement—of *Sable Sellieve* and the black stone. Cleo, though, excused himself from puzzling out its meaning, as he always became drawn to the same conclusion: that Vident Lement's reference was of the black cube in the center of the Convault, under the Tessereum. But that was leagues away. Instead of worrying any further, he stuck Vident Evander with the task of sifting through Vident Lement's book, *Phicantics*, for any clues that it might bring.

Down the spiraling stairs, Cleo trotted slowly, his royal-red cloak skimming past each step as he descended. "Sir," Jones said after he saluted. "Captain Jove should be arriving any moment from his return this morning."

"Thank you, Jones. That will be all."

With an abrupt pause as he exited the meeting room, his steward stuttered like a stag to say, "Your tea—is on the table."

Cleo walked down the long room, one the same size as his own, but without the outstretched balcony at its far end. Along the blackstone walls were torchlit alcoves, spaced far enough apart to spread their light onto the finely engraved table at its center. There he sat, facing the door, tempted to read Vanna's note once more, which he kept folded within his waistband.

Clamorous sounds of erratic sandal steps came from the spiraling staircase, until through the door burst an enthusiastic Captain Jove. Without a salute, he shoved in a man with his arms wrapped tightly behind his back. Following them were four high-ranking guardsmen, all with smiles, who entered to encircle the opposite end of the table. After a moment's pause, the rest of Cleo's council poured in. Captain Ostin, his newest captain, Gregan Igor, who had taken the late Sovano's position, his vice-captains, and Vident Evander all took their seats at the table.

"*Well*," Cleo said, his voice hopeful for the first time in days.

"Commander, allow me to introduce you to one of the two deacons assigned to the temple's shrine in Corlis," Captain Jove stated proudly. "Deacon Ambrose Sengire."

Cleo stood from his chair with a calming smirk and walked toward them. "Captain Jove…you've outdone yourself yet again."

"He's a quiet fella. At first, he wouldn't tell us his name, but his face matched the description—*ugly*," Captain Jove stated with a laugh, causing the others to join in.

Cleo kept his face stern. "Where did you end up finding him?"

"In one of the cabins near the geysers, a few days' hike northeast, up the coast. Old shit tried to run, thinking we wouldn't be able to catch him." Captain Jove shoved the deacon forward again. Cleo walked closer to inspect the old man, to see if he matched the description they were given. His long, gray hair, deep and dark, was parted in the middle and covered most of his puckered face, which was marred by equal parts bruises and dirt.

"From what we gathered around the city, the rich in Corlis used to frequent the hot springs out that way. When we got there, we found an abandoned hold of cabins. And, of course, he was squatting in the biggest," Captain Jove added. "*Scum.*"

"And we're sure it's him?" Cleo asked, pretending to inspect him further.

The guardsman next to Captain Jove threw a bundled robe onto the table, one that was royal red with golden lines of sacred scipyrian stitched in small letters across its centered sash. "It's him, alright." Captain Jove pulled down the collar of the deacon's undergarment to reveal a marking on his chest. Near his heart, in permanent red ink, was the insignia of the Benevolent Sun—a perfect circle with ten rays extending from its rim.

"*Excellent*," Cleo said, finally breaking a smile. "Take him downstairs and see what we can get out of him. Captain Jove, *thank you*. Now we can finally have that meeting with the Black Baron."

Captain Jove nodded at the two guardsmen to his right, giving them both the command to leave the room. To his left, he handed the deacon over to the other two, who escorted him out of the door. "*Commander* …we also found this at his cabin." He handed Cleo a folded piece of parchment, one with a broken seal of Sacrim's insignia.

Cleo took the message and opened it, skimming its contents quickly to find it addressed from the Vice-deacon of the Temple of Sciron. "So, the royals have her?"

"Seems so. The word spread quickly."

Scarlett, Cleo thought. *I haven't forgotten about you.* He passed the note around to his council at the table, then yelled for Jones, who stood beside the door. His steward rushed in, confused, to which Cleo commanded, "Get me our best courier." Cleo returned to his seat at the far end and reached for his parchment, ink, and quill. Unwinding it, he began to write.

"What are you doing?" Captain Ostin asked. "I thought we weren't to do written messages, sir."

"This isn't for any of us. It's for those royal families in the Regent. And that bloody Cathedral. I'm setting up a meeting to exchange our gold for Scarlett."

"But, *sir*...what gold? I thought we'd found Corlis's deacon to help pay the Black Baron for men. How are we to afford the ransom they would require for the girl, too?"

"We did, Ostin. The gold in the vault at Sciron's second temple will help pay our men and the Black Baron's, depending on how many he is willing to provide."

"Then where will we get the gold to exchange for Scarlett? Surely the Calegris have enough to afford her before we ever could," Captain Ostin questioned.

"*Ahh,*" Cleo gasped, finally looking up from writing. "That's exactly where we'll get it. *Their gold,* when we take Sazara. The Cathedral in Bovere has never liked the Temple of Sciron. The two are mortal enemies. Our message will be a way to strong-arm them, to show those hens that we are formidable opposition to the temple. The enemy of their enemy—that it's New Scipyria and its warriors who plan to reign over the Southern Plane, not the Calegris, nor the temple. And we expect to be at that meeting. Not them."

Next to Cleo, Captain Jove scrunched his thick eyebrows and rubbed his reddish beard in confusion. "That courier will take moons to reach Bovere. Their support won't come in time."

"And so will the Calegris' courier. The Regent has closed off the Tannen Bridge since our war began, and it's our men who are stretched between Sazara and the gorge. Unless they take a ship, which is a death sentence in today's waters, we'll beat them there."

"Even then—"

"*Sir.*" Jones slowly cracked open the door to let himself and the courier in.

"Good," Cleo said, folding the parchment. "Jones, thank you. Everyone else, leave us." Without another word, Jones and Cleo's council departed from the room. "*Captain Jove*, stay."

The young courier guardsman stepped forward, saluting nervously as he approached Cleo, who walked to meet him halfway down the table. Like all couriers, in his hands was a satchel, and attached to it was the white flag they were required to post as they rode. "What's your name?"

"Joal."

"Joal, I need you to take this message through the gorge to Bovere. There, at the Cathedral, give it to one of the divine sages. *Them only,*" Cleo commanded. "They'll be in white habits and wearing three circles chained around their necks. Jones will hand you coins for your travels."

The young boy, who must have been only a cagerman, garnered a determined look as he took the message from Cleo. "Yes, sir."

"*Wait,*" Cleo said abruptly. "Before you go through the gorge, I must ask something more of you. Something of high importance. Under the cover of night, I need you to travel to Cignus. Find Commander Kladden and tell him, and only him, this: *Fire burns half-past autumn's end.*"

The courier's green face grew firm. "*Understood, sir.*" He gave his pledge of loyalty, saluted, and then rushed out the door.

Captain Jove turned to Cleo and asked, "So, the note is only a cover if he's stopped?"

"Yes. And who knows what the council would leak for the right price, especially here. But I don't think anyone would bother haggling a courier carrying that letter."

"Then that's the day we attack Sazara?"

"Yes. The most important message I'll send."

"That's soon. But your guardsmen will be ready."

"Good," Cleo said with a smile. "*Commandant* Jove. For you, I have something else. But it will have to wait until after this meeting with the Black Baron."

"*Commandant?* You honor me, sir."

"You've earned that honor, Kenrick," Cleo responded with a smile, shaking his wrist. "I trust you."

For the first time in many days, Cleo ventured out of the blackstone castle of his own accord. Covering himself with his cloak to shield the rain, he followed his newly appointed commandant to the right of the coast, down Corlis's only stone-laid street. People drifted in and around the inter-webbed blocks of homes and buildings, watching Cleo as he passed, headed toward the only busy area of the city—the Port of Corlis.

At the edge of the closest pier stood the Black Baron in his long black coat and muddied black boots. The Baron was young, likely the same age as Cleo, if not younger, but the two couldn't have looked any more distinct. With long and wet honey-colored hair, he stood nearly a head-length taller than Cleo. He was frail and pale, like a *slimy potworm*, as his guardsmen would sometimes joke inside the castle walls. His demeanor, however, was anything but.

"I'm glad you could finally make it," the Baron said, his voice rumbling with mockery. He held out his arm to shake Cleo's wrist.

"It was only a matter of time."

"*Come*," he requested, turning to walk down the pier, toward its end.

Docked at its farthest post was a wooden boat, just larger than a skiff, with six oars at each of its sides. "Where are we going?" Cleo asked, trying not to seem concerned. Inside, however, he was fuming. For as long as he could remember, Cleo hated the sea, even before his training as a cagerman, where he was forced to learn how to swim.

"Across the Silver Sea. To Leghorn Island. The largest of the first rift. It shouldn't take too long."

Shouldn't take too long, Cleo scoffed.

He wasn't as worried about how long it would take, rather that they were taking this passage at all, especially with the rain drizzling down on top of them. Before following the Black Baron onward, he looked out at the sea and watched the whitecaps of violent waves crashing in the distance. His stomach was already turning. But again, trying to seem unfazed, Cleo followed Commandant Jove onto the boat and took the bench seat beside him in the front row. The men to Cleo's left pushed off from the pier and began rowing their way to Leghorn Island.

The farther they traveled, the more Cleo wished they could have just met somewhere in the city or within Corlis's castle. Wave after wave, the boat pitched from bow to stern. On each side, the two rows of men struggled to row in unison with the rising and dipping crests. To Cleo, the waves here were much larger, below and beside them, than they had ever been from his view atop the castle.

For what felt like an eternity, they rode across the Silver Sea. Just as Cleo was beginning to feel nauseous, a dark slab of land rose above the bow's spray. The closer the boat rowed toward it, the tighter Cleo grasped the edge of the bench beside his soaked thighs. The rain had slowed to a halt as they glided with the tide toward the island's shore. Two of the Baron's men had jumped into the water to pull the boat to its lone pier.

"*Welcome to Leghorn Island,*" the Black Baron stated proudly.

Cleo didn't want to turn around and reveal his pale face. He scrunched his nose and nodded to keep his dignity, then calmly followed Commandant Jove toward the white-sand beach. After a short hike through the island's tall grass and around its curving trees, they were brought to a tiny hut. Cleo couldn't tell whether its tilt came from its driftwood design or his nausea. But either way, he wasn't pleased.

He followed the Baron and his assortment of ragtag men inside the hut's steaming single room. At the center of its empty space was a molding, circular table. "This is where we conducted our operations in the past," the Baron said as he walked around its curve, scraping his fingers along its fringe.

"So, we've arrived," Cleo sneered. The Baron and his men sat down and invited Cleo and Jove to do the same. To Cleo's bewilderment, the Baron didn't take the largest chair at the opposite end but, instead, had left it open. "What sort of operations get done in a place like this?"

"Building."

"Building what?"

"I'll show you for a cost. Do you have the gold?"

"For the men we discussed, yes," Cleo said.

"I think you might just like what I've brought you here for a little more," the Black Baron grumbled. "So, do you have the gold to find out, or not?"

"I do," Cleo lied.

"Last time we met, you didn't. What changed?"

"*Access,*" Cleo said slowly.

"Access to what, exactly?"

"My men have one of Corlis's two deacons. A man by the name of Ambrose, who can get us access to the temple's vault."

The Baron looked around the room suddenly, checking the reactions of the ragged-haired men beside him. A snarky smirk crept across his pale face. "That's the *people* of Corlis's *gold*. And the temple is sacred, is it not? You dare to defile the Benevolent Sun?"

Cleo paused, unsure of how to react. He and Jove were outnumbered ten to two and stood almost no chance of making it back to the Port of Corlis alive should a fight break loose. Cleo fumbled with his thoughts as he reached for the grip of his sword. *No, we can't fight.* "I don't believe in that mystic smoke," Cleo stated with his chest out. "If the temple's gold is yours, as you say, then I plan to be the one to deliver it to you."

Across the table, the Black Baron's face was unmoved, blank as the bark of a thousand-solurn-old tree. He sat angrily, or so Cleo thought, with a forehead that steeped to bulge above his narrow cheeks. Cleo waited, thinking only of how to react if he needed to pull his sword, counting the men he could take, *one...three...six...*

As if an axe had been swung into his bark, the Black Baron burst into laughter—silly laughter, as if he meant to mock or scare Cleo. "Commander Scordisci...you impress me," he said, wiping his face as his crackly laugh slowed. "I don't believe in that nonsense either. And neither does my father, who runs this operation. He isn't a Sacrimian like you all."

Cleo's tense hands softened as he wiped his sweat onto the feathered spades of his skirt. "Where is he from?"

"*The north.* That temple is a parasite to Corlis and Sacrim. It collects, collects, and collects, but never gives. I'd be glad to finally take from it. And to help you on your path of eliminating them," the Baron said bluntly.

"Well, then, we have an alignment. Now, what is it you brought me all the way to this forsaken island for?"

"My father has worked between here and Corlis in secret for the past half-decade, if not more, building these weapons."

"What kind of weapons need to be hidden on an island?"

"The kind that can strike the air from the sea," he replied with a smirk.

The Baron stood up and walked out of the hut, telling Cleo and Jove to follow. They left along a side path and walked farther inland, down a sandy trail. Shell-like bugs and others that flew and crawled on their bent legs nagged at the men as they walked through the fan-like leaves. Off in the distance, Cleo noticed three massive storage buildings hidden in the brush. The Baron walked toward the closest one's large doors, unlocked its chain, and slid it open.

"*Ballistas.*"

Cleo's eyes shot open as if he were a kid again, receiving a gift on the day of the Midsun Festival. He walked inside the dirt-floored room, where two large wooden ballistas stood tall, just behind the door. With his mouth hanging open, Cleo moved to inspect the two long rows lined from front to back, stretching to the barn's far end. Two of the Baron's men walked to the side wall and returned with a bolt that was as big as they were. "*They're massive,*" Cleo said, his thoughts leaking aloud.

"More than triple the size of those last used in the Amulonic War," the Baron stated with a prideful grin.

"What are you doing with these?" Cleo asked.

"My father was commissioned to make them. Well, really, to make a fleet of ships that had these as their primary weapons. To usurp those aging ones from Marredom."

"Commissioned by whom?"

"*Clyus Calegri,*" the Baron remarked with a rumbling of disdain. "Watch. Sam will demonstrate." One of his men climbed three steps and reached for the levered wheel. With simple turns around its spoke, the cord attached to its arms pulled back until there was a click. The two men with the bolt helped Sam slide it into the ballista's chamber. With his chest pressed against the curve of its back cavity, Sam rotated its aim out of the barn door. He angled it up, down, and then back toward the way they had come. After a loud click from the releasing lever, the bolt was slung quickly into the trees, splitting two in half before it struck soundly into the third.

No wonder there's a war with Marredom, Cleo thought. *Ships with these to compete with their own. They could sink their whole fleet... Clyus was ages ahead of everyone.* But above all of Cleo's thoughts, one rang the loudest: *These would be perfect for fighting those rook riders.*

"What do you think?" the Black Baron asked with a beaming grin.

Without a moment's hesitation, Cleo replied, "I'll take them all."

"Good. There are twenty-two currently completed, waiting for their ships to be finished. But with your payments, I am willing to forgo those for now. We'll bring them back to the Port of Corlis and have wheels put on them all, so you can march with them wherever you please."

"How much?"

"Fifty golds each," the Black Baron responded.

Cleo shook the pale man's wrist. "*Deal.*"

CHAPTER 34

SEA

Viridian maple trees with foliage that rivaled the sun in their scale of shades were scattered among the Northwoods' coastal line of wet pines. Dane pushed off on the last small boat to leave its rocky shore. As he lifted himself in and helped Caji and two of the mates, Wilkin and Jorgi, to row, he looked out at the cloud-splitting sky and watched the sun shed its midday light onto the cove's bristling water.

Part of him wished they could stay here for a moon's pass longer. The Northwoods was rich in its range of vibrant colors, painting its trees to life and stirring memories of his hometown with a pang of envy. And the people, though few in number, like Niven, were all warm and welcoming. Ruth and Roth, along with their family and friends, had taken him in as one of their own and shown him what it meant to live within the bounds of the Regent's cantons and its freeing covenants. As Dane looked out along its rocky stretch of shore one last time, he couldn't think of a more perfect place to lay his late captain to rest.

But with Ruth having left for Bovere nearly a quarter-moon ago, Dane knew it was time for their fleet to depart. He did his best to help row their wooden boat out into the calm waters of Cubby Cove until they came upon the broadside of his ship in command—the *Freebird*. With a wide-brimmed smile, he drifted his gaze away from the russet and virescent coast to the new white-lettered name painted along the fore of its hull.

Dane, though—being the new captain that he was—noticed that a range of doubts seemed to fester nearly every time one of the mates, or especially one of the other three captains, asked something of him. Their concerns were often menial. They debated new watch stations, crew quarters, and cleaning duties, or even the meals they would have in the following days. Dane found that his mind labored when making any final

432

decision. To him, he was still one of their own—just another oarsman turned mate, scooped from the bottom of the barrel.

It was in those moments that Dane thought the highest of Captain Noreas, a man he admired more so now than he ever had before. With endless decisions and task lists that each required his attuned attention in order to get their fleet back underway, Dane came to understand the burden his late captain had endured. Not just with his daily duties or those of the fleet as a whole, but while also keeping each of the mates and their attitudes in tranquil check. With each resolution Dane came to, he found himself grasping Captain Noreas's leafed necklace tightly, thinking only of what he might say or do.

Dane was a quick learner, however. And he always had a keen sense of structure and timeliness. They were traits that he had learned from his father during his earliest days in Niven. From their time fishing near the knee, cleaning and cooking, building things for his mother and siblings, or even their treks east to Minoska, his father, Domus, had always instilled in him the old and traditional ethics of a true northern man—that nature was order, and order was necessary to survive within it. Though it was a saying that rang true more so in the Northern Plane than it did here in the east, the free fleet was now readying itself to embark that way. And so, Dane held true to what he knew.

From the rope-tied ladder that hung off the *Freebird*'s side, Dane climbed up to the main deck. His head was still hatless, so he brushed his short blond hair off to the side as he passed the mates, mocking the King's Navy and their officers' salutes. It was a communal joke to him and those who had once been oarsmen. The simple tip of the curved brim cap, if he had one, tended to bring them a smile.

Dane walked aft between the mates who scattered throughout the deck, still making their final preparations for their galleon's departure. Up to the quarterdeck he continued, watching as Galen, the deck chief from the *Widow*, and now his own, inspected the helm's winch-wrapped line for precision. Dane gave him a brief comment of support, then walked through the door of the aftcastle, up the stairs, and into his own captain's quarters.

"What took you so long?" Markas asked from one of the four chairs beside his desk.

"Probably waiting to see if Ruth would come back before we left," Caji said with a laugh, standing behind his tall chair.

"Something like that, sure," Dane replied, his voice mellowed to dampen their jesting manner. He walked behind Sonny and Jalek, who sat in two of the other chairs, and then pulled out the charts tucked inside his desk's top drawer. "Now, Caji, you said there was something we needed to see."

"It would be better if you heard it from him directly. I'll go grab him from below deck."

"Good. The last thing we want is Caji trying to recall anything himself," Markas said with a laugh as Dane's first mate departed.

Dane unrolled the largest chart he had onto his desk and went about tracing their route by rule up north, then west, to Nordheim. The three other captains had a few questions on formation particulars and the fleet's signaling before Caji returned with a middle-aged mate and former oarsman, whom he introduced as Dermot.

"Take a seat, please," Dane told the man with fraying hair and glazed eyes. He was thinner than most, at least after their fruitful port stay in the Regent, and had pale skin splotched with bruises and scabs. Dermot moved one of the empty chairs in front of Dane's desk and took off the saber around his black-twine trousers before he sat. "Caji tells me you've been to Nordheim. Is that right?"

"Yes—*sir*," Dermot stuttered nervously, his eye twitching.

"What was it like?" Markas asked bluntly.

"My first sentence was on a war galley. The *Frejma*. We did a few patrols out that way, if I can remember right."

"Anything more you can share?" Dane asked.

"Common patrol…back and forth was all, really."

"Was there just one galley on patrol, then? How many piers? Rotations …anything?"

"Oh, right. Yes—just one of us typically out there. I got a look out when I cleaned the decks some days. If I can remember right, I think there may have been ten piers…but they weren't all that busy. Bare, for the most."

"And your own galley, what was that like?" Dane asked the man whose face looked duller than his mind.

"Smaller than most. Maybe twenty or so marines and officers on board. If not less. Seemed like a vacation to them lot."

"Sounds practical enough," Jalek commented.

"Is there anywhere else that your galley might have gone? Around that region?" Markas questioned him, his voice grumbling with frustration. Dane looked over and saw his long-bearded, swollen face beginning to glisten red.

Dermot twitched his eyes profusely in thought. "There was…actually. We would stop to drop anchor and scrape the hull after a patrol. It was two of us who would switch—back and forth."

"So two, not one. That helps," Dane said, rubbing his thin chin. "Where was this anchorage at, exactly?"

"I couldn't tell ya. I was usually down—down in the oar deck whenever we would go that way."

"Anything you've heard, then?"

"Now that you mention it, those scum above would speak of three—three rocks. Like islands of an extra nipple, they'd say."

"*Perfect*," Dane responded, scanning the chart on his desk. "And the yard itself was usually empty, you said?"

"From what I would see—yeah."

"Thank you. You're free to go," Dane told him. As the scrawny mate got up and turned to leave, Dane stopped him to add, "Dermot, one more thing. Go below deck and have Piney write you down for extra rations. If he gives you any trouble, come back and see me."

"Thank you, *Captain*."

Just as soon as the mate had left, Markas stood from his chair and stretched his gaze onto Dane's desk. "Well, that was almost useless. Caji, even you could have remembered that."

"We did get some good information… The anchorage," Dane said, thinking aloud.

"Will we check there first?" Sonny asked.

"Not just check, no. We'll need to clear it out first. Or at least you two will, Sonny and Jalek. You'll be towing the two cargo galleys and the lumber for masts anyway, so a galley at anchor should be easier picking," Dane said. He scanned the chart for the three rocky islands Dermot had mentioned. "Looks like it's there, just east of the yard around that slender passage."

Jalek stood up and checked the location on the map for himself. "Works for me."

"Me too," Sonny added.

"And that leaves both of us free to hit the yard," Dane said, nodding at Markas.

"Hit that war galley on patrol, yes," Markas corrected. "In one of our last meetings with Captain Noreas, after our battle in the North Sea, he brought up the nork navy's yards. After you mentioned that plan to him, he went on about how he began building his own, back on the islands of the Silver Sea. He spoke about it as if I weren't there with him the entire time."

"Well, what did he say?" Dane asked.

"Noreas used whatever information and books he could find on theirs to model his own after. Sonny, you might remember better than me…but he said something of the sort, that the King and his navy don't waste their crew on ships being docked for repairs or refits."

"Who's the forgetful one now?" Caji shoved the shoulder of their fleet's oldest captain.

"Oh, hush," Markas snarled back.

"Sounds about right," Sonny commented.

"So, what you're saying is that those galleys docked in the yard won't have any marines or officers?" Dane asked, ignoring their bickering.

"It will have yard workers, I'd assume. But not a full crew to take the ships out. At least not enough for every ship."

"That should make this easier, then," Jalek said.

Dane stood with his other three captains. "We can hope."

"Might be why there are no oarsmen we've come across that have actually been there…other than Dermot," Jalek added.

"Our plan sounds good, but I still want reassurance. We can't have anyone leave the yard, or even the island, who has spotted us. It might take another half-moon, or more, to fit the masts and ballistas on the two we have. If our location is given away to anyone back at that main island—*Marredom*—we might as well be docked in a sea of blood."

"If we want this to go smoothly, we'll need tight lips," Sonny added.

"*Right*." Markas ruffled his tangled hair. "From that anchorage, the *Rithron* and *Baroness* could put feet on land. How far away is that? No more than a half day's hike, by the look of it."

"Yes—*that's it*," Dane said with growing enthusiasm. "Sonny and Jalek, we'll place both of our strongest mates with you two. When you clear that anchorage, have the boats take them in. We'll send our best warriors into the yard from around its backside. They'll set the border and take any captives that try to flee. While we take care of the galley on patrol, you'll pinch them in from behind."

"Captives?" Sonny asked.

"Yes. The yard workers. We'll need their experience to refit the ships quickly," Markas replied.

"Markas, you sure you don't want to be captain of the fleet?" Caji asked with a snarky laugh.

"I'd rather swim back to shore and live with those hens and their elk, and sleep in their bloody woods for the rest of my life, than wear Dane's boots," Markas responded, releasing a deep-gutted sigh.

"*Thanks*," Dane sneered.

Markas was shorter than Dane, like Sonny and Jalek, and most of the other mates from the Southern Plane. He had boulders for shoulders and a rounded, swollen gut fit for guzzling wine. With Cowen gone, Dane was glad to still have Markas by his side. From what he had heard from Piney, Markas had been one of Captain Noreas's closest friends since he had first arrived in Corlis. He was once a smuggler himself, who had worked with Noreas under their boss, Casari, just as Cowen and Simion had.

"Sounds good to everyone?" Dane asked. After they all agreed, he turned to his first mate. "Caji, once we're underway, round up half of our strongest men and let them know they'll be sent over to the *Rithron* when we're a few days out from Nordheim."

"*Aye.*"

"Magnus, you do the same when we get back to the *Bessie*. After that, I'm good—set to get underway. I could sure use a nice meal back in my own quarters," Markas said as he walked slowly toward the door. Jalek and Sonny, along with their first mates, Saul and Sidrus, all made similar comments, then followed him toward the door.

"Oh, there's one other thing," Dane said, pausing to collect his thoughts. "The payroll."

"What of it?" Markas asked. "If you're thinking about adding those oarsmen to the tally, we don't have the funds."

"To them, it seems like their freedom is enough," Sonny added.

"It isn't that. Though, that discussion will need to happen later," Dane said.

"Then what is it?"

This was a difficult conversation for Dane, but one he knew he needed to address. "Rigel told me the coffers down below are missing. Simion must have taken it all with him when he joined Cowen on the *Widow*. I don't have the funds to pay the mates this moon's silvers…or any of the moons after that."

Markas walked back to Dane's desk. "We'll find a way. Don't worry about it."

"I'll talk to my chief of the hold and see what we can do, too," Jalek said.

"When we reach Nordheim, I'll do the same," Sonny added. "With our funds pulled together, we should be able to cover it."

They still haven't fully accepted the oarsmen as mates, Dane realized. Despite his concern, he nodded with gratitude and said, "Thank you."

As the captains dismissed themselves back to their galleons, Caji left Dane alone to spend time with his eyes fixated on the blue of his chart. He breathed a sigh of relief as he read the sea's plotted depths and side notes of weather patterns. It was his first passage as captain of the free fleet, and he needed, more than anything, for their mission to go flawlessly if he wanted it to remain that way.

The bell strung from the quarterdeck rang twice as a last call to the mates for their midday meal. Dane had eaten a few bites of roasted whitefish earlier, back on shore, and so he chose to skip the meal. But, in realizing that it was Piney, his new chief of the mess, who had likely rung the bell, Dane made his way out of his captain's quarters to check with him one final time before they departed.

"Piney!" Dane shouted. He hurried out of the aftcastle's door to catch his scrawny friend scampering back below. On the main deck near the stairs was a group of mates huddled in a circle around Roth, listening as he told the stories of his fights back at the Tessereum. "*Piney*," Dane said again, tapping his shoulder to break him away from the outer ring of mates.

Piney whipped his tilted shoulders around in an annoyed fashion before realizing who it was that disturbed him. "Oh, Dane—*Captain*," he replied with a sarcastic salute, as if he, too, were a silver-capped officer. "What is it you need now?"

"Final checks?" Dane asked. The mates, wearing their ragged gray and white garments, began to turn around as soon as they heard Dane speak.

One by one, they scattered from the huddled circle, speaking in low, ominous whispers as they made their way back to work.

"Oh, right. Still working on that. Mind you, we've been doing more organizing than anything, and still cooking, at that, and trying to bring everything back in from ashore. But the shelves are stuffed—that much, I can tell you."

"Okay, just get me an inventory when you can. We're going to need to know just how long we can last out there before we have to stop again."

"Well, if that's all it takes, I take back what I said. Shelves were empty the last time I checked." Piney let out a quirky laugh. His eyes bugged from his head, and he scrunched his thin neck down like a turtle, waiting for Dane to laugh.

"If that's the case, then you'll be the one who has to tell the mates they're going to starve. *Not me*," Dane replied sternly instead. "We're going to be at sea for a bit."

Piney winced at the thought of any mate being angered with him. "I'll have you the list later."

"Thank you."

Roth, who was still spouting his proud tales to the last few mates listening, finally broke away from his chatter to roam over by the bulwark railing beside them.

"I can't get enough of this fella. Have you heard some of the stuff this man did, Dane? A champion of the Plane...on our ship. Who woulda thought?" Piney pointed to the bear-like man. "If the shelves ever do turn up empty, I know who I'll be howling at first."

Roth laughed a bit as he joined their conversation. "You won't have to worry about that. I've found the food on this boat to be quite terrible."

"*Galleon*," Dane corrected.

"This bloke hasn't been to sea a single day, and he's already upset with us cooks. Can you believe that? You're lucky you're a fighter, you know."

"Well, if you feed him well enough, he might just be on your side should those shelves actually turn up empty," Dane commented, more lighthearted than before.

"Now that, I'd have to agree with. Anything you need, big boy... Come find me first, and I'll make sure you're taken care of." Piney tried to reach higher than he could to pat Roth on his shoulders.

"You bet."

"Well, I'll be off to get you that list you asked for," Piney told Dane, already drifting toward the stairs that led below deck.

Dane turned back to Roth and asked, "Have you had a good look around the ship yet?"

"Yeah. I took a few strolls during the past two days to get my bearings before we left."

"Good. You'll have to pick things up quickly. Rigel, downstairs in the hold, can get you any clothes you might need."

"I think I'll just stick to my shawl," Roth replied as he patted his clover-colored top.

Dane scanned the main deck and saw most of the mates dressed the same—in white garments or gray coats, with black-twine trousers tucked into their boots. His first instinct was to be tough on Roth, to tell him that he needed to dress like the rest of the mates did to help with their cohesion. But then, at that moment, he thought back to Ruth and realized that she, too, had always stuck to wearing what she knew—her forest-green plaid skirt. "*Fine.*"

"I'm sorry, I just can't get over your hair." Roth let out a laugh as he ruffled his hand atop Dane's head. "Who did that to you?"

"Did what?" Dane stepped back and rubbed his own hand through his short hair, which now hung like a bowl from ear to ear.

"Man, that needs some work."

"I'll get Piney to cut it again, shorter," Dane responded, not really caring about what Roth had said.

"Again?"

"I had him cut it last night before we left. It was getting long."

"No way would I trust that tiny man with a pair of shears," Roth said with a laugh.

"He's got knives in the kitchens and will be the one cooking your food," Dane reminded him. "But Piney talks too much to have any ill intentions. And even if he did, he'd probably be the first to tell you."

"I can see what you mean."

"But I can assure you, he's a good man to have on your side. He saved me back on my old ship. And Ruth did, as well. If it weren't for that trouble you got yourself in back on that beach in Roverra, I'd probably be dead. So…thank you, too."

"I don't deserve any thanks for that," Roth told him, turning his gaze to the coast.

"Either way, I'm just glad to have you on board."

Roth shifted his chin as if he were sifting through his thoughts. "*You bet.*"

Dane found his remarks to be quite odd, almost as if he were unwilling to consider himself equal to the mates.

"Captain," Galen said as he walked down from the quarterdeck. "Checked the aft mast, and she's good to go. All the ship's sails and rigging are ready."

"Aye," Dane replied. He turned back to Roth and added, "This here is Galen, the deck chief. You'll be sticking with him. He'll give you your watches and show you the ropes."

Roth looked over at the tan, ink-skinned man, whose receding hair left his larger forehead exposed. He then stretched his gaze back out to the shoreline, almost unamused by what Dane had told him. Galen was a calm and simple man, which made for the perfect deck chief. For as long as Dane had known him, Galen had always kept his chin down and did whatever it was Captain Noreas had asked. He was respected by all the mates for his rigorous work and rugged, yet fair-mannered temperament.

Again, Dane caught a glimpse of Roth's face, who seemed to think he might have been joking. His glances at Galen alone were louder than any words he could have spoken. It was clear that Roth looked down on the southern man, considering Galen to be below himself or, even, the work below his worth. Roth's nose bent as he smiled with arrogance, clearly just expecting to be along for the ride.

Ruth had given Dane a summary of her family, as well as what to expect from them before they laid anchor in Cubby Cove. Most of what she had mentioned regarding Roth wasn't pleasant—that he was cheeky and favored time with stout and women over any sort of discipline, work, or rules. He liked to tussle and fight and wasn't one to be told how to act. Dane's initial thought was that her twin brother seemed like any young man across the Plane. But in the past few days he had spent with him, Dane came to realize just how correct Ruth's description was and just how different they both were.

Roth was cocky and almost too big—or too admired, even—to do the menial things that most others took pride in. Even back at their coastal camp, when lumber for the masts and their shorter cross-yards were being brought on board the *Rithron* and *Baroness*, Roth never really took part in any of their lifting and lugging. And when it was time to pack everything up, Dane couldn't remember seeing him anywhere near the coast.

As much as Dane complained about how much Piney liked to talk, Roth seemed to enjoy it just the same. The few times when he could be found, Dane tended to see him within a circle of mates, boasting about all that he had seen or done back at the Isle of Azil. He'd reenact his fights with his hands or axe flailing in the air and talk of all the women he had slept with, just as he had with his ranger friends back in the Northwoods.

But Dane knew from the stories of his fights at the Tessereum—or, really, because of his sheer size alone—that Roth wasn't a man to be teething with it. He stood more than a head-length taller than Dane and had arms and legs as thick as the trunks of wet pines from the deepest parts of the Northwoods. As the awkward moment continued, Dane thought about whether or not he should poke the bear. But the more he questioned himself, the more he remembered one of the last things Ruth had mentioned—that he should work Roth hard. *He needed it.*

"*Actually*, I know just the thing to get you started." Dane walked over to the side railing of the quarterdeck. He picked up a bucket of sandy water and a sandstone, then returned to Roth and handed it to him.

"What is this?"

"Sandy water for the decks. To scrub."

"Oh, no. I can't do that."

"Can't, or won't?" Dane asked.

"*Both*," Roth replied, scuffing his short hair behind his broad ears.

"You know, you remind me of someone—my brother, Maven, back home in Niven. The two of you would make great friends," Dane told him, turning to face the water. But before he said anything he might regret, he decided to hold his tongue. "Here, *in this fleet*, every man is equal. This work is nothing compared to what we oarsmen had to go through."

"I hate to be the one to break it to you, but I'm not an oarsman. And never was."

"But you are a mate, now. And as long as you're with us, you're one of us," Dane responded, thinking back to what Captain Noreas had told

Ruth when he'd given her her saber. "Speaking of which, every mate in this fleet has the right to wield a saber. I have one for you back in my quarters, if you'll take it."

"I'll just stick to my axe, thank you," Roth replied, as if he were still too haughty to wield the same weapon the others did.

"You know, you're just as stubborn as Ruth was when she first came aboard." Dane chuckled to ease the tension. He needed to think of something that might get under Roth's skin—something that might make him crack, without it being Dane, himself, who started the *Freebird*'s first real fight. *Got it.* "Only, Ruth always cleaned the decks with the rest of us…without anyone having to ask. And she took extra watches to help, down below. Everyone on board loved her and the way she worked and helped. You wouldn't want to be shown up by your sister, now, would you?"

Roth rolled his eyes with a disconcerting smirk and took the bucket. "Just don't expect me to be in the kitchens."

"You'll do fine up here. We set sail soon. And then, the fun stuff will come."

Roth finally moved to follow Galen near the opposite railing. "Somehow, I don't believe you."

You probably shouldn't, Dane thought to himself as he watched Roth leave. He cracked his knuckles and made his way back up the stairs to the quarterdeck, where he found his new first mate, Caji, by the navigation table in its far corner.

"All checks are complete," Caji told him. "The crew might not be ready to be back out at sea, but the *Freebird* sure is."

"Good. You'll give the order to raise the anchor." As Dane moved toward the quarterdeck's forward rail, he nodded over to the main deck and added, "Caji, keep a close eye on the big one, there. I have a feeling we're going to need his best on our side."

Caji looked over at Roth, who stood with his bucket in hand, wiping down one of the railing's posts. But just as soon as they both had glanced his way, Roth turned to the mate beside him and returned to chatting. "Empty barrels make the most noise, sir."

"Just make sure he's on one of the boarding parties when we take Nordheim."

"Consider it done."

"Oh, and one more thing. Take down that flag of Corlis at the top of the mast and have the others do the same. We'll make and raise our own when we dock in the north."

"*Aye.*"

CHAPTER 35

SKY

Vanna's breath was dense and heavy, like the air she used to breathe back in the high mountains of the Astrian Range. For as high up as Mersi would take her, Vanna only wished she could fly higher. High enough to break past the heaviest clouds and rise to the stars in the sky so that she could watch as they did, away from the dread of the Plane they glimmered upon.

Mother Moon and her Sister Stars have a thousand eyes looking down on me, and they're probably all laughing at my miserable life—at how naive I've been. Gullible enough to convince myself I was doing something right for once.

Hidden above the clouds, Vanna flew restlessly for the past two nights. She flew high enough to be shrouded from any Sisters scouting below, searching for enemy movements like birchbees sent out of a hive at the behest of their queen. Each flap of Mersi's tired wings in the break of morning lifted Vanna closer to Sazara, a city she was returning to against her earlier will. Any prior objection she once held had left her that night in Cleo's bed, within the highest room of Corlis's castle. Sazara was the place Vanna now felt she needed to be, as Cleo had first asked. With guilt consuming her, she hoped that by fulfilling his task, she could make things right.

Vanna also hoped that night would be the last time she saw him. With her out of his life, Cleo would never discover the truth or feel the pain of being betrayed by someone he trusted. And Vanna, herself, would never have to look him in the eyes again and be reminded of what she had done. Vanna just wanted to forget it all as she had in the Vypores with Arzak and Juni and leave her past behind. And so, she knew that Cleo could never learn the truth.

It would break him like it's broken me—like he would break me.

Cleo had gone to war over the death of his father. Vanna only knew what more he would do if he ever found out that she was the one who had committed that heinous act. He would have her killed, or more likely, he would do it himself.

Despite Vanna's hope of escaping him, Cleo's face was all she could see. His sharp smile and hardened touch were shaped in every cloud she flew past. The guilt she felt never ceased to crawl across her skin each time she looked ahead and painted his face within the white-swashing sky. He was strong at a time when she was weak, and a leader when she had none. Cleo had become her friend, someone she gave her love to and had let inside. To make peace with her guilt, she needed to be there for him, without actually being there with him, and deliver his letter to Vident Maedrick in Sazara. And then, maybe after, she could travel back to Mount Matron, or even to the Eastern Plane, to create a peaceful life for herself. Vanna knew the possibilities were endless. She could be where people lived freely and become someone new among them. Someone different. Someone real.

Her flight with Mersi, though, had been rough. The high altitudes and coarse, early-winter wind hadn't helped to ease her discomfort. But Vanna didn't care. Part of her felt like she deserved it. And being with Mersi in the sky, escaping her past once more, was where Vanna knew she belonged. Having freed the rook during their stay at Corlis, the two had bonded enough for it to follow Vanna's commands without putting up too much of a fight. And she hoped that their bond was strong enough for the rook to stay near her, outside the city's walls, or to return to her when it was time to escape again.

Vanna knew she couldn't stay long in Sacrim's capital city. It was Cleo's target—a city soon to be at war. And she had seen too much bloodshed already, including by her own hands. If Cleo were coming, she needed to leave. Her plan was the same as the last time she'd flown to Sazara with the Brazen Talons—to fly east along the tall coast and enter the city under its wall, through their elaborate maze of aqueduct tunnels.

So, she flew, shedding tears, until she could see the faintest hint of the city's outline, far out and away from the lifeless dirt that surrounded it. Mersi followed the two screeching notes from her flute to descend, and Vanna yanked the saddle to the left, toward the water's edge.

She spotted the same skeleton trees that grew from the sea-shaven rocky cliff. Vanna scanned the coast until she found the enclave where she had left Little Wing once before, then dropped Mersi into it. Without chaining the rook up, she dressed in one of the sleeveless robes she had packed in her sack. But as she readied herself for the long trek, a single tear fell from her eye. Looking down, she realized her sack was all she had. Vanna had never needed much as a Sister or as a Child of the Sisters. And with Cleo's brigade, their supplies and access within the city had been sufficient. But now, it was only her and her sack. Deep within, Vanna felt alone.

With her sandals sifting up clouds of red-shaded dirt, she left Mersi for Sazara. She wrapped her head and hair with extra cloth to shield herself from the southern winter's sun. Near the cliff's edge, Vanna journeyed until she came upon a crevice that dipped below. Just faintly, she could hear water streaming into the Barren Sea. Vanna hurried to it, moving along the tall coastline until she reached the limestone tunnel buried beneath the ground. On her stomach, she peered in.

No. Her breath released.

Iron bars had been fashioned inside the aqueduct tunnel to block entry for what Vanna presumed to be a wartime measure. Possibilities about what to do next paced throughout her mind, leading her to jump in and shake the tight gate. But it came to no avail. *I could fly in…or find a boat heading into the harbor. Or try the obvious: the western gate. It'd be heavily manned, but likely not closed.* Even in war, Vanna knew the people of Sazara still needed supplies.

And so, she walked southeast, back across the lifeless dirt. The occasional breeze sifted dried twigs over her toes, and the lizards she came across greeted her with watchful eyes. Beetle bugs scattered into their holes as the sun followed her in the sky, headed toward the gate. There, Vanna spotted a large caravan of people and wagons traveling along the trail into Sazara.

Vanna kept calm as she joined them, not wanting to be ousted as a foreign straggler. She walked with the caravan, keeping her distance and doing her best to fit in with the travelers. Voices from the front soon rasped with gossiping shouts as the line slowly came to a halt. Vanna looked up, around their amassment, and saw the western gate. Its tower stood out like an armored fort from Sazara's wall, with thick iron bars above its arched opening and bronze shields swarming all around.

Vanna shuffled her way to get a better look ahead, attempting to hide her concern from the crowd's whispers. The line in front of them was at a near-standstill and clogged at the entrance. As the caravan began to move along slowly, she tried to skip closer. But before she could, she felt a tap on the shoulder. A voice from behind asked, "Can you see the men?"

Startled, Vanna's shoulders tensed, readying to turn in defense, until she realized it was just an innocent old woman dressed in a conservative white shawl. "The guardsmen?"

"Who else, dear?"

"*Right.* Yes, they're there." Vanna shrugged the lady off, trying not to let her see her face or continue the conversation as she moved back in line.

"*Oh,* I bet it'll be a long one for them today," the short lady said, following after her.

A long one for what? Again, out of confusion, Vanna lifted her gaze to view the gate. There, a few wagons ahead, were two guardsmen on each side walking down the line, pointing their fingers as if they were counting. Vanna quickly turned back to the old lady and asked, "What's going on?"

The lady's face became more confused than her own, her eyes carrying a swirling bout of judgment. "Don't you know? *The wedding.*"

What wedding? But before Vanna could even react or respond, she knew. *Clyus Calegri and Queen Helera—their wedding.*

"Everyone in the First Partition was recalled to be here. As well as many more in the surrounding."

Of all days.

Vanna's first instinct was to run back to Mersi. She turned quickly, but behind her were crowds of people funneling in from the nearby villages and towns. In a panic, she pivoted again sharply and saw one of the guardsmen directly in front of her, counting and bellowing: "*Keep it moving. You'll all get your view.*"

A view was the opposite of what Vanna wanted. She wanted to retreat, to fly away from this abomination and escape this amassment of a crowd. But there she was, being dragged along with them, pushed closer and closer toward the gate. In front of it was a company of guardsmen swarming the wagons and people, forcing some out to the side to be probed. The black cloth she had wrapped around her head had become moistened with nervous sweat. She couldn't turn back now; it was too late. She was surrounded, being shuffled like a black sheep within the herd into Sazara.

But at that moment, just as Vanna knew she'd have to pass through the gate, her heart plummeted to the lifeless dirt. *My sack.* The guardsmen ahead were searching through everyone's bags and would soon do the same with hers. Vanna had forgotten that her telson was still stored in there, as well as the banned vilovian nectar. *What should I do?* she questioned, knowing she couldn't hold onto either of them any longer. Her only belongings could now cost Vanna her cover—or, more importantly, her life.

Knowing she had no other option than to leave her sack behind, Vanna reached in and grabbed Cleo's message and Zell's flute, then tucked them both inside her waistband. She kept her head forward as she pushed past families of travelers, old and young, creeping her way to the back end of the closest wagon. There, she slid off her bag and tucked it inside its canvas cover.

Vanna's heart pounded as she forced herself ahead, bumping through women and children alike to escape anyone who might have seen her or what she'd done. *Breathe. This is no different than those days in the streets of Mount Matron. They don't know who I am,* she reminded herself, thinking back to the training she had as a Child.

"*You,*" she heard one of the guardsmen shout near the side of the gate. Vanna kept her head down. "Next," the guardsman said. With her chest tensed, she walked forward. Vanna could smell his rotting breath and feel him staring her down, his eyes scanning her for more than the prohibited items she once held.

Despite her concern, Vanna walked through.

From the other side of the gate's shadow, guardsmen in bronze and leather vests aligned on each side of the path, funneling the crowd forward and yelling at them to hurry along. Just as Vanna thought she was in the clear, a flurry of screams and commotion broke out behind her, near the gate's entrance. Guardsmen from all around rushed toward the disturbance, pushing the crowd aside with their shields and spears as they forced their way through the throng of people.

Vanna stopped to look back at the wall. From the other side of the gate, she saw the wagon—the same one she had dropped her sack in, with the old lady in the white shawl standing beside it. The lady was pleading with the guardsmen, her sons being restrained in a tussle. At that moment, Vanna saw it. One of the guardsmen with a spiked bronze helmet held her sack in his hands. He reached inside it and pulled out her telson, holding it to the sunlight for inspection. Vanna knew she needed to leave.

But as she began to move, the old lady's eyes met her own. Vanna turned with the stream of people and rushed forward. Yelling soon surrounded her, but she was quick to sidestep the shoulders of the smelly Sazarans being guided downhill. When she reached the first street of buildings, Vanna discarded the cloth around her head and untied her long hair, letting it flow freely. She glanced to her left and right, looking for an exit. All she saw were guardsmen directing the droves, unbeknownst to the searching eyes of their fellow guardsmen behind her. Every so often, she heard one of them yell and scream above the chaos, pushing her to move forward, faster than before. Down into the dense streets of Sazara, she hurried, catching glimpses of the harbor and twin-pillared lighthouses to her left as she moved with the crowd toward the main square. Vanna peeked her head up and saw a gigantic platform erected in front of the Temple of Sciron.

Lines of guardsmen in red and gold capes surrounded the temple, sweeping around the platform to keep the crowd back. On one side of the platform, magistrates and magnates sat in chairs, dressed in the same outfits they'd worn the last time Vanna had been undercover in the Consolate Chamber. On the other side, mostly women sat, dressed in shades of black and gowns of crisp purple. *Women from Astria,* Vanna knew. Thousands of people were forced to stand and watch, filling the square and the surrounding streets that branched from it. Vanna continued to shoulder forward, trying to escape the guardsmen behind her and get a better sight of the situation.

Near the statue of Claros Sciron, she finally felt somewhat safe, hidden within the sprawl of the crowd and concealed by the statue's long shadow. The men, women, and children of Sazara, dressed in dirty rags, stood fidgeting, crammed shoulder to shoulder as they waited for the ceremony to begin. To Vanna, most seemed somewhat jubilant to be there, awaiting with naive smiles to celebrate the man they envied. Others seemed hypnotized by the square's grand display. Streams of flowers flung between the buildings and draped from the tall platform, while banners of gold and royal red hung from the temple's dome roof.

A young girl with dark hair stood beside Vanna. She couldn't have been older than twelve and seemed as if she had come to the square alone. The longer Vanna stood near the statue in hiding, the more she saw herself in the child—not just by her looks, but also by her demeanor. She was alone at such a young age, unbothered by the feverous crowd. Vanna smiled at the young girl, who broke her innocent gaze to smile back.

Drums began to beat and rumble. Men dressed in ceremonial royal-red vests and golden-laced robes marched onto the platform, playing deep tunes from their bronze horns that wrapped around their arms like snakes. From their line, they separated into two, forming a path for people to walk through as they came up the stairs from the temple doors. For quite a while, Vanna scanned the wide platform in search of her target. *There.* On the left side, she found a bald man dressed in a burnt-orange vestment sitting behind a high chamberman, who matched the description of the man Cleo had spoken of—*Vident Maedrick.*

Two little girls dressed in the finest red silk entered between the horns, followed by several of the temple's deacons. The heavy drumming intensified as men with bronze-spiked helmets and gold cloaks marched forward. When they reached the platform's edge, they saluted the statue, then turned sharply to the left. Behind them came a younger man, one Vanna quickly recognized—the boy she had seen back in the chamber, *Cayen Calegri.*

A long gold cloak flowed from the lion's mane that wrapped around his shoulders. His red vest had white fur along its seams and was laced with the insignia of the Benevolent Sun and its ten rays. He proudly held up the Sunspear, tipped by gold-azilian. From the far corners of the crowd came echoing cheers. The people near Vanna, though, whispered in flutters of uncertainty, as if they rarely saw the young boy and were surprised that he had shown his face.

Behind the young man came a woman dressed in a tight black outfit. Vanna knew immediately who she was. *The Grand Dame.* Her eyes were squared away with anger, and like those around her, Vanna was tempted to scoff at the foreign eminence. As the crowd's clatter rose with discontent, Vanna used the commotion to glance back at the street she had entered from, searching for anyone who might still be giving her chase.

Out from between the playing lines of horns came two deacons of the Temple of Sciron, one of whom Vanna had seen before. *The Vice-deacon.* The other, she couldn't recognize. He looked young, with red strands of curling hair protruding from under his conical, crimson cap. The two men's robes were noticeably finer than the other deacons', laced with a wide sash down their center that displayed the golden-stitched sun. As they walked slowly toward the platform's edge, the younger one moved near the corner, still standing, while the Vice-deacon took his seat.

The horns and drums stopped; a whispering clamor from the crowd broke the long silence. Clashes of silver bells soon broke the air, charming the square with soft hymns played by Astrian flutes near the stage. Out from between the horns pranced Queen Helera.

Her dark hair was pressed tightly against her scalp, split down the middle to conceal her strong and protruding forehead. Vanna could barely see the Skybow she held clasped in her hand. The Queen of Astria wore a long, violet-colored gown of silk fitted with ruffles of diamonds that outlined the splitting crease at her broad chest. In all their magnificence, the gems shimmered in the sunlight as she walked toward the corner to stand beside the young deacon. Around her neck, the Queen wore the same half-moon necklace Vanna had seen in Mudin Spring when she became a Sister of the Silo.

As the hymns came to a halt, the intense drumming resumed below the platform. Moments passed with the crowd held silent until an old man with white hair walked slowly toward the platform's edge. *Clyus Calegri,* Vanna recognized. He wore a vest of gold, hemmed by crimson threads, and a greatcoat of the finest silk to match. Clyus's strong, shaven, freckled face was steadfast and silent as he walked to kiss Queen Helera on her cheek.

The deacon who stood beside them took to the center of the stage, and as soon as the drumming ended, he began to speak. *"By the light of the Benevolent Sun, we are gathered here today to celebrate the joining of spirits in the greatest of cities, Sazara, to be witnessed by all."*

To his right, the man motioned for Clyus and the Queen to come forward. *"I, Archdeacon Cronas Solona Sciarra, shall proclaim thee, Clyus Calegri and Madam Queen Helera Palvini, to be wedded this day and every day under the light of the Benevolent Sun."* A young boy and girl slowly walked up from the back of the platform, each holding a cushioned pillow with a golden crown resting on its top. Vanna watched on in horror. *"Kneel before the sun and sky."*

Turning to face the temple, they each obliged. The Archdeacon chanted words indiscernible for periods longer than the Sazarans liked. He then took the crowns from the pillows and gently placed them on their heads. The Vice-deacon rose from his seat and left the platform. He returned with a chalice, which he then handed to the Archdeacon. Vanna couldn't tell what was within, but she could see smoke rising from its brim.

The Archdeacon held the chalice between Clyus and Queen Helera, and they stretched out their clasped hands above its smoke. "*Rise now, as a conjoined spirit—two stars having become one, to reign over the Southwestern Plane in peace and with prosperity!*"

The Southwestern Plane? Vanna questioned, her eyes fluttering with concern. She understood that the two would become married and align for war, but the two regions of the Plane becoming one was never a possibility she had considered. As Vanna looked around, she found that the crowd shared her worry. The Western and Southern Planes had always been separate entities of their own. Vanna felt as if she were witnessing a massive shift in the sky, just as the Archdeacon had stated. A new sun and sky above them all, which made her and the thousands of Sazarans in the square question whether the real one would rise again in the morning.

A tug came at Vanna's arm. She looked down and saw the young dark-haired girl from before, pointing to her left, out into the crowd. Vanna's eyes were plastered in fright. She looked above the fray and saw the old lady from the western gate being dragged through the crowd, led by five guardsmen with swords and shields, who held out their fingers and pointed them right where Vanna stood.

Vanna panicked, having nowhere else to run or hide. People swarmed to surround her from every direction. Not knowing what else to do, she reached down to the little girl and handed her Cleo's message. "*Please*, I need your help," she urged.

The little girl nodded, so Vanna continued, "There's a bald man up there on the platform, the only one up there wearing burnt-orange drapes—the vestment of a vident. A man by the name of Maedrick. Take this to him, and only him. *Please.* I need you." Vanna struggled to let out a smile as she pushed the girl off into the crowd, watching as she scurried through the sea of Sazarans.

Looking back again, Vanna saw the group of guardsmen closing in, shouldering the crowd out of the way. Her head swirled around for any opening to escape, but none came. But to her fortune, atop the platform, she saw the Archdeacon turn to face the crowd and declare, "*To sanctify this new union, the Temple of Sciron will return to exalting its ceremonies of old. At midday, in the chalice at the altar, the Temple of Sciron shall make a sacrifice to our Benevolent Sun. With honor, these two children have chosen to offer their lifeblood as the first of many tributes. May the youth of their blood be burned for the fortune and blessing of our newly conjoined star, so that they may shine above us all!*"

As soon as the Archdeacon had finished his declaration, all those who stood around Vanna whirled their heads in confusion. Growing groups began to shout aloud, roaring against the temple's decision. It took a second for Vanna to realize what the Archdeacon had said. *Sacrificing children? That's been prohibited for over a millennium.* She knew the temple used its altar at times to sacrifice animals, like the sacred Scipyrians did, but never did she think that this ceremony would return to sacrificing people, let alone children. *Or at least that they'd announce it to all of Sazara.*

Chaos continued to erupt inside the square, as if the Temple of Sciron had managed to resurrect itself as one of those Vyporean volcanoes, spewing its molten tempers in every screaming direction. Arms from the crowd were being thrown up in a feast of anger. Vanna looked around in a panic and tried to run through the first open pathway she could find. *At least this should help me escape,* she knew, trying to gain composure.

People in rags, screaming on her left and right in a rioting fit, began throwing rocks and undiscernible objects onto the platform, at the temple, and at the guardsmen. Instinctually, Vanna ran toward the square's eastern side, heading toward the redbrick home on the harbor the Brazen Talons had used as their first converge. But a company of guardsmen had slammed their bronze shields together to form a wall, forcing the herd of people away from the temple and the platform. Vanna rushed in and around the shoulders of the crowd, looking behind constantly to see if she had lost those who chased her. Up ahead, she caught a glimpse of the harbor and one of the pillared lighthouses between an open split of buildings.

With vigor, she pressed toward it, pushing her way forward until she became locked shoulder to shoulder again with the enraged crowd. The only direction Vanna could tilt her head was up. There, she saw it. Waves of heat, rippling in flames above the horde, blazed in long scorches. Vanna could feel its warmth emanating to coat her skin. She glanced to her left and saw Cayen Calegri at the edge of the platform, whipping the tip of the Sunspear uncontrollably from side to side. Flames of deep red proceeded like rapids from its tip, flinging like a loosened whip above the chaos to create a barrier between the temple and the mob.

Shouts of anger turned into screams of perilous agony—voices of men, women, and children crying out in burning pain. Vanna did all she could not to look their way. Instead, she tucked her chin and pushed forward, out of the wild blaze. Just ahead, she glanced and saw the wall of guardsmen beginning to break.

Vanna shoved her way through and began running as fast as she could toward the opening when she felt it—her cheek slapping hard against the warm limestone ground of the square. Her feet had been yanked out from beneath her. Her only thought was to stand back up and run, to escape the riot lit to fire and its growing stench of burning bodies. But when Vanna lifted herself from the ground, she looked up. Standing above her shoulders was the Grand Dame, glaring at her with rays for eyes that pierced from the sky like black suns of death.

CHAPTER 36

STONE

"*Why did I ever come to this damned place?*" Roth clattered through his teeth in the cold. His breath frosted in plump clouds; his hands stirred in shaking quivers to grip his tiny oar. There he sat, taking up the full length of a bench seat on one of the *Rithron*'s small boats, helping to row their way toward the rock-laden shore that was smothered by the whitest blanket of snow.

The heaving clouds coming from the mates in front of him brought Roth to think of Ludwyn and the rest of his ranger friends and the time they spent together back in the Northwoods. *The good days,* he thought, when they would sit in the crisp air between the wet pines, puffing on redleaf around a warm fire. *Those clouds, I can deal with.*

Roth had only been at sea on the *Freebird* for a quarter-moon when he was given the order to join the *Rithron* and its captain, Sonny Selukos. With this move came the promise of a task away from a mate's duties at sea. The deck watches spent mending the sails and constant cleaning to wipe the wooden planks free from the sea's rub of salt had all become quite dreary in the short span he'd been on board. And the recurring meals of salted fish and bricks for biscuits had grown quite tiresome since the hold ran out of the fresh produce it had taken from the Regent.

Roth had only smiled once since the fleet had left Cubby Cove, when Caji called a group of selected men down to the mess to tell them of their new assignment. The youngest and strongest of the *Freebird* were all gathered and informed that they would lead the fleet's ground assault on Nordheim's shipyard. Roth thought it fitting for him to see real action and felt that anything would be better than trying to learn those entangling lines of rigging that set the sails of the ship. But that feeling quickly washed away when he arrived in the north and felt the frigid sting of its winter air.

"That bastard has a pair on him," one of the mates, Jorgi, turned to tell Roth. Sonny had jumped from the bow of their small boat into the waist-high water to guide it by rope through the pulling waves.

Roth, at the rear, waited for the rest of the mates to hop off, then grabbed his axe and stepped shin-deep into the crashing cold. "A shriveled pair, now."

"Men, brace your boots," Sonny told them as he scourged through his sack to pull out a torn corner of a map. "We'll wait for the others, then head that way, toward the shipyard." As he pointed up the white hill, Roth turned back to the anchored galleons and watched as the other five small boats rowed in a staggered formation toward them.

"If I had known how cold this damned place would be, I would have brought two more coats," Roth told Jorgi and the mates around them as he knocked his boots against a rock, trying to get out the puddle of slosh.

"And a second pair of trousers," Jorgi said. "To keep my own pair from shriveling."

"Do we have time to make a fire?" Marlow, a tall, blond-haired mate, asked. At first, Roth just laughed, but then he moved closer to Sonny and urged him to consider the droll suggestion.

Instead of amusing the mates and their grievances, the young captain simply looked at them and said, "*No*. No fires. We were lucky not to come upon anyone anchored here. And we'd be unlucky if we gave that surprise away. But if you need something to do, go help the others bring the rest of those boats in."

Not a chance, Roth thought to himself, though a few of the other mates took their captain's words seriously. He stood shivering by the gradual coast, staring out under the gloomy clouds of the gray sky, while the rest of the boats were pulled in from the tide's reach. Flurries of ice and sleet began to fall by the time the last of the mates had joined them.

Through the wet and white-powdered snow, they hiked, stomping boot by boot behind the slush of the man in front of them, as they made their way west across Nordheim. More than two hundred mates in total, who were too cold to chat, followed Captain Sonny for what Roth had assumed to be an eternity. The captain of the *Baroness*, Jalek, had stayed behind with a few of the mates to guard the four vessels at anchor. But with each step he took through the knee-deep snow, Roth only wished he could take back that lone smile he had in the *Freebird*'s mess and join the others in their dry warmth.

"Just up this last hill, men," Sonny said, turning back to encourage them. When they were close to the top of the final mound, he waved for them to crouch and spread out wide.

Roth flopped onto his belly and crawled with the rest of the mates toward the peak. Down below, he saw the shipyard from its easternmost side. On the shoreside to the right were five timber buildings with their long roofs covered by snow, stretched evenly along the span of the harbor. Dozens of smaller cabins, linked by cleared trails, were scattered behind them. To Roth's left, across the shoreline gap of muddy land, were ten long piers with, what Roth had counted, fifteen galleys moored among them.

"*Shit*." He heard Sonny gulp. "That's way more than we were expecting."

"Captain—*the sea*," one of the mates on the opposite side of him whispered aloud.

Outside the protection of the harbor, Roth could barely see the sails of the *Freebird* and *Bessie* at full breadth, storming their way through the rolling waves. In front of them were two smaller galleys, struggling to row with any speed as they dipped into the troughs of the waves that then sloshed across their decks.

"There was only supposed to be one," Sonny grumbled, pulling out his spyglass to scan the torrential sea.

"Sir, there's movement at the piers," his first mate, Sidrus, noted.

"It seems as if we weren't the only ones to notice them." Sonny backed away from the mound and stood up to take the saber out from his waist. Roth glanced back down at the central pier and watched as men in black coats and silver-bowled helmets rushed down its planks to board one of the larger war galleys. He and some of the mates beside him turned over to place their backs in the snow, sliding so their heads couldn't be spotted from the shoreline.

Roth's hands and feet grew numb, and so, too, did his courage. In his head, he tried to remind himself that he was a fighter, the champion of the Plane. But every thought had become numbed back to reality by the frigid cold, reminding him that he was just a ranger from Tergona. Roth was no soldier and certainly no mate of the fleet. For all he had talked and told about his glory in the pit, those fights had been different. There, it was just him and one other, and the crowd around them to cheer their battle on. It had been easy, then, to drown it all out. With all the howls and roars and songs of celebration, Roth would become lost in the pit and its pageantry. But on this forsaken island, surrounded by its frozen misery and people from a foreign region of the Plane, his nerves flooded like the curling waves of the North Sea under his skin. This was war. And with war came chaos. Here, there would be no rules—no mutual understanding of combat. There would be no crowd to bring him confidence, and no prize to lift in front of the masses. No. Here, there would be only the coldness of death.

Think, Roth...think...focus. His mind churned in circles as he tried to prepare for what was to come. He peeked over the mound and saw dozens of men wearing black coats and shiny silver helmets still scattering along the central pier with sabers at their waists. They soon took to the decks of the two larger galleys, preparing to get them underway. Roth turned back around once more and closed his eyes.

Roth the Bear, he thought to himself. *The Northwoods...the wet pines... where I am calm and in control.* Within his mind, he saw himself alone, standing within the heart of the woods, where darkness sprawled between the wet pines. Only, in it, he was no longer the bear but was now fighting one. Snow covered its black coat as it growled, its fierce fangs bared as it stood up on its hind legs. The longer Roth stared into its silver eyes, the taller the bear grew to tower over him. Its claws stretched into the sky, readying to strike him down.

Think, Roth...think. But inside, he was panicking. *How do you fight a bear?*

That's it.

His eyes sprang open, and his ears drowned out Sonny's commands. Roth picked his axe up from the snow and charged over the top of the mound, screaming like you were supposed to when facing down a bear in the woods.

"*SHIT—Roth. I never gave the order!*" he heard Sonny yell behind him. "*FOLLOW HIM... CHARGE!*"

Through the flurries, Roth ran, hearing only yells from the other mates as they followed him from behind. He lifted each knee high above the powdered snow as he rushed downhill, letting out his own groaning roar of battle. Off in the distance, and to his left, he saw bolts from the *Freebird* arcing through the air to strike the small galley it chased. Jorgi's raspy voice shouted behind him, and he was drawn back below by the sight of silver-capped men scattering back onto the pier.

Jorgi ran faster down the snowy hill to catch up to his side. "*Roth— you bloody bear!*"

With one hand on his axe, Roth breached the mud along the coastline of the nearest pier, sprinting down the length of its seafront to clash with the few black-coated officers that dared to face him. Each swing he took came with a terrifying yell as he slashed through two arms of nork men that had stuck their sabers out to attack him. Limbs flew in bloodied spurts as he continued to swing his axe, facing the scrawny men in pairs until the rest of the mates from behind could catch up. Most, he could tell, were officers of that nork King's Navy, not trained fighters like those he had faced back in the pit. They were of all ages, from old to young, some fit and others out of shape. But all shared the same terrified look that widened the white around their light eyes as soon as they saw Roth heading their way.

He continued to lead the mates' charge, driving his felling axe into the nork men's bodies, arms, and legs as they swung helplessly to try and attack him. More silver-capped norks flooded down from the galleys onto the pier as he swashed through the muddied ice to keep his footing. In flashes of black and filled with pure rage, he fought two or three, or even four, at a time, slicing through most of the nork men with ease. In his mind, he was chasing prey. He turned to look behind him and saw the rest of the mates struggling to catch up. Roth had made it nearly halfway down the shoreline while the last of their assault had barely broken past the first pier.

Sonny rushed forward to catch up to Roth and Jorgi, yelling, "*Roth, you really are a crazy bastard!*"

A smile broke through the sleet that smothered his face as he spun back around and continued to fight. But just as soon as he had done so, he felt a sharp pain pierce through the meat and bone of his left leg. He looked down and saw a curved blade sticking straight through his thigh. His leg, numbed with agony, collapsed to the ground, unable to hold his weight.

His head whipped around as much as his body would allow, and he saw a short, scrawny officer backing away slowly with his hands in the air. The heat of anger filled him with fury, drowning out the cold pain of the blade stuck in his leg. Overcome by rage, Roth stood up with the saber still piercing him below and rushed right at the tinier man, who trembled in fear.

But just as Roth was about to lift his axe into the air, the nork man's face had changed. All he saw from beneath the crest of the man's silver helmet was the face of Lady Lomberg. Her eyes were bulging, and her plump face smirked as if she were mocking him for what he had done or even questioning him for what he was about to do. Roth paused and blinked his eyes quickly, trying to make her taunting face disappear.

Amid his hesitation, Sonny had slid past him atop the icy mud to block an attack from the lone officer who dared to stop him. Roth opened his eyes and sharpened his sight back to focus. As he stared into the blue eyes of the officer, Roth realized he had a choice. But his pulsating anger had already decided for him. He became that snow-coated bear in the woods and let out his own terrifying growl to prove it. Roth lifted the sharp head of his axe with both hands and drove it down into the scrawny man's head, slicing it straight through his silver helmet.

All around him, the officers in their black coats let out gasps cold enough to freeze the air in its place. Some tried to run, while others threw their sabers to the ground and backed away, their faces filled with a communal look of terror. Roth growled once more, trying to charge at them, the saber in his left leg swinging back and forth with every step he took.

Behind him, Sonny commanded, *"Not one of them gets away!"*

Past Roth ran several mates as they chased any norks trying to flee. Those who had dropped their sabers were forced to their knees and had their hands tied behind their backs. Orders came to search the galleys for more men, and Roth's rage had finally settled. He looked down at his left leg and saw it covered by blood, soaking his trousers and drenching down into the sole of his boot. With a sigh, Roth collapsed to the ground. His vision began to fade with each beat of his heart. He turned onto his back and saw flurries of snow falling from the gray smear in the sky. In single pieces, their cold drifted down slowly to land on him, quenching the anger that had once engulfed his face. With every blink Roth took, the numbing vacancy of black grew thin.

So be the fate of a bear…

"Roth, wake up…you're going to be okay."

Roth opened his eyes and saw the blur of a pale face looking down at him. He rubbed his eyelids to remove the fog. The face cleared to reveal a pair of icy-blue orbs staring back at him with concern. Panicked, he threw his shoulders up from where he had once been lying and turned his face from side to side, half expecting to see a group of men in black coats attacking him.

But instead, it was only Dane. "Roth, you're going to be okay."

Roth's breath heaved in gasps as he looked around the candlelit room. *A cabin?*

"This man, here, did the best he could to save your leg. And your life."

Roth looked at the corner of the room where Dane had pointed and saw two men, both with light-gray hair and pale faces, standing with the sleeves of their garments rolled above their elbows. "*My leg?*" His gaze wandered down to the bed, where a cloth sheet covered him from the waist down. He threw it aside and saw his left leg, from calf to hip, wrapped tightly in bandages.

"It's still intact," the taller man with narrow cheeks told him. "My assistant, here, did the best he could to stitch it up."

"You struck a crucial nerve," the shorter man with a bulging waistline added. "And you lost a lot of blood. But I did all I could."

"*Who are you people?*"

"This is Eriksen," Dane said, pointing to the taller man. "Chief shipwright of the yard and his clinical specialist, Ivar. They saved your life."

Roth ignored Dane's comment, looked down at his leg, and tried to lift it.

"Oh, I wouldn't do that," Ivar clamored, though Roth continued. "With the nerve you hit, you may never regain feeling in your leg. It may eventually be possible to move, but you need to rest."

Feeling? Regain? Move? Roth's thoughts withered with questions that emptied his knotted gut.

"Listen to the man, Roth. He saved your life," Dane told him again.

Instead, Roth ignored their comments and used his arms to lift his leg off the side of the bed. On his good right leg, he lifted himself to stand, struggling to control his balance. Dane moved swiftly to his side, catching him before he could fall over. "Get me something to lean on."

"I've never seen a hen so big. Ivar, go grab the man's walking stick," Eriksen ordered, making the shorter man scamper out of the room.

"What happened? Everything just went black."

"Your friend here, Captain Daneus, took my yard is what happened," Eriksen said, his voice ringing from his thin neck.

"*We* took the yard," Dane corrected, turning behind him to nod at the four mates who stood in the dark corner of the cabin. "The officers are all confined, and the shipwrights have said they will take up our work. Roth, you've been out for a few days now."

"A few days? Where am I?"

"In one of my housing cabins behind my third shop," Eriksen answered.

Roth sat back down and waited for Ivar to return. "And the rest of the mates?"

"Most made it out okay...or, at least, better than you did. We lost eighteen in total."

"Sonny? Jorgi?"

"Jorgi didn't make it," Dane said with regret.

Roth slumped his back against the bed and sighed in despair. "I shouldn't have been so foolish... I rushed down that mound before we were ready—before we had any sort of plan."

"You probably saved us, Roth. Sonny told me he counted fifteen of those officers you killed alone. And if you hadn't come down that mound when you did, those war galleys might have gotten off the pier and attacked us or even slipped away."

"Did the two galleons make it?"

"We're all pier side now. Jalek and Sonny brought the other four around, too."

Ivar made his way back through the cabin's door, his black coat covered with specks of snow. He handed Roth a tall stick and said, "I had one of the men in the shop chop and carve this one up. It should do for now."

Roth took the stick and tried to lift his body to stand, using Dane's thick gray coat to yank himself upright. "It will have to." As he tried to take a step, moving the stick along with the weight of his heavy body, his left leg again collapsed from under him. Dane grabbed him by the arm and lifted him back to stand.

"You need to rest and regain your strength," Ivar told him.

"Nope," Roth replied, taking another step only to collapse again.

"You hens sure are stubborn," Eriksen said.

With each scrape his bandaged leg took forward, he placed more of his weight onto the walking stick until he began to slide across the room. "And you norks can't fight. Want me to make it sixteen?"

"Roth, Eriksen and his men have said they will help us," Dane told him sternly.

"You should listen to your friend. Ivar could have easily left you to die. You should be showing us your gratitude, not your scorn," Eriksen told him.

"*Thanks*," Roth sneered.

"He's right," Dane added. "We spent the last two days setting the border, securing our new captives, and unloading all the lumber. Tomorrow, or whenever the snowfall finally clears, Eriksen said he'd survey our vessels and get started on refitting them. You should listen to Ivar and rest. We can handle the work in the meantime."

Roth made several loops, sliding around the lone room of the cabin before he finally returned to sit on his bed. "Just come get me tomorrow when you go. I need to keep moving."

"*Fine*," Dane replied. There was an awkward silence in the cabin before the two workers of the yard and the mates had all left, leaving the two of them alone. Dane drifted toward the door. Instead of leaving with the others, he turned to Roth and said, "You know, when I was young, growing up in Niven when my family was starving and struggling to survive, I had so many questions. For days, we didn't have a meal to eat. And the winters were harsh enough to freeze our bones from moving. Before the King took my father, I would ask him these things… *Why does life have to be so cruel? Why me? Why us?* And with every question I asked him, he would always respond with the same answer—an answer I hated until I grew older and understood its meaning. *Sometimes, it's necessary to suffer.*"

"*Suffer*," Roth snarled under his breath.

"I'm just happy you're alive," Dane told him.

"*Thanks*."

Dane looked down at his leg one last time, then left through the door. For the rest of the night, Roth paced in circles around the room, trying his best to regain any feeling or strength in his left leg. He stopped only to feed the cabin's fire with chopped wood and to eat the meal brought to him by one of Piney's assistants. As daylight fell, Roth struggled to sleep. His mind scattered in flashes, with short memories of what he had done those few days before. And as he was lying down, his hip ached in pain, unable to turn over or find any semblance of comfort.

The morning light from the cabin's lone window greeted his eyes as he lay there, still wide awake. Flat on his back in bed, covered by a wool blanket to keep him warm, Roth's mind fluttered with never-ending thoughts of everything he had done to lead him there, crippled and alone. *Fighting,* he realized. *From Tergona and Bovere to the Isle of Azil and now here... That's all I'm good for. Fighting for others without an understanding of what I was fighting for.* The longer he lay alone, still hurting from what he was told of his leg, the more he thought back to Dane's anecdote.

Sometimes, it's necessary to suffer.

From it, he came to realize that the feeling of suffering was not his own. That deep pain and all the questions that came with it were feelings many had felt before. But Roth knew that the harshest reality to accept was that he was the one who had brought that same suffering to many.

Remorse washed over him for all he had done, filling him with pain everywhere but his left leg—a leg that now felt nothing. For most of Roth's young life, he may as well have been as lame as his leg now was—useless and numb, constrained without any sort of feeling or use. It was a leg that once did what his mind always assumed it could do, instructed to follow the rest of his body's movements, just as he had always done for everyone else.

The deeper Roth reflected, the more he realized how brash his actions had been on that day of battle. He could have died alone on that forsaken and freezing shoreline without his sister or his family and friends there by his side. And he, just the same, had killed those fifteen men without their own families or loved ones there to weep over what they had lost. As Roth closed his eyes, the memory of the men he had killed continued to flash in vivid images. And accompanying each one, he saw Lady Lomberg's face smirking right back at him. Sorrow smothered him like a blanket of northern snow.

What have I done? And what use am I now because of it?

The pain of his actions had struck him deeper than any sword or saber could have. It was sharp yet eternal, as if all the suffering he had caused to others had imprinted itself deep into his heart with the loneliest feeling of regret.

I need a new purpose, he knew. Deep in thought, he was taken back to Ruth and his parents. He thought long and hard about how caring and loving they always were. *Why so?* he questioned. The answer, though, Roth knew, was one he had always managed to avoid.

Until now.

For the first time in his life, Roth prayed. With his eyes still closed, he tried to remember the words his mother had taught him when he and his sister were both young: "*May the spirit of the Divine One forgive me for the terrible things that I have done. For the killings…for the glory…for the women I have chased after and spoiled. For the pain I have caused others…and caused myself. May your spirit protect my family and friends…and teach me to know and do what is right by you. May the Divine One give me purpose in this life that you have spared…*"

"*Roth,*" a drawling voice yelled to break the blackness of his sleep. Three knocks struck the door beside the window. He opened his eyes and watched it creak ajar.

"I must have drifted asleep," Roth explained to himself as he sat up and watched Dane enter the cabin's only room.

"It's midday, and the snowfall has stopped. Still think you can take that stroll to the yard?" Dane asked. "Eriksen and his shipwrights are down there now."

"Yes," he replied, struggling to raise his leg to the bed's side. "Just help me up." Dane moved to lift his shoulders. As Roth grabbed his walking stick, his leg collapsed again. "Morning rust is all. I was moving just fine last night."

"Take your time," Dane said. But Roth's leg was as frigid as ice. "I brought you some new boots, too. Ivar ripped the old ones to shreds when he was fixing you up." Dane lifted a large pair of boots by their straps. Roth sat back down on the bed again while Dane helped him into them. By Dane's brace, Roth stood.

"Thank you. Now, let's go."

Dane walked slowly beside Roth as he limped his way down the muddy and snow-cleared trail. He lifted the hood of his clover shawl to keep warm.

Step by agonizing step, he followed Dane between two tall lumber warehouses. Roth spotted a group of men near the piers. Beside them were two of the other captains, Markas and Jalek. He looked out at the calmer sea and saw the sails of what must have been the *Rithron* out on patrol.

"I'm surprised you made it this far," Eriksen said as soon as the two of them walked closer.

"*Me too.*" Markas and Jalek walked over to him, each making brief comments about all that had happened and expressing their remorse, helping him to limp along.

"I, along with one of my brightest shipwrights, Niels Pilliam, took the liberty to walk your galley here and check its lines. The *Freebird*, that is. I hope that's okay with you, *Captain*."

"*Galleon*," Dane corrected the stern-faced, older man. "Of course."

"Sorry—*galleon*."

"She's got fine lines, Captain, and planks made of strong grain. It's foreign wood to me but it looks sturdy enough," Niels said. "Sleek at the bow, and it carries its weight well amidship, where your thickest mast is mounted."

"These cargo galleys should have enough strength to hold the masts, right?" Markas asked.

"Should be stable enough, yes. These two you have weren't built in our yard, but they look crafted from the same plans," Niels replied. "I'm well familiar with them." He looked the youngest of the six men but was brawnier than Eriksen and stood taller than the rest.

"What about the others you have here?" Dane asked him.

Niels ran his fingers through his slick, oiled-back blond hair as he scanned the piers. "Less than half are the cargo galleys you're looking for—six in total, by my count. The war galleys might be too sleek to carry the weight."

Roth looked over at Dane and watched as his narrow face slumped in thought. He limped down the muddy line of piers to take a closer look, then added to their conversation by saying, "That's perfect. We only brought enough lumber from the Northwoods for eight masts and their cross-yards anyway."

"The *Northwoods?*" Eriksen asked. Dane looked over at Roth with anger in his eyes, as if he had let slip something he wasn't supposed to. "You know, when I first heard rumors of this phantom pirating fleet, I didn't think they would have come from the Regent. Those royals have always been a thorn in the foot of Plane. But I was under the assumption that those merchants preferred their peace."

"They like their power and control," Markas grumbled.

"We wouldn't be norks if we didn't hold true to our old ways," Dane said, breaking his stare from Roth.

"If we're going to refit all these cargo galleys, we'll need to split the ballistas as well. But only eight of the total fleet will be armed for distance," Markas told them.

"I, for one, find what you're doing to be quite admirable, *Captain*," Niels said to the other shipwrights' discontent. "And the sails you've got crafted here are truly brilliant."

"It'll bring war here, is what it'll do," one of the other shipwrights growled, turning back from facing the harbor.

"It already has," another said.

Dane ignored the comments and asked, "So, do you think it can be done? Eight refits?"

"With just one mast a piece?" Eriksen replied, before answering his question by saying, "They'll be slower, especially with their wide lines, but it can be done. We have three of our shops open now, and another that can be cleared."

"Twelve total makes for a solid fleet," Markas noted.

"How soon?" Dane asked.

"A moon's pass at the earliest, possibly two or three more for this many."

"It'll need to be completed in half that time," Dane responded sternly. "My mates will help to provide labor."

"*Half?*" Eriksen gasped and rolled his eyes. The other shipwrights around him either groaned or laughed at his lofty expectation—all but one.

"*Consider it done*," Niels said with a smile, reaching out to shake Dane's hand.

CHAPTER 37

SUN

"Sir, the Black Baron is at the gate. He said he's here for Commandant Jove."

"Commandant Jove is away, Jones," Cleo responded without looking up from his stack of maps. "Send him up."

"Right away, *sir*."

Cleo reordered his desk in a swift manner and stood to pin his royal-red cloak to the right shoulder of his vest. He made his way toward the balcony and peered down to confirm that only the Baron had been let in. Half hidden behind the starless haze was the moon, far past midnight, dancing its rounded edge between the clouds' soft glow.

A younger Cleo would have been bothered to have company this late at night. These days, however, Cleo rarely slept. While ensnared inside the blackstone walls of the castle, he often found himself doing what he liked the least—straining over his desk, occupied by planning the movements and order of his guardsmen. Most of his time was spent arranging his brigade's numbers into various formations, keeping account of their logistics and supplies, or coordinating the distance and timing of their marches. While he labored over each of these arduous tasks, Cleo found that his thoughts had become erratic and scattered, just like the messy piles of parchment that always ended up sprawled out across his desk.

Staring at his maze of a mess was where Cleo saw his father in himself. He was a man who had little time for anything, except the minute details that kept the wheels of the Guard turning. Those days of thankless work, which Cleo now found himself toiling over, made him understand the weight his father carried on his shoulders every day and just how heavy that weight was. But it was necessary work, Cleo knew, if he wanted to usurp the Calegris in Sazara. Cleo's only hope was that his men didn't look at him the same way he once looked at his father.

"*Sir*, the Baron," Jones said from the opposite end of Cleo's long room.

Jones shut the door behind the Black Baron as he made his way in, tracing his pale fingers along Cleo's table, his stern face drifting into a cold smirk. "I'm surprised a man such as yourself is still up this late…perched above Corlis like one of those king birds."

Cleo moved slowly toward him to shake the Baron's wrist. "I like being up this high so I can watch for those birds, not be one. I was burned by them once before."

"So I've heard," the Baron said, glancing over at Cleo's desk. He moved to rummage through one of the corner piles Cleo hadn't had the time to straighten out, picking up a few sheets to stare at them with a confused look. "Tactics are a waste," he scoffed.

Cleo snatched the parchment away from the taller man. "The history of the Guard would disagree."

"Sacrim's Guard hasn't fought a real war in how many solurns?"

"They're fighting one now," Cleo answered boldly.

"*Oh*, that's right." The Baron's voice dripped with sarcasm. "But these tactics still seem as useless as ever. There is only one maneuver any commander needs to use for victory—strike with your largest force at their weakest point, and it will always keep them on their toes. *Never let them settle*, as my father would put it. Everything else is just waste."

Cleo paused and took a long breath to think about what the Baron had said, pacing his way back toward the long table. *He's not wrong. And, of course, I've done the opposite.* Cleo's shoulders were stooped low, though he tried not to let the Baron see. *I've split my brigade in half. Maybe if Kladden were still with me, we wouldn't have taken those losses at the fort. And maybe Vident Lement might still be alive…* "Sure," Cleo admitted against his own accord. "But finding their weakest point is the hard part. Which is where tactics become necessary."

"Necessary *waste of time*, sure," the Baron said as he continued to wander around Cleo's room. "But I've come to bring good news, not to give you lessons in war. Hopefully, I can take one item off that desk of yours. The last ballista made its way to the port tonight and will have its wheels set by tomorrow."

"*Great.*"

"And the gold?"

"The gold—*right*." Cleo scanned the blackstone walls of his room as if to look for an answer, though he knew he had none. His smile from the Baron's earlier statement had mangled into a confused sneer. "My men are working on it."

"What men might that be? Your steward just told me Jove left Corlis a quarter moon ago."

"He did."

"And you haven't gotten any more information from that deacon since, is that right?" Cleo looked down again without an answer. This time, the slump of his shoulders was obvious. The Baron drifted toward the balcony, peeked down, and then added, "Maybe being perched up here this high has blinded you from the happenings below."

"I have an entire brigade to command," Cleo said sternly.

"Last time I checked, your brigade was down there, becoming more like my men of Corlis with each passing day."

"I'm not oblivious to their doings."

"Give it a few more moons, and they might just be following me, not you."

"Watch yourself."

"I, at least, wouldn't force them to wear those ridiculous skirts," the Baron said, smiling as he rummaged through one of Cleo's burrows.

"They ease our movement in battle. And my guardsmen behave with honor, unlike your own," Cleo responded.

"My men follow their hearts, not some contrived, ritualistic practice."

"Your men follow gold."

"If that's what's in their hearts, then sure. But don't we all?" the Baron asked, his narrow chin forming a cold smirk. "Only a naive fool would claim otherwise. Speaking of which, I want mine."

"I told you I would have it."

"Then where is it?"

Cleo met his question with silence.

The Baron stopped rummaging. "Well, what are we waiting for? Let's go talk to the man."

"The deacon?"

"Who else?"

As if he had no choice, Cleo nodded in agreement. He grabbed his father's sword and laced it around the belt over the band of his feathered spades. Cleo pinned his cloak to his leather vest, then followed the Black Baron down the castle's tall tower, brushing off the guardsmen who moved to their escort. At the bottom step, he took a torch from the sconce and walked across the empty vastness of the main floor, turning toward its annex at the rear. Dark and wide, the blackstone ceiling stood tall over the lone sculpture in the room's center, one of a woman with long hair and the tail of a fish splashing above the curling waves. Behind it was an old door crafted from thick planks of driftwood. On each of its sides were guardsmen with spears in their hands and shields at their backs.

Cleo and the Baron's echoing sandal steps roused the watchstanders to startle awake and render a sloppy salute. The one to Cleo's right unlocked the door, while the other moved to lead them in. Cleo again brushed the guardsman aside, took the keys, and entered into the long and dark hallway with only the Baron. Iron cells filled with forgotten webs and desolate mats were littered behind both rows of empty bars. In the last hold on the right, they reached the man marked with ash and blood, wearing nothing but a rag around his waist, chained with his hands clasped together, hanging over his head.

"*Deacon Ambrose?*" Cleo asked into the darkened holding cell.

The deacon looked up slowly with whatever dwindling strength he had. "The commander has finally come to torture me himself."

"Unlock his cell and help me take him down," the Baron said earnestly.

Cleo obliged, against his hardened instinct. *Putrid.* The cell stunk of dried feces, like an animal a breath away from death. He placed the torch aside and unshackled the deacon's wrists from the wall. The man quickly collapsed to his knees, then stomach, before falling over, unable to hold the weight of his gaunt body. Cleo, himself, felt a few shivers from the deacon's cries of agony as he watched the Baron lift the man back up, sitting him against the blackstone sidewall. The Baron then stuck out his hand to reveal a rolled-up bundle of bread crisps. With his other, he fed the decrepit deacon the broken pieces, giving him sips from his waterskin and moving his chin upright so he could chew. "We're here for answers, not for pain."

With a rough cough, Deacon Ambrose said, "I already told your men—I'm not a smith."

"*A smith?* What do you mean?" Cleo asked.

"A Smith of Sciron," the deacon struggled to say. "Is that not why you've taken me? Are you not after the Sunspear?"

"No," Cleo responded.

"*Then you should be.*"

"We're here about the gold," the Baron stated.

"I haven't eaten in days. I don't give a damn about your gold," the deacon spat aloud. Cleo moved the torch closer and crouched beside him, staring into his eyes. "I tried to tell your men—over and over again."

"Tried to tell them what?"

"*That he left,*" the deacon's broken voice answered angrily. "He left for Sazara moons ago."

The Baron took back his bread and curled it into the side pocket of his long overcoat. "Who left?"

"The other deacon that shared my seat in Corlis."

"Why would we need him?" Cleo asked. "If you help us, I'll set you free."

Deacon Ambrose snarled, then looked up and stared deep into Cleo's eyes. "*Help you,*" he muttered. "I can't help anyone who chooses to war against the Calegris, the family that links their lineage to that of Claros— the richest in Sacrim. *No...no.* You'll need more help than mine as long as you're their enemy."

Cleo's patience waned. "They bleed the same color as my father. And their blood will be spilled in his justice."

"And who might that be?"

"Consolar General Sepatus Scordisci."

"*Ah,* a fool that man was. For once, he had something they'd always controlled. And he was a fool to give it right back to them."

The Sunspear, Cleo understood.

"They've been embarrassed since the day he was voted in as Consolar General. It was a position of power those families always controlled. You aren't just fighting the Calegris, *boy.* They have blood everywhere— especially in our temple. Sciarra...Garsina...Sarnesi...even the bloody Rosenari family claims a finger to their hand. They own *everything.*"

"Soon, they will learn there is something they'll never own," Cleo scowled back.

Deacon Ambrose broke out into laughter, coughing up blood as his strength dwindled. "And what might that be?"

"*Smite.*"

"You can wish all you want, *boy*, but it won't change your circumstances."

The Baron stepped back toward the cell's door and turned in a circle. "Do you know where the keys are or not?"

"*Keys?*"

"To the temple's vault?"

"There are no keys to that vault," the deacon replied, struggling to smirk.

"So, there is a vault." The Black Baron wasted no time lifting the old man to his feet and dragging him by his shoulders toward the door of the cell against his moaning peril. "Well, let's go find it."

"Wait—wait," the deacon pleaded, though the Baron held his bulwark resolve. Both guardsmen at the door rushed down the hall to help after hearing Cleo's order. They wrapped the deacon's arms around their shoulders and used rags to wipe him clean. Beneath the silence of the night sky, they dragged the deacon out of the castle and onto the muddied blackstone streets of Corlis. They walked slowly through the city, passing the port to head northeast until the domed roof of the Second Partition's temple emerged in the darkened distance.

Its tall columns encircled the curve of its outer wall and were covered by tangled vines, with chips and chunks of pale marble missing from their bases. At the peak of the dome stood the temple's stained-glass ornament of the Benevolent Sun, barely visible through the dense fog. The entirety of the temple's circular structure was stained by growing clumps of mold and splotches of dried dirt, unkempt and half abandoned, nearly as bad as the magistrate's castle had been. Cleo led them inside and used the few torches they had to wave away the rats that scurried around and under the vastness of the empty tapestry. When the doors were shut behind them, the Baron ungagged the deacon and reiterated his earlier question.

After gasping for air and releasing his pants of pain, the deacon finally grunted, "*There*—at the altar." Deacon Ambrose struggled to point to the center of the temple. Directly under the peak of the vaulted dome roof stood a circular plateau with three steps. Atop it was a small group of chairs and a large marble basin.

When they reached the first step, the Baron asked, "Well, where is it?"

"*Below*," the deacon coughed, still hanging from the arms of the two guardsmen.

"Help me move it," Cleo commanded. Together, the four of them labored to push the large marble basin toward the edge of the altar's top step. Under where it once stood was a rug of royal red laced by gold, woven thick and stretched wide with patterns of fine scipyrian lettering. Again, the four of them worked together to pull it aside.

He was right, Cleo thought. Once hidden by the rug at the altar's center was an iron-topped manhole set smooth with the floor, just wide enough to fit a segment of stairs below it. Cleo moved closer and inspected the circular cutout, hovering the flame of his torch low. At the center of the manhole was a ruby-colored gem, one larger than his fist, that glistened finer than any jewel he had ever seen before. "Now what?"

"Now, we wait," the deacon answered.

"Wait for what?"

"For the Benevolent Sun to strike center-day." The deacon looked up slowly and pointed to the peak of the dome ceiling. There, at its center, was a similarly round stained-glass piece that protruded down from the ornamentation above. Though this one was much larger, Cleo traced the symmetry of its path with the light from his torch.

"That will take forever," the Black Baron grumbled in annoyance.

"Agreed," Cleo added. He moved some of the chairs near the manhole while the Baron attempted to wedge its iron door open.

"That's no use," Deacon Ambrose told him.

"You two, go and find us food and water. Tell no one we are here besides Jones," Cleo ordered. The two guardsmen nodded, moved the deacon onto one of the chairs, and then saluted before heading off toward the temple's tall, wooden doors.

When the Black Baron finally gave up, he helped himself to a chair. "*How much longer?*"

"Quite a while. When the guardsmen get back, I'll have them stand watch over the deacon so we can rest."

"I don't need rest," the Baron responded, kicking his feet up.

"*I do.*"

"I haven't dragged you all the way to this damned temple for you to rest."

"When you've traveled as far across Sacrim as I have, rest becomes precious."

"Precious enough that you were skipping it late into the night," the Baron snarled, his pale face carving a smirk.

"I'm a busy man with a war to win."

"And if you do win that war, what next? Have you figured that part out, *Commander*?"

Cleo met his question with silence.

"How exactly would a Vizar Cleo rule?"

"I haven't gotten that far yet."

"If I were you, I'd be more worried about that than winning. You're a smart man. You should know this better than most. What's the point of victory if you can't rule over what you've won?"

Cleo sat upright in his chair and adjusted his cloak to the side. "Well, for one, I'd clean up Sazara and make it beautiful like it once was—like I knew it to be. *New Scipyria*, as we'd call it. Not Sacrim. I'd rid the streets of those criminals...the rich who hoard their gold in these temples and the thieves in the alleys who steal from the poor. Like smoke to a hive of beetle wasps, I'd drive them all out and set them ablaze."

"So...like a tyrant?" the Black Baron asked, laughing to mock Cleo's answer.

"It might seem so from the perspective of a criminal. But no one punished would go unjustly."

"Unjustly...judged by whom? Yourself?"

"Who else?"

"*The people*," the Baron answered. "This is their land. The people of Sacrim should decide, of course."

"The same people who let this happen today? The powerful who allowed Sazara to fall into chaos so they could stack their gold? Or the people who feed off their scraps at the bottom like parasites? Those too afraid to take life by their own hands—hands and feet they can't even keep washed, let alone use to better their own city. Or even, at the very least, keep their family fed."

"That's rich coming from the son of the general."

"You heard what that old man said," Cleo replied, glancing over at the deacon, who was already asleep in his chair. "My father didn't grow up rich, and he wasn't a Sazaran. He was from Cignus, like me. A beautiful place, one that those families he mentioned had burned to the ground. We aren't them. And I'd do everything I could to bring Cignus back to its rightful glory, the same as Sazara, where they both belong."

"I believe you. I'm no fan of the temple or those families either. I'm as critical of them as you are. But the Plane doesn't need another Rexam."

"No. But the Plane does need a leader—someone to guide our people onto the path of prosperity," Cleo responded.

"Sure. But the Plane doesn't need war to bring it there," the Baron retorted.

"No, but it needs it."

"I'm sure all those past kings of the east would agree."

"I'm not some tyrant like they were."

"No tyrant thinks he's a tyrant, Cleo. But every one of them dreams of power. My father taught me from my earliest days that no man who desires to rule over another deserves the chance to do so."

"He sounds like my old preceptor—a man of ideals," Cleo said with a faint smile. "*Men only ever dream of being worshiped like the sun*, as he would often put it. My father believed that, too. And both of their spirits sit atop my shoulders everywhere I go. They would never allow that to happen."

The Baron's smirk grew cold. "Never say never."

Cleo rolled his eyes. "I only want to protect and help the people of Sacrim—of New Scipyria. And not leave them vulnerable and blind as they are led toward their own demise."

"What sort of demise could be worse than war?" the Baron asked.

Cleo sat still and contemplated his answer. "*Losing.*"

"Very wise of you, Deacon Cleo," the Baron said, chuckling at his own mockery.

"*To have died for nothing,*" Cleo added, correcting himself.

The Black Baron smothered his narrow smirk as if, for once, he agreed with Cleo.

"We all deserve a purpose, and we all deserve to have our purpose protected. But men don't respect virtue. They respect power. And protection requires power. No deacon, or their mystic smoke, will ever be able to deliver that for them."

"Wise, indeed." The Baron jostled with the curved blade sheathed at his waist. "I met him, you know. *Your father*. When I was young. He came only for a day and stayed the night at that fort near Corlis. He had a meeting with my father, and then the next day he was gone."

"Sounds about right," Cleo said, struggling to keep his eyes open.

"Seeing the Sunspear in person… That was really something. The streams of light glowing from its tip…and the heat it gave off. *True power*. I got close enough to almost touch it."

"Good thing you didn't. You'd probably be serving your life away right now in some heat mine in Sineaqe…or worse—*dead*."

The Baron laughed a little. "I'm not that dumb, Cleo."

"What was he doing in Corlis?"

The Baron looked down at Cleo's waist and pointed to his sword. "That pommel—the black pearl. I knew I recognized it back at Leghorn. You can only find those near the coastal waters by the Vypores. My father sold him that black stone. It was the biggest one he had. And the biggest one I've ever seen."

Cleo reached for his smooth, shiny pommel. When he looked down at it, it clicked. *The black stone—Vident Lement's last words. It can't be, can it?* As his sleep-deprived mind wandered, Cleo asked, "Is that why they call you the *Black* Baron?"

"No, not quite," he answered with a laugh. "Some even think it comes from this." The Black Baron lifted his hand to show Cleo the ring of black glass on his long finger.

"What's that for?"

"I don't really know. It was my grandfather's. Or at least, that's what my father always claimed. He was the real baron—my father—and I, just his bastard. Hence *black*. He came from an old nork family named Galobaron. That's where I got the name."

"A bastard in Corlis? Who would have thought?"

"Very funny." The Black Baron smirked. "But even my father admitted as much. It was why he decided to stay in Corlis, so that I'd have a place to fit in and hide among the scoundrels here. But, as you could probably expect, strange-blooded bastards are easier to spot. And even here, they are looked down on by the normal ones," he explained.

"How did that come to be?" Cleo asked, his voice drifting with intrigue.

"My father once served in the norks' navy. He was one of the few who escaped and found himself in Corlis, where he met my mother and settled. Over time, he cornered most of the city's market when he took their smuggling to the sea...a place where no one could catch him. Those islands are our real home."

"Is your father gone now? Where is he? And your mother?"

"My mother, Bessie, passed when I was young. My father always called her his true star—"

"I'm sorry to hear that," Cleo interjected, offering his condolences.

"Thank you. But he took off nearly a solurn ago, captaining that fleet Clyus commissioned, one I've been helping to build on those islands since I was a boy. *A real fleet.*"

"That must be him, then, causing all that trouble in the north. Why didn't you go with him?"

"Someone had to keep the work going. That was his excuse, at least. I haven't heard anything back from him yet, but I would assume so. Those ships were taken to sea nearly half a decade before they were ready. Or even fully manned. But he'll be okay. He's always taken care of his mates."

"I don't hear much about anything anymore, being on this side of the Southern Plane. But if I do hear anything new, I'll be sure to pass it along to you."

"I think I'm more worried about how he'll react when he gets back and finds out that I've sold you all our ballistas," the Black Baron said with a laugh. "But thank you, Cleo. I would appreciate that."

"They'll be put to good use, that I can assure him."

"He wouldn't argue with you there. He'd just scrape my ass for not charging you more."

"Well, once I take Sazara, the gold of Corlis below us will be just a drop in the barrel."

"Don't tell my father that. He might leave the north and come work for you."

"I'd be happy to have him," Cleo replied with a broad-chinned smile.

Time passed with stories of their past before the two guardsmen returned with a sack of food and skins of water and wine. Cleo shared his food with the deacon, then ordered the two guardsmen back on watch.

He began to fade asleep, his eyes closing as he slumped in his chair, eager to recover whatever rest he could find.

"*Commander.*"

Cleo awoke to one of the guardsmen in a bronze helmet shaking his shoulder. "It's almost midday, sir."

He rubbed his eyes with his knuckles, then jolted himself up after realizing he'd fallen asleep sprawled out on the temple's altar. Light filtered in from the stained-glass windows, but not as much as it did from directly above. A solid band of sunlight streamed straight down, moving slowly toward the gem situated in the center of the vault's iron door. Cleo rubbed his eyes again and looked to his left to find the deacon awake, watching in silence for the light to smudge closer. To his right, the Black Baron did the same, waiting discerningly to see what would happen.

Yes…yes. The light from the stained glass above struck the altar with streams of red and orange, moving slowly across its marble floor until it reached the gem at the manhole's center. Cleo could feel the tension in the room become broken by several clicks of iron against iron, like cogs, followed by the movement of bars underneath that slid with scraping screeches. When the sounds had stopped, the edges of the door popped open like a bubble, relieving whatever air had been trapped below.

Without waiting, the Black Baron grabbed one of the handles and slung the manhole's door open. Down below, there was only darkness. Cleo walked closer and could see a few marble steps wrapping around themselves in a spiral. "Torch," he commanded his guardsmen.

Cleo led them down the spiraling staircase, his left hand holding the relit torch and his right hand grasping the hilt of his sword. Slowly, he crept a few levels down until he reached the bottom step. Cleo could feel his breath dissipate throughout the black space, which extended far beyond their spiraling tunnel. Deacon Ambrose hadn't lied. The Temple of Sciron in Corlis had a broad vault. The Black Baron moved past him to walk farther within. He took the torch from Cleo and lit another that hung beside the bottom of the stairs. Together, they waved their light around the room, searching for their sacks of gold.

"*It's empty,*" the Black Baron gasped, skipping toward the wall's corners to find only bricks of bare blackstone.

This can't be…

Cleo's despair emptied the well of hope he had promised for himself and the Black Baron. His mind recoiled in thought, questioning how he would pay for the ballistas, the scoundrels of Corlis, or even his own guardsmen. *There I was, laughing about drops of water without realizing I stood in a drought.*

Before Cleo could think of a solution, the Black Baron rushed back toward the stairs, headed straight for the deacon. "*WHERE'S MY GOLD?*" he demanded, then threw the torch down and grabbed the deacon by his rag of a collar, shoving him against the wall. "*WHERE IS IT? WHERE?*"

Cleo moved closer, shining the light between the two of them. The Baron's sharp brows and piercing hazel eyes were only a hand's length from the stained teeth of the deacon, who smiled to show his bruised and black gums. "I told you already," he said, turning his head only to cough to the side. "The deacon who shared my seat had already left for Sazara."

"*WHERE IS MY GOLD?*" the Baron asked again.

"*He must have taken it all with him.*"

"It's no use," Cleo said, depleted.

The deacon turned to Cleo. "I showed you the vault. Now, where's my freedom?"

Again, the Black Baron shoved the old man's shoulders hard against the wall, forcing his head to crack against the flat brick. With his right hand, he shifted his long coat aside and unsheathed the sword from his belt. In one quick thrust, he turned the deacon away from the wall and drove the curved blade into his chest. The Baron pulled it out and watched as the decrepit deacon collapsed to the ground. "There's your freedom, *you scum.*"

"I don't know what to say," Cleo struggled to put his thoughts into words. He scanned the vault in circles, checking to see if any gold would appear. "I didn't know they had the gold moved."

"I didn't either... *Damn* that temple. And *damn* Sazara."

"I can pay you back when we take the city. Like the deacon said, the gold is all there. I can even pay you double. You have my word."

"I don't need your word... *I'll be there beside you to take it myself.*"

"You'll come with me to fight?" Cleo asked, his jaw hanging open in relief.

"Those sun-worshiping families are all bastards—*true bastards.* It's *our* gold they took. So I want to be there to take it back myself. And I'm sure my men will want to as well." Cleo saw the anger in his eyes and nodded in agreement. He held out his wrist, and the Black Baron shook it.

The four of them left the temple in an angry silence after locking the deacon's body below in the vault. Cleo ordered his guardsmen to reset the rug and basin, and to swear an oath of loyalty that they'd tell no one about what they'd seen. As they walked back to the old magistrate's castle under the next day's light, the people of Corlis showered them with glances and stares. Just as soon as they had entered through the castle's grand doors, Vident Evander stood up from a side bench and rushed their way, his burnt-orange vestment flapping disparagingly behind his chunky legs. "Sir, Jones said you were busy and that I couldn't bother you, but this requires your urgent attention."

"What is it?"

"A letter from Sazara—from a fellow vident." Evander handed the folded parchment to Cleo. "It arrived early this morning."

Cleo took the letter and read:

I hope this message finds trusted hands. We have decided to comply with your proposal. The girl who delivered your message to me has since been taken captive within Sazara. Queen Helera of Astria has wed Clyus Calegri. The two have announced a joint rulership over the new Southwestern Plane. That very day, Sazara fell into chaos. The city's streets are now closed to all, making your request a difficult one. But we will try.

V.M.

Vanna? Captive? Cleo turned to the Black Baron and handed him the letter. "Have your men ready. We leave for Sazara the day after the morrow."

CHAPTER 38

SEA

"The blue one," Dane said from inside his captain's quarters.

"*Aye.*"

After the mate from the hold was dismissed, Markas and Sonny entered, sidestepping the nervous man as he exited. They patted the wet slosh off their gray overcoats and walked toward Dane at his desk. "What was that about?" Markas asked.

"Just changing things up, is all... Speaking of which." Dane stood up and threw his coat on.

"Finally ready, are we?" Sonny asked.

"Sort of. I wanted to show you both something first." The two captains followed Dane out of the door and down the steps of the *Freebird's* aftcastle, wading their way past the working mates that scattered across the main deck. When they made it to the bow, Dane reached over the forward peak and pulled the canvas cover off the bowsprit. Under the forwardmost rigging was a wooden sculpture of a bird with its wings spread wide, flaring to follow the curve of the hull. "Like it?" Dane asked with a proud smile.

"*That's brilliant*," Sonny said, stretching his waist across the bulwark to inspect its beauty. "What is it?"

"A snow pelican," Dane replied with a laugh, forgetting that type of bird could only be found in the Northern Plane.

"The *Bessie* is going to need one of those," Markas added. "Maybe a fine young blonde broad from Marredom...that's what I'll make her."

"Me and some of the mates carved it up while we were out on patrol. Spent three days on it, then had them polish it nice and pretty when we came back last night. Should be dry enough now to show it off."

"And show it off, you should," Sonny stated after finally bending back upright.

"Ready to take the tour?"

"If you finally are," Markas sneered. "Today marks a half-moon's pass since the yard started their work."

"Well, let's go see what they've finished since I left." Dane led them toward the gangway and off the pier. He and his two captains walked east along the shoreline, from where the *Freebird* was docked at the central pier, past the *Bessie*, which shared its moorings. Farther along the muddy shoreline were the *Baroness* and two other cargo galleys that had already completed their oar-to-sail refits. Atop the two galleys' wide cross-yards were mates preparing their sets of sails, scrambling to fight the frigid wind as they rigged the lifting lines up their masts. Dane counted four more cargo vessels at the pier that had their main masts fitted firmly in place and were each in the process of lifting and assembling their cross-yards.

At mid-sun each day, all three of the available captains would come together to rove the shipyard's progress. They would start at the vessels docked, then walk their way outward, talking to the mates and yard's crew that worked day and night to notch the planks of every mast, boom, and ballista into their proper places. From there, they would rove the border of the yard to probe the mates on containment watch and bring them their daily meals.

Out west, far across the island, was Nordheim's only town, a quarter-moon's hike through the snow to a place the norks called Nismar. Though it was small and sparsely populated, Dane had made sure his mates watched that no one entered or, more importantly, left the yard's premises. The galleons on patrol had only one run-in during their rotating rounds, with a tiny tribute galley that was making passage east after its typical stop at Nismar. The *Baroness* had made quick work of drowning the galley and recovering any oarsmen or officers they found at sea.

When the news had come back ashore, Dane took his galleon to personally patrol the harbor, while the rest of the mates worked tirelessly to finish their refit on schedule. His urgency to leave the yard had heightened since that encounter just a few days prior. And with the *Freebird*'s return to the pier came Dane's hope that the newest ships of the free fleet would be near completion. But as the three of them rounded the shipyard's outer boundary and came to the other side of the shoreline's piers, Dane found the last two cargo galleys docked side-by-side, without their masts. "*Where are they?*"

"Niels said just yesterday, on our last rove, that they'd be in by the morning," Sonny tried to explain.

But Dane had already left the two of them to scamper down the rickety planks of their pier. He climbed aboard one of the galleys and greeted a few of the mates at work. Station by station, he inspected their progress. At the center of the main deck, he found a round hole carved where the mast should have been, with a similar one cut through each deck straight down to the galley's keel. Dane grabbed the closest mate at work. "Have you seen anyone out here today? Any of the shipwrights?"

"No, sir—I haven't."

Dane turned back to Markas and Sonny. "Then it seems we must be the ones to see them."

He reaffixed the buckle at his waistband, cracked his knuckles, and held the grip of his saber tight as he walked between the center of the two long and tall lumber-framed shops. Markas and Sonny both strove to keep up with his pace as he marched through the muddy slosh into the largest cabin on the left. Without a knock, Dane opened the door and demanded, "*Where is Niels?*"

"In his office, sir," one of the young assistants answered, jumping up from his desk. Dane scanned the back wall of its large, open room, moving from left to right to look inside each of the individual office spaces. "Back right, sir," the assistant added.

Between the shipwrights' polished desks he went, stomping his muddy boots along their clean rug to find Niels hunched over his broad desk. He hovered with a quill in hand, tracing its tip along curved splines held in place by weights. Dane stood still and watched quietly, then knocked his dry knuckles against the office's open door.

"Oh, *Captain*—I wasn't expecting you." Niels took the rounded sight glass out from the nook where it sat, nuzzled in the crest between his nose and eye. "Is it that time already?"

"It's that *day* already," Dane corrected. "Where are the masts for my last two ships?"

"They were supposed to be in by this morning. Are they not?" he asked, looking over Dane's shoulder from left to right at the other rugged captains, Sonny and Markas, who stood behind him.

"You're the one leading this project. You haven't had a look yourself?" Markas asked, his voice taut with toughness.

"I was just at the pier last night, actually. But I've been busy, as you could probably see," Niels replied, slicking back his oily blond hair.

"Busy making sure our last two ships are finished, I hope," Markas said.

"No, something better." Niels took the weights off his desk, then wrapped the curved splines together and placed them gently back into his desk's drawer. "Ever since I went with you and the rest of the shipwrights on that sea trial, the day I took on your project, I became enamored with your fleet and with ideas for its innovation. It was as if a light after a long winter's dark had been lit inside my mind that day, with its sails and speed and shape…and power for what could be."

Dane watched as Niels lifted the large sheet of parchment from his desk. "What about my last two ships? We're supposed to leave this island and be back underway tomorrow."

"You will have your ships, Captain. But here, in this office, and on this sheet, is something much, much better. Shut the door, if you don't mind."

After Sonny and Markas squeezed in and shut the door behind them, Dane asked, "And that is?"

"Plans for a vessel, one more than twice the size of your own. The speed from this sail plan will best any other across the Plane's waters."

Dane crunched his way over to the side of Niels's desk. With his arms outstretched, he lifted the broad parchment into the air and held it up to the back window's light. The two captains joined Dane in scanning the softly brushed curves and lines that formed the drawings of a ship's hull.

"She looks beautiful," Sonny said, dipping his head the closest to peer at the design.

"Can she be built by tomorrow?" Markas asked.

"No, it might take a solurn or two," Niels responded.

"Or more. Look at the size of this thing," Dane said as he scanned the proportions of the sails and the broadness of the deck.

"You could have four, or even six, ballistas—two or three at each, the fore and bow. And I have the plans for the decks and hold below, and plans for the masts and—"

"*We need my masts in place first*," Dane stated sternly to cut off his rambling.

"I will personally be there throughout the rest of the day and night, *sir*, to ensure that the foundations for the rest of the masts will be notched and leafed into each of those last two steps."

"*Good*," Dane said after he riffled through the rest of the ship's plans. His eyes were captivated by the sheer size of the vessel and all the capabilities it could bring. It was a ship that would undoubtedly push the tide of seafaring further, one that his fleet might need if it wanted to compete with the King's Navy. *A true flagship,* he thought. "This is impressive…and brilliant, Niels— truly brilliant."

"Thank you, sir."

"We'll need more crew if we're going to add a ship like this to our fleet," Markas stated.

"And the wood to build it," Dane added, placing the thin white parchment back on his desk.

"Yes, that is one of the issues of my design. We would need wagon loads of that lightweight wood for the hull's planks, the same that your galleon has. And tall, continuous pieces of heavy lumber for its masts."

"The masts we can do," Dane said. "But the wood for the hull might make for a challenge."

"Why would that be?"

Dane looked back to make sure the door was still shut. "Our fleet didn't originate in the Regent. It came from the Southern Plane."

"Ah, that makes much more sense to me now. None of your mates are hens," Niels said, rubbing the crest between his pale chin.

"Keep that between us."

"*Of course.* I will see what alterations can be made with that heavy cedar and wet pine should the lighter wood be a challenge."

"Great."

"How much?" Markas asked.

"How much for what?" Niels asked in return, his lean face posturing a confused look.

"For one of these ships… How much will it cost?"

"*Cost?*" Niels asked again. He turned to look at Dane for any sort of answer. "I'm sorry, I don't understand."

"The people of Marredom don't receive any gold or silver, or even copper, for their work like the rest of the Plane does. They are expected to take pride in their work. Their payment comes in the form of food, a place to sleep, and honor in serving their King," Dane explained.

"So, they'll just work for free?" Markas asked, his swollen face scrunching as if he were now the one who didn't understand. "Well, that makes our job a whole lot easier."

"*No*," Dane said. "That's not the way I want to handle things—"

"*Sir*," Niels interjected. "There are issues with doing this, as you might imagine, besides finding the crew and gathering the supplies to build this ship for your fleet. King Mordin would never allow Nordheim to go forth with this project, or any future work, should he ever discover you were here."

"That was the first thing that crossed my mind, Niels. Which is why we can't stay docked here any longer than we already have," Dane told him.

"And the other shipwrights might not be as inclined as I am to take such a risk after you leave, sir. They are already concerned for their lives. As you would know better than anyone—*Marredom is apt to reward loose lips*," Niels uttered, just above the hint of a whisper.

"I know that all too well," Dane said, thinking back to Niven, where his family was ousted to the tributars. "The King is a real concern. The other shipwrights, I will deal with. Whether it be payment by gold or by blood, we will handle it," Dane said.

"And the crew and supplies?" Niels asked.

Dane glanced at Sonny and Markas and saw them nod in support. "We should be able to get you what you need. But it might be another moon's pass before we return here again. And when we do, we'll have what we can of our fleet protect Nordheim so we can put these plans into action. *And* we will pay you and the shipyard's crew for it."

"That's excellent, Captain," Niels responded with a gleaming smile.

"Just have my fleet ready to get underway by tomorrow," Dane told him, sharpening his voice back to sternness.

"*Aye*."

As the night darkened, the air grew colder from the easterly gusts that blustered into Nordheim's harbor. Dane sat with Markas and Sonny inside the cover of his captain's quarters as they ate their last evening meal along the frigid and snowy shore.

"Pass some more of that wine, will ya," Markas told Sonny, who then filled his mug from the nob at the bottom of their half cask.

"So, have we decided?" Dane asked them both.

"The first mates deserve it. The other four will be hard to choose from," Sonny said.

Markas took a sip of wine, then added, "And those other four ships will be the ones without ballistas."

"And slower, too. They will just have to tag behind, like mules almost, to carry our supplies back from the Northwoods," Dane said.

"Four groupings of three, then?" Sonny asked.

"Yes, each of us will take the lead of one grouping. We'll put the mule in the middle, and the first mates will captain those at the rear," Dane said.

"Our crews will be stretched thin."

"Their watches will have to be switched to port and starboard," Dane responded.

"That still doesn't solve our problem. How will we get that lightwood from those scattered islands near Corlis?" Markas grumbled to ask, stroking his long, mossy beard.

"We'll worry about the lumber from the Northwoods first. Once we deliver it here to Nordheim, half the fleet could stay put to protect the shipyard and continue to free whatever oarsmen it can. The other half could head back south."

"I call rights to that passage south…where the sun actually shines, and the women show their skin," Sonny said with a smirk.

"*Same for me,*" Markas added, lifting a lofty smirk at the thought.

"We can make those arrangements later. In the meantime, we'll have to continue scrapping what we can from the King and his cargo galleys to pay for it," Dane said. Just as he went to take a sip, a knock came at his door. "*Enter.*"

The door to his quarters creaked open, and there stood Roth, limping in, still dressed in his blood-stained, clover shawl. "I heard we were still leaving tomorrow?" he asked with a crooked grin.

"Roth, what a pleasant surprise. Yes—yes, we are," Dane said with a welcoming smile, waving him over to the chair on his left side. "Here, take a seat with us and have some wine."

"No more wine for me," he replied as he clanked his walking stick along the deck, ducking his way over to the open seat. "Those stairs were brutal. And the gangway was worse."

"How are you feeling?" Sonny asked.

"There is no feeling, Sonny. That's the problem," Roth said, his tone lingering with scorn. "I can move it now, at least a little, but most of that is from my hip." Dane glanced down at his left leg, which stuck out from the side of the table. His thigh was thinly wrapped in bandages above and below his trousers.

Roth had practically become a different person in the half-moon since they had arrived at Nordheim. He could no longer do the one thing he was known for or be that same person the mates and everyone else around him had admired. He had become almost a hermit now, a man who stayed inside that same cabin behind the workshops, seeing only the sparse light of day. Before Dane had left with the *Freebird* to patrol the harbor, he had strolled with Roth up and down Nordheim's shoreline. While in the cover of the night, they would talk. And after their very first conversation, Dane knew that Roth's injury had affected him in more ways than just his hurt leg. Part of him felt like he was talking to Ruth again, the way he had grown quiet and spoke with consideration for others rather than his typical hubris. And when he did speak of himself, he shared the same desire Ruth had—to return home to Tergona as soon as possible.

"You're still young, Roth—you'll have the time to recover," Markas reassured him.

"That's what stings the most. I'm only in my nineteenth solurn, and I have to deal with this for the rest of my life," Roth said with a disparaging frown.

"Back when I was a cagerman in Sacrim, there was a boy I knew who had a similar problem," Sonny said. "He ended up walking again, just fine."

"I doubt I will share that fortune."

"Cagerman?" Dane asked.

"Junior guardsmen for us young boys of the south," Sonny responded. "It's where we were taught to fight. Caji was one too, you didn't know?"

"No, I didn't. But that explains why both of you are so good with a saber. Young as in…what age?"

"You're too old for that now, Dane. Though, you probably could use some of that training," Markas responded with a drunken laugh.

"Twelve or so," Sonny replied. "How old are you anyway? I've always wondered."

"I'm not sure, really. There isn't much to go by in Marredom, or records for my parents to keep and reference."

"Well, you look younger than me," Roth said.

"I'm going on my twenty-ninth, next solurn, and you definitely don't look there yet either," Sonny added.

"So, no gold for work and no records kept. It's no wonder that nork King can get away with doing whatever he wants," Markas grumbled.

"Not anymore, he won't. I'm at least old enough to know that." Dane went to take a long gulp from his mug when a knock came from the door to his quarters again. In walked Caji, alongside Magnus and Sidrus, the first mates to Markas and Sonny. "*They're ready.*"

"*Perfect*," Dane said. As he stood up to grab his coat, he looked over at Roth and asked, "Care to join us?"

"Where are we going?"

"You'll see." Markas grinned between his fattened cheeks and swallowed whatever was left in his mug with a contented sigh.

Dane followed the captains and their first mates off the *Freebird* and onto the pier, helping Roth as he limped after them. They walked along the edge of the last workshop, through the wind-spurring cold that hissed with growing flurries, to reach the first cabin at the yard's easternmost corner.

"You should have brought your axe," Dane told Roth through the dense gusts and teeth-chattering cold.

"I've retired it," he shouted back as Caji opened the door to the warm, fire-lit cabin.

In the center of the open room were six chairs. In each sat a shipwright with their arms and legs tied at their sides. "Take those gags out of their mouths," Dane ordered. "They aren't animals. They're our friends. *For now*, at least."

The stronger of the mates, who was standing behind the chairs to guard the men, complied with Dane's command. The shipwrights all groaned in a mess of incoherent shouts as soon as they were able to speak, demanding that they be untied. Eriksen's voice screamed the loudest. "*How dare you, after all we've done!*"

"Relax, this is only—"

"*You expect me to relax? We've just been dragged out of our beds into the cold, blinded by hoods, and then tied to these chairs... We are men of craft, not some warriors or marines to be your prisoners of war.*"

"This was only a precaution," Dane tried to explain. "You see, I'm a nork, just like all of you and many of the free mates with me." He nodded over to the three younger blonds who had, like himself, once been oarsmen: Marlow, Marreck, and Oresen. "Which means I, like them, and like all of you, understand how Marredom works. We're aware of the reward your King would give if any of you were to let slip about what's happened here."

"*That would be a death sentence for us, you imbecile,*" Eriksen continued to shout. From the corner of his eye, Dane saw Markas pull his saber out from the sheath at his waist and inspect the curve of its blade.

"I guess that leaves you with a choice, then—death from your King...or death from *us*," Dane said, lowering his voice to sound intimidating.

"*We won't say a word. I swear it,*" one of the cowardly shipwrights cried aloud.

"And your crew?"

"*They won't either,*" another to the far right added.

"Good. But, as much as it may not look like it, we came here to offer you something worthwhile—a job *with pay* that might make each of you among the richest men in the Northern Plane."

Eriksen's thin face still looked angered and unamused by Dane's suggestion. "I already know what this is about—the only one of us not here today. *Niels.*"

"That's right. With his plans, we're going to build the grandest ship ever to embrace the sea right here at this yard."

"As if King Mordin would ever let that happen. As if *I* would ever let that happen in *my yard*," Eriksen stated angrily. "You've kept us here like prisoners since you and those foreign dogs arrived. And you've been littered across the King's north for far too long—"

At that moment, Dane no longer listened. His mind blurred in thoughts to drown out the frantic man's spits and shouts and rampant whistling of insults. Dane questioned what he should do, before realizing instead that he should be asking what Captain Noreas would do. *He would never let this man free again…or let him mock and insult his own, just like he had when he'd dealt with those officers or marines of Marredom. Eriksen's no different,* Dane thought, having already decided on what needed to be done.

Dane grabbed the handle of his saber with his right hand and swung it out from the belt at his waist. In a single jab, he lunged across the floorboard and stuck the blade straight through Eriksen's chest. The shipwrights who sat beside him gasped aloud as Dane rooted it back out like a pesky weed. Eriksen's deep blue eyes gaped in despair, his mouth gurgling to cough up spurts of warm blood in place of that cold, annoying spit of words. His white undergarment began to soak with warm puddles of red as his hands, still tied to the sides of the chair, shook in fits.

"*That should keep him quiet,*" Dane stated. He turned back around to see Roth standing in front of the door with his head turned, unable to look at the dying stirs of the frantic old shipwright. "Marlow. You and the other mates take his body out to the sea and let the fish have him." Dane turned back to the other five shipwrights and added, "Anyone else have anything they wish to say?" None answered. Each of the men still tied to the chairs stared in silence as the mates cut Eriksen's body free and carried it out of the cabin's door.

"Easy enough," Markas said.

"Captain Caji, Captain Magnus, and Captain Sidrus, please escort these fine men back to their cabins. And double the watches at their doors," Dane ordered.

"*Captain?*" Caji replied, inflated with a surprised grin.

"*You've earned it.* You three, along with Saul on the *Baroness*, will take command of the first four refits," Dane explained.

Caji rushed to hug Dane.

"You heard the man," Sonny said, splitting the two apart. "Get these men out. We still leave tomorrow."

† † †

Surfing swells of fury broke in every direction, billowing to crash onto the main deck of the *Freebird*. The sky hammered down with cold rain to match the sea and its daunting hue of ash and slate. At the bow, the *Freebird* dipped and dodged between the hurling troughs. The gale tugged taut at the lines of the sails, snapping them like shattering bones.

We've only been out to sea for a day. Myrph must want me, Dane thought as the wet cold pounded his face and hands. "*BRACE THE RAILINGS… I WANT EVERY MAN ON DECK TIED UP! HELMSMAN, BRING US BEARING SOUTHEAST! GALEN, PORT-QUARTER TACK,*" he commanded from the front railing of the quarterdeck.

"*Sir, I think Galen may have gone overboard,*" a mate shouted back from below.

Damn it. Dane's eyes squandered the dark horizon, looking for any sign of a man or motion that wasn't the deathly roll of breaking waves in the North Sea. Far out, he could barely distinguish the smallest hint of the other galleons still following him. Anguish overtook any feeling he could muster, with regret for having dragged his newest eight captains out into this torrential storm on their very first passage after leaving Nordheim. *We can't keep fighting against this wind to go east toward Cubby Cove,* he knew. *We'll have to turn with it and head west, then south.*

"*Helmsman, turn us around. West, on my signal.*" Dane rushed toward the railing and released the line that was wrapped around his waist. "*MARLOW, JERAD, HELP ME TACK THE YARD,*" he cried out as he flew down the stairs onto the main deck, holding tight to the railing as the bow of his ship breached the air between waves. Only five mates were near the opposite side of the deck, struggling to keep their grip on the *Freebird*'s side railings. "*Where is everyone?*"

"*Sick below, sir,*" Marlow yelled back through the storm. The three of them tugged at the rigging along the starboard bulwark. They fought their way through the wind, sliding over to the mast, where Dane ordered them to help turn the *Freebird*'s cross-yards around, signaling the helmsman up at the quarterdeck to spin the ship's wheel.

With the wind and the waves, they turned. Dane did all he could to signal his change of course to the other galleons, knowing it would be of little avail. But as the *Freebird* sailed west, fast with the swirling wind and surfing waves, it passed each of the vessels it had once led. Dane had taken over the helm himself, maneuvering them close enough so the other captains could see him and his lanterns and ensure that they were still afloat.

Time passed in moments of counted breaths as the rain and waves continued to douse the deck and confine most of the mates inside below. The eleven other ships of the free fleet all followed to turn west as soon as the *Freebird* had passed, picking up speed as they sailed with the wind now at their backs. Their detour might have cost them another day at sea, but

Dane knew that the only way to defeat the storm was to keep every ship of his fleet afloat. And every man kept alive to man it.

As time passed with the wind in their favor, the waves began to calm to half their height, and the rain soon settled into a trickle. The storm had traveled with the trade winds north, curling around their fleet just enough for Dane to spot the calmest edge of its extent. He ordered an account to be taken of every man on board, and the mates soon filtered back above. From what he could see, though, most had returned to the main deck so they could hurl the wrench in their stomachs back into the sea.

Dane was happy to see his deck chief, Galen, walk up from below, too, despite the look of pale death plastered across his quiet face. Whispers from some of the mates claimed that he had hidden with them down in the hold, gripped to a barrel, praying to that southern sun for a saving light. Even Roth had limped his way up to the quarterdeck to breathe its fresh air and sigh in relief that they had finally made it through.

Dane took out his spyglass to scan the sea from the railing. In their mess of a following line, he counted the rest of his fleet to make sure, once again, that they were all still behind him. He gave the order to turn back south and flashed the lantern at the crow's nest for them to follow. As he moved back toward the helm, he saw a faint glimpse of a brown object far west, below the much clearer western sky. "Roth, do you see that?"

"See what?" he asked, limping to join Dane at the railing.

"It almost looks like a ship," Dane said. He unwound his spyglass once more to get a better look.

"It's too far away." Roth took the spyglass and looked at it himself. "But it—it almost looks like it has sails."

Dane looked closer again, leaning to see its tiny shape rolling with the waves. "And a man…*hanging from the top of its mast*. That can't be…can it?"

But he knew that it was. *The Widow…and Maris…and Cowen. But they should have been long gone from the North Sea by now. It's been nearly a moon*, Dane thought with a confused look draped across his pale face. For a brief moment, he questioned whether he should continue west and sail closer to find out why the *Widow* was still in the North Sea. *Something must have gone wrong. Maybe slits in their sails, or lack of food, or they might be taking on water.* Unsure, Dane's mind rattled off the possibilities. *Or perhaps he just wanted to parade Maris's body past the King. But either way, that bastard didn't want to stay and help me.*

495

"Keep our track south then east," Dane commanded the helmsman. "We're going back to Cubby Cove."

CHAPTER 39

SKY

M y life was a lie.
  My life was not mine. It was for the duty I was taught only to provide. It was of obligation—that I should owe my life to someone or something other than myself. A hollow feeling chasing an ever-elusive comfort, for I was scared.

  My life is guilt. It is of servitude that I was raised with this inescapable indignity. It is of the past and present, blinded by the same promise—one that has left me captured here, motionless in this moment. A hollow comfort chasing an ever-elusive resolution, for I was alone.

  My life should be honest. It should be sincere like the people I've met along my way. It should be bound to a devotion of understanding—to know people, their past and their future, and our shared existence. A hollow resolution chasing an ever-elusive answer, for I was ignorant.

  My life will be free. It will be relieved through truth. It will be honest in my actions and thoughts, and rise with love rather than bury with guilt—free to pardon myself for what I've done and hope that others might return the same. A fulfilling answer that has chased an ever-elusive woman. For I will forgive.

Vanna sat still in a dark room the size of a small grot, chained to a stone wall by the shackles around her wrists and ankles. For just shy of a moon's pass, she had been left alone with her thoughts—those of regret and of sorrow for where she now found herself, a prisoner in Sazara.

An empty wooden bucket sat in the corner of her holding room, and a single window, one no bigger than her face, was cast into the wall overlooking the harbor. It was all Vanna had. She'd been left to rot in sequences of sitting and standing, or pacing around in what little space she could, which was barely enough to lie across the stone floor. With every movement she made, her chains clattered like a shadow she wished would vanish with the dark. The only thing there to keep her sane was the view of the twin-pillared lighthouses that stood ever-burning at the harbor's inlet.

From the lighthouses alone, Vanna knew exactly where she was being held. Her room was on the top floor of a series of buildings just west of the First Partition's court, which housed prisoners across Sacrim. She'd seen these same small windows before during her walks with Lora, just two streets away from the harbor's coastline. Its thick walls of limestone formed bland blocks, and its blank facade stood out from all the others.

Every day, only once at random intervals, two guardsmen would bring her a bowl of rice and a few sips of water from the communal waterskin. The men were often harsh and quick, eager to return to their posts and rejoin their company and amusement. Some, though, attempted to stay beyond their welcome and came close to stripping her bare for an indulgence of fun. But Vanna's screaming and wailing always managed to ward off those despicable cowards, who seemed fearful over how their supervising officers might react if caught—or even what Vanna might do if they came within arm's reach.

But none were as cruel to Vanna as the Sisters who had visited her when she was first taken. For five days straight, they had pinned her arms and legs to a flattened board they'd brought into her hold. With her body splayed, they'd turn the board upside down and prod their long needles into the most painful of places. Vanna had been gagged, unable to scream, as her blood slowly dripped into buckets below. And each day they came, the Sisters of the Silo drained her life until the last drops of her vitality were left. The following mornings, she'd awaken from the darkness, unsure how or why she had survived.

On the sixth day, however, it was the Grand Dame who had entered her hold. Her time within was briefer than the Sisters' had been, and she refused to look Vanna in the eyes. But the words she had spoken would last with Vanna forever. *From today forward, you are no longer a Sister of the Silo. Your blood bond has been settled, and you will die a prisoner of Sacrim.*

And since that day, there was only silence.

The Silo taught Vanna how to be alone—to live in the shadows, hidden from the Plane and its people. Silence away from the commotion was where Vanna was most herself. Instead of her studies, she now reflected. The walls around her even felt like her old grot. They were dark and silent and filled with impending death—a way of life Vanna was no stranger to. But in her brooding over forgiveness, there was still a single thought that gave her hope. Neither the Sisters of the Silo nor Sacrim's Guard had discovered her connection to Cleo, or his message, which she hoped had been successfully delivered. Otherwise, Vanna knew she would have been given a swift death.

Vanna pressed her nose against the glass window as the sun rose to midday. Below, the waves rippled with fierce troughs between the harbor's entrance and its seawalls. She stepped back and used the light to adjust the rags that hung loosely around the bones of her pale body. Behind her, the iron-clad door stood still. She closed her eyes, waiting to hear the rattling of keys from the other side. It was a sound she slowly came to know as sustenance rather than pain. And as she hadn't had anything to eat or drink for a turn of the day, Vanna was growing desperate and weak.

She slumped down under the light from the window, leaning her back against the stone wall as she stared at the patterned overlay on the door. A circle resembling the temple's Benevolent Sun was pressed in iron at its top. Out of boredom, Vanna followed its circle with her eyes, tracing its pattern up, down, and then around again.

A faint noise of coughs or sandal steps, or even the rattling of keys, came from its other side. Her first instinct was to stop and look away from the door. But as soon as she did, the brisk sounds of swaying breath ceased. *Different guardsmen?* she questioned.

No. Vanna moved close to the sidewall and pressed her ear against the cold iron. The footsteps grew louder, but they were different from any that had come before. They fluttered in light taps instead of flat, slapping pounds. The tapping rose until she heard the rattling of keys on the other side of the door's lock. Vanna threw herself back under the window, her chains clanking louder than anything else. Still, she stood, her heart slapping like the footsteps once had as the edge of the door swung toward her. On the other side stood a woman dressed in black. Vanna didn't dare move. Her first thought was to fight—to not give in to whatever torture that Sister was about to bring. They would have to drag her body, limp and dead, to that temple if they were going to at all.

499

But instead, a familiar face turned her way.

Elaine.

Vanna stood up, less scared than she had been before, but still just as cautious.

"You look awful," Elaine said, her voice a harbor of despair.

Vanna rubbed her eyes with her dirty fists, not believing what she was seeing. Elaine was still as short as Vanna remembered but was thinner than she had been when they had gone their separate ways as Sisters nearly a solurn ago. Her round face remained, though, as well as her bulbous eyes. And her hair was still cut short, braided in dark webs oiled tightly to her scalp. "*What are you doing here?*"

"Saving you, of course. Here, this is yours," Elaine told her. She walked into the hold and handed Vanna the flute that had been taken from around her neck after the wedding.

"Why are you doing this?" Vanna asked.

"Because you're my sister."

"But I'm not anymore. And I'm not sure if I ever was. My life as a Sister was taken. I was betrayed by the Grand Dame after my very first mission—they left me to die."

"*No,*" Elaine said after peeking back down the hallway. "You were more of a sister to me than any of them ever were. A real *sister.*"

Vanna smiled for the first time since she had left Corlis. Elaine, whom she had known from her earliest memories—someone who was often ridiculed as an outcast and didn't meet the mold thought capable of handling the duties of a Sister—had come to save her.

"When I heard the whispers of you being locked in here, tortured, and stripped of your status as a Sister, I tried to ask questions. But no one could give me an answer. There was no way the Vanna I knew deserved this. You were kind to me when everyone else was cruel."

"Elaine…you risk yourself coming here. *Thank you.*"

"The guardsmen in Sacrim are weak and occupied. It's the other Sisters that worry me. *Come,* let's get you out of here." Elaine used a pair of levered short shears to cut her chains and shackles free, tossing them back by the door before she checked the exits again.

Vanna followed her down the narrow hallway toward the stairs at the far end. After hurrying down its three flights, they reached the main entrance door. Along the way, Vanna saw several guardsmen lying flat, motionless on the floor, with blood still leaking from their bodies. She felt overcome with sorrow that her justice had required their deaths. Though some were the worst of menaces, most had been cordial and were only carrying out their duty. And now their lives were gone, a cost Elaine had paid to save her own, which Vanna felt she didn't deserve.

Free to forgive, she reminded herself as she entered the day's light.

Elaine rushed toward a side alley, west of the coast. Vanna hadn't felt the sun's heat coat her pale skin, or the hot limestone beneath her bare feet, for three-quarters of a moon. Both burned as she followed Elaine through and across alleys and side streets, most of which were scarce of any life. As they moved along, they were cautious and diligent, sure to stay in the shadows. Elaine led her into a doddery home just outside the denser buildings of the city. As soon as they entered, Vanna crashed to the ground, out of breath and exhausted, and filled with thankfulness that she had escaped from her hold.

"Here, drink this," Elaine said, handing her a full waterskin. "You need it. And there's some food I brought here last night." In the corner of the small home was a table, and on it was the plate covered in cloth that Elaine had pointed to.

Vanna struggled to lift herself to the table, sitting to eat and drink, and fill her empty and depleted body. "You planned all of this for me?"

"I needed an opening, but yes."

"An opening?"

"Yes—like this war."

"*War?*" Vanna asked.

"As of two days ago, yes. After Queen Helera's wedding, hundreds, if not thousands, of Sazarans were locked away... They turned that Consolate Hall into a mass prison, and the city's been shut down since. No one was allowed on the streets unless they were escorted by a guardsman. There wasn't a chance that I could have saved you then."

"What changed?"

"Like I said—*war.*" Vanna paused her eating, waiting for Elaine to continue. "Most of the guardsmen have been moved to the fort by the western gate, just outside the city. Which is why the streets of Sazara are practically empty. Sacrim is a mess right now, far worse than Astria is. Another army arrived two nights prior and is camped a distance outside the wall."

"*Cleo…*" Vanna whispered to herself. She stood up and joined Elaine to look out of the lone window. She hadn't expected to miss this much while being locked away. "What's happened?"

"Nothing yet. At least, not that I'm aware of. I'm with the second fleet of Sisters. The first is up with the guardsmen on the front line. We haven't been given any orders yet, but we've been told to expect them sometime today."

"And the Queen? She's still here?"

"From what I hear, yes. But no one knows where. We rarely see her. From what I've heard, she and that man she married haven't left the temple since their wedding day." Vanna returned to the table and continued eating. "Astria's been different since that wedding, too. *Really*, since we were first ordered into Sacrim. Who knows what Mount Matron is like now, with the Queen gone and most of the Sisters here defending this foreign land. The whole Plane just feels off, as if the times are changing right in front of us. I can't even begin to explain it."

"*Time is only life's shadow*," Vanna again whispered to herself, thinking back to Vident Lement's last words of wisdom. "People are what's changing."

"I think you're right. The only Sisters still dedicated to this fight are the older ones—the ones who have nothing to lose. And they're in command of us all."

"Will you fight, then?"

"Of course. It's still my duty. Just because I've freed you doesn't mean I'm no longer a Sister."

Vanna looked her way and noticed the black half cape still wrapped around Elaine's broad shoulders. It reminded her of what she used to be and all that she had been raised to know. *The darkness that is duty, smothering the guilt underneath. A shadow within itself.* But instead of trying to convince Elaine to change and follow the same path she had, Vanna simply smiled softly and said, "I hope you stay safe."

"I'll try my best," Elaine replied as she peeked again out of the window. "Speaking of which, I need to be off. They might start asking questions if I'm gone for too long. *But* I believe this is yours." From a closet around the side room's corner, Elaine reached in and pulled out Vanna's sack. "This was locked away in the Sisters' storage."

Vanna smiled just as much as she had when she first saw Elaine walk through the door. She took her sack and searched it to ensure everything was still inside. "I don't know how I could ever thank you, Elaine—*my sister*."

"All we have is each other." Elaine slowly walked toward the door. She opened it, pointed out to the sky, and added, "That way is west, toward Astria."

Vanna nodded with another soft smile. "*Home*."

After Elaine had said her goodbyes and left, Vanna finished her meal and washed the dirt stains off her pale skin. She dressed in the last outfit from her sack: a short-skirted black robe pinned at her right shoulder by a winged brooch. Applying the oil and paste, she did her best to blend back in, hoping that a change in appearance would leave her unrecognizable. She slid her telson into the waistband at her lower back and shoved Zell's flute into its side. In the closet, Vanna found spare sandals and strapped them to her raw feet.

With cautious steps, she left the doddery home and headed toward the coastline of Sazara's harbor. Once she entered back under the cover of its denser buildings, she blew one long and high-pitched note into the flute around her neck. "*Come on, Mersi*," she whispered, continuing with caution. When she was close enough to hear the waves of the harbor splashing against the seawalls, she gave the flute another long and high-pitched note, hoping Mersi would hear it and obey.

After a long while waiting in the shade, Vanna spotted a faint speck of black in the sky's far distance, moving quickly toward her. Mersi came from the north, over the Barren Sea, flying between the twin flames of the two lighthouses erected at each edge of the curving breakwaters. Vanna hurried to give two screeching commands so she'd fly low, just above the waves, to avoid being spotted.

Mersi hovered to land on the western edge of the rounding harbor front. Vanna rushed to mount the rook quickly, took one look over at the domed temple, and then directed Mersi to take off and fly west. Up and down, its wings thrashed harshly above the crashing water to lift them into the sky.

"*Quiet, Mersi*," Vanna whispered rhetorically, hoping they wouldn't be spotted. She intended to return to the mountains of Astria and hide away in a place where she could survive in peace, alone. The last thing she needed was a trail of Sisters following her as she tried to escape.

And so, Vanna flew on saddleback, rising to glide above Sazara's lowest buildings. She turned Mersi west to pass over the last cluster erected along the coast, and then ordered it to ascend again into the sky. She wanted to break into the clouds and be hidden as they passed over the wall. But the higher Vanna went, the more she became tempted to turn and see what lay outside the city. *One last look,* she thought as she twisted her shoulders to the left. Thousands of men in a field of bronze and red stood just beyond Sazara's outermost western wall, aligned in formations atop the lifeless red dirt.

There are so many of them.

Vanna brought Mersi to a hover and scanned the ground below for any sight of Cleo and the West Brigade. But all she could see was the vastness of the Calegris' forces. Thousands were aligned in long columns, their backs facing the limestone wall. While she continued to search for Cleo's brigade, flames of orange and red erupted from their center and spread out like a tidal wave across the bronze formation. Vanna squinted and saw the swords of Cayen's guardsmen being lit to flame, spreading one by one like fire in the wild.

Inside, Vanna was conflicted. Her urge to help weighed as heavily as her guilt, both feelings rising deep from within her heart. She still felt ashamed for what she had done to Cleo, and she knew that killing his father had caused this war. But below her heart, her legs trembled. With it came the desire to run and hide like she had decided on earlier—so she might survive.

But just surviving isn't freedom, Vanna knew.

Forgiveness, she thought. *That's freedom. It wasn't my fault I was never given the chance to live and be free. I need to forgive myself and not let what I've done grip me forever. And hope that if Cleo finds out, he will forgive me, too. I need to help him, not because I owe him, but because I once gave him my love and I care for him,* she decided. *It's the right thing to do.*

In her rashness, Vanna yanked the saddle of Mersi to the left, back toward the western gate of Sazara's curving wall. She commanded the rook to fly fast around the Calegris' formation in a winding circle to join Cleo's from behind.

Far out, Vanna could see his West Brigade tightened shield to shield, marching directly at the clumped mass of flaming swords in front of Sazara's wall. From the western gate, the flames stretched farther than Vanna could see. And from what she could discern, Cleo's men were outnumbered nearly five to one. Even as tightly together as they were, forming their own wall of shields and spears, the West Brigade was vastly outmatched. *I can't worry now. I need to find him,* she thought, scanning the fray.

There. In the very center of their marching formation, she spotted a tiny bronze speck wearing a royal-red cloak. Surrounded by cloaks of gold was Cleo, riding his warhorse. Behind him was a battalion of cavalry and large wooden structures pulled on wheels by horses and mules.

But to her left and far out near Sazara's large central gate, Vanna witnessed dozens of dark specks breaching the sky. Dread filled the air around her, slapping across her face with frights of worry. *The first fleet of Sisters,* Vanna recognized from what Elaine had told her earlier. There, the Sisters were, taking off for war on the backs of their rooks, heading right at Cleo's brigade.

Flashes of their ambush at Fort Saxoram raced through Vanna's mind. *The bloodshed those rooks caused Cleo's men,* her shivers remembered. Though they were on the opposite end of the Calegris' formation, Vanna could tell that the number in the air now was double that of then. And Vanna knew she was no match for that many of them, let alone a few, especially with the condition she was in. *I can't do this,* she thought, pulling her rook to a stop. *But maybe I can just help Cleo. To protect him, or maybe even rescue him and take him away from the death he was marching himself toward. To be of some use.* But Vanna knew he would never leave. Cleo would fight until the final sword fell.

Just as Vanna slowed to hover over the point where Sazara's wall met the harbor's breakwater, she heard a swirling whistle whiz over her head. She looked back and nearly collapsed under her saddle. Vanna felt like she had been thrust back into her cell, splayed again to that board, and turned upside down, ready to bleed once more. More than thirty rooks were in the air, having taken off near the square, tailing her from behind.

That must be the second fleet, the one Elaine is in, Vanna knew.

She needed to move and move quickly. Vanna did her best to gain as much speed as possible, whipping the saddle of Mersi with ferocity, pushing her to flap her wings faster. *They must be the two wings of Cayen's vanguard, sent to collapse onto Cleo from each end, above. And now I've been caught between them both.* Arrows began to fly past her as she guided Mersi

505

to zig and zag in order to avoid being level with their falling path. Vanna turned again to check her distance and saw the same large rook she'd seen back at the Vypores closing in—and fast.

What can I do? How do I even escape this? There was nowhere left for her to flee. Vanna didn't have time for answers, only reactions. Once she broke past the corner edge of Cayen's line of flaming swords, she blew into her flute with two smooth, high-pitched notes, followed by a single one. Mersi turned to the left and flew right into the vast valley of reddened dirt that still separated the two warring sides. Down, they swept, until Mersi was gliding above the ground in the open space between them both.

Vanna had hoped that the Sisters and their rooks would keep their course to the sides of the Calegris' men. She didn't think they would dare dip into the middle of the two formations' crossfire, with each marching closer to clash in war. But even then, arrows continued to rain in from behind. Vanna turned and saw the Sisters still following her, closing in faster than before, and entering the midst of battle.

I'm so dumb. I've led both fleets of Sisters right at Cleo.

Vanna looked up above Mersi's head and saw a long wall of bronze shields smashed tightly together. Between each were the spears of Cleo's guardsmen pointing forward. She pulled up on the hitch of her saddle, forcing Mersi to gain height above the first line of Cleo's brigade. She shifted her feet again and pushed Mersi to fly above the field of guardsmen. As she soared above them, Vanna caught a quick glimpse of Cleo, and their eyes connected. At that moment, she wanted to apologize for it all—for murdering his father, for leaving his side, and for leading the Grand Dame and her flock of rooks right at his brigade.

But instead of witnessing his despair, Vanna saw Cleo adopt a mischievous grin. He turned around and lifted his arm, pointing to the back of his brigade's formation. Vanna peered that way and heard sounds of clicking, before the large wooden arms began to slap against their wide strings.

Bolts flung from the tall wooden structures flew past her through the air, headed straight for the rooks that tailed her. Almost as quickly as they had been released, she heard the Sisters' rooks begin to screech aloud in the worst cries of pain. Vanna glanced back and saw that most of the long-arrowed bolts had hit. Many had even pierced the rooks' chests, causing them to flail helplessly as they swirled in injured screeches and thumped loudly to the ground. The others managed to strike through a few of their wings, causing them to flap and lash around in chaos, dissipating their formation and scattering them in all directions through the sky.

Vanna flew past the back end of Cleo's brigade with a far-warmer smile than she had before. She directed Mersi to fly high again, so they could turn back around. But as soon as she touched her lips to the flute, Mersi's saddle whipped her body forward. An arrow from the Sisters had pierced her wing.

Curling with dreadful screeches, Vanna looked to her left and saw Mersi tucking itself in out of pain, struggling to keep the two of them in a hover. Behind her, Vanna looked in a panic and saw the Grand Dame's square face staring at her with the most demented of glares.

"*I can't ever escape her,*" Vanna whispered to herself in agony.

She yanked Mersi's saddle to the side, hoping her right wing would be enough to turn the two of them around—back toward Cleo. Vanna yelled at Mersi to keep pushing, to carry on, and to fight forward. But the Grand Dame was relentless and continued to fire arrow after arrow as she pursued from behind.

The sky above the battlefield had become chaotic. And Vanna had directed Mersi to fly straight into it. The rooks flew in every direction, fleeing from Cleo's barrage of bolted arrows, while still trying to fire their own much smaller ones down at his guardsmen. Her flute was useless. Terrible screeches rang in echoes above, burying the clashing of steel on steel below, and men and women screaming alike. But Vanna knew that the chaos was her best chance to lose the shadow of death that still followed her.

Into it, she went. With one wing, Mersi did her best to weave through the madness, escaping arrows from all directions. In front of Vanna and the gliding Mersi grew the flaming swords of Cayen's men, who had stormed forward to march against the tight shields and spears of Cleo's brigade.

Almost there, Vanna thought as she held tight to the hitch of the saddle. Just as she began to pass them, she felt the weight beneath her legs suddenly drop. Vanna had almost reached the edge of the chaos when the talons of the Grand Dame's rook latched onto Mersi from above. Clasped together, the two rooks clawed at each other in the air. Higher and higher, the Grand Dame dragged the two of them up into the sky, away from the warring havoc. Vanna's legs were still strapped to Mersi's saddle as the two of them were being flung left and right and carried toward Sazara's wall.

I'm helpless, Vanna thought as her body shook with every flap from the Grand Dame's giant black rook. Mersi's neck and back end were both grasped by its talons in the tightest of grips. Her mind instantly drifted back to that night above the Vypores with Little Wing. She could see herself again, falling into the black and being pierced by flashes of lightning. Only now, the storm was war.

As soon as they breached the top bulwark of Sazara's wall, Vanna heard the growing sound of a loud whistle once more. Out of nowhere, a large and long object flew above her head, as if lightning had flashed again through the sky. But this time, it had sprung through the air and struck the chest of the Grand Dame's rook.

The heaviest of all cries bellowed aloud in brazen pain. The rook's broad black wings swept out to its sides, shadowing the wall below before they contracted back within. Vanna looked up and saw its talons release the grip on Mersi's body. Mersi tried all it could to flap its lone wing as they descended helplessly to the ground.

The Grand Dame's rook whirled as it fell from the sky. With a squall of pain, it let out its last fainting screech before it thumped behind the wall near the western gate. Spinning in circles, Mersi tried to break their fall, hovering as they collapsed to the ground beside it.

One of Cleo's bolts must have freed me...

But Vanna didn't have time to think. Her blood rushed under her skin like a waterfall released from a dam. She hurried to unlatch herself from the saddle. Mersi's wing twitched, buckling in pain as it struggled to move. Vanna thanked the rook for saving her, patting it on its trembling head. *The Grand Dame,* Vanna thought of in defense, spinning her dizzying head around in search of her. *There.*

The two of them had landed within the confines of Sazara, separated from the battle outside the wall. The Grand Dame's giant rook was embedded into the red dirt like a lifeless whale, beached from the waves of war. All Vanna could hear were the Grand Dame's own deepening groans of pain. Vanna grabbed her sack and telson and cautiously crept toward them.

"*You,*" the voice from behind the dead rook screamed aloud.

Vanna limped slowly around it and saw the top half of the Grand Dame sprawled with her back braced crookedly against the ground. The legs below her waist were squashed under her rook, still strapped to the overturned saddle. Blood and splotches of bruised dirt covered her pale skin.

"You...*how dare you.* The Sisters gave you everything. All you know and have ever had is because of us—*because of me,*" the Grand Dame scorned as she lashed her shoulders around, trying to lift herself out from under the dead rook. "You swore to give your life for duty—*for the Queen and for Astria.* I should have just killed you *myself* when I had the chance. *You traitor...*"

The Grand Dame tried to spit clumps of blood at her as she walked closer. Vanna crouched beside the crushed old woman and said, "I have given my life to the Queen and to Astria. But now, the life of that girl is no more. I'm no longer a Sister, *remember?*"

Vanna took one look at the telson in her right hand and thought about shoving it into the chest of the Grand Dame—to give her the justice she deserved. But the closer she looked at its short, flat blade, the more she could see in it the reflection of her own eyes. Eyes that were big and gray. *My mother's eyes,* she thought, staring into the very blade she had once used to kill her. *No—forced to kill her.*

But I will forgive.

"You're no mother of mine," Vanna said as she stood up. She tossed her telson to the ground, out of the outstretched reach of the Grand Dame, who continued to yell aloud and thrash out in fits of fury.

Thank you, Cleo, for killing the worst part of me.

Vanna turned her back to the Grand Dame and faced the tall wall that stood to separate Sazara and its war. Just as she closed her eyes and exhaled in relief, a thunderous wave of marching stomps came from her left, silencing the Grand Dame's cries for help. Vanna turned and saw thousands of guardsmen being led by four men, marching straight toward the western gate along the inside of the wall. In their hands, the flags of New Scipyria waved.

CHAPTER 40

STONE

"I'm proud of you, Ruth," Edmon said while wrapping his arm around Ruth's shoulder to hug her. "And I'm proud of your new friend here, too. Regardless of what your mother might think."

On the ground beside Ruth's feet was Ozzy, her tiny otter friend, who had already doubled in size since the day they'd left Stamford together. Ruth looked down at it and smiled, watching as it squirmed between the legs of the three horses and the tied-together grouping of mules she and her father had borrowed from their neighbors. "*Or refuse to say*," Ruth said. "She's barely talked to me since I've come home."

"You know how your mother can be. She's just worried, is all. Bringing an army of six hundred sentinels to our little town would do that to anyone," Edmon said.

Ruth looked up at her father and saw that his sly smile matched her own. "She could at least talk to me."

"Your mother has been busy, like us all. I know you don't mean to burden us, but, in fairness, she's been at work, making food and collecting supplies to bring out here to them in the Northwoods."

"No one asked her to do that."

"No, but like I said, you know how your mother can be. It's her way of helping."

"*Helping* isn't the right word. She's scared of them and the royals, is what it is."

"Well, Ruth, I can't say I blame her. We've only ever known our quiet little life out here."

"And it's me who's changed that," Ruth drawled.

"*And your brother*," her father replied quickly to ease her disdain.

"I'm just trying to do what's right. Not just for myself, or for us, but for those who need it the most."

"Which is what I admire most about you, Ruth. And always have. You have a heart bigger than both of ours. And you've grown to embrace it. You know, it'd be an easy life to just stay here, like us, and grow old in Tergona. But from my experience, I can tell you it wouldn't be an interesting one. Your heart was always too big to confine itself here, hidden away in these woods."

"Thank you," Ruth said with a smile. She paused their walk through the wet pines to hug her father again.

Since the days when she was just a little girl, Ruth had always found peace in confiding in her father. He was a quiet old man, at least compared to her mother and Roth, and had never been one for small talk, which Ruth certainly appreciated. Edmon had always been there to listen to her and share his wisdom, regardless of how menial her troubles seemed then compared to now. And anytime she was home, Ruth felt content, knowing she had her father to lean on.

Ozzy scampered its way back onto Ruth's shoulders, and they made their way down the narrow trail. Behind them, the horses and mules whimpered as they snapped twigs and had to be guided over fallen branches to break past the Northwoods' outer tree line. Ruth and her father had walked down Tergona's only road and tied up the mules at the neighbor's stable when Edmon had spotted Ludwyn standing on their cabin's porch. "It's your friend again," he stated, almost with annoyance.

"*As if I haven't already spent enough time with you,*" Ruth sneered under her breath.

Ludwyn came rushing down their porch's three creaky steps, his shawl wrapped tightly around himself to keep warm in the crisp cold of winter. "Ruth—they're back!"

"*Who?*"

"The ships! They pulled back into Cubby Cove, just after midday!"

Ruth rushed to hand the reins of the horses to her father, then released her squirming otter back to the ground. She hurried east toward the pebbled trail. Ludwyn and Ozzy followed behind the best they could as Ruth stomped her leather boots in a hurry to breach the shoreline of the cove.

"There are so many..." she said aloud, catching her breath. Ruth stepped down cautiously, rock by jagged rock. *Dane must have done well for them to come back here with this many ships.*

"Twelve, by my count," Ludwyn shouted from behind as he followed her down toward the flat piece of shore.

A fleet of small boats was being pulled in from the low tide, with mates anchoring their lines to the closest trunk of wet pine. Ruth made her way down to the coast with a brimming smile, rushing to meet her old friends, while Ozzy darted straight for the water. When she got closer, she spotted Roth's tall frame sticking out from the group of mates huddling near a boat, waving their hands in chatter. Dane turned his pale face and shaggy blond hair to her as soon as Roth had glanced their way.

Rashly, Ruth ran right past Dane's ear-to-ear smile and bobbed forward to hug her brother. "You'll never guess what I've brought!" she said just as Roth's weight collapsed from under him. "Roth! *Are you okay? What happened?*"

He released a hiss of groans to make her let go, then grunted to lift himself back up and regain his balance. "It's nothing," he replied, adjusting a walking stick from outside her view.

"That doesn't look like *nothing*."

"Is Scarlett okay?" he asked.

"Yes, of course. It's *you* who doesn't look okay. *Dane*, what happened?"

Dane looked at her with a squeamish face, almost too afraid to speak. "Roth was injured when we stormed the shipyard at Nordheim."

To her left, Roth limped away from their group, clearly trying to avoid her reaction. Ludwyn followed him closely, whispering words she couldn't hear. "*How'd you let this happen?*" Ruth asked Dane.

"Roth's a grown man," Caji said from behind his shoulder.

"It isn't Dane's fault. He wasn't even on the island with him when it happened. I was," Sonny, a captain she'd met briefly, told her.

"Shouldn't you have been on that island then, too? I told you to work him hard—*not get him nearly killed*," Ruth stammered, her complexion growing darker with every word she spoke.

"Look, lady—Roth ran ahead of us by himself," Sonny continued. Ludwyn walked back their way to try to soothe the situation.

"He's telling the truth," Roth said, slowly limping over to join them. "It was my own fault. And something I regret doing."

"Well, then, what's wrong with you?" Ruth asked.

"It's my left leg. I just don't have much feeling in it—or any feeling, really."

Ruth reached her arms around his taller shoulders and hugged him as tightly as her father had just hugged her, making sure, this time, that he didn't topple over. "Roth, I'm so sorry."

"I'll be okay."

"No, I should have been there. I shouldn't have let you go alone."

"There's nothing you could have done."

"Roth's right, Ruth. Even if you did come, you would have been on the ship with me. Your safety is important, too," Dane told her.

"*My safety?* I'm the one who brought an army of sentinels back with me from Bovere."

"*An army?*" Dane asked, his eyebrows raised.

Ruth looked over at her brother and saw his broad forehead crunch and his cheeks become taut with concern. Regardless of what those royals had said back in Bovere, part of her had forgotten that he was still a warranted man. "Six hundred sentinels that the royal families have lent to me," she explained.

"We've come back here for lumber…but, *Ruth*, that's so much better," Dane said. With his back to the anchored fleet, his icy-blue eyes widened with excitement as he scanned the coast for any sight of them.

"Where are they?" Roth asked in a more serious tone.

"None are in Tergona. They're camped out in the Northwoods, hidden away. They've been waiting there for you all to come back."

Roth nodded in affirmation.

Dane turned to the captains behind him and said, "The mates we left behind to guard Niels and the others may not last long. And we can't stay here with Nordheim left unprotected. If we bring these six hundred men to the yard, it'll free our entire fleet up to take to the seas."

Ruth shuffled her way to stand between them. "Dane, there's just one thing—they are only sworn to protect me."

"What?" Captain Markas asked, tilting his head behind the weight of his stubby neck to get a clearer look at her.

"It was a part of my deal with the royals for Scarlett. None of you are from here, so they won't listen to any of you. And they certainly won't follow you."

Roth's head turned back around faster than his body would let him. "*Ruth*, you aren't thinking about going north to Nordheim, are you?"

"I am. And before you even say anything to object, you aren't my father," she replied, thinking back to the advice Edmon had just given her about staying in Tergona.

"*Ruth*, that place is a wasteland…and it's freezing, and everyone there is miserable. And it's dangerous," Roth rambled in pleading spouts.

"So, then you aren't going back either?" Ludwyn asked him.

"Not a chance. I have somewhere else I need to be," Roth responded.

"And where's that?"

"*West*. Go if you want, Ruth, but don't say I didn't warn you." Roth collected himself and began to limp back toward the cove's curving line of wet pines.

Ruth turned back to Dane and his captains with an expression of surprise as if she meant to ask why they weren't trying to stop him. She could tell that the brother she had known her entire life was different than the one who now stood before her. Roth was calmer and more collected than he'd ever been. And, for the first time that she could remember, he seemed to be genuinely concerned for her well-being—at least since that fateful day at the Applewood Tavern.

"*Roth…wait*," she yelled, chasing after him toward the trees, where Ludwyn was helping Roth to limp up the jagged slope of rocks. Ruth could hear him asking Ludwyn about his mother's wagon and mules. "Roth, what's west? You don't plan to turn yourself in, do you?"

"*No*, not quite. There's something that I need to take care of," he answered. "If you choose to go to Nordheim, then go. Lud, you as well. You both will have my prayers."

"*Prayers? From you?*" Ruth questioned in confusion. The brother she knew was never one to dutifully believe in the Divine One, or the Cathedral and its teachings. Let alone, pray.

"If you aren't coming, I'm not going back on that damned ship. I'll go west with you," Ludwyn said.

"This is something I need to do by myself—alone, Lud." Roth stepped over a rock blanketed by mold as Ozzy scampered past them, worried that she was leaving too. "That's a cute friend you've got there."

"Scarlett was the one who convinced me to keep him. His name is Ozzy," Ruth told him.

Roth broke his cool smile as soon as she mentioned Scarlett's name. "I'm just glad the two of you are safe."

"You can thank me for that," Ludwyn said, causing them both to laugh.

Once Roth collected his breath, he said, "I think that otter might have done more than you ever could."

"Did more to keep us happy, that's for sure," Ruth added.

"Look, Ruth," Roth said in a more serious tone. "Whatever happens out there, just don't forget about me."

"Why would I forget about you?" she asked, her voice pitching with concern. "You'll come back, right?"

"If you have anything for me, just get a message to the Cathedral in Bovere."

"*Cathedral? Bovere?* What do you mean? Why would you be there?"

But Roth didn't answer. He gave her a brief hug, then turned back toward the woods. Ruth watched on in silence as Ludwyn helped guide him back down the pebbled path. She could tell he was hurt in more ways than just his limp leg and knew it would have been a futile effort to argue with him in the condition he was in. And so, she watched him leave, with only Ozzy still there, hugging her side. She made her way slowly back to the coast to find Dane still chatting with his captains and the other mates.

"*Ruth*," Dane said, almost surprised that she had returned.

"So, I take it you're the captain, now?"

"Yes—the captain among captains," Dane replied with a deep voice after breaking a cough to clear his throat.

"Good. I've decided to come with you. And I'm bringing those sentinels with me wherever it is you need the help."

"*Perfect.*"

"But under one condition," she said, flattening his narrow smile. "You'll have to dedicate time with me on this island, so I can finally teach you to read and write in roalish."

Some of the other captains around him laughed at his expense, but Dane just straightened his back with that same ear-to-ear smile from before and said, "*Deal.*"

"Well, aren't you a young one."

"Dane, this is Rory Gravelot, second son to Favian Gravelot and second sentinel-in-command to the Gravelot coat," Ruth explained. Dane moved to shake his hand, then turned to the woman beside him to do the same. "And this is Rougina Damas, younger sister to Elvina Damas and commanding sentinel to the Damas coat."

"You can call me Rouge," she told him.

Dane stood facing the cove. "Pleasure. We can fit fifty of your men on each of our ships, since we won't be carrying lumber. You two are welcome to join me and Ruth on board the *Freebird* for our passage back north to Nordheim."

"If that's what's needed," Rory replied, moving his hand to wave the sentinels in from the pebbled path. With all their belongings, they moved in lines down to Cubby Cove's flat piece of shore. Ruth watched Dane scan the men as they walked toward the small boats, inspecting their chain-mail under-suits, longswords, and various colors and coats that were embroidered onto their vested tabards. "I don't know why I did, but I expected the captain of such a fleet to be much older than you are," Rory remarked snobbishly, turning back to their small group. "What is it that they say—that a ship is only as strong as its captain? Must be quite a young ship, then."

"A young *fleet*," Dane corrected. Rory, himself, was a young man, which prompted Ruth and Dane to give each other a questioning look. "But they're still strong, that much, I can assure you. And the mates we have on board don't dress like colorful children, as your own do."

"*Ah*, leave it to a nork to think he knows anything about tradition and beauty. The only beautiful thing the Northern Plane has is its blonde-haired women. And even then, they deprive them to their bones and cover them with rags. Personally, I'm looking forward to this passage north. I'd love to get my hands and eyes on one someday. Do you happen to have any sisters, *Captain*?"

Ruth saw Dane's pale face begin to flush with frustration. The Gravelots were one of the most powerful families in the Regent, which forced Ruth to feel like she needed to calm Dane from saying something he'd regret. Or, more truthfully, something she'd regret.

From what Ruth had gathered during their talks as they traveled to Tergona, the Gravelots originally hailed from Partha—the oldest city in the east and thus the oldest of the Plane. They began as a family of builders, architects of the great Martelmont Castle, which the Martelmont family is still seated in today. The Gravelot coat was awarded kingship upon its completion and granted the canton of Casselton as their own. Within its vast riverfront meadows, their town flourished.

When Rexam ruled across the Plane, the royal families lost many of their members to war. The following Amulonic Age brought a period of intermarriage between the ruling kings and queens to recover what was lost and strengthen their alliances. The Gravelots and Martelmonts wedded many together, as did the Franclares with the Mantises and the Clovins with the Boveres. These unions fostered an age of immense regrowth and renewed competition. As the families and their unions expanded, they no longer warred solely with their knights, lancers, and troopers, but with their assets and in trade.

The Martelmonts used their wealth to engross the livestock market, which constituted large swaths of ranches now granted to the Ockmans. For the Clothars and Furths in Roverra, it was that of sheep and their wool. Some, like the Arsurs in Tammon, grew their wealth by dominating the market for grain. Others, like the Kilgors and the Orlaiths, controlled the market for ore and precious minerals, and the tools needed to excavate them. For the Decanan and Damas families, it was the market of spices and silk, and the production of glass, that expanded their fortune. Even the fore-family of knighthood—the Mantises of Florington—grew in wealth due to their access to Roark's River. But for the Gravelots, their specialty in building was admired by all, and by none greater than Tohen the Second.

With a wave of popular support, the Divine One was declared Supreme King of the Regent in 212 A.D., causing all the kings and queens of the Eastern Plane to relinquish their titles, convert, and pledge their loyalty to the Council of the Divine Sages and the Covenant of the Divine Tomes. The coalition of royal families in favor of the change had forced the Boveres to cede the Stonehammer to the Divine One's protection, settling all feuds and easing the growing tension of war. But as a compromise, their amulon was to remain in Bovere, and the Cathedral was to be built upon its central plaza. With their combined wealth, the royal families established a grant for its construction, offering their gold toward the creation of a cathedral. And with that fortune, the divine sages commissioned the Gravelot coat to build the Cathedral of the Divine One in all its deserved beauty.

From everything Rory had spoken of, that honor was the distinct pride of their family. And though Ruth listened intently when he spoke of the Regent's past, she couldn't stand listening to him speak of much else. He was arrogant and pompous and carried a scathing demeanor that belittled everyone he encountered. The sentinels he commanded were too afraid to challenge him or speak out against his denigrating manners. But Ruth was glad she had Rouge there beside her as they traveled northeast. Any time Rory lifted his tongue to make a rude remark, which was as often as the breeze blew, Rouge pointed her hawk-like eyes his way and corrected his behavior.

For as much as Ruth didn't want to admit it, Rory was a handsome young man. He had bronze locks of hair that shimmered perfectly when settled under the sun, which he kept groomed back smoothly behind his head and ears. He was much shorter than her or Dane, but had a face chiseled fine like a marble bust, eyes of the warmest amber, and a nose that curved like the perfect arches of the Tannen Bridge.

Rouge was also in a class of beauty second only to her sister. Her figure and features were similar to Elvina's, whom Ruth had met briefly back in Bovere. She was taller than her older sister, though, and had broader shoulders, which seemed necessary for a woman who had chosen a life of fighting among men. Being from Damasa, Rouge's skin was tanner than most across the Regent, and her mannerisms matched those mates from the south more than they did anyone Ruth had met from the Eastern Plane.

"Don't worry about him," Ruth told Dane as soon as Rory scampered off to instruct the sentinels on which small boat they were to take to which vessel.

"He's been a pestilent bitch his entire life. Don't let him get to you," Rouge said.

"It's okay," Dane replied, constantly glancing back and forth at the longsword strapped to her waist. Ruth still wore a saber around her own, but it in no way matched the dangerous disposition Rouge carried upon her shoulders, embodied by the golden-laced tabard that was embroidered with her family's coat of a red bull. Ruth could tell that Dane was just as cautious of Rouge as he was of Rory. "The sea will right him as it does with everyone," he said. "*Let's just hope he can swim.*"

For the rest of the day, the fleet's small boats carried groupings of sentinels back and forth from the shoreline to the galleons until they were split nearly even, fifty a ship. Dane commanded the mates of his fleet to stay aboard and let only those who worked in the hold leave to gather fresh produce from the town. Ruth had squandered most of the day alongside

Piney, wandering through the fields and markets nearby as they filled their baskets and shared laughs over each other's stories, which they had missed during their separate journeys.

That night, she, Piney, and his group of mates returned to the shore to catch one of the last boats back to the *Freebird*. Most on board had gone below deck to help set up the sentinels' hammocks and get them situated, or were sitting around the mess enjoying the food and wine Piney had provided to celebrate the night before they planned to get underway. Ruth wandered back up to the main deck and found Dane standing alone near the bow, watching the water like he had the night before they'd first arrived in Cubby Cove.

"A captain with his own ship," Ruth said, moving to lean beside him on the railing of the foredeck. "*I like it.*"

"If you like that, then you'll love this." Dane scooted forward and pointed to show her the sculpture just below the bowsprit. "It's a snow pelican."

Ruth drifted closer to inspect its engravings under the lantern's light. "It's beautiful. This must be the *free* bird it's named after, then. Right?"

"Same one—a snow pelican. It was the last bird I saw the morning I went fishing with my brother back in Niven. Before my life changed. And the same one I saw the night you saved me on that beach in Roverra."

"A snow pelican *in the Regent?*"

"*No,*" Dane replied with a laugh. "Just the vision of one. I could see it as clear as day, though. It had the whitest of wings, and it flew so freely and gracefully. It's been stuck in my head ever since."

"And you've been free ever since," Ruth said with a soft, crooked smile.

Dane leaned his head back behind her shoulder to make sure none of the other mates were close enough to hear them talk. "If I'm being honest, I don't think any captain can call themself free. Part of me wishes I never even corralled them all to let me do it—that I could still be just another one of the mates."

"Don't sell yourself so short," Ruth said, walking back toward the railing, beside him. "As the captain, you're the one who gets to make the decisions and can go wherever or do whatever you want. That sounds freeing to me."

"It isn't that easy. There are things I want to do—to free all the oarsmen and help everyone back home and give them a chance at life like you all do here. But with that comes challenges. We need more mates and more ships —and bigger ones—if we want to survive and compete. I feel responsible for them all. The mates have lent me their trust and their lives to give this a chance. And as their captain, all of that trust becomes so heavy, it can start to drown away any dream," Dane said, his face softening as he looked down at the moon's reflection in the water.

"Wouldn't that just make it all more worth it, then?" Ruth asked.

"When it's done, sure. But until then, it's difficult. Especially when there are things you don't want to lose," Dane replied.

"Lose? Like what?"

"*Like you.*"

Ruth's smile broke whatever composure she was trying to keep. "I'm still here. I came back just like I said I was going to."

"You did. But part of me feels like I failed you—for what I let happen to Roth and for letting you go in the first place."

"You won't be able to protect everyone, Dane," Ruth told him when she saw the shimmer in his blue eyes. Their glistening color captured his emotions like a painting that depicted his past struggles and pain. Looking into them, she could see the man Dane had grown to become—and the captain that both the mates and Marredom needed. "All you can do is fight for those who can't."

"And fight, we will," Dane said more sternly, pulling back at his emotions as if the drapes of a curtain had closed to shutter his artwork. He patted the wooden-planked side hull for support. "I just hope she can keep up."

"If she's anything like the *Widow*, I'm sure she will."

"You know, now that you mention it, I think I saw the *Widow* when we breached that storm."

"Piney said the same. What do you think Cowen was doing still this far north?"

"I'm not sure. I've given it some thought, but I still don't know. Whatever it is, though, I wish him the best."

"Even after he left you?" Ruth asked, trying to remember everything Piney had mentioned.

"Even then, yes. But I must admit, I do miss the *Widow* and Captain Noreas. At least far more than I miss Cowen," Dane added, shifting his eyes and cracking a narrow-mouthed smile.

"I just hope the *Freebird*'s cupboard by the kitchens isn't as smelly as the *Widow*'s was," Ruth said with a soft giggle.

She watched as Dane became lost in thought, as if he were contemplating the right words to say. "Don't hate me...but I think that cupboard might still be filled with overflow from the hold."

"Then where am I supposed to sleep? There's no way I'm sleeping in the berth below deck with the rest of the mates," Ruth said as fast as her thin lips would let her.

"We can move everything around and try to clear the cupboard out. But it might take most of the night. And I can't promise we can get rid of the smell." Dane couldn't hide his laugh. He paused and fidgeted his hand across the wool of his gray overcoat, adjusting its collar nervously. "You're welcome to stay with me—in the captain's quarters. I have the room."

Ruth's lips puckered to one side of her chin as she moved a dangling lock of hair behind her ear. She could feel her face blush at the idea of sleeping next to Dane. But it was an idea she knew was wrong, especially since the Cathedral and the people of the Regent had such a strong stance on marriage.

"I mean, *not together*," Dane corrected, almost against his will. "If you wanted, I could rig your hammock up near my bed. I have plenty of space."

"I'd be okay with that, I guess," Ruth said, her eyes wandering nervously. "As long as Ozzy can sleep there too."

"Even better. Bring your stuff back up to the aftcastle, and I can get your hammock situated."

"Just so you know, I've brought it all with me this time. A sack of fresh plaid skirts, all three volumes of the Divine Tomes, and even extra snacks for me and Ozzy."

"Good thing I have room for it all—as long as you're willing to share," Dane said with a boyish grin.

"Only if you prove yourself to be a nice captain," Ruth replied, her smirk now curling into a shy smile to match his own.

"We'll leave that for you to decide."

Ruth kept smiling as she left the main deck to head below and gather the belongings that Piney had been watching for her near the kitchens. The sentinels and mates in the mess were getting along better than she had expected, with tales and stories being shouted aloud, and mugs of stout and wine being passed from table to table across the packed room. Singing broke out as Ruth made her way back up to the quarterdeck and into the aftcastle's lone set of stairs.

When she entered Dane's captain's quarters, she placed her belongings beside his desk and moved to inspect the hammock he was rigging. Light stretched to the center of the room from dimly lit lanterns in each corner, and dark curtains covered all three of the windows. "This is nice—much better than the cupboard, at least," she told him.

"It's not as well kept as the *Widow*'s was, but similar nonetheless," Dane said. His hands were raised to the thick frame of timber that spanned the full breadth of the ship and his quarters. Opposite his desk were two recessed spaces split between the aftcastle's central stairwell. One was filled by cabinetry above and chests below. The other fit his feather-stuffed bed with its privacy curtain left open.

"It could use some freshening up," Ruth told him as she spun around to examine his room. "Maybe some paintings like Captain Noreas had would help."

"You're right. I'd forgotten about those," Dane said from the edge of his bed. "That's exactly what it needs. I would love a painting of the *Freebird* or even one of my own home, just like he had."

"It definitely needs some color, that's for sure."

"Ruth, you paint, don't you?" Dane asked as he continued to work on stringing her hammock to the ceiling.

"I do."

"Then maybe you could paint something for me. We can hang it there, just to the side of my desk."

"It would cost you, though," Ruth said while walking toward him. She sat on one of the chairs against the sidewall. "After Scarlett saw the one I painted of her, she said she could make me rich."

"Is that right?"

"She seemed to think so."

"Well, then, I'm definitely interested," Dane said, pausing his work to look her way.

"Sounds like we have ourselves another deal."

"Did you bring any of that paint here with you? Along with the rest of your belongings you managed to stuff in those sacks?" Dane asked with a smirk. He began drifting back toward his desk where her things lay.

"Yes, I think so. But something that big and nice might take a while."

"That's okay. It'll take about a quarter-moon to reach Nordheim. That's plenty of time, right?" Dane asked. He reached down for one of her sacks.

Wait...no... Ruth's chest collapsed as soon as Dane began to rummage inside it. "*What are you doing?*" she asked. Panicked, she jumped up from where she was sitting and lunged toward him.

"Just getting your painting stuff out so you can get started," he replied nonchalantly. "I want to see all this good work of yours, too."

Before she could reach him, Dane pulled out her tin of paints and a book that was bound with loosened sheets of parchment. He turned toward her with a look of surprise and let her take her belongings. But instead, Ruth had yanked on the book's cover, and the loose sheets of parchment fell to scatter across the floor.

No...no...no, she thought frantically, rushing around quickly to try to pick them all up.

Dane did the same, helping to gather her work. "What's this? Is this *you?*" he asked, his eyes squinching in confusion. He turned over a sheet of parchment that revealed a perfectly painted image of her own bare body leaning against the bark of a tree. She had painted it herself—of herself and for herself. Proportionally, the painting was accurate—exactly how Ruth saw herself, standing there, as naked as could be. Every mole and curve, her wide-set hips and rounded chest, and even the curving angles beneath her waist were all there for Dane to witness.

"*Give me that,*" she snapped.

But Dane had turned and kept staring at it. "*Ruth*...it's you. This is beautiful! You did this?"

"It's *mine*. Give it back," she demanded, raising her voice.

"But I want to keep it... I won't show a person. I swear," Dane pleaded, pulling the parchment away from her reach with a giddy grin.

"*No.*" Ruth lunged closer and finally snatched it away from him. "I'm sorry you had to see that."

"*Sorry?* You shouldn't be sorry at all, Ruth," he said more calmly than before.

Ruth turned her back to him, and her face flushed, splotching redder than it ever had for the entirety of her young life. She was beyond embarrassed. No one had ever seen her that way before—exposed and open. She wanted to leave, to jump over the side of the *Freebird* and into the water, to swim back home as fast as she could. But as soon as she closed her eyes, she heard Dane's boots walking slowly toward her.

He rested his large hand softly on her shoulder. "Ruth…it's okay. I think you're beautiful."

"*Beautiful…*" she said under her breath, filled with doubt. Tears puddled under her eyes, forcing them open. She turned around. "*I'm ashamed of myself…* I should have hidden this back home or burned it so no one could find it."

Dane moved his calloused finger to wipe away one of the tears that trickled down her warm cheek. "*No,*" he said. "On these ships, nothing is allowed to burn anymore." His head slowly began to lean toward her. As his hands braced the sides of her waist, he pulled her body in close. Dane's cold lips traced every thin curve her own gave. Ruth shut her eyes once more, pressed her body against his own, and gave in to Dane's passionate embrace. As he kissed her, all her worries began to wash away.

CHAPTER 41

SUN

Death loomed in the stagnant air above the blood-rusted horizon. Cleo could feel its grip squeeze to strangle each breath he took and see its taunting vastitude reflected in the eyes of every guardsman. He'd been leading their march toward Sazara for the past half-moon with a cold silence. Despite forcing his brigade to stop every other night to set up camp, he knew not one guardsman found rest. They neither drank nor laughed nor chatted over fires like they had in nights prior. Their stories, just like their touch from women, ran as dry as their wine. The day he told his West Brigade they were leaving for Sazara was the day a cloud of death followed their every step.

And Cleo embraced it.

With all the uncertainty over the past half-solurn, his guardsmen knew their fate. They had accepted Cleo's order with silent solace, relying on the trust of their commander, just as they did on the shield and sword of the man beside them. Shoulder to shoulder, they had marched from Corlis to Sazara, the air filled only with the clatter of their bronze greaves and the stomping of their sandals against the rust-colored dirt.

This morning, however, was different from all the others. The West Brigade had marched its final steps from their camp toward the western gate of Sazara. The enemy, once faceless, would soon stand before them. Any angst that once lingered behind the veil of their minds had now been given life, swelling their eyes like a field of blood roses finally blossomed. Most of Cleo's guardsmen now looked as if they regretted not having the wine, the women, or anything to numb the ringing noise and clamor that battered back and forth between their bronze helmets. Though some, like those remaining from the Sixth Brigade, looked ready to kill as if they had become possessed by the opportunity of personal glory.

But Cleo himself stood steadfast and focused. And he had made sure his captains acted accordingly. He rode Dahlia in the center of their march, beside Captain Gregan Igor and the second battalion's sword and spearmen. Ahead was the first battalion, led by Captain Ostin, a man who had just brought the fore of the West Brigade to a sudden halt.

This is it, Cleo knew. All the days and nights of planning, the continuous troughs of emotion, and all the people who came together by his calling had finally culminated in this *day of inevitability.* Cleo closed his eyes and reminded himself why he was here and what he was fighting for. When he opened them, he saw his father's face over his right shoulder and Vident Lement's over his left. Forward was Kladden's.

Cleo pulled on his reins, turning around to check on the Black Baron, who was leading the armament of ballistas pulled at the rear of their formation. With a nod, the Black Baron and Captain Igor brought the rest of the West Brigade to a complete standstill. The line of guardsmen in front of him began to split, turning their shields to face him and rendering their salutes as he passed. Everyone but Cleo, who was directing Dahlia slowly forward, stood at attention. As he rode up to the front line, surrounded by burnt-orange flags bearing the insignia of New Scipyria, Cleo caught sight of the limestone wall that stood three stories tall. In front of it were thousands of discolored and barely perceptible figures spread in a thick line as far as he could see around its curve. Cleo swallowed the dryness in his throat and continued to ride forward.

I've brought you justice, Father.

At the head of the formation, Cleo greeted the stern-faced Captain Ostin, then directed him to split the cavalry behind their wall of shields. Once the dirt below their hooves had settled, Cleo turned back around to face his West Brigade.

"*Men of Sacrim…of the Sixth Brigade, of Andar and Cignus, and those of Corlis who have all joined us,*" Cleo proclaimed aloud to his guardsmen, pacing Dahlia back and forth as his royal-red cloak sifted in the air behind him. "*We stand at the doorstep of glory—at the doorstep of a city that belongs to each of you, more so than it does to any man you will face in battle today. A city fallen to ruin while those magistrates, chambermen, and deacons line their own pockets with gold—our gold and your children's gold!*"

All the guardsmen in front of him clattered their spears into the dry dirt of the ground, grunting in spouts of support and anger. "*Today, they will meet our vengeance and face our justice! They must be brought to their knees and bleed by our bronze and steel for what they have taken from us— taken from me, my father and mother, and all of our brothers!"*

Cleo paused and stared into the eyes of his guardsmen at the front line. They all looked somber but steady, ready for war and for death. *"Today, we will open the door to a new history! Men, show your courage in battle and fight for glory! Fight for your home! This day shall be yours, the day they write your names in history—in the reign of New Scipyria!"*

From every direction, in a sea of bronze, the guardsmen clapped their spears and swords against their shields, shouting in howling yells meant only for war. Cleo unsheathed his father's shortsword and lifted its tip to the sun. He turned Dahlia around and lowered it to point at Sazara's western gate. *"FORWARD!"*

The wall of rounded shields all lifted at his command, clashing as they thrust forward together. Cleo sat still, watching as the moving line of shields split around him. When Captain Igor had reached his side, Cleo directed Dahlia forward in the middle of the formation. He needed to see the entire battlefield—the shields and spears at the fore, swordsmen in the middle, the cavalry that encircled them from each side, and the ballistas and archers notched at their rear. Step by step, under the bright winter sun, the West Brigade marched toward Sazara.

Cleo could barely make out the shape of the men who stood before the wall. Most were dressed in a non-uniform assortment of garments and cloaks in mixed and matched shades of red and brown. Those in the front held their swords and shields like rabid, untrained street dogs needing to be pulled back. The information Cleo had received back in Corlis seemed correct. From what he could tell, the Calegris had pulled every man of fighting age off the streets of Sazara. Though they were untrained and likely lacked any regard for the decorum of battle, Cleo's men were still vastly outnumbered, which was enough to worry any commander.

Cleo could feel the black-leather grip wrapped around his sword's hilt grow sweaty in his palm. To calm himself, he repeated their planned tactics over and over in his mind and thought back to all the groundwork he had done to prepare his brigade for this moment. *Shields of trust,* he thought as they continued to march forward, their sandals stepping in unison.

In a blaze straight ahead, flames of red and orange sprang into the air. *Must be the Sunspear,* he realized. *Cayen is braver than I thought—to be out here with us.* Cleo had expected to meet Sazara's Guard outside the wall, which was their standard tactic to keep the fight away from the city's center. And Cleo knew that any scouts Astria flew in the sky would have spotted their march days in advance. But what he didn't expect was for Cayen himself to be there outside the wall, leading their effort with his father's Sunspear in hand. And in taking that risk, Cleo reveled.

The still mob in front of the wall had ignited into a barrage of fire. The blades of their swords had lit to flame, spreading out to each of the formation's indiscernible, curving ends. The march of Cleo's own brigade quickly slowed, breaking from its prior stomps of unison. Most of the guardsmen around Cleo were caught off guard by the light and heat emanating across the open field of dirt. His captains and vice-captains from each battalion shouted out commands, reminding the guardsmen to stand firm and continue their march forward.

Cleo wasn't concerned about his men's fear but about the uncertainty that came when fighting with fire. *A single scorch can burn everything to the ground if held in the hands of the undisciplined,* he remembered, as Vident Lement would say. And Cayen's amassment of men, which must have numbered north of twenty thousand, was sure to be undisciplined.

Just as his guardsmen began to regather themselves, Cleo's gaze was drawn to the sky, where dozens of gray silhouettes had ascended into the air. He identified them instantly as rook riders from Astria and whipped Dahlia back to face the Black Baron, who nodded in acknowledgment. "*Not this time, you bastards,*" he whispered to himself.

Horrific images of their ambush at Fort Saxoram replayed throughout Cleo's mind, as he remembered the rook riders' arrows that fell like rain from the sky. As he scanned the fray above the wall, he saw two distinct flocks of rooks flying toward them from both sides of Cayen's formation. The closer they flew, the more he was able to count how many there were—far more than he recalled seeing at Fort Saxoram. Cleo only hoped they had enough bolts for their ballistas to match. He turned and motioned for the Black Baron to split the single formation of ballistas into two, waving his hand in each direction. But as their bows shifted in varying trajectories, their wheels had stopped moving.

In the midst of their marching confusion, the Black Baron shouted words Cleo couldn't hear, then pointed for him to look straight ahead. Cleo turned and saw both flocks of rooks merge, dipping low in front of them to glide above the red dirt that separated his brigade from Cayen's own.

What are they doing? Why would they fly right at us after having the advantage of sweeping our sides? But just as quickly as Cleo had questioned, he found the answer.

Flying out ahead of the flocks of rook riders was Vanna. In the stillness of his disbelief, he saw her rook swirling and making abrupt maneuvers to avoid the arrows being slung her way. He gave one final motion to the Black Baron to realign, then turned back forward to face the incoming onslaught.

Cleo was urging his men to push on when he caught sight of Vanna's eyes. He smiled at her worried face as she passed over him from above, as if to thank her for what she'd done in leading the rook riders right toward them. There, sitting atop his saddle, Cleo waited for them to fly within his range. With his father's sword lifted back into the air, he lowered it to point at the birds and then gave the order, *"RELEASE!"*

The sound of tight ropes clanking against iron and wooden beams rang loudly behind him. In front of the West Brigade's front line of shields, bolts from the ballistas blazed through the sky to hit several of the rooks directly in their chests. Others had scattered, damaging their wings and sides, causing a shrieking mess of havoc to echo in the air above them.

Revenge is ripe, Cleo thought with a smirk.

"SHIELDS UP, SPEARS DOWN!" he ordered the guardsmen around him. Captain Igor trotted his horse down their columns and back again, repeating his command over the loud shrills above them. The birds that had been directly hit plummeted to the ground in front of their formation with heavy thumps. Covering his ears to think above their screeching, Cleo turned to make sure the Black Baron's men were reloading for the second barrage. Again, bolts were vaulted into the sky to unfold the oncoming rooks into further turmoil.

He and his captains used their loud shrieks to judge where they might land as they fell from above, commanding the West Brigade to disperse their marching around them. The few rooks that flew past them unleashed their arrows in hopeful throws. Those hit, but not downed, hovered uncontrollably and became easy targets for the Baron's steady return fire. Even with all the commotion above, Cleo's concern led him to scan the sky in search of Vanna.

But after hearing the shouts from Captain Igor beside him, Cleo saw the wall of flaming swords begin to rush from the wall, sprinting to clash in the direction of his brigade. *"PUSH! SHIELDS DOWN, SHIELDS DOWN! ARCHERS AT THE REAR... FIRE!"*

This is it. All my anger and angst for this very moment...my vengeance. After breathless moments of anticipation, the spearmen of Cleo's second battalion clashed their bronze shields together and braced their sandals into the red dirt, forming a wall at the fore. *"HOLDDDDDD!"* Cleo tried to yell to his men on the front line.

High and low, the furor of war bellowed its loudest before being broken by the deafening collision of the two warring sides. Flaming swords slammed against shields far ahead, and arrows raining down from above were all Cleo could see from where he sat in the middle of their tight formation. In short spurts, the guardsmen behind the line of shields did their best to thrust their long spears and swords into the swarm of flaming masses. With each push from the second battalion's holding wall, the West Brigade fought back.

But his guardsmen soon began to drop, their shields lowering, one by one, as they cried out in burning pain. Cleo scanned from left to right in search of the opening. The fire was spreading, catching behind his line of shields until their formation could no longer hold its formidable defense. Cayen's amassment of unrestrained men had broken through. Cleo motioned his sword back into the sky, recalling his cavalry to break in front of him and cover for the exposed spearmen.

From every direction, the battle for Sazara was unfolding. Cleo charged forward on his horse, joining his cavalry to slash his sword down into the bodies of the men dressed in rags with swords caught aflame, trying to fight their way through. The deepening red of blood covered his blade's shimmer as agonizing screams began to surround him from every direction. Cleo's heart thumped, and his head became thoughtless. It was as if war were just a dance to a song played by the heart's heavy drum, beating along to the sound of survival.

With each of his swings, Cleo pictured Kladden there beside him, guiding him along. His instincts from his days of training were still sharp, though Cleo knew he wasn't the strongest or quickest of swordsmen. Instead, he relied on reading the enemy's moves to anticipate those that would come next. *A dance of death,* as Kladden had often put it. But anticipating move-ments surrounded by nothing but chaos was a feat Cleo soon realized to be impossible.

Survival became his only thought.

Burning bodies loomed left and right, and arrows continued to rain down from the sky. Death was no longer the cloud that followed them but the air they breathed, one that poured down with poisonous misery.

Up ahead, Cleo saw an opening and rode forward to fight beside Captain Ostin. Those of the first battalion, still atop their warhorses, were his brigade's best hope for victory. They evaded the touch of fire and moved quickly enough to avoid most of the arrows from above. On the back of Dahlia, Cleo continued to slash up and down, slicing through the shoulders and bodies of Cayen's undisciplined men.

Cayen...

As soon as he found a sight line, Cleo looked out toward the western gate of Sazara's wall. Dread filled every segment of his body. He could barely distinguish Cayen sitting atop his horse, holding his father's Sunspear, with what looked to be half of his men still waiting by his side. And from their bronze armor alone, Cleo realized that they must be the real guardsmen—reserves from the First and Second Brigades.

All around Cleo, in the midst of battle, were the best of his own, tied up in warring fights of steel and flame, colored by bronze and blood, and filled with the worst horrors of hate. If things continued the way they were, Cleo knew his brigade didn't stand a chance. They were vastly outnumbered as it was, and they hadn't yet begun to face Cayen's toughest and most disciplined assault of guardsmen. Out of hope and desperation, waiting for his plan to succeed, Cleo glanced back at Sazara's wall and scanned it once more. A large shadow broke the air between the two. Above it, Cleo saw the rook Vanna had been riding being carried away by the talons of the largest rook of them all.

Cleo immediately turned back to the tail of his broken formation, the ballistas still too far away for him to reach. In a moment of providence, his eyes met the Black Baron's own. Cleo pointed desperately at the largest rook in the sky as it flew toward the wall. The Black Baron jumped onto the ballista he was the nearest to and placed its end against his chest. He used all his might to turn its aim toward the rook that carried Vanna's and notched the bolt back. Cleo held his tense breath, waiting for the sound of its release.

Through all the screeching of pain and the clashing of steel, Cleo only heard the clicking release of the rope and the slamming of the ballista's arms.

He followed the bolt's path through the air, watching as it flew above Cayen's men to plunge itself into the chest of the giant rook that carried Vanna's, just as they were about to cross over the wall. Cleo's face brimmed with a bloody smile. He threw his fist into the air, shouting with satisfaction.

But just then, Cleo felt his saddle collapse from underneath him. He looked down and saw a man in bloodied rags retrieve a once-flaming sword from the leg of the folding Dahlia. Cleo fell to the side with his horse, lunging himself off his saddle so he wouldn't be crushed by its weight. In a burst of anger, Cleo threw himself back up and charged at his attacker, fighting off two swings to slice his father's shortsword straight into the man's chest.

Dahlia... Cleo thought as he looked back at his dying horse. But there was no time to mourn.

Terror filled the air as Cleo continued to fight on foot. He found Captain Ostin and swung by his side, his hope dwindling. The plan he had spent so long sequestered inside to create was now unraveling before his eyes, and he had nothing to show for it. All he could do was trust that his guardsmen wouldn't give up. And trust that the others would arrive.

With bloodied screams, Cleo continued to fight through the masses as he and Captain Ostin, and whatever other guardsmen were near, made quick work of Cayen's force of ragged men. *Trust...* Cleo thought, glancing back toward Sazara's western gate every chance he could.

His West Brigade had fended off most of Cayen's first assault but had taken heavy losses in doing so. In the break of the dwindling action, Cleo looked down at his arms, legs, and shortsword to see them stained the same color as his torn cloak. He spun to scan what was left of the battlefield. A few of the Queen's rook riders who had managed to survive had landed by Cayen's fresh line of guardsmen. From what he could see, they looked to be readying for their next assault, one Cleo knew his brigade couldn't handle.

Dead horses, scorched bodies, and severed limbs were scattered to blacken the blood-rusted dirt they stood upon. Cleo attempted to count the casualties, realizing that he'd lost well over half of his guardsmen. Behind him, he saw the Black Baron stepping over burning bodies to fend off the last few of Cayen's men who surrounded him. Many of the ballistas scattered at the rear were left unmanned, broken, or ablaze. Cleo wiped the blood off his face and turned in circles to search for his captains, trying to organize whatever guardsmen they could into a new formation.

"*Commander,*" he heard a voice say. "*Down here.*"

Cleo glanced down at his feet and saw Captain Ostin lying between bodies of bronze with blood leaking from the lashes across his stomach. "*Captain Ostin.*" Cleo winced as he knelt, tossing the other bodies aside.

"*Cleo.*" Captain Ostin coughed up blood. "*I haven't followed you this far to die in vain. I was wrong about you...you know, in the beginning.*"

"Captain, I'm here. We'll get you some help," Cleo urged as he looked around, waving his arm to catch the attention of anyone nearby.

"*No...no. Just end it for me. Like a warrior deserves. And have my body burned,*" Captain Ostin struggled to utter as he lifted his finger to point at Cleo's sword.

Cleo stood above him, his face stern and his eyes smudged by blood. "The trust of your shield I will keep," he told his dying captain.

Ostin closed his eyes and formed his right hand into a fist. He placed it at his heart, rendering his final salute. "*May the rays of the Benevolent Sun shine on you forever, Cleo.*"

Cleo pointed the tip of his father's shortsword down to the ground. With both hands grasping the handle, he plunged the blade through Captain Ostin's heart-covered fist. Blood spewed out of his mouth as his sword crunched through his captain's bones. Cleo kneeled to his side and whispered, "*I've come to darken that sun, you fanatical fool.*"

Wiping the blood off once more, Cleo spun around, looking for his other captains. What was left of his brigade had formed into groupings at the fore. A patchwork of bronze shields was combining again, readying for Cayen's second wave of attack. Long and loud yells came from the direction of Sazara's wall as the rest of Cayen's guardsmen began their orderly march forward. In the air, the rook riders who survived had taken to the sky. Cleo gulped, knowing he needed to be strong in order to prevail.

To trust.

Just as his guardsmen looked lost and void of any resolution, the iron-clad doors of Sazara's western gate lifted to open. From behind Cayen's marching men was a charging brigade waving the rose-pommeled sword and swan-winged flags of New Scipyria. It was Cleo's East Brigade, with thousands of warhorses at the fore, galloping through the open gate. Cleo could barely make out the brawny man at their lead. "*KLADDEN!*" he yelled aloud in elation.

Vanna and the vidents did it! Thank you.

The West Brigade raised their swords and spears into the air, cheering for their companion guardsmen to charge forward. Cleo smiled from ear to ear. His tactics had finally come to fruition. He turned back to glee at the Black Baron, who had once claimed them to be unnecessary. Cleo joined his guardsmen by raising his sword to the sky, pointing its tip to pierce the sun that hung above Sazara. "*CHARGE!*"

The West Brigade stormed forward, brimming with a revived confidence. Kladden's cavalry had split from behind each side of Cayen's formation while his spearmen and swordsmen pressed ahead, trapping the enemy between Cleo's two brigades. The momentum of war had finally shifted in their favor. Cleo ran fast with his guardsmen as they charged toward the men in bronze, who stood stagnant, unsure of which direction the fight would come from first. Flames began to burst from within the disordered grouping of Cayen's guardsmen. Cleo scanned for the source and saw it come from horseback, frantically rearing in a spooked panic. In rings, the crimson flames spun out high and low like a whip in the hands of a frightened bull.

Some of Cayen's guardsmen tried to flee from their entrapment, running in all directions to disperse and escape the untamed blaze. Many had caught fire and were screaming aloud in burning pain. Cleo ordered his guardsmen to lower their shields and close in. One by one, the flaming bodies that tried to escape were sliced by sword and spear. Those who weaseled through were cut down by Cleo's cavalry, which rode in circles to surround them.

But as time passed, the uncontrollable blaze of whipping flames grew from the center of their entrapment. Most of Cayen's men had no choice but to run from the fire, scattering in every direction, trying to break through their encircling wall of shields. Waving his hands, Cleo ordered Kladden's brigade to move in faster. On horseback, their cavalry rode straight to the center, heading for the flame's source.

Cleo's eyes followed the root of the fire as it sprang away, fleeing in the opposite direction of Kladden's oncoming cavalry, breaking through his encirclement of shields. Galloping to the east, Cayen fled on horseback, racing out in front of the few captains in gold cloaks who trailed him from behind.

They're headed for the central gate, Cleo realized. He hurried to find a steed of his own, making a guardsman from his cavalry render a horse. Once mounted, he scrambled after Cayen and the tall-flailing flames, motioning for anyone he recognized to do the same. They rode fast to the east, kicking up bloodied dirt as Cleo forced the horse he rode to gallop faster. Across the way and closer to the wall, Cleo saw a few familiar faces doing the same. Kladden and Commandant Jove led their troops of warhorses to chase after Cayen, at an angle along the wall that was better than his own to cut them off.

Come on, Cleo urged the horse to gallop faster. The whips of fire continued to flare ahead, licking some of those who chased as they raced across the open field of red dirt. Cleo watched as Kladden's horse took the lead, galloping closer and closer until he was just able to sling his sword into the hind leg of Cayen's horse.

The injured horse collapsed under itself, launching Cayen into the air. He landed harshly on the ground, pillowing the area into a cloud of red-tinted smoke. Kladden's troop of horses turned to circle back around after passing ahead. The fire that once raged high in the air had subsided to short spurts of scorching flames from the Sunspear, which had tumbled to the ground steps away from Cayen's reach. Cleo led his guardsmen to join Kladden's and Jove's as they surrounded Cayen and the lingering cloud of smoke.

"*Look at what I've brought you,*" Kladden shouted with a maniacal laugh. The guardsmen who followed Kladden now held Cayen's captains at sword point.

"*Kladden!*" Cleo shouted back with excitement as he rode beside him. "I've never been happier to see you!"

"I can see why—you look like death."

"One of us had to be the bait. Maybe I should have sent you ahead instead," Cleo said with a haughty grin as they jumped down from their horses and gave each other a welcoming hug. Cleo walked slowly toward Cayen, who was still lying on the ground, slowly twisting to face him. Between them, but closer to Cayen, was the Sunspear tipped by gold-azilian.

Cleo paused as their eyes met. "Don't do it, Cayen."

"*You...order me?*" Cayen coughed aloud as he struggled to stand up. From his right elbow to his hand, Cayen's arm had been burned to a charred crisp. Dirt was smeared across his pale face, and soot colored his once-curly, orange hair black. Cayen was thinner than Cleo had ever seen him before, unrecognizable to the boy he once knew. "Come to lay ruin to your own city, have you now, Cleo?"

"You burned my city to the ground," Cleo responded with anger.

But Cayen only smirked.

Hatred poured out of Cleo's heart. But as he became consumed with rage, Vident Lement's face was all he could see. And in his mind, he could still hear his soothing voice, calming him to choose the path of peace. "Out of respect for your sister, I'd be willing to show you mercy," Cleo said, staring into Cayen's shifting blue eyes. "Mercy, your murderous father never showed mine. Your demise was his doing, not your own. Lay down now like the dog you are, and I'll let you live out your days far away from New Scipyria." But Cayen's eyes continued to circle frantically until they became fixated on the Sunspear, which was still sizzling with sparks between them. *He's too far away,* Cleo thought in desperation. "You're no warrior, Cayen. And you have nothing left to fight for. All your men are now either dead or captured. The city will be mine."

"*New Scipyria*? Sazara will never be yours—you fool," he snarled back. "So long as the Benevolent Sun shines on Sacrim, it shines on the temple and my family."

Kladden walked slowly up to Cleo's side. "It's a disgrace you ever called yourself a general, you scum. You should have just stayed hidden in the temple like the rest of your cowardly family, using the Benevolent Sun as your shield. And after I'm done with this city, none of you will ever see its light again. I'll make *damn* sure of it."

Shit. Cleo knew that Kladden's words would only make things worse. *Damned fanatics.*

"No. Even in the darkest of nights, the Benevolent Sun will always rise again to light the way for our family," Cayen said, laughing with a desperate, hysterical rage.

"Then we'll settle this like men—like true warriors of old Scipyria," Cleo told Cayen. "Save whatever dignity you have left. Duel me, right here, right now, under the light of your sun to see."

But just as Cleo had finished speaking his last word, Cayen lunged for the Sunspear. With his left hand, he grabbed it and charged in their direction. Cleo crouched and tried to shield his eyes from the intense light that was now emanating in front of him. As Cayen and the Sunspear grew in brightness, so too surged their heat, coating his skin in burning waves. The blinding figure soon engulfed Cleo's entire vision, forcing him to sidestep out of the way. As soon as he saw and felt its source begin to pass in front of him, Cleo swept his blade low, swinging it at the moving light.

The heat and light soon dissipated behind him. Cayen stumbled a bit before collapsing to the ground. "That's for my father, you spineless snake."

"It's over," Kladden stated aloud, waving at the others to stop shielding their eyes.

Cleo turned and saw Cayen's thin, blackened body lying flat on the ground, being consumed by embers. He walked over to him and reached down, grasping the long and thin Sunspear from the curl of Cayen's crisped black hand.

Finally. It's mine.

A flooding sense of renewed life flowed throughout his body with each of the Sunspear's heavy pulses. The warmth and light of fire it once radiated were now coddled inside his chest and spinning in all directions, like a storm cloud filled with rolling heat, bursting at his own silver lining to be unleashed. The Sunspear's pulses of power began to match the beating of his heart, flowing back and forth from his firmly clenched grip.

Thrusting its tip into the air, Cleo became the lion, king of war. Its rays of light spilled out of him like a mane of power, and its warmth became his own roar of dominion. With the Sunspear firmly in hand, Cleo turned to face Sazara's wall and proclaimed aloud, *"This is far from over."*

CHAPTER 42

SEA

"It's flying!" Ruth shouted from the quarterdeck's port-side railing.

At the very top of the *Freebird*'s main mast was the flag the ships of the free fleet had all raised just three days prior, the morning they had departed from Cubby Cove. Its navy-blue color rippled with the growing wind, allowing Dane to finally see the snow pelican with its wings spread wide, stitched in white at the center of the flag. Crushed under its short and stubby feet was the outstretched length of a headless silver sea serpent. The pelican's orange beak was lofted open, facing west, and had the serpent's severed head clenched between it, swallowing it as if it had been tossed into the air.

"*It's beautiful,*" Dane said after moving to join Ruth along the railing. What he really wanted to say was that she was beautiful. Ruth's round eyes, the curve of her thin lips, and the way her hair dangled in threads to each side of her face had made him fall for her more and more over the past three days, each and every time he looked her way. In the short time since he'd kissed her in his quarters, the night before the fleet got underway, Dane knew Ruth was the woman he wanted. He adored the way she cared and how her heart was always overflowing with the most genuine feelings of love, shown through her acts of compassion. Ruth had grown to fill a missing void Dane hadn't known was there.

But as he had expected, Ruth set strict boundaries and stipulations for the two of them. On the deck and below, they were to remain as friends, just as they had been, with no conversation about intimacy or displays of affection allowed. Dane agreed and went along with her rules—as he was the captain, after all, and needed to set a proper example for the rest of the fleet. But it was the nights they spent alone, together, in the privacy of his captain's quarters, that he looked forward to the most. Ruth still had her boundaries on what he could do—or, more so, couldn't do. But even then, Dane still tended to melt like the first shine of spring on winter's ice each night she curled up beside him to fall asleep.

"You can see the coast," Ruth said to him. Dane followed her glance off in the distance and saw the roughest outline of the Regent's rigid shore.

"I just hope the other ships can keep up with us in this wind." He moved to the opposite railing on the starboard side to check the formation of his fleet. Four groupings of three ships were spread wide, with the *Freebird, Bessie, Rithron,* and *Baroness* taking the lead of each. Dane moved again to look aft at his own group and saw Caji's and Marreck's single-masted ships struggling to keep up with the *Freebird's* speed.

"Captain, should we prepare to turn west?" Marlow asked from the navigation desk. "We're coming up on the final easternmost stretch."

Dane moved to check his charts, then shouted down below to the main deck, "Galen, pull in the forward sail and prepare the tack to port." At the helm, a mate younger than himself named Wilkin took to Dane's command to turn the ship over. With the easterly winds now at their backs, he gave the command up to the crow's nest to signal for the rest of the fleet to turn. The *Freebird* spun wide around the revolving coast first, setting the way for the rest of the fleet to follow.

"*What is that?*" Ruth asked, her voice pitching with concern.

"Winter storms of the North Sea, I suppose," Dane replied, trying to appear calm after seeing the dark clouds far off in the distance. Internally, however, his mind flashed with images of their passage back to Cubby Cove—of the sea's power and the devastation it had almost caused the fleet and his mates. But they had sailed through it once before, against the wind, and managed to escape. So, Dane stood firm and dug his boots into the planks of the deck. "*STOW FOR SEA...STRIKE IT ALL BELOW! THIS MAY GET ROUGH,*" he commanded down to the crew on watch.

"No, Dane—*that,*" Ruth said, pointing straight at the center of the storm, just off the port bow.

"I don't see anything." He hurried down to the main deck's railing to get a closer look. Most of the mates were scrambling to clear their loose lines and heave at the rigging of the masts on Galen's command. Others carried loose buckets and chests toward the stairs to be stowed in the hold below. Ruth followed closely behind Dane, grasping the bulwark as the waves began to chop and curl the faster the *Freebird* turned west with the wind.

"*Just there*—under the storm," she stuttered, pointing the same way again.

Dane pulled out his spyglass to get a better view. "*A ship?*" he questioned under his breath. "It sort of looks like the *Widow*…again? What are *you* doing this far east?"

"Dane, I don't think this is good," Ruth mumbled. "Something isn't right."

"No. No, it isn't." He checked the tail end of the free fleet's formation to see Jalek and the farthest grouping of three ships still struggling to make their rounding turn west.

"*Captain*," his deck chief, Galen, shouted through the wind. "*That storm is moving at us.*"

"I see it."

"*At us*, sir. As in, against the throw of our wind."

Shit. That definitely isn't right, Dane thought but couldn't bring himself to say. The last thing he wanted was to frighten the mates and lose their confidence. And so, he kept his face stern and strong, just like Captain Noreas would have. "*ALL MEN, AT YOUR STATIONS! EVERYONE, TO YOUR QUARTERS!*" To the helm, he went, moving past the mates who now ran from mast to mast, readying for whatever orders he was about to give. "*LANTERNS, SIGNAL ONE BY ONE. PREPARE US TO LEAD,*" he ordered up to the crow's nest, then back down below. *I need to make us thin.*

With the wind still at their backs, the *Freebird* and its grouping of galleons hurled as they surfed the waves, picking up speed to increase the distance between them and the others in formation. Dane whipped his spyglass back up to his eye once they were close to breaching the edge of the storm. Bow forward, he saw the *Widow* with its course set straight at them, half-hidden by the veil of downpouring rain that covered its sails. The steadier he held his spyglass, the clearer he could see that same man hanging from its main mast.

Maris… "Ruth, come take a look," Dane shouted across the quarterdeck.

When she reached his side, Ruth took the spyglass and veered her view out across the rolling sea. The longer she held it, the larger the waves grew to punch their way onto the *Freebird*'s deck. "Dane, you need to see this."

"What is it?" He yanked the spyglass from her reach and looked back out across the gloomy sea at the *Widow*. Dane's narrow chin dropped from the clench of his cheeks. He couldn't believe what his eyes were seeing. "That isn't Maris hanging—*it's Cowen*," he stuttered, gasping in disbelief. *Maris must have taken the Widow from him. But how? How could I be such a fool,* he asked himself, his heart thumping with each pang of regret. *He must have seen us leave Nordheim and then followed us east. The Widow's been waiting for us...*

"No—*Dane*—that's not it. Look behind it—there are more ships—*so many more,*" Ruth stumbled over her words, her jaw hanging open.

Dane looked out again, past the rain falling from the dark clouds that smeared the smoldering sky. "And Maris has brought the King's Navy with him." His heart skipped faster than his mind could think. Two massive ships trailed on each side of the *Widow*, accompanied by nearly thirty war galleys treading straight at them. All of them moved in a wide line, their oars slapping in unison through the rough sea to break through the veil of falling rain.

"*Captain,*" Marlow shouted from the starboard side. "The others are still lagging behind!"

Dane hurried his way to the *Freebird*'s starboard railing and saw the eight single-masted ships of his fleet struggling to stabilize themselves with the clashing wind and waves. Dane knew he needed a solution, and he needed to find it quickly. "We're going to have to turn north. The easterly wind at our backs will clash with this storm... Riding along that fringe is our only chance of being faster than they are—*our only chance to escape.* We need to lead the rest in line," Dane thought aloud, still looking at Marlow. He quickly moved to the railing overlooking the main deck. "*GALEN, STARBOARD TACK...BRING THE FORWARD AND AFT SAILS TO FULL BEAM. WILKIN, BRING US OVER AT MY SIGNAL!*"

"What's going on?" Rory questioned, rushing up from below alongside Rouge.

"Not now. I don't have a moment to waste," Dane replied, his voice dripping with scorn.

"It's them—" Ruth could barely get out, pointing to the fleet of ships from the King's Navy, which were moving closer and closer to them with each passing moment.

"*Bowmen, at the ballista! I want every bolt on deck and at the ready!*" Dane commanded as the rain began to fall like rocks hurled from an angry sky.

"What are they doing here?" Rouge asked, joining their huddle near the helm.

"Gather all your sentinels and prepare them for battle. I'll try to get a signal to the others to do the same," Dane ordered. Rouge nodded, then scurried away. Rory looked caught with a look of uneasiness and followed Dane to the aft mast. "*Lanterns, break your flashes.*"

Dane stood tall, trying to maintain whatever lookout he could, scanning for any change in the sea or the navy's course. Rory, however, hadn't wandered far from his hip, following him around the quarterdeck until Dane finally looked his way. "That one there, you don't think that's King Mordin's ship, do you?" Rory asked him.

"*Wilkin, now!*" Just as Dane issued the command, the *Freebird* turned hard to alter its course and head north. The clashing wind from the east and west, which had once rippled their sails, now smoothed their course, increasing the speed of the *Freebird* to lead the line for the other vessels of the fleet. Dane moved to the starboard railing and saw Caji's and Marreck's ships turning to follow the *Freebird*'s path. *I just hope the others can still see us.*

"Dane, you might want to listen to Rory," Ruth said, yanking on the long sleeve of his coat.

"What is it?"

"That ship—*there*—it doesn't have any oars."

Dane whipped out his spyglass again and moved to the *Freebird*'s opposite side. The *Widow* and the two larger vessels that trailed it had also turned north, tracking with the *Freebird*'s change in course. The closer he looked, the more he realized that Ruth and Rory were right. The largest of the three approaching ships had a smooth-sided hull, bare of any oars. It tore through the breaking waves with ease and began to lead the other two by a growing gap of sea. Far behind it was the *Widow*, with its sails full in the heavy wind. The third ship at the rear appeared to be the same size as the King's, but seemed to struggle to keep up, even with its three decks of oars.

That must be the King's flagship with the Seatrident, Dane knew, though his eyes trembled in disbelief. King Mordin the Fourth—Myrph himself—had come this far east in the North Sea to lay waste to him and his free fleet. And with him was the largest ship Dane had ever seen, one that even rivaled the plans Niels had shared with him back on Nordheim.

At that moment, Dane felt his power as a captain fade. An emergence of doubt prickled across the cold of his face, dousing it like the rain to cloak his mind with dismay. He had led his mates to their deaths—to sink to the bottom of the ocean and be swallowed whole by the real serpent of the sea.

And they trusted me.

"*Sir, what should we do?*" Marlow screamed aloud in a panic.

But Dane didn't have an answer. His fleet was in no way ready or prepared to face King Mordin and his fleet of war galleys. Dane knew he was beaten. The King of Marredom had come to destroy his fleet before Dane and his mates ever had the chance of growing large enough to compete with him on the seas. Every thought Dane had curdled his mind with despair. He glanced over at Ruth, who was also wordless. Her eyes whispered the softest hint of sorrow. She lowered her head and began to utter words he couldn't hear but assumed were prayers.

Without an answer and desperate for any sign of hope or help, Dane followed her and did the same. He closed his eyes and gripped Captain Noreas's necklace, trying to gather any strength or courage that he could. *May the Divine One help us…give me the strength to defend those who trusted me,* he thought, but didn't have a clue how or what else to pray. *Think, Dane, think… What would Captain Noreas do?*

"*The distance,*" he spoke aloud, yanking his eyes back open and turning toward the aft mast. "That storm seems to follow wherever he goes. As long as we can continue to sail at the edge of its wind, we can keep our distance from the King. That's our only chance to pick the rest of them apart."

"But, sir, the *Widow* has it in their favor, too. And the changes are erratic," Marlow pleaded from beside the helm.

He's right. We need the Widow out of the fight if we want to keep our advantage. "Then we'll have to be as erratic as it is," Dane replied, marching across the quarterdeck. "Ruth, head inside. This might get ugly. Rory, bring every sentinel up to the main deck. We need to be prepared for anything." Ruth swallowed a large gulp of wet air and nodded, then headed inside the aftcastle. "Galen, prepare the sails for a hard tack… Wilkin, turn us back around. *We're going to sink the Widow.*"

The bow of the *Freebird* dipped and dodged with the whirling wind and roiling of the sea, crossing its nose past the path of the King's flagship, which had raced far ahead of the other two. When the *Freebird*'s hull turned in line with the *Widow*'s own, Dane gave the command to tighten the wheel and keep their course. He pulled out his spyglass once more and scanned the bruised horizon that blended the sky and the sea. Far to his left were the King's war galleys that trailed behind, still rowing in their wide formation, bearing east. Behind him were the rest of his own ships, struggling to keep up with his turns as they headed northwest on a course set for collision.

What have I gotten us into? Dane's heart clouded his mind again with remorse, smothering any rational thought.

"*CAPTAIN! FLAME AHEAD!*" he heard one of the mates scream from the main deck. Dane looked out past his bow, under the sails, and saw a flame ignite on the *Widow*'s forward ballista. Before he could even shout a command, the flame had been flung high into the downpouring sky, soaring straight for them.

Dane's eyes gaped open, and his breathing stopped. He ran down to the main deck, squeezing his way past the sentinels in their chainmail and colorful tabards, who clamored up from below to join them in the rain and cold. All the way forward, he peered over the *Freebird*'s bowsprit. The wind from the storm had been enough to break the bolt's speed, slowing its arc through the air. He watched with nervous anticipation as it plunged into the sea, sizzling as it extinguished its flame just three ships' distance from where they sailed.

"*Let the erratic winds be in our favor,*" he whispered to himself, looking up to the sky as if to thank Ruth's Divine One for watching over them. Dane turned toward Galen, who took aim with the ballista behind him, then turned back toward the sea to check the distance once more. After a few moments of tense silence, he shouted: "*RELEASE!*"

The string of the ballista slammed against its arms as the *Freebird*'s flameless bolt was sent into the air. The bolt moved swiftly over the sea, closing the distance between the two ships until it struck the underdeck of the *Widow*'s forward hull. Behind Dane, the mates and sentinels all released gasps, then cheered over their successful strike. "*READY AGAIN,*" Galen yelled louder than Dane had ever heard him before, his hands gripped tight to the ballista's releasing lever.

Dane waited and waited, watching to see how the *Widow* might react. Straight ahead, its bow began to dip with the troughs of the waves, bobbing in and out of the water. The hit had slowed the ship's motion just enough so it couldn't turn and use its aft ballista. "*RELEASE!*" Dane commanded again. Cheers from behind him rang out once more as the second bolt soared through the air and struck the deck just under the *Widow*'s main mast. "Maris, *you bastard*," Dane mumbled with a smirk.

"*CAPTAIN!*" an unfamiliar voice shouted. Dane looked back across the main deck and saw Rouge standing near the port railing, gripping its post and pointing over the side. The massive galley with three decks of oars was closing in fast, at half the *Widow*'s distance, readying itself to ram right into the bow of their port-side hull.

Without any words to speak, Dane ran as fast as he could back across the crowded main deck, shuffling between the men who were scattering away from the railing and under the snapped lines that were squirming like snakes below the cross-yards. As soon as he braced the top stair to the *Freebird*'s quarterdeck, he turned and saw it.

On the side of the ship's hull was a white word written in norkatis that read: *Klitan*.

Captain Noreas's old ship, Dane realized.

"*CAPTAIN, STARBOARD SIDE!*" Marlow shouted with his arms still struggling to hug the aft mast. Panicked, Dane turned and looked to his right. Headed straight for the bow at their starboard broadside was the King's own oarless flagship, with its hull marked in white norkatis lettering that read: *Lazash*.

"We're about to be rammed from both sides...*and there's nothing I can do*," Dane admitted to himself in defeat.

I've failed. He looked up to the sky one last time and felt the rain pounding against his cold face. *Ruth, I'm sorry I brought you along. Captain Noreas, I'm sorry I couldn't take care of your fleet. To the mates who trusted me, to the people of Marredom that I couldn't save, and to my family that I couldn't help...I'm sorry.*

Dane tilted his chin back down and looked forward. He watched in moments of slowed silence as both massive ships barreled their bow rams straight into each side of the *Freebird*'s forward hull. In a sudden halt, the planks below his feet shook. The forwardmost mast snapped in half, the bowsprit sculpture shredded itself from the rest of the ship, and their only ballista fell into the sea. Sounds of splintered shouts and snapping planks of wood broke the air as Dane was thrust forward. His body lunged up and over the quarterdeck's forward railing. Cheek first, he slammed hard onto the wet planks of the main deck. His sight blurred, and his awareness began to fade in and out. All he could see were the black boots of the sentinels and mates storming forward.

Get up…I need to get back up.

Dane groaned in painful spurts to pick his body up off the deck. His eyes blinked with harsh snaps to break whatever daze had befallen him. Wobbling with the waves, Dane could barely see the two ships flooding his own with men who wore silver caps and black coats.

Bastards…

Steel clattered far forward of the main mast, which soon became drowned out by shouts of death and the rumblings of war. Dane squirmed toward the side staircase and used its railing to lift his broken body back up. Spouts of water spinning like the whirls of a whip thrashed near the *Lazash*'s bow. Sentinels and mates alike rushed toward it only to have their limbs severed and sliced into pieces or their entire bodies flung over the side. Dane could feel the power of the sea being swung up from the waves below as the three-pronged tip of the Seatrident moved its fading colors of silver-azilian in twirling swirls of motion. Dane scanned to his left and saw officers and marines jump from the *Klitan*'s bow down onto his own deck.

I need to move, he thought, scraping aside whatever pain lingered to stifle his numb body. The rain continued to pound his face. Dane reached for the saber at his waist and drew it, rushing forward with whatever courage he could muster to join his mates in battle. Body after body, draped in their colorful tabards and chainmail, or those in gray and black overcoats, littered the main deck, pooling it with puddles of darkening blood.

Marines and officers with their black coats and silver helmets filtered toward him, swinging their sabers to fight the mates and sentinels of the *Freebird*. Dane joined in on the action, grunting in pain as he swung his saber at a younger marine, one who looked possessed by the drawing of bloodshed. The marine bobbed and weaved, backing away from each of Dane's blows, until his foot clapped against a dead body lying flat on the deck. Taking advantage of the opening, Dane pierced the curve of his blade straight through the young marine's chest, then yanked it back out to swipe cleanly at his neck. Blood gushed like a fountain onto the body the young marine had tripped over.

Dane glanced down and saw that it was Galen lying there, pale, his white garment soaked by a sea of red. "*Galen,*" Dane pleaded, reaching down to try to shake him back to life. "*I'm sorry.*"

"*Dane—get your head in the fight!*" a voice shouted from the port side. He looked over and saw Rory and Rouge fighting side by side with six marines and officers, gliding in smooth pivots as they pierced the attackers with their longswords. Dane scampered through the crowded deck to get closer to them, fending off marines and their wild swings, helping his mates and the sentinels wherever he could.

"*Stay away from that side,*" Rouge struggled to get out, nudging her chin over to the starboard side, where the *Lazash* had collided. King Mordin was still at its bow, twirling the Seatrident in the air with both hands gripped halfway up its thin handle. With it, he tugged at the sea to pull up swashes of thin-spinning, sharp waves, slicing it at a group of mates who had dared to charge his way. *We're losing so many men,* Dane realized in despair.

While still facing toward the King, Dane saw a ship with a single set of sails hurtling through the sea beside the *Freebird's* starboard railing. *Marreck,* he realized—one of his own. The snubby bow of the galleon rammed straight into the open broadside of the *Lazash*. From the main deck of Marreck's ship, lines were being cast onto the *Lazash's* railings to hold the two together.

"*Dane, look out!*" Rory shouted from his left, slicing through the waist of a marine who had charged to attack him. Dane snapped his focus back to his own fight, where Rory swept left and right with the best footwork he'd ever seen, taking on three marines at a time.

Dane joined Rouge to battle with two marines who held her up as a gust of wind blew right past his ear. He looked to his left and saw the other ship from his formation quickly sailing past his port railing to strike its bow into the *Klitan's* exposed hull. "*Caji!*" Dane shouted with a relieved grin, watching as the mates and sentinels on board threw their lines over to join the fight.

The marines began to scatter off the *Freebird's* main deck, obeying their officers' commands to fall back and defend their war galleys. Rouge and Dane pressed forward, joining Rory to swipe away at anyone who dared to stay and fight. In the break of action, Dane swept back to the railing to check on the rest of his fleet. But all he could make out was the foggy veil of rainfall. Back toward the quarterdeck, he checked again only to find it littered with piles of motionless bodies as well as those with gashes, or even missing limbs, still squirming and screaming. Next to the staircase, Dane saw Piney, of all people, rushing up to him from the stairs that led below, skipping across whatever open planks he could, his saber in hand.

"Dane...*you're alive*," he said with an exasperated gasp of relief.

"Waiting for an opening, were you, Piney? I thought you told Captain Noreas you were good with a saber," Dane replied with a smirk, still trying to catch his breath.

"The *best* fighter is always the *last* fighter."

"Well, *this fight* isn't over yet," Dane replied more solemnly than Piney had expected. He looked down at the mates who were no longer standing with them.

"I told you renaming this ship was shit luck," Piney said.

"*Maybe you were right, Piney.*"

"Dane—*the King*," Rory shouted to get his attention.

Dane whipped his shoulders forward and saw the King of Marredom break across the bow of the *Lazash* to set foot on the fractured deck of the *Freebird*. For the first time in his life, Dane saw the face of his King. He was older and taller than Dane had expected, with stringy white hair and pale, wrinkled skin that sagged in pockets below his eyes. His mouth withered into a narrow pout, and his broad back hunched to support the seams of white fur striping his black overcoat. Atop his head sat a silver crown with several curling points that matched the Seatrident's hooked-prong shape.

Dane moved his gaze over to the *Lazash* and Marreck's clashed vessel to find it void of any moving life. "*You bastard...*" he uttered under his breath.

"*Be smart*," Rory shouted to him. But before Dane could even move, mates from the *Klitan's* bow jumped onto the *Freebird's* deck and ran straight at the King. Some he recognized as mates from Caji's ship, while others fought forward with shackles and chains still draped around their wrists and ankles. Torrents of water from the restless sea surged onto the deck where King Mordin stood. With every movement he made with the Seatrident, lashes of swirling sea struck his attackers down, slicing with a force of power Dane had never witnessed before. One by one, they were cast aside or severed at their limbs before they could ever get close enough to deliver a blow of their own.

Into the storming swell flew Rory, followed closely by Rouge, each moving with sliding steps to hurl themselves away from the King's harrowing attacks. *Shit,* Dane thought as he flung himself forward to follow after them. To his surprise, Piney had followed his lead as well, running at a slower pace. Across the *Freebird*'s main deck, Dane ran past the main mast to see Rory swerving around and under the King's side-winding whips of water. "*He's smooth,*" Dane stated between pants.

As they ran closer, Dane spotted an opening in the King's motion. Rory lifted his longsword over his head and leaped into the air, only to have his legs pulled out from under him. A spout of water had risen from the deck to coil his body like a snake, slinging him down hard against the planks. Rouge moved in to do the same, only to have a wave from the sea strike her chest, hurling her wailing body overboard.

At that moment, Dane's and the King's eyes met. King Mordin whipped the Seatrident to the side once more, then swung it in an arc from one shoulder to the other. A thin-swirling lash of water quickly swept across the entirety of the deck. Dane slid his body flat to the wood as fast as he could, ducking under the water's sharp slash. But when he turned around, Dane saw Piney's body sliced in half. His entrails hung loosely from his stomach, and his legs were steps away, sprawled flat to the deck.

"*NOOOOOOOOO...PINEY, NOOOOOO!*" Dane cried aloud in pain. He looked up and felt his face light into a flame, fanned by pure anger. "*You bastard!*" Dane screamed, charging forward only to see King Mordin let out a mocking laugh. Dane raised his saber to the sky; his boots pounding across the bloodied deck.

"*You fool,*" King Mordin scoffed. He grabbed the Seatrident with both of his hands and slammed the bottom of its staff hard onto the deck. Over each of his shoulders came a rippling torrent of sea, spinning like waterspouts to slam right into Dane's lurching body.

Dane was flung backward into the air. His chest pounded with pain, and his face became smothered by needles of cold water as he struggled to find air. Dane's back landed harshly against the main mast as if he were the dull side of an axe swung hard against the stiffest tree. His eyes began to close, and his bones felt broken from limb to limb.

Get up...get up, he thought. But his body wouldn't move. With his eyes still shut, he turned around to grasp the thick round of lumber he was pressed against. Like the pillar from Norkatis Street, he hugged it tightly. He pressed his cheek flush against the wet wood, just as he had when he was sentenced and stricken with the King's lashes. That pain, like this one now, squeezed the last drops of blood from his pounding heart. But in the blackness, Dane saw Ruth's gentle face, smiling to block out the nightmare of death that surrounded him. Her voice came over him softly, like a feather dropped from a snow pelican, saying, "*Dane…we need you. I need you. I love you.*"

Dane opened his eyes and saw Ruth's image there beside him, placing her hands under his arms to help him stand back up. "This is my ship— *my fleet!*" Dane bellowed.

Walking slowly toward him was King Mordin, gurgling with laughter at all the bloodshed he had caused. "You dare to war against me—against the *sea*. You are nothing. Not a man, not a captain, and certainly not a king."

Be strong, Dane thought, before turning back to where Ruth stood. But that place beside the main mast was now empty. Her image had vanished, becoming just as invisible as that spirit of the Divine One she so often spoke of. *Give me strength,* he thought, trying to piece both of their ghosts together. *For Piney.*

Dane lifted his chin to face the King of Marredom, limping to leave the pillar and retrieve his saber from the deck. Through the dwindling battle, he trudged. But just as he looked up, another harsh whip of water from the sea flung his body back again. Dane yelled out in pain as the scars on his back struck the mast's pillar once more. His knees buckled, and his eyes fluttered open and closed.

"War isn't for the weak, boy. You cause chaos on my seas, and it becomes my duty to deliver order," King Mordin told him. Dane looked up and saw the withered face of his King standing before him. His eyes were as blue as his own, but the black within had a depth that hid the worst haunting of desires.

"*You're the weak one…*" Dane struggled to utter. "Only a weak man would hurt the innocent." Just as the words had left his mouth, the three silver-azilian prongs of the Seatrident lowered so the middle tip was pointed right at Dane's forehead.

"Only the weak claim innocence."

"You are *no* king," Dane struggled to say. "You're a *little* man."

"And you are *no* captain," King Mordin told him, bellowing a deranged laugh. "The sea is *mine.*"

This is it, he thought in despair. *I'm sorry.*

But just then, when Dane thought that all hope was lost, the curved tip of a saber pierced through the center of the King's chest. The black depths of the King's eyes shuddered; the white around them widened as he looked down in disbelief. In front of Dane, the pronged tips of the crown now pointed. Blood began to pool between the white fur and the black leather of his long overcoat. When the saber was pulled out, blood squirted out from the gash, spraying the *Freebird's* main deck. More thrusts of the saber came from behind the King, slicing through his chest with plunges of permanent anger.

King Mordin wobbled his broad shoulders up and down, struggling in silent pain to turn himself around. The hand that had once held the Seatrident moved to cover the gaping holes in his chest. The King's legs collapsed, and his dying body fell to the deck. Dane looked up and saw an oarsman in rags standing directly behind him. His arms and legs were shackled, and his face was narrow, peppered with thick, wild gray hair. Dane looked into his eyes and saw a familiar glimmer.

"*Father?*" he mumbled to ask. Dane's first thought was that the person in front of him was just another ghostly image. He blinked his eyes several times, but the person never vanished. "It can't really be you, *can it?*"

"I believe this is yours, *Captain.*" His father, dressed in the rags of an oarsman, picked the Seatrident up from the deck and held it out, motioning for Dane to take it. But instead of reaching for it, Dane stood up and wrapped his arms tightly around his father's shoulders. As Dane embraced him with the strongest grip of love, they both dropped to their knees, bruised with warm blood and cold tears. "It's me, *Dane*—it's really me, Domus. Your father. *I'm sorry, my son,*" he told him, refusing to let go. "*I'm sorry I ever left you.*"

"I can't believe it's you. *You saved me.*"

"I've finally been freed from the *Klitan,* son. *You* saved *me,* Dane. *Thank you.*"

CHAPTER 43

SKY

B urnt-orange flags waving the white wings of a swan and a sword grown from the pommel of a blood rose advanced toward the wall that Vanna stood upon. Below her feet was the western gate, which she had helped open after seeing Cleo's flanking brigade wave that same flag of New Scipyria, marching toward her from within. Between the battlements of the limestone wall, she had witnessed the battle in its entirety. The two warring sides had clashed in a bloodied fight for Sazara, and she had been there, hidden at a height, to witness it all.

When Vanna had first reached the top path, she wasn't sure if Cleo was still alive. Men in bronze and leather, covered in dirt and blood, were being slaughtered in all directions. At first glance, Cleo's mess of a battle looked unwinnable. That was until she and a few other guardsmen fought their way to the top of the wall and opened the iron gate to release the East Brigade, in their thousands, to storm the battle from behind.

To Vanna, it was satisfying to have witnessed Cleo lead his men to victory with the tactics he'd held close to his chest for so long. Her torn heart felt pieced back together after realizing what the message she had delivered to Vident Maedrick instructed, allowing the other half of his brigade's entry through Sazara's eastern gate. And after she had turned back to help him in the west, of her own volition, she now found Cleo, with the Sunspear in hand, readying to march his joint brigade into Sazara.

Despite her lingering pain, Vanna couldn't help but smile. After having been locked away in the holding cell for as long as she had, then flown straight into the gauntlet of death itself, Vanna was happy to be alive and happy to have helped Cleo survive. But her bruised body had taken a beating. She had exhausted all she could give and was left depleted.

It's time, Vanna realized.

With the battle finally over, now was her chance to leave Sazara and find a new home. She needed to tell Cleo her final goodbye before departing to live a life of freedom away from the hurt and pain of war she'd been forced, or even chosen, to live among. *With a smile,* she thought, *from both of us.*

Vanna turned back toward the city. In the far distance, at the bottom of the sloped hill, was the harbor and its twin-pillared lighthouses. Beyond it, the sun's brightest rays shimmered across the Barren Sea. There, Sacrim's capital city stood for Cleo's taking. Vanna heaved a deep breath and took it all in, then turned left once more to look down at the ground, along the bottom footing of the wall. The two fallen rooks lay motionless there, with the Grand Dame's body still crushed beneath. Vanna knew that neither rook was capable of flying again. In the side strap at her waist, she poked around in search of Zell's flute. Vanna pulled it out and played a long, high-pitched note, hoping that Felix would hear its near-silent tune from wherever it might be, flying free.

"Please, *let me join you,*" she whispered to the sky.

Behind her, Vanna noticed the New Scipyrian flags forming into rows adjacent to the wall below. Cleo took to the center of the formation, and a few other guardsmen in gold cloaks filtered in behind him. Facing them were most of his two brigades, excluding those occupied with corralling their new prisoners or piling the dead bodies to be burned. As they all huddled around Cleo, he pronounced aloud: "*Today, we have earned a great victory!*" Cleo waited a long moment for the cheering to wane. "*But our prize still awaits us. We fought to take Sazara, and so we shall!*"

Vanna scanned the thousands of guardsmen who all praised their commander with rampant enthusiasm. Though she couldn't yet see his face, she knew Cleo was proud of himself and the prowess he'd shown to lead them to victory. This was his moment—a victory he had planned for and delivered. And so, again, she smiled.

"*But first, I must remind you all of one thing: Sazara is your home. And as such, the women and children behind this wall shall be treated as you would your own. They must all be given the highest honor of respect.*" Most waited in silence. A few of the men laughed, while others growled at their commander's restraint. Cleo continued, silencing their lingering howls to say, "*Any man caught harming or dishonoring either of them, and thus himself, will face the justice of my sword. Men, focus instead on our true enemy—those of the old order. The magistrates, chambermen, and guardsmen alike. Bring them to me, or bring them to their knees!"* Cleo lifted the Sunspear into the air, orchestrating their chorus of victory cheers once more.

He was made for this, Vanna realized.

The guardsmen's shouts faded as they scattered back into formations under the direction of the captains in gold cloaks. When the flag bearers behind him had finally split, Cleo turned to face the western gate. He looked up and met Vanna's eyes, offering a bloodied smile to mirror her own. With a wave, he motioned for her to come down and meet him.

She walked down the stairs inside the wall, passing by the unconscious bodies of guardsmen she had put to sleep earlier in order to reach the gate's rope-spool winch. Just outside the door that opened to Sazara, Cleo rushed around the wall and clenched her from behind. He gave her a strong hug with one arm, which Vanna only loosely returned.

"You did it!" he said with excitement.

"*You've* done it, Cleo. This victory is yours," she told him. "And now you have this!" Vanna pointed to the tall, gold-azilian Sunspear in his right hand. She could feel its waves of heat brushing against her bruised skin.

"Isn't it nice?" He lifted it with a warm smile, showing it off. "Vanna, you flew so well up there. And you managed to deliver my message to Vident Maedrick! When you left, I wasn't sure what would happen—if you would even do it. If Kladden's brigade hadn't been let in through the eastern gate, then this battle would have ended very differently. Speaking of which," Cleo said, stringing his words together with excitement as he turned and walked toward the open gate.

I need to make this quick, Vanna knew.

Cleo returned with a few of his captains. "Introductions are needed. This is Kladden Sordin. My first commandant and my father's most trusted man."

Your father, Vanna thought, reminding herself of what she'd done.

"Pleasure," the tall, stocky man growled. His harsh face stood stern, shrouded by stubby black hair.

"Vanna…Sapharo," she said, almost forgetting the last name she had chosen. "*Pleasure.*"

"This is Captain Thorp and Captain Jostell," Cleo told her.

Vanna repeated her pleasantries.

Cleo turned to the young boy behind him, the same one who had helped lead the other half of his forces in from the east. To Vanna, the boy and Cleo shared the same broad forehead, sharp cheeks, and deep, green eyes. Only, the boy's hair was shades lighter, and his face was spotted by freckles. "And this is...?" Cleo turned to ask Kladden.

"Claudius," Kladden said. "He was a cagerman and took to leading those who survived the slaughtering at Cignus."

Cleo looked down at the blood-rusted dirt as they shook wrists, and then glanced back up at the tall man with a gleaming smile. "I've known Kladden my whole life. Where Vident Lement taught me peace, Kladden taught me war."

"Hmm, if this day is any evidence, then you've taught him well," Vanna said.

Kladden ruffled Cleo's mop of copper hair with a bursting smile. "I did my best with what I had to work with."

"Shall we?" Cleo asked them, raising his open palm toward Sazara's square.

There was still quite a distance of sloping land between the city's dense cluster of buildings and the wall they stood beside. A few large villas and isolated plots of trees loomed within the open space that spread from one end of the wall to the other. The last time Vanna had traveled through this same field of open dirt, she was being ushered in to witness Clyus and Queen Helera's wedding. And the time before that, it had been at night, and she had still been a Sister. But seeing it now, especially in the light of day, cast a bright shadow of remembrance—one she wanted, in no part, to relive, especially beside Cleo.

"*I can't*," Vanna let out as soon as Kladden started walking with Claudius and the other two captains toward the marching brigade.

"What do you mean, *you can't*?"

"I need to leave, Cleo."

"*Leave?* And go where? You don't look like you could even make it to the closest town. Why would you want to leave?"

"I just need to go home. But there's something I must tell you, Cleo, before I go," she said nervously.

Cleo was still smiling, full of passion and rushing blood. "Why would you want to go back to the Vypores? You could make Sazara your home. This city will be great—*we could make it great.*"

Vanna looked down without answering him.

"*Come on.* Whatever it is, I'm sure it can wait." Cleo grabbed her hand and began to guide her toward his marching men.

Vanna stopped and pulled away. "*No.*"

"What is it, then? What's on your mind?"

But Vanna couldn't bring herself to say it out loud. She couldn't admit to Cleo what she had done. Instead, she just stared at him in eye-watering silence.

Cleo turned away and looked down at the city. "All the work I've done to get to this day, and you played such a big part in it, Vanna. Whatever you went through, being imprisoned here, I'm sorry. I can see how much it hurt and affected you. But you, more than anyone else, deserve to be there beside me when we take the city and celebrate our victory. *You've earned it.*"

Vanna turned back his way, still depleted and silent.

"You left me once before, without any explanation… I can't let that happen again," Cleo said.

He's right. She looked into his green eyes the same way she had that night at the top of Corlis's castle, enraptured by his charm. By them alone, her cold and broken heart grew warm. But Vanna couldn't bring herself to speak the right words. And she knew she couldn't break him again, especially now, at his highest. "*Okay,*" she stuttered reluctantly, too afraid to hurt him.

"We can talk more tonight. But first, come with us to take the city and celebrate!"

Vanna nodded along, against her earlier intention, and followed Cleo down the sloping dirt at the edge of his marching brigades. A few stewards rushed in from behind to provide each of them with a horse. They rode fast to make it to the fore, where Vanna saw a few familiar faces from her time marching west to Corlis. Though one, Vanna noticed, was missing. "Where is Vident Evander?"

"He stopped at Castill on our way in," Cleo turned to her to reply. "Said he didn't want any part in our fighting. I don't blame him."

"Was that the tubby boy in orange?" a hoarse voice from behind them asked. Vanna turned and saw a young man dressed very differently from the others. He had ruffled blond hair and pale skin and wore a long black overcoat and heavy boots. By his tone alone, Vanna grew wary.

"The vident, yes," she corrected him.

"Well, he wouldn't have been of much use anyway."

"The vidents are the reason we are marching into Sazara now. Without them, the East Brigade would never have passed through the eastern gate. Seems of use to me," she spouted back at him.

"Cleo, you've got yourself a sharp one."

"She's right," he turned to him to say. "Vanna, this is the Black Baron. The Black Baron, Vanna."

Vanna rolled her eyes. "What kind of man calls himself the Black Baron? You don't have a real name?"

"Cleo, I take it back. She's not sharp—she's spicy," he replied, laughing her off. "And I do have a name, miss. It's Malzini—Malzini Galobaron."

Galobaron… Where have I heard that before? Vanna questioned.

Cleo turned back to him again. "Malzini, huh? How come you've never told me that before?"

"You never asked. Most used to call me Mal."

"And there I was, thinking of you as a friend," Cleo said.

"Well, that would have been your first mistake," Malzini responded.

"You could have died in that battle out there without any of us knowing your real name—the real you," Cleo told him.

"But I didn't," the pale young man calling himself the Black Baron snarled. "And here I am, still marching down this open shitscape beside you. My name changes nothing."

Vanna looked out at the open field and pondered. "Why is it that those men fought your brigade outside Sazara's wall instead of fighting behind it and using it to their advantage?"

"The Guard doesn't hide," one of Cleo's captains responded.

Cleo grunted in agreement. "The wall is too long to defend in its entirety. And the slope down to the city is a vulnerability. The Guard would have to fight anyone who breaches past it uphill."

"It isn't a vulnerability—that's its purpose," Malzini stated. "Vizar Servil built that wall in four thirty-six to entrap his own people. To the chamber and that Temple of Sciron, the Sazarans themselves are the enemy, not what lurks outside of it."

But as soon as he had finished speaking, Malzini was silenced by Cleo's urge. Kladden had slowed to ride beside them. From his presence alone,

Vanna could tell that Kladden garnered respect from everyone. Even Malzini looked somewhat frightened to be riding beside the bouldering commandant.

"Look familiar?" Kladden asked Cleo. He pointed far out to the right.

"The general's villa," Cleo replied. "Or what's left of it."

Vanna turned and saw the pile of burnt rubble off in the distance. Again, her memory flashed back to that night. *That was the home,* she recalled, as a rush of guilt filled her from head to toe. *Forgiveness,* she thought, turning away and closing her eyes. *I need to forgive myself.*

"I wish he could have been here to see us today," Cleo said. "All of this was because of him. Our fight was his own."

"He would be proud of you, Cleo," Kladden told him. "I'm sure of it."

Vanna rode the rest of the way in silence. At the direction of the captains, Cleo's battalions split themselves with fervor, marching with sword and spear in decks to branch through all of Sazara's streets and side alleys. His urgent commands intensified as they approached the denser areas of the city. The narrow streets grew bare as the guardsmen went door to door in search of Cleo's mother, sister, and all the suspects needed to be held to account.

At Arcus Street, Cleo ordered half of his guardsmen to split east. Faint shouts or cheers from inside the buildings could be heard echoing from every direction. But Vanna couldn't distinguish between the two. She just kept pressing forward behind Cleo, Kladden, Jove, and Malzini until commands rang aloud from farther ahead.

Spearmen, with their shields at the ready, rushed forward to form an interlocking wall in front of Cleo. Vanna peeked past the corner of the last red-granite-bricked building and saw Sazara's square. A few hundred of the Calegris' guardsmen stood in a tight formation in front of the Temple of Sciron. Vanna was ordered to fall back as Cleo pressed his guardsmen toward them from every opening of Arcus Street. With each resonating stomp, their shields and front-facing spears began to close in on the last remaining men who dared to fight for Sacrim's old guard.

One by one, the men who stood boldly to defend the Temple of Sciron's front doors began to fall. Sounds of spears and swords being thrust clashed with every shout of death. Eventually, the battalions' arched wall of shields fully enclosed the last of the Calegris' guardsmen, encircling them in front of the temple's entrance doors. As they dropped their weapons and began to surrender, Cleo's guardsmen scattered throughout the square, herding the men together with those chambermen they had captured from across Sazara, grouping them to kneel and tying their hands and feet.

Vanna swung off her horse, jumping down to walk toward Cleo and his fellow captains, where they stood huddled in front of the temple's entrance doors. "What's going on?"

"We have word that the Calegris have been hiding in here," Kladden replied above the commotion.

"But the temple's doors are locked," Jove added. Off to the side, Malzini's men were working to find objects they could use as a battering ram. The other captains discussed and planned for what might be awaiting them inside.

"You have the Sunspear. Why don't you just burn the doors down?" Vanna asked.

The temple's two red-oak doors were tall, nearly half the size of Sazara's outer wall, and were finely engraved with patterns of the Benevolent Sun's movement across the sky. The embossed sun was the largest in the middle, with its ten rays spreading wide to the reinforced frame.

With a confused look, Kladden replied, "*What?* Are you insane? We can't desecrate the temple."

"No, she's right," Cleo said. "Everyone get back."

"*Cleo*, listen to me," Kladden pleaded, moving to stand in front of him.

"The Temple of Sciron has already been desecrated by those same people hiding within it. Doors can be replaced, and so can they."

Vanna and the rest of the captains backed away as Cleo continued to ignore Kladden's urge, moving to point the tip of the Sunspear at the thin slit between the two doors. A blinding light flashed at its peak, and harsh streams of blue flames thrashed out forcefully in front of them. Vanna turned and shielded her eyes with her hand as swirls of diffracting fire danced out like the wings of a butterfly from both sides of the temple's entrance. Blanketing waves of heat filled the air, warming her bruised skin and forcing her to step back.

When the heat had subsided, Vanna and those around her timidly turned to look. Between the two doors was an opening shaped like the molten eye of an almond snake. Its ember edges, which were wide enough for two or three men to fit through, continued to collapse as broken pieces of wood fell to join the black ash on the ground. Cleo walked straight through the waning smoke. His royal-red cloak waved through the embers before he disappeared into the slit's darkness. Vanna, Malzini, and Cleo's golden-cloaked captains hurried to follow him in.

Fire lanterns hung by black chains encircled the bounds of the giant, domed roof, which was covered in illustrious paintings. Massive columns of gold and sculpted marble flanked each side of the grand entrance aisle. Along the temple's rounded edge, identical columns mirrored to support the roof at each of the ten aisle-way rugs, which radiated like the sun's rays toward the central altar. Gleaming streams of crimson and orange shone against the temple's curved wall, sparkling down from the stained-glass ornament at the temple's peak.

Cleo led them down the center aisle until Vanna could see a single chair atop the raised altar. On it sat Queen Helera with the Skybow. At the bottom of the altar's three steps were six Sisters of the Silo dressed tightly in black, blocking their path. Vanna followed closely behind Cleo and his captains as they stopped a short distance away from the Sisters, who each held a telson at their side. Vanna couldn't see his face, but she could feel Cleo's anger pulsating with the growing ripples of heat that emanated from the Sunspear.

Queen Helera stood from the chair; her black leather bodysuit stretching to reveal studded diamonds that scattered across her chest like stars in the midnight sky. At her throat was the same half-moon necklace she'd been wearing when Vanna had first become a Sister. Her long black hair was oiled flat, splitting at the center of her forehead like a curtain, opening to reveal her pale face. The Queen of Astria's round black eyes stared blankly at Cleo, void of any discernible emotion. "What is the meaning of this?" she asked, her voice echoing deeply throughout the empty temple.

Vanna's skin shivered, the hairs on her arms prickling taut at the sound of the Queen's voice. "Where is Clyus Calegri? Where is the Archdeacon of this temple?" Cleo asked, his voice echoing as deep as her own. "I've come for their heads—for justice in the murder of my father."

"You won't find any of them here," the Queen replied.

"Where are they, then?"

"I sent them away. War is no place for old men of politics or those of worship."

Cleo turned around to face everyone behind him. "Commandants Kladden and Jove, find me Clyus. Baron and Jostell, the Archdeacon. They shouldn't have gone far. Igor, see to it what you can about my sister and mother." Without offering a reply, they split to leave the temple. Cleo turned to Vanna and the others. "The rest of you should leave as well."

Despite her condition, Vanna's initial thought was to stay and help Cleo. The Queen of Astria was her fight, not his, and she deserved to see Vanna's justice more than his own. But without either of the two amulons, Vanna knew she was outmatched and would be of little help. And she knew this place would become a temple of death should they clash. So, she complied in silence and turned to walk with the other remaining captains back down the aisle.

But before she reached the light that breached between the slit of the entrance doors, Vanna scurried quickly to her right and pressed her back behind one of the broad marble columns near the edge of the long rug. She peeked her head around its golden engraved siding to watch Cleo from afar.

"This is not your home. *You need to leave,*" she heard Cleo demand.

"I am the wife of the Consolar Vizar of Sacrim and dual ruler of the Southwestern Plane. My claim to be here is greater than anyone else's. Who are *you*, again?"

"*Cleo Justinian Scordisci*, son of the Consolar General of Sacrim and Commander of New Scipyria's Guard. Go home to your mountains in Astria where you belong, and I'll pardon you of your wrongdoing. You have my word that my men won't have you and your women harmed."

Vanna could hear the Queen's mocking laugh echo throughout the vaulted dome ceiling that stood high above them. In response, Cleo lifted the bottom of the Sunspear off the ground and tilted its sharp tip, pointing it directly at her.

"*Cleo the Conqueror*, is that what they call you?"

"I'm not here for you. You need to leave."

"But *I* am here for *you*. Well, for that amulon in your hand," Queen Helera told him.

"You will have no further warning, *woman.*"

"I'm no mere woman—I hold the Skybow. The people you search for are nothing compared to me...as the Sisters of the Silo will demonstrate," the Queen said, raising her own amulon. As soon as the last word had left

561

her purple lips, the Sisters in front of the altar rushed at Cleo with the chains of their telsons loosened, swinging their blades wide in slicing circles.

Cleo quickly slung the Sunspear's tip from side to side, and flames shaped like whips lashed out between their brawl. Vanna heard screams of pain ringing from the center of the temple as the Sunspear's scourges of fire threw the Sisters aback. She moved to the other side of the column to get a better view.

The two Sisters who had made it through with only a few burns fought Cleo with their telsons. He backstepped in defense, then thrust the tip of the Sunspear between them both. Vanna saw a spiraling circle of red and orange flames emanate from its tip, spinning fast as it spread wide. Both Sisters were hurled high into the air by the circling burst of flames. Their bodies caught fire as they were thrown in opposite directions, crashing loudly onto the stone floor in the distance.

As soon as the flames had subsided, Vanna saw a strong, whirling tunnel of wind gust directly at Cleo from atop the altar. His body was flung helplessly down the aisle, tumbling over himself until he caught his footing halfway along. Struggling to stand back up, Cleo swung the Sunspear high into the air, throwing spinning segments of fire the Queen's way.

You're too far away, Vanna thought. *Get closer... Go!*

The Queen used streams of strong wind from the Skybow to misdirect the slow-moving flames that drifted toward her. She walked slowly down the aisle in their direction, deflecting every attack from Cleo's burning onslaught. More and more, he continued to thrash, his voice grunting with each spurning flame, until Queen Helera slammed her Skybow fist down into the ground.

A powerful gale blew, causing Cleo to fly backward. Around each of the column's curving sides, Vanna felt the gust roar. As she shielded her eyes from the debris, she heard Cleo's body crash back-first into the same column she was hiding behind. At the opposite side of the aisle, in front of the mirrored column, the Sunspear clanged loudly to the ground.

It's too far away, Vanna panicked, trying to think of how she could help without being seen.

The Queen's heels clanked loudly against the marble floor as she continued to walk their way. Vanna stood tall and pressed her back against the column's furthest side to ensure her thin body was completely concealed.

"I tried to tell you that no one is a match for me," the Queen said sternly, closing her approach.

Cleo's croaking groans punctuated the silence, loud enough for Vanna to know that he was hurting but still alive. From where he stood, on the other side of the broad column, came the sound of a sword breaching its sheath. Sandals soon slapped against the marble floor, headed away from her and toward the Queen. Vanna peeked around the column's side again and saw the Queen of Astria drawing the Skybow as if it had a string. With the strongest gale of tunneling wind, Cleo was again thrown hard against the column. Rubble, caught in the haze of the gust, flew fast past Vanna's head, swirling around the column with enough force to cut through her exposed skin. Again, she pressed her back flush to it, trying to avoid being cast away.

When the gust had waned, Vanna heard Cleo's grunts of pain growling behind her. She could tell he was being lifted from his feet. "You are no conqueror. No, you're just a boy who marched himself into the wings of death."

No—no. Cleo, be strong. Vanna closed her eyes. Her heart thumped as loudly as the debris that fell from the temple's roof, shaking the ground with each plummeting mass of stone. As a sooty haze began to fill the air, Vanna opened her eyes and crouched low to the ground, attempting to peek around the column's side and check on Cleo.

Cleo had dropped his sword below his feet. She could see its black pearl pommel protruding just beyond the curve of the column's base. Without hesitation, Vanna wrapped herself around the marble, grabbed the sword's handle, and moved to point its blade right at Queen Helera.

The Queen of Astria's eyes fluttered as she held Cleo up by the strap of his breastplate. She released her clenched fist, startled. As soon as Cleo fell and the Queen turned her way, Vanna lunged to shove the blade of his sword through her stomach. The Queen tried lifting the Skybow, but it was too late. Vanna kicked it from her hands and watched as it clanked like rubble to the ground. With a grunt, Vanna twisted and turned Cleo's sword, then pulled its blood-stained blade back out.

"*That's for my mother*," Vanna told her with the fiercest of stares.

Queen Helera stumbled backward with both hands over the gash below her chest. She collapsed to her knees and looked up at Vanna. "*You...dare.*"

Cleo struggled to stand back up, whispering words of thanks that Vanna couldn't discern. With cuts all over his exposed face, arms, and legs, he limped across the aisle to retrieve the Sunspear and joined her in pointing its tip at the Queen of Astria. "I tried to warn you," he said.

"You dare betray your own people...*you traitor. You should be dead,*" the Queen scowled, staring only at Vanna.

"*Traitor?*" Cleo asked, whimpering as he turned to look at Vanna, baffled. "You know her?"

"The Grand Dame told me all about you," the Queen told Vanna before turning her gaze to Cleo. "*You don't know?*"

"Don't know *what?*" Cleo clamored again.

Please...no. Vanna's heart pounded harder than it ever had before. She edged closer, as if to strike the Queen again.

But Cleo had moved to cut her path off. "Wait, Vanna, what did you mean—*that's for your mother?*"

Vanna just stood still, staring blankly at Cleo, unsure of what to say or do. The shimmer around his eyes bent like a crescent moon at full beam, glaring at her in disbelief.

"She was once a Daughter to our Mother Moon—*a Sister of the Silo,*" the Queen stated, coughing up blood. "*This Sister was the one I sent to kill your father...the Consolar General—*"

With a stream of tears flowing down her face, Vanna curled around Cleo and slashed his shortsword straight through Queen Helera's chest.

"*Vanna,* what was she saying? *You? A Sister?* Was she telling the truth? *You* murdered *my father?*" Cleo rambled to ask, his voice thundering with rage. "That can't be true...it can't—I trusted you."

Vanna couldn't bring herself to look at him. Instead, she stared straight into Queen Helera's eyes, which were crying their own silent tears of impending death. She could feel the rage behind her back grow, the heat emanating from the most desolate pits of wrath. Vanna pulled the shortsword out from the Queen's chest and yanked at the moon necklace she wore before daring to turn around.

Cleo held the Sunspear with its tip pointed right at Vanna's face. Bright sparks of amber flowed from its gold-azilian blade with ferocity. "*Tell me,*" he demanded, his voice shaking.

"*Cleo*, I'm sorry... *I meant to tell you earlier. It's why I needed to leave*," Vanna pleaded through her downpouring of tears.

In a fit of fury, flames lashed out in stray flashes from the Sunspear, spreading in all directions to surround them. Nearby columns began to topple over as rubble from the roof's collapse fell in large chunks to the ground.

With a stare of certain death, Cleo stormed toward her. Vanna did all she could to backstep away. "So, it's true... *HOW COULD YOU? I TRUSTED YOU, VANNA. HOW COULD YOU DO THIS TO ME?*"

"Cleo...*I'm sorry*. I should have told you myself."

"*ALL THIS TIME, IT WAS YOU WHO MURDERED MY FATHER?*"

"I was different then—that wasn't the real me. *Cleo, I promise.*"

"*DIFFERENT WHEN? No, Vanna. No. I never knew you.*" Cleo stabbed the Sunspear high, pointing its tip toward the toppling roof of the temple. Rapid streams of fire of the sharpest red and brightest blue filled the vastness of the vaulted space, swooping down to engulf every curve of its round wall.

Vanna used the opening to sprint as fast as she could through the slit between the temple's entrance doors. Guardsmen scattered throughout the square, unsure of what was happening. Soon, they began to flee in all directions as bursts of stray fire were cast into the sky from within the temple.

In waves of painful tears, Vanna ran down the coastline of the harbor. At her side, she reached for Zell's flute. She blew into it again in desperation, playing the long, high-pitched note—one of empty sorrow. She sprinted down the harbor's edge as fast as she could with Cleo's sword still clenched tightly in one hand and the Queen's bloody half-moon necklace wrapped around the other.

Just above the western horizon, Vanna saw a speck in the sky flying toward her. *Felix...please be you. I need you.* With heaving breaths, she played the note over and over again. Through her cloud of tears, she barely recognized the rook. *Felix, it's you...thank you.* It flapped its large wings to land near the western edge of Sazara's curved harbor. Vanna hurried to leap onto its saddle-less back, tugging at its dark feathers to take off again into the sky.

"*Fly. Go and fly...*" she pleaded in distress. "*Be free...*" Vanna clenched its feathers as tightly as she could, and the rook lifted them into the air.

Doused in blood and tears, she looked back at the city one last time from high in the sky. Pillows of black smoke piled in columns, masking the light from the sun that began to set in the east. Below, from the Temple of Sciron to Arcus Street, Sazara had become an inferno.

CHAPTER 44

STONE

Three grand bells in towers just below the Cathedral's spires rang in unison to mark the midpoint of the daily Divine Service. Roth swung his limp leg out from the coach seat of the meager wagon that he had bought from Ludwyn's mother back in Tergona. With a deep breath, he raised his gaze and took in the tallest facade of any across the Plane.

Flying buttresses of sandstone stood between the three towers. Engraved under each bell were circular portals of the whitest stained glass that formed the petals of a flower. Atop every sharp angle was a pointed pinnacle, carved to perfection, with rounded bulbs notched at their lower roots. A statuesque tracery of vertical pillars, resembling the bark and branches of trees, was sculpted across the bottom of the sandstone facade. The longer Roth stared at the Cathedral's west-facing frontage, the more he noticed that all its lines and curves took the shape of bushels and leaves, creating the appearance of a forest.

His sight was drawn to the Cathedral's entrance doors, situated at the middle spire, layered by archivolts that soared tall to the immaculate clerestory. In all the days Roth had spent in Bovere, celebrating himself as the Regent's champion after the bondfight, not once had he taken the time to stroll within the central plaza and witness the Cathedral and all its beauty. And deep within his heart, after seeing it in all its perfect magnificence, Roth was overwhelmed with regret.

"*I guess this is it,*" he whispered to himself. Roth hobbled his way to tie up the mules and wagon to a post near one of many creeks that snaked throughout the largest garden in Bovere. With another gasp to gather his courage, he turned back to the Cathedral and limped toward its front doors. The hand that clung to his walking stick grew clammy the closer he got, gaining clarity of its winding vines of decorative ironwork that was joined to the frame's polished planks of carved wood.

You can do this. You need to do this, he reminded himself.

In the center of each front entrance door hung a bronze knocker that was larger than his head and shaped like the horns of a bull. Roth lowered the hood of his shawl and grabbed it to knock three times. A few moments of silence passed before the right half of the grand door was opened from within. In front of him stood a shorter man dressed in a black habit that draped loosely to his wrists and ankles. His left shoulder was covered by a satin sash that hung diagonally across his chest, tucked into a green cord around his waist.

"Can I help you?" the man asked, his hair cut like the bulge of a mushroom.

"I've come to pledge my life in service to the Divine One and join the Sacred College of the Cathedral," Roth replied through the crawl of his nerves.

The man smirked as if he wanted to laugh but couldn't, then looked at Roth with eyes that questioned the sincerity of his faith. "And who might you be?"

"Roth Fendorse of Tergona."

"*Ah.* The stories of the Regent's champion have traveled far across the east—even reaching here, within the walls of our Cathedral. At least your size matches the tales. I pray not the rest."

Roth quietly considered what to say and even thought about turning back to his wagon, to leave and head home to the Northwoods. But within the honesty of his heart and after all the pain he had suffered, as well as the suffering he had caused to others, Roth knew the Cathedral was where he now belonged. "I pray each day to have my offenses absolved."

"The divine sages may grant you entry if your faith remains proper. But the demands and duties of the Cathedral's college are unending. And the covenant one makes to become a novice is one taken for life. Are you willing to sacrifice the life you once knew?"

I already have, Roth thought. He nodded and said, "*I am.*"

The man withdrew into the dark crack between the grand doors, then opened them fully to invite Roth in with an outstretched arm. Light from the windows, which spanned half the height of the towers, flooded in from the Cathedral's inner walls. Each portrayed a stained-glass figure of noble men or women, past supreme sages, or royal dignitaries in every assortment of tint and shade, color and grandeur. To each side of the entranceway, standing tall in the alcove that was recessed into its forwardmost corners, stood marble statues of the Cathedral's founder, Tohen the Second, and his son, Tavhen.

Roth followed the man down the center aisle, where mosaic tiles in the colors of various nuts shone, forming figures of rings that hooked within one another for the entirety of the beige extent. On each of the aisle's sides were weathered bench seats, filled midway with people attending the Cathedral's daily Divine Service.

"Sit here," the man instructed him, pointing to the first open row behind a family of four. Roth shuffled his limp leg to slide onto the bench and placed his walking stick beneath it. At the aisle's end, he saw a man dressed in the same garb as the one he had just met, standing behind a grand pulpit as he read from the Divine Tomes. Suspended from the tall ceiling above the man hung the Divine Crest, with its three interlocking circles stretching the full width of the grand room. Just below the crest, and behind the man who spoke, was the Cathedral's tree of life—a broad-branched oak tree glazed green with leaves, planted and grown above the gravesite of Tohen the Second, whose incorrupt remains are the centerpiece of the vast crypt below. Before the tree stood the Divine One's throne, left unoccupied by man.

For the first few moments, Roth could only sit in awe, staring at the spectacle he found himself within. Hundreds of sconces lined the walls between each of the Cathedral's colorful windows, fitted with unlit candles, sat upon fine bronze prickets. The people around him, both young and old, and dressed in a variety of poor garments and wealthy tunics, sat in silence as they listened to the man behind the raised pulpit speak. Directly in front of him, Roth took notice of two children who sat beside their parents—a boy and a girl, both too young to grasp the history behind the pageantry they were so fortunate to find themselves witnessing.

Seeing the children brought back memories of when he and Ruth had both been their age. Ruth had always kept her nose stuffed between the pages of a book and had preferred to stay inside most days, while he'd be off in the Northwoods, climbing trees and exploring the trails and wilderness. But the more he sat and listened and continued to watch the two children in front of him, the more Roth began to realize that he and Ruth weren't so different after all. They had both been blessed by the Divine One to have such loving parents who cared for them and taught them right from wrong. And they were both privileged to have grown up in the Eastern Plane, where they could decide on the direction of their lives for themselves. Though they had taken different paths, Roth could only smile as he came to the realization that both he and Ruth had arrived at the same destination: the truth of love, for life and for the Divine One, which nestled itself deep within each of their twin spirits.

As the man at the platform closed one volume of the Divine Tomes and finished his interpreted speech, the people around him began to stand up and leave. Roth sat still, listening to the attendees chat among themselves as they departed toward the doors. He was almost too ashamed to show his face and risk having someone recognize him, so he kept his chin tucked low. Like a hammer to an iron pin nail, his eyes became fixated on his injured left leg. It still couldn't move or bend and had to be tucked under the bench seat in front of him. The pain had dissipated, but all the suffering it had caused him still lingered. It was an injury that had destroyed the life he once knew and changed the man he once was. But the longer Roth sat alone on the bench, the more he knew what sort of man he needed to become.

Time passed slowly as the light that threaded through the windows began to fade. Men in the same black habits, some without the white cross sashes, lit the candles along the walls, providing light to the few Boverians who had wandered into the Cathedral to pray. Roth sat still and waited for the man from before to return. But he never came. Instead of becoming frustrated and feeling forgotten, Roth took that time alone, just as he had during his half-moon journey south, to reflect on his past and pray for what was to come. He closed his eyes and repeated his prayers.

The echoing ring of morning bells broke the peace of his darkened slumber. Roth's eyes opened to find himself sprawled out on the same bench inside the Cathedral. After rubbing away the fog from his eyes, he sprang up and noticed the same man who had let him in, sitting beside him in prayer under the light of the new day.

"I'm sorry, I must have fallen asleep," Roth said, trying to gather his thoughts.

"If you still wish to stick true to the path of the Sacred College, then you will find that this will be the first of many. *Come*," the man said. He stood, shifted his way to the wide central aisle, bowed, and then began walking toward the Divine Crest. Roth followed him, struggling to keep up, his leg stiffer than normal in the mornings. They exited through a smaller set of doors to the right and made their way under a sandstone portico held up by columns patterned like the branches of trees, the same as the Cathedral's facade.

Straight ahead was a simple round building, one without any fine engravings or illustrious windows to distinguish itself from the elegance of the Cathedral. Above its plain door was a simple bronze placard that read: *Sceptory of the Divine Sages.* The man sifted through his iron ring of keys to unlock the door and then invited Roth to enter first. The walls of the long foyer were bland, and the floor was marked by the same unevenly scattered beige tiles. A second door had been left open to a darkened room. Again, Roth entered first.

At the center of the sceptory's main room was a white rug in the shape of a hollow circle, lit only by the pendant that hung from the middle of the coffered ceiling. "Come, please. Stand at the center so we can see you," a voice said from the outer ring of darkness. The door was shut behind him as Roth limped his way toward the light at the center. He turned around in circles, trying to grasp where the voice had come from.

In the dim light, he saw thirteen golden-leafed chairs encircling him. Divine Sages occupied most of them, dressed in their white habits and tall headpieces. Opposite the entrance door was the largest chair of them all—an empty throne stitched with white padding along its seat, with the emblem of the Divine Crest carved in gold at its peak. Roth could faintly make out a man standing behind each occupied chair, wearing white surcoats with the same Divine Crest stitched at their chest. *Tohenic knights,* he realized.

"Tell us who you are and why you've come," the same voice spoke aloud.

"I am Roth Fendorse of Tergona. I came to give my life to the Divine One and seek the path of the Sacred College to become a divine sage." A loud silence filled the air as Roth waited for a response.

From the chair to the right of the throne, a voice broke through the long pause to ask: "And why is it, Roth Fendorse of Tergona, that you feel the path of a novitiate of the Sacred College would be right for you?"

"*Maturity*," Roth responded honestly. Though he couldn't see their faces, he could feel their judgment smothering him. He couldn't lie. Not here, at least, in this sacred place, encircled by the most wise and holy of people. "I had an injury. One to my leg, on the island of Nordheim in the Northern Plane. It changed me—it changed everything. I could have died there. And now that I've had the time to look back on it and reflect, I might as well have been dead for the entirety of my life before it."

"We are closest to the Divine Gates in our moments before death and after birth," an older sage to his right said with a raspy voice. "Without the intimacy of both, prayer is *meaningless*."

"You mentioned your life before. What of it?" the sage who'd spoken first asked.

"I pray to the Divine One for my offenses to be absolved. I've lived a life I now take no pride in—one of vices, of women and violence and drunkenness. *Of ignorance*," Roth responded.

"*Of blindness*, it seems," the Divine Sage with the raspy voice stated. "But a flower doesn't get to choose when it blossoms. That's what the Divine Crest we each wear hanging from our necks signifies. The divine and the depraved are at battle within us all. But the link between them both, from which they both hang, is redemption—the ultimate grace of the Divine One."

"Basil the Elder is correct," another Divine Sage said. "Charity is for everyone. Joining our Sacred College will absolve you from all prior entanglements of the Plane you may be involved with."

The sage closest to the door added, "But this is a commitment for life—a covenant we each make with the Divine One in the duty of its service. Novitiates and junioriates alike take no part in the Plane's vices, all of which must be forsworn. Are you prepared to do so?"

"*I am*," Roth replied.

"And there is no guarantee for one to ascend to a seat among the divine sages. Many have passed honorably through the gates as novices and juniors, for it takes the passing of one of our own for a chair to become open. And a cast from all of us within the sceptory, including the supreme sage himself, to fill it."

Roth saw the palm of the sage's hand rise in the direction of the empty throne. "I understand."

"Are there any among us who might reject Roth Fendorse of Tergona's admittance into the Sacred College of the Divine One?"

Roth held his breath as the silence rang.

"*Aye,*" a voice came from the opposite end of the sceptory. As soon as the word was spoken, Roth's stomach turned over, tightening into an empty knot.

"A rejection has been cast by Dassel the Elder. Is there any who might stand beside the proposed and object?" the sage near the door asked.

"*I will stand for Roth Fendorse of Tergona,*" the old Divine Sage with a raspy voice said from his right. "I have met his kin before. A sister, I believe. She is of honorable faith."

"Very well. Basil the Elder has cast his support in favor of your admittance, against a single rejection. By his kindness and through the grace of the Divine One, you will be allowed admittance into our Sacred College and kept under his watchful eye." The sage near the door moved his hand above his chair and motioned with his fingers toward the center where Roth stood. Out from the darkness walked a Tohenic knight, who wore a white cloak that hung from the collar of his surcoat to the back of his knees. His face was stern, and his head was bald and leathery. "The regnant commander of the Tohenic knights will hand you our covenant oath, should you wish to take it."

"*I do.*"

"Then kneel to the crest and pray."

Roth obeyed the Divine Sage's orders and bent his good knee down onto the white rug. He unfolded the parchment and read: "By the spirit of the Divine One, I, *Roth Fendorse,* forsake my life to become consecrated as a novitiate in the Sacred College. By chastity to its allegiance, I vow my spirit to the Council of the Divine Sages. By obedience to its teachings, I vow my spirit to the Covenant of the Divine Tomes. By poverty to its service, I vow my spirit to the Cathedral of the Divine One. It shall no longer be I who lives, but the sagacious spirit of the Divine One who lives within *me.*"

When the final word of the oath had left Roth's lips, he felt the slightest tingle trace his spine. He stood back up and turned around. The door to the sceptory's main room slowly cracked open, and through it scampered the same man from before, dressed in his black habit and white sash. He bowed to the crest, then walked toward the edge of the light to face the Divine Sage closest to the door. "*Sir…*"

"Please speak, John the Junior," the sage told him.

"A ship has arrived from the north and is docked in Lake Gileed."

A ship? Roth's rounded ears perked up, and he smiled, hanging onto the man's every word, waiting to hear of the free fleet's fate.

"What of it?"

"On it, returned those sentinels injured in battle. And the bodies of those passed through the Gates."

Battle? Dead? Roth's thoughts were scattered with concern over all the friends in the fleet he had made. But above all, his concern flared with worry over the fate of his sister.

"And a message," John the Junior added.

"Then we shall dismiss this meeting at once to discuss such matters in the privacy of the sceptory. Roth, you will wait outside for John. After he is finished, he will show you to your new chambers within the college."

"*Actually*, sir, the message is for Roth Fendorse."

Me?

"Shall I?" John asked.

The Divine Sage turned toward the center of the sceptory. "If our newest novice wishes."

Roth just nodded in silence, not knowing what to say or do. The tingling in his spine had disappeared. John the Junior turned to face him and read: "Roth Fendorse, you are cordially invited to Minoska to attend the coronation of King Daneus of Marredom, midday at winter's end. Captain Sonny of the Rithron awaits your travel north. With love, your sister, Ruth."

"Ruth… Dane—*King?*" Roth spoke his thoughts aloud, forgetting where he was standing.

"*Rithron?*" Basil the Elder questioned John the Junior as if he recognized the name.

"That's what it reads, sir," he replied.

"We must remind you that as a novitiate of the Sacred College, though newly planted, your duty is now here," the Divine Sage sitting beside the door told him.

"That's right. He hasn't even decided on his namesake," another Divine Sage noted.

Roth's shoulders slumped. Had he waited just one day longer to take the oath, he'd be free to visit the Northern Plane and celebrate the triumph of his friends. Instead, there he stood, within the Sceptory of the Divine Sages, confined to a life of solitude in service of the Divine One—a life he had willfully chosen. But after all his thoughts and suppositions had settled, Roth simply smiled to know that Ruth was safe and still alive. "I understand," he told them.

"*I will go*," Basil the Elder said. "And I will take the new Novice with me. On his return, he shall decide on his name."

Roth could feel the glares from every eye hidden in the dark turn with tension to face the Divine Sage as soon as the words had left his mouth. Roth didn't know where to look or what to do, but at that moment, his smile, pinned from ear to ear, had grown to the greatest of grins as he awaited what would come next.

"A divine sage has never before left the Regent, *Basil*."

"Thomas is right," the Divine Sage by the door added.

"Then I shall seek the counsel of the Supreme Sage and ask for his allowance," Basil the Elder said. "It was my doing that placed this faithful girl, Ruth, in such dangerous circumstances. I intend to honor her for her courage and commitment to the Cathedral. And by the grace of the Divine One, we may have found a new friend in the north."

† † †

"The White Tower is just there," Sonny told Roth from the bow of the *Rithron*, handing him his spyglass to see the snow-covered speck in the distance.

"*Finally*. I don't think I could have taken this sea for another day."

"I don't blame you. I haven't seen that old man leave my captain's quarters since we broke from Roark's River into the North Sea," Sonny told him.

"Nine days too long, if you ask me," Roth sneered, half dreading the fact that he was returning to the Northern Plane on the same ship he'd been on the day his life had changed forever. "I'll go wake him and tell him we've almost arrived."

By the brace of the bulwark, Roth limped his way aft across the main deck of the *Rithron*. After each step, he waited to move his walking stick in sync with the roll of the waves, lifting the brim of his black habit above the puddles on the deck. On each side of the aftcastle's door were two Tohenic knights, dressed in their white surcoats and chainmail, who shifted to the side to let Roth enter and walk up the stairs.

Roth knocked and entered cautiously. "Sir—you're already up. Great," he sputtered aloud after seeing Basil the Elder hunched behind Sonny's desk. The hairless skin at the top of his round head was splotched with dark marks that blended with the freckles of his furrowed face.

"I had to make a few final preparations," he rasped without looking up from his moving quill.

"We will be arriving any moment."

"Have you finished chapter seven of volume one?"

"Yes, Elder."

"*Good.* On our way back, you will write me your examination. Now, help me out of here. I need to get some fresh air."

Roth moved as quickly as his left leg would let him, helping to lift the much shorter sage from the chair. He led him down to the quarterdeck, where five of the fifteen Tohenic knights who had traveled with them assisted in his care. They moved toward the starboard railing, and Roth and Basil the Elder looked out at the calming sea of Minoska's approaching harbor.

"You're more than lucky, you know—to be coming here."

For many things, Roth thought, before simply replying, "I know."

"This will likely be the last time you ever leave the Regent."

"Just a half-solurn ago, I never thought I'd become a novice of the Sacred College. And in the past moon, I never envisioned that I'd be back on this ship, traveling to the Northern Plane again. My life lately, even before then, in becoming the Regent's champion, has been a series of unexpected events."

"The Divine One works in mysterious ways," Basil the Elder said while scanning the sea.

"That must be true. And if the Divine One could get rid of this cold, I wouldn't mind the north as much," Roth added, trying to make light of their situation.

Basil the Elder let out a rough chuckle, then calmed himself. "The reach of the Divine One doesn't stop at our land. And its spirit lives in this frigid winter the same as it does in the warmth of our harvest. I wish more of the other sages would recognize the truth in that."

"And if anyone needs prayers, it's the norks," Roth said, nodding to the snow-covered piers they were coming upon. To his surprise, most looked empty. "Sir, if I may ask, back in the sceptory, when John the Junior had mentioned the *Rithron*, it seemed as if you had heard of it before. Have you?"

"The name, I have, yes," the Divine Sage replied.

"Where from, if I may ask?"

"It was an old coat in my family—a name I hadn't heard in a very long time. I thought it had died off a long while ago." Roth nodded along, listening through the yells across the deck that rang in preparation for the *Rithron's* docking. "To be honest with you, hearing it was part of the reason I decided it was right for me to leave—a sign from the Divine One, if you will."

"I'm just glad the Supreme Sage allowed it."

"*I, as well,*" Basil the Elder said with another dry cough. "Though I do share your sentiment about this cold."

Roth laughed a little as they continued to chat and point at the other ships that scattered scarcely across Minoska's wide port. He waited impatiently as the short-handed *Rithron* came beside one of the many slips left open. The mates threw their lines to the dock and began securing the gangway to the main deck. The Tohenic knights escorted Basil the Elder off first and led him to one of the three wagons near the shoreline. Roth thanked Sonny, then followed them down the planks of the pier to take his seat in the wagon beside the Divine Sage.

The coachman led them down the lone trail, thudding through mounds of snow and ice until the city of Minoska came into view. A long street, dense with crowds of people, stretched from the road they traveled on to an awkwardly shaped castle curtained by a graystone wall. From afar, Roth was unimpressed by Minoska's buildings. Most were bland and gray, topped with steeple-pitched roofs and scattered unevenly across the snow-smothered ground.

From the back of the procession, some of the Tohenic knights stepped out from the wagon behind them and walked ahead to split the thousands of norks who gathered in the street to see their new King. Most of the men and women Roth saw looked frail and exhausted, with bruises and bony bulges protruding from any skin left exposed to the cold. Most wore black or gray overcoats, with hats to cover their ears and blond-bundled hair. Roth became saddened by the sight as they passed along Minoska's central street. But through their deformity, most smiled and waved as their wagon rode slowly through, almost as if they were allowed to be happy for the first time in far too long. And despite his oath of celibacy, Roth couldn't help but notice that the young women of the north were exceptionally pretty.

When their wagon reached the two towers that connected the wall facing the central street, Roth's gaze was drawn to the people moving at the top. He smiled from ear to ear when he saw Ruth and Dane standing between the corners of the left tower's battlements, mirroring back his same beaming grin. Ruth waved them through the open arch under the wall, motioning for them to climb up and join her and Dane atop the tower. Roth patiently led Basil the Elder and his watchful guard of Tohenic knights up its spiraling inner stairs.

"*Roth!* You made it!" Ruth shouted in excitement as she ran over to hug him. "I didn't know if the message I gave Sonny would get to you in time! Dane was just about to give his speech. But look at you—you're here, you made it!" His sister grabbed a sleeve of his black habit and tilted her shoulders to inspect his new clothing. Her eyes shifted faster than her face, reflecting an endless stream of questions.

"I'm a novice now. So, this is the last time you'll know me as Roth. I'll be taking a new name upon my return to Bovere."

She tugged at the green cord around his waist. "You of all people, huh?"

Roth held his crooked smile firm. "Me, of all people, yes."

"A life spent in the service of the Divine One is an honorable life. I'm proud of you, *brother*." Ruth's eyes grew watery as she hugged him tight once more.

"I'm just glad you're safe," he replied, looking over her shoulder to see Dane dressed in a long cloak of white fur. In his hand, he held the Seatrident, tipped by its three prongs of silver-azilian. "How did he get *that*?" Roth asked.

"You'd have to ask him yourself," Ruth said before noticing Basil the Elder slowly reach the top of the tower's stairs. "That's the same Divine Sage I met with in Bovere!"

"And I'm lucky he let me come," Roth tried to say, though his sister had already left him to hurry his way, bowing before the old sage in his white habit.

Roth limped over to Dane, who stood at the tower's edge. Near him was a set of stairs that led to the curtained wall's top walkway, just above its open gate. "King Dane has a nice ring to it," Roth told him, reaching to shake his hand. When their hands touched, Roth felt a small pulse, almost like a nerve, tingling throughout his body. "*With an amulon.*"

"Pretty, isn't it?" Dane asked with a proud grin.

"*More than pretty.*"

"Roth, I need to introduce you to my family. This is my mother, Amel; my sisters, Ellian and Alva; and my brother, Maven, whom I've mentioned to you before. And this is my father, Domus," Dane explained, pointing to each of them with a gracious smile.

Dane's father looked frailer than most of the norks he had passed on the street below. "Pleasure," Roth told them.

"We weren't expecting to run into King Mordin in the North Sea, but I wouldn't be here today if it weren't for my father. He was an oarsman on the *Klitan.* He's the real hero."

"Thank you," Roth turned to Domus to say, nodding in acknowledgment. "And thank you for keeping Ruth safe. You'll have to share the stories of it with me once everything settles."

"Absolutely." Dane mirrored the nod to his father, then looked out at the masses crowded in the street. "We lost too many men that day—Piney, chief among them. But their deaths will never be in vain."

"I'm sorry, Dane. I know how close the two of you were. He was a good friend and a great man."

"The *greatest,*" Dane said, sniffling his pale nose. "Thank you, Roth. It's been hard trying to recover, but I'm glad you were able to make it. I know how much it means to Ruth for you to be here."

"This will likely be my last visit. But boy, did I make a good one." Roth limped near the edge of the tall tower and peeked between the battlements. Thousands of people packed the street, breathing clouds of white cold into the air.

"It took a half-moon's pass to spread the word across Marredom. Norkatis Street is more crowded today than it has been in many solurns," Dane said.

"I never knew there were this many people this far north," Roth said. He turned and saw Dane's icy eyes glance over his shoulder toward Ruth and Basil the Elder, who were walking their way. Ruth introduced the sage to Dane.

"It's an honor for you to have come all this way to Minoska, sir," Dane told him.

"The honor is mine. We, in the Regent, recognize no king but the Divine One. Though I pray the best for you," Basil the Elder told Dane.

"Thank you," Dane responded. "I will need it."

The Divine Sage stood silently for a moment, watching Dane's eyes shift nervously. "Rulership can be tricky, as you may find. If it helps, I have found the truth in this: sovereignty either rests in the hands of one or in them all. There can be no in-between." Roth watched Dane take a deep breath, listening to every raspy word of wisdom the Divine Sage had spoken. "But there is something else I traveled all this way for." Basil the Elder turned to Ruth and pulled out a sealed piece of parchment from the center crease of his habit. "Ruth, as an emissary on behalf of Furlak's Royal Order and its presiding council, it is my distinct pleasure to bestow upon you the honor of Cathedral Knighthood."

Ruth…an honorary knight? Roth questioned.

Ruth's face flushed red; her cheeks burst through the cold. Her crooked smile widened, and her eyes began to tear up, glistening like a geyser before it blew. For moments longer than Dane or Roth had expected, Ruth stood in silence, rooted with her boots in the snow like a rare flower blossoming in winter. With streams of tears falling down her face, Basil the Elder slowly walked her way. He reached inside his habit again, then pinned a tiny dove flower to the collar of her overcoat. "*Thank you*—this is all too much. I don't know how I could ever thank you—this is the highest of honors," she stuttered with gratitude.

"The thanks are ours," Basil the Elder said while patting her on the shoulder. "But, please, meet with us in Bovere at your earliest convenience." He then turned back to Dane and told him, "Now, son, go give your speech."

Dane nodded nervously, then walked from the tower to the center of the curtained wall with his family and mates patting him on the back along the way for support. He turned to face the crowd, standing directly above the opened arches of the gate. "*People of Marredom…as you may have already heard, King Mordin the Fourth is dead!*"

In a single pillow of white breath, cheers from the full length of Norkatis Street erupted with chants, shouting, "*King Dane! King Dane! King Dane!*"

Dane used the pause to turn and smile at his family and friends. Roth watched his eyes shift until they met Basil the Elder's beside him. At that moment, Dane's expression had returned to a stern focus. Whatever it was he had planned to say seemed to have vanished. "*I come to you all with a new proposition: a free Marredom—free for every man, woman, and child! But there is one change that must take place to secure our freedom... As of today, Marredom shall have no king!*" Roth heard the norks' cheers fade into a clamoring chatter as soon as Dane had finished his proclamation. "*It is not a title I deserve...nor a title I want. And I will do everything in my power to keep it that way. Henceforth...every man and woman in the north shall be sovereign—a king or queen in their own right!*"

After his announcement, Dane raised the prongs of the Seatrident to the sky. The people packed tightly like tinfish within Norkatis Street began to cheer once more. With a powerful smile of liberation, Dane turned and walked back to the tower. In front of Roth and Basil the Elder, he stopped. The Divine Sage leaned close to Dane's ear, and Roth heard him whisper, "*You made the right decision.*"

"Thank you," Dane said back to him in agreement.

But before Dane could move along, Basil the Elder reached for his chest and grabbed the leaf-shaped necklace he wore half-hidden between the seams of his undergarment. With squinting eyes, the Divine Sage stared at it with a look of disbelief, inspecting it for longer than Dane seemed to be comfortable with. "Where did you manage to find *this?*"

"It was my late captain's. *Why?*" Dane asked, stepping back defensively.

"That key belongs to the Supreme Sage of the Cathedral!"

Dane looked down at his chest. "*Key?*"

www.ingramcontent.com/pod-product-compliance
Lightning Source LLC
Chambersburg PA
CBHW021935110726
47901CB00003B/853